LEGENDS II

NEW SHORT NOVELS BY
THE MASTERS OF
MODERN FANTASY

Also edited by Robert Silverberg

Voyager

LEGENDS II

Edited by
Robert Silverberg

ROBIN HOBB

GEORGE R. R. MARTIN

ORSON SCOTT CARD

DIANA GABALDON

ROBERT SILVERBERG

TAD WILLIAMS

ANNE McCAFFREY

RAYMOND E. FEIST

ELIZABETH HAYDON

NEIL GAIMAN

TERRY BROOKS

HarperCollins*Publishers*

Voyager
An Imprint of HarperCollins*Publishers*
77–85 Fulham Palace Road
Hammersmith, London W6 8JB

www.voyager-books.com

Published by *Voyager* 2003
1 3 5 7 9 8 6 4 2

A catalogue record for this book
is available from the British Library

ISNB 0 00 715435 6

Typeset in Stone Serif by
Palimpsest Book Production Limited,
Polmont, Stirlingshire

Printed and bound in Australia by
Griffin Press

For George R.R. Martin
who baited the trap

And Terry Brooks
for valiant help from an unexpected quarter

CONTENTS

INTRODUCTION *Robert Silverberg*   I

REALM OF THE ELDERLINGS: 3
   Homecoming *Robin Hobb*   9

A SONG OF ICE AND FIRE: 75
   The Sworn Sword *George R.R. Martin*   79

TALES OF ALVIN MAKER: 159
   The Yazoo Queen *Orson Scott Card*   163

OUTLANDER: 207
   Lord John and the Succubus *Diana Gabaldon*   211

MAJIPOOR: 291
   The Book of Changes *Robert Silverberg*   297

OTHERLAND: 351
   The Happiest Dead Boy in the World *Tad Williams*   355

PERN: 401
   Beyond Between *Anne McCaffrey*   407

THE RIFTWAR: 441
   The Messenger *Raymond E. Feist*   447

THE SYMPHONY OF AGES: 489
   Threshold *Elizabeth Haydon*   493

AMERICAN GODS: 555
   The Monarch of the Glen *Neil Gaiman*   559

SHANNARA: 603
   Indomitable *Terry Brooks*   607

INTRODUCTION

The first *Legends* anthology, which was published in 1998, contained eleven never-before-published short novels by eleven bestselling fantasy writers, each story set in the special universe of the imagination that its author had made famous throughout the world. It was intended as the definitive anthology of modern fantasy, and – judging by the reception the book received from readers worldwide – it succeeded at that.

And now comes *Legends II*. If the first book was definitive, why do another one?

The short answer is that fantasy is inexhaustible. There are always new stories to tell, new writers to tell them; and no theme, no matter how hoary, can ever be depleted.

As I said in the introduction to the first volume, fantasy is the oldest branch of imaginative literature – as old as the human imagination itself. It is not difficult to believe that the same artistic impulse that produced the extraordinary cave paintings of Altamira and Lascaux and Chauvet, fifteen and twenty and even thirty thousand years ago, also probably produced astounding tales of gods and demons, of talismans and spells, of dragons and werewolves, of wondrous lands beyond the horizon – tales that fur-clad shamans recited to fascinated audiences around the campfires of Ice Age Europe. So, too, in torrid Africa, in the China of prehistory, in ancient India, in the Americas: everywhere, in fact, on and on back through time for thousands or even hundreds of thousands of years. I like to think that the storytelling impulse is universal – that there have been storytellers as long as there have been beings in this world that could be spoken of as 'human' – and that those storytellers have in particular devoted their skills and energies and talents, throughout our long evolutionary path, to the creation of extraordinary marvels and wonders. The Sumerian epic of Gilgamesh is a tale of fantasy; so too is Homer's *Odyssey*, and on and on up through such modern fantasists as E.R. Eddison, A. Merritt, H.P.

Lovecraft, and J.R.R. Tolkien, and all the great science-fiction writers from Verne and Wells to our own time. (I include science fiction because science fiction, as I see it, belongs firmly in the fantasy category: it is a specialized branch of fantasy, a technology-oriented kind of visionary literature in which the imagination is given free play for the sake of making the scientifically impossible, or at least the implausible, seem altogether probable.)

Many of the contributors to the first *Legends* were eager to return to their special worlds of fantasy for a second round. Several of them raised the subject of a new anthology so often that finally I began to agree with them that a second book would be a good idea. And here it is. Six writers – Orson Scott Card, George R.R. Martin, Raymond E. Feist, Anne McCaffrey, Tad Williams, and myself – have returned from the first one. Joining them are four others – Robin Hobb, Elizabeth Haydon, Diana Gabaldon, and Neil Gaiman – who have risen to great fame among fantasy enthusiasts since the first anthology was published, and one grand veteran of fantasy, Terry Brooks, who had found himself unable at the last minute to participate in the first volume of *Legends* but who joins us for this one.

My thanks are due once again to my wife, Karen, and to my literary agent, Ralph Vicinanza, both of whom aided me in all sorts of ways in the preparation of this book, and, of course, to all the authors who came through with such splendid stories. I acknowledge also a debt of special gratitude to Betsy Mitchell of Del Rey Books, whose sagacious advice and unfailing good cheer were essential to the project. Without her help this book most literally would not have come into being.

Robert Silverberg
February, 2003

REALM OF
THE ELDERLINGS

ROBIN HOBB

STOP EATING
CHOLOCLATE WHEN
READING!
ONLY
CHOCOLATE

REALM OF THE ELDERLINGS
ROBIN HOBB

THE FARSEER TRILOGY
Assassin's Apprentice (1995)
Royal Assassin (1996)
Assassin's Quest (1997)

THE LIVESHIP TRADERS TRILOGY:
Ship of Magic (1998)
The Mad Ship (1999)
Ship of Destiny (2000)

THE TAWNY MAN TRILOGY:
Fool's Errand (2002)
The Golden Fool (2003)
Fool's End (2004)

The first Robin Hobb trilogy, the Farseer Trilogy, took place in the Six Duchies. It is the tale of FitzChivalry Farseer. The discovery that this bastard son exists is enough to topple Prince Chivalry's ambition for the throne. He abdicates, ceding the title of heir to the throne to his younger brother Verity and abandoning the child to the care of the stablemaster Burrich. The youngest prince, Regal, has ambitions of his own, and wishes to do away with the bastard. But old King Shrewd sees the value of taking the lad and training him as an assassin. For a bastard can be sent into dangers where a trueborn son could not be risked, and may be given tasks that would soil an heir's hands.

And so FitzChivalry is trained in the secret arts of being a royal assassin. He shows a predilection for the Wit, a beast magic much despised in the Six Duchies. This secret vice in the young assassin is tolerated, for a partnership with an animal may be a useful trait in an assassin. When it is discovered that he may possess the hereditary magic of the Farseers, the Skill, he becomes both the King's weapon, and an obstacle to Prince Regal's ambitions for the throne. At a time when the rivalry for the throne is intense, and the Outislanders and their Red Ship raiders are bringing war to the Six Duchies, FitzChivalry discovers that the fate of the kingdom may very well rest on the actions of a young bastard and the King's Fool. Armed with little more than loyalty and his sporadic talent for the old magic, Fitz follows the fading trail of King Verity, who has travelled beyond the Mountain Kingdom and into the realm of the legendary Elderlings, in what may be a vain hope to renew an old alliance.

The Liveship Traders trilogy takes place in Jamaillia, Bingtown, and the Pirate Isles, on the coast far to the south of the Six Duchies. The war in the north has interrupted the trade that is the lifeblood of Bingtown, and the Liveship Traders have fallen on hard times despite their magic sentient ships. At one time, possession of a Liveship, constructed of magical wizardwood, guaranteed a Trader's family prosperity. Only a Liveship can brave the dangers of the Rain Wild River and trade with the legendary Rain Wild Traders and their mysterious magical goods, plundered from the enigmatic Elderling ruins. Althea Vestrit expects her families to adhere to tradition and pass the family Liveship on to her when it quickens at the death of her father. Instead, the *Vivacia* goes to her sister Keffria and her scheming Chalcedean husband Kyle. The proud Liveship becomes a transport vessel for the despised but highly profitable slave trade.

Althea, cast out on her own, resolves to make her own way in the world and somehow regain control of her family's living ship. Her old shipmate Brashen Trell, the mysterious woodcarver Amber, and the *Paragon*, the notorious mad Liveship, are the only allies she can rally to her cause. Pirates, a slave rebellion, migrating sea serpents, and a newly hatched dragon are but a few of the obstacles she must face on her way to discovering that Liveships are not, perhaps, what they seem to be, and may have dreams of their own to follow.

The Tawny Man trilogy, a work still in progress at this writing, picks up the tale of Fitz and the Fool some fifteen years after the Red Ship wars. Queen Kettricken is determined to secure her son's throne by arranging a marriage between Prince Dutiful and Elliana, the daughter of their old enemies in the Outislands. But the Six Duchies themselves are restless. The Witted are weary of persecution, and may choose to topple the throne of the Farseers by revealing that young Prince Dutiful carries an old taint in his blood. The Narcheska Elliana sets a high price on her hand: Dutiful must present her with the head of Icefyre, the legendary dragon of Aslevjal Island.

Meanwhile, to the south, the Bingtown Traders continue to wage war against the Chalcedeans, and seek to enlist the Six Duchies into the effort to obliterate Chalced. Bingtown's temperamental ally, the dragon Tintaglia, has her own reasons for supporting them in this, reasons that may lead not only to the restoration of the race of dragons but also to the return of Elderling magic to the Cursed Shores.

HOMECOMING

BY ROBIN HOBB

Day the 7th of the Fish Moon
Year the 14th of the reign of the
Most Noble and Magnificent Satrap Esclepius

Confiscated from me this day, without cause or justice, were five crates and three trunks. This occurred during the loading of the ship *Venture*, setting forth upon Satrap Esclepius' noble endeavour to colonize the Cursed Shores. Contents of the crates are as follows: one block fine white marble, of a size suitable for a bust; two blocks Aarthian jade, sizes suitable for busts; one large fine soapstone, as tall as a man and as wide as a man; seven large copper ingots, of excellent quality; three silver ingots, of acceptable quality, and three kegs of wax. One crate contained scales, tools for the working of metal and stone, and measuring equipment. Contents of trunks are as follows: two silk gowns, one blue, one pink, tailored by Seamstress Wista and bearing her mark. A dress-length of mille-cloth, green. Two shawls, one white wool, one blue linen. Several pairs hose, in winter and summer weights. Three pairs of slippers, one silk and worked with rosebuds. Seven petticoats, three silk, one linen and three wool. One bodice frame, of light bone and silk. Three volumes of poetry, written in my own hand. A miniature by Soiji, of myself, Lady Carillion Carrock, née Waljin, commissioned by my mother, Lady Arston Waljin, on the occasion of my fourteenth birthday. Also included were clothing and bedding for a baby, a girl of four years and two boys, of six and ten years, including both winter and summer garb for formal occasions.

I record this confiscation so that the thieves can be brought to justice upon my return to Jamaillia City. The theft was in this manner: as our ship was being loaded for departure, cargo belonging to various nobles aboard the vessels was detained upon the docks. Captain Triops informed us that our possessions would be held, indefinitely, in the

Satrap's custody. I do not trust the man, for he shows neither my husband nor myself proper deference. So I make this record, and when I return this coming spring to Jamaillia City, my father, Lord Crion Waljin, will bring my complaint before the Satrap's Court of Justice, as my husband seems little inclined to do so. This do I swear.

Lady Carillion Waljin Carrock

Day the 10th of the Fish Moon
Year the 14th of the reign of the Most Noble
and Magnificent Satrap Esclepius

Conditions aboard the ship are intolerable. Once more, I take pen to my journal to record the hardship and injustice to preserve a record so that those responsible may be punished. Although I am nobly born, of the house of Waljin, and although my lord husband is not only noble, but heir to the title of Lord Carrock, the quarters given us are no better than those allotted to the common emigrants and speculators, that is, a smelly space in the ship's hold. Only the common criminals, chained in the deepest holds, suffer more than we do.

The floor is a splintery wooden deck, the walls are the bare planks of the ship's hull. There is much evidence that rats were the last inhabitants of this compartment. We are treated no better than cattle. There are no separate quarters for my maid, so I must suffer her to bed almost alongside us! To preserve my children from the common brats of the emigrants, I have sacrificed three damask hangings to curtain off a space. Those people accord me no respect. I believe that they are surreptitiously plundering our stores of food. When they mock me, my husband bids me ignore them. This has had a dreadful effect on my servant's behaviour. This morning, my maid, who also serves as a nanny in our reduced household, spoke almost harshly to young Petrus, bidding him be quiet and cease his questions. When I rebuked her for it, she dared to raise her brows at me.

My visit to the open deck was a waste of time. It is cluttered with ropes, canvas and crude men, with no provisions for ladies and children to take the air. The sea was boring, the view only distant foggy islands. I found nothing there to cheer me as this detestable vessel bears me ever farther away from the lofty white spires of Blessed Jamaillia City, sacred to Sa.

I have no friends aboard the ship to amuse or comfort me in my heaviness. Lady Duparge has called on me once, and I was civil, but the differences in our station make conversation difficult. Lord Dupage is heir to little more than his title, two ships and one estate that borders on Gerfen Swamp. Ladies Crifton and Anxory appear content with one another's company and have not called upon me at all. They are both too young to have any accomplishments to share, yet their mothers should have instructed them in their social responsibility to their betters. Both might have profited from my friendship upon our return to Jamaillia City. That they choose not to court my favour does not speak well of their intellect. Doubtless they would bore me.

I am miserable in these disgusting surroundings. Why my husband has chosen to invest his time and finances in this venture eludes me. Surely men of a more adventurous nature would better serve our Illustrious Satrap in this exploration. Nor can I understand why our children and myself must accompany him, especially in my condition. I do not think my husband gave any thought to the difficulties this voyage would pose for a woman gravid with child. As ever, he has not seen fit to discuss his decisions with me, no more than I would consult him on my artistic pursuits. Yet my ambitions must suffer to allow him to pursue his! My absence will substantially delay the completion of my 'Suspended Chimes of Stone and Metal'. The Satrap's brother will be most disappointed, for the installation was to have honoured his thirtieth birthday.

Day the 15th of the Fish Moon
Year the 14th of the most Noble and Exalted Satrap Esclepius

I have been foolish. No. I have been deceived. It is not foolishness to trust where one has every right to expect trustworthiness. When my father entrusted my hand and my fate to Lord Jathan Carrock, he believed he was a man of wealth, substance and reputation. My father blessed Sa's name that my artistic accomplishments had attracted a suitor of such lofty stature. When I bewailed the fate that wed me to a man so much my senior, my mother counselled me to accept it and to pursue my art and establish my reputation in the shelter of his influence. I honoured their wisdom. For these last ten years, as my youth and beauty faded in his shadow, I have borne him three children, and bear beneath my heart the burgeoning seed of yet another. I have been an ornament and a blessing to him, and yet he has deceived me. When I think of the hours spent managing his household, hours I could have devoted to my art, my blood seethes with bitterness.

Today, I first entreated, and then, in the throes of my duty to provide for my children, demanded that he force the captain to give us better quarters. Sending our three children out on to the deck with their nanny, he confessed that we were not willing investors in the Satrap's colonization plan but exiles given a chance to flee our disgrace. All we left behind, estates, homes, precious possessions, horses, cattle . . . all are forfeit to the Satrap, as are the items seized from us as we embarked. My genteel respectable husband is a traitor to our gentle and beloved Satrap and a plotter against the Throne Blessed by Sa.

I won this admission from him, bit by bit. He kept saying I should not bother about the politics, that it was solely his concern. He said a wife should trust her husband to manage their lives. He said that by the time the ships resupply our settlement next spring, he would have redeemed our fortune and we would return to Jamaillian society. But I kept pressing my silly woman's questions. All your holdings seized? I asked him. All? And he said it was done to save the Carrock name, so that his parents and younger brother can live with dignity, untarnished by the scandal. A small estate remains for his brother to inherit. The Satrap's Court will believe that Jathan Carrock chose to invest his entire fortune in the Satrap's venture. Only those in the Satrap's innermost circle know it was a confiscation. To win this concession, Jathan begged many hours on his knees, humbling himself and pleading forgiveness.

He went on at great length about that, as if I should be impressed. But I cared nothing for his knees. 'What of Thistlebend?' I asked. 'What of the cottage by the ford there, and the monies from it?' This I brought to him as my marriage portion, and humble though it is, I thought to see it passed to Narissa when she wed.

'Gone,' he said. 'All gone.'

'But why?' I demanded. 'I have not plotted against the Satrap. Why am I punished?'

Angrily, he said I was his wife and of course I would share his fate. I did not see why; he could not explain it, and finally told me that such a foolish woman could never understand, and bade me hold my tongue, not flap it and show my ignorance. When I protested that I am not a fool, but a well-known artist, he told me that I am now a colonist's wife, and to put my artistic pretences out of my head.

I bit my tongue to keep from shrieking at him. But within me, my heart screams in fury against this injustice. Thistlebend, where my little sisters and I waded in the water and plucked lilies to pretend we were goddesses and those our white and gold sceptres . . . Gone for Jathan Carrock's treacherous idiocy.

I had heard rumours of a discovered conspiracy against the Satrap. I paid no attention. I thought it had nothing to do with me. I would say that the punishment was just, if I and my innocent babes were not ensnared in the same net that has trapped the plotters. All the confiscated wealth has financed this expedition. The disgraced nobles were forced to join a company composed of speculators and explorers. Worse, the banished criminals in the hold, the thieves and whores and ruffians, will be released to join our company when we disembark. Such will be the society around my tender children.

Our Blessed Satrap has generously granted us a chance to redeem ourselves. Our Magnificent and Most Merciful Satrap has granted each man of the company two hundred leffers of land, to be claimed anywhere along the banks of the Rain Wild River that is our boundary with barbarous Chalced, or along the Cursed Shores. He directs us to establish our first settlement on the Rain Wild River. He chose this site for us because of the ancient legends of the Elder Kings and their Harlot Queens. Long ago, it is said, their wondrous cities lined the river. They dusted their skin with gold and wore jewels above their eyes. So the tales say. Jathan said that an ancient scroll, showing their settlements, has recently been translated. I am sceptical.

In return for this chance to carve out new fortunes for ourselves and redeem our reputations, our Glorious Satrap Esclepius asks only that we cede to him half of all that we find or produce there. In return, the Satrap will shelter us under his protective hand, prayers will be offered for our well-being, and twice yearly his revenue ships will visit our settlement to be sure we prosper. A charter for our company, signed by the Satrap's own hand, promises this.

Lords Anxory, Critton and Duparge share in our disgrace, though as lesser lords, they had less far to fall. There are other nobles aboard the other two ships of our fleet, but no one I know well. I rejoice that my dear friends do not share my fate yet I mourn that I enter exile alone. I will not count upon my husband for comfort in the disaster he has brought upon us. Few secrets are kept long at court. Is that why none of my friends came to the docks to bid me farewell?

My own mother and sister had little time to devote to my packing and farewells. They wept as they bade me farewell from my father's home, not even accompanying me to the filthy docks where this ship of banishment awaited me. Why, oh Sa, did they not tell me the truth of my fate?

At that though, a hysteria fell upon me, so that I trembled and wept, with occasional shrieks bursting from me whether I would or no. Even now, my hands tremble so violently that this desperate scrawl wanders the page. All is lost to me, home, loving parents, and most crushing, the art that gave me joy in life. The half-finished works I left behind will never be completed, and that pains me as much as a child stillborn. I live only for the day that I can return to gracious Jamaillia by the sea. At this moment – forgive me, Sa – I long to do so as a widow. Never will I forgive Jathan Carrock. Bile rises in my throat at the thought that my children must wear this traitor's name.

Day the 24th of the Fish Moon
Year the 14th of the reign of the Most Noble
and Magnificent Satrap Esclepius

Darkness fills my soul; this voyage to exile has lasted an eternity. The man I must call husband orders me to better manage our household, but I scarcely have the spirit to take up my pen. The children weep, quarrel and complain endlessly, and my maid makes no effort to amuse them. Daily her contempt grows. I would slap her disrespectful scowl from her face if I had the strength. Despite my pregnancy, she lets the children tug at me and demand my attention. All know a woman in my condition should experience a serene existence. Yesterday afternoon, when I tried to rest, she left the children napping beside me while she went out to dally with a common sailor. I awoke to Narissa crying and had to arise and sing to her until she calmed. She complains of a painful belly and a sore throat. No sooner was she settled than both Petrus and Carlmin awoke and started some boyish tussling that completely frayed my spirit: I was exhausted and at the edge of hysteria before she returned. When I chided her for neglecting her duties, she saucily replied that her own mother reared nine children with no servants to aid her. As if such common drudgery were something I should aspire to! Were there anyone else to fulfil her duties, I would send her packing.

And where is Lord Carrock through all of this? Why, out on deck, consulting with the very nobles who led him into disgrace.

The food grows ever worse and the water tastes foul, but our cowardly captain will not put in to shore to seek better. My maid says that her sailor has told her that the Cursed Shore is well named, and that evil befalls those who land there as surely as it befell those who once lived there. Can even Captain Triops believe such superstitious nonsense?

Day the 27th of the Fish Moon
Year the 14th of the reign of the Most Noble
and Magnificent Satrap Esclepius

We are battered by storm. The ship reeks of the vomit of the miserable inhabitants of its bowels. The constant lurching stirs the foul waters of the bilge, so that we must breathe their stench. The captain will not allow us out on the deck at all. The air down here is damp and thick, and the beams drip water on us. Surely, I have died and entered some heathen afterlife of punishment.

Yet in all this wet, there is scarcely enough water for drinking, and none for washing. Clothing and bedding soiled with sickness must be rinsed out in seawater that leaves it stiff and stained with salt. Little Narissa has been most miserable of the children. She has ceased vomiting but has scarcely stirred from her pallet today, poor little creature. Please, Sa, let this horrid rocking and sloshing end soon.

Day the 29th of the Fish Moon
Year the 14th of the reign of the Most Noble
and Magnificent Satrap Esclepius

My child is dead. Narissa, my only daughter, is gone. Sa, have mercy upon me, and visit your justice upon treacherous Lord Jathan Carrock, for his evil has been the cause of all my woe! They wrapped my little girl in canvas and sent her and two others into the waters, and the sailors scarce paused in their labours to notice their passing. I think I went a little mad then. Lord Carrock seized me in his arms when I tried to follow her into the sea. I fought him, but he was too strong for me. I remain trapped in this life his treachery has condemned me to endure.

Day the 7th of the Plough Moon
Year the 14th of the reign of the Most Noble and
Magnificent Satrap Esclepius

My child is still dead. Ah, such a foolish thought to write, and yet still it seems impossible to me. Narissa, Narissa, you cannot be gone for ever. Surely this is some monstrous dream from which I will awake!

Today, because I sat weeping, my husband pushed this book at me and said 'Write a poem to comfort yourself. Hide in your art until you feel better. Do anything, but stop weeping!' As if he offered a squalling baby a sugar teat. As if art took you away from life rather than plunging you headlong into it! Jathan reproached me for my grief, saying that my reckless mourning frightens our sons and threatens the babe in my womb. As if he truly cared! Had he cared for us as a husband and a father, never would he have betrayed our dear Satrap and condemned us to this fate.

But, to stop his scowl, I will sit here and write for a time, like a good wife.

A full dozen of the passengers and two crewmen have died of the flux. Of one hundred and sixteen who began this voyage, ninety-two now remain. The weather has calmed but the warm sunlight on the deck only mocks my sorrow. A haze hangs over the sea and to the west the distant mountains smoke.

Day the 18th of the Plough Moon
Year the 14th of the reign of the Most Noble
and Magnificent Satrap Esclepius

I have no spirit to write, yet there is nothing else to occupy my weary mind. I, who once composed the wittiest prose and most soaring poetry, now plod word by word down a page.

Some days ago we reached the river mouth; I did not note the date, such has been my gloom. All the men cheered when we sighted it. Some spoke of gold, others of legendary cities to plunder, and still others of virgin timber and farmland awaiting us. I thought it marked an end to our voyage, but still it drags on.

At first the rising tide aided our upriver progress. Now the crew must labour at their oars for every ship-length we gain. The prisoners have been taken from their chains and utilized as rowers in tiny boats. They row upriver and set anchors and drag us against the current. By night, we anchor and listen to the rush of the water and the shrieks of unseen creatures from the jungle on the shore. Daily the scenery grows both more fantastic and threatening. The trees on the banks stand twice as tall as our mast, and the ones behind them are taller still. When the river narrows, they cast deep shadows over us. Our view is a near impenetrable wall of greenery. Our search for a kindly shore seems folly. I see no sign that any people have ever lived here. The only creatures are bright birds, large lizards that sun themselves on the tree roots at the water's edge, and something that whoops and scuttles in the treetops. There are no gentle meadows or firm shores, only marshy banks and rank vegetation. Immense trees root stilt-like in the water and dangling vines festoon them, trailing in the chalky water. Some have flowers that gleam white even in the night. They hang, fleshy and thick, and the wind carries their sweet, carnal breath. Stinging insects torment us and the oarsmen are subject to painful rashes. The river water is not potable; worse, it eats at both flesh and wood, softening oars and ulcerating flesh. If left to stand in vessels, the top layer of the water becomes drinkable, but the residue swiftly eats into leaks in the bucket. Those who drink it complain of headaches and wild dreams. One criminal raved of 'lovely serpents' and then threw himself overboard. Two crewmen have been confined in chains because of their wild talk.

I see no end to this horrid journeying. We have lost sight of our two companion vessels. Captain Triops is supposed to put us off at a safe landing that offers opportunity for a settlement and farming. The company's hope of open sunny meadows and gentle hills fades with every passing day. The captain says that this fresh water is bad for his ship's hull. He wishes to put us ashore in the swamp, saying that the trees on the shore may be concealing higher land and open forest. Our men argue against this, and often unroll the charter the Satrap has given us and point out what was promised to us. He counters by showing the orders the Satrap gave him. It speaks of landmarks that don't exist, navigable channels that are shallow and rocky, and cities where only jungle crawls. Sa's priests made this translation and they cannot lie. But something is very wrong.

The entire ship broods. Quarrels are frequent, the crew mutters against the captain. A terrible nervousness afflicts me, so that tears are never far away. Petrus suffers from nightmares and Carlmin, always a reclusive child, has become near mute.

Oh, Fair Jamaillia, city of my birth, will I ever again see your rolling hills and graceful spires? Mother, Father, do you mourn me as lost to you for ever?

And this great splotch is Petrus jostling me as he climbs up on my lap, saying he is bored. My maid is next to useless. She does little to earn all the food she devours, and then she is off, to slink about the ship like a cat in heat. Yesterday, I told her that if she got with child from her immoral passions, I would immediately turn her out. She dared to say she did not care, for her days in my service were numbered. Does the foolish slat forget that she is indentured to us for another five years?

Day the 22nd of the Plough Moon
Year the 14th of the reign of the Most Noble
and Magnificent Satrap Esclepius

It has happened as I feared. I crouch on a great knee of root, my writing desk a chest of my meagre possessions. The tree at my back is as big around as a tower. Strands and tangle of roots, some as big around as barrels, anchor it in the swampy ground. I perch on one to save my skirts from the damp and tussocky earth. At least on the ship, in the middle of the river, we were blessed with sunlight from above. Here, the foliage overshadows us, an eternal twilight.

Captain Triops has marooned us here in the swamp. He claimed that his ship was taking on water, and his only choice was to lighten his load and flee this corrosive river. When we refused to disembark, there was violence as the crew forced us from the ship. After one of our men was thrown overboard and swept away, our will to resist vanished. The stock that was to sustain us they kept. One of our men frantically seized the cage of messenger birds and fought for it. In the tussle, the cage broke, and all our birds rose in a flock to disappear. The crew threw off the crates of tools, seed and provisions that were supposed to aid us in establishing our colony. They did it to lighten the ship, not to help us. Many fell in deep water, out of reach. The men have salvaged what they could of those that fell on the soft riverside. The muck has sucked the rest down. Now we are seventy-two souls in this forsaken place, of whom forty are able-bodied men.

Great trees tower over us. The land trembles under our feet like a crust on a pudding, and where the men marched over it to gather our possessions, water now seeps, filling their footprints.

The current swept the ship and our faithless captain swiftly from our sight. Some say we must stay where we are, beside the river, and watch for the other two ships. Surely, they say, they will help us. I think we must move deeper into the forest, seeking firmer land and relief from the biting insects. But I am a woman, with no say in this.

The men hold council now, to decide leadership of our company. Jathan Carrock put himself forward, as being of the noblest birth, but he was shouted down by others, former prisoners, tradesmen and speculators who said that his father's name had no value here. They mocked him, for all seem to know the 'secret' that we are disgraced in Jamaillia. I walked away from watching them, feeling bitter.

My own situation is a desperate one. My feckless maid did not leave the ship with us, but stayed aboard, a sailor's whore. I wish her all she deserves! And now Petrus and Carlmin cling to me, complaining that the water has soaked their shoes and their feet sting from the damp. When I shall have a moment to myself again, I do not know. I curse the artist in me, for as I look up at the slanting beam of sunlight slicing through the intervening layers of branch and leaf, I see a wild and dangerous beauty to this place. Did I give in to it, I fear it could be as seductive as the raw glance of a rough man.

I do not know where such thoughts come from. I simply want to go home.

Somewhere on the leaves above us, it is raining.

Day the 24th of the Plough Moon
Year the 14th of the reign of the Most Noble
and Magnificent Satrap Esclepius

I was jolted from sleep before dawn, thrown out of a vivid dream of a foreign street festival. It was as if the earth leaped sideways beneath us. Then, when the sun was fairly up in the unseen sky, we again felt the land tremble. The earthquake passed through the Rain Wild about us like a wave. I have experienced earthquakes before, but in this gelid region, the tremor seemed stronger and more threatening. It is easy to imagine this marshy ground gulping us down like a yellow carp swallowing a breadcrumb.

Despite our inland trek, the land remains swampy and treacherous beneath our feet. Today, I came face to face with a snake hanging down from a tangle of green. My heart was seized both by his beauty and my terror. How effortlessly he lifted himself from his perusal of me to continue his journey along the intertwining branches overhead. Would that I could cross this land as effortlessly!

Day the 27th of the Plough Moon
Year the 14th of the reign of the Most Noble
and Magnificent Satrap Esclepius

I write while perched in a tree like one of the bright parrots that share the branch with me. I feel both ridiculous and exhilarated, despite hunger, thirst and great weariness. Perhaps my headiness is a side effect of starvation.

For five days, we have trekked ponderously through soft ground and thick brush, away from the river, seeking dryer ground. Some of our party protest about this, saying that when our promised ship comes in spring, it will not be able to find us. I hold my tongue, but I doubt that any ship will come up this river again.

Moving inland did not improve our lot. The ground remains tremulous and boggy. By the time our entire party has passed over it, we leave a track of mud and standing water behind us. The damp inflames our feet and rots the fabric of my skirt. All the women go draggle-hemmed now.

We have abandoned whatever we could not carry. Every one of us, man, woman and child, carries as much as possible. The little ones grow weary. I feel the child inside me grow heavier with each sucking step.

The men have formed a Council to rule us. Each man is to have one vote in it. I regard this ignoring of the natural order as perilous, yet there is no way for the outcast nobles to assert their right to rule. Jathan told me privately that we do best to let this happen, for soon enough the company will see that common farmers, pick-pockets and adventurers are not suited to rule. For now, we heed their rules. The Council has gathered the dwindling food supplies into a common hoard. We are parcelled out a pittance each day. The Council says that all men will share the work equally. Thus Jathan must stand a night watch with his fellows as if he were a common soldier. The men stand watch in pairs, for a sole watchman is more prone to the strange madness that lurks in this place. We speak little of it, but all have had strange dreams, and some of our company seem to be wandering in their minds. The men blame the water.

There is talk of sending out exploring parties to find a good dry site for our settlement.

I have no faith in their brave plans. This wild place does not care for our rules or Council.

We have found little here to sustain us. The vegetation is strange, and the only animal life we have seen moves in the higher reaches of the trees. Yet amid this wild and tangled sprawl, there is still beauty, if one has an eye for it. The sunlight that reaches us through the canopy of the trees is gentle and dappled, illuminating the feathery mosses that drape from the vines. One moment I curse it as we struggle through its clinging nets, and in the next, I see it as dusky green lace. Yesterday, despite my weariness and Jathan's impatience, I paused to enjoy the beauty of a flowering vine. In examining it, I noticed that each trumpet-like flower cupped a small quantity of rainwater, sweetened by the flower's nectar. Sa forgive me that I and my children drank well from many of the blossoms before I told the others of my find. We have also found mushrooms that grow like shelves on the tree trunks, and a vine that has red berries. It is not enough.

It is to my credit that we sleep dry tonight. I dreaded another night of sleeping on the damp ground, awaking wet and itching, or huddled atop our possessions as they slowly sink into the marshy ground. This evening, as the shadows began to deepen, I noticed bird nests dangling like swinging purses from some of the tree limbs. Well do I know how cleverly Petrus can climb furniture and even drapes. Selecting a tree with several stout branches almost at a level, I challenged my son to see if he could reach them. He clung to the vines that draped the tree while his little feet found purchase on the rough bark. Soon he sat high above us on a very thick limb, swinging his feet and laughing to see us stare.

I bade Jathan follow his son, and take with him the damask drapes that I have carried so far. Others soon saw my plan. Slings of all kinds now hang like bright fruit in these dense trees. Some sleep on the wider branches or in the crotches of the trees, others in hammocks. It is precarious rest, but dry.

All praised me. 'My wife has always been clever,' Jathan declared, as if to take the credit from me, and so I reminded him, 'I have a name of my own. I was Carillion Waljin long before I was Lady Carrock! Some of my best-known pieces as an artist, "Suspended Basins" and "Floating Lanterns" required just such a knowledge of balance and support! The difference is one of scale, not property.' At this, several of the women in our party gasped, deeming me a braggart, but Lady

Duparge exclaimed, 'She is right! I have always admired Lady Carrock's work.'

Then one rough fellow was so bold as to add, 'She will be just as clever as Trader Carrock's wife, for we will have no lords and ladies here.'

It was a sobering thought to me and yet I fear he has the right of it. Birth and breeding count for little here. Already they have given a vote to common men, less educated than Lady Duparge or I. A farmer has more say in our plans than I do.

And what did my husband mutter to me? 'You shamed me by calling attention to yourself. Such vanity to boast of your "art accomplishments". Occupy yourself with your children's needs, not bragging of yourself.' And so he put me in my place.

What is to become of us? What good to sleep dry if our bellies are empty and our throats dry? I pity so the child inside me. All the men cried 'Caution!' to one another as they used a hoist and sling to lift me to this perch. Yet all the caution in the world cannot save this babe from the wilderness being his birthplace. I miss my Narissa still, and yet I think her end was kinder than what this strange forest may visit upon us.

Day the 29th of the Plough Moon
Year the 14th of the reign of the Most Noble
and Magnificent Satrap Esclepius

I ate another lizard tonight. It shames me to admit it. The first time, I did it with no more thought than a cat pouncing on a bird. During a rest time, I noticed the tiny creature on a fern frond. It was green as a jewel and so still. Only the glitter of its bright eye and the tiny pulse of life at its throat betrayed it to me. Swift as a snake, I struck. I caught it in my hand, and in an instant I cupped its soft belly against my mouth. I bit into it, and it was bitter, rank and sweet all at once. I crunched it down, bones and all, as if it were a steamed lark from the Satrap's banquet table. Afterwards, I could not believe I had done it. I expected to feel ill, but I did not. Nevertheless, I felt too shamed to tell anyone what I had done. Such food seems unfit for a civilized human, let alone the manner in which I devoured it. I told myself it was the demands of the child growing in me, a momentary aberration brought on by gnawing hunger. I resolved never to do it again, and I put it out of my mind.

But tonight, I did. He was a slender grey fellow, the colour of the tree. He saw my darting hand and hid in a crack of the bark, but I dragged him out by his tail. I held him pinched between my finger and thumb. He struggled wildly and then grew still, knowing it was useless. I looked at him closely, thinking that if I did so, then I could let him go. He was beautiful, his gleaming eyes, his tiny claws and lashing tail. His back was grey and rough as the tree bark, but his soft little belly was the colour of cream. There was a blush of blue on the soft curve of his throat and a pale stripe of it down his belly. The scales of his belly were tiny and smooth when I pressed my tongue against them. I felt the pattering of his tiny heart and smelled the stench of his fear as his little claws scrabbled against my chapped lips. It was all so familiar somehow. Then I closed my eyes and bit into him, holding both my hands over my mouth to be sure no morsel escaped. There was a tiny smear of blood on my palm afterwards. I licked it off. No one saw.

Sa, sweet Lord of all, what am I becoming? What prompts me to behave this way? The privation of hunger or the contagious wildness of this place? I hardly know myself. The dreams that plague my sleep are not those of a Jamaillian lady. The waters of the earth scald my hands and sear my feet, until they heal rough as cobs. I fear what my face and hair must look like.

Day the 2nd of the Greening Moon
Year the 14th of the reign of the Most Noble
and Magnificent Satrap Esclepius

A boy died last night. We were all shocked. He simply did not wake up this morning. He was a healthy lad of about twelve. Durgan was his name, and though he was only a tradesman's son, I share his parents' grief quite strongly. Petrus had followed him about, and seems very shaken by his death. He whispered to me that he dreamed last night that the land remembered him. When I asked what he meant by that, he could not explain, but said that perhaps Durgan had died because this place didn't want him. He made no sense to me, but he repeated himself insistently until I nodded and said perhaps he was right. Sweet Sa, do not let the madness be taking my boy. It frightens me so. Perhaps it is good that my boy will no longer seek the companionship of such a common lad, yet Durgan had a wide smile and a ready laugh that we will miss.

As fast as the men dug a grave, it welled full of murky water. At last his mother had to be taken away while his father condemned his son's body to the water and muck. As we asked Sa's peace on him, the child inside me kicked angrily. It frightened me.

Day the 8th of the Greening Moon
(I think. Marthi Duparge says it is the 9th.)
**Year the 14th of the reign of the Most Noble
and Magnificent Satrap Esclepius**

We have found a patch of dryer ground and most of us will rest here for a few days while a chosen party of men scouts for a better place. Our refuge is little more than a firmer island amid the swamp. We have learned that a certain type of needled bush indicates firmer ground, and here it is quite dense. It is resinous enough to burn even when green. It produces a dense and choking smoke, but it keeps the biting insects at bay.

Jathan is one of our scouts. With our child soon to be born, I thought he should stay here to help me care for our boys. He said he must go, to establish himself as a leader among the company. Lord Duparge is also to go as a scout. As Lady Marthi Duparge is also with child, Jathan said we could help one another. Such a young wife as she cannot be of much use at a birthing, and yet her company will be preferable to none at all. All of us women have drawn closer as privation has forced us to share our paltry resources for the good of our children.

Another of the women, a weaver's wife, has devised a way to make mats from the abundant vines. I have begun to learn this, for there is little else I can do, so heavy have I become. The mats can be used as bed-pallets and also laced together into screens for shelter. All the nearby trees are smooth-barked, with the branches beginning very high, so we must contrive what shelter we can on the ground. Several women joined us and it was pleasant and almost homey to sit together and talk and work with our hands. The men laughed at us as we raised our woven walls, asking what such frail barriers can keep out. I felt foolish, yet as dark fell, we took comfort in our flimsy cottage. Sewet the weaver has a fine singing voice, and brought tears to my eyes as she sang her youngest to sleep with the old song of Praise to Sa in Tribulation. It seems a lifetime since last I heard music. How long must my children live with no culture and no tutors save the merciless judgment of this wild place?

As much as I disdain Jathan Carrock for bringing about our exile, I miss him this evening.

Day the 12th or 13th of the Greening Moon
Year the 14th of the reign of the Most Noble
and Magnificent Satrap Esclepius

A madness came upon our camp last night. It began with a woman starting up in the darkness, shouting, 'Hark! Hark! Does no one else hear their singing?' Her husband tried to quiet her, but then a young boy exclaimed that he had heard the singing for several nights now. Then he plunged off into the darkness as if he knew where he was going. His mother ran after him. Then the woman broke free of her husband, and raced off into the swamp. Three others went after her, not to bring her back but crying, 'Wait, wait, we will go with you!'

I rose and held on to both my sons, lest the madness take them. A peculiar undark suffuses this jungle by night. The fireflies are familiar, but not an odd spider that leaves a glob of glowing spittle in the middle of its web. Tiny insects fly right into it, just as moths will seek a lantern's fire. There is also a dangling moss that gleams pale and cold. I dare not let my lads know how gruesome I find it. I told them I shivered because of the chill, and in concern for those poor benighted wretches lost in the swamp. Yet it chilled me even more to hear little Carlmin speak of how lovely the jungle was by night, and how sweet the scent of the night-blooming flowers. He said he remembered when I used to make cakes flavoured with those flowers. We never had such flowers in Jamaillia City, yet as he said it, I almost recalled little brown cakes, soft in the middle and crispy brown at the edges. Even as I write the words, I almost recall how I shaped them into blossoms before I cooked them in hot bubbling fat.

Never have I done such cooking, I swear.

As of midday, there is no sign of those the night-madness took. Searchers went after them, but the search party returned wet and insect-bitten and disconsolate. The jungle has swallowed them. The woman left behind a small boy who has been wailing for her most of the day.

I have told no one of the music that haunts my dreams.

Day the 14th or 15th of the Greening Moon
Year the 14th of the reign of the Most Noble
and Magnificent Satrap Esclepius

Our scouts still have not returned. By day, we put a fine face on it for the children, but by night Marthi Duparge and I share our fears while my boys sleep. Surely our men should have returned by now, if only to say that they found no better place than this boggy island.

Last night Marthi wept and said that the Satrap deliberately sent us to our deaths. I was shocked. Sa's priests translated the ancient scrolls that told of cities on this river. Men dedicated to Sa cannot lie. But perhaps they erred, and grievously enough to cost our lives.

There is no plenty here, only strangeness that lurks by day and prowls amongst our huts by night. Almost every night, one or two folk awake shrieking from nightmares they cannot recall. A young woman of easy virtue has gone missing for two days now. She was a whore for coin in Jamaillia's streets, and continued her trade here, asking food from the men who used her. We do not know if she wandered off or was killed by one of our own party. We do not know if we harbour a murderer in our midst, or if this terrible land has claimed another victim.

We mothers suffer the most, for our children beg us for more than the meagre rations allotted us. The supplies from the ship are gone. I forage daily, my sons at my side. I found a heaped mound of loosened earth a few days ago, and poking through it, discovered eggs with brown speckled shells. There were almost fifty of them, and though some of the men refused them, saying they would not eat snake or lizard eggs, none of the mothers did. One lily-like plant is difficult to pull from the shallows, for inevitably I am splashed with stinging water and the roots are long and fibrous. There are nodules on the roots, no bigger than large pearls, and these have a pleasantly peppery flavour. Sewet has been working with the roots themselves, making baskets and recently a coarse cloth. That will be welcome. Our skirts are in tatters up to our calves, and our shoes grow thin as paper. All were surprised when I found the lily pearls. Several people asked how I knew they were edible.

I had no answer to that. The flowers looked familiar somehow. I cannot say what made me pull up the roots nor what prompted me to pick the pearly nodules and put them in my mouth.

The men who stayed here constantly complain of standing watches by night and keeping our fires alight, but in truth I think we women work as hard. It is taxing to keep our youngsters safe and fed and clean in these circumstances. I confess I have learned much of managing my boys from Chellia. She was a laundress in Jamaillia, and yet here she has become my friend, and we share a little hut we have built for the five children and ourselves. Her man, one Ethe, is also among the explorers. Yet she keeps a cheerful face and insists that her three youngsters help with the daily tasks. Our older boys we send out together to gather dry dead wood for the fire. We caution them never to go beyond the sounds of the camp, but both Petrus and Olpey complain that no dry wood remains nearby. Her daughters Piet and Likea watch Carlmin while Chellia and I harvest the water from the trumpet flowers and scavenge whatever mushrooms we can find. We have found a bark that makes a spicy tea; it helps to stave off hunger as well.

I am grateful for her company; both Marthi and I will welcome her help when birth comes upon us. Yet her boy Olpey is older than my Petrus and leading him into bold and reckless ways. Yesterday the two were gone until dusk, and then returned with only an armful of firewood each. They told of hearing distant music and following it. I am sure they ventured deeper into this swampy forest than is wise. I scolded them both, and Petrus was daunted but Olpey snidely asked his mother what else should he do, stay here in the mud and grow roots? I was shocked to hear him speak so to his mother. I am sure that he is the influence behind Petrus's nightmares, for Olpey loves telling wild tales full of parasitic spectres that float as night fogs and lizards that suck blood. I do not want Petrus influenced by such superstitious nonsense and yet, what can I do? The boys must fetch wood for us, and I cannot send him alone. All of the older boys of our company are given such chores. It grieves me to see Petrus, the descendant of two illustrious bloodlines, put to such work alongside common boys. I fear he will be ruined long before we return to Jamaillia.

And why has Jathan not returned to us? What has become of our men?

Day the 19th or 20th of the Greening Moon
Year the 14th of the reign of the Most Noble
and Magnificent Satrap Esclepius

Today three muddy men and a woman walked into our campsite. When I heard the hubbub, my heart leapt in excitement, for I thought our men had returned. Instead, I was shocked to discover that this party was from one of the other ships.

Captain, crew and passengers were flung into the river one evening when the ship simply came apart. They had little opportunity to salvage supplies from the foundering ship. They lost more than half the souls aboard it. Of those that made it to shore, many took the madness, and in the days following the shipwreck, ended their own lives or vanished into the wilds.

Many of them died in the first few nights, for they could find no solid ground at all. I covered my ears when they spoke of people falling and literally drowning in the mud. Some woke witless and raving after experiencing strange dreams. Some recovered, but others wandered off into the swamp, never to be seen again. These three were the vanguard of those who remained alive. Minutes later, others began to arrive. They came in threes and fours, bedraggled and bug-bitten, and horribly scalded from prolonged contact with the river water. There are sixty-two of them. A few are disgraced nobles, and others are commoners who thought to find a new life. The specula-tors who invested wealth in this expedition in the hope of making fortunes seem the most bitter.

The captain did not survive the first night. Those sailors who did are distressed and bewildered by their sudden plunge into exile. Some of them hold themselves apart from the 'colonists', as they call us. Others seem to understand they must claim a place among us or perish.

Some of our party drew apart and muttered that we had little enough shelter and victuals for ourselves, but most of us shared readily. I had never thought to see people more desperate than we were. I feel that all profited from it, and Marthi and I perhaps most of all. Ser, an expe-rienced midwife, was of their party. They also had a thatcher, their ship's carpenter, and men with hunting skills. The sailors are fit and hearty creatures and may adapt enough to be useful.

Still no sign of our own men.

Day the 26th of the Greening Moon
Year the 14th of the reign of the Most Noble
and Magnificent Satrap Esclepius

My time came. The child was born. I did not even see her before the midwife took her away. Marthi and Chellia and Ser the midwife all say she was born dead, yet I am sure I heard her wail once. I was weary and close to fainting, but surely I recall what I heard. My babe cried out for me before she died.

Chellia says it is not so, that the babe was born blue and still. I have asked why I could not have held her once before they gave her to the earth? The midwife said I would grieve less that way. But her face goes pale whenever I ask about it. Marthi does not speak of it. Does she fear her own time, or do they keep something from me? Why, Sa, have you taken both my daughters from me so cruelly?

Jathan will hear of it when he returns. Perhaps if he had been here, to help me in my last heavy days, I would not have had to toil so hard. Perhaps my little girl could have lived. But he was not with me then and he is not with me now. And who will watch my boys, find food for them and make sure they return safe each night while I must lie here and bleed for a babe that did not live?

Day the 1st of the Grain Moon
Year the 14th of the reign of the Most Noble
and Magnificent Satrap Esclepius

I have risen from my lying-in. I feel that my heart is buried with my child. Did I carry her so far and through such hardship for nothing?

Our camp is now so crowded with newcomers that one can scarce thread a path through the makeshift shelters. Little Carlmin, separated from me for my lying-in, now follows me like a thin little shadow. Petrus has made fast his friendship with Olpey and pays no mind to my words at all. When I bid him stay close to camp, he defies me by venturing ever deeper into the swamps. Chellia tells me, let him go. The boys are the darlings of the camp for discovering dangling bunches of sour little berries. The tiny fruits are bright yellow and sour as bile, but even such foul food is welcome to folk as hungry as we are. Still, it infuriates me that all encourage my son to disobey me. Do not they listen to the wild tales the boys tell, of strange music, distantly heard? The boys brag they will find the source of it, and my mother's heart knows it is nothing natural and good that lures them ever deeper into this pestilential jungle.

The camp grows worse every day. Paths are churned to muck, and grow wider and more muddy. Too many people do nothing to better our lot. They live as best they can today, making no provision for tomorrow, relying on the rest of us for food. Some sit and stare, some pray and weep. Do they expect Sa himself to swoop down and save them? Last night a family was found dead, all five of them, huddled around the base of a tree under a pitiful drape of mats. There is no sign of what killed them. No one speaks of what we all fear: there is an insidious madness in the water, or perhaps it comes up from the ground itself, creeping into our dreams as unearthly music. I awaken from dreams of a strange city, thinking I am someone else, somewhere else. And when I open my eyes to mud and insects and hunger, sometimes I long to close them again and simply go back to my dream. Is that what befell that hapless family? All their eyes were wide open and staring when we discovered them. We let their bodies go into the river. The Council took what little goods they had and divided them, but many grumble that the Council only distributed the salvage to their own friends and not to those most in need. Discontent grows with this council of a few who impose rule on all of us.

Our doubtful refuge is starting to fail us. Even the paltry weight of our woven huts turns the fragile sod to mud. I used to speak disdainfully of those who lived in squalor, saying, 'They live like animals'. But in truth, the beasts of this jungle live more graciously than we do. I envy the spiders their webs suspended in the shafts of sunlight overhead. I envy the birds whose woven nests dangle over our heads, out of reach of mud and snakes. I envy even the splay-footed marsh-rabbits, as our hunters call the little game animals that scamper so elusively over the matted reeds and floating leaves of the shallows. By day, the earth sucks at my feet with every step I take. By night, our sleeping pallets sink into the earth, and we wake wet. A solution must be found, but all the others say, 'Wait. Our explorers will return and lead us to a better place.'

I think the only better place they have found is the bosom of Sa. So may we all go. Will I ever see balmy Jamaillia again, ever walk in a garden of kindly plants, ever again be free to eat to satiation and drink without regard for the morrow? I understand the temptation to evade my life by dozing away the hours in dreams of a better place. Only my sons keep me anchored in this world.

Day the 16th of the Grain Moon
Year the 14th of the reign of the Most Noble
and Magnificent Satrap Esclepius

What the waking mind does not perceive, the heart already knows. In a dream, I moved like the wind through these Rain Wilds, skimming over the soft ground and then sweeping through the swaying branches of the trees. Unhindered by muck and caustic water, I could suddenly see the many-layered beauty of our surroundings. I balanced, teetering like a bird, on a frond of fern. Some spirit of the Rain Wilds whispered to me, 'Try to master it and it will engulf you. Become a part of it, and live.'

I do not know that my waking mind believes any of that. My heart cries out for the white spires of Jamaillia, for the gentle blue waters of her harbour, for her shady walks and sunny squares. I hunger for music and art, for wine and poetry, for food that I did not scavenge from the crawl and tangle of this forbidding jungle. I hunger for beauty in place of squalor.

I did not gather food or water today. Instead, I sacrificed two pages of this journal to sketch dwellings suitable for this unforgiving place. I also designed floating walkways to link our homes. It will require some cutting of trees and shaping of lumber. When I showed them, some people mocked me, saying the work is too great for such a small group of people. Some pointed out that our tools have rapidly corroded here. I retorted that we must use our tools now to create shelters that will not fail us when our tools are gone.

Some willingly looked at my sketches, but then shrugged, saying what sense to work so hard when our scouts may return any day to lead us to a better location? We cannot, they said, live in this swamp for ever. I retorted they were right, that if we did not bestir ourselves, we would die here. I did not, for fear of provoking fate, utter my darkest fear: That there is nothing but swamp for leagues under these trees, and that our explorers will never return.

Most people stalked away from my scorn, but two men stood and berated me, asking me what decent Jamaillian woman would raise her voice in anger before men. They were only commoners, as were the wives that stood and nodded behind them. Still, I could not restrain my tears, nor how my voice shook as I demanded what sort of men were they, to send my boys into the jungle to forage food for them while they sat on their heels and waited for someone else to solve their problems? They lifted their hands and made the sign for a shamed woman at me, as if I were a street girl. Then all walked away from me.

I do not care. I will prove them wrong.

Day the 24th of the Grain Moon
Year the 14th of the reign of the Most Noble
and Magnificent Satrap Esclepius

I am torn between elation and grief. My baby is dead, Jathan is still missing, and yet today I feel more triumph than I did at any blessing of my artwork. Chellia, Marthi and little Carlmin have toiled alongside me. Sewet the weaver woman has offered refinements to my experiments. Piet and Likea have gathered food in my stead. Carlmin's small hands have amazed me with their agility and warmed my heart with his determination to help. In this effort, Carlmin has shown himself the son of my soul.

We have floored a large hut with a crosshatching of mats atop a bed of reeds and thin branches. This spreads the weight, so that we float atop the spongy ground as gently as the matted reeds float upon the neighbouring waters. While other shelters sink daily and must be moved, ours has gone four days without settling. Today, satisfied that our home will last, we began further improvements. Without tools, we have broken down small saplings and torn their branches from them. Pieces of their trunks, woven with lily root into a horizontal ladder, form the basis for the walkways around our hut. Layers of woven matting to be added tomorrow will further strengthen our flimsy walkways. The trick, I am convinced, is to spread the weight of the traffic out over the greatest possible area, much as the marsh-rabbits do with their splayed feet. Over the wettest section, behind our hut, we have suspended the walkway, anchoring it like a spiderweb from one tree to its neighbours as best we can. It is difficult, for the girth of the trees is great and the bark smooth. Twice it gave way as we struggled to secure it, and some of those watching jeered, but on our third effort, it held. Not only did we cross over it several times in safety, we were able to stand upon our swaying bridge and look out over the rest of the settlement. It was no lofty view, for we were no more than waist high above the ground, but even so, it gave me a perspective on our misery. Space is wasted with wandering paths and haphazard placement of huts. One of the sailors came over to inspect our effort, with much rocking on his heels and chewing on a twig. Then he had the effrontery to change half our knots. 'That'll hold, madam,' he told me. 'But not for long and not under heavy use. We need better rigging to fasten to. Look up. That's where we need to be, rigging on to all those branches up there.'

I looked up to the dizzying heights where the branches begin and told him that, without wings, none of us could reach those heights. He grinned and said, 'I know a man could do it. If anyone thought it worth his trying.' Then he made one of those ridiculous sailor bows and wandered off.

We must soon take action, for this shivering island diminishes daily. The ground is overtrodden and water stands in our paths. I must be mad to try; I am an artist, not an engineer nor a builder. And yet if no one else steps forward, I am driven to the attempt. If I fail, I will fail having tried.

Day the 5th or 6th of the Prayer Moon
Year the 14th of the reign of the Most Noble
and Magnificent Satrap Esclepius

Today one of my bridges fell. Three men were plunged into the swamp, and one broke a leg. He blamed his mishap upon me and declared that this is what happens when women try their knitting skills as construction. His wife joined in his accusations. But I did not shrink before them. I told them that I did not demand that he use my walk-ways, and that any who had not contributed to them and yet dared to walk upon them deserved whatever fate Sa sent them for laziness and ingratitude.

Someone shouted 'Blasphemy!' but someone else shouted 'Truth is Sa's sword.' I felt vindicated. My workforce has grown enough to be split into two parties. I shall put Sewet in charge of the second one, and woe betide any man who derides my choice. Her weaving skills have proven themselves.

Tomorrow we hope to start raising the first supports for my Great Platforms into the trees. I could fail most spectacularly. The logs are heavier, and we have no true rope for the hoisting, but only lines of braided root. The sailor has devised several crude blocks-and-tackles for us. He and my Petrus were the ones who scaled the smooth trunk of a tree to where the immense limbs branch overhead. They tapped in pegs as they went, but even so, my heart shook to see them venture so high. Retyo the sailor says that his tackles will make our strength sufficient for any task. I wait to see that. I fear they will lead only to our woven lines fraying all the more. I should be sleeping and yet I lie here, wondering if we have sufficient line to hoist our beams. Will our rope ladders stand up to the daily use of workers? What have I undertaken? If any fall from such a height, they will surely die. Yet summer must end, and when winter rains come, we must have a dry retreat.

Day the 12th or 13th of the Prayer Moon
Year the 14th of Satrap Esclepius

Failure upon failure upon failure. I scarce have the spirit to write of it. Retyo the sailor says we must count as a success that no one has been injured. When our first platform fell, it sank itself into the soft earth rather than breaking into pieces. He cheerfully said that proved the platform's strength. He is a resourceful young man, intelligent despite his lack of education. I asked him today if he felt bitter that Fate had trapped him into building a colony in the Rain Wilds instead of sailing. He shrugged and grinned. He had been a tinker and a share-farmer before he was a sailor, so he says he has no idea what fate is rightfully his. He feels entitled to take any of them and turn it to his advantage. I wish I had his spirit.

Idlers in our company gawk and mock us. Their scepticism corrodes my strength much as the chalky water sears the skin. Those who complain most about our situation do the least to better it. 'Wait,' they say. 'Wait for our explorers to return and lead us to a better place.' Yet daily our situation worsens. We go almost in rags now, though Sewet experiments daily with what fibres she can pull from the vines or rub from the pith of reeds. We find barely enough food to sustain us daily, and have no reserves for the winter. The idlers eat as much as those who work daily. My boys toil alongside us each day and yet receive the same ration as those who lie about and bemoan our fate. Petrus has a spreading rash at the base of his neck. I am sure it is due to poor diet and the constant damp.

Chellia must feel the same. Her little daughters Piet and Likea are no more than bones, for unlike our boys who eat as they gather, they must be content with what is handed to them at the end of the day. Olpey has become a strange boy of late, so much so that he frightens even Petrus. Petrus still sets out with him each day, but often comes home long before Olpey. Last night, I awoke to hear Olpey softly singing in his sleep. It was a tune and a tongue that I swear I have never heard, and yet it was haunting in its familiarity.

Heavy rains today. Our huts shed the most of it. I pity those who have not made any effort to provide shelter for themselves, even as I wonder at their lack of intelligence. Two women came to our hut with three little children. Marthi and Chellia and I did not want to let them crowd in with us, yet we could not abide the pitiful shivering of the babes. So we let them in, but warned them sternly that they must help with the construction tomorrow. If they do, we will help them build a hut of their own. If not, out they must go. Perhaps we must force folk to act for their own benefit.

Day the 17th or 18th of the Prayer Moon
Year the 14th of Satrap Esclepius

We have raised and secured the first Great Platform. Sewet and Retyo have woven net ladders that dangle to the ground. It was a moment of great triumph for me to stand below and look up at the platform solidly fixed among the tree limbs. The intervening branches almost cloaked it from sight. This is my doing, I thought to myself. Retyo, Crorin, Finsk and Tremartin are the men who have done most of the hoisting and tying, but the design of the platform, how it balances lightly on the branches, putting weight only where it can be borne, and the selection of the location was my doing. I felt so proud.

It did not last long, however. Ascending a ladder made of vines that gives to each step and sways more the higher one goes is not for the faint of heart nor for a woman's meagre strength. Halfway up, my strength gave out. I clung, half swooning, and Retyo was forced to come to my rescue. It shames me that I, a married woman, wrapped my arms about his neck as if I were a little child. To my dismay, he did not take me down, but insisted on climbing up with me, so that I could see the new vista from our platform.

It was both exhilarating and disappointing. We stood far above the swampy land that has sucked at our feet for so long, yet still below the umbrella of leaves that screens out all but the strongest sunlight. I looked down on a deceptively solid-appearing floor of leaves, branches and vines. Although other immense trunks and branches impeded our view, I could suddenly see a distance into the forest in some directions. It appears to go on for ever. And yet, seeing the branches of adjacent trees nearly touching ours filled me with ambition. Our next platform will be based in three adjacent trees. A catwalk will stretch from Platform One to Platform Two. Chellia and Sewet are already weaving the safety nets that will prevent our younger children from tumbling off Platform One. When they are finished with that, I will put them to stringing our catwalks and the netting that will wall them.

The older children are swiftest to ascend and the quickest to adapt to our tree-dwelling. Already, they are horribly careless as they walk out from the platform along the huge branches that support it. After I had warned them often to be careful, Retyo gently rebuked me. 'This is their world,' he said. 'They cannot fear it. They will become as sure-footed as sailors running rigging. The branches are wider than the walkways of some towns I've visited. The only thing that prevents you from walking out along that branch is your knowledge of how far you may fall. Think instead of the wood beneath your feet.'

Under his tutelage, and gripping his arm, I did walk out along one of the branches. When we had gone some way and it began to sway under our weight, I lost my courage and fled back to the platform. Looking down, I could only glimpse the huts of our muddy little settlement below. We had ascended to a different world. The light is greater here, though still diffuse, and we are closer to both fruit and flowers. Bright-coloured birds squawk at us, as if disputing our right to be there. Their nests dangle like baskets hung in the trees. I look at their suspended homes and wonder if I cannot adapt that example to make a safe 'nest' for myself. Already I feel this new territory is mine by right of ambition and art, as if I inhabit one of my suspended sculptures. Can I imagine a town comprised of hanging cottages? Even this platform, bare as it is right now, has balance and grace.

Tomorrow I shall sit down with Retyo the sailor and Sewet the weaver. I recall the cargo nets that lifted heavy loads from the dock on to the deck of the ship. Could not a platform be placed inside such a net, the net thatched for privacy, and the whole hung from a sturdy branch, to become a lofty and private chamber here? How, then, would we provide access to the Great Platforms from such dwellings? I smile as I write this, knowing that I do not wonder if it can be done, but only how.

Both Olpey and Petrus have a rash on their scalps and down their necks. They scratch and complain and the skin is rough as scales to the touch. I can find no way to ease it for either of them, and fear that it is spreading to others. I've seen a number of the children scratching miserably.

Day the 6th or 7th of the Gold Moon
Year the 14th of Satrap Esclepius

Two events of great significance. Yet I am so weary and heartsick I scarce can write of either of them. Last night, as I fell asleep in this swinging birdcage of a home, I felt safe and almost serene. Tonight, all that is taken from me.

The first: last night Petrus woke me. Trembling, he crept under my mats beside me as if he were my little boy again. He whispered to me that Olpey was frightening him, singing songs from the city, and that he must tell me even though he had promised he would not.

Petrus and Olpey, in their ranging for food, discovered an unnaturally square mound in the forest. Petrus felt uneasy and did not wish to approach it. He could not tell me why. Olpey was drawn to it. Day after day, he insisted that they return to it. On the days when Petrus returned alone, it was because he had left Olpey exploring the mound. At some point in his poking and digging, he found a way into it. The boys have entered it several times now. Petrus describes it as a buried tower, though that made no sense to me. He said the walls are cracked and damp seeps in, but it is mostly solid. There are tapestries and old furniture, some sound, some rotted, and other signs that once people lived in it. Yet Petrus trembled as he spoke, saying that he did not think they were people like us. He says the music comes from it.

Petrus had descended only one level into it, but Olpey told him it went much deeper. Petrus was afraid to go down into the dark, but then by some magic, Olpey caused the tower to blossom with light. Olpey mocked Petrus for being fearful, and told tales of immense riches and strange objects in the depths of the tower. He claimed that ghosts spoke to him and told him its secrets, including where to find treasure. Then Olpey began to say that he had once lived in the tower, a long time ago when he was an old man.

I did not wait for morning. I woke Chellia, and after hearing my tale she woke Olpey. The boy was furious, hissing that he would never trust Petrus again and that the tower was his secret and the treasures all his, and he did not have to share it. While the night was still dark, Olpey fled, running off along one of the tree branches that have become footpaths for the children, and thence we knew not where.

When morning finally sifted through the sheltering branches, Chellia and I followed Petrus through the forest to his tower-mound. Retyo and Tremartin went with us, and little Carlmin refused to stay behind with Chellia's girls. When I saw the squared mound thrusting up from the swamp, my courage quailed inside me. Yet I did not wish Retyo to see me as a coward and so I forced myself on.

The top of the tower was heavily mossed and draped with vinery yet it was too regular a shape to blend with the jungle. On one side, the boys had pulled away vines and moss to bare a window in a stone wall. Retyo kindled the torch he had brought, and then, one after another, we cautiously clambered inside. Vegetation had penetrated the room as tendrils and roots. On the grimy floor were the muddy tracks of the boys' feet. I suspect they have both been exploring that place for far longer than Petrus admits. A bedframe festooned with rags of fabric stood in one corner of the room. Insects and mice had reduced the draperies to dangling rags.

Despite the dimness and decay, there were echoes of loveliness in the room. I seized a handful of rotted curtain and scrubbed a swath across a frieze, raising a cloud of dust. Amazement stilled my coughing. My artist's soul soared at the finely shaped and painted tiles and the delicate colours I had uncovered. But my mother's heart stood still at what was revealed. The figures were tall and thin, humans rendered as stick insects. Yet I did not think it was a conceit of the artist. Some held what might have been musical instruments or weaponry. We could not decide. In the background workers tended a reed-bed by a river like farmers harvesting a field. A woman in a great chair of gold overlooked all and seemed pleased with it. Her face was stern and yet kind; I felt I had seen her before. I would have stared longer, but Chellia demanded we search for her son.

With a sternness I did not feel, I bade Petrus show us where they had been playing. He blanched to see that I had guessed the truth, but he led us on. We left the bedchamber by a short flight of downward stairs. On the landing, there was heavy glass in two windows, but when Retyo held our torch close to one, it illuminated long white worms working in the wet soil pressed against it. How the glass has withstood the force of earth, I do not know. We entered a wide hall. Rugs crumbled into damp thread under our tread. We passed doorways, some closed, others open archways gaping with dark maws, but Petrus led us on. We came at last to the top of a stair, much grander than the first. As we descended this open staircase into a pool of darkness, I was grateful to have Retyo at my side. His calmness fostered my poor courage. The ancient cold of the stone penetrated my worn shoes and crept up my legs to my spine as if it reached for my heart. Our torch illuminated little more than our frightened faces and our whispers faded, waking ghostly echoes. We passed one landing, and then a second, but Petrus neither spoke nor faltered as he led us down. I felt as if I had walked into the throat of some great beast and was descending to its belly.

When at last we reached the bottom, our single torch could not penetrate the blackness around us. The flame fluttered in the moving air of a much larger chamber. Even in the dimness, I knew this room would have dwarfed the great ballroom of the Satrap's palace. I slowly groped my way forward, but Carlmin suddenly strode fearlessly beyond the reach of both my hand and the torchlight. I called after him, but his pattering footsteps as he hurried away was my only answer. 'Oh, follow him!' I beseeched Retyo, but as he started to, the room suddenly lit around us as if a horde of spirits had unhooded their lanterns. I gave one shriek of terror and then was struck dumb.

In the centre of the room, a great green dragon was up-reared on its hind legs. Its hind claws were sunk deep in the stone and its lashing tail stretched halfway across the room. Its emerald wings were unfurled wide and supported the ceiling high overhead. Atop its sinuous neck was a head the size of an oxcart. Intelligence glittered in its shining silver eyes. Its smaller forelimbs clutched the handle of a large basket. The basket itself was elaborately beribboned with bows of jade and streamers of ivory. And within the basket, reclining serenely, was a woman of preternatural authority. She was not beautiful; the power expressed in her made beauty irrelevant. Nor was she young and desirable. She was a woman past her middle years; yet the lines the sculptor had graved in her face seemed wisdom-furrows on her brow, and thought-lines at the corners of her eyes. Jewels had been set above her brow-lines and along the tops of her cheeks to mimic the scaling of the dragon. This was no expressionless representation of Sa's female aspect. I knew, without doubt, that this statue had been fashioned to honour a real woman and it shocked me to my bones. The dragon's supple neck was carved so that he twisted to regard her, and even his reptilian countenance showed respect for her that he carried.

I had never seen such a representation of a woman. I had heard foreign tales of Harlot Queens and women rulers, but always they had seemed fabrications of some barbarous and backward country, seductive women of evil intent. She made such legends lies. For a time, she was all I could see. Then my mind came back to me, and with it my duty.

Little Carlmin, all his teeth showing in a wide smile, stood some distance from us, his hand pressed against a panel attached to a column. His flesh looked like ice in the unnatural light. His smallness put the huge chamber into perspective, and I suddenly saw all that the dragon and woman had obscured.

The light flowed in pale stars and flying dragons across the ceiling. It crawled in vines across the walls, framing four distant doorways to darkened corridors. Dry fountains and statuary broke up the huge expanse of dusty floor. This was a great indoor plaza, a place for people to gather and talk or idly stroll among the fountains and statuary. Lesser columns supported twining vines with leaves of jade and carnelian blossoms. A sculpture of a leaping fish denied the dry fountain basin below it. Mouldering heaps of ruin scattered throughout the chamber indicated the remains of wooden structures, booths or stages. Yet neither dust nor decay could choke the chilling beauty of the place. The scale and the grace of the room left me breathless and woke a wary awe in me. Folk who created such a chamber would not perish easily. What fate had overtaken a people whose magic could still light a room years after their passing? Did the danger that destroyed them threaten us? What had it been? Where had they gone?

Were they truly gone?

As in the chamber above, it felt as if the people had simply departed, leaving all their goods behind. Again, the boys' muddy tracks on the floor betrayed that they had been here before. Most led towards a single door.

'I did not realize this place was so big.' Petrus's small voice seemed shrill in the vastness as he stared up at the lady and her dragon. He turned round in a slow circle, staring at the ceiling. 'We had to use torches here. How did you light it, Carlmin?' Petrus sounded uneasy at his small brother's knowledge.

But Carlmin didn't answer. My little one was trotting eagerly across the vast chamber, as if called to some amusement. 'Carlmin!' I cried, and my voice woke a hundred echoing ghosts. As I gawked, he vanished through one of the archways. It lit in a murky, uncertain way. I ran after him, and the others followed. I was breathless by the time I had crossed the plaza. I chased him down a dusty corridor.

As I followed him into a dim chamber, light flickered around me. My son sat at the head of a long table of guests in exotic dress. There was laughter and music. Then I blinked and empty chairs lined both sides of the table. The feast had dwindled to crusty stains in the crystal goblets and plates, but the music played on, choked and strained. I knew it from my dreams.

Carlmin spoke hollowly as he lofted a goblet in a toast, 'To my lady!' He smiled fondly as his childish gaze met unseen eyes. As he started to put it to his lips, I reached him, seized his wrist and shook the glass from his grasp. It fell to shatter in the dust.

He stared at me with eyes that did not know me. Despite how he has grown of late, I snatched him up and held him to me. His head sagged on to my shoulder and he closed his eyes, trembling. The music sagged into silence. Retyo took him from me, saying sternly, 'We should not have allowed the boy to come. The sooner we leave this place and its dying magic, the better.' He glanced about uneasily. 'Thoughts not mine tug at me, and I hear voices. I feel I have been here before, when I know I have not. We should leave this city to the spirits that haunt it.' He seemed shamed to admit his fear, but I was relieved to hear one of us speak it aloud.

Then Chellia cried that we could not leave Olpey here, to fall under whatever enchantment had seized Carlmin. Sa forgive me, all I wanted to do was seize my own children and flee. But Retyo, carrying both our torch and my son, led us on. His friend Tremartin smashed a chair against the stone floor and took up one of the legs for a club. No one asked him what use a club could be against the spiderwebs of alien memory that snagged at us. Petrus moved up to take the lead. When I glanced back, the lights in the chamber had winked out.

Through a hall and then down another flight of stairs that wound down to a smaller hall we went. Statues in niches lined the walls, with the dwindled remnants of dust-grimed candle stubs before them. Many were women, crowned and glorified like kings. Their sculpted robes glittered with tiny inset jewels, and pearls roped their hair.

The unnatural light was blue and uncertain, flickering with the threat of utter darkness. It made me oddly sleepy. I thought I heard whispering and once, as I brushed through a doorway, I heard two women singing in the distance. I shuddered with fear, and Retyo glanced back as if he, too, had heard them. Neither of us spoke. We went on. Some passages blossomed into light around us as we entered. Others remained stubbornly dark and made our failing torch seem a lie. I do not know which was more daunting to me.

We found Olpey at last. He was sitting in a little room on an opulently carved chair before a gentleman's dressing table. The gilt had fallen from the wood to scatter in flakes all round it. He looked into a mirror clouded with age; black spots had blossomed in it. Shell combs and the handle of a brush littered the table before him. A small chest was open on his lap, and looped around his neck were many pendants. His head drooped to one side but his eyes were open and staring. He was muttering to himself. As we drew near, he reached for a scent bottle and mimed dabbing himself with its long-dried perfume as he turned his face from side to side before his hazy reflection. His motions were the preening of a lordly and conceited man.

'Stop it!' his mother hissed in horror. He did not startle and almost I felt that we were the ghosts there. She seized him and shook him. At that he woke, but he woke in a terror. He cried out as he recognized her, glanced wildly about himself, and then fell into a faint. 'Oh, help me get him out of here,' poor Chellia begged.

Tremartin put Olpey's arm across his shoulders and mostly dragged the lad as we fled. The lights quenched as we left each area, as if pursuing darkness were only a step behind us. Once music swelled loudly around us, subsiding as we fled. When we finally clambered out of the window into open air, the swamp seemed a healthful place of light and freshness. I was shocked to see that most of the day had passed while we were below.

Carlmin recovered quickly in the fresh air. Tremartin spoke sharply to Olpey and shook him, at which he angrily came back to his senses. He jerked free of Tremartin, and would not speak sensibly to us. By turns sullen or defiant, he refused to explain why he had fled to the city or what he had been doing. He denied fainting. He was coldly furious with Petrus and extremely possessive of the jewelled necklaces he wore. They glittered with bright gemstones of every colour, and yet I would no more put one around my neck than I would submit to a snake's embrace. 'They are mine,' he kept exclaiming. 'My lover gave them to me, a long time ago. No one will take them from me now!'

It took all of Chellia's patience and motherly wiles to convince Olpey to return with us. Even so, he dawdled grudgingly along. By the time we reached the outskirts of camp, the dwindling light was nearly gone and insects feasted on us.

The platforms high above were humming with excited voices like a disturbed beehive. We climbed the ladders, and I was so exhausted I thought only of my own shelter and bed. But the moment we reached the platform, cries of excitement greeted us. The explorers had returned. At the sight of my husband, thin, bearded and ragged, but alive, my heart leaped. Little Carlmin stood gawking as if at a stranger, but Petrus rushed to greet him. And Retyo gravely bade me farewell and vanished from my side into the crowd.

Jathan did not recognize his son at first. When he did, he lifted his eyes and looked over the crowd. When his eyes had passed me twice, I stepped forward, leading Carlmin by the hand. I think he knew me by the look on my face rather than by my appearance. He came to me slowly, saying, 'Sa's mercy, Carillion, is that you? Have pity on us all.' By which I judged that my appearance did not please him. And why that should hurt so much is something I do not know, nor why I felt shamed that he took my hand but did not embrace me. Little Carlmin stood beside me, staring blankly at his father.

And now I shall leave this wallowing in self-pity and sum up their report. They found only more swamp. The Rain Wild River is the main drainage of a vast network of water that straggles in threads through a wide valley on its way to the sea. The water runs under the land as much as over it. They had found no sound ground, only bogs, marshes and sloughs. They never had clear sight of a horizon since they had left us. Of the twelve men who set out, seven returned. One drowned in quicksand, one vanished during a night and the other three were overtaken by a fever. Ethe, Chellia's husband, did not return.

They could not tell how far inland they had travelled. The tree cover hampered their efforts to follow the stars and eventually they must have made a great circle, for they found themselves standing at the riverside again.

On their journey back to us, they encountered the remnants of those who had been on the third ship. They were marooned down-river from where we were abandoned. Their captain gave up on his mission when he saw wreckage from a ship float past them. Their captain was more merciful than ours, for he saw that all their cargo was landed with them, and even left them one of the ship's boats. Still, their lives were hard and many wished to go home. The jewel of good news was that they still had four messenger birds. One had been dispatched when they were first put ashore. Another was sent back with news of their hardship after the first month.

Our explorers dashed all their hopes. They decided to abandon their effort at a settlement. Seven of their young men came back with our explorers to help us evacuate as well. When we join them, they will send a message bird to Jamaillia, begging for a rescue ship. Then we will journey down the river and to the coast, in hopes of rescue.

When Chellia, Retyo and I returned, our company was sourly predicting that no ship would be sent. Nevertheless, all were packing to leave. Then Chellia arrived with her jewel-draped son. As she tried to tell her story to a crowd of folks too large to hear it, a riot near broke out. Some men wanted to go immediately to the buried tower, despite the growing dark. Others demanded a chance to handle the jewels, and as young Olpey refused to let anyone touch them, this set off a scuffle. The boy broke free, and leaping from the edge of the platform, he sprang from one branch to another like a monkey until his shape was lost in the darkness. I pray he is safe tonight, but fear the madness has taken him.

A different sort of madness has taken our folk. I huddle in my shelter with my two sons. Outside, on the platforms, the night is full of shouting. I hear women pleading to leave, and men saying, yes, yes, we will, but first we will see what treasure the city will offer us. A messenger bird with a jewel attached to its leg would bring a ship swiftly, they laugh. Their eyes are bright, their voices loud.

My husband is not with me. Despite our long separation, he is in the thick of these arguments rather than with his wife and sons. Did he even notice that my pregnancy had passed, yet my arms were empty? I doubt it.

I do not know where Chellia and her daughters have gone. When she discovered that Ethe had not returned, it broke her. Her husband is dead and Olpey may be lost, or worse. I fear for her, and mourn with her. I thought the return of the explorers would fill me with joy. Now I do not know what I feel. But I know it is not joy or even relief.

Day the 7th or 8th of the Gold Moon
Year the 14th of Satrap Esclepius

He came to me in the dark of the night, and despite the soreness of my heart and our two sons sleeping nearby, I let him have what he sought. Part of me hungered only for a gentle touch; part of me mocked myself for that, for he came to me only when his more pressing business was done. He spoke little and took his satisfaction in darkness. Can I blame him? I know I have gone to skin and bones, my complexion rough and my hair dry as straw. The rash that has afflicted the children now crawls like a snake up my spine. I dreaded that he would touch it, mostly because it would remind me that it was there, but he did not. He wasted no caresses. I stared past his shoulder into the darkness and thought not of my husband, but of Retyo, and he a common sailor who speaks with the accents of the waterfront.

What have I become here?

Afternoon
And so I am Lord Jathan Carrock's wife again, and my life is his to command. He has settled our fate. As Olpey has vanished, and neither Retyo nor Tremartin can be found, Jathan has declared that his son's

discovery of the hidden city gives him prime claim to all treasure in it. Petrus will lead him and the other men back to the buried tower. They will search it systematically for treasure that will buy our way back into the Satrap's graces. He is quite proud to claim that Petrus discovered the tower and thus the Carrocks merit a larger share of the treasure. It does not disturb him that Olpey is still missing, and that Chellia and her daughters are distraught with worry. He talks only of how the treasure will secure our glorious return to society. He seems to forget the leagues of swamp and sea between Jamaillia City and us.

I told him that the city was a dangerous place and he should not venture into it thinking only of spoils. I warned him of its unhealthy magic, of lights that brighten and fade, of voices and music heard in the distance, but he disdains it as a 'woman's overwrought fancy'. He tells me to stay out of danger here in my 'little monkey nest' until he returns. Then I spoke bluntly. The company does not have reserves of food or the strength to make a trek to the coast. Unless we better prepare, we will die along the way, treasure or not. I think we should remain here until we are better prepared, or until a ship comes here for us. We need not admit defeat. We might prosper if we put all our men to gathering food and found a way to trap rainwater for our needs. Our tree city could be a thing of grace and beauty. He shook his head as if I were a child prating of pixies in flowery bowers. 'Ever immersed in your art,' he said. 'Even in rags and starving, you cannot see what is real.' Then he said he admired how I had occupied myself in his absence, but that he had returned now and would take charge of his family.

I wanted to spit at him.

Petrus did not wish to lead the men. He believes the tower took Olpey and we shall never see him again. He speaks of the underground with deep dread. Carlmin told his father he had never been to a buried city, and then sat and sucked his thumb, as he has not since he was two.

When Petrus tried to warn Jathan, he laughed and said, 'I'm a different man than the soft noble who left Jamaillia. Your silly mama's goblins don't worry me.' When I told him sharply that I, too, was a different woman than the one he had left alone to cope in the wilds, he stiffly replied that he saw that too clearly, and only hoped that a return to civilization would restore me to propriety. Then he forced Petrus to lead them to the ruins.

No amount of treasure could persuade me to return there, not if there were diamonds scattered on the floor and strands of pearls dangling from the ceiling. I did not imagine the danger, and I hate Jathan for dragging Petrus back to it.

I shall spend the day with Marthi. Her husband returned safely, only to leave her again to hunt treasure. Unlike me, she is overjoyed with his plans, and says that he will return them to society and wealth again. It is hard for me to listen to such nonsense. 'My baby will grow up in Sa's blessed city,' she says. The woman is thin as a string, with her belly like a knot tied in it.

Day the 8th or 9th of the Gold Moon
Year the 14th of Satrap Esclepius

A ridiculous date for us. Here there will be no golden harvest moon, nor does the Satrap mean anything to me any more.

Yesterday Petrus showed them to the tower window, but ran away when the men entered, leaving his father shouting angrily after him. He came back to me, pale and shaking. He says the singing from the tower has become so loud that he cannot think his own thoughts when he is near it. Sometimes, in the corridors of black stone, he has glimpsed strange people. They come and go in flashes, he says, like their flickering light. I hushed him, for his words were upsetting Marthi. Despite Jathan's plans, I spent yesterday preparing for winter. I put a second thatch on both our hanging huts, using broad leaves laced down with vines. I think our shelters, especially the smaller hanging cottages and the little footbridges that connect them to the Great Platforms, will require reinforcement against winter winds and rain. Marthi was little help to me. Her pregnancy has made her ungainly and listless, but the real problem was that she believes we will soon go home to Jamaillia. Most of the women are now only waiting to leave.

Some of the treasure hunters returned last night, with reports of a vast buried city. It is very different from Jamaillia, all interconnected like a maze. Perhaps some parts of it were always underground, for there are no windows or doors in the lowest chambers. The upper reaches of the buildings were homes and private areas and the lower seemed to have been shops and warehouses and markets. Towards the river, a portion of the city has collapsed. In some chambers, the walls are damp and rot is well at work on the furnishings, but others have withstood time, preserving rugs and tapestries and garments. Those who returned brought back dishes and chairs, rugs and jewellery, statues and tools. One man wore a cloak that shimmered like running water, soft and supple. They had discovered amphorae of wine, still sealed and intact in one warehouse. The wine is golden and so potent that the men were almost instantly drunk. They returned laughing and spirit-breathed, bidding us all come to the city and celebrate with wine the wealth that had come to us. There was a wild glitter in their eyes that I did not like.

Others returned haunted and cringing, not wishing to speak of what they had experienced. Those ones began immediately to plan to leave tomorrow at dawn, to travel down river and join the other folk there.

Jathan did not return at all.

Those obsessed with plunder talk loudly, drunk with old wine and mad dreams. Already they gather hoards. Two men came back bruised, having come to blows over a vase. Where will greed take us? I feel alone in my dismal imaginings.

That city is not a conquered territory to be sacked, but more like a deserted temple, to be treated with the respect one should accord any unknown god. Are not all gods but facets of Sa's presence? But these words come to me too late to utter. I would not be heeded. I feel a terrible premonition, that there will be a consequence to this orgy of plundering.

My tree settlement was almost deserted earlier today. Most of our folk had been infected with a treasure fever and gone underground. Only the infirm and the women with the smallest children remain in our village. I look around me and I am suffused with sorrow, for I am seeing the death of my dreams. Shall I wax more eloquent, more dramatic, more poetic as I once would have thought it? No. I shall simply say I am engulfed in disappointment. And shocked to feel it.

It is hard for me to confront what I mourn. I hesitate to commit it to paper, for the words will remain here, to accuse me later. Yet art, above all, is honesty, and I am an artist before I am a wife, a mother or even a woman. So I will write. It is not that there is now a man that I would prefer over my husband. I admit that freely. I care not that Retyo is a common sailor, seven years my junior, without education or bloodlines to recommend him. It is not what he is but who he is that turns my heart and eyes to him. I would take him into my bed tonight, if I could do so without risking my sons' future. That I will write in a clear hand. Can there be shame in saying I would value his regard above my husband's, when my husband has so clearly shown that he values the regard of the other men in this company over his wife's love?

No. What turns my heart to rust this day is that my husband's return, and the discovery of treasure in the buried city and the talk of returning to Jamaillia, dismantles the life I have built here. That grieves me. It is a hard thing to contemplate. When did I change so completely? This life is harsh and hard. This country's beauty is the beauty of the sunning snake. It threatens as it beckons. I fancy that I can master it by giving it my earnest respect. Without realizing it, I had begun to take pride in my ability to survive and to tame some small part of its savagery. And I have shown others how to do that. I did things here, and they were significant.

Now that will be lost to me. I become again Lord Jathan Carrock's wife. My caution will be discarded as a woman's foolish fear, and my ambitions for a beautiful abode built among the trees will be dismissed as a woman's silly fancy.

Perhaps he would be right. Nay, I know he is right. But somehow, I no longer care for what is right and wise. I have left behind the life where I created art for people to admire. Now my art is how I live and it daily sustains me.

I do not think I can set that aside. To be told I must abandon all that I have begun here is more than I can bear. And for what? To return to his world, where I am of no more consequence than an amusing songbird in a filigreed cage.

Marthi was with me today when Chellia came to ask Petrus to help her look for Olpey. Petrus would not look at her. Chellia began to plead, and Petrus covered his ears. She nagged him until he began to weep, frightening Carlmin. Chellia shrieked as if mad, accusing Petrus of not caring anything for his friend, but only for the riches of the city. She lifted a hand as if to strike my boy, and I rushed in and pushed her. She fell, and her girls dragged her to her feet and then pulled her away, begging her simply to 'come home, Mother, come home'. When I turned around, Marthi had fled.

I sit by myself on the limb above my cottage while my boys sleep within tonight. I am ashamed. But my sons are all I have. Is it wrong for me to keep them safe? What good would it do to sacrifice my sons to save hers? We might only lose them all.

8th Day of the City
Year One of the Rain Wilds

I fear we have come through many trials and tribulations, only to perish from our own greed. Last night, three men died in the city. No one will say how; they brought the unmarked bodies back. Some say it was the madness, others speak of evil magic. In the wake of the gruesome development, seventeen people banded together and bade the rest of us farewell. We gave them ropes and woven mats and whatever else we could spare and wished them well as they left. I hope they reach the other settlement safely, and that someday, someone in Jamaillia may hear the tale of what befell us here. Marthi pleaded with them to tell the other folk to wait a day or two longer before they depart for the coast, that soon her husband will be bringing her to join them.

I have not seen Retyo since my husband returned. I did not think he would go to hunt treasure in the city, but it must be so. I had grown accustomed to being without Jathan. I have no claim to Retyo, and yet miss him the more keenly of the two.

I visited Marthi again. She has grown paler and is now afflicted with the rash. Her skin is as dry as a lizard's. She is miserable with her heaviness. She speaks wildly of her husband finding immense wealth and how she will flaunt it to those who banished us. She fantasizes that as soon as the message bird reaches Jamaillia, the Satrap will send a swift ship to fetch us all back to Jamaillia, where her child will be born into plenty and safety. Her husband returned briefly from the city, to bring her a little casket of jewellery. Her dull hair is netted with chained jewels and gleaming bracelets dangle from her thin wrists. I avoid her lest I tell her that she is a fool. She is not, truly, save that she hopes beyond hope. I hate this wealth that we can neither eat nor drink, for all have focused upon it, and willingly starve while they seek to gather ever more.

Our remaining company is divided into factions now. Men have formed alliances and divided the city into claimed territories. It began with quarrels over the heaps and hoards, with men accusing each other of pilfering. Soon it fostered partnerships, some to guard the hoard while the others strip the city of wealth. Now it extends to men arming themselves with clubs and knives and setting sentries to guard the corridors they have claimed. But the city is a maze, and there are many routes through it. The men fight one another for plunder.

My sons and I remain with the infirm, the elderly, the very young and the pregnant here at the platform. We form alliances of our own, for while the men are engrossed in stealing from each other, the gathering of food goes undone. The archers who hunted meat for us now hunt treasure. The men who had set snares for marsh rabbits now set traps for one another. Jathan came back to the hut, ate all that remained of our supplies, and then left again. He laughed at my anger, telling me that I worry about roots and seeds while there are gems and coins to be gathered. I was glad when he went back to the city. May he be devoured by it! Any food I find now, I immediately give to the boys or eat myself. If I can think of a secret place to cache it, I'll begin to do so.

Petrus, forbidden the city, has resumed his gathering duties, to good end. This day he returned with reeds like the ones we saw peasants cultivating in that mosaic in the city. He told me that the city people would not have grown them if they did not have some use, and that we should discover what it was. It was more disturbing to me when he told me that he remembered that this was the season for harvesting them. When I told him that he could not possibly remember any such thing, he shook his head at me, and muttered something about his 'city memories'.

I hope that the influence of that strange place will fade with time.

The rash has worsened on Carlmin, spreading on to his cheeks and brows. I slathered a poultice on to it in the hopes of easing it. My younger son has scarcely spoken a word to me this day, and I fear what occupies his mind.

My life has become only waiting. At any time, my husband may return from the city and announce that it is time for us to begin our trek down the river. Nothing I build now can be of any consequence, when I know that soon we will abandon it.

Olpey has not been found. Petrus blames himself. Chellia is near mad with grief. I watch her from a distance, for she no longer speaks to me. She confronts any man returning from the city, demanding word of her son. Most of them shrug her off; some become angry. I know what she fears, for I fear it, too. I think Olpey returned to the city. He felt entitled to his treasures, but fatherless as he is and of common birth, who would respect his claim? Would they kill the boy? I would give much not to feel so guilty about Olpey. What can I do? Nothing. Why, then, do I feel so bad? What would it benefit any of us to risk Petrus in another visit to the city? Is not one vanished boy tragedy enough?

8th Day of the City
Year One of the Rain Wilds

Jathan returned at noon today. He was laden with a basket of treasure, jewellery and odd ornaments, small tools of a strange metal, and a purse woven of metal links and full of oddly minted gold coins. His face was badly bruised. He abruptly said that this was enough, there was no sense to the greed in the city. He announced that we would catch up with the others who had already left. He declared that the city holds no good for us and that we are wiser to flee with what he has than to strive for more and die there.

He had not eaten since he last left us. I made him spice bark tea and lily-root mush and encouraged him to speak of what is happening underground. At first he spoke only of our own company there and what they did. Bitterly he accused them of treachery and betrayal. Men have come to bloodshed over the treasure. I suspect Jathan was driven off with what he could carry. But there is worse news. Parts of the city are collapsing. Closed doors have been forced open, with disastrous results. Some were not locked, but were held shut by the force of earth behind them. Now slow muck oozes forth from them, gradually flooding the corridors. Some are already nearly impassable, but men ignore the danger as they try to salvage wealth before it is buried for ever. The flowing muck seems to weaken the city's ancient magic. Many chambers are subsiding into darkness. Lights flash brightly, then dim. Music blares forth and then fades to a whisper.

When I asked him if that had frightened him, he angrily told me to be quiet and recall my respect for him. He scoffed at my notion that he would flee. He said it was obvious that the ancient city would soon collapse under the weight of the swamp, and he had no wish to die there. I do not believe that was all of it, but I suppose I am glad he was intelligent enough to leave. He bade me get the children ready to travel and gather whatever food we had

Reluctantly, I began to obey him. Petrus, looking relieved, sprang to the meagre packing. Carlmin sat silently scratching the poultice off his rash. I hastily covered it afresh. I did not want Jathan to see the coppery scaling on his son's skin. Earlier I had tried picking the scab loose, but when I scrape it off, he cries and the flesh beneath is bloody. It looks as if he is growing fish scales. I try not to think of the rash down my spine. I make this entry hastily, and then I will wrap this small book well and add it to my carry basket. There is precious little else to put in it.

I hate to leave what I have built, but I cannot ignore the relief in Petrus's eyes when his father said we would go. I wish we had never ventured into the city. But for that haunted place, perhaps we could have stayed here and made it a home. I dread our journey, but there is no help for it. Perhaps if we take Carlmin away from here, he will begin to speak again.

Later

I will write in haste and then take this book with me into the city. If ever my body is found, perhaps some kind soul will carry this volume back to Jamaillia and let my parents know what became of Carillion Waljin and where she ended her days. Likely it and I will be buried for ever in the muck inside the hidden city.

I had finished our packing when Chellia came to me with Tremartin. The man was gaunt and his clothing caked with mud. He has finally found Olpey, but the lad is out of his wits. He has barricaded a door against them, and will not come out. Retyo and Tremartin had been searching the city for Olpey all this time. Retyo has remained outside the door, striving to keep it clear of the relentlessly creeping muck filling the passageway. Tremartin does not know how long he can keep up with it. Retyo thinks that Petrus could convince Olpey to open the door. Together, Tremartin and Chellia came to us to beg this favour.

I could no longer ignore the desperation in my friend's eyes, and felt shamed that I had for so long. I appealed to Jathan, saying that we could go directly to where the boy is, persuade him to come out, and then we could all leave together. I even tried to be persuasive, saying that such a larger party would do better in facing the Rain Wilds than if we and our sons went alone.

He did not even call me apart or lower his voice as he demanded why he should risk his son and his heir for the sake of a laundress's boy, one we would not even employ as a servant were we still in Jamaillia. He berated me for letting Petrus become attached to such a common lad and then, in a clear voice, said I was very much mistaken if I thought him such a fool that he did not know about Retyo. Many a foul thing he said then, of what a harlot I was to take a common man into a bed by right a Lord's, and treacherously support a low sailor as he made his bid to claim leadership of the company.

I will not record any more of his shameful accusations. In truth, I do not know why he still has the power to make me weep. In the end, I defied him. When he said I must follow him now or not at all, I told him, 'Not at all. I will stay and aid my friend, for I care not what work she used to do, here she is my friend.'

My decision was not without cost to me. Jathan took Petrus with him. I saw that my elder son was torn, and yet wished to flee with his father. I do not blame him. Jathan left Carlmin behind, saying that my poor judgement had turned his son into a moron and a freak. Carlmin had scratched the poultice from his face, baring the scales that now outline his brows and upper cheeks. My little boy did not even wince at his father's words. He showed no reaction at all. I kissed Petrus goodbye and promised him that I would follow as soon as I could. I hope I can keep that promise. Jathan and Petrus took with them as much as they could carry of our goods. When Carlmin and I follow, we will not have much for supplies until we catch up to them.

And now I shall wrap this little book and slip it, pen and inkpot into the little carry basket they left to me, along with materials for torches and fire starting. Who knows when I shall write in it again? If you read this, my parents, know that I loved you until I died.

9th Day of the City, I think
First Year in the Rain Wilds

How foolish and melodramatic my last entry now looks to me.

I pen this hastily before the light fails. My friends wait for me patiently, though Chellia finds it foolish that I insist on writing before we go on.

Less than ten days have passed since I first saw this city, but it has aged years. The passage of many muddy feet was evident when we entered, and everywhere I saw the depredations of the treasure seekers. Like angry boys, they had destroyed what they could not take, prising tiles out of mosaics, breaking limbs off statues too big to carry, and using fine old furniture for firewood. As much as the city frightens me, still I grieve to see it plundered and ravaged. It has prevailed against the swamp for years, only to fall prey to our greed in days.

Its magic is failing. Only portions of the chamber were lit. The dragons on the ceiling had dimmed. The great woman-and-dragon statue bears marks from errant hammers. The jade and ivory of the woman's basket remained out of the reach of the treasure hunters. The rest of the pavilion had not fared so well. The fish fountain was being used as a great dish to hold someone's hoard. A man stood atop the heap of plunder, knife in one hand and club in the other, and shouted at us that he would kill any thieves who came near. His appearance was so wild, we believed him. I felt shamed for him, and looked aside as we hurried past. Fires burn in the room, with treasure and a guard by each one. In the distance we could hear voices, and sometimes challenging shouts and hammering. I caught a glimpse of four men ascending the steps with heavy sacks of loot.

Tremartin kindled one of our torches at an abandoned fire. We left that chamber by the same passage we had used before. Carlmin, mute since morning, began to hum a strange and wandering tune that raised the hair on the back of my neck. I led him on, while Chellia's two girls wept silently in the dimness as they followed us, holding hands.

We passed the shattered door of a chamber. Thick mud-water oozed from the room. I glanced inside the chamber; a wide crack in its back wall had allowed mud to half-fill the room. Still, someone had entered and sought treasure. Mouldy paintings had been pulled loose from the walls and discarded in the rising muck. We hastened on.

At an intersection of corridors, we saw a slowly advancing flow of mud, and heard a deep groaning in the distance, as of timbers slowly giving way. Nevertheless, a guard stood at that juncture, warning us that all behind him belonged to him and his friends. His eyes gleamed like a wild animal's. We assured him that we were only seeking a lost boy and hurried on. Behind him, we heard hammers begin and surmised that his friends were breaking down another door.

'We should hurry,' Tremartin said. 'Who knows what will be behind the next door they break? They won't leave off until they've let in the river. I left Retyo outside Olpey's door. We both feared others might come and think he guarded treasure.'

'I just want my boy. Then I shall gladly leave this place,' Chellia said. So we still hope to do.

I can write little of what else we saw, for the light flickers. We saw men dragging treasure they could never carry through the swamp. We were briefly attacked by a wild-eyed woman shrieking, 'Thieves, thieves!' I pushed her down, and we fled. As we ran, there was first damp, then water, then oozing mud on the floor. The mud sucked at our feet as we passed the little dressing chamber where we had found Olpey the first time. It is wrecked now, the fine dressing table hacked to pieces. Tremartin took us down a side corridor I would not have noticed, and down a narrow flight of stairs. I smelled stagnant water. I tried not to think of the sodden earth ever pressing in, as we descended another, shorter flight of steps and turned down a wide hall. The doors we passed now were metal. A few showed hammer marks, but they had withstood the siege of the treasure seekers.

As we passed an intersection, we heard a distant crack like lightning, and then men shouting in terror. The unnatural veins of light on the walls flickered and then went out. An instant later, men rushed past us, fleeing back the way we had come. A gush of water that damped us to the ankles followed them, spending itself as it spread. Then came a deep and ominous rumbling. 'Come on!' Tremartin ordered us, and we followed, though I think we all knew we were running deeper into danger, not away from it.

We turned two more corners. The stone of the walls suddenly changed from immense grey blocks to a smooth black stone with occasional veins of silver in it. We went down a long flight of shallow steps, and abruptly the corridor was wider and the ceiling higher, as if we had left behind the servants' area and entered the territory of the privileged. The wall niches had been plundered of their statues. I slipped in the damp on the floor. As I put my hand on a wall to catch myself, I suddenly glimpsed people swarming all around us. Their garb and demeanour were strange. It was a market day, rich with light and noise of conversation and the rich smells of baking. The life of a city swirled around me. In the next moment, Tremartin seized my arm and jerked me away from the wall. 'Do not touch the black stone,' he warned us. 'It puts you in the ghosts' world. Come on. Follow me.' In the distance, we saw the brighter flare of a fire gleaming, shaming the uneasily flickering light.

The fire was Retyo's torch. He was grimed from head to foot. Even when he saw us, he continued to scoop mud away from a door with a crude wooden paddle. The watery ooze was a constant flow down the hall; not even a dozen men could hope to keep up with it. If Olpey did not open the door soon, he would be trapped inside as the mud filled the corridor.

I stepped down into the shallow pit Retyo had been keeping clear. Heedless of the mud on him, heedless that my son and friend watched me, I embraced him. If I had had the time, I would have become what my husband had accused me of being. Perhaps, in spirit, I am already a faithless wife. I care little for that now. I have kept faith with my friends.

Our embrace was brief. We had little time. We called to Olpey through the doors, but he kept silent until he heard his little sisters weeping. Then he angrily bade us go away. His mother begged him to come out, saying that the city was giving way and that the flowing mud would soon trap him. He retorted that he belonged here, that he had always lived here and here he would die. And all the while that we shouted and begged, Retyo grimly worked, scraping the advancing muck away from the doorsill. When our pleas did not work, Retyo and Tremartin attacked the door, but the stout wood would not give to boots or fists, and we had no tools. In a dull whisper, Tremartin said we must leave him. He wept as he spoke. The mud was flowing faster than both men could contain, and we had three other children to think of.

Chellia's voice rose in a shriek of denial, but was drowned by an echoing rumble behind us. Something big gave way. The flow of the muck doubled, for now it came from both directions. Tremartin lifted his torch. In both directions, the corridor ended in blackness. 'Open the door, Olpey!' I begged him. 'Or we all perish here, drowned in muck. Let us in, in Sa's name!'

I do not think he heeded my words. Rather it was Carlmin's voice, raised in a command in a language I've never heard, that finally won a reaction. We heard latches being worked, and then the door grated grudgingly outwards through the muck. The lit chamber dazzled our eyes as we tumbled into it. Water and flowing muck tried to follow us on to the richly tiled floor, but Tremartin and Retyo dragged the door shut, though Retyo had to drop to his knees and push mud out of the way to do so. Mud-tinged water crept determinedly under the closed door.

The chamber was the best preserved that I had seen. We were all dazzled by the richness of the chambers and the brief illusion of safety amid the strangeness. Shelves of gleaming wood supported exquisite vases and small stone statues, intricate carvings and silver ornaments gone black with time. A little winding staircase led up and out of sight. Each step of it was lined with light. The contents of the room could have ransomed our entire company back into the Satrap's goodwill, for the objects were both fine and strange. Olpey stooped down protectively to roll back a carpet in danger of being overtaken by the ooze. It was supple in his hands, and as he disturbed the dust, bright colours peeped out. For a few moments, none of us spoke. As Olpey came to his feet and stood before us, I gasped. He wore a robe that rippled with colours when he moved. About his forehead he had bound a band of linked metal discs, and they seemed to glow with their own light. Chellia dared not embrace him. He blinked owlishly, and Chellia hesitantly asked her son if he knew her.

His reply came slowly. 'I dreamed you once.' Then, looking about the room, he said worriedly, 'Or perhaps I have stepped into a dream. It is so hard to tell.'

'He's been touching that black wall too much,' Tremartin growled. 'It wakes the ghosts and steals your mind. I saw a man two days ago. He was sitting with his back to the wall, his head leaned against it, smiling and gesturing and talking to people who weren't there.'

Retyo nodded grimly. 'Even without touching them, it takes a man's full will to keep the ghosts at bay after a time down here in the dark.' Then, reluctantly, he added, 'It may be too late to bring Olpey all the way back to us. But we can try. And we must all guard our minds as best we can, by talking to one another. And get the little ones out of here as quickly as we can.'

I saw what he meant. Olpey had gone to a small table in a corner. A silver pot awaited beside a tiny silver cup. As we watched in silence, he poured nothing from the pot to the cup, and then quickly quaffed it. He wiped his mouth on the back of his hand and made a face, as if he had just drunk liquor too strong for him.

'If we're going to go, we must go now,' Retyo added. He did not need to say, 'Before it's too late.' We were all thinking it.

But it was already too late. There was a steady seepage of water under the door, and when the men tried to open it, they could not budge it. Even when all the adults put our shoulders to it, it would not move. And then the lights began to flicker dismally.

Now the press of muck against the door grows heavier, so that the wood groans with it. I must be short. The staircase leads up into absolute darkness and the torches we have contrived from the articles in the room will not last long. Olpey has gone into a daze, and Carlmin is not much better. He barely responds to us with a mutter. The men will carry the boys, and Chellia will lead her two girls. I will carry our supply of torches. We will go as far as we can, hoping to discover a different way back to the dragon-woman chamber.

Day – I do not know
Year One of the Rain Wilds

So I head this account, for we have no concept of how much time has passed. For me, it seems years. I quiver, but I am not certain if it is from cold, or from striving to remain who I am. Who I was. My mind swims with the differences, and I could drown in them, if I let go. Yet if this account is to be of any use to others, I must find my discipline and put my thoughts into order.

As we ascended the stairs, the last breath of light in the chamber sighed out. Tremartin lifted our torch bravely but it barely illuminated his head and shoulders in the engulfing blackness. Never have I experienced darkness so absolute. Tremartin gripped Olpey's wrist and compelled the boy to follow him. Behind him went Retyo, carrying Carlmin, then Chellia leading her trembling daughters. I came last, burdened with the crude torches created from the furniture and hangings in the chamber. This last act had infuriated Olpey. He attacked Retyo and would not stop until Retyo struck him a hard open-handed blow to the face. It dazed the boy and horrified his mother and sisters, but he became compliant, if not co-operative.

The stair led to a servants' room. Doubtless the privileged noble in the comfortable chamber below would ring a bell, and his servants would spring to satisfy the master's wish. I saw wooden tubs, perhaps for washing, and glimpsed a worktable before Tremartin hurried us on. There was only one exit. Once outside, the corridor offered blackness in both directions.

The noise of the burning torch seemed almost loud; the only other sound was the dripping of water. I feared that silence. Music and ghostly voices lingered at the edge of it.

'The flame burns steadily,' Chellia observed. 'No draughts.'

I had not thought of that, but she was right. 'All that means is that there is a door between us and the outside.' Even I doubted my words. 'One we must find and open.'

'Which way shall we go?' Tremartin asked all of us. I had long ago lost my bearings, so I kept silent.

'That way,' Chellia answered. 'I think it goes back the direction we came. Perhaps we will see something we recognize, or perhaps the light will come back.'

I had no better suggestion to offer. They led and I followed. Each of them had someone to hold tight, to keep the ghosts of the city at bay. I had only the bundled torches in my arms. My friends became shadows between me and the unsteady torch light. If I looked up, the torch blinded me. Looking down, I saw a goblin's dance of shadows around my feet. Our hoarse breathing, the scuff of our feet on the damp stone and the crackling of the torch were the only sounds I perceived at first. Then I began to hear other things, or to think that I did: the uneven drip of water and once a sliding sound as something in the distance gave way.

And music. It was music thin as watered ink, music muffled by thick stone and time, but it reached out to me. I was determined to take the men's advice and ignore it. To keep my thoughts my own, I began to hum an old Jamaillian lullaby. It was only when Chellia hissed, 'Carillion!' at me that I realized my humming had become the haunting song from the stone. I stopped, biting my lip.

'Pass me another torch. We'd best light a fresh one before this one dies completely.' When Tremartin spoke the words, I realized he'd spoken to me twice before. Dumbly I stepped forward, presenting my armload of makeshift torches. The first two he chose were scarves wrapped around table legs. They would not kindle at all. Whatever the scarves were woven from, they would not take the flame. The third was a cushion tied crudely to a chair leg. It burned smokily and with a terrible stench. Still, we could not be fussy, and holding aloft the burning cushion and the dwindling torch, we moved slowly on. When the torch had burned so close to Tremartin's fingers that he had to let it fall, we had only the smouldering glow of the cushion to light our way. The darkness pressed closer than ever and the foul smell of the thing gave me a headache. I trudged along, remembering the annoying way the long coarse hair tangled on my rough-skinned fingers when I bundled the coiled hair in among the pith to make the cushion more springy and longer-lasting.

Retyo shook me, hard, and then Carlmin came into my arms, sniffling. 'Perhaps you should carry your son for a while,' the sailor told me, without rebuke, as he stooped to gather the spare torches that I had dropped. Ahead of us in the dark, the rest of our party was shadows in shadow, with a red smear for our torch. I had just stopped in my tracks. If Retyo had not noted my absence, I wonder what would have happened to me. Even after we spoke, I felt as if I were two people.

'Thank you,' I told him ashamedly.

'It's all right. Just stay close,' he told me.

We went on. The punishing weight of Carlmin in my arms kept me focused. After a time, I set him down and made him walk beside me, but I think that was better for him. Having once been snared by the ghosts, I resolved to be more wary. Even so, odd bits of dreams, fancies, and voices talking in the distance drifted through my mind as I walked, eyes open, through the dark. We trudged on endlessly. Hunger and thirst made themselves known to us. The seeping runnels of water tasted bitter, but we drank sparingly from them anyway.

'I hate this city,' I said to Carlmin. His little hand in mine was becoming chill as the buried city stole our body warmth from us. 'It's full of traps and snares. Rooms full of mud waiting to crush us, and ghosts trying to steal our minds.'

I had been speaking as much to myself as to him. I didn't expect a response. But then he said slowly, 'It wasn't built to be dark and empty.'

'Perhaps not, but that is how it is now. And the ghosts of those who built it try to steal our minds from us.'

I heard more than saw his scowl. 'Ghosts? Not ghosts. Not thieves.'

'What are they, then?' I asked him, mostly to keep him talking.

He was silent for a time. I listened to our footsteps and breathing. Then he said, 'It's not anyone. It's their art.'

Art seemed a far and useless thing to me now. Once I had used it to justify my existence. Now it seemed an idleness and a ploy, something I did to conceal the insignificance of my daily life. The word almost shamed me.

'Art,' he repeated. He did not sound like a little boy as he went on, 'Art is how we define and explain ourselves to ourselves. In this city, we decided that the daily life of the people was the art of the city. From year to year, the shaking of the earth increased, and the storms of dust and ash. We hid from it, closing our cities in and burrowing under the earth. And yet we knew that a time would come when we could not prevail against the earth itself. Some wished to leave, and we let them. No one was forced to stay. Our cities that had burgeoned with life faded to a trickle of souls. For a time, the earth calmed, with only a shiver now and then to remind us that our lives were daily granted to us and could be taken in a moment. But many of us decided that this was where we had lived, for generations. So this would be where we perished. Our individual lives, long as they were, would end here. But not our cities. No. Our cities would live on and recall us. Recall us . . . would call us home again, whenever anyone woke the echoes of us that we stored here. We're all here, all our richness and complexity, all our joys and sorrows . . .' His voice drifted away in contemplation once more.

I felt chilled. 'A magic that calls the ghosts back.'

'Not magic. Art.' He sounded annoyed.

Suddenly Retyo said unsteadily, 'I keep hearing voices. Someone, talk to me.'

I put my hand on his arm. 'I hear them, too. But they sound Jamaillian.'

With pounding hearts our little party hastened towards them. At the next juncture of corridors, we turned right and the voices came clearer. We shouted, and they shouted a reply. Through the dark, we heard their hurrying feet. They blessed our smoky red torch; theirs had burned out. There were four young men and two women from our company. Frightened as they were, they still clutched armloads of plunder. We were overjoyed to find them, until they dashed our relief into despair. The passage to the outside world was blocked. They had been in the dragon-and-woman chamber when they heard heavy pounding from the rooms above. A great crash was followed by the slow groan of timbers giving way. As a grinding noise grew in volume, the lights in the big chamber flickered and watery mud began to trickle down the grand staircase. They had immediately tried to escape, only to find the stairway blocked by collapsed masonry oozing mud.

Perhaps fifty folk had gathered in the dragon-and-woman chamber, drawn back there by the ominous sound. As the lights dimmed and then went out, some had gone one way and some another, seeking for escape. Even in this danger, their suspicion of one another as thieves had prevented them from joining forces. I was disgusted with them, and said as much. To my surprise, they sheepishly agreed. Then, for a time, we stood uselessly in the dark, listening to our torch burn away and wondering what to do.

When no one else spoke, I asked, 'Do you know the way back to the dragon chamber?' I fought to speak steadily.

One man said he did.

'Then we must go back there. And gather all the people we can, and pool what we know of this maze. It is our only hope of finding a way out before our torches are gone. Otherwise, we may wander until we die.'

Grim silence was their assent. The young man led our way back. As we passed plundered rooms, we gathered anything that might burn. Soon those who had joined us must abandon their plunder to carry more wood. I thought they would part from us before surrendering their treasure, but they decided to leave it in one of the rooms. They marked their claim upon the door, with threats against any thieves. I thought this foolishness, for I would have traded every jewel in the city simply to see honest daylight again. Then we went on.

We reached at last the dragon-woman chamber. We knew it more by its echoes than by the view that our failing torch offered. A small fire still smouldered there, with a few hapless folk gathered around it. We added fuel to wake it to flames. It drew others to join us, and we then raised a shout to summon any who might hear us. Soon our little bonfire lit a circle of some thirty muddy and weary people. The flames showed me frightened white faces like masks. Many of them still clutched bundles of plunder, and eyed one another suspiciously. That was almost more frightening than the slow creep of thick mud spreading from the staircase. Heavy and thick, it trickled inexorably down, and I knew that our gathering place would not long be a refuge from it.

We were a pitiful company. Some of these folk had been lords and ladies, and others pickpockets and whores, but in that place, we finally became equals and recognized one another for what we were: desperate people, dependent on each other. We had convened at the foot of the dragon statue. Now Retyo stepped up on to the dragon's tail and commanded us, 'Hush! Listen!'

Voices ebbed away. We heard the crackling of our fire, and then the distant groans of wood and stone, and the drip and trickle of watery muck. They were terrifying sounds and I wondered why he had made us listen to them. When he spoke, his human voice was welcome as it drowned out the threats of the straining walls.

'We have no time to waste in worrying about treasure or theft. Our lives are the only things we can hope to carry out of here, and only if we pool what we know, so we don't waste time exploring corridors that lead nowhere. Are we together on that?'

A silence followed his words. Then a grimy, bearded man spoke. 'My partners and I claimed the corridors from the west arch. We've been exploring them for days now. There are no stairs going up and the main corridor ends in collapse.'

It was dismal news but Retyo didn't let us dwell on it.

'Well. Any others?'

There was some restless shifting.

Retyo's voice was stern. 'You're still thinking of plunder and secrets. Let them go, or stay here with them. All I want is a way out. Now. We're only interested in stairways leading up. Anyone know of any?'

Finally, a man spoke up reluctantly. 'There were two from the east arch. But . . . well, a wall gave way when we opened a door. We can't get to them any more.'

A deeper silence fell on us and the light from the fire seemed to dwindle.

When Retyo spoke again, his voice was impassive. 'Well, that makes it simpler for us. There's less to search. We'll need two large search parties, one that can divide at each intersection. As each group goes, you'll mark your path. On your way, enter every open chamber, and seek always for stairs leading up, for doubtless that is our only way out. Mark every path that you go by, so that you may return to us.' He cleared his throat. 'I don't need to warn you. If a door won't open, leave it alone.'

'This is a pact we must make: that whoever finds a way out will risk their lives again to return and guide the rest of us out. To those who go out, the pact we make is that we who stay here will try to keep this fire burning, so that if you do not find a way out, you can return here, to light and another attempt.' He looked around carefully at all the upturned faces. 'To that end, every one of us will leave here whatever treasure we have found. To encourage any that find a way out to come back, for gain if not to keep faith with us.'

I would not have dared to test them that way. I saw what he did. The mounded hoard would give hope to those who must stay here and tend the fire, as well as encourage any who found an escape to return for the rest of us. To those who insisted they would take their treasure with them, Retyo simply said, 'Do it. But remember well what you choose. No one who stays here will owe you any help. Should you return and find the fire out and the rest of us gone, do not hope that we will return for you.'

Three men, heavily burdened, went aside to argue heatedly among themselves. Other people began to trickle back to the dragon pavilion, and were quickly informed of the pact. These folk, having already tried to find a way out, quickly agreed to the terms. Someone said that perhaps the rest of our company might dig down to free us. A general silence greeted that thought as we all considered the many steps we had descended to reach this place, and all the mud and earth that stood between us and the outside air. Then no one spoke of it again. When finally all agreed to abide by Retyo's plan, we counted ourselves and found that we numbered fifty-two bedraggled and weary men, women and children.

Two parties set out. Most of our firewood went with them, converted to torches. Before they left, we prayed together, but I doubted Sa could hear us, so deep beneath the ground and so far from sacred Jamaillia. I remained with my son, tending the fire. We took turns making short trips to nearby rooms, to drag back whatever might burn. Treasure seekers had already burned most of the close fuel, but still we found items ranging from massive tables it took eight of us to lift to broken bits of rotted chairs and tatters of curtain.

Most of the children had remained by the fire. In addition to my son and Chellia's children, there were four other youngsters. We took it in turns to tell stories or sing songs to them, trying to keep their minds free of the ghosts that clustered closer as our small fire burned lower. We begrudged every stick of wood we fed to it.

Despite our efforts, the children fell silent one by one and slipped into the dreams of the buried city. I shook Carlmin and pinched him, but could not find the will to be cruel enough to rouse him. In truth, the ghosts plucked at my mind as well, until the distant conversations in an unknown language seemed more intelligible than the desperate mutterings of the other women. I dozed off, then snapped awake as the needs of the dying fire recalled me to my duty.

'Perhaps it's kinder to let them dream themselves to death,' one of the women said as she helped me push one end of a heavy table into the fire. She took a deeper breath and added, 'Perhaps we should all just go to the black wall and lean against it.'

The idea was more tempting than I liked to admit. Chellia returned from a wood foraging effort. 'I think we burn more in torch than we bring back as fuel,' she pointed out. 'I'll sit with the children for a while. See what you can find to burn.'

So I took her stub of torch and went off seeking firewood. By the time I returned with my pitiful scraps, a splinter group of one of the search parties had returned. They had swiftly exhausted their possibilities and their torches and returned hoping that others had had better luck.

When a second party returned shortly afterwards, I felt more discouragement. They brought with them a group of seventeen others whom they had discovered wandering in the labyrinth. The seventeen were the 'owners' of that section of the city, and said that days ago they had early discovered that the upper storeys in that section were collapsed. In all the days they had explored it, always the paths had led outwards and downwards. Any further explorations in that direction would demand more torches than we presently had.

Our supply of wood for the bonfire was already dwindling, and we weren't finding much in the pillaged rooms that we could use for torches. Hunger and thirst were already pressing many of us. Too soon we would have to confront an even more daunting shortage. Once our fire failed, we would be plunged into total darkness. If I dared to think of it, my heart thundered and I felt faint. It was hard enough to hold myself aloof from the city's lingering 'art'. Immersed in blackness, I knew I would give way to it.

I was not the only one who realized this. Tacitly, we let the fire die down and maintained it at a smaller size. The flow of mud down the grand stair brought damp that chilled the air. People huddled together for warmth as much as companionship. I dreaded the first touch of water against my feet. I wondered which would overtake me first: total darkness or rising muck.

I don't know how much time passed before the third party returned to us. They had found three staircases that led up. All were blocked before they reached the surface. Their corridor had become increasingly ruined the further they had gone. Soon they had been splashing through shallow puddles and the smell of earth had grown strong. When their torches were nearly exhausted and the water growing deeper and colder about their knees, they had returned. Retyo and Tremartin had been members of that party. I was selfishly glad to have him at my side again, even though it meant that our hope was now whittled to a single search party.

Retyo wished to shake Carlmin out of his daze, but I asked him, 'To what end? That he might stare into the darkness and know despair? Let him dream, Retyo. He does not seem to be having bad dreams. If I can carry him out of here into daylight once more, then I will wake him and try to call him back to me. Until then, I will leave him in peace.' I sat, Retyo's arm around me, and thought silently of Petrus and my erstwhile husband Jathan. Well, he had made one wise decision. I felt oddly grateful to him that he had not allowed me to squander both our sons' lives. I hoped he and Petrus reached the coast safely and eventually returned to Jamaillia. At least one of my children might grow to adulthood.

And so we waited, our hopes dwindling as swiftly as our firewood. Our men had to venture further and further into the darkness in search of fuel. Finally Retyo lifted his voice. 'Either they are still exploring, in hope of finding a way out, or they have found a way out and are too fearful to return for us. In either way, we gain nothing more by sitting here. Let us go where they went, following their marks, while we still have light to see them. Either we will find the same escape route they did, or die together.'

We took every splinter of firewood. The more foolish among us gathered treasure to carry out. No one remonstrated with them, though many laughed bitterly at their hopeful greed. Retyo picked up Carlmin without a word; it moved me that my son was treasure to him. In truth, weakened as I was by hunger, I do not know if I could have carried my son. I do know that I would not have left him there. Tremartin took Olpey slung across his shoulders. The boy was limp as a drowned thing. Drowned in art, I thought to myself. Drowned in memories of the city.

Of Chellia's two daughters, Piet still clung to wakefulness. She stumbled piteously along beside her mother. A young man named Sterren offered to carry Likea for Chellia. She was so grateful, she wept.

And so we trudged off. We had one torch to lead us, and one at the tail of our procession, so that no one would fall victim to the city's allure and be left behind. I walked in the middle of the company, and the darkness seemed to pluck and snag at my senses. There is little to say of that endless walk. We took no rest, for our fire ate our torches at an alarming rate. There was dark, and wet, the mutter of hungry and thirsty and weary folk all around me, and more darkness. I could not really see the halls we walked through, only the smudge of light that we followed. Bit by bit, I gave up my burden of wood to our light-bearers. The last time I moved forward to offer a new torch, I saw that the walls were of shining black stone veined with silver. They were elaborately decorated with silhouettes of people, done in some shining metal. Curious, I reached out a hand to touch one. I had not even realized that Retyo was at my side. He caught my wrist before I could touch the silhouette. 'Don't,' he warned me. 'I brushed against one once. They leap into your mind if you touch them. Don't.'

We followed the marks of the missing search party. They had marked off the dead ends and drawn arrows as they progressed, and so we trudged on, hoping. Then, to our horror, we caught up with them.

They were huddled in the middle of the corridor. Torches exhausted, they had halted there, paralysed by the complete blackness, unable either to go on or to come back to us. Some were insensible. Others whimpered with joy at the sight of us and clustered around our torch as if light were life itself flowing back into them.

'Did you find a way out?' they asked us, as if they had forgotten that they were the searchers. When they finally understood that they had been our last hope, the life seemed to go out of them. 'The corridor goes on and on,' they said. 'But we have not yet found one place where it leads upwards. The chambers we have been able to enter are windowless. We think this part of the city has always been under-ground.'

Grim words. Useless to dwell on them.

And so, we moved on together. We encountered few intersections, and when we did, we made our choice almost randomly. We no longer had torches to explore every possibility. At each intersection, the men in the lead debated and then chose. And we followed, but at each one we had to wonder if we had made a fatal error. Were we walking away from the passage that would have led to light and air? We gave up having a torch at the end of our procession, instead having folk hold hands and come behind us. Even so, too swiftly we had but three torches, and then two. A woman keened as the final torch was kindled. It did not burn well, or perhaps the dread of the dark was so strong in us that no light would have seemed sufficient. I know we crowded closer around our torch-bearer. The corridor had widened and the ceiling retreated. Every now and then, the torch light would catch a

silver silhouette or a vein of silvery mineral in the polished black wall
and it would blink beckoningly at me. Still we marched hopelessly on,
hungry, thirsty and ever more weary. We did not travel fast, but then,
we did not know if we had any destination save death.

The lost spirits of the city plucked at me. Ever stronger grew the
temptation simply to let go of my puny life and immerse myself in
the beckoning remembrance of the city. Snatches of their music,
conversation heard in a distant mutter, even, it seemed to me, whiffs
of strange fragrances assailed me and tempted me. Well, was not that
what Jathan had always warned me? That if I did not take a firmer
grip on my life, my art would immerse and then devour me? But it
was so hard to resist; it tugged at me like a hook in a fish's lip. It knew
that it had me; it but waited for darkness to pull me in.

The torch burned lower with every step we took. Every step we took
might be one more step in the wrong direction. The passage had
widened around us into a hall; I could no longer see the gleaming
black walls, but I could feel them commanding my attention. We
passed a still fountain flanked by stone benches. We watched in vain
for anything that might fuel our fire. Here, these elder folk had built
for eternity, from stone and metal and fired clay. I knew that these
rooms now were the repository of all they had been. They had believed
they would always live here, that the waters of the fountains and the
swirling beams of light would always dance at their touch. I knew that
as clearly as I knew my own name. Like me, they had foolishly thought
to live for ever through their art. Now it was the only part of them
that lingered still.

And in that moment, I knew my decision. It came to me so clearly
that I am not sure it was solely my own. Did some long dead artist
reach out and tug at my sleeve, begging to be heard and seen one last
time before we tumbled into the dark and silence that had consumed
her city?

I put my hand on Retyo's arm. 'I'm going to the wall now,' I said
simply. To his credit, he immediately knew what I meant.

'You would leave us?' he asked me piteously. 'Not just me, but little
Carlmin? You would drown yourself in dreams and leave me to face
death alone?'

I stood on tiptoe to kiss his whiskery cheek and to press my lips
briefly against my son's downy head. 'I won't drown,' I promised him.
It suddenly seemed so simple. 'I know how to swim in those waters.
I have swum in them since my birth, and like a fish, I will follow
them upstream to their source. And you will follow me. All of you.'

'Carillion, I don't understand. Are you mad?'

'No. But I cannot explain. Only follow me, and trust, as I followed you when I walked out on the tree limb. I will feel the path surely; I won't let you fall.'

Then I did the most scandalous thing I've ever done in my life. I took hold of my weary skirts, long tattered halfway up my calf, and tore them free of my stained waistband, leaving only my pantaloons. I bundled them up and pushed them into his shocked hands. Around us, others had halted in their shadowy trudging to watch my strange performance. 'Feed these to the torch, a bit at a time, to keep it alive. And follow me.'

'You will walk near naked before all of us?' he asked me in horror, as if it were of great concern.

I had to smile. 'While my skirts burn, no one will notice the nakedness of her who stripped to give them light. And after they have burned, we will all be hidden in the darkness. Much like the art of these people.'

Then I walked away from him, into the engulfing darkness that framed us. I heard him shout to our torch-bearer to halt, and I heard others say that I had gone mad. But I felt as if I had finally plunged myself into the river that all my life had tantalized my thirst. I went to the city's wall willingly, opening my mind and heart to their art as I approached it, so that by the time I touched the cold stone, I was already walking among them, hearing their gossip and corner musicians and haggling.

It was a market square. As I touched the stone, it roared to life around me. Suddenly my mind perceived light where my closed eyes did not, and I smelled the cooking river fish on the smoky little braziers, and saw the skewers of dripping honeyed-fruit on the tray of a street hawker. Glazed lizards smoked on a low brazier. Children chased one another past me. People paraded the streets, dressed in gleaming fabrics that rippled colour at their every step. And such people, people that befitted such a grand city! Some might have been Jamaillian, but among them moved others, tall and narrow, scaled like fish or with skin as bronzed as polished metal. Their eyes gleamed too, silver and copper and gold. The ordinary folk made way for these exalted ones with joy rather than cold respect. Merchants stepped out from their stalls to offer them their best and gawking children peeped from around their mothers' trousered legs to glimpse their royalty passing. For such I was sure they were.

With an effort, I turned my eyes and my thoughts from this rich pageantry. I groped to recall who and where I truly was. I dragged Carlmin and Retyo back into my awareness. Then, I deliberately looked around myself. Up and sky, I told myself. Up and sky, into the air. Blue sky. Trees.

Fingers lightly touching the wall, I moved forwards.

Art is immersion, and good art is total immersion. Retyo was right. It sought to drown me. But Carlmin was right, too. There was no malice in the drowning, only the engulfing that art seeks. And I was an artist, and as a practitioner of that magic, I was accustomed to keeping my head even when the current ran strongest and swiftest.

Even so, it was all I could do to cling to my two words. Up and sky. I could not tell if my companions followed me or if they had abandoned me to my madness. Surely, Retyo would not. Surely, he would come behind me, bringing my son with him. Then, a moment later, the struggle to remember their names became too great. Such names and such people had never existed in this city, and I was a citizen of the city now.

I strode through its busy market time. Around me people bought and sold exotic and fascinating merchandise. The colours, the sounds, even the smells tempted me to linger, but up and sky were what I clung to.

They were not a folk who cherished the outside world. Here they had built a hive, much of it underground, lit and warm, clean and immune to wind and storm and rain. They had brought inside it such creatures as appealed to them, flowering trees and caged songbirds and little glittering lizards tethered to potted bushes. Fish leaped and flashed in the fountains, but no dogs ran and barked, no birds flew overhead. Nothing was allowed that might make a mess. All was orderly and controlled, save for the flamboyant people who shouted and laughed and whistled in their precisely arranged streets.

Up and sky, I told them. They did not hear me, of course. Their conversations buzzed uselessly around me, and even once I began to understand them, the things they spoke of did not concern me. What could I care about the politics of a queen a thousand years gone, for society weddings and clandestine affairs noisily gossiped about? Up and sky, I breathed to myself, and slowly, slowly, the memories I sought began to flow to me. For there were others in this city for whom art was up and sky. There was a tower, an observatory. It rose above the river mists on foggy nights, and there learned men and women could study the stars and predict what effect they might have on mortals. I focused my mind on it, and soon 'remembered' where it was. Sa blessed us all, in that it was not far from their market-place.

I was halted once, for though my eyes told me that the way ahead of me was well lit and smoothly paved, my groping hands found a cold tumble of fallen stone and earth seeping water. A man shouted by my ear and restrained my hands. Dimly I recalled my other life. How strange to open my eyes to blackness and Retyo gripping my hands in his. Around me in the darkness, I heard people weeping or muttering despairingly that they followed a dreamer to their deaths. I could see nothing at all. The darkness was absolute. I had no idea how much time had passed, but I was suddenly aware of thirst that near choked me. Retyo's hand still clutched at mine, and I knew then of the long chain of people, hands clasped, that trustingly followed me.

I croaked at them, 'Don't give up. I know the way. I do. Follow me.'

Later, Retyo would tell me that the words I uttered were in no tongue he had ever known, but my emphatic shout swayed him. I closed my eyes, and once more the city surged to life around me. Another way, there had to be another way to the observatory. I turned back to the populous corridors, but now as I passed the leaping fountains, they taunted me with their remembered water. The tantalizing memories of food smells lingered in the air and I felt my belly clench on itself in longing. But up and sky were my words, and I walked on, even as I became aware that moving my body was becoming more and more taxing to me. In another place, my tongue was leather in my mouth, my belly a cramped ball of pain. But here, I moved with the city, immersed in it. I understood now the words that flowed past me, I smelled familiar foods, even knew all the words to the songs the corner minstrels were singing. I was home, and the city as art flowed through me; I was home in a deeper way than ever Jamaillia had been home to me.

I found the other stairs that led to the observatory, the back stairs for the servants and cleaners. Up these stairs, humble folk carried couches and trays of wine glasses for nobles who wished to recline and gaze up at the stars. It was a humble wooden door. It swung open at my push. I heard a murmured gasp behind me, and then words of shouted praise that opened my eyes.

Daylight, thin and feeble, crept down to us. The winding stair was wooden, and rickety, but I decided we would trust it. 'Up and sky,' I told my company as I set my foot to the first creaking step. It was a struggle to recall my precious words and speak them aloud. 'Up and sky.' And they followed me.

As we ascended, the light came stronger, and we blinked like moles in that sweet dimness. When at last I reached the stone-floored upper chamber, I smiled so that my dry lips split.

The thick glass panels of the observatory windows had given way to cracks, followed by questing vines that faded to pale writhing things as they left the daylight behind. The light through the windows was greenish and thick, but it was light. The vines became our ladder to freedom. Many of us were weeping dry tears as we made that last painful climb. Unconscious children and dazed people were passed up and out to us. I took a limp Carlmin in my arms and held him in the light and fresh air.

There were rain flowers awaiting us, as if Sa wished us to know it was her will we survive here, enough rain flowers for each of us to wet our mouths and gather our senses. The wind seemed chill and we laughed joyfully to shiver in it. We stood on top of what had been the observatory, and I looked out with love over a land I had once known. My beautiful wide river valley was swamp now, but it was still mine. The tower that had stood so high above all was only a mound now, but around us were the hunched and mossy remains of other structures, making the land firm and dry beneath our feet. There was not much dry land, less than a leffer, and yet after our months in the swamp, it seemed a grand estate. From atop it, we could look out over the slowly moving river where slanting sunlight fell on the chalky waters. My home had changed, but it was still mine.

Every one of us who left the dragon chamber emerged alive and intact. The city had swallowed us, taken us down and made us hers, and then released us, changed, in this kindlier place. Here, by virtue of the city buried beneath us, the ground is firmer. There are great, strong-branched trees nearby, in which we can build a new platform. There is even food here, a plenitude by Rain Wild standards. A sort of climbing vine festoons the trunks of the trees, and is heavy with pulpy fruit. I recall the same fruit sold in the vendor stalls of my city. It will sustain us. For now, we have all we need to survive this night. Tomorrow will be soon enough to think on the rest of it.

Day the 7th of Light and Air
Year One of the Rain Wilds

It took us a full six days to hike downriver to our original settlement. Time in the light and air have restored most of us to our ordinary senses, though all of the children have a more detached air than they used to have. Nor do I think I am alone in my vivid dreams of life in the city. I welcome them now. The land here has changed vastly since the days of the city; once all was solid ground, and the river a silver shining thread. The land was restless in those days, too, and sometimes the river ran milky and acid. Now the trees have taken back the meadows and croplands, but still, I recognize some features of the land. I recognize, too, which trees are good for timber, which leaves make a pleasantly stimulating tea, which reeds can yield both paper and fabric when beaten to thread and pulp, and oh, so many other things. We will survive here. It will not be lush or easy living, but if we accept what the land offers us, it may be enough.

And that is well. I found my tree city mostly deserted. After the disaster that sealed us in the city, most of the folk here gave up all for lost and fled. Of the treasure they collected and mounded on the platform, they took only a pittance. Only a few people remained. Marthi and her husband and her son are among them. Marthi wept with joy at my return.

When I expressed my anger that the others could go on without her, she told me, quite seriously, that they had promised to send back help, and she was quite sure that they would keep their word, as their treasure is still here.

As for me, I found my own treasure. Petrus had remained here, after all. Jathan, stony-hearted man that he is, went on without the boy when Petrus had a last-moment change of heart and declared that he would wait here for his mother to return. I am glad that he did not wait for me in vain.

I was shocked that Marthi and her husband had remained, until she put in my arms her reason. Her child was born, and for his sake, they will dwell here. He is a lithe and lively little thing, but he is as scaled as a snake. In Jamaillia, he would be a freak. The Rain Wilds are where he belongs.

As we all do, now.

I think I was as shocked at the changes in Marthi as she was in the change in me. Around her neck and wrists where she had worn the jewellery from the city, tiny growths have erupted. When she stared at me, I thought it was because she could see how much the city memories had changed my soul. In reality, it was the beginning of feathery scales on my eyelids and round my lips that caught her eye. I have no looking glass, so I cannot say how pronounced they are. And I have only Retyo's word that the line of scarlet scaling down my spine is more attractive than repellent.

I see the scaling that has begun to show on the children, and in truth, I do not find it abhorrent. Almost all of us who went down into the city bear some sign of it, either a look behind the eyes, or a delicate tracing of scales or perhaps a line of pebbled flesh along the jaw. The Rain Wilds have marked us as their own, and welcome us home.

A SONG OF ICE AND FIRE

GEORGE R. R. MARTIN

A SONG OF ICE AND FIRE
GEORGE R. R. MARTIN

A Game of Thrones (1996)
A Clash of Kings (1998)
A Storm of Swords (2000)
A Feast for Crows (2003)
A Dance with Dragons (forthcoming)
The Winds of Winter (forthcoming)

A Song of Ice and Fire began life as a trilogy, and has since expanded to six books. As J. R. R. Tolkien once said, the tale grew in the telling.

The setting for the books is the great continent of Westeros, in a world both like and unlike our own, where the seasons last for years and sometimes decades. Standing hard against the sunset sea at the western edge of the known world, Westeros stretches from the red sands of Dorne in the south to the icy mountains and frozen fields of the north, where snow falls even during the long summers.

The children of the forest were the first known inhabitants of Westeros, during the Dawn of Days: a race small of stature who made their homes in the greenwood, and carved strange faces in the bone-white weirwood trees. Then came the First Men, who crossed a land bridge from the larger continent to the east with their bronze swords and horses, and warred against the children for centuries before finally making peace with the older race and adopting their nameless, ancient gods. The Compact marked the beginning of the Age of Heroes, when the First Men and the children shared Westeros, and a hundred petty kingdoms rose and fell.

Other invaders came in turn. The Andals crossed the narrow sea in ships, and with iron and fire they swept across the kingdoms of the First Men, and drove the children from their forests, putting many of the weirwoods to the axe. They brought their own faith, worshipping a god with seven aspects whose symbol was a seven-pointed star. Only in the far north did the First Men, led by the Starks of Winterfell, throw back the newcomers. Elsewhere the Andals triumphed, and raised kingdoms of their own. The children of the forest dwindled and disappeared, while the First Men intermarried with their conquerors.

The Rhoynar arrived some thousands of years after the Andals, and came not as invaders but as refugees, crossing the seas in ten thousand ships to escape the growing might of the Freehold of Valyria. The lords freeholder of Valyria ruled the greater part of the known world; they were sorcerers, great in lore, and alone of all the races of man they had learned to breed dragons and bend them to their will. Four hundred years before the opening of A Song of Ice and Fire, however, the Doom descended on Valyria, destroying the city in a single night. Thereafter the great Valyrian empire disintegrated into dissension, barbarism and war.

Westeros, across the narrow sea, was spared the worst of the chaos that followed. By that time only seven kingdoms remained where once there had been hundreds – but they would not stand for much longer. A scion of lost Valyria named Aegon Targaryen landed at the mouth of the Blackwater with a small army, his two sisters (who were also his wives), and three great dragons. Riding on dragonback, Aegon and his sisters won battle after battle, and subdued six of the seven Westerosi kingdoms by fire, sword and treaty. The conqueror collected the melted, twisted blades of his fallen foes, and used them to make a monstrous, towering barbed seat: the Iron Throne, from which he ruled henceforth as Aegon, the First of His Name, King of the Andals and the Rhoynar and the First Men, and Lord of the Seven Kingdoms.

The dynasty founded by Aegon and his sisters endured for most of three hundred years. Another Targaryen king, Daeron II, later brought Dorne into the realm, uniting all of Westeros under a single ruler. He did so by marriage, not conquest, for the last of the dragons had died a half century before. 'The Hedge Knight', published in the first *Legends*, takes place in the last days of Good King Daeron's reign, about a hundred years before the opening of the first of the Ice and Fire novels, with the realm at peace and the Targaryen dynasty at its height. It tells the story of the first meeting between Dunk, a hedge knight's squire, and Egg, a boy who is rather more than he seems, and of the great tourney at Ashford Meadow. 'The Sworn Sword', the tale that follows, picks up their story a year or so later.

THE SWORN SWORD

BY GEORGE R. R. MARTIN

In an iron cage at the crossroads, two dead men were rotting in the summer sun.

Egg stopped below to have a look at them. 'Who do you think they were, ser?' His mule Maester, grateful for the respite, began to crop the dry brown devilgrass along the verges, heedless of the two huge wine casks on his back.

'Robbers,' Dunk said. Mounted atop Thunder, he was much closer to the dead men. 'Rapers. Murderers.' Dark circles stained his old green tunic under both arms. The sky was blue and the sun was blazing hot, and he had sweated gallons since breaking camp this morning.

Egg took off his wide-brimmed floppy straw hat. Beneath, his head was bald and shiny. He used the hat to fan away the flies. There were hundreds crawling on the dead men, and more drifting lazily through the still hot air. 'It must have been something bad, for them to be left to die inside a crow cage.'

Sometimes Egg could be as wise as any maester, but other times he was still a boy of ten. 'There are lords and lords,' Dunk said. 'Some don't need much reason to put a man to death.'

The iron cage was barely big enough to hold one man, yet two had been forced inside it. They stood face to face, with their arms and legs in a tangle and their backs against the hot black iron of the bars. One had tried to eat the other, gnawing at his neck and shoulder. The crows had been at both of them. When Dunk and Egg had come around the hill, the birds had risen like a black cloud, so thick that Maester spooked.

'Whoever they were, they look half-starved,' Dunk said. *Skeletons in skin, and the skin is green and rotting.* 'Might be they stole some bread, or poached a deer in some lord's wood.' With the drought entering its second year, most lords had become less tolerant of poaching, and they hadn't been very tolerant to begin with.

'It could be they were in some outlaw band.' At Dosk, they'd heard a harper sing 'The Day They Hanged Black Robin'. Ever since, Egg had been seeing gallant outlaws behind every bush.

Dunk had met a few outlaws while squiring for the old man. He was in no hurry to meet any more. None of the ones he'd known had been especially gallant. He remembered one outlaw Ser Arlan had helped hang, who'd been fond of stealing rings. He would cut off a man's fingers to get at them, but with women he preferred to bite. There were no songs about him that Dunk knew. *Outlaws or poachers, makes no matter. Dead men make poor company.* He walked Thunder slowly around the cage. The empty eyes seemed to follow him. One of the dead men had his head down and his mouth gaping open. *He has no tongue*, Dunk observed. He supposed the crows might have eaten it. Crows always pecked a corpse's eyes out first, he had heard, but maybe the tongue went second. *Or maybe a lord had it torn out, for something that he said.*

Dunk pushed his fingers through his mop of sun-streaked hair. The dead were beyond his help, and they had casks of wine to get to Standfast. 'Which way did we come?' he asked, looking from one road to the other. 'I'm turned around.'

'Standfast is that way, ser.' Egg pointed.

'That's for us, then. We could be back by evenfall, but not if we sit here all day counting flies.' He touched Thunder with his heels and turned the big destrier towards the left-hand fork. Egg put his floppy hat back on and tugged sharply at Maester's lead. The mule left off cropping at the devilgrass and came along without an argument for once. *He's hot as well*, Dunk thought, *and those wine casks must be heavy.*

The summer sun had baked the road as hard as brick. Its ruts were deep enough to break a horse's leg, so Dunk was careful to keep Thunder to the higher ground between them. He had twisted his own ankle the day they left Dosk, walking in the black of night when it was cooler. A knight had to learn to live with aches and pains, the old man used to say. *Aye, lad, and with broken bones and scars. They're as much a part of knighthood as your swords and shields.* If Thunder were to break a leg, though . . . well, a knight without a horse was no knight at all.

Egg followed five yards behind him, with Maester and the wine casks. The boy was walking with one bare foot in a rut and one out, so he rose and fell with every step. His dagger was sheathed on one hip, his boots slung over his backpack, his ragged brown tunic rolled up and knotted round his waist. Beneath his wide-brimmed straw hat, his face was smudged and dirty, his eyes large and dark. He was ten, not quite five feet tall. Of late he had been sprouting fast, though he had a long long ways to grow before he'd be catching up to Dunk. He looked just like the stableboy he wasn't, and not at all like who he really was.

The dead men soon disappeared behind them, but Dunk found himself thinking about them all the same. The realm was full of lawless men these days. The drought showed no signs of ending, and small-folk by the thousands had taken to the roads, looking for some place where the rains still fell. Lord Bloodraven had commanded them to return to their own lands and lords, but few obeyed. Many blamed Bloodraven and King Aerys for the drought. It was a judgment from the gods, they said, for the kinslayer is accursed. If they were wise, though, they did not say it loudly. *How many eyes does Lord Bloodraven have?* ran the riddle Egg had heard in Oldtown. *A thousand eyes, and one.*

Six years ago in King's Landing, Dunk had seen him with his own two eyes, as he rode a pale horse up the Street of Steel with fifty Raven's Teeth behind him. That was before King Aerys had ascended to the Iron Throne and made him the Hand, but even so he cut a striking figure, garbed in smoke and scarlet with Dark Sister on his hip. His pallid skin and bone-white hair made him look a living corpse. Across his cheek and chin spread a winestain birthmark that was supposed to resemble a red raven, though Dunk only saw an odd-shaped blotch of discoloured skin. He stared so hard that Bloodraven felt it. The king's sorcerer had turned to study him as he went by. He had one eye, and that one red. The other was a empty socket, the gift Bittersteel had given him upon the Redgrass Field. Yet it seemed to Dunk that both eyes had looked right through his skin, down to his very soul.

Despite the heat, the memory made him shiver. 'Ser?' Egg called. 'Are you unwell?'

'No,' said Dunk. 'I'm as hot and thirsty as them.' He pointed towards the field beyond the road, where rows of melons were shrivelling on the vines. Along the verges goatheads and tufts of devilgrass still clung to life, but the crops were not faring near as well. Dunk knew just how the melons felt. Ser Arlan used to say that no hedge knight need ever go thirsty. 'Not so long as he has a helm to catch the rain in. Rainwater is the best drink there is, lad.' The old man never saw a summer like this one, though. Dunk had left his helm at Standfast. It was too hot and heavy to wear, and there had been precious little rain to catch in it. *What's a hedge knight do when even the hedges are brown and parched and dying?*

Maybe when they reached the stream he'd have a soak. He smiled, thinking how good that would feel, to jump right in and come up sopping wet and grinning, with water cascading down his cheeks and through his tangled hair and his tunic clinging sodden to his skin. Egg might want a soak as well, though the boy looked cool and dry, more dusty than sweaty. He never sweated much. He liked the heat. In Dorne he went about barechested, and turned brown as a Dornishman. *It is his dragon blood*, Dunk told himself. *Whoever heard of a sweaty dragon?* He would gladly have pulled his own tunic off, but it would not be fitting. A hedge knight could ride bare naked if he chose; he had no one to shame but himself. It was different when your sword was sworn. *When you accept a lord's meat and mead, all you do reflects on him*, Ser Arlan used to say. *Always do more than he expects of you, never less. Never flinch at any task or hardship. And above all, never shame the lord you serve.* At Standfast, 'meat and mead' meant chicken and ale, but Ser Eustace ate the same plain fare himself.

Dunk kept his tunic on, and sweltered.

Ser Bennis of the Brown Shield was waiting at the old plank bridge. 'So you come back,' he called out. 'You were gone so long I thought you'd run off with the old man's silver.' Bennis was sitting on his shaggy garron, chewing a wad of sourleaf that made it look as if his mouth was full of blood.

'We had to go all the way to Dosk to find some wine,' Dunk told him. 'The krakens raided Little Dosk. They carried off the wealth and women and burned half of what they did not take.'

'That Dagon Greyjoy wants for hanging,' Bennis said. 'Aye, but who's to hang him? You see old Pinchbottom Pate?'

'They told us he was dead. The ironmen killed him when he tried to stop them taking off his daughter.'

'Seven bloody hells.' Bennis turned his head and spat. 'I seen that daughter once. Not worth dying for, you ask me. That fool Pate owed me half a silver.' The brown knight looked just as he had when they left; worse, he smelled the same as well. He wore the same garb every day: brown breeches, a shapeless roughspun tunic, horsehide boots. When armoured he donned a loose brown surcoat over a shirt of rusted mail. His swordbelt was a cord of boiled leather, and his seamed face might have been made of the same thing. *His head looks like one of those shrivelled melons that we passed.* Even his teeth were brown, under the red stains left by the sourleaf he liked to chew. Amid all that brownness, his eyes stood out; they were a pale green, squinty small, close set, and shiny-bright with malice. 'Only two casks,' he observed. 'Ser Useless wanted four.'

'We were lucky to find two,' said Dunk. 'The drought reached the Arbor too. We heard the grapes are turning into raisins on the vines, and the ironmen have been pirating –'

'Ser?' Egg broke in. 'The water's gone.'

Dunk had been so intent on Bennis that he hadn't noticed. Beneath the warped wooden planks of the bridge only sand and stones remained. *That's queer. The stream was running low when we left, but it was running.*

Bennis laughed. He had two sorts of laugh. Sometimes he cackled like a chicken, and sometimes he brayed louder than Egg's mule. This was his chicken laugh. 'Dried up while you was gone, I guess. A drought'll do that.'

Dunk was dismayed. *Well, I won't be soaking now.* He swung down to the ground. *What's going to happen to the crops?* Half the wells in the Reach had gone dry, and all the rivers were running low, even the Blackwater Rush and the mighty Mander.

'Nasty stuff, water,' Bennis said. 'Drank some once, and it made me sick as a dog. Wine's better.'

'Not for oats. Not for barleycorn. Not for carrots, onions, cabbages. Even grapes need water.' Dunk shook his head. 'How could it go dry so quick? We've only been six days.'

'Wasn't much water in there to start with, Dunk. Time was, I could piss me bigger streams than this one.'

'Not *Dunk* ,' said Dunk. 'I told you that.' He wondered why he bothered. Bennis was a mean-mouthed man, and it pleased him to make mock. 'I'm called Ser Duncan the Tall.'

'By who? Your bald pup?' He looked at Egg and laughed his chicken laugh. 'You're taller than when you did for Pennytree, but you still look a proper *Dunk* to me.'

Dunk rubbed the back of his neck and stared down at the rocks. 'What should we do?'

'Fetch home the wines, and tell Ser Useless his stream's gone dry. The Standfast well still draws; he won't go thirsty.'

'Don't call him Useless.' Dunk was fond of the old knight. 'You sleep beneath his roof, give him some respect.'

'You respect him for the both o' us, Dunk,' said Bennis. 'I'll call him what I will.'

The silvery-grey planks creaked heavily as Dunk walked out on to the bridge, to frown down at the sand and stones below. A few small brown pools glistened among the rocks, he saw, none larger than his hand. 'Dead fish, there and there, see?' The smell of them reminded him of the dead men at the crossroads.

'I see them, ser,' said Egg.

Dunk hopped down to the streambed, squatted on his heels, and turned over a stone. *Dry and warm on top, moist and muddy underneath.* 'The water can't have been gone long.' Standing, he flicked the stone sidearm at the bank, where it crashed through a crumbling overhang in a puff of dry brown earth. 'The soil's cracked along the banks, but soft and muddy in the middle. Those fish were alive yesterday.'

'Dunk the lunk, Pennytree used to call you, I recall.' Ser Bennis spat a wad of sourleaf on to the rocks. It glistened red and slimy in the sunlight. 'Lunks shouldn't try and think, their heads is too bloody thick for such.'

Dunk the lunk, thick as a castle wall. From Ser Arlan the words had been affectionate. He had been a kindly man, even in his scolding. In the mouth of Ser Bennis of the Brown Shield, they sounded different. 'Ser Arlan's two years dead,' Dunk said, 'and I'm called Ser Duncan the Tall.' He was sorely tempted to put his fist through the brown knight's face, and smash those red and rotten teeth to splinters. Bennis of the Brown Shield might be a nasty piece of work, but Dunk had a good foot and a half on him, and four stone as well. He might be a lunk, but he was big. Sometimes it seemed as though he'd thumped his head on half the doors in Westeros, not to mention every beam in every inn from Dorne up to the Neck. Egg's brother Aemon had measured him in Oldtown, and found he lacked an inch of seven feet, but that was half a year ago. He might have grown since. Growing was the one thing that Dunk did really well, the old man used to say.

He went back to Thunder and mounted up again. 'Egg, get on back to Standfast with the wine. I'm going to see what's happened to the water.'

'Streams dry up all the time,' said Bennis.

'I just want to have a look –'

'Like how you looked under that rock? Shouldn't go turning over rocks, lunk. Never know what might crawl out. We got us nice straw pallets back at Standfast. There's eggs more days than not, and not much to do but listen to Ser Useless go on about how great he used to be. Leave it be, I say. The stream went dry, that's all.'

Dunk was nothing if not stubborn. 'Ser Eustace is waiting on his wine,' he told Egg. 'Tell him where I went.'

'I will, ser.' Egg gave a tug on Maester's lead. The mule twitched his ears, but started off again at once. *He wants to get those wine casks off his back.* Dunk could not blame him.

The stream flowed north and east when it was flowing, so he turned Thunder south and west. He had not ridden a dozen yards before Bennis caught him. 'I best come see you don't get hanged.' He pushed a fresh sourleaf into his mouth. 'Past that clump o' sandwillows, the whole right bank is spider land.'

'I'll stay on our side.' Dunk wanted no trouble with the Lady of the Coldmoat. At Standfast you heard ill things of her. *The Red Widow*, she was called, for the husbands she had put into the ground. Old Sam Stoops said she was a witch, a poisoner, and worse. Two years ago she had sent her knights across the stream to seize an Osgrey man for stealing sheep. 'When m'lord rode to Coldmoat to demand him back, he was told to look for him at the bottom of the moat,' Sam had said. 'She'd sewn poor Dake in a bag o' rocks and sunk him. 'Twas after that Ser Eustace took Ser Bennis into service, to keep them spiders off his lands.'

Thunder kept a slow, steady pace beneath the broiling sun. The sky was blue and hard, with no hint of cloud anywhere to be seen. The course of the stream meandered around rocky knolls and forlorn willows, through bare brown hills and fields of dead and dying grain. An hour upstream from the bridge, they found themselves riding on the edge of the small Osgrey forest called Wat's Wood. The greenery looked inviting from afar, and filled Dunk's head with thoughts of shady glens and chuckling brooks, but when they reached the trees they found them thin and scraggly, with drooping limbs. Some of the great oaks were shedding leaves, and half the pines had turned as brown as Ser Bennis, with rings of dead needles girdling their trunks. *Worse and worse*, thought Dunk. *One spark, and this will all go up like tinder.*

For the moment, though, the tangled underbrush along the Chequy Water was still thick with thorny vines, nettles and tangles of briarwhite and young willow. Rather than fight through it, they crossed the dry streambed to the Coldmoat side, where the trees had been cleared away for pasture. Among the parched brown grasses and faded wildflowers, a few black-nosed sheep were grazing. 'Never knew an animal stupid as a sheep,' Ser Bennis commented. 'Think they're kin to you, lunk?' When Dunk did not reply, he laughed his chicken laugh again.

Half a league further south, they came upon the dam.

It was not large as such things went, but it looked strong. Two stout wooden barricades had been thrown across the stream from bank to bank, made from the trunks of trees with the bark still on. The space between them was filled with rocks and earth and packed down hard. Behind the dam the flow was creeping up the banks and spilling off into a ditch that had been cut through Lady Webber's fields. Dunk stood in his stirrups for a better look. The glint of sun on water betrayed a score of lesser channels, running off in all directions like a spider's web. *They are stealing our stream.* The sight filled him with indignation, especially when it dawned on him that the trees must surely have been taken from Wat's Wood.

'See what you went and did, lunk,' said Bennis. 'Couldn't have it that the stream dried up, no. Might be this starts with water, but it'll end with blood. Yours and mine, most like.' The brown knight drew his sword. 'Well, no help for it now. There's your thrice-damned diggers. Best we put some fear in them.' He raked his garron with his spurs and galloped through the grass.

Dunk had no choice but to follow. Ser Arlan's longsword rode his hip, a good straight piece of steel. *If these ditch diggers have a lick of sense, they'll run.* Thunder's hooves kicked up clods of dirt.

One man dropped his shovel at the sight of the oncoming knights, but that was all. There were a score of the diggers, short and tall, old and young, all baked brown by the sun. They formed a ragged line as Bennis slowed, clutching their spades and picks. 'This is Coldmoat land,' one shouted.

'And that's an Osgrey stream.' Bennis pointed with his longsword. 'Who put that damned dam up?'

'Maester Cerrick made it,' said one young digger.

'No,' an older man insisted. 'The grey pup pointed some and said do this and do that, but it were us who made it.'

'Then you can bloody well unmake it.'

The diggers' eyes were sullen and defiant. One wiped the sweat off his brow with the back of his hand. No one spoke.

'You lot don't hear so good,' said Bennis. 'Do I need to lop me off an ear or two? Who's first?'

'This is Webber land.' The old digger was a scrawny fellow, stooped and stubborn. 'You got no right to be here. Lop off any ears and m'lady will drown you in a sack.'

Bennis rode closer. 'Don't see no ladies here, just some mouthy peasant.' He poked the digger's bare brown chest with the point of his sword, just hard enough to draw a bead of blood.

He goes too far. 'Put up your steel,' Dunk warned him. 'This is not his doing. This maester set them to the task.'

'It's for the crops, ser,' a jug-eared digger said. 'The wheat was dying, the maester said. The pear trees too.'

'Well, maybe them pear trees die, or maybe you do.'

'Your talk don't frighten us,' said the old man.

'No?' Bennis made his longsword whistle, opening the old man's cheek from ear to jaw. 'I said, them pear trees die, or you do.' The digger's blood ran red down one side of his face.

He should not have done that. Dunk had to swallow his rage. Bennis was on his side in this. 'Get away from here,' he shouted at the diggers. 'Go back to your lady's castle.'

'*Run,*' Ser Bennis urged.

Three of them let go of their tools and did just that, sprinting through the grass. But another man, sunburnt and brawny, hefted a pick and said, 'There's only two of them.'

'Shovels against swords is a fool's fight, Jorgen,' the old man said, holding his face. Blood trickled through his fingers. 'This won't be the end of this. Don't think it will.'

'One more word, and I might be the end o' you.'

'We meant no harm to you,' Dunk said, to the old man's bloody face. 'All we want is our water. Tell your lady that.'

'Oh, we'll tell her, ser,' promised the brawny man, still clutching his pick. 'That we will.'

On the way home they cut through the heart of Wat's Wood, grateful for the small measure of shade provided by the trees. Even so, they cooked. Supposedly there were deer in the wood, but the only living things they saw were flies. They buzzed about Dunk's face as he rode, and crept round Thunder's eyes, irritating the big warhorse no end. The air was still, suffocating. *At least in Dorne the days were dry, and at night it grew so cold I shivered in my cloak.* In the Reach the nights were hardly cooler than the days, even this far north.

When ducking down beneath an overhanging limb, Dunk plucked a leaf and crumpled it between his fingers. It fell apart like thousand-year-old parchment in his hand. 'There was no need to cut that man,' he told Bennis.

'A tickle on the cheek was all it was, to teach him to mind his tongue. I should have cut his bloody throat for him, only then the rest would have run like rabbits, and we'd have had to ride down the lot o' them.'

'You'd kill twenty men?' Dunk said, incredulous.

'Twenty-two. That's two more'n all your fingers and your toes, lunk. You have to kill them all, else they go telling tales.' They circled round a deadfall. 'We should have told Ser Useless the drought dried up his little pissant stream.'

'Ser *Eustace*. You would have lied to him.'

'Aye, and why not? Who's to tell him any different? The flies?' Bennis grinned a wet red grin. 'Ser Useless never leaves the tower, except to see the boys down in the blackberries.'

'A sworn sword owes his lord the truth.'

'There's truths and truths, lunk. Some don't serve.' He spat. 'The gods make droughts. A man can't do a bloody buggering thing about the gods. The Red Widow, though . . . we tell Useless that bitch dog took his water, he'll feel honour bound to take it back. Wait and see. He'll think he's got to *do something*.'

'He should. Our smallfolk need that water for their crops.'

'*Our* smallfolk?' Ser Bennis brayed his laughter. 'Was I off having a squat when Ser Useless made you his heir? How many smallfolk you figure you got? Ten? And that's counting Squinty Jeyne's halfwit son that don't know which end o' the axe to hold. Go make knights o' every one, and we'll have half as many as the Widow, and never mind her squires and her archers and the rest. You'd need both hands and both feet to count all them, and your bald-head boy's fingers and toes too.'

'I don't need toes to count.' Dunk was sick of the heat, the flies, and the brown knight's company. *He may have ridden with Ser Arlan once, but that was years and years ago. The man is grown mean and false and craven.* He put his heels into his horse and trotted on ahead, to put the smell behind him.

Standfast was a castle only by courtesy. Though it stood bravely atop a rocky hill and could be seen for leagues around, it was no more than a towerhouse. A partial collapse a few centuries ago had required some rebuilding, so the north and west faces were pale grey stone above the windows, and the old black stone below. Turrets had been added to the roofline during the repair, but only on the sides that were rebuilt; at the other two corners crouched ancient stone grotesques, so badly abraded by wind and weather that it was hard to say what they had been. The pinewood roof was flat, but badly warped and prone to leaks.

A crooked path led from the foot of the hill up to the tower, so narrow it could only be ridden single file. Dunk led the way on the ascent, with Bennis just behind. He could see Egg above them, standing on a jut of rock in his floppy straw hat.

They reined up in front of the little daub-and-wattle stable that nestled at the tower's foot, half hidden under a misshapen heap of purple moss. The old man's grey gelding was in one of the stalls, next to Maester. Egg and Sam Stoops had got the wine inside, it seemed. Hens were wandering the yard. Egg trotted over. 'Did you find what happened to the stream?'

'The Red Widow's dammed it up.' Dunk dismounted, and gave Thunder's reins to Egg. 'Don't let him drink too much at once.'

'No, ser. I won't.'

'*Boy*,' Ser Bennis called. 'You can take my horse as well.'

Egg gave him an insolent look. 'I'm not your squire.'

That tongue of his will get him hurt one day, Dunk thought. 'You'll take his horse, or you'll get a clout in the ear.'

Egg made a sullen face, but did as he was bid. As he reached for the bridle, though, Ser Bennis hawked and spat. A glob of glistening red phlegm struck the boy between two toes. He gave the brown knight an icy look. 'You spat on my foot, ser.'

Bennis clambered to the ground. 'Aye. Next time I'll spit in your face. I'll have none o' your bloody tongue.'

Dunk could see the anger in the boy's eyes. 'Tend to the horses, Egg,' he said, before things got any worse. 'We need to speak with Ser Eustace.'

The only entrance into Standfast was through an oak-and-iron door twenty feet above them. The bottom steps were blocks of smooth black stone, so worn they were bowl-shaped in the middle. Higher up, they gave way to a steep wooden stair that could be swung up like a draw-bridge in times of trouble. Dunk shooed the hens aside and climbed two steps at a time.

Standfast was bigger than it appeared. Its deep vaults and cellars occupied a good part of the hill on which it perched. Above ground, the tower boasted four storeys. The upper two had windows and balconies, the lower two only arrow slits. It was cooler inside, but so dim that Dunk had to let his eyes adjust. Sam Stoops's wife was on her knees by the hearth, sweeping out the ashes. 'Is Ser Eustace above or below?' Dunk asked her.

'Up, ser.' The old woman was so hunched that her head was lower than her shoulders. 'He just come back from visiting the boys, down in the blackberries.'

The boys were Eustace Osgrey's sons: Edwyn, Harrold, Addam. Edwyn and Harrold had been knights, Addam a young squire. They had died on the Redgrass Field fifteen years ago, at the end of the Blackfyre Rebellion. 'They died good deaths, fighting bravely for the king,' Ser Eustace told Dunk, 'and I brought them home and buried them among the blackberries.' His wife was buried there as well. Whenever the old man breached a new cask of wine, he went down the hill to pour each of his boys a libation. 'To the king!' he would call out loudly, just before he drank.

Ser Eustace's bedchamber occupied the fourth floor of the tower, with his solar just below. That was where he would be found, Dunk knew, puttering among the chests and barrels. The solar's thick grey walls were hung with rusted weaponry and captured banners, prizes from battles fought long centuries ago, and now remembered by no one but Ser Eustace. Half of the banners were mildewed, and all were badly faded and covered with dust, their once bright colours gone to grey and green.

Ser Eustace was scrubbing the dirt off a ruined shield with a rag when Dunk came up the steps. Bennis followed fragrant at his heels. The old knight's eyes seemed to brighten a little at the sight of Dunk. 'My good giant,' he declared, 'and brave Ser Bennis. Come have a look at this. I found it in the bottom of that chest. A treasure, though fearfully neglected.'

It was a shield, or what remained of one. That was little enough. Almost half of it had been hacked away, and the rest was grey and splintered. The iron rim was solid rust, and the wood was full of wormholes. A few flakes of paint still clung to it, but too few to suggest a sigil.

'M'lord,' said Dunk. The Osgreys had not been lords for centuries, yet it pleased Ser Eustace to be styled so, echoing as it did the past glories of his House. 'What is it?'

'The Little Lion's shield.' The old man rubbed at the rim, and some flakes of rust came off. 'Ser Wilbert Osgrey bore this at the battle where he died. I am sure you know the tale.'

'No, m'lord,' said Bennis. 'We don't, as it happens. The *Little* Lion, did you say? What, was he a dwarf or some such?'

'Certainly not.' The old knight's moustache quivered. 'Ser Wilbert was a tall and powerful man, and a great knight. The name was given him in childhood, as the youngest of five brothers. In his day there were still seven kings in the Seven Kingdoms, and Highgarden and the Rock were oft at war. The green kings ruled us then, the Gardeners.

They were of the blood of old Garth Greenhand, and a green hand upon a white field was their kingly banner. Gyles the Third took his banners east, to war against the Storm King, and Wilbert's brothers all went with him, for in those days the chequy lion always flew beside the green hand when the King of the Reach went forth to battle.

'Yet it happened that while King Gyles was away, the King of the Rock saw his chance to tear a bite out of the Reach, so he gathered up a host of westermen and came down upon us. The Osgreys were the Marshals of the Northmarch, so it fell to the Little Lion to meet them. It was the fourth King Lancel who led the Lannisters, it seems to me, or mayhaps the fifth. Ser Wilbert blocked King Lancel's path, and bade him halt. *"Come no further,"* he said. *"You are not wanted here. I forbid you to set foot upon the Reach."* But the Lannister ordered all his banners forward.'

'They fought for half a day, the gold lion and the chequy. The Lannister was armed with a Valyrian sword that no common steel can match, so the Little Lion was hard pressed, his shield in ruins. In the end, bleeding from a dozen grievous wounds with his own blade broken in his hand, he threw himself headlong at his foe. King Lancel cut him near in half, the singers say, but as he died the Little Lion found the gap in the king's armour beneath his arm, and plunged his dagger home. When their king died, the westermen turned back, and the Reach was saved.' The old man stroked the broken shield as tenderly as if it had been a child.

'Aye, m'lord,' Bennis croaked, 'we could use a man like that today. Dunk and me had a look at your stream, m'lord. Dry as a bone, and not from no drought.'

The old man set the shield aside. 'Tell me.' He took a seat, and indicated that they should do the same. As the brown knight launched into the tale, he sat listening intently, with his chin up and his shoulders back, as upright as a lance.

In his youth, Ser Eustace Osgrey must have been the very picture of chivalry, tall and broad and handsome. Time and grief had worked their will on him, but he was still unbent, a big-boned, broad-shouldered, barrel-chested man with features as strong and sharp as some old eagle. His close-cropped hair had gone white as milk, but the thick moustache that hid his mouth remained an ashy grey. His eyebrows were the same colour, the eyes beneath a paler shade of grey, and full of sadness.

They seemed to grow sadder still when Bennis touched upon the dam. 'That stream has been known as the Chequy Water for a thousand years or more,' the old knight said. 'I caught fish there as a boy, and my sons all did the same. Alysanne liked to splash in the shallows on hot summer days like this.' Alysanne had been his daughter, who had perished in the spring. 'It was on the banks of the Chequy Water that I kissed a girl for the first time. A cousin, she was, my uncle's youngest daughter, of the Osgreys of Leafy Lake. They are all gone now, even her.' His moustache quivered. 'This cannot be borne, sers. The woman will not have my water. She will not have my *Chequy* Water.'

'Dam's built strong, m'lord,' Ser Bennis warned. 'Too strong for me and Ser Dunk to pull down in an hour, even with the bald-head boy to help. We'll need ropes and picks and axes, and a dozen men. And that's just for the work, not for the fighting.'

Ser Eustace stared at the Little Lion's shield.

Dunk cleared his throat. 'M'lord, as to that, when we came upon the diggers, well . . .'

'Dunk, don't trouble m'lord with trifles,' said Bennis. 'I taught one fool a lesson, that was all.'

Ser Eustace looked up sharply. 'What sort of lesson?'

'With my sword, as it were. A little claret on his cheek, that's all it were, m'lord.'

The old knight looked long at him. 'That . . . that was ill-considered, ser. The woman has a spider's heart. She murdered three of her husbands. And all her brothers died in swaddling clothes. Five, there were. Or six, mayhaps, I don't recall. They stood between her and the castle. She would whip the skin off any peasant who displeased her, I do not doubt, but for *you* to cut one . . . no, she will not suffer such an insult. Make no mistake. She will come for you, as she came for Lem.'

'Dake, m'lord,' Ser Bennis said. 'Begging your lordly pardon, you knew him and I never did, but his name were Dake.'

'If it please m'lord, I could go to Goldengrove and tell Lord Rowan of this dam,' said Dunk. Rowan was the old knight's liege lord. The Red Widow held her lands of him as well.

'Rowan? No, look for no help there. Lord Rowan's sister wed Lord Wyman's cousin Wendell, so he is kin to the Red Widow. Besides, he loves me not. Ser Duncan, on the morrow you must make the rounds of all my villages, and roust out every able-bodied man of fighting age. I am old, but I am not dead. The woman will soon find that the chequy lion still has claws!'

Two, Dunk thought glumly, *and I am one of them.*

*   *   *

Ser Eustace's lands supported three small villages, none more than a handful of hovels, sheepfolds and pigs. The largest boasted a thatched one-room sept with crude pictures of the Seven scratched upon the walls in charcoal. Mudge, a stoop-backed old swineherd who'd once been to Oldtown, led devotions there every seventh day. Twice a year a real septon came through to forgive sins in the Mother's name. The smallfolk were glad of the forgiveness, but hated the septon's visits all the same, since they were required to feed him.

They seemed no more pleased by the sight of Dunk and Egg. Dunk was known in the villages, if only as Ser Eustace's new knight, but not so much as a cup of water was offered him. Most of the men were in the fields, so it was largely women and children who crept out of the hovels at their coming, along with a few grandfathers too infirm for work. Egg bore the Osgrey banner, the chequy lion green and gold, rampant upon its field of white. 'We come from Standfast with Ser Eustace's summons,' Dunk told the villagers. 'Every able-bodied man between the ages of fifteen and fifty is commanded to assemble at the tower on the morrow.'

'Is it war?' asked one thin woman, with two children hiding behind her skirts and a babe sucking at her breast. 'Is the black dragon come again?'

'There are no dragons in this, black or red,' Dunk told her. 'This is between the chequy lion and the spiders. The Red Widow has taken your water.'

The woman nodded, though she looked askance when Egg took off his hat to fan his face. 'That boy got no hair. He sick?'

'It's *shaved*,' said Egg. He put the hat back on, turned Maester's head, and rode off slowly.

The boy is in a prickly mood today. He had hardly said a word since they set out. Dunk gave Thunder a touch of the spur and soon caught the mule. 'Are you angry that I did not take your part against Ser Bennis yesterday?' he asked his sullen squire, as they made for the next village. 'I like the man no more than you, but he *is* a knight. You should speak to him with courtesy.'

'I'm your squire, not his,' the boy said. 'He's dirty and mean-mouthed, and he pinches me.'

If he had an inkling who you were, he'd piss himself before he laid a finger on you. 'He used to pinch me too.' Dunk had forgotten that, till Egg's words brought it back. Ser Bennis and Ser Arlan had been among a party of knights hired by a Dornish merchant to see him safe from Lannisport to the Prince's Pass. Dunk had been no older than Egg, though taller. *He would pinch me under the arm so hard he'd leave a bruise. His fingers felt like iron pincers, but I never told Ser Arlan.* One of the other knights had vanished near Stoney Sept, and it was bruited about that Bennis had gutted him in a quarrel. 'If he pinches you again, tell me and I'll end it. Till then, it does not cost you much to tend his horse.'

'Someone has to,' Egg agreed. 'Bennis never brushes him. He never cleans his stall. He hasn't even *named* him!'

'Some knights never name their horses,' Dunk told him. 'That way, when they die in battle, the grief is not so hard to bear. There are always more horses to be had, but it's hard to lose a faithful friend.' *Or so the old man said, but he never took his own counsel. He named every horse he ever owned.* So had Dunk. 'We'll see how many men turn up at the tower . . . but whether it's five or fifty, you'll need to do for them as well.'

Egg looked indignant. 'I have to serve *smallfolk*? '

'Not serve. Help. We need to turn them into fighters.' *If the widow gives us time enough.* 'If the gods are good, a few will have done some soldiering before, but most will be green as summer grass, more used to holding hoes than spears. Even so, a day may come when our lives depend on them. How old were you when you first took up a sword?'

'I was little, ser. The sword was made from wood.'

'Common boys fight with wooden swords too, only theirs are sticks and broken branches. Egg, these men may seem fools to you. They won't know the proper names for bits of armour, or the arms of the great houses, or which king it was who abolished the lord's right to the first night . . . but treat them with respect all the same. You are a squire born of noble blood, but you are still a boy. Most of them will be men grown. A man has his pride, no matter how lowborn he may be. You would seem just as lost and stupid in their villages. And if you doubt that, go hoe a row and shear a sheep, and tell me the names of all the weeds and wildflowers in Wat's Wood.'

The boy considered for a moment. 'I could teach them the arms of the great houses, and how Queen Alysanne convinced King Jaehaerys to abolish the first night. And they could teach me which weeds are best for making poisons, and whether those green berries are safe to eat.'

'They could,' Dunk agreed, 'but before you get to King Jaehaerys, you'd best help us teach them how to use a spear. And don't go eating anything that Maester won't.'

*　　*　　*

The next day a dozen would-be warriors found their way to Standfast to assemble among the chickens. One was too old, two were too young, and one skinny boy turned out to be a skinny girl. Those Dunk sent back to their villages, leaving eight: three Wats, two Wills, a Lem, a Pate and Big Rob the lackwit. *A sorry lot*, he could not help but think. The strapping handsome peasant boys who won the hearts of high-born maidens in the songs were nowhere to be seen. Each man was dirtier than the last. Lem was fifty if he was a day, and Pate had weepy eyes; they were the only two who had ever soldiered before. Both had been gone with Ser Eustace and his sons to fight in the Blackfyre Rebellion. The other six were as green as Dunk had feared. All eight had lice. Two of the Wats were brothers. 'Guess your mother didn't know no other name,' Bennis said, cackling.

As far as arms went, they brought a scythe, three hoes, an old knife, some stout wooden clubs. Lem had a sharpened stick that might serve for a spear, and one of the Wills allowed that he was good at chucking rocks. 'Well and good,' Bennis said, 'we got us a bloody trebuchet.' After that the man was known as Treb.

'Are any of you skilled with a longbow?' Dunk asked them.

The men scuffed at the dirt, while hens pecked the ground around them. Pate of the weepy eyes finally answered. 'Begging your pardon, ser, but m'lord don't permit us longbows. Osgrey deers is for the chequy lions, not the likes o' us.'

'We will get swords and helms and chainmail?' the youngest of the three Wats wanted to know.

'Why, sure you will,' said Bennis, 'just as soon as you kill one o' the widow's knights and strip his bloody corpse. Make sure you stick your arm up his horse's arse too, that's where you'll find his silver.' He pinched young Wat beneath his arm until the lad squealed in pain, then marched the whole lot of them off to Wat's Wood to cut some spears.

When they came back, they had eight fire-hardened spears of wildly unequal length, and crude shields of woven branches. Ser Bennis had made himself a spear as well, and he showed them how to thrust with the point and use the shaft to parry . . . and where to put the point to kill. 'The belly and the throat are best, I find.' He pounded his fist against his chest. 'Right there's the heart, that will do the job as well. Trouble is, the ribs is in the way. The belly's nice and soft. Gutting's slow, but certain. Never knew a man to live when his guts was hanging out. Now if some fool goes and turns his back on you, put your point between his shoulder blades or through his kidney. That's here. They don't live long once you prick 'em in the kidney.'

Having three Wats in the company caused confusion when Bennis was trying to tell them what to do. 'We should give them village names, ser,' Egg suggested, 'like Ser Arlan of Pennytree, your old master.' That might have worked, only their villages had no names either. 'Well,' said Egg, 'we could call them for their crops, ser.' One village sat among beanfields, one planted mostly barleycorn, and the third cultivated rows of cabbages, carrots, onions, turnips and melons. No one wanted to be a Cabbage or a Turnip, so the last lot became the Melons. They ended up with four Barleycorns, two Melons and two Beans. As the brothers Wat were both Barleycorns, some further distinction was required. When the younger brother made mention of once having fallen down the village well, Bennis dubbed him 'Wet Wat', and that was that. The men were thrilled to have been given 'lord's names', save for Big Rob, who could not seem to remember whether he was a Bean or a Barleycorn.

Once all of them had names and spears, Ser Eustace emerged from Standfast to address them. The old knight stood outside the tower door, wearing his mail and plate beneath a long woollen surcoat that age had turned more yellow than white. On front and back it bore the chequy lion, sewn in little squares of green and gold. 'Lads,' he said, 'you all remember Dake. The Red Widow threw him in a sack and drowned him. She took his life, and now she thinks to take our water too, the Chequy Water that nourishes our crops . . . but she will not!' He raised his sword above his head. 'For Osgrey!' he said ringingly. 'For Standfast!'

'Osgrey!' Dunk echoed. Egg and the recruits took up the shout. 'Ogsrey! Osgrey! For Standfast! '

Dunk and Bennis drilled the little company among the pigs and chickens, while Ser Eustace watched from the balcony above. Sam Stoops had stuffed some old sacks with soiled straw. Those became their foes. The recruits began practising their spear work as Bennis bellowed at them. 'Stick and twist and rip it free. Stick and twist and rip, but *get the damn thing out*! You'll be wanting it soon enough for the next one. Too slow, Treb, too damn slow. If you can't do it quicker, go back to chucking rocks. Lem, get your weight behind your thrust. There's a boy. And in and out and in and out. Fuck 'em with it, that's the way, in and out, rip 'em, rip 'em, *rip 'em* '

When the sacks had been torn to pieces by half a thousand spear thrusts and all the straw spilled out on to the ground, Dunk donned his mail and plate and took up a wooden sword to see how the men would fare against a livelier foe.

Not too well, was the answer. Only Treb was quick enough to get a spear past Dunk's shield, and he did it only once. Dunk turned one clumsy lurching thrust after another, pushed their spears aside, and bulled in close. If his sword had been steel instead of pine, he would have slain each of them half a dozen times. 'You're *dead* once I get past your point,' he warned them, hammering at their legs and arms to drive the lesson home. Treb and Lem and Wet Wat soon learned how to give ground, at least. Big Rob dropped his spear and ran, and Bennis had to chase him down and drag him back in tears. The end of the afternoon saw the lot of them all bruised and battered, with fresh blisters rising on their callused hands from where they gripped the spears. Dunk bore no marks himself, but he was half-drowned by sweat by the time Egg helped him peel his armour off.

As the sun was going down, Dunk marched their little company down into the cellar and forced them all to have a bath, even those who'd had one just last winter. Afterward Sam Stoops's wife had bowls of stew for all, thick with carrots, onions and barley. The men were bone-tired, but to hear them talk every one would soon be twice as deadly as a Kingsguard knight. They could hardly wait to prove their valour. Ser Bennis egged them on by telling them of the joys of the soldier's life: loot and women, chiefly. The two old hands agreed with him. Lem had brought back a knife and a pair of fine boots from the Blackfyre Rebellion, to hear him tell; the boots were two small for him to wear, but he had them hanging on his wall. And Pate could not say enough about some of the camp followers he'd known following the dragon.

Sam Stoops had set them up with eight straw pallets in the under-croft, so once their bellies were filled they all went off to sleep. Bennis lingered long enough to give Dunk a look of disgust. 'Ser Useless should have fucked a few more peasant wenches while he still had a bit o' sap left in them old sad balls o' his,' he said. 'If he'd sown himself a nice crop o' bastard boys back then, might be we'd have some soldiers now.'

'They seem no worse than any other peasant levy.' Dunk had marched with a few such while squiring for Ser Arlan.

'Aye,' Ser Bennis said. 'In a fortnight they might stand their own, 'gainst some other lot o' peasants. Knights, though?' He shook his head, and spat.

Standfast's well was in the undercellar, in a dank chamber walled in stone and earth. It was there that Sam Stoops's wife soaked and scrubbed and beat the clothes before carrying them up to the roof to dry. The big stone washtub was also used for baths. Bathing required drawing water from the well bucket by bucket, heating it over the hearth in a big iron kettle, emptying the kettle into the tub, then starting the whole process once again. It took four buckets to fill the kettle, and three kettles to fill the tub. By the time the last kettle was hot the water from the first had cooled to lukewarm. Ser Bennis had been heard to say that the whole thing was too much bloody bother, which was why he crawled with lice and fleas and smelled like a bad cheese.

Dunk at least had Egg to help him when he felt in dire need of a good wash, as he did tonight. The lad drew the water in a glum silence, and hardly spoke as it was heating. 'Egg?' Dunk asked as the last kettle was coming to a boil. 'Is aught amiss?' When Egg made no reply, he said, 'Help me with the kettle.'

Together they wrestled it from hearth to tub, taking care not to splash themselves. 'Ser,' the boy said, 'what do you think Ser Eustace means to do?'

'Tear down the dam, and fight off the widow's men if they try to stop us.' He spoke loudly, so as to be heard above the splashing of the bath water. Steam rose in a white curtain as they poured, bringing a flush to his face.

'Their shields are woven wood, ser. A lance could punch right through them, or a crossbow bolt.'

'We may find some bits of armour for them, when they're ready.' That was the best they could hope for.

'They might be killed, ser. Wet Wat is still half a boy. Will Barleycorn is to be married the next time the septon comes. And Big Rob doesn't even know his left foot from his right.'

Dunk let the empty kettle thump down on to the hard-packed earthen floor. 'Roger of Pennytree was younger than Wet Wat when he died on the Redgrass Field. There were men in your father's host who'd just been married too, and other men who'd never even kissed a girl. There were hundreds who didn't know their left foot from their right, maybe thousands.'

'That was *different*,' Egg insisted. 'That was war.'

'So is this. The same thing, only smaller.'

'Smaller and *stupider*, ser.'

'That's not for you or me to say,' Dunk told him. 'It's their duty to go to war when Ser Eustace summons them . . . and to die, if needs be.'

'Then we shouldn't have named them, ser. It will only make the grief harder for us when they die.' He screwed up his face. 'If we used my boot –'

'No.' Dunk stood on one leg to pull his own boot off.

'Yes, but my father –'

'No.' The second boot went the way of the first.

'We –'

'No.' Dunk pulled his sweat-stained tunic up over his head, and tossed it at Egg. 'Ask Sam Stoops's wife to wash that for me.'

'I will, ser, but –'

'No, I said. Do you need a clout in the ear to help you hear better?' He unlaced his breeches. Underneath was only him; it was too hot for smallclothes. 'It's good that you're concerned for Wat and Wat and Wat and the rest of them, but the boot is only meant for dire need.' *How many eyes does Lord Bloodraven have? A thousand eyes, and one.* 'What did your father tell you, when he sent you off to squire for me?'

'To keep my hair shaved or dyed, and tell no man my true name,' the boy said, with obvious reluctance.

Egg had served Dunk for a good year and a half, though some days it seemed like twenty. They had climbed the Prince's Pass together and crossed the deep sands of Dorne, both red and white. A poleboat had taken them down the Greenblood to the Planky Town, where they took passage for Oldtown on the galleass *White Lady* . They had slept in stables, inns, and ditches, broken bread with holy brothers, whores and mummers, and chased down a hundred puppet shows. Egg had kept Dunk's horse groomed, his longsword sharp, his mail free of rust. He had been as good a companion as any man could wish for, and the hedge knight had come to think of him almost as a little brother.

He isn't, though. This egg had been hatched of dragons, not of chickens. *Egg* might be a hedge knight's squire, but Aegon of House Targaryen was the fourth and youngest son of Maekar, Prince of Summerhall, himself the fourth son of the late King Daeron the Good, the Second of His Name, who'd sat the Iron Throne for five and twenty years until the Great Spring Sickness took him off.

'So far as most folk are concerned, Aegon Targaryen went back to Summerhall with his brother Daeron after the tourney at Ashford Meadow,' Dunk reminded the boy. 'Your father did not want it known that you were wandering the Seven Kingdoms with some hedge knight. So let's hear no more about your boot.'

A look was all the answer that he got. Egg had big eyes, and somehow his shaven head made them look even larger. In the dimness of the lamplit cellar they looked black, but in better light their true colour could be seen: deep and dark and purple. *Valyrian eyes*, thought Dunk. In Westeros, few but the blood of the dragon had eyes that colour, or hair that shone like beaten gold and strands of silver woven all together.

When they'd been poling down the Greenblood, the orphan girls had made a game of rubbing Egg's shaven head for luck. It made the boy blush redder than a pomegranate. 'Girls are so *stupid*,' he would say. 'The next one who touches me is going into the river.' Dunk had to tell him, 'Then *I'll* be touching you. I'll give you such a clout in the ear you'll be hearing bells for a moon's turn.' That only goaded the boy to further insolence. 'Better bells than stupid *girls*,' he insisted, but he never threw anyone into the river.

Dunk stepped into the tub and eased himself down until the water covered him up to his chin. It was still scalding hot on top, though cooler further down. He clenched his teeth to keep from yelping. If he did the boy would laugh. Egg *liked* his bath water scalding hot.

'Do you need more water boiled, ser?'

'This will serve.' Dunk rubbed at his arms and watched the dirt come off in long grey clouds. 'Fetch me the soap. Oh, and the long-handled scrub brush too.' Thinking about Egg's hair had made him remember that his own was filthy. He took a deep breath and slid down beneath the water to give it a good soak. When he emerged again, sloshing, Egg was standing beside the tub with the soap and long-handled horsehair brush in hand. 'You have hairs on your cheek,' Dunk observed, as he took the soap from him. 'Two of them. There, below your ear. Make sure you get them the next time you shave your head.'

'I will, ser.' The boy seemed pleased by the discovery.

No doubt he thinks a bit of beard makes him a man . Dunk had thought the same when he first found some fuzz growing on his upper lip. *I tried to shave with my dagger, and almost nicked my nose off.* 'Go and get some sleep now,' he told Egg. 'I won't have any more need of you till morning.'

It took a long while to scrub all the dirt and sweat away. Afterwards, he put the soap aside, stretched out as much as he was able, and closed his eyes. The water had cooled by then. After the savage heat of the day, it was a welcome relief. He soaked till his feet and fingers were all wrinkled up and the water had gone grey and cold, and only then reluctantly climbed out.

Though he and Egg had been given thick straw pallets down in the cellar, Dunk preferred to sleep up on the roof. The air was fresher there, and sometimes there was a breeze. It was not as though he need have much fear of rain. The next time it rained on them up there would be the first.

Egg was asleep by the time Dunk reached the roof. He lay on his back with his hands behind his head and stared up at the sky. The stars were everywhere, thousands and thousands of them. It reminded him of a night at Ashford Meadow, before the tourney started. He had seen a falling star that night. Falling stars were supposed to bring you luck, so he'd told Tanselle to paint it on his shield, but Ashford had been anything but lucky for him. Before the tourney ended, he had almost lost a hand and a foot, and three good men had lost their lives. *I gained a squire, though. Egg was with me when I rode away from Ashford. That was the only good thing to come of all that happened.*

He hoped that no stars fell tonight.

There were red mountains in the distance and white sands beneath his feet. Dunk was digging, plunging a spade into the dry hot earth, and flinging the fine sand back over his shoulder. He was making a hole. *A grave*, he thought, *a grave for hope*. A trio of Dornish knights stood watching, making mock of him in quiet voices. Further off the merchants waited with their mules and wayns and sand sledges. They wanted to be off, but he could not leave until he'd buried Chestnut. He would not leave his old friend to the snakes and scorpions and sand dogs.

The stot had died on the long thirsty crossing between the Prince's Pass and Vaith, with Egg upon his back. His front legs just seemed to fold up under him, and he knelt right down, rolled on to his side, and died. His carcass sprawled beside the hole. Already it was stiff. Soon it would begin to smell.

Dunk was weeping as he dug, to the amusement of the Dornish knights. 'Water is precious in the waste,' one said, 'you ought not to waste it, ser.' The other chuckled and said, 'Why do you weep? It was only a horse, and a poor one.'

Chestnut, Dunk thought, digging, *his name was Chestnut, and he bore me on his back for years, and never bucked or bit.* The old stot had looked a sorry thing beside the sleek sand steeds that the Dornishmen were riding, with their elegant heads, long necks and flowing manes, but he had given all he had to give.

'Weeping for a swaybacked stot?' Ser Arlan said, in his old man's voice. 'Why, lad, you never wept for me, who put you on his back.'

He gave a little laugh, to show he meant no harm by the reproach. 'That's Dunk the lunk, thick as a castle wall.'

'He shed no tears for me, either,' said Baelor Breakspear from the grave, 'though I was his prince, the hope of Westeros. The gods never meant for me to die so young.'

'My father was only nine-and-thirty,' said Prince Valarr. 'He had it in him to be a great king, the greatest since Aegon the Dragon.' He looked at Dunk with cool blue eyes. 'Why would the gods take him, and leave *you*?' The Young Prince had his father's light brown hair, but a streak of silver-gold ran through it.

You are dead, Dunk wanted to scream, *you are all three dead, why won't you leave me be*? Ser Arlan had died of a chill, Prince Baelor of the blow his brother dealt him during Dunk's trial of seven, his son Valarr during the Great Spring Sickness. *I am not to blame for that. We were in Dorne, we never even knew.*

'You are mad,' the old man told him. 'We will dig no hole for you, when you kill yourself with this folly. In the deep sands a man must hoard his water.'

'Begone with you, Ser Duncan,' Valarr said. 'Begone.'

Egg helped him with the digging. The boy had no spade, only his hands, and the sand flowed back into the grave as fast as they could fling it out. It was like trying to dig a hole in the sea. *I have to keep digging*, Dunk told himself, though his back and shoulders ached from the effort. *I have to bury him down deep where the sand dogs cannot find him. I have to . . .*

'. . . die?' said Big Rob the simpleton from the bottom of the grave. Lying there, so still and cold, with a ragged red wound gaping in his belly, he did not look very big at all.

Dunk stopped and stared at him. 'You're not dead. You're down sleeping in the cellar.' He looked to Ser Arlan for help. 'Tell him, ser,' he pleaded, 'tell him to get out of the grave.'

Only it was not Ser Arlan of Pennytree standing over him at all, it was Ser Bennis of the Brown Shield. The brown knight only cackled. 'Dunk the lunk,' he said, 'gutting's slow, but certain. Never knew a man to live with his entrails hanging out.' Red froth bubbled on his lips. He turned and spat, and the white sands drank it down. Treb was standing behind him with an arrow in his eye, weeping slow red tears. And there was Wet Wat too, his head cut near in half, with old Lem and red-eyed Pate and all the rest. They had all been chewing sourleaf with Bennis, Dunk thought at first, but then he realized that it was blood trickling from their mouths. *Dead*, he thought, *all dead*, and the brown knight brayed. 'Aye, so best get busy. You've more graves to dig, lunk. Eight for them and one for me and one for old Ser Useless, and one last one for your bald-head boy.'

The spade slipped from Dunk's hands. 'Egg,' he cried, 'run! We have to *run*!' But the sands were giving way beneath their feet. When the boy tried to scramble from the hole, its crumbling sides gave way and collapsed. Dunk saw the sands wash over Egg, burying him as he opened his mouth to shout. He tried to fight his way to him, but the sands were rising all around him, pulling him down into the grave, filling his mouth, his nose, his eyes . . .

Come the break of day, Ser Bennis set about teaching their recruits to form a shield wall. He lined the eight of them up shoulder to shoulder, with their shields touching and their spear points poking through like long sharp wooden teeth. Then Dunk and Egg mounted up and charged them.

Maester refused to go within ten feet of the spears and stopped abruptly, but Thunder had been trained for this. The big warhorse pounded straight ahead, gathering speed. Hens ran beneath his legs and flapped away screeching. Their panic must have been contagious. Once more Big Rob was the first to drop his spear and run, leaving a gap in the middle of the wall. Instead of closing up, Standfast's other warriors joined the flight. Thunder trod upon their discarded shields before Dunk could rein him up. Woven branches cracked and splintered beneath his iron-shod hooves. Ser Bennis rattled off a pungent string of curses as chickens and peasants scattered in all directions. Egg fought manfully to hold his laughter in, but finally lost the battle.

'Enough of that.' Dunk drew Thunder to a halt, unfastened his helm, and tore it off. 'If they do that in a battle, it will get the whole lot of them killed.' *And you and me as well, most like.* The morning was already hot, and he felt as soiled and sticky as if he'd never bathed at all. His head was pounding, and he could not forget the dream he had dreamed the night before. *It never happened that way*, he tried to tell himself. *It wasn't like that.*

Chestnut had died on the long dry ride to Vaith; that part was true. He and Egg rode double until Egg's brother gave them Maester. The rest of it, though . . .

I never wept. I might have wanted to, but I never did. He had wanted to bury the horse as well, but the Dornishmen would not wait. 'Sand dogs must eat and feed their pups,' one of the Dornish knights told him as he helped Dunk strip the stot of saddle and bridle. 'His flesh will feed the dogs or feed the sands. In a year, his bones will be scoured clean. This is Dorne, my friend.' Remembering, Dunk could not help but wonder who would feed on Wat's flesh, and Wat's and Wat's. *Maybe there are chequy fish down beneath the Chequy Water.*

He rode Thunder back to the tower and dismounted. 'Egg, help Ser Bennis round them up and get them back here.' He shoved his helm at Egg and strode to the steps.

Ser Eustace met him in the dimness of his solar. 'That was not well done.'

'No, m'lord,' said Dunk. 'They will not serve.' *A sworn sword owes his liege service and obedience, but this is madness.*

'It was their first time. Their fathers and brothers were as bad or worse when they began their training. My sons worked with them, before we went to help the king. Every day, for a good fortnight. They made soldiers of them.'

'And when the battle came, m'lord?' Dunk asked. 'How did they fare then? How many of them came home with you?'

The old knight looked long at him. 'Lem,' he said at last, 'and Pate and Dake. Dake foraged for us. He was as fine a forager as I ever knew. We never marched on empty bellies. Three came back, ser. Three and me.' His moustache quivered. 'It may take longer than a fortnight.'

'M'lord,' said Dunk, 'the woman could be here upon the morrow, with all her men.' *They are good lads,* he thought, *but they will soon be dead lads, if they go up against the knights of Coldmoat.* 'There must be some other way.'

'Some other way.' Ser Eustace ran his fingers lightly across the Little Lion's shield. 'I will have no justice from Lord Rowan, nor this king . . .' He grasped Dunk by the forearm. 'It comes to me that in days gone by, when the green kings ruled, you could pay a man a blood price if you had slain one of his animals or peasants.'

'A blood price?' Dunk was dubious.

'Some other way, you said. I have some coin laid by. It was only a little claret on the cheek, Ser Bennis says. I could pay the man a silver stag, and three to the woman for the insult. I could, and would . . . if she would take the dam down.' The old man frowned. 'I cannot go to her, however. Not at Coldmoat.' A fat black fly buzzed around his head and lighted on his arm. 'The castle was ours once. Did you know that, Ser Duncan?'

'Aye, m'lord.' Sam Stoops had told him.

'For a thousand years before the Conquest, we were the Marshals of the Northmarch. A score of lesser lordlings did us fealty, and a hundred landed knights. We had four castles then, and watchtowers on the hills to warn of the coming of our enemies. Coldmoat was the greatest of our seats. Lord Perwyn Osgrey raised it. Perwyn the Proud, they called him.

'After the Field of Fire, Highgarden passed from kings to stewards and the Osgreys dwindled and diminished. 'Twas Aegon's son King Maegor who took Coldmoat from us, when Lord Ormond Osgrey spoke out against his suppression of the Stars and Swords, as the Poor Fellows and the Warrior's Sons were called.' His voice had grown hoarse. 'There is a chequy lion carved into the stone above the gates of Coldmoat. My father showed it to me, the first time he took me with him to call on old Reynard Webber. I showed it to my own sons in turn. Addam . . . Addam served at Coldmoat, as a page and squire, and a . . . a certain . . . fondness grew up between him and Lord Wyman's daughter. So one winter day I donned my richest raiment and went to Lord Wyman to propose a marriage. His refusal was courteous, but as I left I heard him laughing with Ser Lucas Inchfield. I never returned to Coldmoat after that, save once, when that woman presumed to carry off one of mine own. When they told me to seek for poor Lem at the bottom of the moat –'

'Dake,' said Dunk. 'Bennis says his name was Dake.'

'Dake?' The fly was creeping down his sleeve, pausing to rub its legs together the way flies did. Ser Eustace shooed it away, and rubbed his lip beneath his moustache. 'Dake. That was what I said. A staunch fellow, I recall him well. He foraged for us, during the war. We never marched on empty bellies. When Ser Lucas informed me of what had been done to my poor Dake, I swore a holy vow that I would never again set foot inside that castle again, unless to take possession. So you see, I cannot go there, Ser Duncan. Not to pay the blood price, or for any other reason. I *cannot.* '

Dunk understood. 'I could go, m'lord. I swore no vows.'

'You are a good man, Ser Duncan. A brave knight, and true.' Ser Eustace gave Dunk's arm a squeeze. 'Would that the gods had spared my Alysanne. You are the sort of man I had always hoped that she might marry. A true knight, Ser Duncan. A true knight.'

Dunk was turning red. 'I will tell Lady Webber what you said, about the blood price, but . . .'

'You will save Ser Bennis from Dake's fate. I know it. I am no mean judge of men, and you are the true steel. You will give them pause, ser. The very sight of you. When that woman sees that Standfast has such a champion, she may well take down that dam of her own accord.'

Dunk did not know what to say to that. He knelt. 'M'lord. I will go upon the morrow, and do the best I can.'

'On the morrow.' The fly came circling back, and lit upon Ser Eustace's left hand. He raised his right and smashed it flat. 'Yes. On the morrow.'

'*Another* bath?' Egg said, dismayed. 'You washed yesterday.'

'And then I spent a day in armour, swimming in my sweat. Close your lips and fill the kettle.'

'You washed the night Ser Eustace took us into service,' Egg pointed out. 'And last night, and now. That's *three times*, ser.'

'I need to treat with a highborn lady. Do you want me to turn up before her high seat smelling like Ser Bennis?'

'You would have to roll in a tub of Maester's droppings to smell as bad as that, ser.' Egg filled the kettle. 'Sam Stoops says the castellan at Coldmoat is as big as you are. Lucas Inchfield is his name, but he's called the Longinch for his size. Do you think he's as big as you are, ser?'

'No.' It had been years since Dunk had met anyone as tall as he was. He took the kettle and hung it above the fire.

'Will you fight him?'

'No.' Dunk almost wished it had been otherwise. He might not be the greatest fighter in the realm, but size and strength could make up for many lacks. *Not for a lack of wits, though.* He was no good with words, and worse with women. This giant Lucas Longinch did not daunt him half so much as the prospect of facing the Red Widow. 'I'm going to talk to the Red Widow, that's all.'

'What will you tell her, ser?'

'That she has to take the dam down.' *You must take down your dam, m'lady, or else . . .* 'Ask her to take down the dam, I mean.' *Please give back our Chequy Water.* 'If it pleases her.' *A little water, m'lady, if it please you.* Ser Eustace would not want him to beg. *How do I say it, then?*

The water soon began to steam and bubble. 'Help me lug this to the tub,' Dunk told the boy. Together they lifted the kettle from the hearth and crossed the cellar to the big wooden tub. 'I don't know how to talk with highborn ladies,' he confessed as they were pouring. 'We both might have been killed in Dorne, on account of what I said to Lady Vaith.'

'Lady Vaith was mad,' Egg reminded him, 'but you could have been more gallant. Ladies like it when you're gallant. If you were to rescue the Red Widow the way you rescued that puppet girl from Aerion . . .'

'Aerion's in Lys, and the widow's not in want of rescuing.' He did not want to talk of Tanselle. *Tanselle Too-Tall was her name, but she was not too tall for me.*

'Well,' the boy said, 'some knights sing gallant songs to their ladies, or play them tunes upon a lute.'

'I have no lute.' Dunk looked morose. 'And that night I drank too much in the Planky Town, you told me I sang like a ox in a mud wallow.'

'I had forgotten, ser.'

'How could you forget?'

'You told me to forget, ser,' said Egg, all innocence. 'You told me I'd get a clout in the ear the next time I mentioned it.'

'There will be no singing.' Even if he had had the voice for it, the only song Dunk knew all the way through was 'The Bear and the Maiden Fair'. He doubted that would do much to win over Lady Webber. The kettle was steaming once again. They wrestled it over to the tub and up-ended it.

Egg drew water to fill it for the third time, then clambered back on to the well. 'You'd best not take any food or drink at Coldmoat, ser. The Red Widow poisoned all her husbands.'

'I'm not like to marry her. She's a highborn lady, and I'm Dunk of Flea Bottom, remember?' He frowned. 'Just how many husbands has she had, do you know?'

'Four,' said Egg, 'but no children. Whenever she gives birth, a demon comes by night to carry off the issue. Sam Stoops's wife says she sold her babes unborn to the Lord of the Seven Hells, so he'd teach her his black arts.'

'Highborn ladies don't meddle with the black arts. They dance and sing and do embroidery.'

'Maybe she dances with demons and embroiders evil spells,' Egg said with relish. 'And how would you know what highborn ladies do, ser? Lady Vaith is the only one you ever knew.'

That was insolent, but true. 'Might be I don't know any highborn ladies, but I know a boy who's asking for a good clout in the ear.' Dunk rubbed the back of his neck. A day in chainmail always left it hard as wood. 'You've known queens and princesses. Did they dance with demons and practise the black arts?'

'Lady Shiera does. Lord Bloodraven's paramour. She bathes in blood to keep her beauty. And once my sister Rhae put a love potion in my drink, so I'd marry her instead of my sister Daella.'

Egg spoke as if such incest was the most natural thing in the world. *For him it is.* The Targaryens had been marrying brother to sister for hundreds of years, to keep the blood of the dragon pure. Though the last actual dragon had died before Dunk was born, the dragonkings went on. *Maybe the gods don't mind them marrying their sisters.* 'Did the potion work?' Dunk asked.

'It would have,' said Egg, 'but I spat it out. I don't want a wife, I want to be a knight of the Kingsguard, and live only to serve and defend the king. The Kingsguard are sworn not to wed.'

'That's a noble thing, but when you're older you may find you'd sooner have a girl than a white cloak.' Dunk was thinking of Tanselle Too-Tall, and the way she'd smiled at him at Ashford. 'Ser Eustace said I was the sort of man he'd hoped to have his daughter wed. Her name was Alysanne.'

'She's dead, ser.'

'I know she's dead,' said Dunk, annoyed. '*If* she was alive, he said. If she was, he'd like her to marry me. Or someone like me. I never had a lord offer me his daughter before.'

'His *dead* daughter. And the Osgreys might have been lords in the old days, but Ser Eustace is only a landed knight.'

'I know what he is. Do you want a clout in the ear?'

'Well,' said Egg, 'I'd sooner have a clout than a *wife*. Especially a dead wife, ser. The kettle's steaming.'

They carried the water to the tub, and Dunk pulled his tunic over his head. 'I will wear my Dornish tunic to Coldmoat.' It was sandsilk, the finest garment that he owned, painted with his elm and falling star.

'If you wear it for the ride it will get all sweaty, ser,' Egg said. 'Wear the one you wore today. I'll bring the other, and you can change when you reach the castle.'

'*Before* I reach the castle. I'd look a fool, changing clothes on the drawbridge. And who said you were coming with me?'

'A knight is more impressive with a squire in attendance.'

That was true. The boy had a good sense of such things. *He should. He served two years as a page at King's Landing.* Even so, Dunk was reluctant to take him into danger. He had no notion what sort of welcome awaited him at Coldmoat. If this Red Widow was as dangerous as they said, he could end up in a crow cage, like those two men they had seen upon the road. 'You will stay and help Bennis with the small-folk,' he told Egg. 'And don't give me that sullen look.' He kicked his breeches off, and climbed into the tub of steaming water. 'Go on and get to sleep now, and let me have my bath. You're not going, and that's the end of it.'

Egg was up and gone when Dunk awoke, with the light of the morning sun in his face. *Gods be good, how can it be so hot so soon*? He sat up and stretched, yawning, then climbed to his feet and stumbled sleepily down to the well, where he lit a fat tallow candle, splashed some cold water on his face, and dressed.

When he stepped out into the sunlight, Thunder was waiting by the stable, saddled and bridled. Egg was waiting too, with Maester his mule.

The boy had put his boots on. For once he looked a proper squire, in a handsome doublet of green and gold checks and a pair of tight white woollen breeches. 'The breeches were torn in the seat, but Sam Stoops's wife sewed them up for me,' he announced.

'The clothes were Addam's,' said Ser Eustace, as he led his own grey gelding from his stall. A chequy lion adorned the frayed silk cloak that flowed from the old man's shoulders. 'The doublet is a trifle musty from the trunk, but it should serve. A knight is more impressive with a squire in attendance, so I have decided that Egg should accompany you to Coldmoat.'

Outwitted by a boy of ten. Dunk looked at Egg and silently mouthed the words *clout in the ear*. The boy grinned.

'I have something for you as well, Ser Duncan. Come.' Ser Eustace produced a cloak, and shook it out with a flourish.

It was white wool, bordered with squares of green satin and cloth of gold. A woollen cloak was the last thing he needed in such heat, but when Ser Eustace draped it about his shoulders, Dunk saw the pride on his face, and found himself unable to refuse. 'Thank you, m'lord.'

'It suits you well. Would that I could give you more.' The old man's moustache twitched. 'I sent Sam Stoops down into the cellar to search through my sons' things, but Edwyn and Harrold were smaller men, thinner in the chest and much shorter in the leg. None of what they left would fit you, sad to say.'

'The cloak is enough, m'lord. I won't shame it.'

'I do not doubt that.' He gave his horse a pat. 'I thought I'd ride with you part of the way, if you have no objection.'

'None, m'lord.'

Egg led them down the hill, sitting tall on Maester. 'Must he wear that floppy straw hat?' Ser Eustace asked Dunk. 'He looks a bit foolish, don't you think?'

'Not so foolish as when his head is peeling, m'lord.' Even at this hour, with the sun barely above the horizon, it was hot. *By afternoon the saddles will be hot enough to raise blisters*. Egg might look elegant in the dead boy's finery, but he would be a boiled Egg by nightfall. Dunk at least could change; he had his good tunic in his saddlebag, and his old green one on his back.

'We'll take the west way,' Ser Eustace announced. 'It is little used these past years, but still the shortest way way from Standfast to Coldmoat Castle.' The path took them around behind the hill, past the graves where the old knight had laid his wife and sons to rest in a thicket of blackberry bushes. 'They loved to pick the berries here, my boys. When they were little they would come to me with sticky faces and scratches on their arms, and I'd know just where they'd been.' He smiled fondly. 'Your Egg reminds me of my Addam. A brave boy, for one so young. Addam was trying to protect his wounded brother Harrold when the battle washed over them. A riverman with six acorns on his shield took his arm off with an axe.' His sad grey eyes found Dunk's. 'This old master of yours, the knight of Pennytree . . . did he fight in the Blackfyre Rebellion?'

'He did, m'lord. Before he took me on.' Dunk had been no more than three or four at the time, running half-naked through the alleys of Flea Bottom, more animal than boy.

'Was he for the red dragon or the black?'

Red or black? was a dangerous question, even now. Since the days of Aegon the Conqueror, the arms of House Targaryen had borne a three-headed dragon, red on black. Daemon the Pretender had reversed those colours on his own banners, as many bastards did. *Ser Eustace is my liege lord*, Dunk reminded himself. *He has a right to ask*. 'He fought beneath Lord Hayford's banner, m'lord.'

'Green fretty over gold, a green pale wavy?'

'It might be, m'lord. Egg would know.' The lad could recite the arms of half the knights in Westeros.

'Lord Hayford was a noted *loyalist* . King Daeron made him his Hand just before the battle. Butterwell had done such a dismal job that many questioned his loyalty, but Lord Hayford had been stalwart from the first.'

'Ser Arlan was beside him when he fell. A lord with three castles on his shield cut him down.'

'Many good men fell that day, on both sides. The grass was not red before the battle. Did your Ser Arlan tell you that?'

'Ser Arlan never liked to speak about the battle. His squire died there too. Roger of Pennytree was his name, Ser Arlan's sister's son.' Even saying the name made Dunk feel vaguely guilty. *I stole his place.* Only princes and great lords had the means to keep two squires. If Aegon the Unworthy had given his sword to his heir Daeron instead of his bastard Daemon, there might never have been a Blackfyre Rebellion, and Roger of Pennytree might be alive today. *He would be a knight somewhere, a truer knight than me. I would have ended on the gallows, or been sent off to the Night's Watch to walk the Wall until I died.*

'A great battle is a terrible thing,' the old knight said, 'but in the midst of blood and carnage, there is sometimes also beauty, beauty that could break your heart. I will never forget the way the sun looked when it set upon the Redgrass Field . . . ten thousand men had died, and the air was thick with moans and lamentations, but above us the sky turned gold and red and orange, so beautiful it made me weep to know that my sons would never see it.' He sighed. 'It was a closer thing than they would have you believe, these days. If not for Bloodraven . . .'

'I'd always heard that it was Baelor Breakspear who won the battle,' said Dunk. 'Him and Prince Maekar.'

'The hammer and the anvil?' The old man's moustache gave a twitch. 'The singers leave out much and more. Daemon was the Warrior himself that day. No man could stand before him. He broke Lord Arryn's van to pieces and slew the Knight of Ninestars and Wild Wyl Waynwood before coming up against Ser Gwayne Corbray of the Kingsguard. For near an hour they danced together on their horses, wheeling and circling and slashing as men died all around them. It's said that whenever Blackfyre and Lady Forlorn clashed, you could hear the sound for a league around. It was half a song and half a scream, they say. But when at last the Lady faltered, Blackfyre clove through Ser Gwayne's helm and left him blind and bleeding. Daemon dismounted to see that his fallen foe was not trampled, and commanded Redtusk to carry him back to the maesters in the rear. And there was his mortal error, for the Raven's Teeth had gained the top of Weeping Ridge, and Bloodraven saw his half-brother's royal standard three hundred yards away, and Daemon and his sons beneath it. He slew Aegon first, the elder of the twins, for he knew that Daemon would never leave the boy while warmth lingered in his body, though white shafts fell like rain. Nor did he, though seven arrows pierced him, driven as much by sorcery as by Bloodraven's bow. Young Aemon took up Blackfyre when the blade slipped from his dying father's fingers, so Bloodraven slew him too, the younger of the twins. Thus perished the black dragon and his sons.

'There was much and more afterwards, I know. I saw a bit of it myself . . . the rebels running, Bittersteel turning the rout and leading his mad charge . . . his battle with Bloodraven, second only to the one Daemon fought with Gwayne Corbray . . . Prince Baelor's hammerblow against the rebel rear, the Dornishmen all screaming as they filled the air with spears . . . but at the end of the day, it made no matter. The war was done when Daemon died.

'So close a thing . . . if Daemon had ridden over Gwayne Corbray and left him to his fate, he might have broken Maekar's left before Bloodraven could take the ridge. The day would have belonged to the black dragons then, with the Hand slain and the road to King's Landing open before them. Daemon might have been sitting on the Iron Throne by the time Prince Baelor could come up with his stormlords and his Dornishmen.

'The singers can go on about their hammer and their anvil, ser, but it was the kinslayer who turned the tide with a white arrow and a black spell. He rules us now as well, make no mistake. King Aerys is his creature. It would not surprise me to learn that Bloodraven had ensorcelled His Grace, to bend him to his will. Small wonder we are cursed.' Ser Eustace shook his head, and lapsed into a brooding silence. Dunk wondered how much Egg had overheard, but there was no way to ask him. *How many eyes does Lord Bloodraven have?* he thought.

Already the day was growing hotter. *Even the flies have fled*, Dunk noted. *Flies have better sense than knights. They stay out of the sun.* He wondered whether he and Egg would be offered hospitality at Coldmoat. A tankard of cool brown ale would go down well. Dunk was considering that prospect with pleasure when he remembered what Egg had said about the Red Widow poisoning her husbands. His thirst fled at once. There were worse things than dry throats.

'There was a time when House Osgrey held all the lands for many leagues around, from Nunny in the east to Cobble Cover,' Ser Eustace said. 'Coldmoor was ours, and the Horseshoe Hills, the caves at Derring Downs, the villages of Dosk and Little Dosk and Brandybottom, both sides of Leafy Lake . . . Osgrey maids wed Florents, Swanns and Tarbecks, even Hightowers and Blackwoods.'

The edge of Wat's Wood had come in sight. Dunk shielded his eyes with one hand, and squinted at the greenery. For once he envied Egg his floppy hat. *At least we'll have some shade.*

'Wat's Wood once extended all the way to Coldmoat,' Ser Eustace said. 'I do not recall who Wat was. Before the Conquest you could find aurochs in his wood, though, and great elks of twenty hands and more. There were more red deer than any man could take in a life-time, for none but the king and the chequy lion were allowed to hunt here. Even in my father's day, there were trees on both side of the stream, but the spiders cleared the woods away to make pasture for their cows and sheep and horses.'

A thin finger of sweat crept down Dunk's chest. He found himself wishing devoutly that his liege lord would keep quiet. *It is too hot for talk. It is too hot for riding. It is just too bloody hot.*

In the woods they came upon the carcass of a great brown tree cat, crawling with maggots. 'Eew,' Egg said, as he walked Maester wide around it, 'that stinks worse than Ser Bennis.'

Ser Eustace reined up. 'A tree cat. I had not known there were any left in this wood. I wonder what killed him.' When no one answered, he said, 'I will turn back here. Just continue on the west way and it will take you straight to Coldmoat. You have the coin?' Dunk nodded. 'Good. Come home with my water, ser.' The old knight trotted off, back the way they'd come.

When he was gone, Egg said, 'I thought how you should speak to Lady Webber, ser. You should win her to your side with gallant compli-ments.' The boy looked as cool and crisp in his chequy tunic as Ser Eustace had in his cloak.

Am I the only one who sweats? 'Gallant compliments,' Dunk echoed. 'What sort of gallant compliments?'

'You know, ser. Tell her how fair and beautiful she is.'

Dunk had doubts. 'She's outlived four husbands, she must be as old as Lady Vaith. If I say she's fair and beautiful when she's old and warty, she will take me for a liar.'

'You just need to find something true to say about her. That's what my brother Daeron does. Even ugly old whores can have nice hair or well-shaped ears, he says.'

'Well-shaped ears?' Dunk's doubts were growing.

'Or pretty eyes. Tell her that her gown brings out the colour of her eyes.' The lad reflected for a moment. 'Unless she only has the one eye, like Lord Bloodraven.'

My lady, that gown brings out the colour of your eye. Dunk had heard knights and lordlings mouth such gallantries at other ladies. They never put it quite so baldly, though. *Good lady, that gown is beau-tiful. It brings out the colour of both your lovely eyes.* Some of the ladies had been old and scrawny, or fat and florid, or pox-scarred and homely, but all wore gowns and had two eyes, and as Dunk recalled, they'd been well pleased by the flowery words. *What a lovely gown, my lady. It brings out the lovely beauty of your beautiful-coloured eyes.* 'A hedge knight's life is simpler,' Dunk said glumly. 'If I say the wrong thing, she's like to sew me in a sack of rocks and throw me in her moat.'

'I doubt she'll have that big a sack, ser,' said Egg. 'We could use my boot instead.'

'No,' Dunk growled, 'we couldn't.'

When they emerged from Wat's Wood, they found themselves well upstream of the dam. The waters had risen high enough for Dunk to take that soak he'd dreamed of. *Deep enough to drown a man*, he thought. On the far side, the bank had been cut through and a ditch dug to divert some of the flow westwards. The ditch ran along the road, feeding a myriad of smaller channels that snaked off through the fields. *Once we cross the stream, we are in the Widow's power.* Dunk wondered what he was riding into. He was only one man, with a boy of ten to guard his back.

Egg fanned his face. 'Ser? Why are we stopped?'

'We're not.' Dunk gave his mount his heels and splashed down into the stream. Egg followed on the mule. The water rose as high as Thunder's belly before it began to fall again. They emerged dripping on the Widow's side. Ahead, the ditch ran straight as a spear, shining green and golden in the sun.

When they spied the towers of Coldmoat several hours later, Dunk stopped to change to his good Dornish tunic and loosen his longsword in its scabbard. He did not want the blade sticking should he need to pull it free. Egg gave his dagger's hilt a shake as well, his face solemn beneath his floppy hat. They rode on side by side, Dunk on the big destrier, the boy upon his mule, the Osgrey banner flapping listlessly from its staff.

Coldmoat came as somewhat of a disappointment, after all that Ser Eustace had said of it. Compared to Storm's End or Highgarden and other lordly seats that Dunk had seen, it was a modest castle . . . but it *was* a castle, not a fortified watchtower. Its crenellated outer walls stood thirty feet high, with towers at each corner, each one half again the size of Standfast. From every turret and spire the black banners of Webber hung heavy, each emblazoned with a spotted spider upon a silvery web.

'Ser?' Egg said. 'The water. Look where it goes.'

The ditch ended under Coldmoat's eastern walls, spilling down into the moat from which the castle took its name. The gurgle of the falling water made Dunk grind his teeth. *She will not have my Chequy Water.* 'Come,' he said to Egg.

Over the arch of the main gate a row of spider banners drooped in the still air, above the older sigil carved deep into the stone. Centuries of wind and weather had worn it down, but the shape of it was still distinct: a rampant lion made of chequered squares. The gates beneath were open. As they clattered across the drawbridge, Dunk made note of how low the moat had fallen. *Six feet at least*, he judged.

Two spearmen barred their way at the portcullis. One had a big black beard and one did not. The beard demanded to know their purpose here. 'My lord of Osgrey sent me to treat with Lady Webber,' Dun told him. 'I am called Ser Duncan, the Tall.'

'Well, I knew you wasn't Bennis,' said the beardless guard. 'We would have smelled him coming.' He had a missing tooth and a spotted spider badge sewn above his heart.

The beard was squinting suspiciously at Dunk. 'No one sees her ladyship unless the Longinch gives his leave. You come with me. Your stableboy can stay with the horses.'

'I'm a squire, not a stableboy,' Egg insisted. 'Are you blind, or only stupid?'

The beardless guard broke into laughter. The beard put the point of his spear to the boy's throat. 'Say that again.'

Dunk gave Egg a clout in the ear. 'No, shut your mouth and tend the horses.' He dismounted. 'I'll see Ser Lucas now.'

The beard lowered his spear. 'He's in the yard.'

They passed beneath the spiked iron portcullis and under a murder hole before emerging in the outer ward. Hounds were barking in the kennels, and Dunk could hear singing coming from the leaded glass windows of a seven-sided wooden sept. In front of the smithy, a black-smith was shoeing a warhorse, with a 'prentice boy assisting. Nearby a squire was loosing shafts at the archery butts, while a freckled girl with a long braid matched him shot for shot. The quintain was spin-ning too, as half a dozen knights in quilted padding took their turns knocking it around.

They found Ser Lucas Longinch among the watchers at the quin-tain, speaking with a great fat septon who was sweating worse than Dunk, a round white pudding of a man in robes as damp as if he'd worn them in his bath. Inchfield was a lance beside him, stiff and straight and very tall . . . though not so tall as Dunk. *Six feet and seven inches*, Dunk judged, *and each inch prouder than the last*. Though he wore black silk and cloth-of-silver, Ser Lucas looked as cool as if he were walking on the Wall.

'My lord,' the guard hailed him. 'This one come from the chicken tower for an audience with her ladyship.'

The septon turned first, with a hoot of delight that made Dunk wonder if he were drunk. 'And what is this? A hedge knight? You have large hedges in the Reach.' The septon made a sign of blessing. 'May the Warrior fight ever at your side. I am Septon Sefton. An unfortunate name, but mine own. And you?'

'Ser Duncan the Tall.'

'A modest fellow, this one,' the septon said to Ser Lucas. 'Were I as large as him, I'd call myself Ser Sefton the Immense. Ser Sefton the Tower. Ser Sefton with the Clouds About His Ears.' His moon face was flushed, and there were wine stains on his robe.

Ser Lucas studied Dunk. He was an older man; forty at the least, perhaps as old as fifty, sinewy rather than muscular, with a remarkably ugly face. His lips were thick, his teeth a yellow tangle, his nose broad and fleshy, his eyes protruding. *And he is angry*, Dunk sensed, even before the man said, 'Hedge knights are beggars with blades at best, outlaws at worst. Be gone with you. We want none of your sort here.'

Dunk's face darkened. 'Ser Eustace Osgrey sent me from Standfast to treat with the lady of the castle.'

'Osgrey?' The septon glanced at Longinch. 'Osgrey of the chequy lion? I thought House Osgrey was extinguished.'

'Near enough as makes no matter. The old man is the last of them. We let him keep a crumbling towerhouse a few leagues east.' Ser Lucas frowned at Dunk. 'If Ser Eustace wants to talk with her ladyship, let him come himself.' His eyes narrowed. 'You were the one with Bennis at the dam. Don't trouble to deny it. I ought to hang you.'

'Seven save us.' The septon dabbed sweat from his brow with his sleeve. 'A brigand, is he? And a big one. Ser, repent your evil ways, and the Mother will have mercy.' The septon's pious plea was undercut when he farted. 'Oh, dear. Forgive my wind, ser. That's what comes of beans and barley bread.'

'I am not a brigand,' Dunk told the two of them, with all the dignity he could muster.

The Longinch was unmoved by the denial. 'Do not presume upon my patience, ser . . . if you are a *ser*. Run back to your chicken tower and tell Ser Eustace to deliver up Ser Bennis Brownstench. If he spares us the trouble of winkling him out of Standfast, her ladyship may be more inclined to clemency.'

'I will speak with her ladyship about Ser Bennis and the trouble at the dam, and about the stealing of our water too.'

'Stealing?' said Ser Lucas. 'Say that to our lady, and you'll be swimming in a sack before the sun has set. Are you quite certain that you wish to see her?'

The only thing that Dunk was certain of was that he wanted to drive his fist through Lucas Inchfield's crooked yellow teeth. 'I've told you what I want.'

'Oh, let him speak with her,' the septon urged. 'What harm could it do? Ser Duncan has had a long ride beneath this beastly sun, let the fellow have his say.'

Ser Lucas studied Dunk again. 'Our septon is a godly man. Come. I will thank you to be brief.' He strode across the yard, and Dunk was forced to hurry after him.

The doors of the castle sept had opened, and worshippers were streaming down the steps. There were knights and squires, a dozen children, several old men, three septas in white robes and hoods . . . and one soft, fleshy lady of high birth, garbed in a gown of dark blue damask trimmed with Myrish lace, so long its hems were trailing in the dirt. Dunk judged her to be forty. Beneath a spun-silver net her auburn hair was piled high, but the reddest thing about her was her face.

'My lady,' Ser Lucas said, when they stood before her and her septas, 'this hedge knight claims to bring a message from Ser Eustace Osgrey. Will you hear it?'

'If you wish it, Ser Lucas.' She peered at Dunk so hard that he could not help but recall Egg's talk of sorcery. *I don't think this one bathes in blood to keep her beauty.* The widow was stout and square, with an oddly pointed head that her hair could not quite conceal. Her nose was too big, and her mouth too small. She did have two eyes, he was relieved to see, but all thought of gallantry had abandoned Dunk by then. 'Ser Eustace bade me talk with you concerning the recent trouble at your dam.'

She blinked. 'The . . . dam, you say?'

A crowd was gathering about them. Dunk could feel unfriendly eyes upon him. 'The stream,' he said, 'the Chequy Water. Your ladyship built a dam across it . . .'

'Oh, I am quite sure I haven't,' she replied. 'Why, I have been at my devotions all morning, ser.'

Dunk heard Ser Lucas chuckle. 'I did not mean to say that your ladyship built the dam herself, only that . . . without that water, all our crops will die . . . the smallfolk have beans and barley in the fields, and melons . . .'

'Truly? I am very fond of melons.' Her small mouth made a happy bow. 'What sort of melons are they?'

Dunk glanced uneasily at the ring of faces, and felt his own face growing hot. *Something is amiss here. Longinch is playing me for a fool.* 'M'lady, could we continue our discussion in some . . . more private place?'

'A silver says the great oaf means to *bed her*!' someone japed, and a roar of laughter went up all around him. The lady cringed away, half in terror, and raised both hands to shield her face. One of the septas moved quickly to her side, and put a protective arm around her shoulders.

'And what is all this merriment?' The voice cut through the laughter, cool and firm. 'Will no one share the jape? Ser knight, why are you troubling my good-sister?'

It was the girl he had seen earlier at the archery butts. She had a quiver of arrows on one hip, and held a longbow that was just as tall as she was, which wasn't very tall. If Dunk was shy an inch of seven feet, the archer was shy an inch of five. He could have spanned her waist with his two hands. Her red hair was bound up in a braid so long it brushed past her thighs, and she had a dimpled chin, a snub nose, and a light spray of freckles across her cheeks.

'Forgive us, Lady Rohanne.' The speaker was a pretty young lord with the Caswell centaur embroidered on his doublet. 'This great oaf took the Lady Helicent for you.'

Dunk looked from one lady to the other. '*You* are the Red Widow?' he heard himself blurt out. 'But you're too –'

'Young?' The girl tossed her longbow to the lanky lad he'd seen her shooting with. 'I am five-and-twenty, as it happens. Or was it *small* you meant to say?'

'– pretty. It was pretty.' Dunk did not know where that came from, but he was glad it came. He liked her nose, and the strawberry-blonde colour of her hair, and the small but well-shaped breasts beneath her leather jerkin. 'I thought that you'd be . . . I mean . . . they said you were four times a widow, so . . .'

'My first husband died when I was ten. He was twelve, my father's squire, ridden down upon the Redgrass Field. My husbands seldom linger long, I fear. The last died in the spring.'

That was what they always said of those who had perished during the Great Spring Sickness two years past. *He died in the spring.* Many tens of thousands had died in the spring, among them a wise old king and two young princes full of promise. 'I . . . I am sorry for all your losses, m'lady.' *A gallantry, you lunk, give her a gallantry.* 'I want to say . . . your gown . . .'

'Gown?' She glanced down at her boots and breeches, loose linen tunic and leather jerkin. 'I wear no gown.'

'Your hair, I meant . . . it's soft and . . .'

'And how would you know that, ser? If you had ever touched my hair, I should think that I might remember.'

'Not soft,' Dunk said miserably. 'Red, I meant to say. Your hair is very red.'

'*Very* red, ser? Oh, not as red as your face, I hope.' She laughed, and the onlookers laughed with her.

All but Ser Lucas Longinch. 'My lady,' he broke in, 'this man is one of Standfast's sellswords. He was with Bennis of the Brown Shield when he attacked your diggers at the dam and carved up Wolmer's face. Old Osgrey sent him to treat with you.'

'He did, m'lady. I am called Ser Duncan, the Tall.'

'Ser Duncan the Dim, more like,' said a bearded knight who wore the threefold thunderbolt of Leygood. More guffaws sounded. Even Lady Helicent had recovered herself enough to give a chuckle.

'Did the courtesy of Coldmoat die with my lord father?' the girl asked. *No, not a girl, a woman grown.* 'How did Ser Duncan come to make such an error, I wonder?'

Dunk gave Inchfield an evil look. 'The fault was mine.'

'Was it?' The Red Widow looked Dunk over from his heels up to his head, though her gaze lingered longest on his chest. 'A tree and shooting star. I have never seen those arms before.' She touched his tunic, tracing a limb of his elm tree with two fingers. 'And painted, not sewn. The Dornish paint their silks, I've heard, but you look too big to be a Dornishman.'

'Not all Dornishmen are small, m'lady.' Dunk could feel her fingers through the silk. Her hand was freckled too. *I'll bet she's freckled all over.* His mouth was oddly dry. 'I spent a year in Dorne.'

'Do all the oaks grow so tall there?' she said, as her fingers traced a tree limb round his heart.

'It's meant to be an elm, m'lady.'

'I shall remember.' She drew her hand back, solemn. 'The ward is too hot and dusty for a conversation. Septon, show Ser Duncan to my audience chamber.'

'It would be my great pleasure, good-sister.'

'Our guest will have a thirst. You may send for a flagon of wine as well.'

'Must I?' The fat man beamed. 'Well, if it please you.'

'I will join you as soon as I have changed.' Unhooking her belt and quiver, she handed them to her companion. 'I'll want Maester Cerrick as well. Ser Lucas, go ask him to attend me.'

'I will bring him at once, my lady,' said Lucas Longinch.

The look she gave her castellan was cool. 'No need. I know you have many duties to perform about the castle. It will suffice if you send Maester Cerrick to my chambers.'

'M'lady,' Dunk called after her. 'My squire was made to wait by the gates. Might he join us as well?'

'Your squire?' When she smiled, she looked a girl of five-and-ten, not a woman five-and-twenty. *A pretty girl full of mischief and laughter.* 'If it please you, certainly.'

'Don't drink the wine, ser,' Egg whispered to him, as they waited with the septon in her audience chamber. The stone floors were covered with sweet-smelling rushes, the walls hung with tapestries of tourney scenes and battles.

Dunk snorted. 'She has no need to poison me,' he whispered back. 'She thinks I'm some great lout with pease porridge between his ears, you mean.'

'As it happens, my good-sister likes pease porridge,' said Septon Sefton, as he reappeared with a flagon of wine, a flagon of water and three cups. 'Yes, yes, I heard. I'm fat, not deaf.' He filled two cups with wine and one with water. The third he gave to Egg, who gave it a long dubious look and put it aside. The septon took no notice. 'This is an Arbor vintage,' he was telling Dunk. 'Very fine, and the poison gives it a special piquance.' He winked at Egg. 'I seldom touch the grape myself, but I have heard.' He handed Dunk a cup.

The wine was lush and sweet, but Dunk sipped it gingerly, and only after the septon had quaffed down half of his in three big, lip-smacking gulps. Egg crossed his arms and continued to ignore his water.

'She does like pease porridge,' the septon said, 'and you as well, ser. I know my own good-sister. When I first saw you in the yard, I half-hoped you were some suitor, come from King's Landing to seek my lady's hand.'

Dunk furrowed his brow. 'How did you know I was from King's Landing, septon?'

'Kingslanders have a certain way of speaking.' The septon took a gulp of wine, sloshed it about his mouth, swallowed and sighed with pleasure. 'I have served there many years, attending our High Septon in the Great Sept of Baelor.' He sighed. 'You would not know the city since the spring. The fires changed it. A quarter of the houses gone, and another quarter empty. The rats are gone as well. That is the queerest thing. I never thought to see a city without rats.'

Dunk had heard that too. 'Were you there during the Great Spring Sickness?'

'Oh, indeed. A dreadful time, ser, dreadful. Strong men would wake healthy at the break of day and be dead by evenfall. So many died so quickly there was no time to bury them. They piled them in the Dragonpit instead, and when the corpses were ten feet deep, Lord Rivers commanded the pyromancers to burn them. The light of the fires shone through the windows, as it did of yore when living dragons still nested beneath the dome. By night you could see the glow all through the city, the dark green glow of wildfire. The colour green still haunts me to this day. They say the spring was bad in Lannisport and worse in Oldtown, but in King's Landing it cut down four of ten. Neither young nor old were spared, nor rich nor poor, nor great nor humble. Our good High Septon was taken, the gods' own voice on earth, with a third of the Most Devout and near all our silent sisters. His Grace King Daeron, sweet Matarys and bold Valarr, the Hand . . . oh, it was a dreadful time. By the end, half the city was praying to the Stranger.' He had another drink. 'And where were you, ser?'

'In Dorne,' said Dunk.

'Thank the Mother for her mercy, then.' The Great Spring Sickness had never come to Dorne, perhaps because the Dornish had closed their borders and their ports, as had the Arryns of the Vale, who had also been spared. 'All this talk of death is enough to put a man off wine, but cheer is hard to come by in such times as we are living. The drought endures, for all our prayers. The kingswood is one great tinder box, and fires rage there night and day. Bittersteel and the sons of Daemon Blackfyre are hatching plots in Tyrosh, and Dagon Greyjoy's krakens prowl the sunset sea like wolves, raiding as far south as the Arbor. They carried off half the wealth of Fair Isle, it's said, and a hundred women too. Lord Farman is repairing his defences, though that strikes me as akin to the man who claps his pregnant daughter in a chastity belt when her belly's big as mine. Lord Bracken is dying slowly on the Trident, and his eldest son perished in the spring. That means Ser Otho must succeed. The Blackwoods will never stomach the Brute of Bracken as a neighbour. It will mean war.'

Dunk knew about the ancient emnity between the Blackwoods and the Brackens. 'Won't their liege lord force a peace?'

'Alas,' said Septon Sefton, 'Lord Tully is a boy of eight, surrounded by women. Riverrun will do little, and King Aerys will do less. Unless some maester writes a book about it, the whole matter may escape his royal notice. Lord Rivers is not like to let any Brackens in to see him. Pray recall, our Hand was born half Blackwood. If he acts at all, it will be only to help his cousins bring the Brute to bay. The Mother marked Lord Rivers on the day that he was born, and Bittersteel marked him once again upon the Redgrass Field.'

Dunk knew he meant Bloodraven. Brynden Rivers was the Hand's true name. His mother had been a Blackwood, his father King Aegon the Fourth.

The fat man drank his wine and rattled on. 'As for Aerys, His Grace cares more for old scrolls and dusty prophecies than for lords and laws. He will not even bestir himself to sire an heir. Queen Aelinor prays daily at the Great Sept, beseeching the Mother Above to bless her with a child, yet she remains a maid. Aerys keeps his own apartments, and it is said that he would sooner take a book to bed than any woman.' He filled his cup again. 'Make no mistake, 'tis Lord Rivers who rules us, with his spells and spies. There is no one to oppose him. Prince Maekar sulks at Summerhall, nursing his grievances against his royal brother. Prince Rhaegal is as meek as he is mad, and his children are . . . well, children. Friends and favourites of Lord Rivers fill every office, the lords of the small council lick his hand, and this new Grand Maester is as steeped in sorcery as he is. The Red Keep is garrisoned by Raven's Teeth, and no man sees the king without his leave.'

Dunk shifted uncomfortably in his seat. *How many eyes does Lord Bloodraven have? A thousand eyes, and one.* He hoped the King's Hand did not have a thousand ears and one as well. Some of what Septon Sefton was saying sounded treasonous. He glanced at Egg, to see how he was taking all of this. The boy was struggling with all his might to hold his tongue.

The septon pushed himself to his feet. 'My good-sister will be a while yet. As with all great ladies, the first ten gowns she tries will be found not to suit her mood. Will you take more wine?' Without waiting for an answer, he refilled both cups.

'The lady I mistook,' said Dunk, anxious to speak of something else, 'is she your sister?'

'We are all children of the Seven, ser, but apart from that . . . dear me, no. Lady Helicent was sister to Ser Rolland Uffering, Lady

Rohanne's fourth husband, who died in the spring. My brother was his predecessor, Ser Simon Staunton, who had the great misfortune to choke upon a chicken bone. Coldmoat crawls with revenants, it must be said. The husbands die yet their kin remain, to drink my lady's wines and eat her sweetmeats, like a plague of plump pink locusts done up in silk and velvet.' He wiped his mouth. 'And yet she must wed again, and soon.'

'Must?' said Dunk.

'Her lord father's will demands it. Lord Wyman wanted grandsons to carry on his line. When he sickened he tried to wed her to the Longinch, so he might die knowing that she had a strong man to protect her, but Rohanne refused to have him. His lordship took his vengeance in his will. If she remains unwed on the second anniversary of her father's passing, Coldmoat and its lands pass to his cousin Wendell. Perhaps you glimpsed him in the yard. A short man with a goitre on his neck, much given to flatulence. Though it is small of me to say so. I am cursed with excess wind myself. Be that as it may. Ser Wendell is grasping and stupid, but his lady wife is Lord Rowan's sister . . . and damnably fertile, that cannot be denied. She whelps as often as he farts. Their sons are quite as bad as he is, their daughters worse, and all of them have begun to count the days. Lord Rowan has upheld the will, so her ladyship has only till the next new moon.'

'Why has she waited so long?' Dunk wondered aloud.

The septon shrugged. 'If truth be told, there has been a dearth of suitors. My good-sister is not hard to look upon, you will have noticed, and a stout castle and broad lands add to her charms. You would think that younger sons and landless knights would swarm about her ladyship like flies. You would be wrong. The four dead husbands make them wary, and there are those who will say that she is barren too . . . though never in her hearing, unless they yearn to see the inside of a crow cage. She has carried two children to term, a boy and a girl, but neither lived to see a name day. Those few who are not put off by talk of poisonings and sorcery want no part of the Longinch. Lord Wyman charged him on his deathbed to protect his daughter from unworthy suitors, which he has taken to mean *all* suitors. Any man who means to have her hand would need to face his sword first.' He finished his wine and set the cup aside. 'That is not to say there has been no one. Cleyton Caswell and Simon Leygood have been the most persistent, though they seem more interested in her lands than in her person. Were I given to wagering, I should place my gold on Gerold Lannister. He has yet to put in an appearance, but they say he is golden-haired and quick of wit, and more than six feet tall . . .'

'. . . and Lady Webber is much taken with his letters.' The lady in question stood in the doorway, beside a homely young maester with a great hooked nose. 'You would lose your wager, good-brother. Gerold will never willingly forsake the pleasures of Lannisport and the splendour of Casterly Rock for some little lordship. He has more influence as Lord Tybolt's brother and adviser than he could ever hope for as my husband. As for the others, Ser Simon would need to sell off half my land to pay his debts and Ser Cleyton trembles like a leaf whenever the Longinch deigns to look his way. Besides, he is prettier than I am. And you, septon, have the biggest mouth in Westeros.'

'A large belly requires a large mouth,' said Septon Sefton, utterly unabashed. 'Else it soon becomes a small one.'

'Are *you* the Red Widow?' Egg asked, astonished. 'I'm near as tall as you are!'

'Another boy made that same observation not half a year ago. I sent him to the rack to make him taller.' When Lady Rohanne settled on to the high seat on the dais, she pulled her braid forward over her left shoulder. It was so long that the end of it lay coiled in her lap, like a sleeping cat. 'Ser Duncan, I should not have teased you in the yard, when you were trying so hard to be gracious. It was only that you blushed so red . . . was there no girl to tease you, in the village where you grew so tall?'

'The village was King's Landing.' He did not mention Flea Bottom. 'There were girls, but . . .' The sort of teasing that went on in Flea Bottom sometimes involved cutting off a toe.

'I expect they were afraid to tease you.' Lady Rohanne stroked her braid. 'No doubt they were frightened of your size. Do not think ill of Lady Helicent, I pray you. My good-sister is a simple creature, but she has no harm in her. For all her piety, she could not dress herself without her septas.'

'It was not her doing. The mistake was mine.'

'You lie most gallantly. I know it was Ser Lucas. He is a man of cruel humours, and you offended him on sight.'

'How?' Dunk said, puzzled. 'I never did him any harm.'

She smiled a smile that made him wish that she was plainer. 'I saw you standing with him. You're taller by a hand, or near enough. It has been a long while since Ser Lucas met anyone he could not look down on. How old are you, ser?'

'Near twenty, if it please m'lady.' Dunk liked the ring of *twenty*, though most like he was a year younger, maybe two. No one knew for certain, least of all him. He must have had a mother and a father like everybody else, but he'd never known them, not even their names, and no one in Flea Bottom had ever cared much when he'd been born, or to whom.

'Are you as strong as you appear?'

'How strong do I appear, m'lady?'

'Oh, strong enough to annoy Ser Lucas. He is my castellan, though not by choice. Like Coldmoat, he is a legacy of my father. Did you come to knighthood on some battlefield, Ser Duncan? Your speech suggests that you were not born of noble blood, if you will forgive my saying so.'

I was born of gutter blood. 'A hedge knight named Ser Arlan of Pennytree took me on to squire for him when I was just a boy. He taught me chivalry and the arts of war.'

'And this same Ser Arlan knighted you?'

Dunk shuffled his feet. One of his boots was half-unlaced, he saw. 'No one else was like to do it.'

'Where is Ser Arlan now?'

'He died.' He raised his eyes. He could lace his boot up later. 'I buried him on a hillside.'

'Did he fall valiantly in battle?'

'There were rains. He caught a chill.'

'Old men are frail, I know. I learned that from my second husband. I was thirteen when we wed. He would have been five-and-fifty on his next name day, had he lived long enough to see it. When he was half a year in the ground, I gave him a little son, but the Stranger came for him as well. The septons said his father wanted him beside him. What do you think, ser?'

'Well,' Dunk said hesitantly, 'that might be, m'lady.'

'Nonsense,' she said, 'the boy was born too weak. Such a tiny thing. He scarce had strength enough to nurse. Still. The gods gave his father five-and-fifty years. You would think they might have granted more than three days to the son.'

'You would.' Dunk knew little and less about the gods. He went to sept sometimes, and prayed to the Warrior to lend strength to his arms, but elsewise he let the Seven be.

'I am sorry your Ser Arlan died,' she said, 'and sorrier still that you took service with Ser Eustace. All old men are not the same, Ser Duncan. You would do well to go home to Pennytree.'

'I have no home but where I swear my sword.' Dunk had never seen Pennytree; he couldn't even say if it was in the Reach.

'Swear it here, then. The times are uncertain. I have need of knights. You look as though you have a healthy appetite, Ser Duncan. How many chickens can you eat? At Coldmoat you would have your fill of warm pink meat and sweet fruit tarts. Your squire looks in need of sustenance as well. He is so scrawny that all his hair has fallen out. We'll have him share a cell with other boys of his own age. He'll like that. My master-at-arms can train him in all the arts of war.'

'I train him,' said Dunk defensively.

'And who else? Bennis? Old Osgrey? The chickens?'

There had been days when Dunk had set Egg to chasing chickens. *It helps make him quicker*, he thought, but he knew that if he said it she would laugh. She was distracting him, with her snub nose and her freckles. Dunk had to remind himself of why Ser Eustace had sent him here. 'My sword is sworn to my lord of Osgrey, m'lady,' he said, 'and that's the way it is.'

'So be it, ser. Let us speak of less pleasant matters.' Lady Rohanne gave her braid a tug. 'We do not suffer attacks on Coldmoat or its people. So tell me why I should not have you sewn in a sack.'

'I came to parley,' he reminded her, 'and I have drunk your wine.' The taste still lingered in his mouth, rich and sweet. So far it had not poisoned him. Perhaps it was the wine that made him bold. 'And you don't have a sack big enough for me.'

To his relief, the jape made her smile. 'I have several that are big enough for Bennis, though. Maester Cerrick says Wolmer's face was sliced open almost to the bone.'

'Ser Bennis lost his temper with the man, m'lady. Ser Eustace sent me here to pay the blood price.'

'The blood price?' She laughed. 'He is an old man, I know, but I had not realized that he was so old as that. Does he think we are living in the Age of Heroes, when a man's life was reckoned to be worth no more than a sack of silver?'

'The digger was not killed, m'lady,' Dunk reminded her. 'No one was killed that I saw. His face was cut, is all.'

Her fingers danced idly along her braid. 'How much does Ser Eustace reckon Wolmer's cheek to be worth, pray?'

'One silver stag. And three for you, m'lady.'

'Ser Eustace sets a niggard's price upon my honour, though three silvers are better than three chickens, I grant you. He would do better to deliver Bennis up to me for chastisement.'

'Would this involve that sack you mentioned?'

'It might.' She coiled her braid around one hand. 'Osgrey can keep his silver. Only blood can pay for blood.'

'Well,' said Dunk, 'it may be as you say, m'lady, but why not send for that man that Bennis cut, and ask him if he'd sooner have a silver stag or Bennis in a sack?'

'Oh, he'd pick the silver, if he couldn't have both. I don't doubt that, ser. It is not his choice to make. This is about the lion and the spider now, not some peasant's cheek. It is Bennis I want, and Bennis I shall have. No one rides on to my lands, does harm to one of mine, and escapes to laugh about it.'

'Your ladyship rode on to Standfast land, and did harm of one of Ser Eustace's,' Dunk said, before he stopped to think about it.

'Did I?' She tugged her braid again. 'If you mean the sheep-stealer, the man was notorious. I had twice complained to Osgrey, yet he did nothing. I do not ask thrice. The king's law grants me the power of pit and gallows.'

It was Egg who answered her. 'On your own lands,' the boy insisted. 'The king's law gives lords the power of pit and gallows on their own lands.'

'Clever boy,' she said. 'If you know that much, you will also know that landed knights have no right to punish without their liege lord's leave. Ser Eustace holds Standfast of Lord Rowan. Bennis broke the king's peace when he drew blood, and must answer for it.' She looked to Dunk. 'If Ser Eustace will deliver Bennis to me, I'll slit his nose, and that will be the end of it. If I must come and take him, I make no such promise.'

Dunk had a sudden sick feeling in the pit of his stomach. 'I will tell him, but he won't give up Ser Bennis.' He hesitated. 'The dam was the cause of all the trouble. If your ladyship would consent to take it down –'

'Impossible,' declared the young maester by Lady Rohanne's side. 'Coldmoat supports twenty times as many smallfolk as does Standfast. Her ladyship has fields of wheat and corn and barley, all dying from the drought. She has half a dozen orchards, apples and apricots and three kinds of pears. She has cows about to calve, five hundred head of black-nosed sheep, and she breeds the finest horses in the Reach. We have a dozen mares about to foal.'

'Ser Eustace has sheep too,' Dunk said. 'He has melons in the fields, beans and barleycorn, and . . .'

'You were taking water for the *moat*!' Egg said loudly.

I was getting to the moat, Dunk thought.

'The moat is essential to Coldmoat's defences,' the maester insisted. 'Do you suggest that Lady Rohanne leave herself open to attack, in such uncertain times as these?'

'Well,' Dunk said slowly, 'a dry moat is still a moat. And m'lady has strong walls, with ample men to defend them.'

'Ser Duncan,' Lady Rohanne said, 'I was ten years old when the black dragon rose. I begged my father not to put himself at risk, or at least to leave my husband. Who would protect me, if both my men were gone? So he took me up on to the ramparts, and pointed out Coldmoat's strong points. "Keep them strong," he said, "and they will keep you safe. If you see to your defenses, no man may do you harm." The first thing he pointed at was the moat.' She stroked her cheek with the tail of her braid. 'My first husband perished on the Redgrass Field. My father found me others, but the Stranger took them too. I no longer trust in men, no matter how *ample* they may seem. I trust in stone and steel and water. I trust in moats, ser, and mine will *not* go dry.'

'What your father said, that's well and good,' said Dunk, 'but it doesn't give you the right to take Osgrey water.'

She tugged her braid. 'I suppose Ser Eustace told you that the stream was his.'

'For a thousand years,' said Dunk. 'It's *named* the Chequy Water. That's plain.'

'So it is.' She tugged again; once, twice, thrice. 'As the river is called the Mander, though the Manderlys were driven from its banks a thousand years ago. Highgarden is still Highgarden, though the last Gardener died on the Field of Fire. Casterly Rock teems with Lannisters, and nowhere a Casterly to be found. The world changes, ser. This Chequy Water rises in the Horseshoe Hills, which were wholly mine when last I looked. The water is mine as well. Maester Cerrick, show him.'

The maester descended from the dais. He could not have been much older than Dunk, but in his grey robes and chain collar he had an air of sombre wisdom that belied his years. In his hands was an old parchment. 'See for yourself, ser,' he said as he unrolled it, and offered it to Dunk.

Dunk the lunk, thick as a castle wall. He felt his cheeks reddening again. Gingerly he took parchment from the maester and scowled at the writing. Not a word of it was intelligible to him, but he knew the wax seal beneath the ornate signature; the three-headed dragon of House Targaryen. *The king's seal.* He was looking at a royal decree of some sort. Dunk moved his head from side to side so they would think that he was reading. 'There's a word here I can't make out,' he muttered, after a moment. 'Egg, come have a look, you have sharper eyes than me.'

The boy darted to his side. 'Which word, ser?' Dunk pointed. 'That one? Oh.' Egg read quickly, then raised his eyes to Dunk's and gave a little nod.

It is her stream. She has a paper. Dunk felt as though he'd been punched in the stomach. *The king's own seal.* 'This . . . there must be some mistake. The old man's sons died in service to the king, why would His Grace take his stream away?'

'If King Daeron had been a less forgiving man, he should have lost his head as well.'

For half a heartbeat Dunk was lost. 'What do you mean?'

'She means,' said Maester Cerrick, 'that Ser Eustace Osgrey is a rebel and a traitor.'

'Ser Eustace chose the black dragon over the red, in hopes that a Blackfyre king might restore the lands and castles that the Osgreys had lost under the Targaryens,' Lady Rohanne said. 'Chiefly he wanted Coldmoat. His sons paid for his treason with their life's blood. When he brought their bones home and delivered his daughter to the king's men for a hostage, his wife threw herself from the top of Standfast tower. Did Ser Eustace tell you that?' Her smile was sad. 'No, I did not think so.'

'The black dragon.' *You swore your sword to a traitor, lunk. You ate a traitor's bread and slept beneath a rebel's roof.* 'M'lady,' he said, groping, 'the black dragon . . . that was fifteen years ago. This is now, and there's a drought. Even if he was a rebel once, Ser Eustace still needs water.'

The Red Widow rose, and smoothed her skirts. 'He had best pray for rain, then.'

That was when Dunk recalled Osgrey's parting words in the wood. 'If you will not grant him a share of the water for his own sake, do it for his son.'

'His son?'

'Addam. He served here as your father's page and squire.'

Lady Rohanne's face was stone. 'Come closer.'

He did not know what else to do, but to obey. The dais added a good foot to her height, yet even so Dunk towered over her. 'Kneel,' she said. He did.

The slap she gave him had all her strength behind it, and she was stronger than she looked. His cheek burned, and he could taste blood in his mouth from a broken lip, but she hadn't truly hurt him. For a moment all Dunk could think of was grabbing her by that long red braid and pulling her across his lap to slap her arse, as you would a spoiled child. *If I do, she'll scream, though, and twenty knights will come bursting in to kill me.*

'You dare appeal to me in *Addam's* name?' Her nostrils flared. 'Remove yourself from Coldmoat, ser. At once.'

'I never meant –'

'*Go*, or I will find a sack large enough for you, if I have to sew one up myself. Tell Ser Eustace to bring me Bennis of the Brown Shield by the morrow, else I will come for him myself with fire and sword. Do you understand me? *Fire and sword!*'

Septon Sefton took Dunk's arm and pulled him quickly from the room. Egg followed close behind them. 'That was most unwise, ser,' the fat septon whispered, and he led them to the steps. '*Most* unwise. To mention Addam Osgrey . . .'

'Ser Eustace told me she was fond of the boy.'

'Fond?' The septon huffed heavily. 'She loved the boy, and him her. It never went beyond a kiss or two, but . . . it was Addam she wept for after the Redgrass Field, not the husband she hardly knew. She blames Ser Eustace for his death, and rightly so. The boy was twelve.'

Dunk knew what it was to bear a wound. Whenever someone spoke of Ashford Meadow, he thought of the three good men who'd died to save his foot, and it never failed to hurt. 'Tell m'lady that it was not my wish to hurt her. Beg her pardon.'

'I shall do all I can, ser,' Septon Sefton said, 'but tell Ser Eustace to bring her Bennis, and *quickly*. Elsewise it will go hard on him. It will go very hard.'

Not until the walls and towers of Coldmoat had vanished in the west behind them did Dunk turn to Egg and say, 'What words were written on that paper?'

'It was a grant of rights, ser. To Lord Wyman Webber, from the king. For his leal service in the late rebellion, Lord Wyman and his descendants were granted all rights to the Chequy Water, from where it rises in the Horseshoe Hills to the shores of Leafy Lake. It also said that Lord Wyman and his descendants should have the right to take red deer and boar and rabbits in Wat's Wood whene'er it pleased them, and to cut twenty trees from the wood each year.' The boy cleared his throat. 'The grant was only for a time, though. The paper said that if

Ser Eustace were to die without a male heir of his body, Standfast would revert to the crown, and Lord Webber's privileges would end.'

They were the Marshals of the Northmarch for a thousand years. 'All they left the old man was a tower to die in.'

'And his head,' said Egg. 'His Grace did leave him his head, ser. Even though he was a rebel.'

Dunk gave the boy a look. 'Would you have taken it?'

Egg had to think about it. 'Sometimes at court I would serve the king's small council. They used to fight about it. Uncle Baelor said that clemency was best when dealing with an honourable foe. If a defeated man believes he will be pardoned, he may lay down his sword and bend the knee. Elsewise he will fight on to the death, and slay more loyal men and innocents. But Lord Bloodraven said that when you pardon rebels, you only plant the seeds of the next rebellion.' His voice was full of doubts. 'Why would Ser Eustace rise against King Daeron? He was a good king, everybody says so. He brought Dorne into the realm and made the Dornishmen our friends.'

'You would have to ask Ser Eustace, Egg.' Dunk thought he knew the answer, but it was not one the boy would want to hear. *He wanted a castle with a lion on the gatehouse, but all he got were graves among the blackberries.* When you swore a man your sword, you promised to serve and obey, to fight for him at need, not to pry into his affairs and question his allegiances . . . but Ser Eustace had played him for a fool. *He said his sons died fighting for the king, and let me believe the stream was his.*

Night caught them in Wat's Wood.

That was Dunk's fault. He should have gone the straight way home, the way they'd come, but instead he'd taken them north for another look at the dam. He had half a thought to try and tear the thing apart with his bare hands. But the Seven and Ser Lucas Longinch did not prove so obliging. When they reached the dam they found it guarded by a pair of crossbowmen with spider badges sewn on their jerkins. One sat with his bare feet in the stolen water. Dunk could gladly have throttled him for that alone, but the man heard them coming and was quick to snatch up his bow. His fellow, even quicker, had a quarrel nocked and ready. The best that Dunk could do was scowl at them threateningly.

After that, there was nought to do but retrace their steps. Dunk did not know these lands as well as Ser Bennis did; it would have been humiliating to get lost in a wood as small as Wat's. By the time they splashed across the stream, the sun was low on the horizon and the first stars were coming out, along with clouds of mites. Among the tall black trees, Egg found his tongue again. 'Ser? That fat septon said my father sulks in Summerhall.'

'Words are wind.'

'My father doesn't sulk.'

'Well,' said Dunk, 'he might. *You* sulk.'

'I do not. Ser.' He frowned. 'Do I?'

'Some. Not too often, though. Elsewise I'd clout you in the ear more than I do.'

'You clouted me in the ear at the gate.'

'That was half a clout at best. If I ever give you a whole clout, you'll know it.'

'The Red Widow gave *you* a whole clout.'

Dunk touched his swollen lip. 'You don't need to sound so pleased about it.' *No one ever clouted your father in the ear, though. Maybe that's why Prince Maekar is the way he is.* 'When the king named Lord Bloodraven his Hand, your lord father refused to be part of his council and departed King's Landing for his own seat,' he reminded Egg. 'He has been at Summerhall for a year, and half of another. What do you call that, if not sulking?'

'I call it being wroth,' Egg declared loftily. 'His Grace should have made my father Hand. He's his *brother*, and the finest battle commander in the realm since Uncle Baelor died. Lord Bloodraven's not even a real lord; that's just some stupid *courtesy* . He's a sorcerer, and base-born besides.'

'Bastard born, not baseborn.' Bloodraven might not be a real lord but he was noble on both sides. His mother had been one of the many mistresses of King Aegon the Unworthy. Aegon's bastards had been the bane of the Seven Kingdoms ever since the old king died. He had legitimized the lot upon his deathbed; not only the Great Bastards like Bloodraven, Bittersteel and Daemon Blackfyre, whose mothers had been ladies, but even the lesser ones he'd fathered on whores and tavern wenches, merchants' daughters, mummers' maidens, and every pretty peasant girl who chanced to catch his eye. *Fire and Blood* were the words of House Targaryen, but Dunk once heard Ser Arlan say that Aegon's should have been, *Wash Her And Bring Her to My Bed.*

'King Aegon washed Bloodraven clean of bastardy,' he reminded Egg, 'the same as he did the rest of them.'

'The old High Septon told my father that kings' laws are one thing, and the laws of the gods another,' the boy said stubbornly. 'Trueborn children are made in a marriage bed and blessed by the Father and the Mother, but bastards are born of lust and weakness, he said. King Aegon decreed that his bastards were not bastards, but he could not change their nature. The High Septon said all bastards are born to betrayal . . . Daemon Blackfyre, Bittersteel, even Bloodraven. Lord Rivers was more cunning than the other two, he said, but in the end he would prove himself a traitor too. The High Septon counselled my father never to put any trust in him, nor in any other bastards, great or small.'

Born to betrayal, Dunk thought. *Born of lust and weakness. Never to be trusted, great or small.* 'Egg,' he said, 'didn't you ever think that I might be a bastard?'

'You, ser?' That took the boy aback. 'You are not.'

'I might be. I never knew my mother, or what became of her. Maybe I was born too big and killed her. Most like she was some whore or tavern girl. You don't find highborn ladies down in Flea Bottom. And if she ever wed my father . . . well, what became of *him*, then?' Dunk did not like to be reminded of his life before Ser Arlan found him. 'There was a pot shop in King's Landing where I used to sell them rats and cats and pigeons for the brown. The cook always claimed my father was some thief or cutpurse. "Most like I saw him hanged," he used to tell me, "but maybe they just sent him to the Wall." When I was squiring for Ser Arlan, I would ask him if we couldn't go up that way some day, to take service at Winterfell or some other northern castle. I had this notion that if I could only reach the Wall, might be I'd come on some old man, a real tall man who looked like me. We never went, though. Ser Arlan said there were no hedges in the north, and all the woods were full of wolves.' He shook his head. 'The long and short of it is, most like you're squiring for a bastard.'

For once Egg had nothing to say. The gloom was deepening around them. Lantern bugs moved slowly through the trees, their little lights like so many drifting stars. There were stars in the sky as well, more stars than any man could ever hope to count, even if he lived to be as old as King Jaehaerys. Dunk need only lift his eyes to find familiar friends: the Stallion and the Sow, the King's Crown and the Crone's Lantern, the Galley, Ghost and Moonmaid. But there were clouds to the north, and the blue eye of the Ice Dragon was lost to him, the blue eye that pointed north.

The moon had risen by the time they came to Standfast, standing dark and tall atop its hill. A pale yellow light was spilling from the tower's upper windows, he saw. Most nights Ser Eustace sought his bed as soon as he had supped, but not tonight, it seemed. *He is waiting for us*, Dunk knew.

Bennis of the Brown Shield was waiting up as well. They found him sitting on the tower steps, chewing sourleaf and honing his longsword in the moonlight. The slow scrape of stone on steel carried a long way. However much Ser Bennis might neglect his clothes and person, he kept his weapons well.

'The lunk comes back,' Bennis said. 'Here I was sharpening my steel to go and rescue you from that Red Widow.'

'Where are the men?'

'Treb and Wet Wat are on the roof standing watch, case the widow comes to call. The rest crawled into bed whimpering. Sore as sin, they are. I worked them hard. Drew a little blood off that big lackwit, just to make him mad. He fights better when he's mad.' He smiled his brown and red smile. 'Nice bloody lip you got. Next time, don't go turning over rocks. What did the woman say?'

'She means to keep the water. And she wants you as well, for cutting that digger by the dam.'

'Thought she might.' Bennis spat. 'Lot o' bother for some peasant. He ought to thank me. Women like a man with scars.'

'You won't mind her slitting your nose, then.'

'Bugger that. If I wanted my nose slit I'd slit it for myself.' He jerked a thumb up. 'You'll find Ser Useless in his chambers, brooding on how great he used to be.'

Egg spoke up. 'He fought for the black dragon.'

Dunk could have given the boy a clout, but the brown knight only laughed. ''Course he did. Just look at him. He strike you as the kind who picks the winning side?'

'No more than you. Else you wouldn't be here with us.' Dunk turned to Egg. 'Tend to Thunder and the Maester and then come up and join us.'

When Dunk came up through the trap, the old knight was sitting by the hearth in his bedrobe, though no fire had been laid. His father's cup was in his hand, a heavy silver cup that had been made for some Lord Osgrey back before the Conquest. A chequy lion adorned the bowl, done in flakes of jade and gold, though some of the jade flakes had gone missing. At the sound of Dunk's footsteps, the old knight looked up and blinked like a man waking from a dream. 'Ser Duncan. You are back. Did the sight of you give Lucas Inchfield pause, ser?'

'Not as I saw, m'lord. More like, it made him wroth.' Dunk told it all as best he could, though he omitted the part about Lady Helicent, which made him look an utter fool. He would have left out the clout too, but his broken lip had puffed up twice its normal size, and Ser Eustace could not help but notice.

When he did, he frowned. 'Your lip . . .'

Dunk touched it gingerly. The broken lip was puffed up to twice its normal size. 'Her ladyship gave me a slap.'

'She *struck* you?' His mouth opened and closed. 'She struck my envoy, who came to her beneath the chequy lion? She dared lay hands upon your person?'

'Only the one hand, ser. It stopped bleeding before we even left the castle.' He made a fist. 'She wants Ser Bennis, not your silver, and she won't take down the dam. She showed me a parchment with some writing on it, and the king's own seal. It said the stream is hers. And . . .' He hesitated. 'She said that you were . . . that you had . . .'

'. . . risen with the black dragon?' Ser Eustace seemed to slump. 'I feared she might. If you wish to leave my service, I will not stop you.' The old knight gazed into his cup, though what he might be looking for Dunk could not say.

'You told me your sons died fighting for the king.'

'And so they did. The *rightful* king, Daemon Blackfyre. The King Who Bore the Sword.' The old man's moustache quivered. 'The men of the red dragon call themselves the *loyalists*, but we who chose the black were just as loyal, once. Though now . . . all the men who marched beside me to seat Prince Daemon on the Iron Throne have melted away like morning dew. Mayhaps I dreamed them. Or more like, Lord Bloodraven and his Raven's Teeth have put the fear in them. They cannot all be dead.'

Dunk could not deny the truth of that. Until this moment, he had never met a man who'd fought for the Pretender. *I must have, though. There were thousands of them. Half the realm was for the red dragon, and half was for the black.* 'Both sides fought valiantly, Ser Arlan always said.' He thought the old knight would want to hear that.

Ser Eustace cradled his wine cup in both hands. 'If Daemon had ridden over Gwayne Corbray . . . if Fireball had not been slain on the eve of battle . . . if Hightower and Tarbeck and Oakheart and Butterwell had lent us their full strength instead of trying to keep one foot in each camp . . . if Manfred Lothston had proved true instead of treacherous . . . if storms had not delayed Lord Bracken's sailing with the

Myrish crossbowmen . . . if Quickfinger had not been caught with the stolen dragon's eggs . . . so many *ifs*, ser . . . had any one come out differently, it could all have turned t'other way. Then we would called be the loyalists, and the red dragons would be remembered as men who fought to keep the usurper Daeron the Falseborn upon his stolen throne, and failed.'

'That's as it may be, m'lord,' said Dunk, 'but things went the way they went. It was all years ago, and you were pardoned.'

'Aye, we were pardoned. So long as we bent the knee and gave him a hostage to ensure our future loyalty, Daeron forgave the traitors and the rebels.' His voice was bitter. 'I bought my head back with my daughter's life. Alysanne was seven when they took her off to King's Landing and twenty when she died, a silent sister. I went to King's Landing once to see her, and she would not even speak to me, her own father. A king's mercy is a poisoned gift. Daeron Targaryen left me life, but took my pride and dreams and honour.' His hand trembled, and wine spilled red upon his lap, but the old man took no notice of it. 'I should have gone with Bittersteel into exile, or died beside my sons and my sweet king. That would have been a death worthy of a chequy lion descended from so many proud lords and mighty warriors. Daeron's mercy made me smaller.'

In his heart the black dragon never died, Dunk realized.

'My lord?'

It was Egg's voice. The boy had come in as Ser Eustace was speaking of his death. The old knight blinked at him as if he were seeing him for the first time. 'Yes, lad? What is it?'

'If it please you . . . the Red Widow says you rebelled to get her castle. That isn't true, is it?'

'The castle?' He seemed confused. 'Coldmoat . . . Coldmoat was promised me by Daemon, yes, but . . . it was not for gain, no . . .'

'Then why?' asked Egg.

'Why?' Ser Eustace frowned.

'Why were you a traitor? If it wasn't just the castle.'

Ser Eustace looked at Egg a long time before replying. 'You are only a young boy. You would not understand.'

'Well,' said Egg, 'I might.'

'Treason . . . is only a word. When two princes fight for a chair where only one may sit, great lords and common men alike must choose. And when the battle's done, the victors will be hailed as loyal men and true, while those who were defeated will be known for evermore as rebels and traitors. That was my fate.'

Egg thought about it for a time. 'Yes, my lord. Only . . . King Daeron was a good man. Why would you choose Daemon?'

'Daeron . . .' Ser Eustace almost slurred the word, and Dunk realized he was half drunk. 'Daeron was spindly and round of shoulder, with a little belly that wobbled when he walked. Daemon stood straight and proud, and his stomach was flat and hard as an oaken shield. And he could *fight*. With axe or lance or flail, he was as good as any knight I ever saw, but with *the sword* he was the Warrior himself. When Prince Daemon had Blackfyre in his hand, there was not a man to equal him . . . not Ulrick Dayne with Dawn, no, nor even the Dragonknight with Dark Sister.

'You can know a man by his friends, Egg. Daeron surrounded himself with maesters, septons and singers. Always there were women whispering in his ear, and his court was full of Dornishmen. How not, when he had taken a Dornishwoman into his bed, and sold his own sweet sister to the Prince of Dorne, though it was Daemon that she loved? Daeron bore the same name as the Young Dragon, but when his Dornish wife gave him a son he named the child Baelor, after the feeblest king who ever sat the Iron Throne.

'Daemon, though . . . Daemon was no more pious than a king need be, and all the great knights of the realm gathered to him. It would suit Lord Bloodraven if their names were all forgotten, so he has forbidden us to sing of them, but *I* remember. Robb Reyne, Gareth the Grey, Ser Aubrey Ambrose, Lord Gormon Peake, Black Byren Flowers, Redtusk, Fireball . . . *Bittersteel*! I ask you, has there ever been such a noble company, such a roll of heroes?

'*Why*, lad? You ask me why? Because Daemon was the better man. The old king saw it too. He gave the sword to Daemon. *Blackfyre*, the sword of Aegon the Conqueror, the blade that every Targaryen king had wielded since the Conquest . . . he put that sword in Daemon's hand the day he knighted him, a boy of twelve.'

'My father says that was because Daemon was a swordsman, and Daeron never was,' said Egg. 'Why give a horse to a man who cannot ride? The sword was not the kingdom, he says.'

The old knight's hand jerked so hard that wine spilled from his silver cup. 'Your father is a fool.'

'He is *not*,' the boy said.

Osgrey's face twisted in anger. 'You asked a question and I answered it, but I will not suffer insolence. Ser Duncan, you should beat this boy more often. His courtesy leaves much to be desired. If I must needs do it myself, I will –'

'No,' Dunk broke in. 'You won't. Ser.' He had made up his mind. 'It is dark. We will leave at first light.'

Ser Eustace stared at him, stricken. 'Leave?'

'Standfast. Your service.' *You lied to us. Call it what you will, there was no honour in it.* He unfastened his cloak, rolled it up, and put it in the old man's lap.

Osgrey's eyes grew narrow. 'Did that woman offer to take you into service? Are you leaving me for that whore's bed?'

'I don't know that she is a whore,' Dunk said, 'or a witch or a poisoner or none of that. But whatever she may be makes no matter. We're leaving for the hedges, not for Coldmoat.'

'The ditches, you mean. You're leaving me to prowl in the woods like wolves, to waylay honest men upon the roads.' His hand was shaking. The cup fell from his fingers, spilling wine as it rolled along the floor. 'Go, then. Go. I want none of you. I should never have taken you on. *Go!* '

'As you say, ser.' Dunk beckoned, and Egg followed.

That last night Dunk wanted to be as far from Eustace Osgrey as he could, so they slept down in the cellar, among the rest of Standfast's meagre host. It was a restless night. Lem and red-eyed Pate both snored, the one loudly and the other constantly. Dank vapours filled the cellar, rising through the trap from the deeper vaults below. Dunk tossed and turned on the scratchy bed, drifting off into a half-sleep only to wake suddenly in darkness. The bites he'd got in the woods were itching fiercely, and there were fleas in the straw as well. *I will be well rid of this place, well rid of the old man, and Ser Bennis, and the rest of them.* Maybe it was time that he took Egg back to Summerhall to see his father. He would ask the boy about that in the morning, when they were well away.

Morning seemed a long way off, though. Dunk's head was full of dragons, red and black . . . full of chequy lions, old shields, battered boots . . . full of streams and moats and dams, and papers stamped with the king's great seal that he could not read.

And *she* was there as well, the Red Widow, Rohanne of the Coldmoat. He could see her freckled face, her slender arms, her long red braid. It made him feel guilty. *I should be dreaming of Tanselle. Tanselle Too-Tall, they called her, but she was not too tall for me.* She had painted arms upon his shield and he had saved her from the Bright Prince, but she vanished even before the trial of seven. *She could not bear to see me die,* Dunk often told himself, but what did he know? He was as thick as a castle wall. Just thinking of the Red Widow was proof enough of that. *Tanselle smiled at me, but we never held each other, never kissed, not even lips to cheek.* Rohanne at least had touched him; he had the swollen lip to prove it. *Don't be daft. She's not for the likes of you. She is too small, too clever, and much too dangerous.*

Drowsing at long last, Dunk dreamed. He was running through a glade in the heart of Wat's Wood, running towards Rohanne, and she was shooting arrows at him. Each shaft she loosed flew true, and pierced him through the chest, yet the pain was strangely sweet. He should have turned and fled, but he ran towards her instead, running slowly as you always did in dreams, as if the very air had turned to honey. Another arrow came, and yet another. Her quiver seemed to have no end of shafts. Her eyes were grey and green and full of mischief. *Your gown brings out the colour of your eyes*, he meant to say to her, but she was not wearing any gown, or any clothes at all. Across her small breasts was a faint spray of freckles, and her nipples were red and hard as little berries. The arrows made him look like some great porcupine as he went stumbling to her feet, but somehow he still found the strength to grab her braid. With one hard yank he pulled her down on top of him and kissed her.

He woke suddenly, at the sound of a shout.

In the darkened cellar, all was confusion. Curses and complaints echoed back and forth, and men were stumbling over one another as they fumbled for their spears or breeches. No one knew what was happening. Egg found the tallow candle and got it lit, to shed some light upon the scene. Dunk was the first one up the steps. He almost collided with Sam Stoops rushing down, puffing like a bellows and babbling incoherently. Dunk had to hold him by both shoulders to keep him from falling. 'Sam, what's wrong?'

'The sky,' the old man whimpered. 'The *sky*!' No more sense could be got from him, so they all went up to the roof for a look. Ser Eustace was there before them, standing by the parapets in his bedrobe, staring off into the distance.

The sun was rising in the west.

It was a long moment before Dunk realized what that meant. 'Wat's Wood is afire,' he said in a hushed voice. From down at the base of the tower came the sound of Bennis cursing, a stream of such surpassing filth that it might have made Aegon the Unworthy blush. Sam Stoops began to pray.

They were too far away to make out flames, but the red glow engulfed half the western horizon, and above the light the stars were vanishing. The King's Crown was half gone already, obscured behind a veil of the rising smoke.

Fire and sword, she said.

The fire burned all through the night. No one in Standfast slept that night. Before long they could smell the smoke, and see flames dancing in the distance like girls in scarlet skirts. They all wondered if the fire would engulf them. Dunk stood behind the parapets, his eyes burning, watching for riders in the night. 'Bennis,' he said, when the brown knight came up, chewing on his sourleaf, 'it's you she wants. Might be you should go.'

'What, run?' He brayed. 'On *my* horse? Might as well try to fly off on one o' these damn chickens.'

'Then give yourself up. She'll only slit your nose.'

'I like my nose how it is, lunk. Let her try and take me, we'll see what gets slit open.' He sat crosslegged with his back against a merlon, and took a whetstone from his pouch to sharpen his sword. Ser Eustace stood above him. In low voices, they spoke of how to fight the war. 'The Longinch will expect us at the dam,' Dunk heard the old knight say, 'so we will burn her crops instead. Fire for fire.' Ser Bennis thought that would be just the thing, only maybe they should put her mill to the torch as well. 'It's six leagues on t'other side o' the castle, the Longinch won't be looking for us there. Burn the mill and kill the miller, that'll cost her dear.'

Egg was listening too. He coughed, and looked at Dunk with wide white eyes. 'Ser, you have to stop them.'

'How?' Dunk asked. *The Red Widow will stop them. Her, and that Lucas Longinch.* 'They're only making noise, Egg. It's that, or piss their breeches. And it's nought to do with us now.'

Dawn came with hazy grey skies and air that burned the eyes. Dunk meant to make an early start, though after their sleepless night he did not know how far they'd get. He and Egg broke their fast on boiled eggs while Bennis was rousting the others outside for more drill. *They are Osgrey men and we are not,* he told himself. He ate four of the eggs. Ser Eustace owed him that much, as he saw it. Egg ate two. They washed them down with ale.

'We could go to Fair Isle, ser,' the boy said as they were gathering up their things. 'If they're being raided by the ironmen, Lord Farman might be looking for some swords.'

It was a good thought. 'Have you ever been to Fair Isle?'

'No, ser,' Egg said, 'but they say it's fair. Lord Farman's seat is fair too. It's called Faircastle.'

Dunk laughed. 'Faircastle it shall be.' He felt as if a great weight had been lifted off his shoulders. 'I'll see to the horses,' he said, when he'd tied his armour up in a bundle, secured with hempen rope. 'Go to the roof and get our bedrolls, squire.' The last thing he wanted this morning was another confrontation with the chequy lion. 'If you see Ser Eustace, let him be.'

'I will, ser.'

Outside, Bennis had his recruits lined up with their spears and shields, and was trying to teach them to advance in unison. The brown knight paid Dunk not the slightest heed as he crossed the yard. *He will lead the whole lot of them to death. The Red Widow could be here any moment.* Egg came bursting from the tower door and clattered down the wooden steps with their bedrolls. Above him, Ser Eustace stood stiffly on the balcony, his hands resting on the parapet. When his eyes met Dunk's his moustache quivered, and he quickly turned away. The air was hazy with blowing smoke.

Bennis had his shield slung across his back, a tall kite shield of unpainted wood, dark with countless layers of old varnish and girded all about with iron. It bore no blazon, only a centre boss that reminded Dunk of some great eye, shut tight. *As blind as he is.* 'How do you mean to fight her?' Dunk asked.

Ser Bennis looked at his soldiers, his mouth running red with sourleaf. 'Can't hold the hill with so few spears. Got to be the tower. We all hole up inside.' He nodded at the door. 'Only one way in. Haul up them wooden steps, and there's no way they can reach us.'

'Until they build some steps of their own. They might bring ropes and grapnels too, and swarm down on you through the roof. Unless they just stand back with their crossbows and fill you full of quarrels while you're trying to hold the door.'

The Melons, Beans and Barleycorns were listening to all they said. All their brave talk had blown away, though there was no breath of wind. They stood clutching their sharpened sticks, looking at Dunk and Bennis and each other.

'This lot won't do you a lick of good,' Dunk said, with a nod at the ragged Osgrey army. 'The Red Widow's knights will cut them to pieces if you leave them in the open, and their spears won't be any use inside that tower.'

'They can chuck things off the roof,' said Bennis. 'Treb is good at chucking rocks.'

'He could chuck a rock or two, I suppose,' said Dunk, 'until one of the widow's crossbowmen puts a bolt through him.'

'Ser?' Egg stood beside him. 'Ser, if we mean to go, we'd best be gone, in case the widow comes.'

The boy was right. *If we linger, we'll be trapped here.* Yet still Dunk hesitated. 'Let them go, Bennis.'

'What, lose our valiant lads?' Bennis looked at the peasants, and brayed laughter. 'Don't you lot be getting any notions,' he warned them. 'I'll gut any man who tries to run.'

'Try, and I'll gut you.' Dunk drew his sword. 'Go home, all of you,' he told the smallfolk. 'Go back to your villages, and see if the fire's spared your homes and crops.'

No one moved. The brown knight stared at him, his mouth working. Dunk ignored him. 'Go,' he told the smallfolk once again. It was as if some god had put the word into his mouth. *Not the Warrior. Is there a god for fools?* 'GO!' he said again, roaring it this time. 'Take your spears and shields, but *go*, or you won't live to see the morrow. Do you want to kiss your wives again? Do you want to hold your children? *Go home!* Have you all gone deaf?'

They hadn't. A mad scramble ensued among the chickens. Big Rob trod on a hen as he made his dash, and Pate came within half a foot of disembowelling Will Bean when his own spear tripped him up, but off they went, running. The Melons went one way, the Beans another, the Barleycorns a third. Ser Eustace was shouting down at them from above, but no one paid him any mind. *They are deaf to him at least,* Dunk thought.

By the time the old knight emerged from his tower and came scrambling down the steps, only Dunk and Egg and Bennis remained among the chickens. 'Come back,' Ser Eustace shouted at his fast-fleeing host. 'You do not have my leave to go. *You do not have my leave!*'

'No use, m'lord,' said Bennis. 'They're gone.'

Ser Eustace rounded on Dunk, his moustache quivering with rage. 'You had no right to send them away. *No right!* I told them not to go, I *forbade* it. I *forbade* you to dismiss them.'

'We never heard you, my lord.' Egg took off his hat to fan away the smoke. 'The chickens were cackling too loud.'

The old man sank down on to Standfast's lowest step. 'What did that woman offer you to deliver me to her?' he asked Dunk in a bleak voice. 'How much gold did she give you to betray me, to send my lads away and leave me here alone?'

'You're not alone, m'lord.' Dunk sheathed his sword. 'I slept beneath your roof, and ate your eggs this morning. I owe you some service still. I won't go slinking off with my tail between my legs. My sword's still here.' He touched the hilt.

'One sword.' The old knight got slowly to his feet. 'What can one sword hope to do against that woman?'

'Try and keep her off your land, to start with.' Dunk wished he was as certain as he sounded.

The old knight's moustache trembled every time he took a breath. 'Yes,' he said at last. 'Better to go boldly than hide behind stone walls. Better to die a lion than a rabbit. We were the Marshals of the Northmarch for a thousand years. I must have my armour.' He started up the steps.

Egg was looking up at Dunk. 'I never knew you had a tail, ser,' the boy said.

'Do you want a clout in the ear?'

'No, ser. Do you want your armour?'

'That,' Dunk said, 'and one thing more.'

There was talk of Ser Bennis coming with them, but in the end Ser Eustace commanded him to stay and hold the tower. His sword would be of little use against the odds that they were like to face, and the sight of him would inflame the widow further.

The brown knight did not require much convincing. Dunk helped him knock loose the iron pegs that held the upper steps in place. Bennis clambered up them, untied the old grey hempen rope, and hauled on it with all his strength. Creaking and groaning, the wooden stair swung upwards, leaving ten feet of air between the top stone step and the tower's only entrance. Sam Stoops and his wife were both inside. The chickens would need to fend for themselves. Sitting below on his grey gelding, Ser Eustace called up to say, 'If we have not returned by nightfall . . .'

'. . . I'll ride for Highgarden, m'lord, and tell Lord Tyrell how that woman burned your wood and murdered you.'

Dunk followed Egg and Maester down the hill. The old man came after, his armour rattling softly. For once a wind was rising, and he could hear the flapping of his cloak.

Where Wat's Wood had stood they found a smoking wasteland. The fire had largely burned itself out by the time they reached the wood, but here and there a few patches were still burning, fiery islands in a sea of ash and cinders. Elsewhere the trunks of burned trees thrust like blackened spears into the sky. Other trees had fallen and lay athwart the west way with limbs charred and broken, dull red fires smouldering inside their hollow hearts. There were hot spots on the forest floor as well, and places where the smoke hung in the air like a hot grey haze. Ser Eustace was stricken with a fit of coughing, and for a few moments Dunk feared the old man would need to turn back, but finally it passed.

They rode past the carcass of a red deer, and later on what might have been a badger. Nothing lived, except the flies. Flies could live through anything, it seemed.

'The Field of Fire must have looked like this,' Ser Eustace said. 'It was there our woes began, two hundred years ago. The last of the green kings perished on that field, with the finest flowers of the Reach around him. My father said the dragonfire burned so hot that their swords melted in their hands. Afterwards the blades were gathered up, and went to make the Iron Throne. Highgarden passed from kings to stewards, and the Osgreys dwindled and diminished, until the Marshals of the Northmarch were no more than landed knights bound in fealty to the Rowans.'

Dunk had nothing to say to that, so they rode in silence for a time, till Ser Eustace coughed, and said, 'Ser Duncan, do you remember the story that I told you?'

'I might, ser,' said Dunk. 'Which one?'

'The Little Lion.'

'I remember. He was the youngest of five sons.'

'Good.' He coughed again. 'When he slew Lancel Lannister, the westermen turned back. Without the king there was no war. Do you understand what I am saying?'

'Aye,' Dunk said reluctantly. *Could I kill a woman?* For once Dunk wished he *were* as thick as that castle wall. *It must not come to that. I must not let it come to that.*

A few green trees still stood where the west way crossed the Chequy Water. Their trunks were charred and blackened on one side. Just beyond, the water glimmered darkly. *Blue and green*, Dunk thought, *but all the gold is gone*. The smoke had veiled the sun.

Ser Eustace halted when he reached the water's edge. 'I took a holy vow. I will not cross that stream. Not so long as the land beyond is *hers*.' The old knight wore mail and plate beneath his yellowed surcoat. His sword was on his hip.

'What if she never comes, ser?' Egg asked.

With fire and sword, Dunk thought. 'She'll come.'

She did, and within the hour. They heard her horses first, and then the faint metallic sound of clinking armour, growing louder. The drifting smoke made it hard to tell how far off they were, until her banner bearer pushed through the ragged grey curtain. His staff was crowned by an iron spider painted white and red, with the black banner of the Webbers hanging listlessly beneath. When he saw them across the water, he halted on the bank. Ser Lucas Inchfield appeared half a heartbeat later, armoured head to heel.

Only then did Lady Rohanne herself appear, astride a coal-black mare decked out in strands of silvery silk, like unto a spider's web. The widow's cloak was made of the same stuff. It billowed from her shoulders and her wrists, as light as air. She was armoured too, in a suit of green enamel scale chased with gold and silver. It fitted her figure like a glove, and made her look as if she were garbed in summer leaves. Her long red braid hung down behind her, bouncing as she rode. Septon Sefton rode red-faced at her side, atop a big grey gelding. On her other side was her young maester, Cerrick, mounted on a mule.

More knights came after, half a dozen of them, attended by as many esquires. A column of mounted crossbowmen brought up the rear, and fanned out to either side of the road when they reached the Chequy Water and saw Dunk waiting on the other side. There were three-and-thirty fighting men all told, excluding the septon, the maester and the widow herself. One of the knights caught Dunk's eye; a squat bald keg of a man in mail and leather, with an angry face and an ugly goitre on his neck.

The Red Widow walked her mare to the edge of the water. 'Ser Eustace, Ser Duncan,' she called across the stream, 'we saw your fire burning in the night.'

'Saw it?' Ser Eustace shouted back. 'Aye, you saw it . . . after you made it.'

'That is a vile accusation.'

'For a vile act.'

'I was asleep in my bed last night, with my ladies all around me. The shouts from the walls awoke me, as they did most everyone. Old men climbed up steep tower steps to look, and babes at the breast saw the red light and wept in fear. And that is all I know of your fire, ser.'

'It was your fire, woman,' insisted Ser Eustace. 'My wood is gone. *Gone*, I say!'

Septon Sefton cleared his throat. 'Ser Eustace,' he boomed, 'there are fires in the kingswood too, and even in the rainwood. The drought has turned all our woods to kindling.'

Lady Rohanne raised an arm and pointed. 'Look at my fields, Osgrey.

How dry they are. I would have been a fool to set a fire. Had the wind changed direction, the flames might well have leapt the stream, and burned out half my crops.'

'Might have?' Ser Eustace shouted. 'It was my woods that burned, and you that burned them. Most like you cast some witch's spell to drive the wind, just as you used your dark arts to slay your husbands and your brothers!'

Lady Rohanne's face grew harder. Dunk had seen that look at Coldmoat, just before she slapped him. 'Prattle,' she told the old man. 'I will waste no more words on you, ser. Produce Bennis of the Brown Shield, or we will come and take him.'

'That you shall not do,' Ser Eustace declared in ringing tones. 'That you shall *never* do.' His moustache twitched. 'Come no further. This side of the stream is mine, and you are not wanted here. You shall have no hospitality from me. No bread and salt, not even shade and water. You come as an intruder. I forbid you to set foot on Osgrey land.'

Lady Rohanne drew her braid over her shoulder. 'Ser Lucas,' was all she said. The Longinch made a gesture, the crossbowmen dismounted, winched back their bowstrings with the help of hook and stirrup, and plucked quarrels from their quivers. 'Now, ser,' her ladyship called out, when every bow was nocked and raised and ready, 'what was it you forbade me?'

Dunk had heard enough. 'If you cross the stream without leave, you are breaking the king's peace.'

Septon Sefton urged his horse forward a step. 'The king will neither know nor care,' he called. 'We are all the Mother's children, ser. For her sake, stand aside.'

Dunk frowned. 'I don't know much of gods, septon . . . but aren't we the Warrior's children, too?' He rubbed the back of his neck. 'If you try to cross, I'll stop you.'

Ser Lucas the Longinch laughed. 'Here's a hedge knight who yearns to be a hedgehog, my lady,' he said to the Red Widow. 'Say the word, and we'll put a dozen quarrels in him. At this distance they will punch through that armour as if it was made of spit.'

'No. Not yet, ser.' Lady Rohanne studied him from across the stream. 'You are two men and a boy. We are three-and-thirty. How do you propose to stop us crossing?'

'Well,' said Dunk, 'I'll tell you. But only you.'

'As you wish.' She pressed her heels into her horse and rode her out into the stream. When the water reached the mare's belly, she halted, waiting. 'Here I am. Come closer, ser. I promise not to sew you in a sack.'

Ser Eustace grasped Dunk by the arm before he could respond. 'Go to her,' the old knight said, 'but remember the Little Lion.'

'As you say, m'lord.' Dunk walked Thunder down into the water. He drew up beside her and said, 'M'lady.'

'Ser Duncan.' She reached up and laid two fingers on his swollen lip. 'Did I do this, ser?'

'No one else has slapped my face of late, m'lady.'

'That was bad of me. A breach of hospitality. The good septon has been scolding me.' She gazed across the water at Ser Eustace. 'I scarce remember Addam any longer. It was more than half my life ago. I remember that I loved him, though. I have not loved any of the others.'

'His father put him in the blackberries, with his brothers,' Dunk said. 'He was fond of blackberries.'

'I remember. He used to pick them for me, and we'd eat them in a bowl of cream.'

'The king pardoned the old man for Daemon,' said Dunk. 'It is past time you pardoned him for Addam.'

'Give me Bennis, and I'll consider that.'

'Bennis is not mine to give.'

She sighed. 'I would as lief not have to kill you.'

'I would as lief not die.'

'Then give me Bennis. We'll cut his nose off and hand him back, and that will be the end of that.'

'It won't, though,' Dunk said. 'There's still the dam to deal with, and the fire. Will you give us the men who set it?'

'There were lantern bugs in that wood,' she said. 'It may be they set the fire off, with their little lanterns.'

'No more teasing now, m'lady,' Dunk warned her. 'This is no time for it. Tear down the dam, and let Ser Eustace have the water to make up for the wood. That's fair, is it not?'

'It might be, if I had burned the wood. Which I did not. I was at Coldmoat, safe abed.' She looked down at the water. 'What is there to prevent us from riding right across the stream? Have you scattered caltrops among the rocks? Hidden archers in the ashes? Tell me what you think is going to stop us.'

'Me.' He pulled one gauntlet off. 'In Flea Bottom I was always bigger and stronger than the other boys, so I used to beat them bloody and steal from them. The old man taught me not to do that. It was wrong, he said, and besides, sometimes little boys have great big brothers.

Here, have a look at this.' Dunk twisted the ring off his finger and held it out to her. She had to let loose of her braid to take it.

'Gold?' she said, when she felt the weight of it. 'What is this, ser?' She turned it over in her hand. 'A signet. Gold and onyx.' Her green eyes narrowed as she studied the seal. 'Where did you find this, ser?'

'In a boot. Wrapped in rags and stuffed up in the toe.'

Lady Rohanne's fingers closed around it. She glanced at Egg and old Ser Eustace. 'You took a great risk in showing me this ring, ser. But how does it avail us? If I should command my men to cross . . .'

'Well,' said Dunk, 'that would mean I'd have to fight.'

'And die.'

'Most like,' he said, 'and then Egg would go back where he comes from, and tell what happened here.'

'Not if he died as well.'

'I don't think you'd kill a boy of ten,' he said, hoping he was right. 'Not *this* boy of ten, you wouldn't. You've got three-and-thirty men there, as you said. Men talk. That fat one there especially. No matter how deep you dug the graves, the tale would out. And then, well . . . might be a spotted spider's bite can kill a lion, but a dragon is a different sort of beast.'

'I would sooner be the dragon's friend.' She tried the ring on her finger. It was too big even for her thumb. 'Dragon or no, I must have Bennis of the Brown Shield.'

'No.'

'You are seven feet of stubborn.'

'Less an inch.'

She gave him back the ring. 'I cannot return to Coldmoat empty-handed. They will say the Red Widow has lost her bite, that she was too weak to do justice, that she could not protect her smallfolk. You do not understand, ser.'

'I might.' *Better than you know.* 'I remember once some little lord in the stormlands took Ser Arlan into service, to help him fight some other little lord. When I asked the old man what they were fighting over, he said, "Nothing, lad. It's just some pissing contest."'

Lady Rohanne gave him a shocked look, but could sustain it no more than half a heartbeat before it turned into a grin. 'I have heard a thousand empty courtesies in my time, but you are the first knight who ever said *pissing* in my presence.' Her freckled face went sombre. 'Those pissing contests are how lords judge one another's strength, and woe to any man who shows his weakness. A woman must needs piss twice as hard, if she hopes to rule. And if that woman should happen to be *small* . . . Lord Stackhouse covets my Horseshoe Hills, Ser Clifford Conklyn has an old claim to Leafy Lake, those dismal Durwells live by stealing cattle . . . and beneath mine own roof I have the Longinch. Every day I wake wondering if this might be the day he marries me by force.' Her hand curled tight around her braid, as hard as if it were a rope, and she was dangling over a precipice. 'He wants to, I know. He holds back for fear of my wroth, just as Conklyn and Stackhouse and the Durwells tread carefully where the Red Widow is concerned. If any of them thought for a moment that I had turned weak and soft . . .'

Dunk put the ring back on his finger, and drew his dagger.

The widow's eyes went wide at the sight of naked steel. 'What are you doing?' she said. 'Have you lost your *wits*? There are a dozen cross-bows trained on you.'

'You wanted blood for blood.' He laid the dagger against his cheek. 'They told you wrong. It wasn't Bennis cut that digger, it was me.' He pressed the edge of the steel into his face, slashed downward. When he shook the blood off the blade some spattered on her face. *More freckles*, he thought. 'There, the Red Widow has her due. A cheek for a cheek.'

'You are quite mad.' The smoke had filled her eyes with tears. 'If you were better born, I'd marry you.'

'Aye, m'lady. And if pigs had wings and scales and breathed flame, they'd be as good as dragons.' Dunk slid the knife back in its sheath. His face had begun to throb. The blood ran down his cheek and dripped on to his gorget. The smell made Thunder snort, and paw the water. 'Give me the men who burned the wood.'

'No one burned the wood,' she said, 'but if some man of mine had done so, it must have been to please me. How could I give such a man to you?' She glanced back at her escort. 'It would be best if Ser Eustace were just to withdraw his accusation.'

'Those pigs will be breathing fire first, m'lady.'

'In that case, I must assert my innocence before the eyes of gods and men. Tell Ser Eustace that I demand an apology . . . or a trial. The choice is his.' She wheeled her horse about to ride back to her men.

The stream would be their battleground.

Septon Sefton waddled out and said a prayer, beseeching the Father Above to look down on these two men and judge them justly, asking the Warrior to lend his strength to the man whose cause was just and true, begging the Mother's mercy for the liar, that he might be forgiven for his sins. When the praying was over and done with, he turned to Ser Eustace Osgrey one last time. 'Ser,' he said, 'I beg you once again, withdraw your accusation.'

'I will not,' the old man said, his moustache trembling.

The fat septon turned to Lady Rohanne. 'Good-sister, if you did this thing, confess your guilt, and offer good Ser Eustace some restitution for his wood. Elsewise blood must flow.'

'My champion will prove my innocence before the eyes of gods and men.'

'Trial by battle is not the only way,' said the septon, waist-deep in the water. 'Let us go to Goldengrove, I implore you both, and place the matter before Lord Rowan for his judgment.'

'*Never*,' said Ser Eustace. The Red Widow shook her head.

Ser Lucas Inchfield looked at Lady Rohanne, his face dark with fury. 'You *will* marry me when this mummer's farce is done. As your lord father wished.'

'My lord father never knew you as I do,' she gave back.

Dunk went to one knee beside Egg, and put the signet back in the boy's hand; four three-headed dragons, two and two, the arms of Maekar, Prince of Summerhall. 'Back in the boot,' he said, 'but if it happens that I die, go to the nearest of your father's friends and have him take you back to Summerhall. Don't try to cross the whole Reach on your own. See you don't forget, or my ghost will come and clout you in the ear.'

'Yes, ser,' said Egg, 'but I'd sooner you didn't die.'

'It's too hot to die.' Dunk donned his helm, and Egg helped him fasten it tightly to his gorget. The blood was sticky on his face, though Ser Eustace had torn a piece off his cloak to help stop the gash from bleeding. He rose and went to Thunder. Most of the smoke had blown away, he saw as he swung up on to the saddle, but the sky was still dark. *Clouds*, he thought, *dark clouds*. It had been so long. *Maybe it's an omen. But is it his omen, or mine*? Dunk was no good with omens.

Across the stream, Ser Lucas had mounted up as well. His horse was a chestnut courser; a splendid animal, swift and strong, but not as large as Thunder. What the horse lacked in size he made up for in armour, though; he was clad in crinet, chanfron, and a coat of light chain. The Longinch himself wore black enamelled plate and silvery ringmail. An onyx spider squatted malignantly atop his helmet, but his shield displayed his own arms: a bend sinister, chequy black and white, on a pale grey field. Dunk watched Ser Lucas hand it to a squire. *He does not mean to use it.* When another squire delivered him a poleaxe, he knew why. The axe was long and lethal, with a banded haft, a heavy head and a wicked spike on its back, but it was a two-handed weapon. The Longinch would need to trust in his armour to protect him. *I need to make him rue that choice.*

His own shield was on his left arm, the shield Tanselle had painted with his elm and falling star. A child's rhyme echoed in his head. *Oak and iron, guard me well, or else I'm dead, and doomed to hell.* He slid his longsword from its scabbard. The weight of it felt good in his hand.

He put his heels into Thunder's flanks, and walked the big destrier down into the water. Across the stream, Ser Lucas did the same. Dunk pressed right, so as to present the Longinch with his left side, protected by his shield. That was not something Ser Lucas was willing to concede him. He turned his courser quickly, and they came together in a tumult of grey steel and green spray. Ser Lucas struck with his poleaxe. Dunk had to twist in the saddle to catch it on his shield. The force of it shot down his arm and jarred his teeth together. He swung his sword in answer, a sideways cut that took the other knight beneath his upraised arm. Steel screamed on steel, and it was on.

The Longinch spurred his courser in a circle, trying to get around to Dunk's unprotected side, but Thunder wheeled to meet him, snapping at the other horse. Ser Lucas delivered one crashing blow after another, standing in his stirrups to get all his weight and strength behind the axehead. Dunk shifted his shield to catch each blow as it came. Half-crouched beneath its oak, he hacked at Inchfield's arms and side and legs, but his plate turned every stroke. Round they went, and round again, the water lapping at their legs. The Longinch attacked, and Dunk defended, watching for a weakness.

Finally he saw it. Every time Ser Lucas lifted his axe for another blow, a gap appeared beneath his arm. There was mail and leather there, and padding underneath, but no steel plate. Dunk kept his shield up, trying to time his attack. *Soon. Soon.* The axe crashed down, wrenched free, came up. *Now!* He slammed his spurs into Thunder, driving him closer, and thrust with his longsword, to drive his point through the opening.

But the gap vanished as quickly as it had appeared. His swordpoint scraped a rondel, and Dunk, overextended, almost lost his seat. The axe descended with a crash, slanting off the iron rim of Dunk's shield, crunching against the side of his helm, and striking Thunder a glancing blow along the neck.

The destrier screamed and reared up on two legs, his eye rolling white in pain as the sharp coppery smell of blood filled the air. He lashed out with his iron hooves just as Longinch was moving in. One caught Ser Lucas in the face, the other on a shoulder. Then the heavy warhorse came down atop his courser.

It all happened in a heartbeat. The two horses went down in a tangle, kicking and biting at each other, churning up the water and the mud below. Dunk tried to throw himself from the saddle, but one foot tangled in a stirrup. He fell face first, sucking down one desperate gulp of air before the stream came rushing into the helm through the eyeslit. His foot was still caught up, and he felt a savage yank as Thunder's struggles almost pulled his leg out of its socket. Just as quickly he was free, turning, sinking. For a moment he flailed helplessly in the water. The world was blue and green and brown.

The weight of his armour pulled him down until his shoulder bumped the streambed. *If that is down the other way is up.* Dunk's steel-clad hands fumbled at the stones and sands, and somehow he gathered his legs up under him and stood. He was reeling, dripping mud, with water pouring from the breath holes in his dinted helm, but he was standing. He sucked down air.

His battered shield still clung to his left arm, but his scabbard was empty and his sword was gone. There was blood inside his helm as well as water. When he tried to shift his weight, his ankle sent a lance of pain right up his leg. Both horses had struggled back to their feet, he saw. He turned his head, squinting one-eyed through a veil of blood, searching for his foe. *Gone*, he thought, *he's drowned, or Thunder crushed his skull in.*

Ser Lucas burst up out of the water right in front of him, sword in hand. He struck Dunk's neck a savage blow, and only the thickness of his gorget kept his head upon his shoulders. He had no blade to answer with, only his shield. He gave ground, and the Longinch came after, screaming and slashing. Dunk's upraised arm took a numbing blow above the elbow. A cut to his hip made him grunt in pain. As he backed away, a rock turned beneath his foot, and he went down to one knee, chest-high in the water. He got his shield up, but this time Ser Lucas struck so hard he split the thick oak right down the middle, and drove the remnants back into Dunk's face. His ears were ringing and his mouth was full of blood, but somewhere far away he heard Egg screaming. 'Get him, ser, get him, get him, he's *right there!* '

Dunk dived forwards. Ser Lucas had wrenched his sword free for another cut. Dunk slammed into him waist-high and knocked him off his feet. The stream swallowed both of them again, but this time Dunk was ready. He kept one arm around the Longinch and forced him to the bottom. Bubbles came streaming out from behind Inchfield's battered, twisted visor, but still he fought. He found a rock at the bottom of the stream and began hammering at Dunk's head and hands. Dunk fumbled at his swordbelt. *Have I lost the dagger too?* he wondered. No, there it was. His hand closed round the hilt and he wrenched it free, and drove it slowly through the churning water, through the iron rings and boiled leather beneath the arm of Lucas the Longinch, turning it as he pushed. Ser Lucas jerked and twisted, and the strength left him. Dunk shoved away and floated. His chest was on fire. A fish flashed past his face, long and white and slender. *What's that?* he wondered. *What's that? What's that?*

He woke in the wrong castle.

When his eyes opened, he did not know where he was. It was blessedly cool. The taste of blood was in his mouth and he had a cloth across his eyes, a heavy cloth fragrant with some unguent. It smelled of cloves, he thought.

Dunk groped at his face, pulled the cloth away. Above him torchlight played against a high ceiling. Ravens were walking on the rafters overhead, peering down with small black eyes and *quork*ing at him. *I am not blind, at least.* He was in a maester's tower. The walls were lined with racks of herbs and potions in earthen jars and vessels of green glass. A long trestle table nearby was covered with parchments, books and queer bronze instruments, all spattered with droppings from the ravens in the rafters. He could hear them muttering at one another.

He tried to sit. It proved a bad mistake. His head swam, and his left leg screamed in agony when he put the slightest weight upon it. His ankle was wrapped in linen, he saw, and there were linen strips around his chest and shoulders too.

'Be still.' A face appeared above him, young and pinched, with dark brown eyes on either side of a hooked nose. Dunk knew that face. The man who owned it was all in grey, with a chain collar hanging loose about his neck, a maester's chain of many metals. Dunk grabbed him by the wrist. 'Where . . . ?'

'Coldmoat,' said the maester. 'You were too badly injured to return to Standfast, so Lady Rohanne commanded us to bring you here. Drink this.' He raised a cup of . . . something . . . to Dunk's lips. The potion had a bitter taste, like vinegar, but at least it washed away the taste of blood.

Dunk made himself drink it all. Afterwards he flexed the fingers of his sword hand, and then the other. *At least my hands still work, and my arms.* 'What . . . what did I hurt?'

'What not?' The maester snorted. 'A broken ankle, a sprained knee, a broken collarbone, bruising . . . your upper torso is largely green and yellow and your right arm is a purply black. I thought your skull was cracked as well, but it appears not. There is that gash in your face, ser. You will have a scar, I fear. Oh, and you had drowned by the time we pulled you from the water.'

'Drowned?' said Dunk.

'I never suspected that one man could swallow so much water, not even a man as large as you, ser. Count yourself fortunate that I am ironborn. The priests of the Drowned God know how to drown a man and bring him back, and I have made a study of their beliefs and customs.'

I drowned. Dunk tried to sit again, but the strength was not in him. *I drowned in water that did not even come up to my neck.* He laughed, then groaned in pain. 'Ser Lucas?'

'Dead. Did you doubt it?'

No. Dunk doubted many things, but not that. He rememberd how the strength had gone out of the Longinch's limbs, all at once. 'Egg,' he got out. 'I want Egg.'

'Hunger is a good sign,' the maester said, 'but it is sleep you need just now, not food.'

Dunk shook his head, and regretted it at once. 'Egg is my squire . . .'

'Is he? A brave lad, and stronger than he looks. He was the one to pull you from the stream. He helped us get that armour off you too, and rode with you in the wain when we brought you here. He would not sleep himself, but sat by your side with your sword across his lap, in case someone tried to do you harm. He even suspected *me*, and insisted that I taste anything I meant to feed you. A queer child, but devoted.'

'Where is he?'

'Ser Eustace asked the boy to attend him at the wedding feast. There was no one else on his side. It would have been discourteous for him to refuse.'

'Wedding feast?' Dunk did not understand.

'You would not know, of course. Coldmoat and Standfast were reconciled after your battle. Lady Rohanne begged leave of old Ser Eustace to cross his land and visit Addam's grave, and he granted her that right. She knelt before the blackberries and began to weep, and he was so moved that he went to comfort her. They spent the whole night talking of young Addam and my lady's noble father. Lord Wyman and Ser Eustace were fast friends, until the Blackfyre Rebellion. His lordship and my lady were wed this morning, by our good Septon Sefton. Eustace Osgrey is the Lord of Coldmoat, and his chequy lion flies beside the Webber spider on every tower and wall.'

Dunk's world was spinning slowly all around him. *That potion. He's put me back to sleep.* He closed his eyes, and let all the pain drain out of him. He could hear the ravens *quork*ing and screaming at each other, and the sound of his own breath, and something else as well . . . a softer sound, steady, heavy, somehow soothing. 'What's that?' he murmured sleepily. 'That sound . . . ?'

'That?' The maester listened. 'That's just rain.'

He did not see her till the day they took their leave.

'This is folly, ser,' Septon Sefton complained, as Dunk limped heavily across the yard, swinging his splinted foot and leaning on a crutch. 'Maester Cerrick says you are not half-healed as yet, and this rain . . . you're like to catch a chill, if you do not drown again. At least wait for the rain to stop.'

'That may be years.' Dunk was grateful to the fat septon, who had visited him near every day . . . to pray for him, ostensibly, though more time seemed to be taken up with tales and gossip. He would miss his loose and lively tongue and cheerful company, but that changed nothing. 'I need to go.'

The rain was lashing down around them, a thousand cold grey whips upon his back. His cloak was already sodden. It was the white wool cloak Ser Eustace had given him, with the green and gold chequered border. The old knight had pressed it on him once again, as a parting gift. 'For your courage and leal service, ser,' he said. The brooch that pinned the cloak at his shoulder was a gift as well: an ivory spider brooch with silver legs. Clusters of crushed garnets made spots upon its back.

'I hope this is not some mad quest to hunt down Bennis,' Septon Sefton said. 'You are so bruised and battered that I would fear for you, if that one found you in such a state.'

Bennis, Dunk thought bitterly, *bloody Bennis*. While Dunk had been making his stand at the stream, Bennis had tied up Sam Stoops and his wife, ransacked Standfast from top to bottom, and made off with every item of value he could find, from candles, clothes and weaponry to Osgrey's old silver cup and a small cache of coins the old man had hidden in his solar behind a mildewed tapestry. One day Dunk hoped to meet

Ser Bennis of the Brown Shield again, and when he did . . .' Bennis will keep.'

'Where will you go?' The septon was panting heavily. Even with Dunk on a crutch, he was too fat to match his pace.

'Fair Isle. Harrenhal. The Trident. There are hedges everywhere.' He shrugged. 'I've always wanted to see the Wall.'

'The Wall?' The septon jerked to a stop. 'I despair of you, Ser Duncan!' he shouted, standing in the mud with outspread hands as the rain came down around him. 'Pray, ser, pray for the Crone to light your way!' Dunk kept walking.

She was waiting for him inside the stables, standing by the yellow bales of hay in a gown as green as summer. 'Ser Duncan,' she said when he came pushing through the door. Her red braid hung down in front, the end of it brushing against her thighs. 'It is good to see you on your feet.'

You never saw me on my back, he thought. 'M'lady. What brings you to the stables? It's a wet day for a ride.'

'I might say the same to you.'

'Egg told you?' *I owe him another clout in the ear.*

'Be glad he did, or I would have sent men after you to drag you back. It was cruel of you to try and steal away without so much as a farewell.'

She had never come to see him while he was in Maester Cerrick's care, not once. 'That green becomes you well, m'lady,' he said. 'It brings out the colour of your eyes.' He shifted his weight awkwardly on the crutch. 'I'm here for my horse.'

'You do not need to go. There is a place for you here, when you're recovered. Captain of my guards. And Egg can join my other squires. No one need ever know who he is.'

'Thank you, m'lady, but no.' Thunder was in a stall a dozen places down. Dunk hobbled towards him.

'Please reconsider, ser. These are perilous times, even for dragons and their friends. Stay until you've healed.' She walked along beside him. 'It would please Lord Eustace too. He is very fond of you.'

'Very fond,' Dunk agreed. 'If his daughter wasn't dead, he'd want me to marry her. Then you could be my lady mother. I never had a mother, much less a *lady* mother.'

For half a heartbeat Lady Rohanne looked as though she was going to slap him again. *Maybe she'll just kick my crutch away.*

'You are angry with me, ser,' she said instead. 'You must let me make amends.'

'Well,' he said, 'you could help me saddle Thunder.'

'I had something else in mind.' She reached out her hand for his, a freckled hand, her fingers strong and slender. *I'll bet she's freckled all over.* 'How well do you know horses?'

'I ride one.'

'An old destrier bred for battle, slow-footed and ill-tempered. Not a horse to ride from place to place.'

'If I need to get from place to place, it's him or these.' Dunk pointed at his feet.

'You have large feet,' she observed. 'Large hands as well. I think you must be large all over. Too large for most palfreys. They'd look like ponies with you perched upon their backs. Still, a swifter mount would serve you well. A big courser, with some Dornish sand steed for endurance.' She pointed to the stall across from Thunder's. 'A horse like her.'

She was a blood bay with a bright eye and a long fiery mane. Lady Rohanne took a carrot from her sleeve and stroked her head as she took it. 'The carrot, not the fingers,' she told the horse, before she turned again to Dunk. 'I call her Flame, but you may name her as you please. Call her Amends, if you like.'

For a moment he was speechless. He leaned on the crutch and looked at the blood bay with new eyes. She was magnificent. A better mount than any the old man had ever owned. You had only to look at those long, clean limbs to see how swift she'd be.

'I bred her for beauty, and for speed.'

He turned back to Thunder. 'I cannot take her.'

'Why not?'

'She is too good a horse for me. Just look at her.'

A flush crept up Rohanne's face. She clutched her braid, twisting it between her fingers. 'I had to marry, you know that. My father's will . . . oh, don't be such a fool.'

'What else should I be? I'm thick as a castle wall and bastard-born as well.'

'Take the horse. I refuse to let you go without something to remember me by.'

'I will remember you, m'lady. Have no fear of that.'

'Take her!'

Dunk grabbed her braid and pulled her face to his. It was awkward with the crutch and the difference in their heights. He almost fell before he got his lips on hers. He kissed her hard. One of her hands went round his neck, and one around his chest. He learned more about kissing in a moment than he had ever known from watching. But when they finally broke apart, he drew his dagger. 'I know what I want to remember you by, m'lady.'

Egg was waiting for him at the gatehouse, mounted on a handsome new sorrel palfrey and holding Maester's lead. When Dunk trotted up to them on Thunder, the boy looked surprised. 'She said she wanted to give you a new horse, ser.'

'Even highborn ladies don't get all they want,' Dunk said, as they rode out across the drawbridge. 'It wasn't a horse I wanted.' The moat was so high it was threatening to overflow its banks. 'I took something else to remember her by instead. A lock of that red hair.' He reached under his cloak, brought out the braid, and smiled.

In the iron cage at the crossroads, the corpses still embraced. They looked lonely, forlorn. Even the flies had abandoned them, and the crows as well. Only some scraps of skin and hair remained upon the dead men's bones.

Dunk halted, frowning. His ankle was hurting from the ride, but it made no matter. Pain was as much a part of knighthood as were swords and shields. 'Which way is south?' he asked Egg. It was hard to know, when the world was all rain and mud and the sky was grey as a granite wall.

'That's south, ser.' Egg pointed. 'That's north.'

'Summerhall is south. Your father.'

'The Wall is north.'

Dunk looked at him. 'That's a long way to ride.'

'I have a new horse, ser.'

'So you do.' Dunk had to smile. 'And why would you want to see the Wall?'

'Well,' said Egg, 'I hear it's tall.'

ALVIN MAKER

ORSON SCOTT CARD

ALVIN MAKER
ORSON SCOTT CARD

THE TALES OF ALVIN MAKER:
Seventh Son (1987)
Red Prophet (1988)
Prentice Alvin (1989)
Alvin Journeyman (1996)
Heartfire (1998)

In the Tales of Alvin Maker series, an alternate-history view of an America that never was, Orson Scott Card postulated what the world might have been like if the Revolutionary War had never happened, and if folk magic actually worked.

America is divided into several provinces, with the Spanish and French still having a strong presence in the New World. The emerging scientific revolution in Europe has led many people with 'talent', that is, magical ability, to emigrate to North America, bringing their prevailing magic with them. The books chronicle the life of Alvin, the seventh son of a seventh son – a fact that marks him right away as a person of great power. It is Alvin's ultimate destiny to become a Maker, an adept being of a kind that has not existed for a thousand years. There exists, however, an Unmaker for every Maker – a being of great supernatural evil – who is Alvin's adversary, and strives to use Alvin's brother Calvin against him.

During the course of his adventures, Alvin explores the world around him and encounters such problems as slavery and the continued enmity between the settlers and the Native Americans who control the western half of the continent. The series appears to be heading towards an ultimate confrontation between Alvin and the Unmaker, with the fate of the entire continent, perhaps even the world, hinging on the outcome.

THE YAZOO QUEEN

BY ORSON SCOTT CARD

Alvin watched as Captain Howard welcomed aboard another group of passengers, a prosperous family with five children and three slaves.

'It's the Nile River of America,' said the captain. 'But Cleopatra herself never sailed in such splendour as you folks is going to experience on the *Yazoo Queen*.'

Splendour for the family, thought Alvin. Not likely to be much splendour for the slaves – though, being house servants, they'd fare better than the two dozen runaways chained together in the blazing sun at dockside all afternoon.

Alvin had been keeping an eye on them since he and Arthur Stuart got here to the Carthage City riverport at eleven. Arthur Stuart was all for exploring, and Alvin let him go. The city that billed itself as the Phoenicia of the West had plenty of sights for a boy Arthur's age, even a half-black boy. Since it was on the north shore of the Hio, there'd be suspicious eyes on him for a runaway. But there was plenty of free blacks in Carthage City, and Arthur Stuart was no fool. He'd keep an eye out.

There was plenty of slaves in Carthage, too. That was the law, that a black slave from the South remained a slave even in a free state. And the greatest shame of all was those chained-up runaways who got themselves all the way across the Hio to freedom, only to be picked up by Finders and dragged back in chains to the whips and other horrors of bondage. Angry owners who'd make an example of them. No wonder there was so many who killed theirselves, or tried to.

Alvin saw wounds on more than a few in this chained-up group of twenty-five, though many of the wounds could have been made by the slave's own hand. Finders weren't much for injuring the property they was getting paid to bring on home. No, those wounds on wrists and bellies were likely a vote for freedom before life itself.

What Alvin was watching for was to know whether the runaways were going to be loaded on this boat or another. Most often runaways were ferried across river and made to walk home over land – there was too many stories of slaves jumping overboard and sinking to the bottom with their chains on to make Finders keen on river transportation.

But now and then Alvin had caught a whiff of talking from the slaves – not much, since it could get them a bit of lash, and not loud enough for him to make out the words, but the music of the language didn't sound like English, not northern English, not southern English, not slave English. It wasn't likely to be any African language. With the British waging full-out war on the slave trade, there weren't many new slaves making it across the Atlantic these days.

So it might be Spanish they were talking, or French. Either way, they'd most likely be bound for Nueva Barcelona, or New Orleans, as the French still called it.

Which raised some questions in Alvin's mind. Mostly this one: how could a bunch of Barcelona runaways get themselves to the state of Hio? That would have been a long trek on foot, especially if they didn't speak English. Alvin's wife, Peggy, grew up in an Abolitionist home, with her papa, Horace Guester, smuggling runaways across river. Alvin knew something about how good the Underground Railway was. It had fingers reaching all the way down into the new duchies of Mizzippy and Alabam, but Alvin never heard of any Spanish- or French-speaking slaves taking that long dark road to freedom.

'I'm hungry again,' said Arthur Stuart.

Alvin turned to see the boy – no, the young man, he was getting so tall and his voice so low – standing behind him, hands in his pockets, looking at the *Yazoo Queen*.

'I'm a-thinking,' said Alvin, 'as how instead of just looking at this boat, we ought to get on it and ride a spell.'

'How far?' asked Arthur Stuart.

'You asking cause you're hoping it's a long way or a short one?'

'This one goes clear to Barcy.'

'It does if the fog on the Mizzippy lets it,' said Alvin.

Arthur Stuart made a goofy face at him. 'Oh, that's right, cause around you that fog's just bound to close right in.'

'It might,' said Alvin. 'Me and water never did get along.'

'When you was a little baby, maybe,' said Arthur Stuart. 'Fog does what you tell it to do these days.'

'You think,' said Alvin.

'You showed me your own self.'

'I showed you with smoke from a candle,' said Alvin, 'and just because I *can* do it don't mean that every fog or smoke you see is doing what I say.'

'Don't mean it ain't, either,' said Arthur Stuart, grinning.

'I'm just waiting to see if this boat's a slave ship or not,' said Alvin.

Arthur Stuart looked over where Alvin was looking, at the runaways. 'Why don't you just turn them loose?' he asked.

'And where would they go?' said Alvin. 'They're being watched.'

'Not all that careful,' said Arthur Stuart. 'Them so-called guards has got jugs that ain't close to full by now.'

'The Finders still got their sachets. It wouldn't take long to round them up again, and they'd be in even more trouble.'

'So you ain't going to do a thing about it?'

'Arthur Stuart, I can't just pry the manacles off every slave in the South.'

'I seen you melt iron like it was butter,' said Arthur Stuart.

'So a bunch of slaves run away and leave behind puddles of iron that was once their chains,' said Alvin. 'What do the authorities think? There was a blacksmith snuck in with a teeny tiny bellows and a ton of coal and lit him a fire that het them chains up? And then he run off after, taking all his coal with him in his pockets?'

Arthur Stuart looked at him defiantly. 'So it's all about keeping you safe.'

'I reckon so,' said Alvin. 'You know what a coward I am.'

Last year, Arthur Stuart would have blinked and said he was sorry, but now that his voice had changed the word 'sorry' didn't come so easy to his lips. 'You can't heal everybody, neither,' he said, 'but that don't stop you from healing *some*.'

'No point in freeing them as can't stay free,' said Alvin. 'And how many of them would run, do you think, and how many drown themselves in the river?'

'Why would they do that?'

'Because they know as well as I do, there ain't no freedom here in Carthage City for a runaway slave. This town may be the biggest on the Hio, but it's more southern than northern, when it comes to slavery. There's even buying and selling of slaves here, they say, flesh markets hidden in cellars, and the authorities know about it and don't do a thing because there's so much money in it.'

'So there's nothing you can do.'

'I healed their wrists and ankles where the manacles bite so deep.

I cooled them in the sun and cleaned the water they been given to drink so it don't make them sick.'

Now, finally, Arthur Stuart looked a bit embarrassed – though still defiant. 'I never said you wasn't *nice*,' he said.

'Nice is all I can be,' said Alvin. 'In this time and place. That and I don't plan to give my money to this captain iffen the slaves are going southbound on his boat. I won't help pay for no slave ship.'

'He won't even notice the price of our passage.'

'Oh, he'll notice, all right,' said Alvin. 'This Captain Howard is a fellow what can tell how much money you got in your pocket by the smell of it.'

'*You* can't even do that,' said Arthur Stuart.

'Money's his knack,' said Alvin. 'That's my guess. He's got him a pilot to steer the ship, and an engineer to keep that steam engine going, and a carpenter to tend the paddlewheel and such damage as the boat takes passing close to the left bank all the way down the Mizzippy. So why is he captain? It's about the money. He knows who's got it, and he knows how to talk it out of them.'

'So how much money's he going to think *you* got?'

'Enough money to own a big young slave, but not enough money to afford one what doesn't have such a mouth on him.'

Arthur Stuart glared. 'You don't own me.'

'I told you, Arthur Stuart, I didn't want you on this trip and I still don't. I hate taking you south because I have to pretend you're my property, and I don't know which is worse, you pretending to be a slave, or me pretending to be the kind of man as would own one.'

'I'm going and that's that.'

'So you keep on saying,' said Alvin.

'And you must not mind because you could force me to stay here iffen you wanted.'

'Don't say "iffen", it drives Peggy crazy when you do.'

'She ain't here and you say it your own self.'

'The idea is for the younger generation to be an improvement over the older.'

'Well, then, you're a mizzable failure, you got to admit, since I been studying makering with you for lo these many years and I can barely make a candle flicker or a stone crack.'

'I think you're doing fine, and you're better than that, anyway, if you just put your mind to it.'

'I put my mind to it till my head feels like a cannonball.'

'I suppose I should have said, Put your heart in it. It's not about *making* the candle or the stone – or the iron chains, for that matter – it's not about *making* them do what you want, it's about *getting* them to do what you want.'

'I don't see you setting down and *talking* no iron into bending or dead wood into sprouting twigs, but they do it.'

'You may not see me or hear me do it, but I'm doing it all the same, only they don't understand words, they understand the plan in my heart.'

'Sounds like making wishes to me.'

'Only because you haven't learned yourself how to do it yet.'

'Which means you ain't much of a teacher.'

'Neither is Peggy, what with you still saying "ain't".'

'Difference is, I know how *not* to say "ain't" when she's around to hear it,' said Arthur Stuart, 'only I can't poke out a dent in a tin cup whether you're there or not.'

'Could if you cared enough,' said Alvin.

'I want to ride on this boat.'

'Even if it's a slave ship?' said Alvin.

'Us staying off ain't going to make it any less a slave ship,' said Arthur Stuart.

'Ain't you the idealist.'

'You ride this *Yazoo Queen*, Master of mine, and you can keep those slaves comfy all the way back to hell.'

The mockery in his tone was annoying, but not misplaced, Alvin decided.

'I could do that,' said Alvin. 'Small blessings can feel big enough, when they're all you got.'

'So buy the ticket, cause this boat's supposed to sail first thing in the morning, and we want to be aboard already, don't we?'

Alvin didn't like the mixture of casualness and eagerness in Arthur Stuart's words. 'You don't happen to have some plan to set these poor souls free during the voyage, do you? Because you know they'd jump overboard and there ain't a one of them knows how to swim, you can bet on that, so it'd be plain murder to free them.'

'I got no such plan.'

'I need your promise you won't free them.'

'I won't lift a finger to help them,' said Arthur Stuart. 'I can make my heart as hard as yours whenever I want.'

'I hope you don't think that kind of talk makes me glad to have your company,' said Alvin. 'Specially because I think you know I don't deserve it.'

'You telling me you *don't* make your heart hard, to see such sights and do nothing?'

'If I could make my heart hard,' said Alvin, 'I'd be a worse man, but a happier one.'

Then he went off to the booth where the *Yazoo Queen*'s purser was selling passages. Bought him a cheap ticket all the way to Nueva Barcelona, and a servant's passage for his boy. Made him angry just to have to say the words, but he lied with his face and the tone of his voice and the purser didn't seem to notice anything amiss. Or maybe all slave owners were just a little angry with themselves, so Alvin didn't seem much different from any other.

Plain truth of it was, Alvin was about as excited to make this voyage as a man could get. He loved machinery, all the hinges, pistons, elbows of metal, the fire hot as a smithy, the steam pent up in the boilers. He loved the great paddlewheel, turning like the one he grew up with at his father's mill, except here it was the wheel pushing the water, stead of the water pushing the wheel. He loved feeling the strain on the steel – the torque, the compression, the levering, the flexing and cooling. He sent out his doodlebug and wandered around inside the machines, so he'd know it all like he knew his own body.

The engineer was a good man who cared well for his machine, but there was things he couldn't know. Small cracks in the metal, places where the stress was too much, places where the grease wasn't enough and the friction was a-building up. Soon as he understood how it ought to be, Alvin began to teach the metal how to heal itself, how to seal the tiny fractures, how to smooth itself so the friction was less. That boat wasn't more than two hours out of Carthage before he had the machinery about as perfect as a steam engine could get, and then it was just a matter of riding with it. His body, like everybody else's, riding on the gently shifting deck, and his doodlebug skittering through the machinery to feel it pushing and pulling.

But soon enough it didn't need his attention any more, and so the machinery moved to the back of his mind while he began to take an interest in the goings-on among the passengers.

There was people with money in the first-class cabins, with their servants' quarters close at hand. And then people like Alvin, with only a little coin, but enough for the second-class cabins, where there was four passengers to the room. All *their* servants, them as had any, was forced to sleep below decks like the crew, only even more cramped, not because there wasn't room to do better, but because the crew was bound to get surly iffen their bed was as bad as a blackamoor's.

And finally there was the steerage passengers, who didn't even have no beds, but just benches. Them as was going only a short way, a day's journey or so, it made plain good sense to go steerage. But a good many was just poor folks bound for some far-off destination, like Thebes or Corinth or Barcy itself, and if their butts got sore on the benches, well, it wouldn't be the first pain they suffered in their life, nor would it be their last.

Still, Alvin felt like it was kind of his duty, being as how it took him so little effort, to sort of shape the benches to the butts that sat on them. And it took no great trouble to get the lice and bedbugs to move on up to the first-class cabins. Alvin thought of it as kind of an educational project, to help the bugs get a taste of the high life. Blood so fine must be like fancy likker to a louse, and they ought to get some knowledge of it before their short lives was over.

All this took Alvin's concentration for a good little while. Not that he ever gave it his whole attention – that would be too dangerous, in their world where he had enemies out to kill him, and strangers as would wonder what was in his bag that he kept it always so close at hand. So he kept an eye out for all the heartfires on the boat, and if any seemed coming a-purpose towards him, he'd know it, right enough.

Except it didn't work that way. He didn't sense a soul anywheres near him, and then there was a hand right there on his shoulder, and he like to jumped clean overboard with the shock of it.

'What the devil are you – Arthur Stuart, don't sneak up on a body like that.'

'It's hard not to sneak with the steam engine making such a racket,' said Arthur, but he was a-grinnin' like old Davy Crockett, he was so proud of himself.

'Why is it the one skill you take the trouble to master is the one that causes me the most grief?' asked Alvin.

'I think it's good to know how to hide my . . . heartfire.' He said the last word real soft, on account of it didn't do to talk about makery where others might hear and get too curious.

Alvin taught the skill freely to all who took it serious, but he didn't put on a show of it to inquisitive strangers, especially because there was no shortage of them as would remember hearing tales of the runaway smith's apprentice who stole a magic golden ploughshare. Didn't matter that the tale was three-fourths fantasy and nine-tenths lie. It could get Alvin kilt or knocked upside the head and robbed all the same, and the one part that was true was that living plough inside his poke, which he didn't want to lose, specially not now after carrying it up and down America for half his life now.

'Ain't nobody on this boat can see your heartfire ceptin' me,' said Alvin. 'So the only reason for you to learn to hide is to hide from the one person you shouldn't hide from anyhow.'

'That's plain dumb,' said Arthur Stuart. 'If there's one person a slave has to hide from, it's his master.'

Alvin glared at him. Arthur grinned back.

A voice boomed out from across the deck. 'I like to see a man who's easy with his servants!'

Alvin turned to see a smallish man with a big smile and a face that suggested he had a happy opinion of himself.

'My name's Travis,' said the fellow. 'William Barret Travis, attorney at law, born, bred and schooled in the Crown Colonies, and now looking for people as need legal work out here on the edge of civilization.'

'The folks on either hand of the Hio like to think of theirselves as mostwise civilized,' said Alvin, 'but then, they haven't been to Camelot to see the King.'

'Was I imagining that I heard you speak to your boy there as "Arthur Stuart"?'

'It was someone else's joke at the naming of the lad,' said Alvin, 'but I reckon by now the name suits him.' All the time Alvin was thinking, what does this man want, that he'd trouble to speak to a sun-browned, strong-armed, thick-headed-looking wight like me?

He could feel a breath for speech coming up in Arthur Stuart, but the last thing Alvin wanted was to deal with whatever fool thing the boy might take it into his head to say. So he gripped him noticeably on the shoulder and it just kind of squeezed the air right out of him without more than a sigh.

'I noticed you've got shoulders on you,' said Travis.

'Most folks do,' said Alvin. 'Two of 'em, nicely matched, one to an arm.'

'I almost thought you might be a smith, except smiths always have one huge shoulder, and the other more like a normal man's.'

'Except such smiths as use their left hand exactly as often as their right, just so they keep their balance.'

Travis chuckled. 'Well, then, that solves the mystery. You *are* a smith.'

'When I got me a bellows, and charcoal, and iron, and a good pot.'

'I don't reckon you carry that around with you in your poke.'

'Sir,' said Alvin, 'I been to Camelot once, and I don't recollect as how it was good manners there to talk about a man's poke or his shoulders neither, upon such short acquaintance.'

'Well, of course, it's bad manners all around the world, I'd say, and I apologize. I meant no disrespect. Only I'm recruiting, you see, them as has skills we need, and yet who don't have a firm place in life. Wandering men, you might say.'

'Lots of men a-wanderin',' said Alvin, 'and not all of them are what they claim.'

'But that's why I've accosted you like this, my friend,' said Travis. 'Because you weren't claiming a blessed thing. And on the river, to meet a man with no brag is a pretty good recommendation.'

'Then you're new to the river,' said Alvin, 'because many a man with no brag is afraid of gettin' recognized.'

'Recognized,' said Travis. 'Not "reckonize". So you've had you some schooling.'

'Not as much as it would take to turn a smith into a gentleman.'

'I'm recruiting,' said Travis. 'For an expedition.'

'Smiths in particular need?'

'Strong men good with tools of all kinds,' said Travis.

'Got work already, though,' said Alvin. 'And an errand in Barcy.'

'So you wouldn't be interested in trekking out into new lands, which are now in the hands of bloody savages, awaiting the arrival of Christian men to cleanse the land of their awful sacrifices?'

Alvin instantly felt a flush of anger mixed with fear, and as he did whenever so strong a feeling came over him, he smiled brighter than ever and kept hisself as calm as could be. 'I reckon you'd have to brave the fog and cross to the west bank of the river for that,' said Alvin. 'And I hear the reds on that side of the river has some pretty powerful eyes and ears, just watching for whites as think they can take war into peaceable places.'

'Oh, you misunderstood me, my friend,' said Travis. 'I'm not talking about the prairies where one time trappers used to wander and now the reds won't let no white man pass.'

'So what savages did you have in mind?'

'South, my friend, south and west. The evil Mexica tribes, that vile race that tears the heart out of a living man upon the tops of their ziggurats.'

'That's a long trek indeed,' said Alvin. 'And a foolish one. What the might of Spain couldn't rule, you think a few Englishmen with a lawyer at their head can conquer?'

By now Travis was leaning on the rail beside Alvin, looking out over the water. 'The Mexica have become rotten. Hated by the other reds they rule, dependent on trade with Spain for second-rate weaponry – I tell you it's ripe for conquest. Besides, how big an army can they put in the field, after killing so many men on their altars for all these centuries?'

'It's a fool as goes looking for a war that no one brought to him.'

'Aye, a fool, a whole passel of fools. The kind of fools as wants to be as rich as Pizarro, who conquered the great Inca with a handful of men.'

'Or as dead as Cortez?'

'They're all dead now,' said Travis. 'Or did you think to live for ever?'

Alvin was torn between telling the fellow to go pester someone else and leading him on so he could find out more about what he was planning. But in the long run, it wouldn't do to become too familiar with this fellow, Alvin decided. 'I reckon I've wasted your time up to now, Mr Travis. There's others are bound to be more interested than I am, since I got no interest at all.'

Travis smiled all the more broadly, but Alvin saw how his pulse leapt up and his heartfire blazed. A man who didn't like being told no, but hid it behind a smile.

'Well, it's good to make a friend all the same,' said Travis, sticking out his hand.

'No hard feelings,' said Alvin, 'and thanks for thinking of me as a man you might want at your side.'

'No hard feelings indeed,' said Travis, 'and though I won't ask you again, if you change your mind I'll greet you with a ready heart and hand.'

They shook on it, clapped shoulders, and Travis went on his way without a backwards glance.

'Well, well,' said Arthur Stuart. 'What do you want to bet it isn't no invasion or war, but just a raiding party bent on getting some of that Mexica gold?'

'Hard to guess,' said Alvin. 'But he talks free enough, for a man proposing to do something forbidden by King and by Congress. Neither the Crown Colonies nor the United States would have much patience with him if he was caught.'

'Oh, I don't know,' said Arthur Stuart. 'The law's one thing, but what if King Arthur got it in his head that he needed more land and more slaves and didn't want a war with the USA to get it?'

'Now there's a thought,' said Alvin.

'A pretty smart thought, I think,' said Arthur Stuart.

'It's doing you good, travelling with me,' said Alvin. 'Finally getting some sense into your head.'

'I thought of it first,' said Arthur Stuart.

In answer, Alvin took a letter out of his pocket and showed it to the boy.

'It's from Miz Peggy,' said Arthur. He read for a moment. 'Oh, now, don't tell me you knew this fellow was going to be on the boat.'

'I most certainly did not have any idea,' said Alvin. 'I figured my inquiries would begin in Nueva Barcelona. But now I've got a good idea *whom* to watch when we get there.'

'She talks about a man named Austin,' said Arthur Stuart.

'But he'd have men under him,' said Alvin. 'Men to go out recruiting for him, iffen he hopes to raise an army.'

'And he just happened to walk right up to you.'

'He just happened to listen to you sassing me,' said Alvin, 'and figured I wasn't much of a master, so maybe I'd be a natural follower.'

Arthur Stuart folded up the letter and handed it back to Alvin. 'So if the King *is* putting together an invasion of Mexico, what of it?'

'Iffen he's fighting the Mexica,' said Alvin, 'he can't be fighting the free states, now, can he?'

'So maybe the slave states won't be so eager to pick a fight,' said Arthur Stuart.

'But someday the war with Mexico will end,' said Alvin. 'Iffen there is a war, that is. And when it ends, either the King lost, in which case he'll be mad and ashamed and spoilin' for trouble, or he won, in which case he'll have a treasury full of Mexica gold, able to buy him a whole navy iffen he wants.'

'Miz Peggy wouldn't be too happy to hear you sayin' "iffen" so much.'

'War's a bad thing, when you take after them as haven't done you no harm, and don't mean to.'

'But wouldn't it be good to stop all that human sacrifice?'

'I think the reds as are prayin' for relief from the Mexica don't exactly have slavers in mind as their new masters.'

'But slavery's better than death, ain't it?'

'Your mother didn't think so,' said Alvin. 'And now let's have done with such talk. It just makes me sad.'

'To think of human sacrifice? Or slavery?'

'No. To hear you talk as if one was better than the other.' And with that dark mood on him, Alvin walked to the room that so far he had all to himself, set the golden plough upon the bunk, and curled up around it to think and doze and dream a little and see if he could understand what it all meant, to have this Travis fellow acting so bold about his project, and to have Arthur Stuart be so blind, when so many people had sacrificed so much to keep him free.

It wasn't till they got to Thebes that another passenger was assigned to Alvin's cabin. He'd gone ashore to see the town – which was being touted as the greatest city on the American Nile – and when he came back, there was a man asleep on the very bunk where Alvin had been sleeping.

Which was irksome, but understandable. It was the best bed, being the lower bunk on the side that got sunshine in the cool of the morning instead of the heat of the afternoon. And it's not as if Alvin had left any possessions in the cabin to mark the bed as his own. He carried his poke with him when he left the boat, and all his worldly goods was in it. Lessen you counted the baby that his wife carried inside her – which, come to think of it, she carried around with her about as constantly as Alvin carried that golden plough.

So Alvin didn't wake the fellow up. He just turned and left, looking for Arthur Stuart or a quiet place to eat the supper he'd brought on board. Arthur had insisted he wanted to stay aboard, and that was fine with Alvin, but he was blamed if he was going to hunt him down before eating. It wasn't no secret that the whistle had blowed the signal for everyone to come aboard. So Arthur Stuart should have been watching for Alvin, and he wasn't.

Not that Alvin doubted where he was. He could key right in on Arthur's heartfire most of the time, and he doubted the boy could hide from him if Alvin was actually seeking him out. Right now he knew that the boy was down below in the slave quarters, a place where no one would ask him his business or wonder where his master was. What he was about was another matter.

Almost as soon as Alvin opened up his poke to take out the cornbread and cheese and cider he'd brought in from town, he could see Arthur start moving up the ladderway to the deck. Not for the first time, Alvin wondered just how much the boy really understood of makering.

Arthur Stuart wasn't a liar by nature, but he could keep a secret, more or less, and wasn't it just possible that he hadn't quite got around to telling Alvin all that he'd learned how to do? Was there a chance the boy picked that moment to come up because he *knew* Alvin was back from town, and *knew* he was setting hisself down to eat?

Sure enough, Alvin hadn't got but one bite into his first slice of bread and cheese when Arthur Stuart plunked himself down beside him on the bench. Alvin could've eaten in the dining room, but there it would have given offence for him to let his 'servant' set beside him. Out on the deck, it was nobody's business. Might make him look low-class, in the eyes of some slave owners, but Alvin didn't much mind what slave owners thought of him.

'What was it like?' asked Arthur Stuart.

'Bread tastes like bread.'

'I didn't mean the bread, for pity's sake!'

'Cheese is pretty good, despite being made from milk that come from the most measly, mangy, scrawny, fly-bit, sway-backed, half-blind, bony-hipped, ill-tempered, cud-pukin', sawdust-fed bunch of cattle as ever teetered on the edge of the grave.'

'So they don't specialize in fine dairy, is what you're saying.'

'I'm saying that if Thebes is spose to be the greatest city on the American Nile, they might oughta start by draining the swamp. I mean, the reason the Hio and the Mizzippy come together here is because it's low ground, and being low ground it gets flooded a lot. It didn't take no scholar to figure that out.'

'Never heard of a scholar who knowed low ground from high, anyhow.'

'Now, Arthur Stuart, it's not a requirement that scholars be dumb as mud about . . . well, mud.'

'Oh, I know. Somewhere there's bound to be a scholar who's got book-learnin' *and* common sense, both. He just hasn't come to America.'

'Which I spose is proof of the common sense part, bein' as this is the sort of country where they build a great city in the middle of a bog.'

They chuckled together and then filled up their mouths too much for talking.

When the food was gone – and Arthur had et more than half of it, and looked like he was wishing for more – Alvin asked him, pretending to be all casual about it, 'So what was so interesting down with the servants in the hold?'

'The slaves, you mean?'

'I'm trying to talk like the kind of person as would own one,' said

Alvin very softly. 'And you ought to try to talk like the kind of person as was owned. Or don't come along on trips south.'

'I was trying to find out what language those score-and-a-quarter chained-up runaways was talking.'

'And?'

'Ain't French, cause there's a cajun what says not. Ain't Spanish, cause there's a fellow grew up in Cuba what says not. Nary a soul knew their talk.'

'Well, at least we know what they're not.'

'I know more than that,' said Arthur Stuart.

'I'm listening.'

'The Cuba fellow, he takes me aside and he says, Tell you what, boy, I think I hear me their kind talk afore, and I says, What's their language, and he says, I think they be no kind runaway.'

'Why's he think that?' said Alvin. But inside, he's noticing the way Arthur Stuart picks up exactly the words the fellow said, and the accent, and he remembers how it used to be when Arthur Stuart could do any voice he heard, a perfect mimic. And not just human voices, neither, but bird calls and animal cries, and a baby crying, and the wind in the trees or the scrape of a shoe on dirt. But that was before Alvin changed him, deep inside, changed the very smell of him so that the Finders couldn't match him up to his sachet no more. He had to change him in the smallest, most hidden parts of him. Cost him part of his knack, it did, and that was a harsh thing to do to a child. But it also saved his freedom. Alvin couldn't regret doing it. But he could regret the cost.

'He says, I hear me their kind talk aforeday, long day ago, when I belong a massuh go Mexico.'

Alvin nodded wisely, though he had no idea what this might mean.

'And I says to him, How come black folk be learning Mexica talk? And he says, They be black folk all over Mexico, from aforeday.'

'That would make sense,' said Alvin. 'The Mexica only threw the Spanish out fifty years ago. I reckon they was inspired by Tom Jefferson getting Cherriky free from the King. Spanish must've brought plenty of slaves to Mexico up to then.'

'Well, sure,' said Arthur Stuart. 'So I was wondering, if the Mexica kill so many sacrifices, why didn't they use up these African slaves first? And he says, Black man dirty, Mexica no can cook him up for Mexica god. And then he just laughed and laughed.'

'I guess there's advantages to having folks think you're impure by nature.'

'Heard a lot of preachers in America say that God thinks *all* men is filthy at heart.'

'Arthur Stuart, I know that's a falsehood, because in your life you never been to hear a *lot* of preachers say a blame thing.'

'Well, I heard *of* preachers saying such things. Which explains why our God don't hold with human sacrifice. Ain't none of us worthy, white or black.'

'Except I don't think that's the opinion God has of his children,' said Alvin, 'and neither do you.'

'I think what I think,' said Arthur Stuart. 'Ain't always the same thing as you.'

'I'm just happy you've taken up thinkin' at all,' said Alvin.

'As a hobby,' said Arthur Stuart. 'I ain't thinkin' of takin' it up as a trade or nothin'.'

Alvin gave a chuckle, and Arthur Stuart settled back to enjoy it.

Alvin got to thinking out loud. 'So. We got us twenty-five slaves who used to belong to the Mexica. Only now they're going down the Mizzippy on the very same boat as a man recruiting soldiers for an expedition *against* Mexico. That's a downright miraculous coincidence.'

'Guides?' said Arthur Stuart.

'I reckon that's likely. Maybe they're wearing chains for the same reason you're pretending to be a slave. So people will think they're one thing, when actually they're another.'

'Or maybe somebody's so dumb he thinks that chained-up slaves will be good guides through uncharted land.'

'So you're saying maybe they won't be reliable.'

'I'm saying maybe they think starving to death all lost in the desert ain't a bad way to die, if they can take some white slave owners with them.'

Alvin nodded. The boy did understand that slaves might prefer death, after all. 'Well, I don't speak Mexica, and neither do you.'

'Yet,' said Arthur Stuart.

'Don't see how you'll learn it,' said Alvin. 'They don't let nobody near 'em.'

'Yet,' said Arthur Stuart.

'I hope you ain't got some damn fool plan going on in your head that you're not going to tell me about.'

'Don't mind telling you. I already got me a turn feeding them and picking up their slop bucket. The pre-dawn turn, which nobody belowdecks is hankering to do.'

'They're guarded day and night. How you going to start talking to them anyway?'

'Come on now, Alvin, you know there must be at least one of them speaks English, or how would they be able to guide anybody anywhere?'

'Or one of them speaks Spanish, and one of the slave owners speaks it too, you ever think of that?'

'That's why I got the Cuba fellow to teach me Spanish.'

That was brag. 'I was only gone into town for six hours, Arthur Stuart.'

'Well, he didn't teach me *all* of it.'

That set Alvin to wondering once again if Arthur Stuart had more of his knack left than he ever let on. Learn a language in six hours? Of course, there was no guarantee that the Cuban slave knew all that much Spanish, any more than he knew all that much English. But what if Arthur Stuart had him a knack for languages? What if he'd never been a mimic at all, but instead a natural speaker-of-all-tongues? There was tales of such – of men and women who could hear a language and speak it like a native right from the start.

Did Arthur Stuart have such a knack? Now that the boy was becoming a man, was he getting a real grasp of it? For a moment Alvin caught himself being envious. And then he had to laugh at himself – imagine a fellow with *his* knack, envying somebody else. I can make rock flow like water, I can make water as strong as steel and as clear as glass, I can turn iron into living gold, and I'm jealous because I can't also learn languages the way a cat learns to land on its feet? The sin of ingratitude, just one of many that's going to get me sent to hell.

'What're you laughing at?' asked Arthur Stuart.

'Just appreciating that you're not a mere boy any more. I trust that if you need any help from me – like somebody catches you talking to them Mexica slaves and starts whipping you – you'll contrive some way to let me know that you need some help?'

'Sure. And if that knife-wielding killer who's sleeping in your bed gets troublesome, I expect you'll find some way to let me know what you want written on your tombstone?' Arthur Stuart grinned at him.

'Knife-wielding killer?' Alvin asked.

'That's the talk belowdecks. But I reckon you'll just ask him your-self, and he'll tell you all about it. That's how you usually do things, isn't it?'

Alvin nodded. 'I spose I do start out asking pretty direct what I want to know.'

'And so far you mostly haven't got yourself killed,' said Arthur Stuart.

'My average is pretty good so far,' said Alvin modestly.

'Haven't always found out what you wanted to know, though,' said Arthur Stuart.

'But I always find out something useful,' said Alvin. 'Like, how easy it is to get some folks riled.'

'If I didn't know you had another, I'd say that *was* your knack.'

'Rilin' folks.'

'They do get mad at you pretty much when you say hello, some-times,' said Arthur Stuart.

'Whereas nobody ever gets mad at you.'

'I'm a likeable fellow,' said Arthur Stuart.

'Not always,' said Alvin. 'You got a bit of brag in you that can be annoying sometimes.'

'Not to my friends,' said Arthur, grinning.

'No,' Alvin conceded. 'But it drives your family insane.'

By the time Alvin got to his room, the 'knife-wielding killer' had woke up from his nap and was somewhere else. Alvin toyed with sleeping in the very same bed, which had been his first, after all. But that was likely to start a fight, and Alvin just plain didn't care all that much. He was glad to have a bed at all, come to think of it, and with four bunks in the room to share between two men, there was no call to be provoking anybody over who got to which one first.

Drifting off to sleep, Alvin reached out as he always did, seeking Peggy, making sure from her heartfire that she was all right. And then the baby, growing fine inside her, had a heartbeat now. Not going to end like the first pregnancy, with a baby born too soon so it couldn't get its breath. Not going to watch it gasp its little life away in a couple of desperate minutes, turning blue and dying in his arms while he frantically searched inside it for some way to fix it so's it could live. What good is it to be a seventh son of a seventh son if the one person you can't heal is your own firstborn baby?

Alvin and Peggy clung together for the first days after that, but then over the weeks to follow she began to grow apart from him, to avoid him, until he finally realized that she was keeping him from being with her to make another baby. He talked with her then, about how you couldn't hide from it, lots of folks lost babies, and half-growed children too, the thing to do was try again, have another, and another, to comfort you when you thought about the little body in the grave.

'I grew up with two graves before my eyes,' she said, 'and knowing how my parents looked at me and saw my dead sisters with the same name as me.'

'Well, you was a torch, so you knew more than children ought to know about what goes on inside folks. Our baby most likely won't be a torch. All she'll know is how much we love her and how much we wanted her.'

He wasn't sure he so much persuaded her to want another baby as she decided to try again just to make him happy. And during this pregnancy, just like last time, she kept gallivanting up and down the country, working for abolition even as she tried to find some way to bring about freedom short of war. While Alvin stayed in Vigor Church or Hatrack River, teaching them as wanted to learn the rudiments of makery.

Until she had an errand for him, like now. Sending him downriver on a steamboat to Nueva Barcelona, when in his secret heart he just wished she'd stay home with him and let him take care of her.

Course, being a torch she knew perfectly well that was what he wished for, it was no secret at all. So she must need to be apart from him more than he needed to be with her, and he could live with that.

Couldn't stop him from looking for her on the skirts of sleep, and dozing off with her heartfire and the baby's, so bright in his mind.

He woke in the dark, knowing something was wrong. It was a heartfire right up close to him; then he heard the soft breath of a stealthy man. With his doodlebug he got inside the man and felt what he was doing – reaching across Alvin towards the poke that was tucked in the crook of his arm.

Robbery? On board a riverboat was a blame foolish time for it, if that was what the man had in mind. Unless he was a good enough swimmer to get to shore carrying a heavy golden ploughshare.

The man carried a knife in a sheath at his belt, but his hand wasn't on it, so he wasn't looking for trouble.

So Alvin spoke up soft as could be. 'If you're looking for food, the door's on the other side of the room.'

Oh, the man's heart gave a jolt at that! And his first instinct was for his hand to fly to that knife – he was quick at it, too, Alvin could see that it didn't much matter whether his hand was on the knife or not, he was always ready with that blade.

But in a moment the fellow got a hold of hisself, and Alvin could pretty much guess at his reasoning. It was a dark night, and as far as this fellow knew, Alvin couldn't see any better than him.

'You was snoring,' said the man. 'I was looking to jostle you to get you to roll over.'

Alvin knew that was a flat lie. When Peggy had mentioned a snoring problem to him years ago, he studied out what made people snore and fixed his palate so it didn't make that noise any more. He had a rule about not using his knack to benefit himself, but he figured curing his snore was a gift to other people. *He* always slept through it.

Still, he'd let the lie ride. 'Why, thank you,' said Alvin. 'I sleep pretty light, though, so all it takes is you sayin' "roll over" and I'll do it. Or so my wife tells me.'

And then, bold as brass, the fellow as much as confesses what he was doing. 'You know, stranger, whatever you got in that sack, you hug it so close to you that somebody might get curious about what's so valuable.'

'I've learned that folks get just as curious when I *don't* hug it close, and they feel a mite freer about groping in the dark to get a closer look.'

The man chuckled. 'So I reckon you ain't planning to tell me much about it.'

'I always answer a well-mannered question,' said Alvin.

'But since it ain't good manners to ask about what's in your sack,' said the man, 'I reckon you don't answer such questions at all.'

'I'm glad to meet a man who knows good manners.'

'Good manners and a knife that don't break off at the stem, that's what keeps me at peace with the world.'

'Good manners has always been enough for me,' said Alvin. 'Though I admit I would have liked that knife better back when it was still a file.'

With a bound the man was at the door, his knife drawn. 'Who are you, and what do you know about me?'

'I don't know nothing about you, sir,' said Alvin. 'But I'm a black-smith, and I know a file that's been made over into a knife. More like a sword, if you ask me.'

'I haven't drawn my knife aboard this boat.'

'I'm glad to hear it. But when I walked in on *you* asleep, it was still daylight enough to see the size and shape of the sheath you keep it in. Nobody makes a knife that thick at the haft, but it was right propor-tioned for a file.'

'You can't tell something like that just from looking,' said the man. 'You heard something. Somebody's been talking.'

'People are always talking, but not about you,' said Alvin. 'I know my trade, as I reckon you know yours. My name's Alvin.'

'Alvin Smith, eh?'

'I count myself lucky to have a name. I'd lay good odds that you've got one too.'

The man chuckled and put his knife away. 'Jim Bowie.'

'Don't sound like a trade name to me.'

'It's a Scotch word. Means light-haired.'

'Your hair is dark.'

'But I reckon the first Bowie was a blond Viking who liked what he saw while he was busy raping and pillaging in Scotland, and so he stayed.'

'One of his children must have got that Viking spirit again and found his way across another sea.'

'I'm a Viking through and through,' said Bowie. 'You guessed right about this knife. I was witness at a duel at a smithy just outside Natchez a few years ago. Things got out of hand when they both missed – I reckon folks came to see blood and didn't want to be disappointed. One fellow managed to put a bullet through my leg, so I thought I was well out of it, until I saw Major Norris Wright setting on a boy half his size and half his age, and that riled me up. Riled me so bad that I clean forgot I was wounded and bleeding like a slaughtered pig. I went berserk and snatched up a blacksmith's file and stuck it clean through his heart.'

'You got to be a strong man to do that.'

'Oh, it's more than that. I didn't slip it between no ribs. I jammed it right *through* a rib. We Vikings get the strength of giants when we go berserk.'

'Am I right to guess that the knife you carry is that very same file?'

'A cutler in Philadelphia reshaped it for me.'

'Did it by grinding, not forging,' said Alvin.

'That's right.'

'Your lucky knife.'

'I ain't dead yet.'

'Reckon that takes a lot of luck, if you got the habit of reaching over sleeping men to get at their poke.'

The smile died on Bowie's face. 'Can't help it if I'm curious.'

'Oh, I know, I got me the same fault.'

'So now it's your turn,' said Bowie.

'My turn for what?'

'To tell your story.'

'Me? Oh, all I got's a common skinning knife, but I've done my share of wandering in wild lands and it's come in handy.'

'You know that's not what I'm asking.'

'That's what I'm telling, though.'

'I told you about my knife, so you tell me about your sack.'

'You tell everybody about your knife,' said Alvin, 'which makes it so you don't have to use it so much. But I don't tell nobody about my sack.'

'That just makes folks more curious,' said Bowie. 'And some folks might even get suspicious.'

'From time to time that happens,' said Alvin. He sat up and swung his legs over the side of his bunk and stood. He had already sized up this Bowie fellow and knew that he'd be at least four inches taller, with longer arms and the massive shoulders of a blacksmith. 'But I smile so nice their suspicions just go away.'

Bowie laughed out loud at that. 'You're a big fellow, all right! And you ain't afeared of nobody.'

'I'm afraid of lots of folks,' said Alvin. 'Especially a man can shove a file through a man's rib and ream out his heart.'

Bowie nodded at that. 'Well, now, ain't that peculiar. Lots of folks been afraid of me in my time. But the more scared they was, the less likely they was to admit it. You're the first one actually said he was afraid of me. So does that make you the *most* scared? Or the least?'

'Tell you what,' said Alvin. 'You keep your hands off my poke, and we'll never have to find out.'

Bowie laughed again – but his grin looked more like a wildcat snarling at its prey than like an actual smile. 'I like you, Alvin Smith.'

'I'm glad to hear it,' said Alvin.

'I know a man who's looking for fellows like you.'

So this Bowie was part of Travis's company. 'If you're talking about Mr Travis, he and I already agreed that he'll go his way and I'll go mine.'

'Ah,' said Bowie.

'Did you just join up with him in Thebes?'

'I'll tell you about my knife,' said Bowie, 'but I won't tell you about my business.'

'I'll tell you mine,' said Alvin. 'My business right now is to get back to sleep and see if I can find the dream I was in before you decided to stop me snoring.'

'Well, that's a good idea,' said Bowie. 'And since I haven't been to sleep at all yet tonight, on account of your snoring, I reckon I'll give it a go before the sun comes up.'

Alvin lay back down and curled himself around his poke. His back was to Bowie, but of course he kept his doodlebug in him and knew every move he made. The man stood there watching Alvin for a long time, and from the way his heart was beating and the blood rushed around in him, Alvin could tell he was upset. Angry? Afraid? Hard to tell when you couldn't look at a man's face, and not so easy even then. But his heartfire blazed and Alvin figured the fellow was making some kind of decision about him.

Won't get to sleep very soon if he keeps himself all agitated like that, thought Alvin. So he reached inside the fellow and gradually calmed him down, got his heart beating slower, steadied his breathing. Most folks thought that their emotions caused their bodies to get all agitated, but it was the other way around, Alvin knew. The body leads, and the emotions follow.

In a couple of minutes Bowie was relaxed enough to yawn. And soon after, he was fast asleep. With his knife still strapped on, and his hand never far from it.

This Travis fellow had him some interesting friends.

Arthur Stuart was feeling way too cocky. But if you *know* you feel too cocky, and you compensate for it by being extra careful, then being cocky does you no harm, right? Except maybe it's your cockiness makes you feel like you're safer than you really are.

That's what Miz Peggy called 'circular reasoning' and it wouldn't get him nowhere. Anywhere. One of them words. Whatever the rule was. Thinking about Miz Peggy always got him listening to the way he talked and finding fault with himself. Only what good would it do him to talk right? All he'd be is a half-black man who somehow learned to talk like a gentleman – a kind of trained monkey, that's how they'd see him. A dog walking on its hind legs. Not an *actual* gentleman.

Which was why he got so cocky, probably. Always wanting to prove something. Not to Alvin, really.

No, *expecially* to Alvin. Cause it was Alvin still treated him like a boy when he was a man now. Treated him like a son, but he was no man's son.

All this thinking was, of course, doing him no good at all, when his job was to pick up the foul-smelling slop bucket and make a slow and lazy job of it so's he'd have time to find out which of them spoke English or Spanish.

'Quien me compreende?' he whispered. 'Who understands me?'

'Todos te compreendemos, pero calle la boca,' whispered the third man. We all understand you, but shut your mouth. 'Los blancos piensan que hay solo uno que hable un poco de ingles.'

Boy howdy, he talked fast, with nothing like the accent the Cuban had. But still, when Arthur got the feel of a language in his mind, it wasn't that hard to sort it out. They all spoke Spanish, but they were pretending that only one of them spoke a bit of English.

'Quieren fugir de ser esclavos?' Do you want to escape from slavery?

'La unica puerta es la muerta.' The only door is death.

'Al otro lado del rio,' said Arthur, 'hay rojos que son amigos nuestros.' On the other side of the river there are reds who are friends of ours.

'Sus amigos no son nuestros,' answered the man. Your friends aren't ours.

Another man near enough to hear nodded in agreement. 'Y ya no puedo nadar.' And I can't swim anyway.

'Los blancos, que van a hacer?' What are the whites going to do?

'Piensan en ser conquistadores.' Clearly these men didn't think much of their masters' plans. 'Los Mexicos van comer sus corazones.' The Mexica will eat their hearts.

Another man chimed in. 'Tu hablas como cubano.' You talk like a Cuban.

'Soy americano,' said Arthur Stuart. 'Soy libre. Soy . . .' He hadn't learned the Spanish for 'citizen'. 'Soy igual.' I'm equal. But not really, he thought. Still, I'm more equal than you.

Several of the Mexica blacks sniffed at that. 'Ya hay visto, tu dueño.' All Arthur understood was 'dueño', owner.

'Es amigo, no dueño.' He's my friend, not my master.

Oh, they thought that was hilarious. But of course their laughter was silent, and a few of them glanced at the guard, who was dozing as he leaned against the wall.

'Me de promesa.' Promise me. 'Cuando el ferro quiebra, no se maten. No salguen sin ayuda.' When the iron breaks, don't kill yourselves. Or maybe it meant don't get killed. Anyway, don't leave without help. Or that's what Arthur thought he was saying. They looked at him with total incomprehension.

'Voy quebrar el ferro,' Arthur repeated.

One of them mockingly held out his hands. The chains made a noise. Several looked again at the guard.

'No con la mano,' said Arthur. 'Con la cabeza.'

They looked at each other with obvious disappointment. Arthur knew what they were thinking – this boy is crazy. Thinks he can break iron with his head. But he didn't know how to explain it any better.

'Mañana,' he said.

They nodded wisely. Not a one of them believed him.

So much for the hours he'd spent learning Spanish. Though maybe the problem was that they just didn't know about makery and couldn't think of a man breaking iron with his mind.

Arthur Stuart knew he could do it. It was one of Alvin's earliest lessons, but it was only on this trip that Arthur had finally understood what Alvin meant. About getting inside the metal. All this time, Arthur had thought it was something he could do by straining real hard with his mind. But it wasn't like that at all. It was easy. Just a sort of turn of his mind. Kind of the way language worked for him. Getting the taste of the language on his tongue, and then trusting how it felt. Like knowing somehow that even though *mano* ended in *o*, it still needed *la* in front of it instead of *el*. He just knew how it ought to be.

Back in Carthage City, he gave two bits to a man selling sweet bread, and the man was trying to get away with not giving him change. Instead of yelling at him – what good would that do, there on the levee, a half-black boy yelling at a white man? – Arthur just thought about the coin he'd been holding in his hand all morning, how *warm* it was, how right it felt in his own hand. It was like he understood the metal of it, the way he understood the music of language. And thinking of it warm like that, he could see in his mind that it was getting warmer.

He encouraged it, thought of it getting warmer and warmer, and all of a sudden the man cried out and started slapping at the pocket into which he'd dropped the quarter.

It was burning him.

He tried to get it out of his pocket, but it burned his fingers and finally he flung off his coat, flipped down his suspenders, and dropped his trousers, right in front of everybody. Tipped the coin out of his pocket on to the sidewalk, where it sizzled and made the wood start smoking.

Then all the man could think about was the sore place on his leg where the coin had burned him. Arthur Stuart walked up to him, all the time thinking the coin cool again. He reached down and picked it up off the sidewalk. 'Reckon you oughta give me my change,' he said.

'You get away from me, you black devil,' said the man. 'You're a wizard, that's what you are. Cursing a man's coin, that's the same as thievin'!'

'That's awful funny, coming from a man who charged me two bits for a five-cent hunk of bread.'

Several passers-by chimed in.

'Trying to keep the boy's quarter, was you?'

'There's laws against that, even if the boy is black.'

'Stealin' from them as can't fight back.'

'Pull up your trousers, fool.'

A little later, Arthur Stuart got change for his quarter and tried to give the man his nickel, but he wouldn't let Arthur get near him.

Well, I tried, thought Arthur. I'm not a thief.

What I am is, I'm a maker.

No great shakes at it like Alvin, but dadgummit, I thought a quarter hot and it dang near burned its way out of the man's pocket.

If I can do that, then I can learn to do it all, that's what he thought, and that's why he was feeling cocky tonight. Because he'd been practising every day on anything metal he could get his hands on. Wouldn't do no good to turn the iron hot enough to melt, of course – these slaves wouldn't thank him if he burned their wrists and ankles up in the process of getting their chains off.

No, his project was to make the metal soft without getting it hot. That was a lot harder than hetting it up. Lots of times he'd caught himself straining again, trying to *push* softness on to the metal. But when he relaxed into it again and got the feel of the metal into his head like a song, he gradually began to get the knack of it again. Turned his own belt buckle so soft he could bend it into any shape he wanted. Though after a few minutes he realized the shape he wanted it in was like a belt buckle, since he still needed it to hold his pants up.

Brass was easier than iron, since it was softer in the first place. And it's not like Arthur Stuart was fast. He'd seen Alvin turn a gun barrel soft while a man was in the process of shooting it at him, that's how quick *he* was. But Arthur Stuart had to ponder on it first. Twenty-five slaves, each with an iron band at his ankle and another at his wrist. He had to make sure they all waited till the last one was free. If any of them bolted early, they'd all be caught.

Course, he could ask Alvin to help him. But he already had Alvin's answer. Leave 'em slaves, that's what Alvin had decided. But Arthur wouldn't do it. These men were in his hands. He was a maker now, after his own fashion, and it was up to him to decide for himself when it was right to act and right to let be. He couldn't do what Alvin did, healing folks and getting animals to do his bidding and turning water into glass. But he could soften iron, by damn, and so he'd set these men free.

Tomorrow night.

Next morning they passed from the Hio into the Mizzippy, and for the first time in years Alvin got a look at Tenskwa Tawa's fog on the river.

It was like moving into a wall. Sunny sky, not a cloud, and when you looked ahead it really didn't look like much, just a little mist on the river. But all of a sudden you couldn't see more than a hundred yards ahead of you – and that was only if you were headed up or down the river. If you kept going straight across to the right bank, it was like you went blind, you couldn't even see the front of your own boat.

It was the fence that Tenskwa Tawa had built to protect the reds who moved west after the failure of Ta-Kumsaw's war. All the reds who didn't want to live under white man's law, all the reds who were done with war, they crossed over the water into the west, and then Tenskwa Tawa . . . closed the door behind them.

Alvin had heard tales of the west from trappers who used to go there. They talked of mountains so sharp with stone, so rugged and high that they had snow on them clear into June. Places where the ground itself spat hot water fifty feet into the sky, or higher. Herds of buffalo so big they could pass by you all day and night, and next morning it still looked like there was just as many as yesterday. Grassland and desert, pine forest and lakes like jewels nestled among mountains so high that if you climbed to the top you ran out of air.

And all that was now red land, where whites would never go again. That's what this fog was all about.

Except for Alvin. He knew that if he wanted to, he could dispel that fog and cross over. Not only that, but he wouldn't be killed, neither. Tenskwa Tawa had said so, and there'd be no red man who'd go against the Prophet's law.

A part of him wanted to put to shore, wait for the riverboat to move on, and then get him a canoe and paddle across the river and look for his old friend and teacher. It would be good to talk to him about all that was going on in the world. About the rumours of war coming, between the United States and the Crown Colonies – or maybe between the free states and slave states within the USA. About rumours of war with Spain to get control of the mouth of the Mizzippy, or war between the Crown Colonies and England.

And now this rumour of war with the Mexica. What would Tenskwa Tawa make of that? Maybe he had troubles of his own – maybe he was working even now to make an alliance of reds to head south and defend their lands against men who dragged their captives to the tops of their ziggurats and tore their hearts out to satisfy their god.

Anyway, that's the kind of thing going through Alvin's mind as he leaned on the rail on the right side of the boat – the stabberd side, that was, though why boatmen should have different words for right and left made no sense to him. He was just standing there looking out into the fog and seeing no more than any other man, when he noticed something, not with his eyes, but with that inward vision that saw heartfires.

There was a couple of men out on the water, right out in the middle where they wouldn't be able to tell up from down. Spinning round and round, they were, and scared. It took only a moment to get the sense of it. Two men on a raft, only they didn't have drags under the raft and had it loaded front-heavy. Not boatmen, then. Had to be a homemade raft, and when their tiller broke they didn't know how to get the raft to keep its head straight downriver. At the mercy of the current, that's what, and no way of knowing what was happening five feet away.

Though it wasn't as if the *Yazoo Queen* was quiet. Still, fog had a way of damping down sounds. And even if they heard the riverboat, would they know what the sound was? To terrified men, it might sound like some kind of monster moving along the river.

Well, what could Alvin do about it? How could he claim to see what no one else could make out? And the flow of the river was too strong and complicated for him to get control of it, to steer the raft closer.

Time for some lying. Alvin turned around and shouted. 'Did you hear that? Did you see them? Raft out of control on the river! Men on a raft, they were calling for help, spinning around out there!'

In no time the pilot and captain both were leaning over the rail of the pilot's deck. 'I don't see a thing!' shouted the pilot.

'Not *now*,' said Alvin. 'But I saw 'em plain just a second ago, they're not far.'

Captain Howard could see the drift of things and he didn't like it. 'I'm not taking the *Yazoo Queen* any deeper into this fog than she already is! No sir! They'll fetch up on the bank farther downriver, it's no business of ours!'

'Law of the river!' shouted Alvin. 'Men in distress!'

That gave the pilot pause. It *was* the law. You had to give aid.

'I don't see no men in distress!' shouted Captain Howard.

'So don't turn the big boat,' said Alvin. 'Let me take that little rowboat and I'll go fetch 'em.'

Captain didn't like that either, but the pilot was a decent man and pretty soon Alvin was in the water with his hands on the oars.

But before he could fair get away, there was Arthur Stuart, leaping over the gap and sprawling into the little boat. 'That was about as clumsy a move as I ever saw,' said Alvin.

'I ain't gonna miss this,' said Arthur Stuart.

There was another man at the rail, hailing him. 'Don't be in such a hurry, Mr Smith!' shouted Jim Bowie. 'Two strong men is better than one on a job like this!' And then he, too, was leaping – a fair job of it, too, considering he must be at least ten years older than Alvin and a good twenty years older than Arthur Stuart. But when he landed, there was no sprawl about it, and Alvin wondered what this man's knack was. He had supposed it was killing, but maybe the killing was just a sideline. The man fair to flew.

So there they were, each of them at a set of oars while Arthur Stuart sat in the stern and kept his eyes peeled.

'How far are they?' he kept asking.

'The current might of took them farther out,' said Alvin. 'But they're there.'

And when Arthur started looking downright sceptical, Alvin fixed him with such a glare that Arthur Stuart finally got it. 'I think I see 'em,' he said, giving Alvin's lie a boost.

'You ain't trying to cross this whole river and get us kilt by reds,' said Jim Bowie.

'No sir,' said Alvin. 'Got no such plan. I saw those boys, plain as day, and I don't want their death on my conscience.'

'Well where are they now?'

Of course Alvin knew, and he was rowing towards them as best he could. Trouble was that Jim Bowie didn't know where they were, and he was rowing too, only not quite in the same direction as Alvin. And seeing as how both of them had their backs to where the raft was, Alvin couldn't even pretend to see them. He could only try to row stronger than Bowie in the direction he wanted to go.

Until Arthur Stuart rolled his eyes and said, 'Would you two just stop pretending that anybody believes anybody, and row in the right direction?'

Bowie laughed. Alvin sighed.

'You didn't see nothin',' said Bowie. 'Cause I was watching you looking out into the fog.'

'Which is why you came along.'

'Had to find out what you wanted to do with this boat.'

'I want to rescue two lads on a flatboat that's spinning out of control on the current.'

'You mean that's *true*?'

Alvin nodded, and Bowie laughed again. 'Well I'm jiggered.'

'That's between you and your jig,' said Alvin. 'More downstream, please.'

'So what's your knack, man?' said Bowie. 'Seeing through fog?'

'Looks like, don't it?'

'I think not,' said Bowie. 'I think there's a lot more to you than meets the eye.'

Arthur Stuart looked Alvin's massive blacksmith's body up and down. 'Is that *possible*?'

'And you're no slave,' said Bowie.

There was no laugh when he said *that*. That was dangerous for any man to know.

'Am so,' said Arthur Stuart.

'No slave would answer back like that, you poor fool,' said Bowie. 'You got such a mouth on you, there's no way you ever had a taste of the lash.'

'Oh, it's a *good* idea for you to come with me on this trip,' said Alvin.

'Don't worry,' said Bowie. 'I got secrets of my own. I can keep yours.'

Can – but will you? 'Not much of a secret,' said Alvin. 'I'll just have to take him back north and come down later on another steamboat.'

'Your arms and shoulders tell me you really are a smith,' said Bowie. 'But. Ain't no smith alive can look at a knife in its sheath and say it used to be a file.'

'I'm good at what I do,' said Alvin.

'Alvin Smith. You really ought to start travelling under another name.'

'Why?'

'You're the smith what killed a couple of Finders a few years back.'

'Finders who murdered my wife's mother.'

'Oh, no jury would convict you,' said Bowie. 'No more than I got convicted for *my* killing. Looks to me like we got a lot in common.'

'Less than you might think.'

'Same Alvin Smith who absconded from his master with a particular item.'

'A lie,' said Alvin. 'And he knows it.'

'Oh, I'm sure it is. But so the story goes.'

'You can't believe these tales.'

'Oh, I know,' said Bowie. 'You aren't slacking off on your rowing, are you?'

'I'm not sure I want to overtake that raft while we're still having this conversation.'

'I was just telling you, in my own quiet way, that I think I know what you got in that sack of yours. Some powerful knack you got, if the rumours are true.'

'What do they say, that I can fly?'

'You can turn iron to gold, they say.'

'Wouldn't that be nice,' said Alvin.

'But you didn't deny it, did you?'

'I can't make iron into anything but horseshoes and hinges.'

'You did it once, though, didn't you?'

'No sir,' said Alvin. 'I told you those stories were lies.'

'I don't believe you.'

'Then you're calling me a liar, sir,' said Alvin.

'Oh, you're not going to take offence, are you? Because I have a way of winning all my duels.'

Alvin didn't answer, and Bowie looked long and hard at Arthur Stuart. 'Ah,' said Bowie. 'That's the way of it.'

'What?' said Arthur Stuart.

'You ain't askeered of me,' said Bowie, exaggerating his accent.

'Am so,' said Arthur Stuart.

'You're scared of what I know, but you ain't a-scared of me taking down your "master" in a duel.'

'Terrified,' said Arthur Stuart.

It was only a split second, but there were Bowie's oars a-dangling, and his knife out of its sheath and his body twisted around with his knife right at Alvin's throat.

Except that it wasn't a knife any more. Just a handle.

The smile left Bowie's face pretty slow when he realized that his precious knife-made-from-a-file no longer had any iron in it.

'What did you do?' he asked.

'That's a pretty funny question,' said Alvin, 'coming from a man who meant to kill me.'

'Meant to scare you is all,' said Bowie. 'You didn't have to do that to my knife.'

'I got no knack for knowing a man's intentions,' said Alvin. 'Now turn around and row.'

Bowie turned around and took hold of the oars again. 'That knife was my luck.'

'Then I reckon you just run out of it,' said Alvin.

Arthur Stuart shook his head. 'You oughta take more care about who you draw against, Mr Bowie.'

'You're the man we want,' said Bowie. 'That's all I wanted to say. Didn't have to wreck my knife.'

'Next time you look to get a man on your team,' said Alvin, 'don't draw a knife on him.'

'And don't threaten to tell his secrets,' said Arthur Stuart.

And now, for the first time, Bowie looked more worried than peeved. 'Now, I never said I *knew* your secrets. I just had some guesses, that's all.'

'Well, Arthur Stuart, Mr Bowie just noticed he's out here in the middle of the river, in the fog, on a dangerous rescue mission, with a couple of people whose secrets he threatened to tell.'

'It's a position to give a man pause,' said Arthur Stuart.

'I won't go out of this boat without a struggle,' said Bowie.

'I don't plan to hurt you,' said Alvin. 'Because we're not alike, you and me. I killed a man once, in grief and rage, and I've regretted it ever since.'

'Me too,' said Bowie.

'It's the proudest moment of your life. You saved the weapon and called it your luck. We're not alike at all.'

'I reckon not.'

'And if I want you dead,' said Alvin, 'I don't have to throw you out of no boat.'

Bowie nodded. And then took his hands off the oar. His hands began to flutter around his cheeks, around his mouth.

'Can't breathe, can you?' said Alvin. 'Nobody's blocking you. Just do it, man. Breathe in, breathe out. You been doing it all your life.'

It wasn't like Bowie was choking. He just couldn't get his body to do his will.

Alvin didn't keep it going till the man turned blue or nothing. Just long enough for Bowie to feel real helpless. And then he remembered how to breathe, just like that, and sucked in the air.

'So now that we've settled the fact that you're in no danger from me here on this boat,' said Alvin, 'let's rescue a couple of fellows got themselves on a homemade raft that got no drag.'

And at that moment, the whiteness of the fog before them turned into a flatboat not five feet away. Another pull on the oars and they bumped it. Which was the first time the men on the raft had any idea that anybody was coming after them.

Arthur Stuart was already clambering to the bow of the boat, holding on to the stern rope and leaping on to the raft to make it fast.

'Lord be praised,' said the smaller of the two men.

'You come at a right handy time,' said the tall one, helping Arthur make the line fast. 'Got us an unreliable raft here, and in this fog we wasn't even seeing that much of the countryside. A second-rate voyage by any reckoning.'

Alvin laughed at that. 'Glad to see you've kept your spirits up.'

'Oh, we was both praying and singing hymns,' said the lanky man.

'How tall *are* you?' said Arthur Stuart as the man loomed over him.

'About a head higher than my shoulders,' said the man, 'but not quite long enough for my suspenders.'

The fellow had a way about him, right enough. You just couldn't help but like him.

Which made Alvin suspicious right off. If that was the man's knack, then he couldn't be trusted. And yet the most cussed thing about it was, even while you wasn't trusting him, you still had to like him.

'What are you, a lawyer?' asked Alvin.

By now they had manoeuvred the boat to the front of the raft, ready to tug it along behind them as they rejoined the riverboat.

The man stood to his full height and then bowed, as awkward-looking a manoeuvre as Alvin had ever seen. He was all knees and elbows, angles everywhere, even his face, nothing soft about him, as bony a fellow as could be. No doubt about it, he was ugly. Eyebrows like an ape's, they protruded so far out over his eyes. And yet . . . he wasn't bad to look at. Made you feel warm and welcome, when he smiled.

'Abraham Lincoln of Springfield, at your service, gentlemen,' he said.

'And I'm Cuz Johnston of Springfield,' said the other man.

'Cuz for "Cousin",' said Abraham. 'Everybody calls him that.'

'They do *now*,' said Cuz.

'*Whose* cousin?' asked Arthur Stuart.

'Not mine,' said Abraham. 'But he looks like a cousin, don't he? He's the epitome of cousinhood, the quintessence of cousiniferosity. So when I started calling him Cuz, it was just stating the obvious.'

'Actually, I'm his father's second wife's son by her first husband,' said Cuz.

'Which makes us step-strangers,' said Abraham. 'In-law.'

'I'm particularly grateful to you boys for pickin' us up,' said Cuz, 'on account of now old Abe here won't have to finish the most obnoxious tall tale I ever heard.'

'It wasn't no tall tale,' said old Abe. 'I heard it from a man named Taleswapper. He had it in his book, and he didn't never put anything in it lessen it was true.'

Old Abe – who couldn't have been more than thirty – was quick of eye. He saw the glance that passed between Alvin and Arthur Stuart.

'So you know him?' asked Abe.

'A truthful man, he is indeed,' said Alvin. 'What tale did he tell you?'

'Of a child born many years ago,' said Abe. 'A tragic tale of a brother who got kilt by a treetrunk carried downstream by a flood, which hit him while he was a-saving his mother, who was in a waggon in the middle of the stream, giving birth. But doomed as he was, he stayed alive long enough on that river that when the baby was born, it was the seventh son of a seventh son, and all the sons alive.'

'A noble tale,' said Alvin. 'I've seen that one in his book my own self.'

'And you believe it?'

'I do,' said Alvin.

'I never said it wasn't true,' said Cuz. 'I just said it wasn't the tale a man wants to hear when he's spinning downstream on a flapdoodle flatboat in the midst of the Mizzippy mist.'

Abe Lincoln ignored the near-poetic language of his companion. 'So I was telling Cuz here that the river hadn't treated us half bad, compared to what a much smaller stream done to the folks in that story. And now here *you* are, saving us – so the river's been downright kind to a couple of second-rate raftmakers.'

'Made this one yourself, eh?' said Alvin.

'Tiller broke,' said Abe.

'Didn't have no spare?' said Alvin.

'Didn't know I'd need one. But if we ever once fetched up on shore, I could have made another.'

'Good with your hands?'

'Not really,' said Abe. 'But I'm willing to do it over till it's right.'

Alvin laughed. 'Well, time to do this raft over.'

'I'd welcome it if you'd show me what we done wrong. I can't see a blame thing here that isn't good raftmaking.'

'It's what's under the raft that's missing. Or rather, what ought to be there but ain't. You need a drag at the stern, to keep the back in back. And on top of that you've got it heavy-loaded in front, so it's bound to turn around any old way.'

'Well I'm blamed,' said Abe. 'No doubt about it, I'm not cut out to be a boatman.'

'Most folks aren't,' said Alvin. 'Except my friend Mr Bowie here. He's just can't keep away from a boat, when he gets a chance to row.'

Bowie gave a tight little smile and a nod to Abe and his companion. By now the raft was slogging along behind them in the water, and it was all Alvin and Bowie could do to move it forward.

'Maybe,' said Arthur Stuart, 'the two of you could stand at the *back* of the raft so it didn't dig so deep in front and make it such a hard pull.'

Embarrassed, Abe and Cuz did so at once. And in the thick fog of midstream, it made them mostly invisible and damped down any sound they made so that conversation was nigh impossible.

It took a good while to overtake the steamboat, but the pilot, being a good man, had taken it slow, despite Captain Howard's ire over time lost, and all of a sudden the fog thinned and the noise of the paddle-wheels was right beside them as the *Yazoo Queen* loomed out of the fog.

'I'll be plucked and roasted,' shouted Abe. 'That's a right fine steam-boat you got here.'

'Tain't our'n,' said Alvin.

Arthur Stuart noticed how little time it took Bowie to get himself up on deck and away from the boat, shrugging off all the hands clapping at his shoulder like he was a hero. Well, Arthur couldn't blame him. But it was a sure thing that however Alvin might have scared him out on the water, Bowie was still a danger to them both.

Once the dinghy was tied to the *Yazoo Queen*, and the raft lashed alongside as well, there was all kinds of chatter from passengers wanting to know obvious things like how they ever managed to find each other in the famous Mizzippy fog.

'It's like I said,' Alvin told them. 'They was right close, and even then, we still had to search.'

Abe Lincoln heard it with a grin, and didn't say a word to contradict him, but he was no fool, Arthur Stuart could see that. He knew that the raft had been nowheres near the riverboat. He also knew that Alvin had steered straight for the *Yazoo Queen* as if he could see it.

But what was that to him? In no time he was telling all who cared to listen about what a blame fool job he'd done a-making the raft, and how dizzy they got spinning round and round in the fog. 'It twisted me up into such a knot that it took the two of us half a day to figure out how to untie my arms from my legs and get my head back out from my armpit.' It wasn't all that funny, really, but the way he told it, he got such a laugh. Even though the story wasn't likely to end up in Taleswapper's book.

Well, that night they put to shore at a built-up rivertown and there was so much coming and going on the *Yazoo Queen* that Arthur Stuart gave up on his plan to set the twenty-five Mexica slaves free that night.

Instead, he and Alvin went to a lecture being held that night in the dining room of the riverboat. The speaker was none other than Cassius Marcellus Clay, the noted anti-slavery orator, who persisted in his mad course of lecturing against slavery right in the midst of slave country. But listening to him, Arthur Stuart could see how the man got away with it. He didn't call names or declare slavery to be a terrible sin. Instead he talked about how much harm slavery did to the owners and their families.

'What does it do to a man, to raise up his children to believe that their own hands never have to be set to labour? What will happen when he's old, and these children who never learned to work freely spend his money without heed for the morrow?

'And when these same children have seen their fellow human, however dusky of hue his skin might be, treated with disdain, their labour dispraised and their freedom treated as nought – will they hesitate to treat their ageing father as a thing of no value, to be discarded when he is no longer useful? For when one human being is treated as a commodity, why should children not learn to think of all humans as either useful or useless, and discard all those in the latter category?'

Arthur Stuart had heard plenty of Abolitionists speak over the years, but this one took the cake. Because instead of stirring up a mob of slave owners wanting to tar and feather him, or worse, he got them looking all thoughtful and glancing at each other uneasily, probably thinking on their own children and what a useless set of grubs they no doubt were.

In the end, though, it wasn't likely Clay was doing all that much good. What were they going to do, set their slaves free and move north? That would be like the story in the Bible, where Jesus told the rich young man, Sell all you got and give it unto the poor and come follow me. The wealth of these men was measured in slaves. To give them up was to become poor, or at least to join the middling sort of men who have to pay for what labour they hire. Renting a man's back, so to speak, instead of owning it. None of them had the courage to do it, at least not that Arthur Stuart saw.

But he noticed that Abe Lincoln seemed to be listening real close to everything Clay said, eyes shining. Especially when Clay talked about them as wanted to send black folks back to Africa. 'How many of you would be glad to hear of a plan to send *you* back to England or Scotland or Germany or whatever place your ancestors came from? Rich or poor, bond or free, we're Americans now, and slaves whose grandparents were born on this soil can't be sent *back* to Africa, for it's no more their home than China is, or India.'

Abe nodded at that, and Arthur Stuart got the impression that up to now, the lanky fellow probably thought that the way to solve the black problem was exactly that, to ship 'em back to Africa.

'And what of the mulatto? The light-skinned black man who partakes of the blood of Europe and Africa in equal parts? Shall such folk be split in two like a rail, and the pieces divvied up between the lands of their ancestry? No, like it or not we're all bound together in this land, yoked together. When you enslave a black man, you enslave yourself as well, for now you are bound to him as surely as he is bound to you, and your character is shaped by his bondage as surely as his own is. Make the black man servile, and in the same process you make yourself tyrannical. Make the black man quiver in fear before you, and you make yourself a monster of terror. Do you think your children will not see you in that state, and fear you too? You cannot wear one face to the slave and another face to your family, and expect either face to be believed.'

When the talk was over, and before Arthur and Alvin separated to their sleeping places, they had a moment together at the rail over-looking the flatboat. 'How can anybody hear that talk,' said Arthur Stuart, 'and go home to their slaves, and not set them free?'

'Well, for one thing,' said Alvin, 'I'm not setting *you* free.'

'Because you're only pretending I'm a slave,' whispered Arthur.

'Then I *could* pretend to set you free, and be a good example for the others.'

'No you can't,' said Arthur Stuart, 'because then what would you do with me?'

Alvin just smiled a little and nodded, and Arthur Stuart got his point. 'I didn't say it would be easy. But if everybody would do it –'

'But everybody won't do it,' said Alvin. 'So them as free their slaves, they're suddenly poor, while them as don't free them, they stay rich. So now who has all the power in slavery country? Them as keep their slaves.'

'So there's no hope.'

'It has to be all at once, by law, not bit by bit. As long as it's permitted to keep slaves anywhere, then bad men will own them and get advantage from it. You have to ban it outright. That's what I can't get Peggy to understand. All her persuasion in the end will come to nothing, because the moment somebody stops being a slave owner, he loses all his influence among those who have kept their slaves.'

'Congress can't ban slavery in the Crown Colonies, and the King can't ban it in the States. So no matter what you do, you're gonna have one place that's got slaves and the other that doesn't.'

'It's going to be war,' said Alvin. 'Sooner or later, as the free states get sick of slavery and the slave states get more dependent on it, there'll be a revolution on one side of the line or the other. I think there won't be freedom until the King falls and his Crown Colonies become states in the union.'

'That'll never happen.'

'I think it will,' said Alvin. 'But the bloodshed will be terrible. Because people fight most fiercely when they dare not admit even to themselves that their cause is unjust.' He spat into the water. 'Go to bed, Arthur Stuart.'

But Arthur couldn't sleep. Having Cassius Clay speaking on the riverboat had got the belowdecks folk into a state, and some of them were quite angry at Clay for making white folks feel guilty. 'Mark my words,' said a fellow from Kenituck. 'When they get feelin' guilty, then the only way to feel better is to talk theirself into believing we *deserve* to be slaves, and if we deserve to be slaves, we must be very bad and need to be punished all the time.'

It sounded pretty convoluted to Arthur Stuart, but then he was only a baby when his mother carried him to freedom, so it's not like he knew what he was talking about in an argument about what slavery was really like.

Even when things finally quieted down, though, Arthur couldn't sleep, until finally he got up and crept up the ladderway to the deck.

It was a moonlit night, here on the east bank, where the fog was only a low mist and you could look up and see stars.

The twenty-five Mexica slaves were asleep on the stern deck, some of them mumbling softly in their sleep. The guard was asleep, too.

I meant to free you tonight, thought Arthur. But it would take too long now. I'd never be done by morning.

And then it occurred to him that maybe it wasn't so. Maybe he could do it faster than he thought.

So he sat down in a shadow and after a couple of false starts, he got the nearest slave's ankle iron into his mind and began to sense the metal the way he had that coin. Began to soften it as he had softened his belt buckle.

Trouble was, the iron ring was thicker and had more metal in it than either the coin or the buckle had had. By the time he got one part softened up, another part was hard again, and so it went. It began to feel like the story Peggy read them about Sisyphus, whose time in Hades was spent pushing a stone up a mountain, but for every step up, he slid two steps back, so after working all day he was farther from the top than he was when he began.

And then he almost cussed out loud at how stupid he had been.

He didn't have to soften the whole ring. What were they going to do, slide it off like a sleeve? All he had to do was soften it at the hinge, where the metal was thinnest and weakest.

He gave it a try and it was getting all nice and soft when he realized something.

The hinges weren't connected. The one side wasn't joined to the other. The pin was gone.

He took one fetter after another into his mind and discovered they were all the same. Every single hinge pin was missing. Every single slave was already free.

He got up from the shadows and walked out to stand among the slaves.

They weren't asleep. They made tiny hand gestures to tell Arthur to go away, to get out of sight.

So he went back into the shadows.

As if at a signal, they all opened their fetters and set the chains gently on the deck. It made a bit of racket, of course, but the guard didn't stir. Nor did anyone else in the silent boat.

Then the black men arose and swung themselves over the side away from shore.

They're going to drown. Nobody taught slaves to swim, or let them learn it on their own. They were choosing death.

Except that, come to think of it, Arthur didn't hear a single splash.

He stood up when all the slaves were gone from the deck and walked to another part of the rail. Sure enough, they were overboard all right – all gathered on the raft. And now they were carefully loading Abe Lincoln's cargo into the dinghy. It wasn't much of a dinghy, but it wasn't much of a cargo, either, and it didn't take long.

What difference did it make, not to steal Abe's stuff? They were all thieves, anyway, since they were stealing themselves by running away. Or that was the theory, anyway. As if a man, by being free, thereby stole something from someone else.

They laid themselves down on the raft, all twenty-five, making a veritable pile of humanity, and with those at the edges using their hands as paddles, they began to pull away out into the current. Heading out into the fog, towards the red man's shore.

Someone laid a hand on his shoulder and he near jumped out of his skin.

It was Alvin, of course.

'Let's not be seen here,' Alvin said softly. 'Let's go below.'

So Arthur Stuart led the way down into the slave quarters, and soon they were in whispered conversation in the kitchen, which was dark but for a single lantern that Alvin kept trimmed low.

'I figured you'd have some blame fool plan like that,' said Alvin.

'And I thought you was going to let them go on as slaves like you didn't care, but I should've knowed better,' said Arthur Stuart.

'I thought so, too,' said Alvin. 'But I don't know if it was having Jim Bowie guess too much, or him trying to kill me with that knife – and no, Arthur Stuart, he did *not* stop in time, if there'd been a blade in that knife it would have cut right through my throat. Could have been the fear of death made me think that I didn't want to face God knowing I could have freed twenty-five men, but chose to leave them slaves. Then again, it might have been Mr Clay's sermon tonight. Converted me as neat as you please.'

'Converted Mr Lincoln,' said Arthur Stuart.

'Might be,' said Alvin. 'Though he doesn't look like the sort who ever sought to own another man.'

'I know why you had to do it,' said Arthur Stuart.

'Why is that?'

'Because you knew that if you didn't, I would.'

Alvin shrugged. 'Well, I knew you'd made up your mind to try.'

'I could have done it.'

'Very slowly.'

'It was working, once I realized I only had to go after the hinge.'

'I reckon so,' said Alvin. 'But the real reason I chose tonight was that the raft was here. A gift to us, don't you think? Would have been a shame not to use it.'

'So what happens when they get to the red man's shore?'

'Tenskwa Tawa will see to them. I gave them a token to show to the first red they meet. When they see it, they'll get escorted straight to the Prophet, wherever he might be. And when *he* sees it, he'll give them safe passage. Or maybe let them dwell there.'

'Or maybe he'll need them, to help him fight the Mexica. If they're moving north.'

'Maybe.'

'What was the token?' asked Arthur Stuart.

'A couple of these,' said Alvin. He held up a tiny shimmering cube that looked like the clearest ice that had ever been, or maybe glass, but no glass had ever shimmered.

Arthur Stuart took it in his hand and realized what it was. 'This is water. A box of water.'

'More like a *block* of water. I decided to it today out on the river, when I came so close to having my blood spill into the water. That's partly how they're made. A bit of my own self has to go into the water to make it strong as steel. You know the law. "The maker is the one . . ."'

'The maker is the one who is part of what he makes,' said Arthur Stuart.

'Get to sleep,' said Alvin. 'We can't let nobody know we was up tonight. I can't keep them all asleep for ever.'

'Can I keep this?' said Arthur Stuart. 'I think I see something in it.'

'You can see everything in it, if you look long enough,' said Alvin. 'But no, you can't keep it. If you think what I got in my poke is valuable, think what folks would do to have a solid block of water that showed them true visions of things far and near, past and present.'

Arthur reached out and offered the cube to Alvin.

But instead of taking it, Alvin only smiled, and the cube went liquid all at once and dribbled through Arthur Stuart's fingers. Arthur looked at the puddle on the table, feeling as forlorn as he ever had.

'It's just water,' said Alvin.

'And a little bit of blood.'

'Naw,' said Alvin. 'I took that back.'

'Good night,' said Arthur Stuart. 'And . . . thank you for setting them free.'

'Once you set your heart on it, Arthur, what else could I do? I looked at them and thought, somebody loved them once as much as your mama loved you. She died to set you free. I didn't have to do that. Just inconvenience myself a little. Put myself at risk, but not by much.'

'But you saw what I did, didn't you? I made it soft without getting it hot.'

'You done good, Arthur Stuart. There's no denying it. You're a maker now.'

'Not much of one.'

'Whenever you got two makers, one's going to be more of a maker than the other. But lessen that one starts gettin' uppity, it's good to remember that there's always a third one who's better than both of them.'

'Who's better than you?' asked Arthur Stuart.

'You,' said Alvin. 'Because I'll take an ounce of compassion over a pound of tricks any day. Now go to sleep.'

Only then did Arthur let himself feel how very, very tired he was. Whatever had kept him awake before, it was gone now. He barely made it to his cot before he fell asleep.

Oh, there was a hullabaloo in the morning. Suspicions flew every which way. Some folks thought it was the boys from the raft, because why else would the slaves have left their cargo behind? Until somebody pointed out that with the cargo still on the raft, there wouldn't have been room for all the runaways.

Then suspicion fell on the guard who had slept, but most folks knew that was wrong, because if he had done it then why didn't he run off, instead of lying there asleep on the deck till a crewman noticed the slaves was gone and raised the alarm.

Only now, when they were gone, did the ownership of the slaves become clear. Alvin had figured Mr Travis to have a hand in it, but the man most livid at their loss was Captain Howard hisself. That was a surprise. But it explained why the men bound for Mexico had chosen this boat to make their journey downriver.

To Alvin's surprise, though, Travis and Howard both kept glancing at him and young Arthur Stuart as if they suspected the truth. Well, he shouldn't have been surprised, he realized. If Bowie told them what had happened to his knife out on the water, they'd naturally wonder if a man with such power over iron might have been the one to slip the hinge pins out of all the fetters.

Slowly the crowd dispersed. But not Captain Howard, not Travis. And when Alvin and Arthur made as if to go, Howard headed straight for them. 'I want to talk to you,' he said, and he didn't sound friendly.

'What about?' said Alvin.

'That boy of yours,' said Howard. 'I saw how he was doing their slops on the morning watch. I saw him talking to them. That made me suspicious, all right, since not one of them spoke English.'

'Pero todos hablaban espanol,' said Arthur Stuart.

Travis apparently understood him, and looked chagrined. 'They *all* of them spoke Spanish? Lying skunks.'

Oh, right, as if slaves owed you some kind of honesty.

'That's as good as a confession,' said Captain Howard. 'He just admitted he speaks their language and learned things from them that even their master didn't know.'

Arthur was going to protest, but Alvin put a hand on his shoulder. He did *not*, however, stop his mouth. 'My boy here,' said Alvin, 'only just learned to speak Spanish, so naturally he seized on an opportunity to practise. Unless you got some evidence that those fetters was opened by use of a slop bucket, then I think you can safely leave this boy out of it.'

'No, I expect he *wasn't* the one who popped them hinge pins,' said Captain Howard. 'I expect he was somebody's spy to tell them blacks about the plan.'

'I didn't tell nobody no plan,' said Arthur Stuart hotly.

Alvin clamped his grip tighter. No slave would talk to a white man like that, least of all a boat captain.

Then from behind Travis and Howard came another voice. 'It's all right, boy,' said Bowie. 'You can tell them. No need to keep it secret any more.'

And with a sinking feeling, Alvin wondered what kind of pyrotechnics he'd have to go through to distract everybody long enough for him and Arthur Stuart to get away.

But Bowie didn't say at all what Alvin expected. 'I got the boy to tell me what he learned from them. They were cooking up some evil Mexica ritual. Something about tearing out somebody's heart one night when they were pretending to be our guides. A treacherous bunch, and so I decided we'd be better off without them.'

'*You* decided!' Captain Howard growled. 'What right did *you* have to decide.'

'Safety,' said Bowie. 'You put me in charge of the scouts, and that's what these were supposed to be. But it was a blame fool idea from the start. Why do you think them Mexica left those boys alive instead of taking their beating hearts out of their chests? It was a trap. All along, it was a trap. Well, we didn't fall into it.'

'Do you know how much they cost?' demanded Captain Howard.

'They didn't cost *you* anything,' said Travis.

That reminder took a bit of the dudgeon out of Captain Howard. 'It's the principle of the thing. Just setting them free.'

'But I didn't,' said Bowie. 'I sent them across river. What do you think will happen to them there – *if* they make it through the fog?'

There was a bit more grumbling, but some laughter, too, and the matter was closed.

Back in his room, Alvin waited for Bowie to return.

'Why?' he demanded.

'I told you I could keep a secret,' said Bowie. 'I watched you and the boy do it, and I have to say, it was worth it to see how you broke their irons without ever laying a hand on them. To think I'd ever see a knack like that. Oh, you're a maker all right.'

'Then come with me,' said Alvin. 'Leave these men behind. Don't you know the doom that lies over their heads? The Mexica aren't fools. These are dead men you're travelling with.'

'Might be so,' said Bowie, 'but they need what I can do, and you don't.'

'I do so,' said Alvin. 'Because I don't know many men in this world can hide their heartfire from me. It's your knack, isn't it? To disappear from all men's sight, when you want to. Because I never saw you watching us.'

'And yet I woke you up just reaching for your poke the other night,' said Bowie with a grin.

'Reaching for it?' said Alvin. 'Or putting it back?'

Bowie shrugged.

'I thank you for protecting us and taking the blame on yourself.'

Bowie chuckled. 'Not much blame there. Truth is, Travis was getting sick of all the trouble of taking care of them blacks. It was only Howard who was so dead set on having them, and he ain't even going with us, once he drops us off on the Mexica coast.'

'I could teach you. The way Arthur Stuart's been learning.'

'I don't think so,' said Bowie. 'It's like you said. We're different kind of men.'

'Not so different but what you can't change iffen you've a mind to.'

Bowie only shook his head.

'Well, then, I'll thank you the only way that's useful to you,' said Alvin.

Bowie waited. 'Well?'

'I just did it,' said Alvin. 'I just put it back.'

Bowie reached down to the sheath at his waist. It wasn't empty. He drew out the knife. There was the blade, plain as day, not a whit changed.

You'd've thought Bowie was handling his long-lost baby.

'How'd you get the blade back on it?' he asked. 'You never touched it.'

'It was there all along,' said Alvin. 'I just kind of spread it out a little.'

'So I couldn't see it?'

'And so it wouldn't cut nothing.'

'But now it will?'

'I think you're bound to die, when you take on them Mexica, Mr Bowie. But I want you to take some human sacrificers with you on the way.'

'I'll do that,' said Bowie. 'Except for the part about me dying.'

'I hope I'm wrong and you're right, Mr Bowie,' said Alvin.

'And I hope you live for ever, Alvin Maker,' said the knife-wielding killer.

That morning Alvin and Arthur Stuart left the boat, as did Abe Lincoln and Cuz, and they made their journey down to Nueva Barcelona together, all four of them, swapping impossible stories all the way. But that's another tale, not this one.

OUTLANDER

DIANA GABALDON

OUTLANDER
DIANA GABALDON

Outlander (1991*)
Dragonfly in Amber (1992)
Voyager (1994)
Drums of Autumn (1997)
The Outlandish Companion (nonfiction) (1999)
The Fiery Cross (2001)
A Breath of Snow and Ashes (in progress)

The Lord John Grey books:
Hellfire (short story – published in UK anthology, Past Poisons, 1998)
Lord John and the Private Matter (2003)
Lord John and the Brotherhood of the Blade (in progress)

In 1946, just after World War II, a young woman named Claire Beauchamp Randall goes to the Scottish Highlands on a second honeymoon. She and her husband, Frank, have been separated by the war, he as a British army officer, she as a combat nurse, and are now becoming reacquainted, rekindling their marriage, and thinking of starting a family. These plans hit a snag when Claire, walking by herself one afternoon, walks through a circle of standing stones and disappears.

The first person she meets, upon regaining possession of her faculties, is a man in the uniform of an eighteenth-century English army officer – a man who bears a startling resemblance to her husband, Frank. This is not terribly surprising, as Captain Johnathan Randall is her husband's six-times-great-grandfather. However, Black Jack, as he's called, does not resemble his descendant in terms of personality, being a sadistic bisexual pervert, and while attempting to escape from him, Claire falls into the hands of a group of Highland Scots, who are also eager to avoid the Captain for reasons of their own.

---

* All dates are first US hardcover publication, unless otherwise noted.

Events culminate in Claire's being obliged to marry Jamie Fraser, a young Highlander, in order to stay out of the hands of Black Jack Randall. Hoping to escape from the Scots long enough to get back to the stone circle and Frank, Claire agrees – only to find herself gradually falling in love with Jamie.

The *Outlander* books are the story of Claire, Jamie, and Frank, and a complicated double marriage that occupies two separate centuries. They are also the story of the Jacobite Rising under Bonnie Prince Charlie, the end of the Highland clans, and the flight of the Highlanders after the slaughter of Culloden, to the refuge and promise of the New World – a world that promises to be just as dangerous as the old one. And along the way, the *Outlander* series is an exploration of the nuances, operation, and moral complexities of time-travel – and history.

The series encompasses hundreds of characters. Among these, one of the most complex and interesting is Lord John Grey, whom we meet originally in *Dragonfly in Amber*, and who appears again in the succeeding books of the series. A gay man in a time when that particular predilection could get one hanged, Lord John is a man accustomed to keeping secrets. He's also a man of honour and deep affections – whether returned or not.

Lord John's adventures are interpolations within the storyline of the main *Outlander* novels; following the same timeline (complex as that may be), and involving the same universe and people – but focused on the character of Lord John Grey.

LORD JOHN
AND THE SUCCUBUS

BY DIANA GABALDON

Historical note: Between 1756 and 1763, Great Britain joined with her allies, Prussia and Hanover, to fight against the combined forces of Austria, Saxony – and England's ancient foe, France. In the autumn of 1757, the Duke of Cumberland was obliged to surrender at Kloster-Zeven, leaving the allied armies temporarily shattered, and the forces of Frederick the Great of Prussia encircled by French and Austrian troops.

1
Death Rides a Pale Horse

Grey's spoken German was improving by leaps and bounds, but found itself barely equal to the present task.

After a long, boring day of rain and paperwork, there had come the sound of loud dispute in the corridor outside his office, and the head of Lance-Korporal Helwig appeared in his doorway, wearing an apologetic expression.

'Major Grey?' he said *'Ich habe ein kleine Englische-Problem.'*

A moment later, Lance-Korporal Helwig had disappeared down the corridor like an eel sliding into mud, and Major John Grey, English liaison to the First Regiment of Schwabian Foot, found himself adjudicating a three-way dispute among an English private, a gypsy prostitute, and a Prussian tavern owner.

'A little English problem,' Helwig had described it as. The problem, as Grey saw it, was rather the *lack* of English.

The tavern owner spoke the local dialect with such fluency and speed that Grey grasped no more than one word in ten. The English private, who normally probably knew no more German than '*Ja*', '*Nein*', and the two or three crude phrases necessary to accomplish immoral transactions, was so stricken with fury that he was all but speechless in his own tongue as well.

The gypsy, whose abundant charms were scarcely impaired by a missing tooth, had German that most nearly matched Grey's own in terms of grammar – though her vocabulary was immensely more colourful and detailed.

Using alternate hands to quell the sputterings of the private and the torrents of the Prussian, Grey concentrated his attention carefully on the gypsy's explanations – meanwhile taking care to consider the source, which meant discounting the factual basis of most of what she said.

'. . . and then the disgusting pig of an Englishman, he put his (incomprehensible colloquial expression) into my (unknown Gypsy word)! And then . . .'

'She said, she said, she'd do it for sixpence, sir! She did, she said so – but, but, but then . . .'

'These-barbarian-pig-dogs-did-revolting-things-under-the-table-and-made-it-fall-over-so-the-leg-of-the-table-was-broken-and-the-dishes-broken-too-even-my-large-platter-which-cost-six-thalers-at-St. Martin's-Fair-and-the-meat-was-ruined-by-falling-on-the-floor-and-even-if-it-was-not-the-dogs-fell-upon-it-snarling-so-that-I-was-bitten-when-I-tried-to-seize-it-away-from-them-and-all-the-time-these -vile-persons-were-copulating-like-filthy-foxes-on-the-floor-and-THEN . . .'

At length, an accommodation was reached, by means of Grey demanding that all three parties produce what money was presently in their possession. A certain amount of shifty-eyed reluctance and dramatic pantomimes of purse- and pocket-searching having resulted in three small heaps of silver and copper, he firmly rearranged these in terms of size and metal value, without reference as to the actual coinage involved, as these appeared to include the currency of at least six different principalities.

Eyeing the gypsy's ensemble, which included both gold earrings and a crude but broad gold band round her finger, he assigned roughly equitable heaps to her and to the private, whose name, when asked, proved to be Bodger.

Assigning a slightly larger heap to the tavern owner, he then scowled fiercely at the three combatants, jabbed a finger at the money, and jerked a thumb over his shoulder, indicating that they should take the coins and leave while he was still in possession of his temper.

This they did, and storing away a most interesting gypsy curse for future reference, Grey returned tranquilly to his interrupted correspondence.

26 September, 1757
To Harold, Earl of Melton
From Lord John Grey
Gurgelwitz, Kingdom of Prussia

My Lord –

In reply to your request for information regarding my situation, I beg to say that I am well-suited. My duties are . . . [He paused, considering, then wrote, 'interesting', smiling slightly to himself at thought of what interpretation Hal might put upon that] . . . and the conditions comfortable. I am quartered with several other English and German officers in the house of a Princess von Lowenstein, the widow of a minor Prussian noble, who possesses a fine estate near the town.

We have two English regiments quartered here: Sir Peter Hicks's 35th, and half of the 52nd Artillery – I am told Colonel Ruysdale is in command, but have not yet met him, the 52nd having arrived only days ago. As the Schwabians to whom I am attached and a number of Prussian troops are occupying all the suitable quarters in the town, Hicks's men are encamped some way to the south; Ruysdale to the north.

French forces are reported to be within twenty miles, but we expect no immediate trouble. Still, so late in the year, the snow will come soon, and put an end to the fighting; they may try for a final thrust before the winter sets in. Sir Peter begs me send his regards.

He dipped his quill again, and changed tack.

My grateful thanks to your good wife for the small-clothes, which are superior in quality to what is available here.

At this point, he was obliged to transfer the pen to his left hand in order to scratch ferociously at the inside of his left thigh. He was wearing a pair of the local German product under his breeches, and while they were well laundered and not infested with vermin, they were made of coarse linen and appeared to have been starched with some substance derived from potatoes, which was irritating in the extreme.

Tell mother I am still intact, and not starving, [he concluded, transferring the pen back to his right hand.] Quite the reverse, in fact; Princess von Lowenstein has an excellent cook.

Your Most Affec't. Brother,

J.

Sealing this with a brisk stamp of his half-moon signet, he then took down one of the ledgers and a stack of reports, and began the mechanical work of recording deaths and desertions. There was an outbreak of bloody flux among the men; more than a score lost to it in the last two weeks.

The thought brought the gypsy woman's last remarks to mind. Blood and bowels had both come into that, though he feared he had missed some of the refinements. Perhaps she had merely been trying to curse him with the flux?

He paused for a moment, twiddling the quill. It was rather unusual for the flux to occur in the cold weather; it was more commonly a disease of hot summer, while winter was the season for consumption, catarrh, influenza and fever.

He was not at all inclined to believe in curses, but did believe in poison. A whore would have ample opportunity to administer poison to her customers . . . but to what end? He turned to another folder of reports and shuffled through them, but saw no increase in the report of robbery or missing items – and the dead soldiers' comrades would certainly have noted anything of the kind. A man's belongings were sold by auction at his death, the money used to pay his debts and – if anything were left – to be sent to his family.

He put back the folder and shrugged, dismissing it. Illness and death trod closely in a soldier's footsteps, regardless of season or gypsy curse. Still, it might be worth warning Private Bodger to be wary of what he ate, particularly in the company of light-frigates and other dubious women.

A gentle rain had begun to fall again outside, and the sound of it against the windowpanes combined with the soothing shuffle of paper and scratch of quill to induce a pleasant sense of mindless drowsiness. He was disturbed from this trance-like state by the sound of footsteps on the wooden stair.

Captain Stephan von Namtzen, Landgrave von Erdberg, poked his handsome blond head through the doorway, ducking automatically to avoid braining himself on the lintel. The gentleman following him had no such difficulty, being a foot or so shorter.

'Captain von Namtzen,' Grey said, standing politely. 'May I be of assistance?'

'I have here Herr Blomberg,' Stephan said in English, indicating the small, round, nervous-looking individual who accompanied him. 'He wishes to borrow your horse.'

Grey was sufficiently startled by this that he merely said, 'Which one?' rather than 'Who is Herr Blomberg?' or 'What does he want with a horse?'

The first of these questions was largely academic in any case; Herr Blomberg wore an elabourate chain of office about his neck, done in broad, flat links of enamel and chased gold, from which depended a seven-pointed starburst, enclosing a plaque of enamel on which was painted some scene of historic interest. Herr Blomberg's engraved silver coat-buttons and shoe-buckles were sufficient to proclaim his wealth; the chain of office merely confirmed his importance as being secular, rather than noble.

'Herr Blomberg is buergermeister of the town,' Stephan explained, taking matters in a strictly logical order of importance, as was his habit. 'He requires a white stallion, in order that he shall discover and destroy a succubus. Someone has told him that you possess such a horse,' he concluded, frowning at the temerity of whoever had been bandying such information.

'A succubus?' Grey asked, automatically rearranging the logical order of this speech, as was *his* habit.

Herr Blomberg had no English, but evidently recognized the word, for he nodded vigorously, his old-fashioned wig bobbing, and launched into impassioned speech, accompanied by much gesticulation.

With Stephan's assistance, Grey gathered that the town of Gurgelwitz had recently suffered a series of mysterious and disturbing events, involving a number of men who claimed to have been victimized in their sleep by a young woman of demonic aspect. By the time these events had made their way to the attention of Herr Blomberg, the situation was serious; a man had died.

'Unfortunately,' Stephan added, still in English, 'the dead man is ours.' He pressed his lips tightly together, conveying his dislike of the situation.

'Ours?' Grey asked, unsure what this usage implied, other than that the victim had been a soldier.

'Mine,' Stephan clarified, looking further displeased. 'One of the Prussians.'

The Landgrave von Erdberg had three hundred Schwabian foot-troops, raised from his own lands, equipped and funded from his personal fortune. In addition, Captain von Namtzen commanded two additional companies of Prussian horse, and was in temporary command of the fragments of an artillery company whose officers had all died in an outbreak of the bloody flux.

Grey wished to hear more details regarding both the immediate death and – most particularly – the demoniac visitations, but his questions along these lines were interrupted by Herr Blomberg, who had been growing more restive by the moment.

'It grows soon dark,' the buergermeister pointed out in German. 'We do not wish to fall into an open grave, so wet as it is.'

'*Ein offnen Grab*?' Grey repeated, feeling a sudden chill draught on the back of his neck.

'This is true,' Stephan said, with a nod of moody acquiescence. 'It would be a terrible thing if your horse were to break his leg; he is a splendid creature. Come then, let us go.'

'What *is* a s-succubus, me lord?' Tom Byrd's teeth were chattering, mostly from chill. The sun had long since set, and it was raining much harder. Grey could feel the wet seeping through the shoulders of his officer's greatcoat; Byrd's thin jacket was already soaked through, pasted to the young valet's stubby torso like butcher's paper round a joint of beef.

'I believe it is a sort of female . . . spirit,' Grey said, carefully avoiding the more evocative term 'demon'. The churchyard gates yawned before them like open jaws, and the darkness beyond seemed sinister in the extreme. No need to terrify the boy unnecessarily.

'Horses don't like ghosts,' Byrd said, sounding truculent. 'Everybody knows that, me lord.'

He wrapped his arms round himself, shivering, and huddled closer to Karolus, who shook his mane as though in agreement, showering water liberally over both Grey and Byrd.

'Surely you don't believe in ghosts, Tom?' Grey said, trying to be jocularly reassuring. He swiped a strand of wet fair hair out of his face, wishing Stephan would hurry.

''Tisn't a matter what *I* don't believe in, me lord,' Byrd replied. 'What if this lady's ghost believes in *us*? Who is she, anyway?' The lantern he carried was sputtering fitfully in the wet, despite its shield. Its dim light failed to illumine more than a vague outline of boy and horse, but perversely caught the shine of their eyes, lending them a disturbingly supernatural appearance, like staring wraiths.

Grey glanced aside, keeping an eye out for Stephan and the Buergermeister, who had gone to assemble a digging party. There was some movement outside the tavern, just visible at the far end of the street. That was sensible of Stephan. Men with a fair amount of beer on board were much more likely to be enthusiastic about the current prospect than were sober ones.

'Well, I do not believe that it is precisely a matter of ghosts,' he said. 'The German belief, however, seems to be that the succubus . . . er . . . the feminine spirit . . . may possess the body of a recently dead person, however.'

Tom cast a look into the inky depths of the churchyard, and glanced back at Grey.

'Oh?' he said.

'Ah,' Grey replied.

Byrd pulled the slouch hat low on his forehead and hunched his collar up round his ears, clutching the horse's halter-rope close to his chest. Nothing of his round face now showed save a downturned mouth, but that was eloquent.

Karolus stamped one foot and shifted his weight, tossing his head a little. He didn't seem to mind either rain or churchyard, but was growing restive. Grey patted the stallion's thick neck, taking comfort from the solid feel of the cold firm hide and massive body. Karolus turned his head and blew hot breath affectionately into his ear.

'Almost ready,' he said soothingly, twining a fist in the horse's soggy mane. 'Now, Tom. When Captain von Namtzen arrives with his men, you and Karolus will walk forward very slowly. You are to lead him back and forth across the churchyard. Keep a few feet in front of him, but leave some slack in the rope.'

The point of this procedure, of course, was to keep Karolus from stumbling over a gravestone or falling into any open graves, by allowing Tom to do it first. Ideally, Grey had been given to understand, the horse should be turned into the churchyard and allowed to wander over the graves at his own will, but neither he nor Stephan was willing to risk Karolus's valuable legs in the dark.

He had suggested waiting until the morning, but Herr Blomberg was insistent. The succubus must be found, without delay. Grey was more than curious to hear the details of the attacks, but had so far been told little more than that a Private Koenig had been found dead in the barracks, the body bearing marks that made his manner of death clear. What marks? Grey wondered.

Classically educated, he had read of succubi and incubi, but had been taught to regard such references as quaintly superstitious, of a piece with other medieval Popish nonsense like saints who strolled about with their heads in their hands or statues of the Virgin whose tears healed the sick. His father had been a rationalist, an observer of the ways of nature and a firm believer in the logic of phenomena.

His two months' acquaintance with the Schwabians, though, had shown him that they were deeply superstitious; more so even than the English common soldiers. Even Stephan kept a small, carved image of some pagan deity about his person at all times, to guard against being struck by lightning, and the Prussians seemed to harbour similar notions, judging from Herr Blomberg's behaviour.

The digging party was making its way up the street now, bright with sputtering torches and emitting snatches of song. Karolus snorted and pricked his ears; Karolus, Grey had been told, was fond of parades.

'Well, then.' Stephan loomed suddenly out of the murk at his side, looking pleased with himself under the broad shelf of his slouch hat. 'All is ready, Major?'

'Yes. Go ahead then, Tom.'

The diggers – mostly labourers, armed with spades, hoes and mattocks – stood back, lurching tipsily and stepping on each others' shoes. Tom, lantern held delicately before him in the manner of an insect's feeler, took several steps forward – then stopped. He turned, tugging on the rope.

Karolus stood solidly, declining to move.

'I told you, me lord,' Byrd said, sounding more cheerful. 'Horses don't like ghosts. Me uncle had an old carthorse once, wouldn't take a step past a churchyard. We had to take him clear round two streets to get him past.'

Stephan made a noise of disgust.

'It is not a ghost,' he said, striding forward, prominent chin held high. 'It is a succubus. A demon. That is quite different.'

'*Daemon?*' one of the diggers said, catching the English word and looking suddenly dubious. '*Ein Teufel?*'

'Demon?' said Tom Byrd, and gave Grey a look of profound betrayal.

'Something of the kind, I believe,' Grey said, and coughed. 'If such a thing should exist, which I doubt it does.'

A chill of uncertainty seemed to have overtaken the party with this demonstration of the horse's reluctance. There was shuffling and murmuring, and heads turned to glance back in the direction of the tavern.

Stephan, magnificently disregarding this tendency to pusillanimity in his troops, clapped Karolus on the neck and spoke to him encouragingly in German. The horse snorted and arched his neck, but still resisted Tom Byrd's tentative yanks on his halter. Instead, he swivelled his enormous head towards Grey, jerking Byrd off his feet. The boy lost his grip on the rope, staggered off-balance, trying vainly to keep hold of the lantern, and finally slipped on a stone submerged in the mud, landing on his buttocks with a rude splat.

This mishap had the salutary effect of causing the diggers to roar with laughter, restoring their spirits. Several of the torches had by now been extinguished by the rain, and everyone was thoroughly wet, but goatskin flasks and pottery jugs were produced from a number of pockets and offered to Tom Byrd by way of restorative, being then passed round the company in sociable fashion.

Grey took a deep swig of the fiery plum liquor himself, handed back the jug, and came to a decision.

'I'll ride him.'

Before Stephan could protest, Grey had taken a firm grip on Karolus's mane and swung himself up on the stallion's broad back. Karolus appeared to find Grey's familiar weight soothing; the broad white ears, which had been pointing to either side in suspicion, rose upright again, and the horse started forward willingly enough at Grey's nudge against his sides.

Tom, too, seemed heartened, and ran to pick up the trailing halter-rope. There was a ragged cheer from the diggers, and the party moved awkwardly after them, through the yawning gates.

It seemed much darker in the churchyard than it had looked from outside. Much quieter, too; the jokes and chatter of the men died away into an uneasy silence, broken only by an occasional curse as someone knocked against a tombstone in the dark. Grey could hear the patter of rain on the brim of his hat, and the suck and thump of Karolus's hooves as he plodded obediently through the mud.

He strained his eyes to see what lay ahead, beyond the feeble circle of light cast by Tom's lantern. It was black-dark, and he felt cold, despite the shelter of his greatcoat. The damp was rising, mist coming up out of the ground; he could see wisps of it purling away from Tom's boots, disappearing in the lantern-light. More of it drifted in an eerie fog round the mossy tombstones of neglected graves, leaning like rotted teeth in their sockets.

The notion, as it had been explained to him, was that a white stallion had the power to detect the presence of the supernatural. The horse would stop at the grave of the succubus, which could then be opened, and steps taken to destroy the creature.

Grey found a number of logical assumptions wanting in this proposal, chief among which – putting aside the question of the existence of succubi, and why a sensible horse should choose to have anything to do with one – was that Karolus was not choosing his own path. Tom was doing his best to keep slack in the rope, but as long as he held it, the horse was plainly going to follow him.

On the other hand, he reflected, Karolus was unlikely to stop anywhere, so long as Tom kept walking. That being true, the end result of this exercise would be merely to cause them all to miss their suppers and to render them thoroughly wet and chilled. Still, he supposed they would be still more wet and chilled, if obliged actually to open graves and perform whatever ritual might follow –

A hand clamped itself on his calf, and he bit his tongue – luckily, as it kept him from crying out.

'You are all right, Major?' It was Stephan, looming up beside him, tall and dark in a woollen cloak. He had left aside his plumed helmet, and wore a soft-brimmed wide hat against the rain, which made him look both less impressive and more approachable.

'Certainly,' Grey said, mastering his temper. 'How long must we do this?'

Von Namtzen lifted one shoulder in a shrug.

'Until the horse stops, or until Herr Blomberg is satisfied.'

'Until Herr Blomberg begins wanting his supper, you mean.' He could hear the buergermeister's voice at a distance behind them, lifted in exhortation and reassurance.

A white plume of breath floated out from under the brim of von Namtzen's hat, the laugh behind it barely audible.

'He is more . . . resolute? . . . than you might suppose. It is his duty, the welfare of the village. He will endure as long as you will, I assure you.'

Grey pressed his bitten tongue against the roof of his mouth, to prevent any injudicious remarks.

Stephan's hand was still curled about his leg, just above the edge of his boot. Cold as it was, he felt no warmth from the grasp, but the pressure of the big hand was both a comfort and something more.

'The horse – he goes well, *nicht wahr?*'

'He is wonderful,' Grey said, with complete sincerity. 'I thank you again.'

Von Namtzen flicked his free hand in dismissal, but made a pleased sound, deep in his throat. He had – against Grey's protests – insisted upon making the stallion a gift to Grey, 'in token of our alliance and our friendship', he had said firmly, clapping Grey upon both shoulders and then seizing him in fraternal embrace, kissing him formally upon both cheeks and mouth. At least Grey was obliged to consider it a fraternal embrace, unless and until circumstance might prove it otherwise.

But Stephan's hand still curled round his calf, hidden under the skirt of his greatcoat.

Grey glanced towards the squat bulk of the church, a black mass that loomed beyond the churchyard.

'I am surprised that the minister is not with us. Does he disapprove of this – excursion?'

'The minister is dead. A fever of some kind, *ein flus*, more than a month since. They will send another, from Strausberg, but he has not come yet.' Little wonder; a large number of French troops lay between Strausberg and the town; travel would be difficult, if not impossible.

'I see.' Grey glanced back over his shoulder. The diggers had paused to open a fresh jug, torches tilting in momentary distraction.

'Do you believe in this – this succubus?' he asked, careful to keep his voice low.

Rather to his surprise, von Namtzen didn't reply at once. At last, the Schwabian took a deep breath and hunched his broad shoulders in a gesture not quite a shrug.

'I have seen . . . strange things from time to time,' von Namtzen said at last, very quietly. 'In this country, particularly. And a man is dead, after all.'

The hand on his leg squeezed briefly and dropped away, sending a small flutter of sensation up Grey's back.

He took a deep breath of cold, heavy air, tinged with smoke, and coughed. It was like the smell of grave-dirt, he thought, and then wished the thought had not occurred to him.

'One thing I confess I do not quite understand,' he said, straightening himself in the saddle. 'A succubus is a demon, if I am not mistaken. How is it, then, that such a creature should take refuge in a churchyard, in consecrated ground?'

'Oh,' von Namtzen said, sounding surprised that this was not obvious. 'The succubus takes possession of the body of a dead person, and rests within it by day. Such a person must of course be a corrupt and wicked sort, filled perhaps with depravity and perversion. So that even within the churchyard, the succubus suitable refuge will find.'

'How recently must the person have died?' Grey asked. Surely it would make their perambulations more efficient, were they to go directly to the more recent graves. From the little he could see in the swaying light of Tom's lanterns, most of the stones nearby had stood where they were for decades, if not centuries.

'That I do not know,' von Namtzen admitted. 'Some people say that the body itself rises with the succubus; others say that the body remains in the grave, and by night the demon rides the air as a dream, seeking men in their sleep.'

Tom Byrd's figure was indistinct in the gathering fog, but Grey saw his shoulders rise, nearly touching the brim of his hat. He coughed again, and cleared his throat.

'I see. And . . . er . . . what, precisely, do you intend to do, should a suitable body be located?'

Here von Namtzen was on surer ground.

'Oh, that is simple,' he assured Grey. 'We will open the coffin, and drive an iron rod through the corpse's heart. Herr Blomberg has brought one.'

Tom Byrd made an inarticulate noise, which Grey thought it wiser to ignore.

'I see,' he said. His nose had begun to run with the cold, and he wiped it on his sleeve. At least he no longer felt hungry.

They paced for a little in silence. The buergermeister had fallen silent, too, though the distant sounds of squelching and glugging behind them indicated that the digging party was loyally persevering, with the aid of more brandy.

'The dead man,' Grey said at last. 'Private Koenig. Where was he found? And you mentioned marks upon the body – what sort of marks?'

Von Namtzen opened his mouth to answer, but was forestalled. Karolus glanced suddenly to the side, nostrils flaring. Then he flung up his head with a great *Harrumph!* of startlement, nearly hitting Grey in the face. At the same moment, Tom Byrd uttered a high, thin scream, dropped the rope, and ran.

The big horse flexed his hindquarters, slewed round and took off, leaping a small stone angel that stood in his path; Grey saw it as a looming pale blur, but had no time to worry about it before it passed beneath the stallion's outstretched hooves, its stone mouth gaping as though in astonishment.

Lacking reins and unable to seize the halter-rope, Grey had no recourse but to grip the stallion's mane in both hands, clamp his knees, and stick like a burr. There were shouts and screams behind him, but he had no attention to spare for anything but the wind in his ears and the elemental force between his thighs.

They bounded like a skipping cannonball through the dark, striking the ground and rocketing upwards, seeming to cover leagues at a stride. He leaned low and held on, the stallion's mane whipping like stinging nettles across his face, the horse's breath loud in his ears – or was it his own?

Through streaming eyes, he glimpsed light flickering in the distance, and realized they were heading now for the village. There was a six-foot stone wall in the way; he could only hope the horse noticed it in time.

He did; Karolus skidded to a stop, divots of mud and withered grass shooting up around him, sending Grey lurching up on to his neck. The horse reared, came down, then turned sharply, trotted several yards, and slowed to a walk, shaking his head as though to try and free himself of the flapping rope.

Legs quivering as with ague, Grey slid off, and with cold-stiff fingers, grasped the rope.

'You big white *bastard*,' he said, filled with the joy of survival, and laughed. 'You're bloody marvellous!'

Karolus took this compliment with tolerant grace, and shoved at him, whickering softly. The horse seemed largely over his fright, whatever had caused it; he could but hope Tom Byrd fared as well.

Grey leaned against the wall, panting until his breath came back and his heart slowed a bit. The exhilaration of the ride was still with him, but he had now a moment's heed to spare for other things.

At the far side of the churchyard, the torches were clustered close together, lighting the fog with a reddish glow. He could see the digging party, standing in a knot shoulder to shoulder, all in attitudes of the most extreme interest. And towards him, a tall black figure came through the mist, silhouetted by the torch-glow behind him. He had a moment's turn, for the figure looked sinister, dark cloak swirling about him – but it was, of course, merely Captain von Namtzen.

'Major Grey!' von Namtzen called. 'Major Grey!'

'Here!' Grey shouted, finding breath. The figure altered course slightly, hurrying towards him with long, stilted strides that zigged and zagged to avoid obstacles in the path. How in God's name had Karolus managed on that ground, he wondered, without breaking a leg or both their necks?

'Major Grey,' Stephan said, grasping both his hands tightly. 'John. You are all right?'

'Yes,' he said, gripping back. 'Yes, of course. What has happened? My valet – Mr Byrd – is he all right?'

'He has into a hole fallen, but he is not hurt. We have found a body. A dead man.'

Grey felt a sudden lurch of the heart.

'What –'

'Not in a grave,' the Captain hastened to assure him. 'Lying on the ground, leaning against one of the tombstones. Your valet saw the corpse's face most suddenly in the light of his lantern, and was frightened.'

'I am not surprised. Is he one of yours?'

'No. One of yours.'

'What?' Grey stared up at the Schwabian. Stephan's face was no more than a dark oval in the dark. He squeezed Grey's hands gently and let them go.

'An English soldier. You will come?'

He nodded, feeling the cold air heavy in his chest. It was not impossible; there were English regiments to the north and to the south of the town, no more than an hour's ride away. Men off-duty would often come into town in search of drink, dice and women. It was, after all, the reason for his own presence here – to act as liaison between the English regiments and their German allies.

The body was less horrible in appearance than he might have supposed; while plainly dead, the man seemed quite peaceful, slumped half-sitting against the knee of a stern stone matron holding a book. There was no blood nor wound apparent, and yet Grey felt his stomach clench with shock.

'You know him?' Stephan was watching him intently, his own face stern and clean as those of the stone memorials about them.

'Yes.' Grey knelt by the body. 'I spoke to him only a few hours ago.'

He put the backs of his fingers delicately against the dead man's throat – the slack flesh was clammy, slick with rain, but still warm. Unpleasantly warm. He glanced down, and saw that Private Bodger's breeches were opened, the stuff of his shirt-tail sticking out, rumpled over the man's thighs.

'Does he still have his dick, or did the she-thing eat it?' said a low voice in German. A faint, shocked snigger ran through the men. Grey pressed his lips tight together and jerked up the soggy shirt-tail. Private Bodger was somewhat more than intact, he was glad to see. So were the diggers; there was an audible sigh of mass relief behind him.

Grey stood, conscious all at once of tiredness and hunger, and of the rain pattering on his back.

'Wrap him in a canvas; bring him . . .' Where? The dead man must be returned to his own regiment, but not tonight. 'Bring him to the Schloss. Tom? Show them the way; ask the gardener to find you a suitable shed.'

'Yes, me lord.' Tom Byrd was nearly as pale as the dead man, and covered with mud, but once more in control of himself. 'Will I take the horse, me lord? Or will you ride him?'

Grey had forgotten entirely about Karolus, and looked blankly about. Where had he gone?

One of the diggers had evidently caught the word 'horse', and understood it, for a murmur of *'Das Pferd'* rippled through the group, and the men began to look round, lifting the torches high and craning their necks.

One man gave an excited shout, pointing into the dark. A large white blur stood a little distance away.

'He's on a grave! He's standing still! He's found it!'

This caused a stir of sudden excitement; everyone pressed forwards together, and Grey feared lest the horse should take alarm and run again.

No such danger; Karolus was absorbed in nibbling at the soggy remnants of several wreaths, piled at the foot of an imposing tombstone. This stood guard over a small group of family graves – one very recent, as the wreaths and raw earth showed. As the torchlight fell upon the scene, Grey could easily read the name chiselled black into the stone.

'BLOMBERG,' it read.

2
But What, Exactly, Does a Succubus *Do?*

They found Schloss Lowenstein alight with candles and welcoming fires, despite the late hour of their return. They were far past the time for dinner, but there was food in abundance on the sideboard, and Grey and von Namtzen refreshed themselves thoroughly, interrupting their impromptu feast periodically to give particulars of the evening's adventures to the house's other inhabitants, who were agog with curiosity.

'No! Herr Blomberg's *mother*?' The Princess von Lowenstein pressed fingers to her mouth, eyes wide in delighted shock. 'Old Agathe? I don't believe it!'

'Nor does Herr Blomberg,' von Namtzen assured her, reaching for a leg of roast pheasant. 'He was most . . . vehement?' He turned towards Grey, eyebrows raised, then turned back to the Princess, nodding with assurance. 'Vehement.'

He had been. Grey would have chosen 'apoplectic' as the better description, but was reasonably sure that none of the Germans present would know the term, and had no idea how to translate it. They were all speaking English, as a courtesy to the British officers present, who included a Captain of Horse named Billman, Colonel Sir Peter Hicks and a Lieutenant Dundas, a young Scottish officer in charge of an ordnance survey party.

'The old woman was a saint, absolutely a saint!' protested the Dowager Princess Lowenstein, crossing herself piously. 'I do not believe it, I cannot!'

The younger Princess cast a brief glance at her mother-in-law, then away – meeting Grey's eyes. The Princess had bright blue eyes, all the brighter for candlelight, brandy – and mischief.

The Princess was a widow of a year's standing. Grey judged from the large portrait over the mantelpiece in the drawing room that the late Prince had been roughly thirty years older than his wife; she bore her loss bravely.

'Dear me,' she said, contriving to look winsome, despite her anxiety. 'As if the French were not enough! Now we are to be threatened with nightmare demons?'

'Oh, you will be quite safe, madam, I assure you,' Sir Peter assured her. 'What-what? With so many gallant gentlemen in the house?'

The ancient Dowager glanced at Grey, and said something about gentlemen in highly accented German that Grey didn't quite catch, but the Princess flushed like a peony in bloom, and von Namtzen, within earshot, choked on a swallow of wine.

Captain Billman smote the Schwabian helpfully on the back.

'Is there news of the French?' Grey asked, thinking that perhaps the conversation should be guided back to more earthly concerns before the party retired to bed.

'Look to be a few of the bastards, milling round,' Billman said casually, cutting his eyes at the women in a manner suggesting that the word 'few' was a highly discreet euphemism. 'Expect they'll be moving on, heading for the west within a day or so.'

Or heading for Strausberg, to join with the French regiment reported there, Grey thought. He returned Billman's meaningful look. Gurgelwitz lay in the bottom of a river valley – directly between the French and Strausberg.

'So,' Billman said, changing the subject with a heavy jocularity, 'your succubus got away, did she?'

Von Namtzen cleared his throat.

'I would not say that, particularly,' he said. 'Herr Blomberg refused to allow the men to disturb the grave, of course, but I have men ordered to guard it.'

'That'll be popular duty, I shouldn't think,' said Sir Peter, with a glance at a nearby window, where even several thicknesses of silk and woollen draperies and heavy shutters failed to muffle the thrum of rain and occasional distant boom of thunder.

'A good idea,' one of the German officers said, in heavily accented but very correct English. 'We do not wish to have rumours fly about, that there is a succubus behaving badly in the vicinity of the soldiers.'

'But what, exactly, does a succubus *do*?' the Princess inquired, looking expectantly from face to face.

There was a sudden massive clearing of throats and gulping of wine, as all the men present tried to avoid her eye. A explosive snort from the Dowager indicated what *she* thought of this cowardly behaviour.

'A succubus is a she-demon,' the old lady said, precisely. 'It comes to men in dreams, and has congress with them, in order to extract from them their seed.'

The Princess's eyes went perfectly round. She *hadn't* known, Grey observed.

'Why?' she asked. 'What does she do with it? Demons do not give birth, do they?'

Grey felt a laugh trying to force its way up under his breastbone, and hastily took another drink.

'Well, no,' said Stephan von Namtzen, somewhat flushed, but still self-possessed. 'Not exactly. The succubus procures the . . . er . . . essence,' he gave a slight bow of apology to the Dowager at this, 'and then will mate with an incubus – this being a male demon, you see?'

The old lady looked grim, and placed a hand upon the religious medal she wore pinned to her gown.

Von Namtzen took a deep breath, seeing that everyone was hanging upon his words, and fixed his gaze upon the portrait of the late Prince.

'The incubus then will seek out a human woman by night, couple with her, and impregnate her with the stolen seed – thus producing demon-spawn.'

Lieutenant Dundas, who was very young and likely a Presbyterian, looked as though he were being strangled by his stock. The other men, all rather red in the face, attempted to look as though they were entirely familiar with the phenomenon under discussion and thought little of it. The Dowager looked thoughtfully at her daughter-in-law, then upwards at the picture of her deceased son, eyebrows raised as though in silent conversation.

'Ooh!' Despite the late hour and the informality of the gathering, the Princess had a fan, which she spread now before her face in shock, big blue eyes wide above it. These eyes swung towards Grey, and blinked in pretty supplication.

'And do you really think, Lord John, that there is such a creature . . .' she shuddered, with an alluring quiver of the bosom, '. . . prowling near?'

Neither eyes nor bosom swayed him, and it was clear to him that the Princess found considerably more excitement than fear in the notion, but he smiled reassuringly, an Englishman secure in his rationality.

'No,' he said. 'I don't.'

As though in instant contradiction of this stout opinion, a blast of wind struck the Schloss, carrying with it a burst of hail that rattled off the shutters and fell hissing down the chimney. The thunder of the hailstorm upon roof and walls and outbuildings was so great that for a moment it drowned all possibility of conversation.

The party stood as though paralysed, listening to the roar of the elements. Grey's eyes met Stephan's; the Schwabian lifted his chin a little in defiance of the storm, and gave him a small, private smile. Grey smiled back, then glanced away – just in time to see a dark shape fall from the chimney and plunge into the flames with a piercing shriek.

The shriek was echoed at once by the women – and possibly by Lieutenant Dundas, though Grey could not quite swear to it.

Something was struggling in the fire, flapping and writhing, and the stink of scorched skin came sharp and acrid in the nose. Acting by sheer instinct, Grey seized a poker and swept the thing out of the fire and on to the hearth, where it skittered crazily, emitting sounds that pierced his eardrums.

Stephan lunged forward and stamped on the thing, putting an end to the unnerving display.

'A bat,' he said calmly, removing his boot. 'Take it away.'

The footman to whom he addressed this command came hastily,

and flinging a napkin over the blackened corpse, scooped it up and carried it out on a tray, this ceremonial disposal giving Grey a highly inappropriate vision of the bat making a second appearance at breakfast, roasted and garnished with stewed prunes.

A sudden silence had fallen upon the party. This was broken by the sudden chiming of the clock, which made everyone jump, then laugh nervously.

The party broke up, the men standing politely as the women withdrew, then pausing for a few moments' conversation as they finished their wine and brandy. With no particular sense of surprise, Grey found Sir Peter at his elbow.

'A word with you, Major?' Sir Peter said quietly.

'Of course, sir.'

The group had fragmented into twos and threes; it was not difficult to draw aside a little, under the pretext of examining a small, exquisite statue of Eros that stood on one of the tables.

'You'll be taking the body back to the 52nd in the morning, I expect?' The English officers had all had a look at Private Bodger, declaring that he was none of theirs; by elimination, he must belong to Colonel Ruysdale's 52nd Foot, presently encamped on the other side of Gurgelwitz.

Without waiting for Grey's nod, Sir Peter went on, touching the statue abstractedly.

'The French are up to something; had a scout's report this afternoon, great deal of movement among the troops. They're preparing to move, but we don't yet know where to or when. I should feel happier if a few more of Ruysdale's troops were to move to defend the bridge at Aschenwald, just in case.'

'I see,' Grey said cautiously. 'And you wish me to carry a message to that effect to Colonel Ruysdale.'

Sir Peter made a slight grimace.

'I've sent one. I think it might be helpful, though, if you were to suggest that von Namtzen wished it, as well.'

Grey made a noncommittal noise. It was common knowledge that Sir Peter and Ruysdale were not on good terms. The Colonel might well be more inclined to oblige a German ally.

'I will mention it to Captain von Namtzen,' he said, 'though I expect he will be agreeable.' He would have taken his leave then, but Sir Peter hesitated, indicating that there was something further.

'Sir?' Grey said.

'I think . . .' Sir Peter said, glancing round and lowering his voice still further, '. . . that perhaps the Princess should be advised – cautiously; no need to give alarm – that there is some slight possibility . . . if the French *were* in fact to cross the valley . . .' He rested a hand thoughtfully upon the head of Eros, and glanced at the other furnishings of the room, which included a number of rare and costly items. 'She might wish to withdraw her family to a place of safety. Not amiss to suggest a few things be put safely away in the meantime. Shouldn't like to see a thing like that decorating a French general's desk, eh?'

'That' was the skull of an enormous bear – an ancient cave-bear, the Princess had informed the party earlier – that stood by itself upon a small, draped table. The skull was covered with gold, hammered flat and etched in primitive designs, with a row of semi-precious stones running up the length of the snout, then diverging to encircle the empty eye sockets. It was a striking object.

'Yes,' Grey said, 'I quite . . . oh. You wish me to speak with the Princess?'

Sir Peter relaxed a little, having accomplished his goal.

'She seems quite taken by you, Grey,' he said, his original joviality returning. 'Advice might be better received from you, eh? Besides, you're a liaison, aren't you?'

'To be sure,' Grey said, less than pleased, but aware that he had received a direct order. 'I shall attend to it as soon as I may, sir.' He took leave of the others remaining in the drawing room, and made his way to the staircase that led to the upper floors.

The Princess von Lowenstein *did* seem most taken with him; he wasn't surprised that Sir Peter had noticed her smiles and languishings. Fortunately, she seemed equally taken with Stephan von Namtzen, going so far as to have Maulthausen, a sort of spicy Schwabian dumpling, served regularly at dinner in his honour.

At the top of the stair, he hesitated. There were three corridors opening off the landing, and it always took a moment to be sure which of the stone-floored halls led to his own chamber. A flicker of movement to the left attracted his eye, and he turned that way, to see someone dodge out of sight behind a tall armoire that stood against the wall.

'*Wo ist das?*' he asked sharply, and got a stifled gasp in reply.

Moving cautiously, he went and peered round the edge of the armoire, to find a small, dark-haired boy pressed against the wall, both hands clasped over his mouth and eyes round as saucers. The boy wore a nightshirt and cap, and had plainly escaped from his nursery. He recognized the child, though he had seen him only once or twice before; it was the Princess's young son – what was the boy's name? Heinrich? Reinhardt?

'Don't be afraid,' he said gently to the boy, in his slow, careful German. 'I am your mother's friend. Where is your room?'

The boy didn't reply, but his eyes flicked down the hallway and back. Grey saw no open doors, but held out a hand to the boy.

'It is very late,' he said. 'Shall we find your bed?'

The boy shook his head so hard that the tassel of his nightcap slapped against the wall.

'I don't want to go to bed. There is a bad woman there. *Eine Hexe.*'

'A witch?' Grey repeated, and felt an odd *frisson* run down his back, as though someone had touched his nape with a cold finger. 'What did this witch look like?'

The child stared back at him, uncomprehending.

'Like a witch,' he said.

'Oh,' said Grey, momentarily stymied. He rallied, though, and beckoned, curling his fingers at the boy. 'Come, then; show me. I am a soldier, I am not afraid of a witch.'

'You will kill her and cut out her heart and fry it over the fire?' the boy asked eagerly, peeling himself off the wall. He reached out to touch the hilt of Grey's dagger, still on his belt.

'Well, perhaps,' Grey temporized. 'Let us go and find her first.' He picked the boy up under the arms and swung him up; the child came willingly enough, curling his legs around Grey's waist and cuddling close to him for warmth.

The hallway was dark; only a rush-light sputtered in a sconce near the farther end, and the stones emanated a chill that made the child's own warmth more than welcome. Rain was still coming down hard; a small dribble of moisture had seeped in through the shutters at the end of the hall, and the flickering light shone on the puddle.

Thunder boomed in the distance, and the child threw his arms around Grey's neck with a gasp.

'It is all right.' Grey patted the small back soothingly, though his own heart had leapt convulsively at the sound. No doubt the noise of the storm had wakened the boy.

'Where is your chamber?'

'Upstairs.' The boy pointed vaguely towards the far end of the hallway; presumably there were back stairs somewhere near. The Schloss was immense and sprawling; Grey had learned no more of its geography than what was necessary to reach his own quarters. He hoped that the boy knew the place better, so they were not obliged to wander the chilly hallways all night.

As he approached the end of the hall, the lightning flashed again, a vivid line of white that outlined the window – and showed him clearly that the window was open, the shutters unfastened. With the boom of thunder came a gust of wind, and one loose shutter flung back suddenly, admitting a freezing gust of rain.

'Oooh!' The boy clutched him tightly round the neck, nearly choking him.

'It is all right,' he said, as calmly as possible, shifting his burden in order to free one hand.

He leaned out to seize the shutter, trying at the same time to shelter the boy with his body. A soundless flash lit up the world in a burst of black and white, and he blinked, dazzled, a pinwheel of stark images whirling at the back of his eyes. Thunder rolled past, with a sound so like an oxcart full of stones that he glanced up, involuntarily, half-expecting to see one of the old German gods go past, driving gleefully through the clouds.

The image he saw was not of the storm-tossed sky, though, but of something seen when the lightning flashed. He blinked hard, clearing his sight, and then looked down. It *was* there. A ladder, leaning against the wall of the house. Well, then. Perhaps the child *had* seen someone strange in his room.

'Here,' he said to the boy, turning to set him down. 'Stay out of the rain while I fasten the shutter.'

He turned back, and leaning out into the storm, pushed the ladder off, so that it fell away into the dark. Then he closed and fastened the shutters, and picked up the shivering boy again. The wind had blown out the rush-light, and he was obliged to feel his way into the turning of the hall.

'It's very dark,' said the boy, with a tremor in his voice.

'Soldiers are not afraid of the dark,' he reassured the child, thinking of the graveyard.

'I'm not afraid!' The little boy's cheek was pressed against his neck.

'Of course you are not. How are you called, young sir?' he asked, in hopes of distracting the boy.

'Siggy.'

'Siggy,' he repeated, feeling his way along the wall with one hand. 'I am John. Johannes, in your tongue.'

'I know,' said the boy, surprising him. 'The servant-girls think you are good-looking. Not so big as Landgrave Stephan, but prettier. Are you rich? The Landgrave is very rich.'

'I won't starve,' Grey said, wondering how long the blasted hallway was, and whether he might discover the staircase by falling down it in the dark.

At least the boy seemed to have lost some of his fear; he cuddled close, rubbing his head under Grey's chin. There was a distinct smell about him; nothing unpleasant – rather like the smell of a month-old litter of puppies, Grey thought; warmly animal.

Something occurred to him, then; something he should have thought to ask at once.

'Where is your nurse?' A boy of this age would surely not sleep alone.

'I don't know. Maybe the witch ate her.'

This cheering suggestion coincided with a welcome flicker of light in the distance, and the sound of voices. Hastening towards these, Grey at last found the nursery stairs, just as a wild-eyed woman in nightgown, cap and shawl popped out, holding a pottery candle-stick.

'Siegfried!' she cried. 'Master Siggy, where have you been? What has – oh!' At this point, she realized that Grey was there, and reared back as though struck forcefully in the chest.

'*Guten Abend, Madam,*' he said, politely. 'Is this your nurse, Siggy?'

'No,' said Siggy, scornful of such ignorance. 'That's just Hetty. Mama's maid.'

'Siggy? Siegfried, is it you? Oh, my boy, my boy!' The light from above dimmed as a fluttering body hurtled down the stairs, and the Princess von Lowenstein seized the boy from his arms, hugging her son and kissing him so passionately that his nightcap fell off.

More servants were coming downstairs, less precipitously. Two footmen and a woman who might be a parlour-maid, all in varying degrees of undress, but equipped with candles or rush-lights. Evidently, Grey had had the good fortune to encounter a search party.

There was a good deal of confused conversation, as Grey's attempt at explanation was interrupted by Siggy's own rather disjointed account of his adventures, punctuated by exclamations of horror and surprise from the Princess and Hetty.

'Witch?' the Princess was saying, looking down at her son in alarm. 'You saw a witch? Did you have an evil dream, child?'

'No. I just woke up and there was a witch in my room. Can I have some marzipan?'

'Perhaps it would be a good idea to search the house,' Grey managed to get in. 'It is possible that the . . . witch . . . is still inside.'

The Princess had very fine, pale skin, radiant in the candlelight, but at this, it went a sickly colour, like toadstools. Grey glanced meaningfully at Siggy, and the Princess at once gave the child to Hetty, telling the maid to take him to his nursery.

'Tell me what is happening,' she said, gripping Grey's arm, and he did, finishing the account with a question of his own.

'The child's nurse? Where is she?'

'We don't know. I went to the nursery to look at Siegfried before retiring –' the Princess's hand fluttered to her bosom, as she became aware that she was wearing a rather unbecoming woollen nightgown and cap, with a heavy shawl and thick, fuzzy stockings. 'He wasn't there; neither was the nurse. Jakob, Thomas –' She turned to the footmen, suddenly taking charge. 'Search! The house first, then the grounds.'

A distant rumbling of thunder reminded everyone that it was still pouring with rain outside, but the footmen vanished with speed.

The sudden silence left in the wake of their departure gave Grey a slightly eerie feeling, as though the thick stone walls had moved subtly closer. A solitary candle burned, left behind on the stairs.

'Who would do this?' said the Princess, her voice suddenly small and frightened. 'Did they mean to take Siegfried? Why?'

It looked very much to Grey as though kidnapping had been the plan; no other possibility had entered his mind, until the Princess seized him by the arm again.

'Do you think – do you think it was . . . her?' she whispered, eyes dilated to pools of horror. 'The succubus?'

'I think not,' Grey said, taking hold of her hands for reassurance. They were cold as ice – hardly surprising, in view of the temperature inside the Schloss. He smiled at her, squeezing her fingers gently. 'A succubus would not require a ladder, surely?' He forbore to add that a boy of Siggy's age was unlikely to have much that a succubus would want, if he had correctly understood the nature of such a creature.

A little colour came back into the Princess's face, as she saw the logic in this.

'No, that's true.' The edge of her mouth twitched, in an attempt at a smile, though her eyes were still fearful.

'It might be advisable to set a guard near your son's room,' Grey suggested. 'Though I expect the . . . person . . . has been frightened off by now.'

She shuddered, whether from cold, or at the thought of roving intruders, he couldn't tell. Still, she was clearly steadier at the thought of action, and that being so, he rather reluctantly took the opportunity to share with her Sir Peter Hicks's cautions, feeling that perhaps a solid enemy such as the French would be preferable to phantasms and shadowy threats.

'Ha, those frog-eaters,' she said, proving his supposition by drawing herself up with a touch of scorn in her voice. 'They have tried before, the Schloss to take. They have never done it; they will not do it now.' She gestured briefly at the stone walls surrounding them, by way of justification in this opinion. 'My husband's great-great-great-grandfather built the Schloss; we have a well inside the house, a stable, food-stores. This place was built to withstand siege.'

'I am sure you are right,' Grey said, smiling. 'But you will perhaps take some care?' He let go of her hands, willing her to draw the interview to a close. Excitement over, he was very much aware that it had been a long day, and that he was freezing.

'I will,' she promised him. She hesitated a moment, not quite sure how to take her leave gracefully, then stepped forward, rose on to her toes, and with her hands on his shoulders, kissed him on the mouth.

'Good night, Lord John,' she said softly, in English. '*Danke.*' She turned and hurried up the stairs, picking up her skirts as she went.

Grey stood for a startled moment looking after her, the disconcerting feel of her uncorseted breasts still imprinted on his chest. Then he shook his head and went to pick up the candlestick she had left on the stair for him.

Straightening up, he was overtaken by a massive yawn, the fatigues of the day coming down upon him like a thousand-weight of grapeshot. He only hoped he could find his own chamber again, in this ancient labyrinth. Perhaps he should have asked the Princess for directions.

He made his way back down the hallway, his candle flame seeming puny and insignificant in the oppressive darkness cast by the great stone blocks of Schloss Lowenstein. It was only when the light gleamed on the puddle on the floor that the thought suddenly occurred to him: someone had to have opened the shutters – from the inside.

Grey made his way back as far as the head of the main stairs, only to find Stephan von Namtzen coming up them. The Schwabian was a little flushed with brandy, but still clear-headed, and listened to Grey's account of events with consternation.

'*Schmutzen!*' he said, and spat on the floor to emphasize his opinion of kidnappers. 'The servants are searching, you say – but you think they will find nothing?'

'Perhaps they will find the nurse,' Grey said. 'But if the kidnapper has an ally inside the house – and he must . . . or she, I suppose,' he added. 'The boy did say he saw a witch.'

'*Ja*, I see.' Von Namtzen looked grim. One big hand fisted at his side, but then relaxed. 'I will perhaps go and speak to the Princess. My men, I will have them come to guard the house. If there is a criminal within, he will not get out.'

'I'm sure the Princess will be grateful.' Grey felt all at once terribly tired. 'I must take Bodger – the body – back to his regiment in the morning. Oh – in that regard . . .' He explained Sir Peter's wishes, to which von Namtzen agreed with a flip of the hand.

'Have you any messages for me to carry, to the troops at the bridge?' Grey asked. 'Since I will be going in that direction, anyway.' One English regiment lay to the south of the town, the other – Bodger's – to the north, between the town and the river. A small group of the Prussian artillery under Stephan's command was stationed a few miles beyond, guarding the bridge at Aschenwald.

Von Namtzen frowned, thinking, then nodded.

'*Ja*, you are right. It is best they hear officially of the –' He looked suddenly uneasy, and Grey was slightly amused to see that Stephan did not want to speak the word 'succubus'.

'Yes, better to avoid rumours,' he agreed, saving Stephan's awkwardness. 'Speaking of that – do you suppose Herr Blomberg will let the villagers exhume his mother?'

Stephan's broad-boned face broke into a smile at that.

'No,' he said. 'I think he would make them drive an iron rod through his own heart, first. Better, though,' he added, the humour fading from his face, 'if someone finds who plays these tricks, and a stop to it makes. Quickly.'

Stephan was tired, too, Grey saw; his English grammar was slipping. They stood together for a moment, silent, listening to the distant hammer of the rain, both feeling still the chill touch of the graveyard in their bones.

Von Namtzen turned to him suddenly, and put a hand on his shoulder, squeezing.

'You will take care, John,' he said, and before Grey could speak or move, Stephan pulled him close and kissed his mouth. Then he smiled, squeezed Grey's shoulder once more, and with a quiet 'Guten Abend,' went up the stairs towards his own room.

Grey shut the door of his chamber behind him and leaned against it, in the manner of a man pursued. Tom Byrd, curled up asleep on the hearth-rug, sat up and blinked at him.

'Me lord?'

'Who else?' Grey asked, made jocular from the fatigues and excitements of the evening. 'Did you expect a visit from the succubus?'

Tom's face lost all its sleepiness at that, and he glanced uneasily at the window, closed and tightly shuttered against the dangers of the night.

'You oughtn't jest that way, me lord,' he said reproachfully. 'It's an Englishman what's dead now.'

'You are right, Tom; I beg pardon of Private Bodger.' Grey found some justice in the rebuke, but was too much overtaken by events to be stung by it. 'Still, we do not know the cause of his death. Surely there is no proof as yet that it was occasioned by any sort of supernatural interference. Have you eaten?'

'Yes, me lord. Cook had gone to bed, but she got up and fetched us out some bread and dripping, and some ale. Wanting to know all about what I found in the churchyard,' he added practically.

Grey smiled to himself; the faint emphasis on 'I' in this statement indicating to him that Tom's protests on behalf of the late Private Bodger sprang as much from a sense of proprietorship as from a sense of propriety.

Grey sat down, to let Tom pull off his boots and still damp stockings. The room he had been given was small, but warm and bright, the shadows from a well tended fire flickering over striped damask wallpaper. After the wet cold of the churchyard and the bleak chill of the Schloss's stone corridors, the heat upon his skin was a gratifying feeling – much enhanced by the discovery of a pitcher of hot water for washing.

'Shall I come with you, me lord? In the morning, I mean.' Tom undid the binding of Grey's hair and began to comb it, dipping the comb occasionally in a cologne of bay-leaves and chamomile, meant to discourage lice.

'No, I think not. I shall ride over and speak to Colonel Ruysdale first; one of the servants can follow me with the body.' Grey closed his eyes, beginning to feel drowsy, though small jolts of excitement still pulsed through his thighs and abdomen. 'If you would, Tom, I should like you to talk with the servants; find out what they are saying about things.' God knew, they would have plenty to talk about.

Clean, brushed, warmed and cosily ensconced in nightshirt, cap and banyan, Grey dismissed Tom, the valet's arms piled high with filthy uniform bits.

He shut the door behind the boy, and hesitated, staring into the polished surface of the wood as though to look through it and see who might be standing on the other side. Only the blur of his own face met his gaze, though, and only the creak of Tom's footsteps was audible, receding down the corridor.

Thoughtfully, he touched his lips with a finger. Then he sighed, and bolted the door.

Stephan had kissed him before – kissed innumerable people, for that matter, the man was an inveterate *embrasseur*. But surely this had been somewhat more than the fraternal embrace of a fellow soldier or particular friend. He could still feel the grip of Stephan's hand, curled around his leg. Or was he deluded by fatigue and distraction, imagining more to it than there was?

And if he were right?

He shook his head, took the warming-pan from his sheets, and crawled between them, reflecting that, of all the men in Gurgelwitz that night, he at least was safe from the attentions of any roving succubi.

3

A Remedy for Sleeplessness

Regimental headquarters for the 52nd were in Bonz, a small hamlet that stood some ten miles from Gurgelwitz. Grey found Colonel Ruysdale in the central room of the largest inn, in urgent conference with several other officers, and indisposed to take time to deal with an enlisted body.

'Grey? Oh, yes, know your brother. You found what? Where? Yes, all right. See, um . . . Sergeant-Major Sapp. Yes, that's it. Sapp will know who . . .' The Colonel waved a vague hand, indicating that Grey would doubtless find whatever assistance he required elsewhere.

'Yes, sir,' Grey said, settling his boot-heels into the sawdust. 'I shall do so directly. Am I to understand, though, that there are developments of which our allies should be informed?'

Ruysdale stared at him, eyes cold and upper lip foremost.

'Who told you that, sir?'

As though he needed telling. Troops were being mustered outside the village, drummers beating the call to arms and corporals shouting through the streets, men pouring out from their quarters like an anthill stirred with a stick.

'I am a liaison officer, sir, seconded to Captain von Namtzen's Schwabian foot,' Grey replied, evading the question. 'They are at present quartered in Gurgelwitz; will you require their support?'

Ruysdale looked grossly offended at the notion, but a captain wearing an artillery cockade coughed tactfully.

'Colonel, shall I give Major Grey such particulars of the situation as may seem useful? You have important matters to deal with . . .' He nodded round at the assembled officers, who seemed attentive, but hardly on the brink of action.

The Colonel snorted briefly and made a gesture somewhere between gracious dismissal and the waving away of some noxious insect, and Grey bowed, murmuring, 'Your servant, sir.'

Outside, the clouds of last night's storm were making a hasty exodus, scudding away on a fresh, cold wind. The artillery captain clapped a hand to his hat, and jerked his head towards a pot-house down the street.

'A bit of warmth, Major?'

Gathering that the village was in no danger of imminent invasion, Grey nodded, and accompanied his new companion into a dark, smoky womb, smelling of pigs' feet and fermented cabbage.

'Benjamin Hiltern,' the Captain said, putting back his cloak and holding up two fingers to the barman. 'You'll take a drink, Major?'

'John Grey. I thank you. I collect we shall have time to drink it, before we are quite overrun?'

Hiltern laughed, and sat down across from Grey, rubbing a knuckle under a cold-reddened nose.

'We should have time for our gracious host –' he nodded at the wizened creature fumbling with a jug, '– to hunt a boar, roast it, and serve it up with an apple in its mouth, if you should be so inclined.'

'I am obliged, Captain,' Grey said, with a glance at the barman, who upon closer inspection, appeared to have only one leg, the other being supported by a stout peg of battered aspect. 'Alas, I have breakfasted but recently.'

'Too bad. I haven't. *Bratkartoffeln mit Rührei*,' Hiltern said to the barman, who nodded and disappeared into some still more squalid den to the rear of the house. 'Potatoes, fried with eggs and ham,' he explained, taking out a kerchief and tucking it into the neck of his shirt. 'Delicious.'

'Quite,' Grey said politely. 'One would hope that your troops are fed as well, after the effort I saw being expended.'

'Oh, that.' Hiltern's cherubic countenance lost a little of its cheerfulness, but not much. 'Poor sods. At least it's stopped raining.'

In answer to Grey's raised brows, he explained.

'Punishment. There was a game of bowls yesterday, between a party of men from Colonel Bampton-Howard's lot and our lads – local form of skittles. Ruysdale had a heavy wager on with Bampton-Howard, see?'

'And your lot lost. Yes, I see. So your lads are –'

'Ten-mile run to the river and back, in full kit. Keep them fit and out of trouble, at least,' Hiltern said, half-closing his eyes and lifting his nose at the scent of frying potatoes that had begun to waft through the air.

'I see. One assumes that the French have moved, then? Our last intelligence reported them as being a few miles north of the river.'

'Yes, gave us a bit of excitement for a day or two; thought they might come this way. They seem to have sheered off, though – gone round to the west.'

'Why?' Grey felt a prickle of unease go down his spine. There was a bridge at Aschenwald, a logical crossing point – but there was another several miles north, at Gruneberg. The eastern bridge was defended by a company of Prussian artillery; a detachment of grenadiers, under Colonel Bampton-Howard, presumably held the western crossing.

'There's a mass of Frenchies beyond the river,' Hiltern replied. 'We think they have it in mind to join up with that lot.'

That was interesting. It was also information that should have been shared with the Schwabian and Prussian commanders by official despatch – not acquired accidentally by the random visit of a liaison officer. Sir Peter Hicks was scrupulous in maintaining communications with the allies; Ruysdale evidently saw no such need.

'Oh!' Hiltern said, divining his thought. 'I'm sure we would have let you know, only for things here being in a bit of confusion. And truly, it didn't seem urgent; scouts just said the French were shining their gear, biffing up the supplies, that sort of thing. After all, they've got to go *somewhere* before the snow comes down.'

He raised one dark brow, smiling in apology – an apology that Grey accepted with no more than a second's hesitation. If Ruysdale was going to be erratic about despatches, it would be as well for Grey to keep himself informed by other means – and Hiltern was obviously well-placed to know what was going on.

They chatted casually until the host came out with Hiltern's breakfast, but Grey learned no more of interest – save that Hiltern was remarkably *un*interested in the death of Private Bodger. He was also vague about the 'confusion' to which he had referred, dismissing it with a wave of the hand as 'bit of a muddle in the commissary – damn' bore'.

The sound of hooves and wheels, moving slowly, came from the street outside, and Grey heard a loud voice with a distinctly Schwabian accent, requesting direction to '*Der InglischerKamp.*'

'What is *that*?' Hiltern asked, turning on his stool.

'I expect that will be Private Bodger coming home,' Grey replied, rising. 'I'm obliged to you, sir. Is Sergeant-Major Sapp still in camp, do you know?'

'Mmm . . . no.' Hiltern spoke thickly, through a mouthful of potatoes and eggs. 'Gone to the river.'

That was inconvenient; Grey had no desire to hang about all day, waiting for Sapp's return in order to hand over the corpse and responsibility for it. Another idea occurred to him, though.

'And the regimental surgeon?'

'Dead. Flux.' Hiltern spooned in more egg, concentrating. 'Mmp. Try Keegan. He's the surgeon's assistant.'

With most of the men emptying out of camp, it took some time to locate the surgeon's tent. Once there, Grey had the body deposited on a bench, and at once sent the waggon back to the Schloss. He was taking no chances on Private Bodger's being left in his custody.

Keegan proved to be a scrappy Welshman, equipped with rimless spectacles and an incongruous mop of reddish ringlets. Blinking through the spectacles, he bent close to the corpse and poked at it with a smudgy exploratory finger.

'No blood.'

'No.'

'Fever?'

'Probably not. I saw the man several hours before his death, and he seemed in reasonable health then.'

'Hmmm.' Keegan bent and peered keenly up Bodger's nostrils, as though suspecting that the answer to the Private's untimely death might be lurking there.

Grey frowned at the fellow's grubby knuckles and the thin crust of blood that rimmed his cuff. Nothing out of the way for a surgeon, but the dirt bothered him.

Keegan tried to thumb up one of the eyelids, but it resisted him. Bodger had stiffened during the night, and while the hands and arms had gone limp again, the face, body, and legs were all hard as wood. Keegan sighed and began tugging off the corpse's stockings. These were greatly the worse for wear, the soles stained with mud; the left one had a hole worn through and Bodger's great toe poked out like the head of an inquisitive worm.

Keegan rubbed a hand on the skirt of his already grubby coat, leaving further streaks, then rubbed it under his nose, sniffing loudly. Grey had an urge to step away from the man. Then he realized, with a small sense of startlement mingled with annoyance, that he was thinking of the Woman. Fraser's wife. Fraser had spoken of her very little – but that reticence only added to the significance of what he *did* say.

One late night, in the governor's quarters at Ardsmuir Prison, they had sat longer than usual over their chess game – a hard-fought draw, in which Grey took more pleasure than he might have taken in victory over a lesser opponent. They usually drank sherry, but not that night; he had a special claret, a present from his mother, and had insisted that Fraser must help him to finish it, as the wine would not last, once opened.

It was a strong wine, and between the headiness of it and the stimulation of the game, even Fraser had lost a little of his formidable reserve.

Past midnight, Grey's orderly had come to take away the dishes from their repast, and stumbling sleepily on the threshold in his leaving, had sprawled full-length, cutting himself badly on a shard of glass. Fraser had leapt up like a cat, snatched the boy up, and pressed a fold of his shirt to the wound to stop the bleeding. But then, when Grey would have sent for a surgeon, had stopped him, saying tersely that Grey could do so if he wished to kill the lad, but if not, had best allow Fraser to tend him.

This he had done with skill and gentleness, washing first his hands, and then the wound, with wine, then demanding needle and silk thread – which he had astonished Grey by dipping into the wine as well, and passing the needle through the flame of a candle.

'My wife would do it so,' he'd said, frowning slightly in concentration. 'There are the wee beasties, called germs, d'ye see, and if they –'

He set his teeth momentarily into his lip as he made the first stitch, then went on.

'If they should be getting into a wound, it will suppurate. So ye must wash well before ye tend the wound, and put flame or alcohol to your instruments, to kill the germs.' He smiled briefly at the orderly, who was white-faced and wobbling on his stool. 'Never let a surgeon wi' dirty hands touch ye, she said. Better to bleed to death quickly than die slow of the pus, aye?'

Grey was as sceptical of the existence of germs as of succubi, but ever afterwards had glanced automatically at the hands of any medical man – and it did seem to him that perhaps the more cleanly of the breed tended to lose fewer patients, though he had made no real study of the matter.

In the present instance, though, Mr Keegan offered no hazard to the late Private Bodger, and in spite of his distaste, Grey made no protest as the surgeon undressed the corpse, making small interested 'Tut!' noises in response to the postmortem phenomena thus revealed.

Grey was already aware that the private had died in a state of arousal. This state appeared to be permanent, even though the limbs had begun to relax from their rigor, and was the occasion of a surprised 'Tut!' from Mr Keegan.

'Well, he died happy, at least,' Keegan said, blinking. 'Sweet God Almighty.'

'Is this a . . . normal manifestation, do you think?' Grey inquired. He had rather expected Private Bodger's condition to abate post-mortem. If anything, it seemed particularly pronounced, viewed by daylight. Though of course that might be merely an effect of the colour, which was now a virulent dark purple, in stark contrast to the pallid flesh of the body.

Keegan prodded the condition cautiously with a forefinger.

'Stiff as wood,' he said, unnecessarily. 'Normal? Don't know. Mind, what chaps I see here have mostly died of fever or flux, and men what are ill aren't mostly of a mind to . . . hmm.' He relapsed into a thoughtful contemplation of the body.

'What did the woman say?' he asked, shaking himself out of this reverie after a moment or two.

'Who, the woman he was with? Gone. Not that one might blame her.' Always assuming that it had been a woman, he added to himself. Though given Private Bodger's earlier encounter with the gypsy, one *would* assume . . .

'Can you say what caused his death?' Grey inquired, seeing that

Keegan had begun to inspect the body as a whole, though his fasci-nated gaze kept returning to . . . colour notwithstanding, it really was remarkable.

The assistant surgeon shook his ringlets, absorbed in wrestling off the corpse's shirt.

'No wound that I can see. Blow to the head, perhaps?' He bent close, squinting at the corpse's head and face, poking here and there in an exploratory fashion.

A group of men in uniform came towards them at the trot, hastily doing up straps and buttons, hoiking packs and muskets into place, and cursing as they went. Grey removed his hat and placed it strate-gically abaft the corpse, not wishing to excite public remark – but no one bothered to spare a glance at the tableau by the surgeon's tent; one dead man was much like another.

Grey reclaimed his hat and watched them go, grumbling like a miniature thunderstorm on the move. Most of the troops were already massed on the parade-ground. He could see them in the distance, moving in a slow, disorderly mill that would snap into clean forma-tion at the sergeant-major's shout.

'I know Colonel Ruysdale by reputation,' Grey said, after a thoughtful pause, 'though not personally. I have heard him described as "a bit of a Gawd-'elp-us", but I have not heard that he is altogether an ass.'

Keegan smiled, keeping his eyes on his work.

'Shouldn't think he is,' he agreed. 'Not altogether.'

Grey kept an inviting silence, to which invitation the surgeon acqui-esced within moments.

'He means to wear them out, see. Bring them back so tired they fall asleep in their suppers.'

'Oh, yes?'

'They been a-staying up all night, you see? Nobody wanting to fall asleep, lest the thing – a sucky-bus, is it? – should come round in their dreams. Mind, it's good for the tavern owners, but not so good for discipline, what with men falling asleep on sentry-go, or in the midst of drill . . .'

Keegan glanced up from his inspections, observing Grey with interest.

'Not sleeping so well yourself, Major?' He tapped a dirty finger beneath his eye, indicating the presence of dark rings, and chuckled.

'I kept rather late hours last night, yes,' Grey replied equably. 'Owing to the discovery of Private Bodger.'

'Hm. Yes, I see.' Keegan said, straightening up. 'Seems as though the sucky-bus had her fill of him, then.'

'So you do know about the rumours of a succubus?' Grey asked, ignoring the attempt at badinage.

'Of course I do.' Keegan looked surprised. 'Everybody knows. Aren't I just telling you?'

Keegan did not know how the rumour had reached the encampment, but it had spread like wildfire, reaching every man in camp within twenty-four hours. Original scoffing had become sceptical attention, and then reluctant belief, as more stories began to circulate of the dreams and torments suffered by men in the town – and had become outright panic, with the news of the Schwabian soldier's death.

'I don't suppose you saw that body?' Grey asked, interested.

The Welshman shook his head.

'The word is that the poor bugger was drained of blood – but who's to know the truth of it? Perhaps it was an apoplexy; I've seen 'em taken so, sometimes – the blood comes bursting from the nose, so as to relieve the pressure on the brain. Messy enough to look at.'

'You seem a rational man, sir,' Grey said, in compliment.

Keegan gave a small, huffing sort of laugh, dismissing it, and straightened up, brushing his palms once more against his coat-skirts.

'Deal with soldiers for as long as I have, Major, and you get used to wild stories, that's all I can say. Men in camp, 'specially. Not enough to keep them busy, and a good tale will spread like butter on hot toast. And when it comes to dreams –!' He threw up his hands.

Grey nodded, acknowledging the truth of this. Soldiers put great store in dreams.

'So you can tell me nothing regarding the cause of Private Bodger's death?'

Keegan shook his head, scratching at a row of flea-bites on his neck as he did so.

'Don't see a thing, sir, I'm sorry to say. Other than the . . . um . . . obvious,' he nodded delicately toward the corpse's mid-region, 'and that's not generally fatal. You might ask the fellow's friends, though. Just in case.'

This cryptic allusion made Grey glance up in question, and Keegan coughed.

'I did say the men didn't sleep, sir? Not wanting to give any sucky-bus an invitation, so to speak. Well, some went a bit further than that, and took matters – so to speak – into their own hands.'

A few bold souls, Keegan said, had reasoned that if what the succubus desired was the male essence, safety lay in removing this temptation – 'so to speak, sir.' While most of those choosing this expedient had presumably chosen to take their precautions in privacy, the men lived in very close quarters. It was in fact complaints from more than one citizen of gross mass indecency by the soldiers quartered on his premises that had provoked General Ruysdale's edict.

'Only thinking, sir, as a wet graveyard is maybe not the place I'd choose for romance, was the opportunity to come my way. But I could see, maybe, a group of men thinking they'd face down the sucky-bus on her own ground, perhaps? And if Private . . . Bodger, you said was his name, sir? . . . was to have keeled over in the midst of such proceedings . . . well, I expect his comrades would have buggered off smartly, not hung about to answer questions.'

'You have a very interesting turn of mind, Mr Keegan,' Grey said. 'Highly rational. I don't suppose it was you who suggested this particular . . . precaution?'

'Who, me?' Keegan tried – and failed – to exhibit outrage. 'The idea, Major!'

'Quite,' Grey said, and took his leave.

In the distance, the troops were departing the parade-ground in orderly fashion, each rank setting off in turn, to the clank and rattle of canteens and muskets and the staccato cries of corporals and sergeants. He stopped for a moment to watch them, enjoying the warmth of the autumn sun on his back.

After the fury of the night's storm, the day had dawned clear and calm, and promised to be mild. Very muddy underfoot, though, he noted, seeing the churned earth of the parade-ground, and the spray of clods flying off the feet of the runners, spattering their breeches. It would be heavy going, and the devil of a sweat to clean up afterwards. Ruysdale might not have intended this exercise principally as punishment, but that's what it would be.

Artilleryman that he was, Grey automatically evaluated the quality of the terrain for the passage of caissons. Not a chance. The ground was soft as sodden cheese. Even the mortars would bog down in nothing flat.

He turned, eyeing the distant hills where the French were said to be. If they had cannon, chances were that they were going nowhere for the moment.

The situation still left him with a lingering sense of unease, loath though he was to admit it. Yes, the French likely were intending to move towards the north. No, there was no apparent reason for them to cross the valley; Gurgelwitz had no strategic importance, nor was it of sufficient size to be worth a detour to loot. Yes, Ruysdale's troops were between the French and the town. But he looked at the deserted parade-ground, and the troops vanishing in the distance, and felt a tickle between the shoulderblades, as though someone stood behind him with a loaded pistol.

'I should feel a little happier if an additional detachment could be sent to guard the bridge.' Hicks's words echoed in memory. So Sir Peter felt that itch, as well. It was possible, Grey reflected, that Ruysdale *was* an ass.

4
The Gun-Crew

It was past midday by the time he reached the river. From a distance, it was a tranquil landscape under a high, pale sun, the river bordered by a thick growth of trees in autumn leaf, their ancient golds and bloody reds a-shimmer, in contrast to the black-and-dun patchwork of fallow fields and meadows gone to seed.

A little closer, though, and the river itself dispelled this impression of pastoral charm. It was a broad, deep stream, turbulent and fast moving, much swollen by the recent rains. Even at a distance, he could see the tumbling forms of uprooted trees and bushes, and the occasional carcass of a small animal, drowned in the current.

The Prussian artillery were placed upon a small rise of ground, concealed in a copse. Only one ten-pounder, he saw, with a sense of unease, and a small mortar – though there were sufficient stores of shot and powder, and these were commendably well kept, with a Prussian sense of order, tidily sheltered under canvas against the rain.

The men greeted him with great cordiality; any diversion from the boredom of bridge-guarding was welcome – the more welcome, if it came bearing beer, which Grey did, having thoughtfully procured two large ale-skins before leaving camp.

'You will with us eat, Major,' said the Schwabian Lieutenant in charge, accepting both beer and despatches, and waving a gracious hand towards a convenient boulder.

It was a long time since breakfast, and Grey accepted the invitation with pleasure. He took off his coat and spread it over the boulder, rolled up his sleeves, and joined companionably in the hard biscuit, cheese, and beer, accepting with gratitude a few bites of chewy, spicy sausage.

Lieutenant Dietrich, a middle-aged gentleman with a luxuriant beard and eyebrows to match, opened the despatches and read them while Grey practised his German with the gun-crew. He kept a careful eye upon the Lieutenant as he chatted, though, curious to see what the artilleryman would make of von Namtzen's despatch.

The Lieutenant's eyebrows were an admirable indication of his interior condition; they remained level for the first moments of reading, then rose to an apex of astonishment, where they remained suspended for no little time, returning to their original position with small flutters of dismay, as the Lieutenant decided how much of this information it was wise to impart to his men.

The Lieutenant folded the paper, shooting Grey a sharp interrogative glance. Grey gave a slight nod; yes, he knew what the despatch said.

The Lieutenant glanced round at the men, then back over his shoulder, as though judging the distance across the valley to the British camp and the town beyond. Then he looked back at Grey, thoughtfully chewing his moustache, and shook his head slightly. He would not mention the matter of a succubus.

On the whole, Grey thought that wise, and inclined his head an inch in agreement. There were only ten men present; if any of them had already known of the rumours, all would know. And while the Lieutenant seemed at ease with his command, the fact remained that these were Prussians, and not his own men. He could not be sure of their response.

The Lieutenant folded away his papers and came to join the conversation. However, Grey observed with interest that the substance of the despatch seemed to weigh upon the Lieutenant's mind, in such a way that the conversation turned – with no perceptible nudge in that direction, but with the inexorable swing of a compass-needle – to manifestations of the supernatural.

It being a fine day, with golden leaves drifting gently down around them, the gurgle of the river nearby, and plenty of beer to hand, the varied tales of ghosts, bleeding nuns and spectral battles in the sky were no more than the stuff of entertainment. In the cold shadows of the night, it would be different – though the stories would still be told. More than cannon-shot, bayonets or disease, boredom was a soldier's greatest enemy.

At one point, though, an artilleryman told the story of a fine house in his town, where the cries of a ghostly child echoed in the rooms at night, to the consternation of the householders. In time, they traced the sound to one particular wall, chipped away the plaster, and discovered a bricked-up chimney, in which lay the remains of a young boy, next to the dagger which had cut his throat.

Several of the soldiers made the sign of the horns at this, but Grey saw distinct expressions of unease on the faces of two of the men. These two exchanged glances, then looked hurriedly away.

'You have heard such a story before, perhaps?' Grey asked, addressing the younger of the two directly. He smiled, doing his best to look harmlessly engaging.

The boy – he could be no more than fifteen – hesitated, but such was the press of interest from those around him that he could not resist.

'Not a story,' he said. 'I – we –' he nodded at his fellow, '– last night, in the storm. We heard a child crying, near the river. We went to look, with a lantern, but there was nothing there. Still, we heard it. It went on and on, though we walked up and down, calling and searching, until we were wet through, and nearly frozen.'

'Oh, is that what you were doing?' a fellow in his twenties interjected, grinning. 'And here we thought you and Samson were just buggering each other under the bridge.'

Blood surged up into the boy's face with a suddenness that made his eyes bulge, and he launched himself at the older man, knocking him off his seat and rolling with him into the leaves in a ball of fists and elbows.

Grey sprang to his feet and kicked them apart, seizing the boy by the scruff of the neck and jerking him up. The Lieutenant was shouting at them angrily in idiomatic German, which Grey ignored. He shook the boy slightly, to bring him to his senses, and said, very quietly, 'Laugh. It was a joke.'

He stared hard into the boy's eyes, willing him to come to his senses. The thin shoulders under his hands vibrated with the need to strike out, to hit something – and the brown eyes were glassy with anguish and confusion.

Grey shook him harder, then released him, and under the guise of slapping dead leaves from his uniform, leaned closer. 'If you act like this, they will know,' he said, speaking in a rapid whisper. 'For God's sake, laugh!'

Samson, experienced enough to know what to do in such circumstances, was doing it – pushing at joking comrades, replying to crude jests with cruder ones. The young boy glanced at him, a flicker of awareness coming back into his face. Grey let him go, and turned back to the group, saying loudly, 'If I were going to bugger someone, I would wait for good weather. A man must be desperate, to swive *anything* in such rain and thunder!'

'It's been a long time, Major,' said one of the soldiers, laughing. He made crude thrusting gestures with his hips. 'Even a sheep in a snow-storm would look good now!'

'Haha. Go fuck yourself, Wulfie. The sheep wouldn't have you.' The boy was still flushed and damp-eyed, but back in control of himself. He rubbed a hand across his mouth and spat, forcing a grin as the others laughed.

'You *could* fuck yourself, Wulfie – if your dick is as long as you say it is.' Samson leered at Wulf, who stuck out an amazingly long tongue in reply, waggling it in derision.

'Don't you wish you knew!'

The discussion was interrupted at this point by two soldiers who came puffing up the rise, wet to the waist and dragging with them a large dead pig, fished out of the river. This addition to supper was greeted with cries of approbation, and half the men fell at once to the work of butchery, the others returning in desultory fashion to their conversation.

The vigour had gone out of it, though, and Grey was about to take his leave, when one of the men said something, laughing, about gypsy women.

'What did you say? I mean – *was ist das Du hast sprechen?*' He groped for his German. 'Gypsies? You have seen them recently?'

'Oh, *ja*, Major,' said the soldier, obligingly. 'This morning. They came across the bridge, six waggons with mules. They go back and forth. We've seen them before.'

With a little effort, Grey kept his voice calm.

'Indeed?' He turned to the Lieutenant. 'Does it not seem possible that they may have dealings with the French?'

'Of course.' The Lieutenant looked mildly surprised, then grinned. 'What are they going to tell the French? That we're here? I think they know that, Major.'

He gestured towards a gap in the trees. Through it, Grey could see the English soldiers of Ruysdale's regiment, perhaps a mile away, their ranks piling up on the bank of the river like driftwood as they flung down their packs and waded into the shallows to drink, hot and mud-caked from their run.

It was true; the presence of the English and Schwabian regiments could be a surprise to no one; anyone on the cliffs with a spyglass could likely count the spots on Colonel Ruysdale's dog. As for information regarding their movements . . . well, since neither Ruysdale nor Hicks had any idea where they were going or when, there wasn't any great danger of that intelligence being revealed to the enemy.

He smiled, and took gracious leave of the Lieutenant, though privately resolving to speak to Stephan von Namtzen. Perhaps the gypsies were harmless – but they should be looked into. If nothing else, the gypsies were in a position to tell anyone who cared to ask them how few men were guarding that bridge. And somehow, he thought that Ruysdale was not of a mind to consider Sir Peter's request for reinforcement, though he had delivered it.

He waved casually to the artillerymen, who took little notice, elbow-deep in blood and pig guts. The boy was by himself, chopping green wood for the spit.

Leaving the artillery camp, he rode up to the head of the bridge and paused, reining Karolus in as he looked across the river. The land was flat for a little way, but then broke into rolling hills that rose to a steep promontory. Above, on the cliffs, the French presumably still lurked. He took a small spyglass from his pocket, and scanned the cliff-tops, slowly. Nothing moved on the heights; no horses, no men, no swaying banners – and yet a faint grey haze drifted up there, a cloud in an otherwise cloudless sky. The smoke of campfires; many of them. Yes, the French were still there.

He scanned the hills below, looking carefully – but if the gypsies were there as well, no rising plume of smoke betrayed their presence.

He should find the gypsy camp and question its inhabitants himself – but it was growing late, and he had no stomach for that now. He reined about and turned the horse's head back towards the distant town, not glancing at the copse that hid the cannon and its crew.

The boy had best learn – and quickly – to hide his nature, or he would become in short order bumboy to any man who cared to use him. And many would. Wulf had been correct; after months in the field, soldiers were not particular, and the boy was much more appealing than a sheep, with those soft red lips and tender skin.

Karolus tossed his head, and he slowed, uneasy. Grey's hands were trembling on the reins, gripped far too tightly. He forced them to relax, stilled the trembling, and spoke calmly to the horse, nudging him back to speed.

He had been attacked once, in camp somewhere in Scotland, in the days after Culloden. Someone had come upon him in the dark, and taken him from behind with an arm across his throat. He had thought he was dead, but his assailant had something else in mind. The man had never spoken, and was brutally swift about his business, leaving him moments later, curled in the dirt behind a waggon, speechless with shock and pain.

He had never known who it was: officer, soldier, or some anonymous intruder. Never known whether the man had discerned something in his own appearance or behaviour that led to the attack, or had only taken him because he was there.

He *had* known the danger of telling anyone about it. He washed himself, stood straight and walked firmly, spoke normally and looked men in the eye. No one had suspected the bruised and riven flesh beneath his uniform, or the hollowness beneath his breastbone. And if his attacker sat at meals and broke bread with him, he had not known it. From that day, he had carried a dagger at all times, and no one had ever touched him again, against his will.

The sun was sinking behind him, and the shadow of horse and rider stretched out far before him, flying, and faceless in their flight.

5
Dark Dreams

Once more he was late for dinner. This time, though, a tray was brought for him, and he sat in the drawing room, taking his supper while the rest of the company chatted.

The Princess saw to his needs, and sat with him for a time, flatteringly attentive. He was worn out from a day of riding, though, and his answers to her questions were brief. Soon enough, she drifted away and left him to a peaceful engagement with some cold venison and a tart of dried apricots.

He had nearly finished, when he felt a large, warm hand on his shoulder.

'So, you have seen the gun-crew at the bridge? They are in good order?' von Namtzen asked.

'Yes, very good,' Grey replied. No point – not yet – in mentioning the young soldier to von Namtzen. 'I told them more men will come, from Ruysdale's regiment. I hope they will.'

'The bridge?' The Dowager, catching the word, turned from her conversation, frowning. 'You have no need to worry, Landgrave. The bridge is safe.'

'I am sure it will be safe, madam,' Stephan said, clicking his heels gallantly as he bowed to the old lady. 'You may be assured, Major Grey and I will protect you.'

The old lady looked faintly put out at the notion.

'The bridge is safe,' she repeated, touching the religious medal on the bodice of her gown, and glancing pugnaciously from man to man. 'No enemy has crossed the bridge at Aschenwald in three hundred years. No enemy will ever cross it!'

Stephan glanced at Grey, and cleared his throat slightly. Grey cleared his own throat and made a gracious compliment upon the food.

When the Dowager had moved away, Stephan shook his head behind her back, and exchanged a brief smile with Grey.

'You know about that bridge?'

'No, is there something odd about it?'

'Only a story.' Von Namtzen shrugged, with a tolerant scorn for the superstition of others. 'They say that there is a guardian; a spirit of some kind that defends the bridge.'

'Indeed,' Grey said, with an uneasy memory of the stories told by the gun-crew stationed near the bridge. Were any of them local men, he wondered, who would know the story?

'*Mein Gott*,' Stephan said, shaking his massive head as though assailed by gnats. 'These stories! How can sane men believe such things?'

'I collect you do not mean that particular story?' Grey said. 'The succubus, perhaps?'

'Don't speak to me of that thing,' von Namtzen said gloomily. 'My men look like scarecrows and jump at a bird's shadow. Every one of them is scared to lay his head upon a pillow, for fear that he will turn and look into the night-hag's face.'

'Your chaps aren't the only ones.' Sir Peter had come to pour himself another drink. He lifted the glass and took a deep swallow, shuddering slightly. Billman, behind him, nodded in glum confirmation.

'Bloody sleep-walkers, the lot.'

'Ah,' said Grey thoughtfully. 'If I might make a suggestion . . . not my own, you understand. A notion mentioned by Ruysdale's surgeon . . .'

He explained Mr Keegan's remedy, keeping his voice discreetly low. His listeners were less discreet in their response.

'What, Ruysdale's chaps are all boxing the Jesuit and begetting cock-roaches?' Grey thought Sir Peter would expire from suffocated laughter. Just as well Lieutenant Dundas wasn't present, he thought.

'Perhaps not all of them,' he said. 'Evidently enough, though, to be of concern. I take it you have not experienced a similar phenomenon among your troops . . . yet?'

Billman caught the delicate pause and whooped loudly.

'Boxing the Jesuit?' Stephan nudged Grey with an elbow, and raised thick blond brows in puzzlement. 'Cockroaches? What does this mean, please?'

'Ahhh . . .' Having no notion of the German equivalent of this expression, Grey resorted to a briefly graphic gesture with one hand, looking over his shoulder to be sure that none of the women was watching.

'Oh!' Von Namtzen looked mildly startled, but then grinned widely. 'I see, yes, very good!' He nudged Grey again, more familiarly, and dropped his voice a little. 'Perhaps wise to take some such precaution personally, do you think?'

The women and the German officers, heretofore intent on a card game, were looking towards the Englishmen in puzzlement. One man called a question to von Namtzen, and Grey was fortunately saved from reply.

Something occurred to him, though, and he grasped von Namtzen by the arm, as the latter was about to go and join the others at a hand of bravo.

'A moment, Stephan. I had meant to ask – that man of yours who died – Koenig? Did you see the body yourself?'

Von Namtzen was still smiling, but at this, his expression grew more sombre, and he shook his head.

'No, I did not see him. They said, though, that his throat was most terribly torn – as though a wild animal had been at him. And yet he was not outside; he was found in his quarters.' He shook his head again, and left to join the card game.

Grey finished his meal amid cordial conversation with Sir Peter and Billman, though keeping an inconspicuous eye upon the progress of the card game.

Stephan was in dress uniform tonight. A smaller man would have been overwhelmed by it; Schwabian taste in military decoration was grossly excessive, to an English eye. Still, with his big frame and leonine blond head, the Landgrave von Erdberg was merely . . . eye-catching.

He appeared to have caught the eye not only of the Princess Louisa, but of three other young women friends of the Princess. These surrounded him like a moony triplet, caught in his orbit. Now he reached into the breast of his coat and withdrew some small object, causing them to cluster round to look at it.

Grey turned to answer some question of Billman's, but then turned back, trying not to look too obviously.

He had been trying to suppress the feeling Stephan roused in him, but in the end, such things were never controllable – they rose up. Sometimes like the bursting of a mortar shell, sometimes like the inexorable green spike of a crocus pushing through snow and ice – but they rose up.

Was he in love with Stephan? There was no question of that. He liked and respected the Schwabian, but there was no madness in it, no yearning. Did he *want* Stephan? A soft warmth in his loins, as though his blood had begun somehow to simmer over a low flame, suggested that he did.

The ancient bear's skull still sat in its place of honour, below the old Prince's portrait. He moved slowly to examine it, keeping half an eye on Stephan.

'Surely you have not eaten enough, John!' A delicate hand on his elbow turned him, and he looked down into the Princess's face, smiling up at him with pretty coquetry. 'A strong man, out all day – let me call the servants to bring you something special.'

'I assure you, your Highness . . .' But she would have none of it, and tapping him playfully with her fan, she scudded away like a gilded cloud, to have some special dessert prepared for him.

Feeling obscurely like a fatted calf being readied for the slaughter, Grey sought refuge in male company, coming to rest beside von Namtzen, who was folding up whatever he had been showing to the women, who had all gone to peer over the card players' shoulders and make bets.

'What is that?' Grey asked, nodding at the object.

'Oh –' Von Namtzen looked a little disconcerted at the question, but with only a moment's hesitation, handed it to Grey. It was a small leather case, hinged, with a gold closure. 'My children.'

It was a miniature, done by an excellent hand. The heads of two children, close together, one boy, one girl, both blonde. The boy, clearly a little older, was perhaps three or four.

Grey felt momentarily as though he had received an actual blow to the pit of the stomach; his mouth opened, but he was incapable of speech. Or at least he thought he was. To his surprise, he heard his own voice, sounding calm, politely admiring.

'They are very handsome indeed. I am sure they are a consolation to your wife, in your absence.'

Von Namtzen grimaced slightly, and gave a brief shrug.

'Their mother is dead. She died in childbirth when Elise was born.'
A huge forefinger touched the tiny face, very gently. 'My mother looks
after them.'

Grey made the proper sounds of condolence, but had ceased to hear
himself, for the confusion of thought and speculation that filled his
mind.

So much so, in fact, that when the Princess's special dessert – an enormous concoction of preserved raspberries, brandy, sponge-cake and cream
– arrived, he ate it all, despite the fact that raspberries made him itch.

He continued to think, long after the ladies had left. He joined the
card game, bet extensively, and played wildly – winning, with Luck's
usual perversity, though he paid no attention to his cards.

Had he been entirely wrong? It was possible. All of Stephan's gestures
towards him had been within the bounds of normalcy – and yet . . .

And yet it was by no means unknown for men such as himself
to marry and have children. Certainly men such as von Namtzen,
with a title and estates to bequeath, would wish to have heirs. That
thought steadied him, and though he scratched occasionally at chest
or neck, he paid more attention to his game – and finally began to
lose.

The card game broke up an hour later. Grey loitered a bit, in hopes
that Stephan might seek him out, but the Schwabian was detained in
argument with Kaptain Steffens, and at last Grey went upstairs, still
scratching.

The halls were well lit tonight, and he found his own corridor
without difficulty. He hoped Tom was still awake; perhaps the young
valet could fetch him something for the itching. Some ointment,
perhaps, or – he heard the rustle of fabric behind him, and turned to
find the Princess approaching him.

She was once again in a nightdress – but not the homely woollen
garment she had worn the night before. This time, she wore a flowing
thing of diaphanous lawn, which clung to her bosom and rather clearly
revealed her nipples through the thin fabric. He thought she must be
very cold, in spite of the lavishly embroidered robe thrown over the
nightgown.

She had no cap, and her hair had been brushed out, but not yet
plaited for the night; it flowed becomingly in golden waves below her
shoulders. Grey began to feel somewhat cold, too, in spite of the
brandy.

'My Lord,' she said. 'John,' she added, and smiled. 'I have something for you.' She was holding something in one hand, he saw; a small box of some sort.

'Your Highness,' he said, repressing the urge to take a step backwards. She was wearing a very strong scent, redolent of tuberoses – a scent he particularly disliked.

'My name is Louisa,' she said, taking another step towards him. 'Will you not call me by my name? Here, in private?'

'Of course. If you wish it – Louisa.' Good God, what had brought this on? He had sufficient experience to see what she was about – he was a handsome man, of good family, and with money; it had happened often enough – but not with royalty, who tended to be accustomed to taking what they wanted.

He took her outstretched hand, ostensibly for the purpose of kissing it; in reality, to keep her at a safe distance. What did she want? And why?

'This is – to thank you,' she said as he raised his head from her beringed knuckles. She thrust the box into his other hand. 'And to protect you.'

'I assure you, madam, no thanks are necessary. I did nothing.' Christ, was that it? Did she think she must bed him, in token of thanks – or rather, had convinced herself that she must, because she wanted to? She did want to; he could see her excitement, in the slightly widened blue eyes, the flushed cheeks, the rapid pulse in her throat. He squeezed her fingers gently and released them, then tried to hand back the box.

'Really, madam – Louisa – I cannot accept this; surely it is a treasure of your family.' It certainly looked valuable; small as it was, it was remarkably heavy – made either of gilded lead or of solid gold – and sported a number of crudely cut cabochon stones, which he feared were precious.

'Oh, it is,' she assured him. 'It has been in my husband's family for hundreds of years.'

'Oh, well, then certainly –'

'No, you must keep it,' she said vehemently. 'It will protect you from the creature.'

'Creature. You mean the –'

'*Die Nacht Toter*,' she said, lowering her voice and looking involuntarily over one shoulder, as though fearing that some vile thing hovered in the air nearby.

Nacht Toter. 'Night-killer', it meant. Despite himself, a brief shiver tightened Grey's shoulders. The halls were better lighted, but still harboured draughts that made the candles flicker, and shadows flow like moving water down the walls.

He glanced down at the box. There were letters etched into the lid, in Latin, but of so ancient a sort that it would take close examination to work out what they said.

'It is a reliquary,' she said, moving closer, as though to point out the inscription. 'Of St Orgevald.'

'Ah? Er . . . yes. Most interesting.' He thought this mildly gruesome. Of all the objectionable Popish practices, this habit of chopping up saints and scattering their remnants to the far ends of the earth was possibly the most reprehensible. But why should the Princess have such an item? The von Lowensteins were Lutheran. Of course, it *was* very old – no doubt she regarded it as no more than a family talisman.

She was very close, her perfume cloying in his nostrils. How was he to get rid of the woman? The door to his room was only a foot or two away; he had a strong urge to open it, leap in, and slam it shut, but that wouldn't do.

'You will protect me, protect my son,' she murmured, looking trustfully up at him from beneath golden lashes. 'So I will protect you, dear John.'

She flung her arms about his neck, and once more glued her lips to his in a passionate kiss. Sheer courtesy required him to return the embrace, though his mind was racing, looking feverishly for some escape. Where the devil were the servants? Why did no one interrupt them?

Then someone did interrupt them. There was a gruff cough near at hand, and Grey broke the embrace with relief – a short-lived emotion, as he looked up to discover the Landgrave von Erdberg standing a few feet away, glowering under heavy brows.

'Your pardon, Your Highness,' Stephan said, in tones of ice. 'I wished to speak to Major Grey; I did not know anyone was here.'

The Princess was flushed, but quite collected. She smoothed her gown down across her body, drawing herself up in such a way that her fine bust was strongly emphasized.

'Oh,' she said, very cool. 'It's you, Erdberg. Do not worry, I was just taking my leave of the Major. You may have him now.' A small, smug smile twitched at the corner of her mouth. Quite deliberately, she laid a hand along Grey's heated cheek, and let her fingers trail along his skin as she turned away. Then she strolled – curse the woman, she *strolled!* – away, switching the tail of her robe.

There was a profound silence in the hallway.

Grey broke it, finally.

'You wished to speak with me, Captain?'

Von Namtzen looked him over coldly, as though deciding whether to step on him.

'No,' he said at last. 'It will wait.' He turned on his heel and strode away, making a good deal more noise in his departure than had the Princess.

Grey pressed a hand to his forehead, until he could trust his head not to explode, then shook it, and lunged for the door to his room before anything else should happen.

Tom was sitting on a stool by the fire, mending a pair of breeches that had suffered injury to the seams while Grey was demonstrating sabre lunges to one of the German officers. He looked up at once when Grey came in, but if he had heard any of the conversation in the hall, he made no reference to it.

'What's that, me lord?' he asked instead, seeing the box in Grey's hand.

'What? Oh, that.' Grey put it down, with a faint feeling of distaste. 'A relic. Of St Orgevald, whoever he might be.'

'Oh, I know him!'

'You do?' Grey raised one brow.

'Yes, me lord. There's a little chapel to him, down the garden. Ilse – she's one of the kitchen maids – was showing me. He's right famous hereabouts.'

'Indeed.' Grey began to undress, tossing his coat across the chair and starting on his waistcoat buttons. His fingers were impatient, slipping on the small buttons. 'Famous for what?'

'Stopping them killing the children. Will I help you, me lord?'

'What?' Grey stopped, staring at the young valet, then shook his head and resumed twitching buttons. 'No, continue. Killing what children?'

Tom's hair was standing up on end, as it tended to do whenever he was interested in a subject, owing to his habit of running one hand through it.

'Well, d'ye see, me lord, it used to be the custom, when they'd build something important, they'd buy a child from the gypsies – or just take one, I 'spose – and wall it up in the foundation. Specially for a bridge. It keeps anybody wicked from crossing over, see?'

Grey resumed his unbuttoning, more slowly. The hair prickled uneasily on his nape.

'The child – the murdered child – would cry out, I suppose?'

Tom looked surprised at his acumen.

'Yes, me lord. However did you know that?'

'Never mind. So St Orgevald put a stop to this practice, did he? Good for him.' He glanced, more kindly, at the small gold box. 'There's a chapel, you say – is it in use?'

'No, me lord. It's full of bits of stored rubbish. Or, rather – 'tisn't in use for what you might call devotions. Folk do go there.' The boy flushed a bit, and frowned intently at his work. Grey deduced that Ilse might have shown him another use for a deserted chapel, but chose not to pursue the matter.

'I see. Was Ilse able to tell you anything else of interest?'

'Depends upon what you call interesting, me lord.' Tom's eyes were still fixed upon his needle, but Grey could tell from the way in which he caught his upper lip between his teeth that he was in possession of a juicy bit of information.

'At this point, my chief interest is in my bed,' Grey said, finally extricating himself from the waistcoat, 'but tell me anyway.'

'Reckon you know the nursemaid's still gone?'

'I do.'

'Did you know her name was Koenig, and that she was wife to the Hun soldier what the succubus got?'

Grey had just about broken Tom of calling the Germans 'Huns', at least in their hearing, but chose to overlook this lapse.

'I did not.' Grey unfastened his neckcloth, slowly. 'Was this known to all the servants?' More importantly, did Stephan know?

'Oh, yes, me lord.' Tom had laid down his needle, and now looked up, eager with his news. 'See, the soldier, he used to do work here, at the Schloss.'

'When? Was he a local man, then?' It was quite usual for soldiers to augment their pay by doing work for the local citizenry in their off-hours, but Stephan's men had been *in situ* for less than a month. But if the nursery-maid was the man's wife –

'Yes, me lord. Born here, the both of them. He joined the local regiment some years a-gone, and came here to work –'

'What work did he do?' Grey asked, unsure whether this had any bearing on Koenig's demise, but wanting a moment to encompass the information.

'Builder,' Tom replied promptly. 'Part of the upper floors got the wood-worm, and had to be replaced.'

'Hm. You seem remarkably well informed. Just how long did you spend in the chapel with young Ilse?'

Tom gave him a look of limpid innocence, much more inculpatory than an open leer.

'Me lord?'

'Never mind. Go on. Was the man working here at the time he was killed?'

'No, me lord. He left with the regiment two years back. He did come round a week or so ago, Ilse said, only to visit his friends among the servants, but he didn't work here.'

Grey had now got down to his drawers, which he removed with a sigh of relief.

'Christ, what sort of perverse country is it where they put starch in a man's small-clothes? Can you not deal with the laundresses, Tom?'

'Sorry, me lord.' Tom scrambled to retrieve the discarded drawers. 'I didn't know the word for starch. I thought I did, but whatever I said just made 'em laugh.'

'Well, don't make Ilse laugh too much. Leaving the maid-servants with child is an abuse of hospitality.'

'Oh, no, me lord,' Tom assured him earnestly. 'We was too busy talking to, er . . .'

'To be sure you were,' Grey said equably. 'Did she tell you anything else of interest?'

'Mebbe.' Tom had the nightshirt already aired and hanging by the fire to warm; he held it up for Grey to draw over his head, the wool flannel soft and gratifying as it slid over his skin. 'Mind, it's only gossip.'

'Mm?'

'One of the older footmen, who used to work with Koenig – after Koenig came to visit, he was talkin' with one of the other servants, and he said in Ilse's hearing as how little Siegfried was growing up to be the spit of him – of Koenig, I mean, not the footman. But then he saw her listening and shut up smart.'

Grey stopped in the act of reaching for his banyan, and stared.

'Indeed,' he said. Tom nodded, looking modestly pleased with the effect of his findings.

'That's the Princess's old husband, isn't it, over the mantelpiece in the drawing room? Ilse showed me the picture. Looks a proper old bugger, don't he?'

'Yes,' said Grey, smiling slightly. 'And?'

'He ain't had – hadn't, I mean – any children more than Siegfried, though he was married twice before. And Master Siegfried was born six months to the day after the old fellow died. That kind of thing always causes talk, don't it?'

'I should say so, yes.' Grey thrust his feet into the proffered slippers. 'Thank you, Tom. You've done more than well.'

Tom shrugged modestly, though his round face beamed as though illuminated from within.

'Will I fetch you tea, me lord? Or a nice syllabub?'

'Thank you, no. Find your bed, Tom, you've earned your rest.'

'Very good, me lord.' Tom bowed; his manners were improving markedly, under the example of the Schloss's servants. He picked up the clothes Grey had left on the chair, to take away for brushing, but then stopped to examine the little reliquary, which Grey had left on the table.

'That's a handsome thing, me lord. A relic, did you say? Isn't that a bit of somebody?'

'It is.' Grey started to tell Tom to take the thing away with him, but stopped. It was undoubtedly valuable; best to leave it here. 'Probably a finger or a toe, judging from the size.'

Tom bent, peering at the faded lettering.

'What does it say, me lord? Can you read it?'

'Probably.' Grey took the box, and brought it close to the candle. Held thus at an angle, the worn lettering sprang into legibility. So did the drawing etched into the top, which Grey had to that point assumed to be merely decorative lines. The words confirmed it.

'Isn't that a . . . ?' Tom said, goggling at it.

'Yes, it is.' Grey gingerly set the box down.

They regarded it in silence for a moment.

'Ah . . . where did you get it, me lord?' Tom asked, finally.

'The Princess gave it me. As protection from the succubus.'

'Oh.' The young valet shifted his weight to one foot, and glanced sidelong at him. 'Ah . . . d'ye think it will work?'

Grey cleared his throat.

'I assure you, Tom, if the phallus of St Orgevald does not protect me, nothing will.'

Left alone, he sank into the chair by the fire, closed his eyes, and tried to compose himself sufficiently to think. The conversation with Tom had at least allowed him a little distance, from which to contemplate matters with the Princess and Stephan – save that they didn't bear contemplation.

He felt mildly nauseated, and sat up to pour a glass of plum brandy from the decanter on the table. That helped, settling both his stomach and his mind.

He sat slowly sipping it, gradually bringing his mental faculties to bear on the less personal aspects of the situation.

Tom's discoveries cast a new and most interesting light on matters. If Grey had ever believed in the existence of a succubus – and he was sufficiently honest to admit that there had been moments, both in the graveyard and in the dark-flickering halls of the Schloss – he believed no longer.

The attempted kidnapping was plainly the work of some human agency, and the revelation of the relationship between the two Koenigs – the vanished nursemaid and her dead husband – just as plainly indicated that the death of Private Koenig was part of the same affair, no matter what hocus-pocus had been contrived around it.

Grey's father had died when he was twelve, but had succeeded in instilling in his son his own admiration for the philosophy of reason. In addition to the concept of Occam's Razor, his father had also introduced him to the useful doctrine of *Cui bono*?

The plainly obvious answer there was the Princess Louisa. Granting for the present that the gossip was true, and that Koenig had fathered little Siegfried . . . the last thing the woman could want was for Koenig to return and hang about where awkward resemblances could be noted.

He had no idea of the German law regarding paternity. In England, a child born in wedlock was legally the offspring of the husband, even when everyone and the dog's mother knew that the wife had been openly unfaithful. By such means, several gentlemen of his acquaintance had children, even though he was quite sure that the men had never even thought of sharing their wives' beds. Had Stephan perhaps –

He caught that thought by the scruff of the neck and shoved it aside. Besides, if the miniaturist had been faithful, Stephan's son was the spitting image of his father. Though painters naturally would produce what image they thought most desired by the patron, in spite of the reality –

He picked up the glass and drank from it until he felt breathless and his ears buzzed.

'Koenig,' he said firmly, aloud. Whether the gossip was true or not – and having kissed the Princess, he rather thought it was; no shrinking violet, she! – and whether or not Koenig's reappearance might threaten Siggy's legitimacy, the man's presence must certainly be unwelcome.

Unwelcome enough to have arranged his death?

Why, when he would be gone again soon? The troops were likely to move within the week – surely within the month. Had something happened that made the removal of Private Koenig urgent? Perhaps Koenig himself had been in ignorance of Siegfried's parentage – and upon discovering the boy's resemblance to himself on his visit to the castle, determined to extort money or favour from the Princess?

And bringing the matter full circle . . . had the entire notion of the succubus been introduced merely to disguise Koenig's death? If so, how? The rumour had seized the imagination of both troops and townspeople to a marked extent – and Koenig's death had caused it to reach the proportions of a panic – but how had that rumour been started?

He dismissed that question for the moment, as there was no rational way of dealing with it. As for the death, though . . .

He could without much difficulty envision the Princess Louisa conspiring in the death of Koenig; he had noticed before that women were quite without mercy where their offspring were concerned. Still . . . the Princess had presumably not entered a soldier's quarters and done a man to death with her own lily-white hands.

Who had done it? Someone with great ties of loyalty to the Princess, presumably. Though, upon second thought, it need not have been anyone from the Castle. Gurgelwitz was not the teeming boil that London was, but the town was still of sufficient size to sustain a reasonable number of criminals; one of these could likely have been induced to perform the actual murder – if it was a murder, he reminded himself. He must not lose sight of the null hypothesis, in his eagerness to reach a conclusion.

And further . . . even if the Princess had in some way contrived both the rumour of the succubus *and* the death of Private Koenig – who was the witch in Siggy's room? Had someone truly tried to abduct the child? Private Koenig was already dead; clearly he could have had nothing to do with it.

He ran a hand through his hair, rubbing his scalp slowly to assist thought.

Loyalties. Who was most loyal to the Princess? Her butler? Stephan?

He grimaced, but examined the thought carefully. No. There were no circumstances conceivable, under which Stephan would have conspired in the murder of one of his own men. Grey might be in doubt of many things concerning the Schwabian, but not his honour.

This led back to the Princess's behaviour towards himself. Did she act from attraction? Grey was modest about his own endowments, but also honest enough to admit that he possessed some, and that his person was reasonably attractive to women.

He thought it more likely, if the Princess had indeed conspired in Koenig's removal, that her actions towards himself were intended as distraction. Though there *was* yet another explanation.

One of the minor corollaries to Occam's Razor that he had himself derived suggested that quite often, the observed result of an action really was the intended end of that action. The end result of that encounter in the hallway was that Stephan von Namtzen had discovered him in embrace with the Princess, and been noticeably annoyed by said discovery.

Had Louisa's motive been the very simple one of making von Namtzen jealous?

And if Stephan *were* jealous . . . of whom?

The room had grown intolerably stuffy, and he rose, restless, and went to the window, unlatching the shutters. The moon was full, a great, fecund yellow orb that hung low above the darkened fields, and cast its light over the slated roofs of Gurgelwitz and the paler sea of canvas tents that lay beyond.

Did Ruysdale's troops sleep soundly tonight, exhausted from their healthful exercise? He felt as though he would profit from such exercise himself. He braced himself in the windowframe and pushed, feeling the muscles pop in his arms, envisioning escape into that freshening night, running naked and silent as a wolf, soft earth cool, yielding to his feet.

Cold air rushed past his body, raising the coarse hairs on his skin, but his core felt molten. Between the heat of fire and brandy, the nightshirt's original gratifying warmth had become oppressive; sweat bloomed upon his body, and the woollen cloth hung limp upon him.

Suddenly impatient, he stripped it off, and stood in the open window, fierce and restless, the cold air caressing his nakedness.

There was a whir and rustle in the ivy nearby, and then something – several somethings – passed in absolute silence so close and so swiftly by his face that he had not even time to start backwards, though his heart leapt to his throat, strangling his involuntary cry.

Bats. The creatures had disappeared in an instant, long before his startled mind had collected itself sufficiently to put a name to them.

He leaned out, searching, but the bats had disappeared at once into the dark, swift about their hunting. It was no wonder that legends of succubi abounded, in a place so bat-haunted. The behaviour of the creatures indeed seemed supernatural.

The bounds of the small chamber seemed at once intolerably confining. He could imagine himself some demon of the air, taking wing to haunt the dreams of a man, seize upon a sleeping body and ride it – could he fly as far as England? he wondered. Was the night long enough?

The trees at the edge of the garden tossed uneasily, stirred by the wind. The night itself seemed tormented by an autumn restlessness, the sense of things moving, changing, fermenting.

His blood was still hot, having now reached a sort of full, rolling boil, but there was no outlet for it. He did not know whether Stephan's anger was on his own behalf – or Louisa's. In neither case, though, could he make any open demonstration of feeling towards von Namtzen, now; it was too dangerous. He was unsure of the German attitude towards sodomites, but felt it unlikely to be more forgiving than the English stance. Whether stolid Protestant morality, or a wilder Catholic mysticism – he cast a brief look at the reliquary – neither was likely to have sympathy with his own predilections.

The mere contemplation of revelation, and the loss of its possibility, though, had shown him something important.

Stephan von Namtzen both attracted and aroused him, but it was not because of his own undoubted physical qualities. It was, rather, the degree to which those qualities reminded Grey of James Fraser.

Von Namtzen was nearly the same height as Fraser, a powerful man with broad shoulders, long legs, and an instantly commanding presence. However, Stephan was heavier, more crudely constructed and less graceful than the Scot. And while Stephan warmed Grey's blood, the fact remained that the Schwabian did not burn his heart like living flame.

He lay down finally upon his bed, and put out the candle. Lay watching the play of firelight on the walls, seeing not the flicker of wood-flame, but the play of sun upon red hair, the sheen of sweat on a pale bronzed body . . .

A brief and brutal dose of Mr Keegan's remedy left him drained, if not yet peaceful. He lay staring upwards into the shadows of the carved wooden ceiling, able at least to think once more.

The only conclusion of which he was sure was that he needed very much to talk to someone who had seen Koenig's body.

6
Hocus-pocus

Finding Private Koenig's last place of residence was simple. Thoroughly accustomed to having soldiers quartered upon them, Prussians sensibly built their houses with a separate chamber intended for the purpose. Indeed, the populace viewed such quartering not as an imposition, but as a windfall, since the soldiers not only paid for board and lodging, and would often do chores such as fetching wood and water – but were also better protection against thieves than a large watch-dog might be, without the expense.

Stephan's records were of course impeccable; he could lay hands on any one of his men at a moment's notice. And while he received Grey with extreme coldness, he granted the request without question, directing Grey to a house towards the western side of the town.

In fact, von Namtzen hesitated for a moment, clearly wondering whether duty obliged him to accompany Grey upon his errand – but Lance-Korporal Helwig appeared with a new difficulty – he averaged three per day – and Grey was left to carry out the errand on his own.

The house where Koenig had lodged was nothing out of the ordinary, so far as Grey could see. The owner of the house was rather remarkable, though, being a dwarf.

'Oh, the poor man! So much blood you have before not seen!'

Herr Huckel stood perhaps as high as Grey's waist – a novel sensation, to look down so far to an adult conversant. Herr Huckel was none the less intelligent and coherent, which was also novel in Grey's experience; most witnesses to violence tended to lose what wits they had and either to forget all details, or to imagine impossible ones.

Herr Huckel, though, showed him willingly to the chamber where the death had occurred, and explained what he had himself seen.

'It was late, you see, sir, and my wife and I had gone to our beds. The soldiers were out – or at least we supposed so.' The soldiers had just received their pay, and most were busy losing it in taverns or brothels. The Huckels had heard no noises from the soldiers' room, and thus assumed that all four of the soldiers quartered with them were absent on such business.

Somewhere in the small hours, though, the good-folk had been awakened by terrible yells coming from the chamber. These were not produced by Private Koenig, but by one of his companions, who had returned in a state of advanced intoxication, and stumbled into a blood-soaked shambles.

'He lay here, sir. Just so?' Herr Huckel waved his hands to indicate the position the body had occupied at the far side of the cosy room. There was nothing there now, save irregular dark blotches that stained the wooden floor.

'Not even lye would get it out,' said Frau Huckel, who had come to the door of the room to watch. 'And we had to burn the bedding.'

Rather to Grey's surprise, she was not only of normal size, but quite pretty, with bright, soft hair peeking out from under her cap. She frowned at him in accusation.

'None of the soldiers will stay here, now. They think the *Nacht-Toter* will get them, too!' Clearly, this was Grey's fault. He bowed apologetically.

'I regret that, madam,' he said. 'Tell me, did you see the body?'

'No,' she said promptly, 'but I saw the night-hag.'

'Indeed,' Grey said, surprised. 'Er . . . what did it – she – it look like?' He hoped he was not going to receive some form of Siggy's logical but unhelpful description, '*Like a night-hag.*'

'Now, Margarethe, said Herr Huckel, putting a warning hand up to his wife's arm. 'It might not have been –'

'Yes, it was!' She transferred the frown to her husband, but did not shake off his hand, instead putting her own over it, before returning her attention to Grey.

'It was an old woman, sir, with her white hair in braids. Her shawl slipped off in the wind, and I saw. There are two old women who live nearby, this is true – but one walks only with a stick, and the other does not walk at all. This . . . thing, she moved very quickly, hunched a little, but light on her feet.'

Herr Huckel was looking more and more uneasy as this description progressed, and opened his mouth to interrupt, but was not given the chance.

'I am sure it was old Agathe!' Frau Huckel said, her voice dropping to a portentous whisper. Herr Huckel shut his eyes with a grimace.

'Old Agathe?' Grey asked, incredulous. 'Do you mean Frau Blomberg – the buergermeister's mother?'

Frau Huckel nodded, face fixed in grave certainty.

'Something must be done,' she declared. 'Everyone is afraid at night – either to go out, or to stay in. Men whose wives will not watch over them as they sleep are falling asleep as they work, as they eat . . .'

Grey thought briefly of mentioning Mr Keegan's patent preventative, but dismissed the notion, instead turning to Herr Huckel to inquire for a close description of the state of the body.

'I am told that the throat was pierced, as with an animal's teeth,' he said, at which Herr Huckel made a quick sign against evil and nodded, going a little pale. 'Was the throat torn quite open – as though the man were attacked by a wolf? Or –' But Herr Huckel was already shaking his head.

'No, no! Only two marks – two holes. Like a snake's fangs.' He poked two fingers into his own neck in illustration. 'But so much blood!' He shuddered, glancing away from the marks on the floorboards.

Grey had once seen a man bitten by a snake, when he was quite young – but there had been no blood, that he recalled. Of course, the man had been bitten in the leg, too.

'Large holes, then?' Grey persisted, not liking to press the man to recall vividly unpleasant details, but determined to obtain as much information as possible.

With some effort, he established that the tooth-marks had been size-able – perhaps a bit more than a quarter-inch or so in diameter – and located on the front of Koenig's throat, about half-way up. He made Huckel show him, repeatedly, after ascertaining that the body had shown no other wound, when undressed for cleansing and burial.

He glanced at the walls of the room, which had been freshly white-washed. Nevertheless, there was a large dark blotch showing faintly, down near the floor – probably where Koenig had rolled against the wall in his death-throes.

He had hoped that a description of Koenig's body would enable him to discover some connection between the two deaths – but the only similarity between the deaths of Koenig and Bodger appeared to be that both men were indeed dead, and both dead under impossible circumstances.

He thanked the Huckels and prepared to take his leave, only then realizing that Frau Huckel had resumed her train of thought and was speaking to him quite earnestly.

'. . . call a witch to cast the runes,' she said.

'I beg your pardon, madam?'

She drew in a breath of deep exasperation, but refrained from open rebuke.

'Herr Blomberg,' she repeated, giving Grey a hard look. 'He will call a witch to cast the runes. Then we will discover the truth of every-thing!'

'He will do *what*?' Sir Peter squinted at Grey in disbelief. 'Witches?'

'Only one, I believe, sir,' Grey assured Sir Peter. According to Frau Huckel, matters had been escalating in Gurgelwitz. The rumour that Herr Blomberg's mother was custodian to the succubus was rampant in the town, and public opinion was in danger of overwhelming the little buergermeister.

Herr Blomberg, however, was a stubborn man, and most devoted to his mother's memory. He refused entirely to allow her coffin to be dug up and her body desecrated.

The only solution, which Herr Blomberg had declared out of desperation, seemed to be to discover the true identity and hiding place of the succubus. To this end, the buergermeister had summoned a witch, who would cast runes –

'What are those?' Sir Peter asked, puzzled.

'I am not entirely sure, sir,' Grey admitted. 'Some object for divination, I suppose.'

'Really?' Sir Peter rubbed his knuckles dubiously beneath a long, thin nose. 'Sounds very fishy, what? This witch could say anything, couldn't she?'

'I suppose Herr Blomberg expects that if he is paying for the . . . er . . . ceremony, the lady is perhaps more likely to say something favourable to his situation,' Grey suggested.

'Hmm. Still don't like it,' Sir Peter said. 'Don't like it at all. Could be trouble, Grey, surely you see that?'

'I do not believe you can stop him, sir.'

'Perhaps not, perhaps not.' Sir Peter ruminated fiercely, brow crinkled under his wig. 'Ah! Well, how's this, then – you go round and fix it up, Grey. Tell Herr Blomberg he can have his hocus-pocus, but he must do it here, at the Schloss. That way we can keep a lid on it, what, see there's no untoward excitement?'

'Yes, sir,' Grey said, manfully suppressing a sigh, and went off to execute his orders.

By the time he reached his room to change for dinner, Grey felt dirty, irritable, and thoroughly out of sorts. It had taken most of the afternoon to track down Herr Blomberg and convince him to hold his . . . Christ, what was it? His rune-casting? . . . at the Schloss. Then he had run across the pest Helwig, and before he was able to escape, had been embroiled in an enormous controversy with a gang of mule drovers who claimed not to have been paid by the army.

This in turn had entailed a visit to two army camps, an inspection of thirty-four mules, trying interviews with both Sir Peter's paymaster and von Namtzen's – and involved a further cold interview with Stephan, who had behaved as though Grey were personally responsible for the entire affair, and then turned his back, dismissing Grey in mid-sentence, as though unable to bear the sight of him.

He flung off his coat, sent Tom to fetch hot water, and irritably tugged off his stock, wishing he could hit someone.

A knock sounded on the door, and he froze, irritation vanishing upon the moment. What to do? Pretend he wasn't in, was the obvious course, in case it was Louisa, in her sheer lawn shift or something worse. But if it were Stephan, come either to apologize or to demand further explanation?

The knock sounded again. It was a good, solid knock. Not what one would expect of a female – particularly not of a female intent on dalliance. Surely the Princess would be more inclined to a discreet scratching?

The knock came again, peremptory, demanding. Taking an enormous breath and trying to still the thumping of his heart, Grey jerked the door open.

'I wish to speak to you,' said the Dowager, and sailed into the room, not waiting for invitation.

'Oh,' said Grey, having lost all grasp of German on the spot. He closed the door, and turned to the old lady, instinctively rebuttoning his shirt.

She ignored his mute gesture towards the chair, but stood in front of the fire, fixing him with a steely gaze. She was completely dressed, he saw, with a faint sense of relief. He really could not have borne the sight of the Dowager *en dishabille.*

'I have come to ask you,' she said without preamble, 'if you have intentions to marry Louisa.'

'I have not,' he said, his German returning with miraculous promptitude. '*Nein.*'

One sketchy grey brow twitched upwards.

'*Ja*? That is not what she thinks.'

He rubbed a hand over his face, groping for some diplomatic reply – and found it, in the feel of the stubble on his own jaw.

'I admire Princess Louisa greatly,' he said. 'There are few women who are her equal –' *And thank God for that*, he added to himself, '– but I regret that I am not free to undertake any obligation. I have . . . an understanding. In England.' His understanding with James Fraser was that if he were ever to lay a hand on the man or speak his heart, Fraser would break his neck instantly. It was, however, certainly an understanding, and clear as Irish crystal.

The Dowager looked at him with a narrow gaze of such penetration that he wanted to take several steps backwards. He stood his ground, though, returning the look with one of patent sincerity.

'Hmph!' she said at last. 'Well, then. That is good.' Without another word, she turned on her heel. Before she could close the door behind her, he reached out and grasped her arm.

She swung round to him, surprised and outraged at his presumption. He ignored this, though, absorbed in what he had seen as she turned.

'Pardon, Your Highness,' he said. He touched the medal pinned to the bodice of her gown. He had seen it a hundred times, and assumed it always to contain the image of some saint – which, he supposed, it did, but certainly not in the traditional manner.

'St Orgevald?' he inquired. The image was crudely embossed, and could easily be taken for something else – if one hadn't seen the larger version on the lid of the reliquary.

'Certainly.' The old lady fixed him with a glittering eye, shook her head, and went out, closing the door firmly behind her.

For the first time, it occurred to Grey that whoever Orgevald had been, it was entirely possible that he had not originally been a saint. Pondering this, he went to bed, scratching absent-mindedly.

7

Ambush

The next day dawned cold and windy. Grey saw pheasants huddling under the cover of shrubs as he rode, crows hugging the ground in the stubbled fields, and slate roofs thick with shuffling doves, feathered bodies packed together in the quest for heat. In spite of their reputed brainlessness, he had to think that the birds were more sensible than he.

Birds had no duty – but it wasn't quite duty that propelled him on this ragged, chilly morning. It was in part simple curiosity, in part official suspicion. He wished to find the gypsies; in particular, he wished to find *one* gypsy; the woman who had quarrelled with Private Bodger, soon before his death.

If he were quite honest – and he felt that he could afford to be, so long as it was within the privacy of his own mind – he had another motive for the journey. It would be entirely natural for him to pause at the bridge for a cordial word with the artillerymen, and perhaps see for himself how the boy with the red lips was faring.

While all these motives were undoubtedly sound, though, the real reason for his expedition was simply that it would remove him from the Schloss. He did not feel safe in a house containing the Princess Louisa, let alone her mother-in-law. Neither could he go to his usual office in the town, for fear of encountering Stephan.

The whole situation struck him as farcical in the extreme; still, he could not keep himself from thinking about it – about Stephan.

Had he been deluding himself about Stephan's attraction to him? He was as vain as any man, he supposed, and yet he could swear . . . his thoughts went round and round in the same weary circle. And yet, each time he thought to dismiss them entirely, he felt again the overwhelming sense of warmth and casual possession with which Stephan had kissed him. He had not imagined it. And yet . . .

Embrangled in this tedious but inescapable coil, he reached the bridge by mid-morning, only to find that the young soldier was not in camp.

'Franz? Gone foraging, maybe,' said the Schwabian lieutenant, with a shrug. 'Or got home-sick and run. They do that, the young ones.'

'Got scared,' one of the other men suggested, overhearing.

'Scared of what?' Grey asked sharply, wondering whether in spite of everything, word of the succubus had reached the bridge.

'Scared of his shadow, that one,' said the man he recalled as Samson, making a face. 'He keeps talking about the child, he hears a crying child at night.'

'Thought you heard it too, eh?' said the Schwabian, not sounding entirely friendly. 'The night it rained so hard?'

'Me? I didn't hear anything then but Franz's squealing.' There was a rumble of laughter at that, the sound of which made Grey's heart drop to his boots. *Too late*, he thought. 'At the lightning,' Samson added blandly, catching his glance.

'He's run for home,' the Schwabian declared. 'Let him go; no use here for a coward.'

There was a small sense of disquiet in the man's manner that belied his confidence, Grey thought – and yet there was nothing to be done about it. He had no direct authority over these men; could not order a search to be undertaken.

As he crossed the bridge, though, he could not help but glance over. The water had subsided only a little; the flood still tumbled past, choked with torn leaves and half-seen sodden objects. He did not want to stop, to be caught looking, and yet looked as carefully as he could, half-expecting to see little Franz's delicate body broken on the rocks, or the blind eyes of a drowned face trapped beneath the water.

He saw nothing but the usual flood debris, though, and with a slight sense of relief, continued on towards the hills.

He knew nothing save the direction the gypsy waggons had been going when last observed. It was long odds that he would find them, but he searched doggedly, pausing at intervals to scan the countryside with his spyglass, or to look for rising plumes of smoke.

These last occurred sporadically, but proved invariably to be peasant huts or charcoal burners, all of whom either disappeared promptly when they saw his red coat, or stared and crossed themselves, but none of whom admitted to having heard of the gypsies, let alone seen them.

The sun was coming down the sky, and he realized that he must turn back soon, or be caught in open country by night. He had a tinder-box and a bottle of ale in his saddle-bag, but no food, and the prospect of being marooned in this fashion was unwelcome, particularly with the French forces only a few miles to the west. If the British army had scouts, so did the frogs, and he was lightly armed, with no more than a pair of pistols, a rather dented cavalry sabre, and his dagger to hand.

Not wishing to risk Karolus on the boggy ground, he was riding another of his horses, a thickset bay who went by the rather unflattering name of Hognose, but who had excellent manners and a steady foot. Steady enough that Grey could ignore the ground, trying to focus his attention, strained from prolonged tension, into a last look round. The foliage of the hills around him faded into patchwork, shifting constantly in the roiling wind. Again and again, he thought he saw things – human figures, animals moving, the briefly seen corner of a waggon – only to have them prove illusory when he ventured towards them.

The wind whined incessantly in his ears, adding spectral voices to the illusions that plagued him. He rubbed a hand over his face, gone numb from the cold, imagining momentarily that he heard the wails of Franz's ghostly child. He shook his head to dispel the impression – but it persisted.

He drew Hognose to a stop, turning his head from side to side, listening intently. He was sure he heard it – but what was it? No words were distinguishable above the moaning of the wind, but there *was* a sound, he was sure of it.

At the same time, it seemed to come from nowhere in particular; try as he might, he could not locate it. The horse heard it, too, though – he saw the bay's ears prick and turn nervously.

'Where?' he said softly, laying the rein on the horse's neck. 'Where is it? Can you find it?'

The horse apparently had little interest in finding the noise, but some in getting away from it; Hognose backed, shuffling on the sandy ground, kicking up sheaves of wet yellow leaves. Grey drew him up sharply, swung down, and wrapped the reins around a bare-branched sapling.

With the horse's revulsion as guide, he saw what he had overlooked; the churned earth of a badger's sett, half-hidden by the sprawling roots of a large elm. Once focused on this, he could pinpoint the noise as coming from it. And damned if he'd ever heard a badger carry on like that!

Pistol drawn and primed, he edged towards the bank of earth, keeping a wary eye on the nearby trees.

It was certainly crying, but not a child; a sort of muffled whimpering, interspersed with the kind of catch in the breath that injured men often made.

'*Wo ist das*?' he demanded, halting just short of the opening to the sett, pistol raised. 'You are injured?'

There was a gulp of surprise, followed at once by scrabbling sounds.

'Major? Major Grey? It is you?'

'Franz?' he said, flabbergasted.

'*Ja*, Major! Help me, help me, please!'

Uncocking the pistol and thrusting it back in his belt, he knelt and peered into the hole. Badger setts are normally deep, running straight down for six feet or more before turning, twisting sideways into the badger's den. This one was no exception; the grimy, tear-streaked face of the young Prussian soldier stared up at him from the bottom, his head a good foot below the rim of the narrow hole.

The boy had broken his leg in falling, and it was no easy matter to lift him straight up. Grey managed it at last by improvising a sling of his own shirt and the boy's, tied to a rope anchored to Hognose's saddle.

At last he had the boy laid on the ground, covered with his coat and taking small sips from the bottle of ale.

'Major –' Franz coughed and spluttered, trying to rise on one elbow.

'Hush, don't try to talk.' Grey patted his arm soothingly, wondering how best to get him back to the bridge. 'Everything will be –'

'But Major – the red coats! *Der Inglischeren*!'

'What? What are you talking about?'

'Dead Englishmen! It was the little boy, I heard him, and I dug, and –' The boy's story was spilling out in a torrent of Prussian, and it took no little time for Grey to slow him down sufficiently to disentangle the threads of what he was saying.

He had, Grey understood him to say, repeatedly heard the crying near the bridge, but his fellows either didn't hear or wouldn't admit to it, instead teasing him mercilessly about it. At last he determined to go by himself and see if he could find a source for the sound – wind moaning through a hole, as his friend Jurgen had suggested.

'But it wasn't.' Franz was still pale, but small patches of hectic colour glowed in the translucent skin of his cheeks. He had poked about the base of the bridge, discovering eventually a small crack in the rocks at the foot of a pillar on the far side of the river. Thinking that this might indeed be the source of the crying, he had inserted his bayonet and pried at the rock – which had promptly come away, leaving him face to face with a cavity inside the pillar, containing a small, round, very white skull.

'More bones, too, I think. I didn't stop to look.' The boy swallowed. He had simply run, too panicked to think. When he stopped at last, completely out of breath and with legs like jelly, he had sat down to rest and think what to do.

'They couldn't beat me more than once for being gone,' he said, with the ghost of a smile. 'So I thought I would be gone a little longer.'

This decision was enhanced by the discovery of a grove of walnut trees, and Franz had made his way up into the hills, gathering both nuts and wild blackberries – his lips were still stained purple with the juice, Grey saw.

He had been interrupted in this peaceful pursuit by the sound of gunfire. Throwing himself flat on the ground, he had then crept a little forwards, until he could see over the edge of a little rocky escarpment. Below, in a hollow, he saw a small group of English soldiers, engaged in mortal combat with Austrians.

'Austrians? You are sure?' Grey asked, astonished.

'I know what Austrians look like,' the boy assured him, a little tartly. Knowing what Austrians were capable of, too, he had promptly backed up, risen to his feet, and run as fast as he could in the opposite direction – only to fall into the badger's sett in his haste.

'You were lucky the badger wasn't at home,' Grey remarked, teeth beginning to chatter. He had reclaimed the remnants of his shirt, but this was insufficient shelter against dropping temperature and probing wind. 'But you said dead Englishmen.'

'I think they were all dead,' the boy said. 'I didn't go see.'

Grey, however, must. Leaving the boy covered with his coat and a mound of dead leaves, he untied the horse and turned his head in the direction Franz had indicated.

Proceeding with care and caution in case of lurking Austrians, it was nearly sunset before he found the hollow.

It was Dundas and his survey party; he recognized the uniforms at once. Cursing under his breath, he flung himself off his horse and scrabbled hurriedly from one body to the next, hoping against hope as he pressed shaking fingers against flaccid cheeks and cooling breasts.

Two were still alive: Dundas and a corporal. The Corporal was badly wounded and unconscious; Dundas had taken a gun-butt to the head and a bayonet through the chest, but the wound had fortunately sealed itself. The Lieutenant was disabled and in pain, but not yet on the verge of death.

'Hundreds of the buggers,' he croaked breathlessly, gripping Grey's arm. 'Saw . . . whole battalion . . . guns. Going to . . . the French. Fanshawe – followed them. Spying. Heard. Fucking succ – succ –' he coughed hard, spraying a little blood with the saliva, but it seemed to ease his breath temporarily.

'It was a plan. Got whores – agents. Slept with men, gave them o-opium. Dreams. Panic, aye?' He was half-sitting up, straining to make words, make Grey understand.

Grey understood, only too well. He had been given opium once, by a doctor, and remembered vividly the weirdly erotic dreams that had ensued. Do the same to men who had likely never heard of opium, let alone experienced it – and at the same time, start rumours of a demoness who preyed upon men in their dreams? Particularly with a flesh-and-blood avatar, who could leave such marks as would convince a man he had been so victimized?

Only too effective, and one of the cleverest notions he had ever come across, for demoralizing an enemy before attack. It was that alone that gave him some hope, as he comforted Dundas, piling him with coats taken from the dead, dragging the corporal to lie near the Lieutenant for the sake of shared warmth, digging through a discarded rucksack for water to give him.

If the combined force of French and Austrians were huge, there would be no need for such subtleties – the enemy would simply roll over the English and their German allies. But if the numbers were closer to equal – and it was still necessary to funnel them across that narrow bridges . . . then yes, it was desirable to face an enemy who had not slept for several nights, whose men were tired and jumpy, whose officers were not paying attention to possible threat, being too occupied with the difficulties close at hand.

He could see it clearly; Ruysdale was busy watching the French, who were sitting happily on the cliffs, moving just enough to keep attention diverted from the Austrian advance. The Austrians would come down on the bridge – likely at night – and then the French on their heels.

Dundas was shivering, eyes closed, teeth set hard in his lower lip against the pain of the movement.

'Christopher, can you hear me? Christopher!' Grey shook him, as gently as possible. 'Where's Fanshawe?' He didn't know the members of Dundas's party; if Fanshawe had been taken captive, or – but Dundas was shaking his head, gesturing feebly towards one of the corpses, lying with his head smashed open.

'Go on,' Dundas whispered. His face was grey, and not only from the waning light. 'Warn Sir Peter.' He put his arm about the unconscious corporal, and nodded to Grey. 'We'll . . . wait.'

8
The Witch

Grey had been staring with great absorption at his valet's face for some moments, before he realized even what he was looking at, let alone why.

'Uh?' he said.

'I *said*,' Tom repeated, with some emphasis, 'you best drink this, me lord, or you're going to fall flat on your face, and that won't do, will it?'

'It won't? Oh. No. Of course not.' He took the cup, adding a belated, 'Thank you, Tom. What is it?'

'I told you twice, I'm not going to try and say the name of it again. Ilse says it'll keep you on your feet, though.' He leaned forwards and sniffed approvingly at the liquid, which appeared to be brown and foamy, indicating the presence in it of eggs, Grey thought.

He followed Tom's lead and sniffed, too, recoiling only slightly at the eye-watering reek. Hartshorn, perhaps? It had quite a lot of brandy, no matter what else was in it. And he did need to stay on his feet. With no more than a precautionary clenching of his belly-muscles, he put back his head and drained it.

He had been awake for nearly forty-eight hours, and the world around him had a tendency to pass in and out of focus, like the scene in a spyglass. He had also a proclivity to go intermittently deaf, not hearing what was said to him – and Tom was correct, that wouldn't do.

He had taken time, the night before, to fetch Franz, put him on the horse – with a certain amount of squealing, it must be admitted, as Franz had never been on a horse before – and take him to the spot where Dundas lay, feeling that they would be better together. He had pressed his dagger into Franz's hands, and left him guarding the Corporal and the Lieutenant, who was by then passing in and out of consciousness.

Grey had then donned his coat and come back to raise the alarm, riding a flagging horse at the gallop over pitch-black ground, by the light of a sinking moon. He'd fallen twice, when Hognose stumbled, jarring bones and jellying kidneys but luckily escaped injury both times.

He had alerted the artillery crew at the bridge, ridden on to Ruysdale's encampment, roused everyone, seen the Colonel in spite of all attempts to prevent him waking the man, gathered a rescue party, and ridden back to retrieve Dundas and the others, arriving in the hollow near dawn to find the Corporal dead and Dundas nearly so, with his head in Franz's lap.

Captain Hiltern had of course sent someone with word to Sir Peter at the Schloss, but it was necessary for Grey to report personally to Sir Peter and von Namtzen, when he returned at midday with the rescue party. After which, officers and men had flapped out of the place like a swarm of bats, the whole military apparatus moving like the armature of some great engine, creaking, groaning, but coming to life with amazing speed.

Which left Grey alone in the Schloss at sunset, blank in mind and body, with nothing further to do. There was no need for liaison; couriers were flitting to and from all the regiments, carrying orders. He had no duty to perform; no one to command, no one to serve.

He would ride out in the morning with Sir Peter Hicks, part of Sir Peter's personal guard. But there was no need for him now; everyone was about his own business; Grey was forgotten.

He felt odd; not unwell, but as though objects and people near him were not quite real, not entirely firm to the touch. He should sleep, he knew – but could not, not with the whole world in flux around him, and a sense of urgency that hummed on his skin, yet was unable to penetrate to the core of his mind.

Tom was talking to him; he made an effort to attend.

'Witch,' he repeated, awareness struggling to make itself known. 'Witch. You mean Herr Blomberg still intends to hold his – ceremony?'

'Yes, me lord.' Tom was sponging Grey's coat, frowning as he tried to remove a pitch stain from the skirt. 'Ilse says he won't rest until he's cleared his mother's name, and damned if the Austrians will stop him.'

Awareness burst through Grey's fog like a pricked soap bubble.

'Christ! He doesn't know!'

'About what, me lord?' Tom turned to look at him curiously, sponging cloth and vinegar in hand.

'The succubus. I must tell him – explain.' Even as he said it, though, he realized how little force such an explanation would have upon Herr Blomberg's real problem. Sir Peter and Colonel Ruysdale might accept the truth – the townspeople would be much less likely to accept having been fooled – and by Austrians!

Grey knew enough about gossip and rumour to realize that no amount of explanation from him would be enough. Still less, if that explanation were to be filtered through Herr Blomberg, whose bias in the matter was clear.

Even Tom was frowning doubtfully at him as he rapidly explained the matter. *Superstition and sensation are always so much more appealing than truth and rationality.* The words echoed as though spoken in his ear, with the same humorously rueful intonation with which his father had spoken them, many years before.

He rubbed a hand vigorously over his face, feeling himself come back to life. Perhaps he had one more task to complete, in his role as liaison.

'This witch, Tom – the woman who is to cast the runes – whatever in God's name that might involve. Do you know where she is?'

'Oh, yes, me lord.' Tom had put down his cloth now, interested. 'She's here – in the Schloss, I mean. Locked up in the larder.'

'Locked up in the larder? Why?'

'Well, it has a good lock on the door, me lord, to keep the servants from – oh, you mean why's she locked up at all? Ilse says she didn't want to come; dug in her heels entire, and wouldn't hear of it. But Herr Blomberg wouldn't hear of her *not*, and had her dragged up here, and locked up 'til this evening. He's fetching up the Town Council, and the Magistrate, and all the big-wigs he can lay hands on, Ilse says.'

'Take me to her.'

Tom's mouth dropped open. He closed it with a snap and looked Grey up and down.

'Not like *that*. You're not even shaved!'

'Precisely like this,' Grey assured him, tucking in the tails of his shirt. 'Now.'

*   *   *

The game-larder was locked, but as Grey had surmised, Ilse knew where the key was kept, and was not proof against Tom's charm. The room itself was in an alcove behind the kitchens, and it was a simple matter to reach it without detection.

'You need not come further, Tom,' Grey said, low-voiced. 'Give me the keys; if anyone finds me here, I'll say I took them.'

Tom, who had taken the precaution of arming himself with a toasting fork, merely clutched the keys tighter in his other hand, and shook his head.

The door swung open silently on leather hinges. Someone had given the captive woman a candle; it lit the small space and cast fantastic shadows on the walls, from the hanging bodies of swans and pheasants, ducks and geese.

The drink had restored a sense of energy to Grey's mind and body, but without quite removing the sense of unreality that had pervaded his consciousness. It was therefore with no real surprise that he saw the woman who turned towards him, and recognized the gypsy prostitute who had quarrelled with Private Bodger, a few hours before the soldier's death.

She obviously recognized him, too, though she said nothing. Her eyes passed over him with cool scorn, and she turned away, evidently engrossed in some silent communion with a severed hog's head that sat upon a china plate.

'Madam,' he said softly, as though his voice might rouse the dead fowl to sudden flight, 'I would speak with you.'

She ignored him, and folded her hands elaborately behind her back. The light winked gold from the rings in her ears and the rings on her fingers – and Grey saw that one was a crude circlet, with the emblem of St Orgevald's protection.

He was overcome with a sudden sense of premonition, though he did not believe in premonition. He felt things in motion around him, things that he did not understand and could not control, things settling of themselves into an ordained and appointed position, like the revolving spheres of his father's orrery – and he wished to protest about this state of affairs, but could not.

'Me lord.' Tom's hissed whisper shook him out of this momentary disorientation, and he glanced at the boy, eyebrows raised. Tom was staring at the woman, who was still turned away, but whose face was visible in profile.

'Hanna,' he said, nodding at the gypsy. 'She looks like Hanna, Siggy's nursemaid. You know, me lord, the one what disappeared?'

The woman had swung round abruptly at mention of Hanna's name, and stood glaring at them both.

Grey felt the muscles of his back loosen, very slightly, as though some force had picked him up and held him by the scruff of the neck. As though he, too, was one of the objects being moved, placed in the spot ordained for him.

'I have a proposition for you, madam,' he said calmly, and pulled a cask of salted fish out from beneath a shelf. He sat on it, and reaching behind him, pulled the door closed.

'I do not wish to hear anything you say, *Schwein-hund*,' she said, very coldly. 'As for you, piglet . . .' Her eyes darkened with no very pleasant light as she looked at Tom.

'You have failed,' Grey went on, ignoring this digression. 'And you are in considerable danger. The Austrian plan is known; you can hear the soldiers preparing for battle, can't you?' It was true; the sounds of drums and distant shouting, the shuffle of many marching feet, were audible even here, though muffled by the stone walls of the Schloss.

He smiled pleasantly at her, and his fingers touched the silver gorget that he had seized before leaving his room. It hung about his neck, over his half-buttoned shirt, the sign of an officer on duty.

'I offer you your life, and your freedom. In return . . .' He paused. She said nothing, but one straight black brow rose, slowly.

'I want a bit of justice,' he said. 'I want to know how Private Bodger died. Bodger,' he repeated, seeing her look of incomprehension, and realizing that she had likely never known his name. 'The English soldier who said you had cheated him.'

She sniffed contemptuously, but a crease of angry amusement lined the edge of her mouth.

'Him. God killed him. Or the Devil, take your choice. Or, no –' the crease deepened, and she thrust out the hand with the ring on it, nearly in his face. 'I think it was my saint. Do you believe in saints, Pig-soldier?'

'No,' he said calmly. 'What happened?'

'He saw me, coming out of a tavern, and he followed me. I didn't know he was there; he caught me in an alley, but I pulled away and ran into the churchyard. I thought he wouldn't follow me there, but he did.'

Bodger had been both angry and aroused, insisting that he would take the satisfaction she had earlier denied him. She had kicked and struggled, but he was stronger than she.

'And then –' she shrugged. 'Poof. He stops what he is doing, and makes a sound.'

'What sort of sound?'

'How should I know? Men make all kinds of sounds. Farting, groaning, belching . . . pff.' She bunched her fingers and flicked them sharply, disposing of men and all their doings with the gesture.

At any rate, Bodger had then dropped heavily to his knees, and still clinging to her dress, had fallen over. The gypsy had rapidly pried loose his fingers and run, thanking the intercession of St Orgevald.

'Hmm.' A sudden weakness of the heart? An apoplexy? Keegan had said such a thing was possible – and there was no evidence to belie the gypsy's statement. 'Not like Private Koenig, then,' Grey said, watching carefully.

Her head jerked up and she stared hard at him, lips tight.

'Me lord,' said Tom softly behind him. 'Hanna's name is Koenig.'

'It is not!' the gypsy snapped. 'It is Mulengro, as is mine!'

'First things first, if you please, madam,' Grey said, repressing the urge to stand up, as she leaned glowering over him. 'Where *is* Hanna? And what is she to you? Sister, cousin, daughter . . . ?'

'Sister,' she said, biting the word off like a thread. Her lips were tight as a seam, but Grey touched his gorget once again.

'Life,' he said. 'And freedom.' He regarded her steadily, watching indecision play upon her features like the wavering shadows on the walls. She had no way of knowing how powerless he was; he could neither condemn nor release her – and nor would anyone else, all being caught up in the oncoming maelstrom of war.

In the end, he had his way, as he had known he would, and sat listening to her in a state that was neither trance nor dream; just a tranquil acceptance as the pieces fell before him, one upon one.

She was one of the women recruited by the Austrians to spread the rumours of the succubus – and had much enjoyed the spreading, judging from the way she licked her lower lip while telling of it. Her sister Hanna had been married to the soldier Koenig, but had rejected him, he being a faithless hound, like all men.

Bearing in mind the gossip regarding Siegfried's paternity, Grey nodded thoughtfully, motioning to her with one hand to go on.

She did. Koenig had gone away with the army, but then had come back, and had had the audacity to visit the Schloss, trying to rekindle the flame with Hanna. Afraid that he might succeed in seducing her sister again –'She is weak, Hanna,' she said with a shrug, 'she *will* trust men!' – she had gone to visit Koenig at night, planning to drug him with wine laced with opium, as she had done with the others.

'Only this time, a fatal dose, I suppose.' Grey had propped his elbow upon his crossed knee, hand under his chin. The tiredness had come back; it hovered near at hand, but was not yet clouding his mental processes.

'I meant it so, yes.' She uttered a short laugh. 'But he knew the taste of opium. He threw it at me, and grabbed me by the throat.'

Whereupon she had drawn the dagger she always carried at her belt and stabbed at him – striking upwards into his open mouth, and piercing his brain.

'You never saw so much blood in all your life,' the gypsy assured Grey, unconsciously echoing Herr Huckel.

'Oh, I rather think I have,' Grey said politely. His hand went to his own waist – but of course, he had left his dagger with Franz. 'But pray go on. The marks, as of an animal's fangs?'

'A nail,' she said, and shrugged.

'So, was it him – Koenig, I mean – was it him tried to snatch little Siggy?' Tom, deeply absorbed in the revelations, could not keep himself from blurting out the question. He coughed and tried to fade back into the woodwork, but Grey indicated that this was a question which he himself found of some interest.

'You did not tell me where your sister is. But I assume that it was you the boy saw in his chamber?' *'What did she look like?' he had asked. 'Like a witch,' the child replied.* Did she? She did not look like Grey's conception of a witch – but what was that, save the fabrication of a limited imagination?

She was tall for a woman, dark, and her face mingled an odd sexuality with a strongly forbidding aspect – a combination that many men would find intriguing. Grey thought it was not something that would have struck Siggy, but something else about her evidently had.

She nodded. She was fingering her ring, he saw, and watching him with calculation, as though deciding whether to tell him a lie.

'I have seen the Dowager Princess's medal,' he said politely. 'Is she an Austrian, by birth? I assume that you and your sister are.'

The woman stared at him, and said something in her own tongue, which sounded highly uncomplimentary.

'And you think *I* am a witch!' she said, evidently translating the thought.

'No, I don't,' Grey said. 'But others do, and that is what brings us here. If you please, madam, let us conclude our business. I expect someone will shortly come for you.' The Schloss was at dinner; Tom had brought Grey a tray, which he was too tired to eat. No doubt the rune casting would be the after-dinner entertainment, and he must make his desires clear before that.

'Well, then.' The gypsy regarded him, her awe at his perspicacity fading back into the usual derision. 'It was your fault.'

'I beg your pardon?'

'It was Princess Gertrude – the Dowager, so you call her. She saw Louisa – that slut –' she spat casually on the floor, almost without pausing, and went on, '– making sheep's eyes at you, and was afraid she meant to marry you. Louisa thought she would marry you and go to England, to be safe and rich. But if she did, she would take with her her son.'

'And the Dowager did not wish to be parted from her grandson,' Grey said slowly. Whether the gossip was true or not, the old woman loved the boy.

The gypsy nodded. 'So she arranged that we would take the boy – my sister and me. He would be safe with us, and after a time, when the Austrians had killed you all or driven you away, we would bring him back.'

Hanna had gone down the ladder first, meaning to comfort Siggy if he woke in the rain. But Siggy had wakened before that, and bollocksed the scheme by running out of the room. Hanna had no choice but to flee when Grey had tipped the ladder over, leaving her sister to hide in the Schloss, and make her way out at daybreak, with the help of the Dowager.

'She is with our family,' the gypsy said, with another shrug. 'Safe.'

'The ring,' Grey said, nodding at the gypsy's circlet. 'Do you serve the Dowager? Is that what it means?'

So much confessed, the gypsy evidently felt now at ease. Casually, she pushed a platter of dead doves aside, and sat down upon the shelf, feet dangling.

'We are Rom,' she said, drawing herself up proudly. 'The Rom serve no one. But we have known the Trauchtenbergs – the Dowager's family – for generations, and there is tradition between us. It was her great-great-grandfather who bought the child who guards the bridge – and that child was the younger brother of my own four times great-grandfather. The ring was given to my ancestor then, as a sign of the bargain.'

Grey heard Tom grunt slightly with confusion, but took no heed. The words struck him as forcefully as a blow, and he could not speak for a moment. The thing was too shocking. He took a deep breath, fighting the vision of Franz's words – the small, round, white skull, looking out at him from the hollow in the bridge.

Sounds of banging and clashing dishes from the scullery nearby brought him to himself, though, and he realized that time was growing short.

'Very well,' he said, as briskly as he could. 'I want one last bit of justice, and our bargain is made. Agathe Blomberg.'

'Old Agathe?' The gypsy laughed, and in spite of her missing tooth, he could see how attractive she could be. 'How funny! How could they suppose such an old stick might be a demon of desire? A hag, yes, but a night-hag?' She went off into peals of laughter, and Grey jumped to his feet, seizing her by the shoulder to silence her.

'Be quiet,' he said, 'someone will come.'

She stopped, then, though she still snorted with amusement.

'So, then?'

'So, then,' he said firmly. 'When you do your hocus-pocus – whatever it is they've brought you here to do – I wish you particularly to exonerate Agathe Blomberg. I don't care what you say or how you do it – I leave that to your own devices, which I expect are considerable.'

She looked at him for a moment, looked down at his hand upon her shoulder, and shrugged it off.

'That's all, is it?' she asked sarcastically.

'That's all. Then you may go.'

'Oh, I may go? How kind.' She stood smiling at him, but not in a kindly way. It occurred to him quite suddenly that she had required no assurances from him; had not asked for so much as his word as a gentleman – though he supposed she would not have valued that, in any case.

She did not care, he realized, with a small shock. She had not told him anything for the sake of saving herself – she simply wasn't afraid. Did she think the Dowager would protect her, for the sake either of their ancient bond, or because of what she knew about the failed kidnapping?

Perhaps. Perhaps she had confidence in something else. And if she had, he chose not to consider what that might be. He rose from the cask of fish, and pushed it back under the shelves.

'Agathe Blomberg was a woman, too,' he said.

She rose, too, and stood looking at him, rubbing her ring with apparent thought.

'So she was. Well, perhaps I will do it, then. Why should men dig up her coffin and drag her poor old carcass through the streets?'

He could feel Tom behind him, vibrating with eagerness to be gone; the racket of the dinner clearing was much louder.

'For you, though –'

He glanced at her, startled by the tone in her voice, which held something different. Neither mockery nor venom, nor any other emotion that he knew.

Her eyes were huge, gleaming in the candlelight, but so dark that they seemed void pools, her face without expression.

'You will never satisfy a woman,' she said softly. 'Any woman who shares your bed will leave after no more than a single night, cursing you.'

Grey rubbed a knuckle against his stubbled chin, and nodded.

'Very likely, madam,' he said. 'Good night.'

Epilogue: Among the Trumpets

The order of battle was set. The autumn sun had barely risen, and the troops would march within the hour to meet their destiny at the bridge of Aschenwald.

Grey was in the stable-block, checking Karolus's tack, tightening the girth, adjusting the bridle, marking second by second the time until he should depart, as though each second marked an irretrievable and most precious drop of his life.

Outside the stables, all was confusion, as people ran hither and thither, gathering belongings, searching for children, calling for wives and parents, strewing away objects gathered only moments before, heedless in their distraction. His heart beat fast in his chest, and intermittent small thrills coursed up the backs of his legs and curled between them, tightening his scrotum.

The drums were beating in the distance, ordering the troops. The thrum of them beat in his blood, in his bone. Soon, soon, soon. His chest was tight; it was difficult to draw full breath.

He did not hear the footsteps approaching through the straw of the stables. Keyed up as he was, though, he felt the disturbance of air nearby, that intimation of intrusion that now and then had saved his life, and whirled, hand on his dagger.

It was Stephan von Namtzen, gaudy in full uniform, his great plumed helmet underneath one arm – but with a face sober by contrast to his clothing.

'It is nearly time,' the Schwabian said quietly. 'I would speak with you – if you will hear me.'

Grey slowly let his hand fall away from the dagger, and took the full breath he had been longing for.

'You know that I will.'

Von Namtzen inclined his head in acknowledgement, but did not speak at once, seeming to need to gather his words – although they were speaking German now.

'I will marry Louisa,' he said, finally, formally. 'If I live until Christmas. My children –' He hesitated, free hand flat upon the breast of his coat. 'It will be good they should have a mother once more. And –'

'You need not give reasons,' Grey interrupted. He smiled at the big Schwabian, with open affection. Caution was no longer necessary. 'If you wish this, then I wish you well.'

Von Namtzen's face lightened a bit. He ducked his head a little, and took a breath.

'*Danke*. I say, I will marry, if I am alive. If I am not . . .' His hand still rested on his breast, above the miniature of his children.

'If I live, and you do not, then I will go to your home in Schwabia,' Grey said. 'I will tell your son what I have known of you. Is this your desire?'

The Schwabian's graveness did not alter, but a deep warmth softened his grey eyes.

'It is. You have known me, perhaps, better than anyone.'

He stood still, looking at Grey, and all at once, the relentless marking of fleeting time stopped. Confusion and danger still hastened without, and drums beat loud, but inside the stables, there was a great peace.

Stephan's hand left his breast, and reached out. Grey took it, and felt love flow between them. He thought that heart and body must be entirely melted – if only for that moment.

Then they parted, each drawing back, each seeing the flash of desolation in the other's face, both smiling ruefully to see it.

Stephan was turning to go, when Grey remembered.

'Wait!' he called, and turned to fumble in his saddle-bag.

'What is this?' Stephan turned the small, heavy box over in his hands, looking puzzled.

'A charm,' Grey said, smiling. 'A blessing. My blessing – and St Orgevald's. May it protect you.'

'But –' Von Namtzen frowned with doubt, and tried to give the reliquary back, but Grey would not accept it.

'Believe me,' he said in English, 'it will do you more good than me.'

Stephan looked at him for a moment longer, then nodded, and

tucking the little box away in his pocket, turned and left. Grey turned back to Karolus, who was growing restive, tossing his head and snorting softly through his nose.

The horse stamped, hard, and the vibration of it ran through the long bones of Grey's legs.

'Hast thou given the horse strength?' he quoted softly, hand stroking the braided mane that ran smooth and serpent-like down the great ridge of the stallion's neck. 'Hast thou clothed his neck with thunder? He paweth in the valley, and rejoiceth in his strength: he goeth on to meet the armed men. He mocketh at fear, and is not affrighted; neither turneth he back from the sword.'

He leaned close and pressed his forehead against the horse's shoulder. Huge muscles bulged beneath the skin, warm and eager, and the clean musky scent of the horse's excitement filled him. He straightened then, and slapped the taut, twitching hide.

'He saith among the trumpets, Ha, ha; and he smelleth the battle afar off, the thunder of the captains, and the shouting.'

Grey heard the drums again, and his palms began to sweat.

Historical note: In October of 1757, the forces of Frederick the Great and his allies moved swiftly, crossing the country to defeat the gathering French and Austrian army at Rossbach, in Saxony. the town of Gurgelwitz was left undisturbed; the bridge at Aschenwald has never been crossed by an enemy.

MAJIPOOR

ROBERT SILVERBERG

MAJIPOOR
ROBERT SILVERBERG

Lord Valentine's Castle (1980)
Majipoor Chronicles (1981)
Valentine Pontifex (1983)
The Mountains of Majipoor (1995)

THE PRESTIMION TRILOGY:
Sorcerers of Majipoor (1997)
Lord Prestimion (1999)
The King of Dreams (2001)

The giant world of Majipoor, with a diameter at least ten times as great as that of our own planet's, was settled in the distant past by colonists from Earth, who made a place for themselves amid the Piurivars, the intelligent native beings, known to the intruders from Earth as 'Shapeshifters' or 'Metamorphs' because of their ability to alter their bodily forms. Majipoor is an extraordinarily beautiful planet, with a largely benign climate, and is a place of astonishing zoological, botanical and geographical wonders. Everything on Majipoor is large-scale – fantastic, marvellous.

Over the course of thousands of years friction between the human colonists and the Metamorphs eventually led to a lengthy war and the defeat of the natives, who were penned up in huge reservations in remote regions of the planet. During those years, also, species from various other worlds came to settle on Majipoor – the tiny gnomish Vroons, the great shaggy four-armed Skandars, the two-headed Su-Suheris race, and several more. Some of these – notably the Vroons and the Su-Suheris – were gifted with extrasensory mental powers that permitted them to practise various forms of wizardry. But throughout the thousands of years of Majipoor history the humans remained the dominant species. They flourished and expanded and eventually the human population of Majipoor came to number in the billions, mainly occupying huge and distinctive cities of ten to twenty million people.

The governmental system that evolved over those years was a kind of non-hereditary dual monarchy. Upon coming to power the senior ruler, known as the Pontifex, selects his own junior ruler, the Coronal. Technically the Coronal is regarded as the adoptive son of the Pontifex, and upon the death of the Pontifex takes his place on the senior throne, naming a new Coronal as his own successor. Both of these rulers make their homes on Alhanroel, the largest and most populous of Majipoor's three continents. The imperial residence of the Pontifex is in the lowest level of a vast subterranean city called the Labyrinth, from which he emerges only at rare intervals. The Coronal lives in an enormous castle at the summit of Castle Mount, a thirty-mile-high peak whose atmosphere is maintained in an eternal springtime by elaborate machinery. From time to time the Coronal descends from the opulence of the Castle to travel across the face of the world in a Grand Processional, an event designed to remind Majipoor of the might and power of its rulers. Such a journey, which in Majipoor's vast distances could take several years, invariably brings the Coronal to Zimroel, the second continent, a place of gigantic cities interspersed among tremendous rivers and great unspoiled forests. More rarely he goes to the torrid third continent in the south, Suvrael, largely a wasteland of Sahara-like deserts.

Two other functionaries became part of the Majipoor governmental system later on. The development of a method of worldwide telepathic communication made possible nightly sendings of oracular advice and occasional therapeutic counsel, which became the responsibility of the mother of the incumbent Coronal, under the title of Lady of the Isle of Sleep. Her headquarters are situated on an island of continental size midway between Alhanroel and Zimroel. Later, a second telepathic authority, the King of Dreams, was set in place. He employs more powerful telepathic equipment in order to monitor and chastise criminals and other citizens whose behaviour deviates from accepted Majipoor norms. This office is the hereditary property of the Barjazid family of Suvrael.

The first of the Majipoor novels, *Lord Valentine's Castle*, tells of a conspiracy that succeeds in overthrowing the legitimate Coronal, Lord Valentine, and replacing him with an impostor. Valentine, stripped of all his memories, is set loose in Zimroel to live the life of a wandering juggler, but gradually regains an awareness of his true role and launches a successful campaign to reclaim his throne. In the sequel, *Valentine Pontifex*, the now mature Valentine, a pacifist at heart, must deal with an uprising among the Metamorphs, who are determined to drive the hated human conquerors from their world at last. Valentine defeats them and restores peace with the help of the giant maritime beasts known as sea-dragons, whose intelligent powers were not previously suspected on Majipoor.

The story collection *Majipoor Chronicles* depicts scenes from many eras and social levels of Majipoor life, providing detailed insight into a number of aspects of the giant world not described in the novels. The short novel *The Mountians of Majipoor*, set five hundred years after Valentine's reign, carries the saga into the icy northlands, where a separate barbaric civilization has long endured. And the most recent of the Majipoor books, *The Prestimion Trilogy*, set a thousand years prior to Valentine's time, tells of an era in which the powers of sorcery and magic have become rife on Majipoor. The Coronal Lord Prestimion, after being displaced from his throne by the usurping son of the former Coronal with the assistance of mages and warlocks, leads his faction to victory in a civil war in which he too makes use of necromantic powers.

The story presented here offers an episode dating back to a time before any of the Majipoor novels published so far – a period more than four thousand years before Valentine's time, more than three thousand years before Prestimion. But its setting is ten thousand years after the time of the first human settlement, and the early history of Majipoor is already becoming legendary.

THE BOOK OF CHANGES

BY ROBERT SILVERBERG

Standing at the narrow window of his bedchamber early on the morning of the second day of his new life as a captive, looking out at the blood-red waters of the Sea of Barbirike far below, Aithin Furvain heard the bolt that sealed his apartment from the outside being thrown back. He glanced quickly around and saw the lithe catlike form of his captor, the bandit chief Kasinibon, come sidling in. Furvain turned towards the window again.

'As I told you last night, it truly is a beautiful view, isn't it?' Kasinibon said. 'There's nothing like that scarlet lake anywhere else in all Majipoor.'

'Lovely, yes,' said Furvain, in a remote, affectless way.

With the same relentless good cheer Kasinibon went on, addressing himself to Furvain's back, 'I do hope you slept well, and that in general you're finding your lodgings here comfortable, Prince Aithin.'

Out of some vestigial sense of courtesy – courtesy, even to a bandit! – Furvain turned to face the other man. 'I don't ordinarily use my title,' he said, stiffly, coolly.

'Of course. Neither do I, as a matter of fact. I come from a long line of east-country nobility, you know. Minor nobility, perhaps, yet nobility never the less. But they are such archaic things, titles!' Kasinibon grinned. It was a sly grin, almost conspiratorial, a mingling of mockery and charm. Despite everything Furvain found it impossible to dislike the man. 'You haven't answered my question, though. Are you comfortable here, Furvain?'

'Oh, yes. Quite. It's absolutely the most elegant of prisons.'

'I do wish to point out that this is not actually a prison but merely a private residence.'

'I suppose. Even so, I'm a prisoner here, is that not true?'

'I concede the point. You are indeed a prisoner, for the time being. My prisoner.'

'Thank you,' said Furvain. 'I appreciate your straightforwardness.'

He returned his attention to the Barbirike Sea, which stretched, long and slender as a spear, for fifty miles or so through the valley below the grey cliff on which Kasinibon's fortress-like retreat was perched. Long rows of tall sharp-tipped crescent dunes, soft as clouds from this distance, bordered its shores. They too were red. Even the air here had a red reflected shimmer. The sun itself seemed to have taken on a tinge of it. Kasinibon had explained yesterday, though Furvain had not been particularly interested in hearing it at the time, that the Sea of Barbirike was home to untold billions of tiny crustaceans whose fragile bright-coloured shells, decomposing over the millennia, had imparted that bloody hue to the sea's waters and given rise also to the red sands of the adjacent dunes. Furvain wondered whether his royal father, who had such an obsessive interest in intense colour effects, had ever made the journey out here to see this place. Surely he had. Surely.

Kasinibon said, 'I've brought you some pens and a supply of paper.' He laid them neatly out on the little table beside Furvain's bed. 'As I said earlier, this view is bound to inspire poetry in you, that I know.'

'No doubt it will,' said Furvain, still speaking in that same distant, uninflected tone.

'Shall we take a closer look at the lake this afternoon, you and I?'

'So you don't intend to keep me penned up all the time in these three rooms?'

'Of course I don't. Why would I be so cruel?'

'Well, then. I'll be pleased to be taken on a tour of the lake,' Furvain said, as indifferently as before. 'Its beauty may indeed stir a poem or two in me.'

Kasinibon gave the stack of paper an amiable tap. 'You also may wish to use these sheets to begin drafting your ransom request.'

Furvain narrowed his eyes. 'Tomorrow, perhaps, for that. Or the day after.'

'As you wish. There's no hurry, you know. You are my guest here for as long as you care to stay.'

'Your prisoner, actually.'

'That too,' Kasinibon said. 'My guest, but also my prisoner, though I hope you will see yourself rather more as guest than prisoner. You will excuse me now. I have my dreary administrative duties to deal with. Until this afternoon, then.' And grinned once more, and bowed and took his leave.

Furvain was the fifth son of the former Coronal Lord Sangamor, whose best-known achievement had been the construction of the remarkable tunnels on Castle Mount that bore his name. Lord Sangamor was a man of a strong artistic bent, and the tunnels, whose walls were fashioned from a kind of artificial stone that blazed with inherent radiant colour, were considered by connoisseurs to be a supreme work of art. Furvain had inherited his father's aestheticism but very little of his strength of character: in the eyes of many at the Mount he was nothing more than a wastrel, an idler, even a rogue. His own friends, and he had many of them, were hard pressed to find any great degree of significant merit in him. He was an unusually skilful writer of light verse, yes; and a genial companion on a journey or in a tavern, yes; and a clever hand with a quip or a riddle or a paradox, yes; and otherwise – otherwise –

A Coronal's son has no significant future in the administration of Majipoor, by ancient constitutional tradition. No function is set aside for him. He can never rise to the throne himself, for the crown is always adoptive, never hereditary. The Coronal's eldest son would usually establish himself on a fine estate in one of the Fifty Cities of the Mount and live the good life of a provincial duke. A second son, or even a third, might remain at the Castle and become a councillor of the realm, if he showed any aptitude for the intricacies of government. But a fifth son, born late in his father's reign and thereby shouldered out of the inner circle by all those who had arrived before him, would usually face no better destiny than a drifting existence of irresponsible pleasure and ease. There is no role in public life for him to play. He is his father's son, but he is nothing at all in his own right. No one is likely to think of him as qualified for any kind of serious duties, nor even to have any interest in such things. Such princes are entitled by birth to a permanent suite of rooms at the Castle and a generous and irrevocable pension, and it is assumed of them that they will contentedly devote themselves to idle amusements until the end of their days.

Furvain, unlike some princes of a more restless nature, had adapted very well to that prospect. Since no one expected very much of him, he demanded very little of himself. Nature had favoured him with good looks: he was tall and slender, a graceful, elegant man with wavy golden hair and finely chiselled features. He was an admirable dancer, sang quite well in a clear, light tenor voice, excelled at most sports that did not require brute physical force, and was a capable hand at swordsmanship and chariot-racing. But above all else he excelled at the making of verse. Poetry flowed from him in torrents, as rain falls from the sky. At any moment of the day or night, whether he had just been awakened after a long evening of drunken carousing or was in the midst of that carousing itself, he could take pen in hand and compose, almost extemporaneously, a ballad or a sonnet or a villanelle or a jolly rhyming epigram, or quick thumping short-legged doggerel, or even a long skein of heroic couplets, on any sort of theme. There was no profundity to such hastily dashed-off stuff, of course. It was not in his nature to probe the depths of the human soul, let alone to want to set out his findings in the form of poetry. But everyone knew that Aithin Furvain had no master when it came to the making of easy, playful verse, minor verse that celebrated the joys of the moment, the pleasures of the bed or of the bottle, verse that poked fun without ever edging into sour malicious satire, or that demonstrated a quick verbal interplay of rhythm and sound without actually being about anything at all.

'Make a poem for us, Aithin,' someone of his circle would call out, as they sat at their wine in one of the brick-walled taverns of the Castle. 'Yes!' the others would cry. 'A poem, a poem!'

'Give me a word, someone,' Furvain would say.

And someone, his current lover, perhaps, would say at random, 'Sausage.'

'Splendid. And you, give me another, now. The first that comes to mind.'

'Pontifex,' someone else would say.

'One more,' Furvain would beg. 'You, back there.'

'Steetmoy,' the reply would come, from someone at the back of the group. And Furvain, glancing for just a moment into his wine-bowl as though some poem might be lurking there, would draw a deep breath and instantaneously begin to recite a mock epic, in neatly balanced hexameter and the most elaborate of anapestic rhythms, about the desperate craving of a Pontifex for sausage made of steetmoy meat, and the sending of the laziest and most cowardly of the royal courtiers on a hunting expedition to the snowbound lair of that ferocious white-furred creature of northern Zimroel. Without pausing he would chant for eight or ten minutes, perhaps, until the task was done, and the tale, improvised though it was, would have a beginning and a middle and an uproariously funny end, bringing him a shower of enthusiastic applause and a fresh flask of wine.

The collected works of Aithin Furvain, had he ever bothered to collect them, would have filled many volumes; but it was his custom to toss his poems aside as quickly as he had scribbled them, nor were many of them ever written down in the first place, and it was only through the prudence of his friends that some of them had been saved and copied and circulated through the land. But that was of no importance to him. Making poetry was as easy for him as drawing breath, and he saw no reason why his quick improvisations should be saved and treasured. It was not, after all, as though they had been intended as enduring works of art, such as his royal father's tunnels had been meant to be.

The Coronal Lord Sangamor had reigned long and generally successfully as Majipoor's junior monarch for nearly thirty years under the Pontifex Pelxinai, until at last the venerable Pelxinai had been gathered to the Source by the Divine and Sangamor had ascended to the Pontificate himself. As Pontifex it was mandatory for him to leave Castle Mount and relocate himself in the subterranean Labyrinth, far to the south, that was the constitutional home of the elder ruler. For the remainder of his life he would rarely be seen in the outside world. Aithin Furvain had dutifully visited his father at the Labyrinth not long after his investiture as Pontifex, as he and his brothers were supposed to do now and then, but he doubted that he would ever make another such journey. The Labyrinth was a dark and gloomy place, very little to his liking. It could not be very pleasing for old Sangamor either, Furvain suspected; but, like all Coronals, Sangamor had known from the start that the Labyrinth was where he must finish his days. Furvain was under no such obligation to reside there, nor even to go there at all if he chose not to. And so Furvain, who had never known his father particularly well, did not see any reason why the two of them would ever meet again.

He had effectively separated himself from the Castle as well by then, too. Even while Lord Sangamor still reigned there, Furvain had set up a second residence for himself at Dundilmir, one of the Slope Cities far down towards the base of the gigantic upthrusting fang of rock that was Castle Mount. A schoolmate and close friend of his named Tanigel had now come into his inheritance as Duke of Dundilmir, and had offered Furvain some property there, a relatively modest estate overlooking the volcanic region known as the Fiery Valley. Furvain would in essence be Duke Tanigel's court jester, a boon companion and maker of comic verse on demand. It was mildly irregular for a Coronal's son to accept a gift of land from a mere duke, but Tanigel understood that fifth sons of Coronals rarely were men of independent wealth, and he knew also that Furvain had grown weary of his listless life at the Castle and was looking to shift the scene of his idleness elsewhere. Furvain, who was not one to stand overmuch on dignity, had gladly acceded to Tanigel's suggestion, and spent most of the next few years at his Dundilmir estate, enjoying raucous times among Tanigel and his prosperous hard-drinking friends and going up to the great Castle at the summit of the Mount only on the most formal of occasions, such as his father's birthday, but scarcely returning to it at all after his father had become Pontifex and moved along to the Labyrinth.

Even the good life at Dundilmir had palled after a time, however. Furvain was entering his middle years now, and he had begun to feel something that he had never experienced before, a vague gnawing dissatisfaction of some unspecifiable kind. Certainly he had nothing specific to complain about. He lived well, surrounded by amusing and enjoyable friends who admired him for the one minor skill that he practised so well; his health was sound; he had sufficient funds to meet the ordinary expenses of his life, which were basically reasonable ones; he was rarely bored and never lacked for companions or lovers. And yet there was that odd ache in his soul from time to time, now, that inexplicable and unwarranted pang of malaise. It was a new kind of mood for him, disturbing, incomprehensible.

Perhaps the answer lay in travel, Furvain thought. He was a citizen of the largest and grandest and most beautiful world in all the universe, and yet he had seen very little of it: only Castle Mount, and no more than a dozen or so of the Mount's Fifty Cities at that, and the pleasant but not very interesting Glayge Valley through which he had passed on his one journey to his father's new home in the Labyrinth. There was so much more out there to visit: the legendary cities of the south, places like Sippulgar and golden Arvyanda and many-spired Ketheron, and the stilt-legged villages around silvery Lake Roghoiz, and hundreds, even thousands of others spread like jewels across this enormous continent of Alhanroel, and then there was the other major continent too, fabulous Zimroel, about which he knew practically nothing, far across the sea, abounding in marvellous attractions that sounded like places out of fable. It would be the task of several lifetimes to travel to all of those places.

But in the end he went in a different direction entirely. Duke Tanigel, who was fond of travel, had begun speaking of making a journey to the east-country, that empty and virtually unknown territory that lay between Castle Mount and the shores of the unexplored Great Sea. It was ten thousand years now, since the first human settlers had come to dwell on Majipoor, which would have been time enough for filling up any world of normal size; but so large was Majipoor that even a hundred centuries of steady population growth had not been sufficient for the settlers to establish footholds in all its far-flung territories. The path of development had led steadily westwards from the heart of Alhanroel, and then across the Inner Sea that separated Alhanroel from Zimroel to the other two. Scarcely anyone but a few inveterate wanderers had ever bothered to go east. There was a scruffy little farming town out there, Vrambikat, in a misty valley lying practically in the shadow of the Mount, and beyond Vrambikat there were, apparently, no settlements whatever, or at least none that could be found in the roster of the Pontifical tax-collectors. Perhaps an occasional tiny settlement existed out there; perhaps not. In that sparsely populated region, though, lay an assortment of natural wonders known only from the memoirs of bold explorers. The scarlet Sea of Barbirike – the group of lakes known as the Thousand Eyes – the huge serpentine chasm called the Viper Rift, three thousand miles or more long and of immeasurable depth; and ever so much more – the Wall of Flame, the Web of Jewels, the Fountain of Wine, the Dancing Hills – much of it, perhaps, purely mythical, the inventions of imaginative but untrustworthy adventurers. Duke Tanigel proposed an expedition into these mysterious realms. 'On and on, even to the Great Sea itself!' he cried. 'We'll take the whole court with us. Who knows what we'll find? And you, Furvain – you'll write an account of everything we see, setting it all down in an unforgettable epic, a classic for the ages!'

But Duke Tanigel, though he was good at devising grand projects and planning them down to the finest detail, was less diligent in the matter of bringing them into the realm of actuality. For months the Duke and his courtiers pored over maps and explorers' narratives, hundreds and even thousands of years old, and laid out grandiose charts of their own intended route through what was, in fact, a trackless wilderness. Furvain found himself completely caught up in the enterprise, and in his dreams often imagined himself hovering like a great bird over some yet-to-be-discovered landscape of inconceivable beauty and strangeness. He yearned for the day of departure. The journey to the east-country, he came to realize, met some inner need of his that he had not previously known existed. The Duke continued planning endlessly for the trip, but never actually announced a date for setting forth, and finally Furvain came to see that no such expedition ever would take place. The Duke had no need actually to go, only to plan. And so one day Furvain, who had never gone any large distance by himself and usually found the whole idea of solitary travel a bit unpleasant, resolved to set out alone into the east-country.

Even so, he needed one last push, and it came to him from an unexpected quarter.

During the tense and bothersome period of hesitation and uncertainty that preceded his departure he paid a visit to the Castle, on the pretext of consulting certain explorers' charts said to be on deposit at the royal library. But once at the Castle he found himself unwilling to approach the library's unthinkable, almost infinite vastness, and instead paid a call on his father's famous tunnels, over on the western face of the Mount within a slim rocky spire that jutted hundreds of feet upwards from the Mount's own bulk.

Lord Sangamor had caused his tunnels to be constructed in a long coiling ramp that wound upwards through the interior of that elongated stony spire. In the forges of the secret chambers of the royal artisans, deep beneath the Castle of the Coronal, Sangamor's workmen had devised the radiant synthetic stone out of which the tunnels were to be built, and smelted it into big dazzling slabs; then, under the Coronal's personal direction, teams of masons had shaped those raw slabs of glowing matter into rectangular paving blocks of uniform size, which they fastidiously mortared into the walls and roofs of each chamber according to a carefully graded sequence of colours. As one walked along, one's eyes were bombarded with throbbing, pulsing emanations: sulphur-yellow in this room, saffron in the next, topaz in the one after that, emerald, maroon, and then a sudden staggering burst of urgent red, with quieter tones beyond, mauve, aquamarine, a soft chartreuse. It was a symphony of colours, an unfailing outpouring of glowing light every moment of the day. Furvain spent two hours there, moving from room to room in mounting fascination and pleasure, until suddenly he could take no more. Some unexpected eruption was taking place within him. Sensations of vertigo and nausea swept through him. His mind felt numbed by the tremendous power and intensity of the display. He began to tremble, and there was a pounding in his chest. Obviously a quick retreat was necessary. He rushed towards the exit. Another half-minute within those tunnels, Furvain realized, and he would have been forced to his knees.

Once outside, Furvain clung to a parapet, sweating, dazed, until in a little while something like calmness returned. The strength of his reaction perplexed him. The physical distress was over, but something else still remained, some sort of free-floating disquiet, at first hard to comprehend, but which he came quickly to understand for what it was: the splendour of the tunnels had kindled in him at first a sense of admiration verging on awe, but that had gone moving swiftly onwards through his soul to become a crushing, devastating sensation of personal inadequacy.

He had always regarded this thing that the old man had built as nothing much other than a pleasant curiosity. But today, apparently having entered once more into that strangely oversensitized, almost neurasthenic state that had been typical of his recent moods, he had been overwhelmed by a new awareness of the greatness of his father's work. Through Furvain now was running a surge of something he was forced to recognize as humility, an emotion with which he had never been particularly well acquainted. And why should he not feel humble? His father had achieved something rare and wonderful here. Amid all the exhausting cares and distractions of state, Lord Sangamor had found the strength and inspiration to create a masterpiece of art.

Whereas he himself – whereas he –

The impact of the tunnels was still reverberating in him that evening. Rather than going on to the library afterwards he arranged to dine with an old lover, the Lady Dolitha, in the airy restaurant that hung just above the Grand Melikand Court. She was a delicate-looking woman, very beautiful, dark-haired, olive-skinned, keen-witted. They had had a tempestuous affair for six months, ten years before. Eventually a certain unfettered sharpness about her, an excessive willingness to utter truths that one did not ordinarily utter, an overly sardonic way in which she sometimes chose to express her opinions, had cooled his desire for her. But Furvain had always prized the companionship of intelligent women, and the very quality of terrifying truthfulness that had driven him from her bed had made her appealing to him as a friend. So he had taken pains to preserve the friendship he had enjoyed with Dolitha even after the other sort of intimacy had been severed. She was as close as a sister to him now.

He told her of his experience in the tunnels. 'Who would have expected such a thing?' he asked her. 'A Coronal who's also a great artist!'

The Lady Dolitha's eyes sparkled with the ironic amusement that was her speciality. 'Why do you think the one should exclude the other? The artistic gift's something an artist is born with. Later, perhaps, one can also choose the path that leads towards the throne. But the gift remains.'

'I suppose.'

'Your father sought power, and that can absorb one's entire energies. But he also chose to exercise his gift.'

'The mark of his greatness, that he had breadth enough of soul to
do both.'

'Or confidence enough in himself. Of course, other people make
different choices. Not always the right ones.'

Furvain forced himself to meet her gaze directly, though he would
rather have looked away. 'What are you saying, Dolitha? That it was
wrong of me not to go into the government?'

She put the back of her small hand to her lips to conceal, only
partly, her wry smile.

'Hardly, Aithin.'

'Then what? Come on. Spell it out! It isn't much of a secret, you
know, even to me. I've fallen short somewhere, haven't I? You think
I've misused my gift, is that it? That I've frittered away my talents
drinking and gambling and amusing people with trivial little jingling
rhymes, when I should have been closeted away somewhere writing
some vast, profound philosophical masterpiece, something sombre and
heavy and pretentious that everybody would praise but no one would
want to read?'

'Oh, Aithin, Aithin –'

'Am I wrong?'

'How can I tell you what you should have been writing? All I can
tell you is that I see how unhappy you are, Aithin. I've seen it for a
long time. Something's wrong within you – even you've finally come
to recognize that, haven't you? – and my guess is it must have something to do with your art, your poetry, since what else is there that's
important to you, really?'

He stared at her. How very characteristic of her it was to say a thing
like that.

'Go on.'

'There's very little more to say.'

'But there's something, eh? Say it, then.'

'It's nothing that I haven't said before.'

'Well, say it again. I can be very obtuse, Dolitha.'

He saw the little quiver of her nostrils that he had been expecting,
the tiny movement of the tip of her tongue between her closed lips.
It was clear to him from that that he could expect no mercy from her
now. But mercy was not the commodity for which he had come to
her this evening.

Quietly she said, 'The path you've taken isn't the right path. I don't know what the right path would be, but it's clear that you aren't on it. You need to reshape your life, Aithin. To make something new and different out of it for yourself. That's all. You've gone along this path as far as you can, and now you need to change. I knew ten years ago, even if you didn't, that something like this was going to come. Well, now it has. As you finally have come to realize yourself.'

'I suppose I have, yes.'

'It's time to stop hiding.'

'Hiding?'

'From yourself. From your destiny, from whatever that may be. From your true essence. You can hide from all those, Aithin, but you can't hide from the Divine. So far as the Divine is concerned, there's no place where you can't be seen. Change your life, Aithin. I can't tell you how.'

He looked at her, stunned.

'No. Of course you can't.' He was silent a moment. 'I'll start by taking a trip,' he said. 'Alone. To some distant place where there'll be no one but myself, and I can meet myself face to face. And then we'll see.'

In the morning, dismissing all thought of the royal library and whatever maps it might or might not contain – the time for planning was over; it was the time simply to go – he returned to Dundilmir and spent a week putting his house in order and arranging for the provisions he would need for his journey into the east-country. Then he set out, unaccompanied, saying nothing to anyone about where he was going. He had no idea what he would find, but he knew he would find something, and that he would be the better for it. This would be, he thought, a serious venture, a quest, even: a search for the interior life of Aithin Furvain, which somehow he had misplaced long ago. *You have to change your life*, Dolitha had said, and, yes, yes, that was what he would do. It would be a new thing for him. He had never embarked on anything serious before. He set out now in a strangely optimistic mood, alert to all vibrations of his consciousness. And was barely a week beyond the small dusty town of Vrambikat when he was captured by a party of roving outlaws and taken to Kasinibon's hilltop stronghold.

That there should be anarchy of this sort in an outlying district like the east-country was something that had never occurred to him, but it was no major surprise. Majipoor was, by and large, a peaceful place, where the rulers had for thousands of years ruled by the freely given consent of the governed; but the distances were so vast, the writ of the Pontifex and Coronal so tenuous in places, that quite probably there were many districts where the central government existed only in name. When it took months for news to travel between the centres of the administration and remote Zimroel or sun-blasted Suvrael in the south, was it proper to say that the arm of the government actually reached those places? Who could know, up there at the summit of Castle Mount, or in the depths of the Labyrinth, what really went on in those distant lands? Everyone generally obeyed the law, yes, because the alternative was chaos; but it was quite conceivable that in many districts the citizens did more or less as they pleased most of the time, while maintaining staunchly that they were faithful in their obedience to the commandments of the central government.

And out here, where no one dwelled anyway, or hardly anyone, and the government did not so much as attempt to maintain a presence – what need was there for a government at all, or even the pretence of one?

Since leaving Vrambikat Furvain had been riding quietly along through the quiet countryside, with titanic Castle Mount still a mighty landmark behind him in the west but now beginning to dwindle a little, and a dark range of hills starting to come into view ahead of him. Every prospect before him appeared to go on for a million miles. He had never seen open space such as this, with no hint anywhere that human life might be present on this world. The air was clear as glass here, the sky cloudless, the weather gentle, springlike. Broad rolling meadows of bright golden grass, short-leaved, fleshy-stemmed, dense as a tightly woven carpet, stretched out before him. Here and there some beast of a sort unknown to Furvain browsed on the grass, paying no heed to him. This was the ninth day of his journey. The solitude was refreshing. It cleansed the soul. The deeper he went into this silent land, the greater was his sense of inner healing, of purification.

He paused at noon at a place where little rocky hills jutted from the blunt-stalked yellow grass to rest his mount and allow it to graze. He had brought an elegant beast with him, high-spirited and beautiful, a racing mount, really, not perfectly suited for long plodding marches. It was necessary to halt frequently while the animal gathered its strength.

Furvain did not mind that. With no special destination in mind, there was no reason to adopt a hurried pace.

His mind roved ahead into the emptiness and tried to envision the marvels that awaited him. The Viper Rift, for example: what would that be like, that colossal cleft in the bosom of the world? Vertical walls that gleamed like gold, so steep that one could not even think of descending to the rift floor, where a swift green river, a serpent that seemed to have neither head nor tail, flowed towards the sea. The Great Sickle, said to be a slender, curving mass of shining white marble, a sculpture fashioned by the hand of the Divine, rising in superb isolation to a height of hundreds of feet above a tawny expanse of flat desert, a fragile arc that sighed and twanged like a harp when strong winds blew across its edge: an account dating from Lord Stiamot's time, four thousand years before, said that the sight of it, limned against the night sky with a moon or two glistening near its tip, was so beautiful it would make a Skandar drayman weep. The Fountains of Embolain, where thunderous geysers of fragrant pink water smooth as silk went rushing upwards every fifty minutes, day and night – and then, a year's journey away, or perhaps two or three, the towering cliffs of black stone, riven by dazzling veins of white quartz, that guarded the shore of the Great Sea, the unbroken and unnavigable expanse of water that covered nearly half of the giant planet –

'Stand,' a harsh voice suddenly said. 'You are trespassing here. Identify yourself.'

Furvain had been alone in this silent wilderness for so long that the grating sound ripped across his awareness like a blazing meteor's jagged path across a starless sky. Turning, he saw two glowering men, stocky and roughly dressed, standing atop a low outcropping of rock just a few yards behind him. They were armed. A third and a fourth, farther away, guarded a string of a dozen or so mounts roped together with coarse yellow cord.

He remained calm. 'A trespasser, you say? But this place belongs to no one, my friend! Or else to everyone.'

'This place belongs to Master Kasinibon,' said the shorter and surlier-looking of the two, whose eyebrows formed a single straight black line across his furrowed forehead. He spoke in a coarse, thick-tongued way, with an unfamiliar accent that muffled all his consonants. 'You'll need his permission to travel here. What is your name?'

'Aithin Furvain of Dundilmir,' answered Furvain mildly. 'I'll thank you to tell your master, whose name is unknown to me, that I mean no harm to his lands or property, that I'm a solitary traveller passing quickly through, who intends nothing more than –'

'Dundilmir?' the other man muttered. The thick eyebrow rose. 'That's a city of the Mount, if I'm not mistaken. What's a man of Castle Mount doing wandering around in these parts? This is no place for you.' And, with a guffaw: 'Who are you, anyway, the Coronal's son?'

Furvain smiled. 'As long as you ask,' he said, 'I might as well inform you that in point of fact I *am* the Coronal's son. Or I was, anyway, until the death of the Pontifex Pelxinai. My father's name is –'

A quick backhand blow across the face sent Furvain sprawling to the ground. He blinked in amazement. The blow had been a light one, merely a slap; it was the utter surprise of it that had cost him his balance. He could not remember any occasion in his life when someone had struck him, even when he was a boy.

'– Sangamor,' he went on, more or less automatically, since the words were already in his mouth. 'Who was Coronal under Pelxinai, and now is Pontifex himself –'

'Do you value your teeth, man? I'll hit you again if you keep on mocking me!'

In a wondering tone Furvain said, 'I told you nothing but the simple truth, friend. I am Aithin of Dundilmir, the son of Sangamor. My papers will confirm it.' It was beginning to dawn on him now that announcing his royal pedigree to men like this might not have been the most intelligent possible course to take, but he had never given any thought before this to the possibility that there might be places in the world where revealing such a thing could be unwise. In any case it was too late now for him to take it back. He had no way of preventing them from examining his papers; they plainly stated who he was; it was best to assume that no one, even out here, would presume to interfere with the movements of a son of the Pontifex, mere fifth son though he might be. 'I forgive you for that blow,' he said to the one who had struck him. 'You had no idea of my identity. I'll see that no harm comes to you for it. And now, if you please, with all respect to your Master Kasinibon, the time has come for me to continue on my way.'

'Your way, at the moment, leads you to Master Kasinibon,' replied the man who had knocked him down. 'You can pay your respects to him yourself.'

They prodded him roughly to his feet and indicated with a gesture that he was to get astride his mount, which the other two – grooms, evidently – tied to the last of the string of mounts they had been leading. Furvain saw now what he had not noticed earlier, that what he had taken for a small hummock at the highest ridge of the hill just before him was actually a low structure of some sort; and as they went upwards, following a steep path that was hardly a path at all, a mere thin scuffing of hoofprints through the grass, all but invisible at times, it became clear to him that the structure was in fact a substantial hilltop redoubt, virtually a fortress, fashioned from the same glossy grey stone as the hill itself. Though apparently only two storeys high, it spread on and on for a surprising distance along the ridge, and, as the path they were following began to curve around to the side, giving Furvain a better view, he saw that the structure extended down the eastern front of the hill for several additional levels facing into the valley beyond. He saw, too, the red shimmer of the sky above the valley, and then, as they attained the crest, the startling red slash of a long narrow lake that could only be the famed Sea of Barbirike, flanked by parallel rows of dunes whose sand was of the same brilliant red hue. Master Kasinibon, whoever he might be, this outlaw chieftain, had seized for the site of his citadel one of the most spectacular vantage-points in all of Majipoor, a site of almost unworldly splendour. One had to admire the audacity of that, Furvain thought. The man might be an outlaw, yes, a bandit, even, but he must also be something of an artist.

The building, when they finally came over the top of the hill and around to its front, turned out to be a massive thing, square-edged and heavy-set, designed for solidity rather than elegance, but not without a certain rustic power and presence. It had two long wings, radiating from a squat central quadrangle, that bent forwards to reach a considerable way down the Barbirike Valley side of the hill. Its designer must have had impregnability in mind more than anything else. There was no plausible way to penetrate its defences. The building could not be approached at all from its western side, because the final stretch of the hillside up which Furvain and his captors had just come was wholly vertical, a bare rock face impossible to ascend, and the building itself showed only a forbidding windowless façade on that side. The path from below, once it had brought them to that point of no ascent, made a wide swing off to the right, taking them over the ridge at the hill's summit and around to the front of the building, where any wayfarer would be fully exposed to the weaponry of the fortress above. Here it was guarded by watchtowers. It was protected also by a stockade, a portcullis, a formidable rampart. The building had only one entrance, not a large one. All its windows were constricted vertical slits, invulnerable to attack but useful to the defenders in case attack should come.

Furvain was conducted unceremoniously within. There was no

shoving or pushing; no one actually touched him at all; but the effect was one of being hustled along by Kasinibon's men, who doubtless would shove him quite unhesitatingly if he made it necessary for them to do so. He found himself being marched down a long corridor in the left-hand wing, and then up a single flight of stairs and into a small suite of rooms, a bedroom and a sitting room and a room containing a tub and a washstand. It was a stark place. The walls were of the same blank grey stone as the exterior of the fortress, without decoration of any kind. The windows of all three rooms, like all those in the rest of the building, were mere narrow slits, facing out towards the lake. The place was furnished simply, with a couple of spare util-itarian tables and chairs and a small, uninviting bed, a cupboard, a set of empty shelves, a brick-lined fireplace. They deposited his baggage with him and left him alone, and when he tried the door he discov-ered that it was bolted from without. So, then, it was a suite main-tained for the housing of unwilling guests, Furvain thought. And doubtless he was not the first.

Not for many hours did he have the pleasure of meeting the master of this place. Furvain spent the time pacing from room to room, surveying his new domain until he had seen it all, which did not take very long. Then he stared out at the lake for a while, but its loveli-ness, remarkable though it was, eventually began to pall. Then he constructed three quick verse epigrams that made ironic fun of his new predicament, but in all three instances he was oddly unable to find an adequate closing line, and he eradicated all three from his memory without completing them.

He felt no particular annoyance at having been captured like this. At this point he saw it as nothing more than an interesting novelty, a curious incident of his journey into the east-country, an episode with which to amuse his friends after his return. There was no reason to feel apprehensive. This Master Kasinibon was, most likely, some petty lordling of the Mount who had grown tired of his coddled, stable life in Banglecode or Stee or Bibiroon, or wherever it was he came from, and had struck out for himself into this wild region to carve out a little principality of his own. Or perhaps he had been guilty of some minor infraction of the law, or had given offence to a powerful kinsman, and had chosen to remove himself from the world of conven-tional society. Either way, Furvain saw no reason why he should come to harm at Kasinibon's hands. No doubt Kasinibon wanted merely to impress him with his own authority as master of this territory, and to storm and bluster a bit at Furvain's temerity in entering the district without the permission of its self-appointed overlord, and then he would be released.

The shadows over the red lake were lengthening now as the sun proceeded on its journey towards Zimroel. Restlessness began to grow in Furvain with the coming of the day's end. Eventually a servant appeared, an expressionless puffy-faced Hjort with great staring batrachian eyes, who set before him a tray of food and departed without saying a word. Furvain inspected his meal: a flask of pink wine, a plate of some pallid soft meat, a bowl filled with what looked like unopened flower-buds. Simple fare for rustic folk, he thought. But the wine was supple and pleasant, the meat was tender and bathed in a subtle aromatic sauce, and the flower-buds, if that was what they were, released an agreeable sweetness when he bit into them, and left an interesting subtaste of sharp spiciness behind.

Not long after he was done, the door opened again and a small, almost elfin man of about fifty, grey-eyed and thin-lipped, garbed in a green leather jerkin and yellow tights, came in. From his swagger and stance it was plain that he was a person of consequence. He affected a clipped moustache and a short, pointed beard and wore his long hair, which was a deep black liberally streaked with strands of white, pulled tightly back and knotted behind. There was a look of slyness about him, of a playful slipperiness, that Furvain found pleasing and appealing.

'I am Kasinibon,' he announced. His voice was soft and light but had the ring of authority to it nevertheless. 'I apologize for any deficiencies in our hospitality thus far.'

'I have noticed none,' said Furvain coolly. 'Thus far.'

'But surely you must be accustomed to finer fare than I'm able to offer here. My men tell me you are the son of Lord Sangamor.' Kasinibon offered Furvain a quick cool flicker of a smile, but nothing that could be interpreted as any sort of gesture of respect, let alone obeisance. 'Or did they misunderstand something you said?'

'There was no misunderstanding. I'm indeed one of Sangamor's sons. The youngest one. I am called Aithin Furvain. If you'd like to see my papers –'

'That's scarcely necessary. Your bearing alone reveals you for who and what you are.'

'And if I may ask –' Furvain began.

But Kasinibon spoke right over Furvain's words, doing it so smoothly that it seemed almost not to be discourteous. 'Do you, then, have an important role in His Majesty's government?'

'I have no role at all. You are aware, I think, that high office is never awarded on the basis of one's ancestry. A Coronal's sons do the best they can for themselves, but nothing is guaranteed to them. As I was growing up I discovered that my brothers had already taken advantage of most of the available opportunities. I live on my pension. A modest one,' Furvain added, because it was beginning to occur to him that Kasinibon might have a ransom in mind.

'You hold no official post whatever, is that what you're saying?'

'None.'

'What is it that you do, then? Nothing?'

'Nothing that could be considered work, I suppose. I spend my days as companion to my friend, the Duke of Dundilmir. My role is to provide amusement for the Duke and his court circle. I have a certain minor gift for poetry.'

'Poetry!' Kasinibon exclaimed. 'You are a poet? How splendid!' A new light came into his eyes, a look of eager interest that had the unexpected effect of transforming his features in such a way as to strip him of all his slyness for a moment, leaving him looking strangely youthful and vulnerable. 'Poetry is my great passion,' Kasinibon said, in an almost confessional tone. 'My comfort and my joy, living out here as I do on the edge of nowhere, so far from civilized pursuits. Tuminok Laskil! Vornifon! Dammiunde! Do you know how much of their work I've committed to memory?' And he struck a schoolboy pose and began to recite something of Dammiunde's, one of his most turgid pieces, a deadly earnest piece of romantic fustian about star-crossed lovers that Furvain, even as a boy, had always found wildly ludicrous. He struggled now to maintain a straight face as Kasinibon quoted an extract from one of its most preposterous sequences, the wild chase through the swamps of Kajith Kabulon. Perhaps Kasinibon came to suspect, in time, that his guest did not have the highest respect for Dammiunde's famous work, because a glow of embarrassment spread across his cheeks, and he broke the recitation off abruptly, saying, 'A little old-fashioned, perhaps. But I've loved it since my boyhood.'

'It's not one of my favourites,' Furvain conceded. 'But Tuminok Laskil, now –'

'Ah, yes. Tuminok Laskil!' At once Kasinibon treated Furvain to one of Laskil's soppiest lyrics, a work of the Ni-moyan poet's extreme youth for which Furvain could not even pretend to hide his contempt, and then, reddening once again and again leaving the poem unfinished, switched hastily to a much later verse, the third of the dark *Sonnets of Reconciliation*, which he spoke with surprising eloquence and depth of emotion. Furvain knew the poem well and cherished it, and recited it silently along with Kasinibon to the finish, and found himself unexpectedly moved at the end, not only by the poem itself but by the force of Kasinibon's admiration for it and the deftness of his reading.

'That one is much more to my taste than the first two,' said Furvain after a moment, feeling that something had to be said to break the awkward stillness that the poem's beauty had created in the room.

Kasinibon seemed pleased. 'I see: you prefer the deeper, more sombre work, is that it? Perhaps those first two misled you, then. Let me not do that: please understand that for me as it is for you, late Laskil is much to be preferred. I won't deny that I have a hearty appreciation for plenty of simple stuff, but I hope you'll believe me when I say that I turn to poetry for wisdom, for consolation, for instruction, even, far more often than I do for light entertainment. Your own work, I take it, is of the serious kind? A man of your obvious intelligence must be well worth reading. How strange that I don't know your name.'

'I said I had a minor gift,' Furvain replied, 'and minor is what it is, and my verse as well. Light entertainment is the best I can do. And I've published none of it. My friends think that I should, but such trifling pieces as I produce hardly seem worth the trouble.'

'Would you favour me by quoting one?'

This seemed entirely absurd, to be standing here discussing the art of poetry with a bandit chieftain whose minions had seized him without warrant and who now had locked him up in this grim frontier fortress, for what Furvain just now was beginning to suspect might be an extended imprisonment. And at the moment nothing would come to mind, anyway, except some of his silliest piffle, the trivial lyrics of a trivial-minded courtier. He could not bear, suddenly, to reveal himself to this strange man as the empty, dissolute spinner of idle verse that he knew he was. And so he begged off, claiming that the fatigue of his day's adventures had left him too weary to be able to do a proper recitation.

'Tomorrow, then, I hope,' Kasinibon said. 'And it would give me much pleasure not only if you would allow me to hear some of your finest work, but also for you to compose some memorable new poems during your stay under my roof.'

'Ah,' said Furvain. He gave Kasinibon a long, piercing look. 'And just how long, do you think, is that stay likely to be?'

'That will depend,' Kasinibon said, and the slippery glint of slyness, not so pleasing now, was back in his eyes, 'on the generosity of your family and friends. But we can talk more about that tomorrow, Prince Aithin.' Then he gestured towards the window. Moonlight now glittered on the breast of the scarlet lake, carving a long ruby track running off towards the east. 'That view, Prince Aithin: it certainly must be inspiring to a man of your poetic nature.' Furvain did not reply. Kasinibon, undeterred, spoke briefly of the origin of the lake, the multitude of small organisms whose decaying shells had given it its extraordinary colour, like any proud host explaining a famed local wonder to an interested guest. But Furvain had little interest, just now, in the beauty of the lake or the role its inhabitants had played in its appearance. Kasinibon seemed to perceive that, after a bit. 'Well,' he said, finally. 'I bid you goodnight, and a good night's rest.'

So he was indeed a prisoner, being held here for ransom. What a lovely, farcical touch! And how appropriate that a man who could in his middle years still love that childish, idiotic romantic epic of Dammiunde's would come up with the fanciful idea, straight out of Dammiunde, of demanding a ransom for his release!

But for the first time since being brought here Furvain felt some uneasiness. This was a serious business. Kasinibon might be a romantic, but he was no fool. His impregnable stone fortress alone testified to that. Somehow he had managed to set himself up as the independent ruler of a private domain, less than two weeks' journey from Castle Mount itself, and very probably he ruled that domain as its absolute master, beholden to no one in the world, a law unto himself. Obviously his men had had no idea that they would be kidnapping a Coronal's son when they had come upon a lone wayfarer in that meadow of golden grass, but all the same they had not hesitated to take him to Kasinibon after Furvain had revealed his identity to them, and Kasinibon himself did not seem to regard himself as running any serious risk by making Lord Sangamor's youngest son his prisoner.

A prisoner held for ransom, then.

And who was going to pay that ransom? Furvain had no significant assets himself. Duke Tanigel did, of course. But Tanigel, most likely, would think the ransom note was one of Furvain's pleasant jests, and would chuckle and throw it away. A second, more urgent request would in all probability meet the same fate, especially if Kasinibon asked some ridiculous sum as the price of Furvain's freedom. The Duke was a wealthy man, but would he deem it worth, say, ten thousand royals to have Furvain back at his court again? That was a very high price to pay for a spinner of idle verse.

To whom, then, could Furvain turn? His brothers? Hardly. They were, all four of them, mean-souled, purse-pinching men who clutched tight at every coin. And in their eyes he was only a useless, frivolous nullity. They'd leave him to gather dust here forever rather than put up half a crown to rescue him. And his father the Pontifex? Money would not be an issue for him. But Furvain could easily imagine his father shrugging and saying, 'This will do Aithin some good, I think. He's had an easy ride through life: let him endure a little hardship, now.'

On the other hand, the Pontifex could scarcely condone Kasinibon's lawlessness. Seizing innocent travellers and holding them for ransom? It was a deed that struck at the very core of the social contract that allowed a civilization so far-flung as Majipoor's to hold together. But a military scout would come out and see that the citadel was unassailable, and they would decide not to waste lives in the attempt. A stern decree would be issued, ordering Kasinibon to release his captive and desist from taking others, but nothing would be done by way of enforcing it. I will stay here the rest of my life, Furvain concluded gloomily. I will finish my days as a prisoner in this stone fortress, endlessly pacing these echoing halls. Master Kasinibon will award me the post of court poet and we will recite the collected works of Tuminok Laskil to each other until I lose my mind.

A bleak prospect. But there was no point in fretting further over it tonight, at any rate. Furvain forced himself to push all these dark thoughts aside and made himself ready for bed.

The bed, meagre and unresilient, was less comfortable than the one he had left behind in Dundilmir, but was, at least, to be preferred to the simple bedroll laid out on the ground under a canopy of stars that he had used these past ten days of his journey through the east-country. As he dropped towards sleep, Furvain felt a sensation he knew well, that of a poem knocking at the gates of his mind, beckoning to him to allow it to be born. He saw it only dimly, a vague thing without form, but even in that dimness he was aware that it would be something unusual, at least for him. More than unusual, in fact: something unique. It would be, he sensed, a prodigious work, unprecedented, a poem that would somehow be of far greater scope and depth than anything he had ever produced, though what its subject was was something he could not yet tell. Something magnificent, of that he felt certain, as the knocking continued and became more insistent. Something mighty. Something to touch the soul and heart and mind: something that would transform all who approached it. He was a little frightened of the size of it. He scarcely knew what to make of it, that something like this had come into his mind. There was great power to it, and soaring music, sombre and jubilant all at once. But of course the poem had *not* come into his mind – only its dimensions, not the thing itself. The actual poem would not come into clear view at all, at least not of its own accord, and when he reached through to seize it, it eluded him with the swiftness of a skittish bilantoon, dancing back beyond his reach, vanishing finally into the well of darkness that lay beneath his consciousness, nor would it return even though he lay awake a long while awaiting it.

At last he abandoned the effort and tried to compose himself for sleep once again. Poems must never be seized, he knew; they came only when they were willing to come, and it was futile to try to coerce them. Furvain could not help wondering, though, about its theme. He had no idea of what the poem had been about, nor, he suspected, had he been aware of it even in the instant of the dream. There was no specificity to it, no tangible substance. All he could say was that the poem had been some kind of mighty thing, a work of significant breadth and meaning, and a kind of majesty. Of that he was sure, or reasonably sure, anyway: it had been the major poem of which everyone but he himself was certain he was capable, offering itself to his mind at last. Teasing him, tempting him. But never showing anything more of itself to him than its aura, its outward gleam, and then dancing away, as though to mock him for the laziness of all his past years. An ironic tragedy: the great lost poem of Aithin Furvain. The world would never know, and he would mourn its loss for ever.

Then he decided that he was simply being foolish. What had he lost? His drowsy mind had been playing with him. A poem that is only a shadow of a shadow is no poem at all. To think that he had lost a masterpiece was pure idiocy. How did he know how good the poem, had he been granted any clear sight of it, would have been? What means did he have to judge the quality of a poem that had refused to come into being? He was flattering himself to think that there had been any substance there. The Divine, he knew, had not chosen to give him the equipment that was necessary for the forging of major poems. He was a shallow, idle man, meant to be the maker of little jingling rhymes, of light-hearted playful verse, not of master-pieces. That beckoning poem had been a mere phantom, he thought, the delusion of a weary mind at the edge of sleep, the phantasmagoric aftermath of his bizarre conversation with Master Kasinibon. Furvain let himself drift downwards again into slumber, and slipped away quickly this time.

When he woke, with vague fugitive memories of the lost poem still troubling his mind like a dream that will not let go, he had no idea at first where he was. Bare stone walls, a hard narrow bed, a mere slit of a window through which the morning sun was pouring with merciless power? Then he remembered. He was a prisoner in the fortress of Master Kasinibon. He was angry, at first, that what he had intended as a journey of private discovery, the purifying voyage of a troubled soul, had been interrupted by a band of marauding ruffians; then he was once more amused at the novelty of having been seized in such a fashion; and then he became angry again over the intrusion on his life. But anger, Furvain knew, would serve no useful purpose. He must remain calm, and look upon this purely as an adventure, the raw material for anecdotes and poems with which to regale his friends when he was home at last in Dundilmir.

He bathed and dressed and spent some time studying the effects of morning light on the still surface of the lake, which at this early hour seemed crimson rather than scarlet, and then grew irritable again, and was pacing from room to room once more when the Hjort appeared with his breakfast. In mid-morning Kasinibon paid his second visit to him, but only for a few minutes, and then the morning stretched on interminably until the Hjort came by to bring him lunch. For a time he plumbed his consciousness for some vestige of that lost poem, but the attempt was hopeless, and only instilled in him pangs of regret for he knew not what. Which left him with nothing to do but stare at the lake; and though the lake was indeed exquisite, and of the sort of beauty that changed from hour to hour with the changing angles of the sunlight, Furvain could study those changes only so long before even such beauty as this ceased to stir a response in him.

He had brought some books with him on this journey, but he found that he had no interest in reading now. The words seemed mere meaningless marks on the page. Nor was he able to find distraction in poetry of his own making. It was as if the vanishing of that imaginary masterpiece of the night had taken the ability even to write light verse from him. The fountain that had flowed in a copious gush all his life had gone mysteriously dry: just now he was as empty of poetry as the walls of these rooms were of ornament. So there he was without solace for his solitude. Solitude had never been this much of a problem for him before. Not that he had ever had to put up with any great deal of it, but he had always been able to divert himself with versifying or word-games when he did, and that, for some reason he failed to comprehend, was cut off from him now. While he was still travelling on his own through the east-country he had found being alone to be no burden at all, in fact an interesting and stimulating and instructive new experience; but out there he had had the strangeness of the landscape to appreciate, the unusual new flora and fauna that each day brought, and also he had been much absorbed by the whole challenge of solitary travel, the need to manage his own meals, to find an adequate place to make camp at night, a suitable source of water, and all that. Here, though, locked up in these barren little rooms, he was thrown back on his own resources, and the only resource he had, really, was the boundless fertility of his poetic imagination; and, although he had no idea why, he seemed no longer to have any access to that.

Kasinibon returned for him not long after lunch.

'To the lake, then?' he asked.

'To the lake, yes.'

The outlaw chieftain led him grandly through the clattering stone hallways of the fortress, down and down and down, and ultimately to a corridor on the lowest level, through which they emerged on to a little winding path covered with tawny gravel that curved off in a series of gentle switchbacks to the red lake far below. To Furvain's surprise Kasinibon was unaccompanied by any of his men: the party consisted only of the two of them. Kasinibon walked in front, completely untroubled, apparently, by the possibility that Furvain might choose to attack him.

I could snatch his knife from its scabbard and put it to his throat, Furvain thought, and make him swear to release me. Or I could simply knock him down and club his head against the ground a few times, and run off into the wilderness. Or I could –

It was all too inane to contemplate. Kasinibon was a man of small stature but he looked quick and strong. Doubtless he would instantly make Furvain regret any sort of physical attack. Probably he had bodyguards lurking in the bushes, besides. And even if Furvain did somehow succeed in overpowering him and getting away, what good would it do? Kasinibon's men would hunt him down and take him prisoner again within an hour.

I am his guest, Furvain told himself. He is my host. Let us leave it at that, at least for now.

Two mounts were waiting for them at the edge of the lake. One was the fine, high-spirited creature, with fiery red eyes and flanks of a deep maroon, that Furvain had brought with him from Dundilmir; the other, a short-legged, yellowish beast, looked like a peasant's dray-mount. Kasinibon vaulted up into its saddle and gestured to Furvain to follow suit.

'Barbirike Sea,' said Kasinibon, in a tour-guide's mechanical voice, as they started forwards, 'is close to three hundred miles long, but no more than two thousand feet across at its widest point. It is closed at each end by virtually unscalable cliffs. We have never been able to find any spring that flows into it: it replenishes itself entirely through rainfall.' Seen at close range, the lake seemed more than ever like a great pool of blood. So dense was the red hue that the water had no transparency whatever. From shore to shore it presented itself as an impenetrable sheet of redness, with no features visible below the surface. The reflected face of the sun burned like a sphere of flame on the still waters.

'Can anything live in it?' Furvain asked. 'Other than the crustaceans that give it its colour?'

'Oh, yes,' said Kasinibon. 'It's only water, you know. We fish it every day. The yield is quite heavy.'

A path barely wide enough for their two mounts side by side separated the lake's edge from the towering dunes of red sand that ran alongside it. As they rode rode eastwards along the lake, Kasinibon, still playing the guide, pointed out tidbits of natural history to Furvain: a plant with short, purplish, plumply succulent finger-shaped leaves that was capable of flourishing in the nearly sterile sand of the dunes and dangled down over the crescent slopes in long ropy strands, and a yellow-necked beady-eyed predatory bird that hovered overhead, now and again plunging with frightful force to snatch some denizen of the water out of the lake, and furry little round-bodied crabs that scuttered around like mice along the shore, digging in the scarlet mud for hidden worms. He told Furvain the scientific name of each one, but the names went out of his mind almost at once. Furvain had never troubled to learn very much about the creatures of the wild, although he found these creatures interesting enough, in their way. But Kasinibon, who seemed to be in love with this place, evidently knew everything there was to know about each one. Furvain, though he listened politely enough to his disquisitions, found them distracting and bothersome.

For Furvain the overwhelming redness of the Barbarike Valley was the thing that affected him most deeply. This was beauty of an astounding sort. It seemed to him that all the world had turned scarlet: there was no way to see over the tops of the dunes, so that the view to his left consisted entirely of the red lake itself and the red dunes beyond it, with nothing else visible, and on his right side everything was walled in by the lofty red barrier of the dunes that rose just beside their riding track, and the sky overhead, drawing reflected colour from what lay below it, was a shimmering dome of a slightly paler red. Red, red and red: Furvain felt cloaked in it, contained in it, sealed tight in a realm of redness. He gave himself up to it entirely. He let it engulf and possess him.

Kasinibon seemed to take notice of Furvain's long silence, his air of deepening concentration. 'What we see here is the pure stuff of poetry, is it not?' Kasinibon said proudly, making a sweeping gesture that encompassed both shore and sky and the distant dark hulk of his own fortress, looming at the top of the cliff that lay at their backs. They had come to a halt half a league up the valley. It looked much the same here as at the place where they had begun their ride: red everywhere, before and behind, an unchanging scarlet world. 'I draw constant inspiration from it, and surely you will as well. You will write your masterpiece here. That much I know.'

The sincerity in his voice was unmistakable. He wants that poem very much, Furvain realized. But he resented the little man's jarring invasion of his thoughts and he winced at that reference to a 'masterpiece'. Furvain had no wish to hear anything further about masterpieces, not after last night's painful quasi-dream, in which his own mind seemed to have been mocking him for the deficiencies of his ambitions, pretending to lead him towards some noble work that was not within his soul to create.

Curtly he said, 'Poetry seems to have deserted me for the moment, I'm afraid.'

'It will return. From what you've told me, I know that making poems is something that's innate to your nature. Have you ever gone very long without producing something? As much as a week, say?'

'Probably not. I couldn't really say. The poems happen when they happen, according to some rhythm of their own. It's not something I've paid much conscious attention to.'

'A week, ten days, two weeks – the words will come,' said Kasinibon. 'I know they will.' He seemed strangely excited. 'Aithin Furvain's great poem, written while he is the guest of Master Kasinibon of Barbirike! I might even dare to hope for a dedication, perhaps. Or is that too bold of me?'

This was becoming intolerable. Would it never end, the world's insistence that he must pull some major enterprise from his unwilling mind?

Furvain said, 'Shall I correct you yet again? I am your prisoner, Kasinibon, not your guest.'

'At least you say that, I think, without rancour.'

'What good is rancour, eh? But when one is being held for ransom –'

'Ransom is such an ugly word, Furvain. All that I require is that your family pay the fee I charge for crossing my territory, since you appear to be unable to pay it yourself. Call it ransom, if you like. But the term does offend me.'

'Then I withdraw it,' said Furvain, still concealing his irritation as well as he could beneath a forced lightness of tone. 'I am a man of breeding, Kasinibon. Far be it from me to offend my host.'

In the evening they dined together, just the two of them, in a great echoing candlelit hall where a platoon of silent Hjorts in gaudy livery did the serving, stalking in and out with the absurd grandeur that the people of that unattractive race liked to affect. The banquet was a rich one, first a compote of fruits of some kind unknown to Furvain, then a poached fish of the most delicate flavour, nestling in a dark sauce that must have been based in honey, and then several sorts of grilled meats on a bed of stewed vegetables. The wines for each course were impeccably chosen. Occasionally Furvain caught sight of some of the other outlaws moving about in the corridor at the lower end of the hall, shadowy figures far away, but none entered the room.

Flushed with drink, Kasinibon spoke freely of himself. He seemed very eager, almost pathetically so, to win his captive's friendship. He was, he said, a younger son himself, third son of the Count of Kekkinork. Kekkinork was not a place known to Furvain. 'It lies two hours' march from the shores of the Great Sea,' Kasinibon explained. 'My ancestors came there to mine the handsome blue stone known as seaspar, which the Coronal Lord Pinitor of ancient times used in decorating the walls of the city of Bombifale. When the work was done some of the miners chose not to return to Castle Mount. And there at Kekkinork they have lived ever since, in a village at the edge of the Great Sea, a free people, beyond the ken of Pontifex and Coronal. My father, the Count, was the sixteenth holder of that title in the direct line of succession.'

'A title conferred by Lord Pinitor?'

'A title conferred by the first Count upon himself,' said Kasinibon. 'We are the descendants of humble miners and stonemasons, Furvain. But, of course, if one only goes back far enough, which of the lords of Castle Mount would be seen to be free of the blood of commoners?'

'Indeed,' Furvain said. That part was unimportant. What he was struggling to assimilate was the knowledge that this small bearded man sitting elbow to elbow with him had beheld the Great Sea with his own eyes, had grown to manhood in a remote part of Majipoor that was widely looked upon as the next thing to mythical. The notion of the existence of an actual town of some sort out there, a town unknown to geographers and census-keepers, situated in an obscure location at Alhanroel's easternmost point many thousands of miles from Castle Mount, strained credibility. And that this place had a separate aristocracy of its own creation, counts and marquises and ladies and all the rest, which had endured for sixteen generations there – that, too, was hard to believe.

Kasinibon refilled their wine-bowls. Furvain had been drinking as sparingly as he could all evening, but Kasinibon was merciless in his generosity, and Furvain felt flushed, now, and a little dizzy. Kasinibon had taken on the glossy-eyed look of full drunkenness.

He had begun to speak, in a rambling, circuitous way that Furvain found difficult to follow, of some bitter family quarrel, a dispute with one of his older brothers over a woman, the great love of his life, perhaps, and an appeal laid before their father in which the father had taken the brother's side. It sounded familiar enough to Furvain: the grasping brother, the distant and indifferent noble father, the younger son treated with offhand disdain. But Furvain, perhaps because he had never been a man of much ambition or drive, had not allowed the disappointments of his early life ever to stir much umbrage in his mind. He had always felt that he was more or less invisible to his dynamic father and his rapacious, aggressive brothers. He expected indifference from them, at best, and was not surprised when that was what he got, and had gone on to construct a reasonably satisfactory life for himself even so, founded on the belief that the less one expected out of life, the less one was likely to feel dissatisfied with what came one's way.

Kasinibon, though, was of another kind, hot-blooded and determined, and his dispute with his brother had mounted to something of shattering acrimony, leading finally to an actual violent assault by Kasinibon on – whom? – his brother? – his father? – Furvain was not entirely sure which. It finally came to pass that Kasinibon had found it advisable to flee from Kekkinork, or perhaps had been exiled from it – again, Furvain did not know which – and had gone roaming for many years from one sector of the east-country to another until, here at Barbirike, he had found a place where he could fortify himself against anyone who might attempt to offer a challenge to his truculent independence. 'And here I am to this day,' he concluded. 'I have no dealings with my family, nor any with Pontifex or Coronal, either. I am my own master, and the master of my little kingdom. And those who wander across my territory must pay the price. More wine, Furvain?'

'Thank you, no.'

He poured, as though he had not heard. Furvain began to brush his hand aside, then halted and let Kasinibon fill the bowl.

'I like you, you know, Furvain. I hardly know you, but I'm as good a judge of men as you'll ever find, and I see the depth of you, the greatness in you.'

And I see the drunkenness in you, Furvain thought, but he said nothing.

'If they pay the fee, I'll have to let you go, I suppose. I'm an honourable man. But I'd regret it. I've had very little intelligent company here. Very little company of any sort, as a matter of fact. It's the life I chose, of course. But still –'

'You must be very lonely.'

It occurred to Furvain that he had not seen any women at the fortress, nor even any sign of a female presence: only the Hjort servants, and the occasional glimpse of some of Kasinibon's followers, all of them men. Was Kasinibon that rarity, the one-woman man? And had that woman of Kekkinork, the one his brother had taken from him, been that woman? It must be a grim existence for him, then, in this desolate keep. No wonder he sought the consolations of poetry; no wonder he was still capable, at this advanced age, of finding so much to admire in the nonsensical puerile effusions of Dammiunde or Tuminok Laskil.

'Lonely, yes. I can't deny that. Lonely – lonely –' Kasinibon turned a bloodshot gaze on Furvain. His eyes had taken on a glint as red as the waters of the Barbirike Sea. 'But one learns to live with loneliness. One makes one's choices in life, does one not, and although they are never perfect choices, they are, after all, one's own, eh? Ultimately, we choose what we choose because – we choose – because – because –'

Kasinibon's voice grew less distinct and trailed off into incoherence. Furvain thought he might have fallen asleep; but no, no, Kasinibon's eyes were open, his lips were slowly moving, he was searching still for the precise phrase to explain whatever it was he was trying to explain. Furvain waited until it became clear that the bandit chieftain was never going to find that phrase. Then he touched Kasinibon lightly on the arm. 'You must forgive me,' he said. 'The hour is very late.' Kasinibon nodded vaguely. A Hjort in livery showed Furvain to his rooms.

In the night Furvain dreamed a dream of such power and lucidity that he thought, even as he was experiencing it, that it must be a sending of the Lady of the Isle, who visits millions of the sleepers of Majipoor each night to bring them guidance and comfort. If indeed it were a sending, it would be his first: the Lady did not often visit the minds of the princes of the Castle, and in any case she would not have been likely to visit that of Furvain, for it was the ancient custom for the mother of the current Coronal to be chosen as Lady of the Isle, and thus, for most of Furvain's life, the reigning Lady had been his own grandmother. She would not enter the mind of a member of her own family except at some moment of high urgency. Now, of course, with Lord Sangamor having moved on to become Sangamor Pontifex, there was a new Coronal at the Castle and a new Lady at the helm of the Isle of Sleep. But even so – a sending? For *him*? Here? Why?

As he was drifting back into sleep once the dream had left him, he decided that it had not been a sending at all, but merely the workings of his own agitated mind, stirred to frantic excitation by his evening with Master Kasinibon. It had been too personal, too intimate a vision to have been the work of the stranger who now was Lady of the Isle. Yet Furvain knew it to have been no ordinary dream, but rather one of those strange dreams by which one's whole future life is determined.

For in it his sleeping mind had been lifted up out of Kasinibon's stark sanctuary and carried from it over the night-shrouded plains of the east-country, off to the other side of the blue cliffs of Kekkinork where the Great Sea began, stretching forth into the immeasurable and incomprehensible distances that separated Alhanroel from the continent of Zimroel half a world away. Here, far to the east of any place he had ever known, he could see the light of the dawning day gleaming on the breast of the ocean, which was a gentle pink in colour at the sandy shore, then pale green, and a deeper green farther out, and then deepening by steady gradation to the azure grey of the unfathomable depths.

The Spirit of the Divine lingered high above that mighty ocean, Furvain perceived: impersonal, unknowable, infinite, all-seeing.

Though the Spirit was without form or feature, Furvain recognized it for what it was, and the Spirit recognized him, touching his mind, gathering it in, linking it, for one stunning moment, to the vastness that was itself. And in that infinitely long moment the greatest of all poems was dictated to him, poured into him in one tremendous cascade, a poem that only a god could create, the poem that encompassed the meaning of life and of death, of the destiny of all worlds and all the creatures that dwelled upon them. Or so Furvain thought, later, when he had awakened and lay shivering, feverish with bewilderment, contemplating the vision that had been thrust upon him.

No shard of that vision remained, not a single detail by which he could try to reconstruct it. It had shattered like a soap-bubble and vanished into the darkness. Once again he had been brought to the presence of a sublime poem of the greatest beauty and profundity and then it had been snatched away again.

Tonight's dream, though, was different in its deepest essence from the one of the night before. That other dream had been a sad cruel joke, a bit of mere harsh mockery. It had flaunted a poem before him but had given him no access to it, only the humiliating awareness that a major poem of some sort lurked somewhere within him but would be kept for ever beyond his reach. This time he had had the poem itself. He had lived it, line by line, stanza by stanza, canto by canto, through all its grand immensity. Although he had lost it upon waking, perhaps it could be found again. The first dream had told him, *Your gift is an empty one and you are capable of nothing but the making of trivialities.* The second dream had told him, *You contain godlike greatness within you and you must now strive to find a way to draw it forth.*

Though the content of that great vision was gone, Furvain realized in the morning that one aspect of it still remained, as though burned into his mind: its framework, the container for the mighty poem itself; the metric pattern, the rhyme-scheme, the method of building verses into stanzas and the grouping of stanzas into cantos. A mere empty vessel, yes. But if the container, at least, was left to him, there might be hope of rediscovering the awesome thing that it had contained.

The structural pattern was such a distinctive one that he knew he was unlikely to forget it, but even so he would not take the risk. He reached hastily for his pen and a blank sheet of paper and scribbled it down. Rather than attempting at this point to recapture even a fragment of what would be no small task to retrieve, Furvain used mere nonsense syllables to provide a shape for the vessel, meaningless dum-de-dum sounds that provided the basic rhythmic outline of one extended passage. When he was done he stared in wonder at it, murmuring it to himself over and over again, analysing consciously now what he had set down as a sort of automatic transcription of his dream-memory. It was a remarkable structure, yes, but almost comically extreme. As he counted out its numbers he asked himself whether anything so intricate had ever been devised by poet's mind before, and whether any poet in the long history of the universe would ever have been able to carry off a long work using prosody of such an extravagant kind.

It was a marvel of complexity. It made no use of the traditional stress-patterned metrics he knew so well, the iambs and trochees and dactyls, the spondees and anapests, out of which Furvain had always built his poems with such swiftness and ease. Those traditional patterns were so deeply ingrained in him that it seemed to others that he wrote without thinking, that he simply exhaled his poems rather than creating them by conscious act. But this pattern – he chanted it over and over to himself, struggling to crack its secret – was alien to all that he understood of the craft of poetry.

At first he could see no sort of regularity to the rhythms whatever, and was at a loss to explain the strangely compelling power of them. But then he realized that the metric of his dream-poem must be a quantitative one, based not on where the accents fell but on the length of syllables, a system that struck Furvain at first as disconcertingly arbitrary and irregular but which, he saw after a while, could yield a wondrously versatile line in the hands of anyone gifted enough to manipulate its intricacies properly. It would have the force almost of an incantation; those caught up in its sonorous spell would be held as if by sorcery. The rhyme-scheme too was a formidable one, with stanzas of seventeen lines that allowed of only three different rhymes, arranged in a pattern of five internal couplets split by a triolet and balanced by four seemingly unrhymed lines that actually were reaching into adjacent stanzas.

Could a poem actually be written according to such a structure? Of course, Furvain thought. But what poet could possibly have the patience to stay with it long enough to produce a work of any real scope? The Divine could, of course. By definition the Divine could do anything: what difficulties would a mere arrangement of syllables and rhymes offer to the omnipotent force that had brought into being the stars and worlds? But it was not just blasphemous for a mere mortal to set himself up in competition with the Divine, he thought, it was contemptible folly. Furvain knew he could write three or four stanzas in this kind of scheme, if he turned himself properly to the task, or perhaps seven, that made some kind of poetic sense. But a whole canto? And a series of cantos that would constitute a coherent work of epic magnitude? No, he thought. No. No. That would drive him out of his mind. No doubt of it, to undertake a task of such grandeur would be to invite madness.

Still, it had been an extraordinary dream. The other one had left him with nothing but the taste of ashes in his mouth. This one showed him that he – not the Divine, but *he*, for Furvain was not a very religious man and felt sure that it was his own dreaming mind that had invented it, without supernatural assistance – was able to conceive a stanzaic system of almost impossible difficulty. It must have been in him all along, he thought, gestating quietly, finally erupting from him as he slept. The tensions and pressures of his captivity, he decided, must have aided in the birth. No longer was he as amused as he once had been about spending his days in Kasinibon's custody. It was becoming harder to take a comic view of the affair. The rising anger he felt at being held prisoner here, the frustrations, his growing restlessness: all that must be altering the chemistry of his brain, forcing his thoughts into new channels, his inner torment bringing out new aspects of his poetic skill.

Not that he had the slightest idea of trying to make actual use of such a system as the night just past had brought him; but it was pleasing enough to know that he was capable of devising such a thing. Perhaps that portended a return of his ability to write light verse, at least. Furvain knew that he was never going to give the world the deathless masterpiece that Kasinibon was so eager to have from him, but it would be good at least to regain the pleasant minor skill that had been his until a few days before.

But the days went by and Furvain remained unaccountably unproductive. Neither Kasinibon's urgings nor Furvain's own attempts at inducing the presence of the muse were in any way helpful, and his old spontaneous facility was so far from being in evidence that he could almost persuade himself that it had never existed.

His captivity, now, was weighing on him with increasing discomfort. Accustomed as he was to a life of idleness, this kind of forced inactivity was nothing he had ever had to endure before, and he longed to be on his way. Kasinibon tried his best, of course, to play the part of the charming host. He took Furvain on daily rides through the scarlet valley, he brought forth the finest wines from his surprisingly well-stocked cellar for their nightly dinners, he provided him with whatever book he might fancy – his library was well stocked, also – and lost no opportunity to engage him in serious discussion of the literary arts.

But the fact remained that Furvain was here unwillingly, penned up in this dour, forbidding mausoleum of a place, snared midway through a crisis of his own and compelled, before he had reached any resolution of that, to live as the prisoner of another man, and a limited man at that. Kasinibon now allowed him to roam freely through the building and its grounds – if he tried to escape, where could he hope to go, after all? – but the long echoing halls and mainly empty rooms were far from congenial. There was nothing really congenial about Kasinibon's company, either, however much Furvain pretended that there was, and there was no one else here to keep company with Furvain than Kasinibon. The outlaw chieftain, walled about by his hatred for his own family and stunted by his long isolation here, was as much a prisoner at Barbirike as Furvain himself, and behind his superficial amiability, that elfin playfulness of his, some hidden fury lurked and seethed. Furvain saw that fury and feared it.

He had still done nothing about sending out a ransom request. It seemed utterly futile, and embarrassing as well: what if he asked, and no one complied? But the growing probability that he was going to remain here for ever was starting to engender a sense of deep desperation in him.

What was particularly hard to bear was Kasinibon's fondness for poetry. Kasinibon seemed to want to talk about nothing else. Furvain had never cared much for conversation about poetry. He was content to leave that to the academic folk, who had no creative spark themselves but found some sort of fulfilment in endless discussions of the thing that they were themselves unable to produce, and to those persons of culture who felt that it was incumbent on them to be seen carrying some slim volume of poetry about, and even to dip into it from time to time, and to utter praise for some currently acclaimed poet's work. Furvain, from whom poems by the ream had always emerged with only the slightest of efforts and who had had no lofty view of what he had achieved, had no interest in such talk. For him poetry was something to make, not something to discuss. What a horror it was, then, to be trapped like this in the presence of the most talkative of amateur connoisseurs of the art, and an ignorant one at that!

Like most self-educated men, Kasinibon had no taste in poetry at all – he gobbled everything omnivorously, indiscriminately, and was uncritically entranced by it all. Stale images, leaden rhymes, bungled metaphors, ridiculous similes – he had no difficulty overlooking such things, perhaps did not even notice them. The one thing he demanded was a bit of emotional power in a poem, and if he could find it there, he forgave all else.

And so Furvain spent most nights in the first weeks of his stay at the outlaw's keep listening to Kasinibon's readings of his favourite poems. His extensive library, hundreds and hundreds of well-thumbed volumes, some of them practically falling apart after years of constant use, seemed to contain the work of every poet Furvain had ever heard of, and a good many that he had not. It was such a wide-ranging collection that its very range argued for its owner's lack of discernment. Kasinibon's passionate love of poetry struck Furvain as mere promiscuity. 'Let me read you this!' Kasinibon would cry, eyes aglow with enthusiasm, and he would intone some incontestibly great work of Gancislad or Emmengild; but then, even as the final glorious lines still were echoing in Furvain's mind, Kasinibon would say, 'Do you know what it reminds me of, that poem?' And he would reach for his beloved volume of Vortrailin, and with equal enthusiasm declaim one of the tawdriest bits of sentimental trash Furvain had ever heard. He seemed unable to tell the difference.

Often he asked Furvain to choose poems that he would like to read, also, wanting to hear how a practitioner of the art handled the ebb and flow of poetic rhythms. Furvain's own tastes in poetry had always run heavily to the sort of light verse at which he excelled himself, but, like any cultivated man, he appreciated more serious work as well, and on these occasions he took a deliberate malicious pleasure in selecting for Kasinibon the knottiest, most abstruse modern works he could find on Kasinibon's shelves, poems that he himself barely understood and should have been mysteries to Kasinibon also. These, too, Kasinibon loved. 'Beautiful,' he would murmur, enraptured. 'Sheer music, is it not?'

I am going to go mad, Furvain thought.

At some point during nearly every one of these nightly sessions of poetic discourse Kasinibon would press Furvain to recite some of his own work. Furvain could no longer claim, as he had on the first day, that he was too tired to comply. Nor could he pretend very plausibly that he had forgotten every poem he had ever written. So in the end he yielded and offered a few. Kasinibon's applause was hearty in the extreme, and seemed unfeigned. And he spoke at great length in praise not just of Furvain's elegance of phrasing but his insight into human nature. Which was all the more embarrassing; Furvain himself was abashed by the triviality of his themes and the glibness of his technique; it took every ounce of his aristocratic breeding to hold himself back from crying out, 'But don't you see, Kasinibon, what hollow word-spinning that is!' That would have been cruel, and discourteous besides. Both men now had entered into a pretence of friendship, which might not even have been a pretence on Kasinibon's part. One may not call one's friend a fool to his face, Furvain thought, and expect him to go on being your friend.

The worst part of all was Kasinibon's unfeigned eagerness to have Furvain write something new, and important, while a guest under his roof. There had been nothing playful about that wistfully expressed hope of his that Furvain would bring into being here some masterpiece that would for ever link his name and Kasinibon's in the archives of poetry. Behind that wistfulness, Furvain sensed, lay ferocious need. He suspected that matters would not always remain so amiable here: that indirection would turn to blunt insistence, that Kasinibon would squeeze him and squeeze him until Furvain brought forth the major work that Kasinibon so hungrily yearned to usher into existence. Furvain replied evasively to each of Kasinibon's inquiries about new work, explaining, truthfully enough, that inspiration was still denied to him. But there was a mounting intensity to Kasinibon's demands.

The question of ransom, which Furvain had continued to push aside, needed to be squarely faced. Furvain saw that he could not remain here much longer without undergoing some kind of inner explosion. But the only way he was going to get out of this place, he knew, was with the help of someone else's money. Was there anyone in the world willing to put up money to rescue him? He suspected he knew the answer to that, but shied away from confirming his fears. Still, if he never so much as asked, he would spend the remaining days of his life listening to Master Kasinibon's solemn, worshipful readings of the worst poetry human mind had ever conceived, and fending off Kasinibon's insistence that Furvain write for him some poem of a grandeur and majesty that was not within Furvain's abilities to produce.

'How much, would you say, should I ask as the price of my freedom?' Furvain asked one day, as they rode together beside the shore of the scarlet sea.

Kasinibon told him. It was a stupendous sum, more than twice Furvain's own highest guess. But he had asked, and Kasinibon had answered, and he was in no position to haggle with the bandit over the amount.

Duke Tanigel, he supposed, was the first one he should try. Furvain knew that his brothers were unlikely to care much whether he stayed here for ever or not. His father might take a gentler position, but his father was far away in the Labyrinth, and appealing to the Pontifex carried other risks, too, for if it came to pass that a Pontifical army were dispatched to Barbirike to rescue the captive prince, Kasinibon might react in some unpleasant and possibly fatal way. The same risk would apply if Furvain were to turn to the new Coronal, Lord Hunzimar. Strictly speaking, it was the Coronal's responsibility to deal with such matters as banditry in the outback. But that was exactly what Furvain was afraid of, that Hunzimar would send troops out here to teach Kasinibon a lesson, a lesson that might have ugly consequences for Kasinibon's prisoner. Even more probably, Hunzimar, who had never shown much affection for any of his predecessor's sons, would do nothing at all. No, Tanigel was his only hope, faint though that hope might be.

Furvain did have some notion of the extent of Duke Tanigel's immense wealth, and suspected that the whole gigantic amount of his ransom would be no more than the cost of one week's feasting and revelry at the court in Dundilmir. Perhaps Tanigel would deign to help, out of fond memories of happy times together. Furvain spent half a day writing and revising his note to the Duke, working hard to strike the proper tone of amused, even waggish chagrin over his plight, while at the same time letting Tanigel know that he really did have to come through with the money if ever he hoped to see his friend Furvain again. He turned the letter over to Kasinibon, who sent one of his men off to Dundilmir to deliver it.

'And now,' said Kasinibon, 'I propose we turn our attention this evening to the ballads of Garthain Hagavon –'

At the beginning of the fourth week of his captivity Furvain made the dream-journey to the Great Sea once again, and again took dictation from the Divine, who appeared to him in the guise of a tall, broad-shouldered, golden-haired man of cheerful mien, wearing a Coronal's silver band about his head. And when he woke it was all still in his mind, every syllable of every verse, every verse of every stanza, every stanza of what appeared to be a third of a canto, as well as he could judge the proportions of such things. But it began to fade almost at once. Out of fear that he might lose it all he set about the work of transcribing as much of it as he could, and as the lines emerged on to the paper he saw that they followed the inordinately intricate metrical pattern and rhyming scheme of the poem that had been given to him by the hand of the Divine that other time weeks before: appeared to be, indeed, a fragment of that very poem.

A fragment was all that it was. What Furvain had managed to get down began in the middle of a stanza, and ended, pages later, in the middle of another one. The subject was warfare, the campaign of the great Lord Stiamot of thousands of years before against the rebellious aboriginal people of Majipoor, the shapeshifting Metamorph race. The segment that lay before him dealt with Stiamot's famous march through the foothills of Zygnor Peak in northern Alhanroel, the climactic enterprise of that long agonizing struggle, when he had set fire to the whole district, parched by the heat of the long dry summer, in order to drive the final bands of Metamorph guerrillas from their hiding places. It broke off at the point where Lord Stiamot found himself confronting a recalcitrant landholder, a man of the ancient northern gentry who refused to pay heed to Stiamot's warning that all this territory was going to be put to the torch and that it behoved every settler to flee at once.

When it became impossible for Furvain to go any further with his transcription he read it all back, astounded, even bemused. The style and general approach, the bizarre schemes of rhyme and metre apart, were beyond any doubt his own. He recognized familiar turns of phrase, similes of a kind that had always come readily to him, choices of rhyme that declared themselves plainly as the work of Aithin Furvain. But how, if not by direct intervention of the Divine, had anything so complicated and deep sprung from his own shallow mind? This was majestic poetry. There was no other word for it. He read it aloud to himself, revelling in the sonorities, the internal assonances, the sinewy strength of the line, the inevitability of each stanza's form. He had never written anything remotely like this before. He had had the technique for it, very likely, but he could not imagine ever making so formidable a demand on that technique.

And also there were things in here about Stiamot's campaign that Furvain did not in fact believe he had ever known. He had learned about Lord Stiamot from his tutors, of course. Everyone did; Stiamot was one of the great figures of Majipoor's history. But Furvain's schooling had taken place decades ago. Had he ever really heard the names of all these places – Milimorn, Hamifieu, Bizfern, Kattikawn? Were they genuine place-names, or his own inventions?

His inventions? Well, yes, anyone could make up names, he supposed. But there was too much here about military procedure, lines of supply and chains of command and order of march and such, that read like the work of some other hand, someone far more knowledgeable about such things than he had ever been. How, then, could he possibly claim this poem as his own? Yet where had it come from, if not from him? Was he truly the vehicle through which the Divine had chosen to bring this fragment into existence? Furvain found his slender fund of religious feeling seriously taxed by such a notion. And yet – and yet –

Kasinibon saw at once that something out of the ordinary had happened. 'You've begun to write, haven't you?'

'I've begun a poem, yes,' said Furvain uneasily.

'Wonderful! When can I see it?'

The blaze of excitement in Kasinibon's eyes was so fierce that Furvain had to back away a few steps. 'Not just yet, I think. This is much too soon to be showing it to anyone. At this point it would be extremely easy for me to lose my way. A casual word from someone else might be just the one that would deflect me from my path.'

'I swear that I'll offer no comment at all. I simply would like to –'

'No. Please.' Furvain was surprised by the steely edge he heard in his own voice. 'I'm not sure yet what this is a part of. I need to examine, to evaluate, to ponder. And that has to be done on my own. I tell you, Kasinibon, I'm afraid that I'll lose it altogether if I reveal anything of it now. Please: let me be.'

Kasinibon seemed to understand that. He grew instantly solicitous. Almost unctuously he said, 'Yes. Yes, of course, it would be tragic if my blundering interference harmed the flow of your creation. I withdraw my request. But you will, I hope, grant me a look at it just as soon as you feel that the time has come when you –'

'Yes. Just as soon as the time has come,' said Furvain.

He retreated to his quarters and returned to work, not without trepidation. This was new to him, this business of setting down formally to work. In the past poems had always found *him* – taking a direct and immediate line from his mind to his fingertips. He had never needed to go searching for *them*. Now, though, Furvain self-consciously sat himself at his little bare table, he laid out two or three pens at his side, he tapped the edges of his stack of blank paper until every sheet was perfectly aligned, he closed his eyes and waited for the heat of inspiration.

Quickly he discovered that inspiration could not simply be invited to arrive, at least not when one was embarked on an enterprise such as this. His old methods no longer applied. For what he had to do now, one had to go out in quest of the material; one had to fix it in one's gaze and seize it firmly; one had to compel it to do one's bidding. He was writing, it seemed, a poem about Lord Stiamot. Very well: he must focus every atom of his being on that long-ago monarch, must reach out across the ages and enter into a communion of a sort with him, must touch his soul and follow his path.

That was easy enough to say, not so easy to accomplish. The inadequacies of his historical knowledge troubled him. With nothing more than a schoolboy's knowledge of Stiamot's life and career, and that knowledge, such as it ever had been, now blurred by so many years of forgetfulness, how could he presume to tell the tale of the epochal conflict that had ended for all time the aboriginal threat to the expansion of the human settlements on Majipoor?

Abashed at his own lack of learning, he prowled Kasinibon's library, hoping to come upon some works of historical scholarship. But history, it seemed, was not a subject that held any great interest for his captor. Furvain found no texts of any consequence, just a brief history of the world, which seemed to be nothing more than a child's book. From an inscription on its back cover he saw that it was in fact a relic of Kasinibon's own childhood in Kekkinork. It contained very little that was useful: just a brief, highly simplified recapitulation of Lord Stiamot's attempts to seek a negotiated peace with the Metamorphs, the failure of those attempts, and the Coronal's ultimate decision to put an end once and for all to Metamorph depredations against the cities of the human settlers by defeating them in battle, expelling them from human-occupied territories, and confining them for all time in the rain-forests of southern Zimroel. Which had, of course, entangled the world in a generation-long struggle that ended ultimately in success and made possible the explosive growth of civilization on Majipoor and prosperity everywhere on the giant world. Stiamot was one of the key figures of Majipoor's history. But Kasinibon's little history-book told only the bare outlines of the story, the politics and the battles, not a word about Stiamot as a man, his inner thoughts and emotions, his physical appearance, anything of that sort.

Then Furvain realized that he had no real need to know those things. He was writing a poem, not a historical text or a work of biography. He was free to imagine any detail he liked, so long as he remained faithful to the broad outline of the tale. Whether the actual Lord

Stiamot had been short or tall, plump or thin, cheerful of nature or a dyspeptic brooder, would make no serious difference to a poet intent only on re-creating the Stiamot legend. Lord Stiamot, by now, had become a mythical figure. And myth, Furvain knew, has a power that transcends mere history. History could be as arbitrary as poetry, he told himself: what is history, other than a matter of choice, the picking and choosing of certain facts out of a multitude to elicit a meaningful pattern, which was not necessarily the true one? The act of selecting facts, by definition, inherently involved discarding facts as well, often the ones most inconvenient to the pattern that the historian was trying to reveal. Truth thus became an abstract concept: three different historians, working with the same set of data, might easily come up with three different 'truths'. Whereas myth digs deep into the fundamental reality of the spirit, into that infinite well that is the shared consciousness of the entire race, reaching the levels where truth is not an optional matter, but the inescapable foundation of all else. In that sense myth could be truer than history; by creating imaginative episodes that clove to the essence of the Stiamot story, a poet could reveal the truth of that story in a way that no historian could claim to do. And so Furvain resolved that his poem would deal with the myth of Stiamot, not with the historical man. He was free to invent as he pleased, so long as what he invented was faithful to the inner truth of the story.

After that everything became easier, although there was never anything simple about it for him. He developed a technique of meditation that left him hovering on the border of sleep, from which he could slip readily into a kind of trance. Then – more rapidly with each passing day – Furvain's guide would come to him, the golden-haired man wearing a Coronal's silver diadem, and lead him through the scenes and events of his day's work.

His guide's name, he discovered, was Valentine: a charming man, patient, affable, sweet-tempered, always ready with an easy smile, the absolute best of guides. Furvain could not remember any Coronal named Valentine, nor did Kasinibon's boyhood history text mention one. Evidently no such person had ever existed. But that made no difference. For Furvain's purposes, it was all the same whether this Lord Valentine had been a real historical figure or was just a figment of Furvain's imagination: what he needed was someone to take him by the hand and lead him through the shadowy realms of antiquity, and that was what his golden-haired guide was doing. It was almost as though he were the manifestation in a readily perceptible form of the will of the Divine, whose vehicle Furvain had become. It is through the voice of this imaginary Lord Valentine, Furvain told himself, that the shaping spirit of the cosmos is inscribing this poem on my soul.

Under Valentine's guidance Furvain's dreaming mind traversed the deeds of Lord Stiamot, beginning with his first realization that the long poisonous struggle with the Metamorphs must be brought to a conclusive end and going on through the sequence of increasingly bloody battles that had culminated in the burning of the northlands, the surrender of the last aboriginal rebels, and the establishment of the province of Piurifayne in Zimroel as the permanent home and place of eternal confinement of the Shapeshifters of Majipoor. When Furvain emerged from his trance each day the details of what he had learned would still be with him, and had the balance and shape and the tragic rhythm that great poetry requires. He saw not only the events but the inexorable and inescapable conflicts out of which they arose, driving even a man of good will like Stiamot into the harsh necessity of making war. The pattern of the story was there; Furvain had merely to set it all down on paper: and here his innate technical skill was fully at his command, as much so as it had ever been in the old days, so that the intricate stanza and complex rhythmic scheme that he had carried back from his first dreaming encounters with the Divine soon became second nature to him, and the poem grew by a swift process of accretion.

Sometimes it came a little *too* easily. Now that Furvain had mastered that strange stanza he was able to reel off page after page with such effortless fluency that he would on occasion wander on into unexpected digressions that concealed and muddled the main thrust of his narrative. When that happened he would halt, rip the offending sections out, and go on from the point where he had begun to diverge from his proper track. He had never revised before. At first it seemed wasteful to him, since the discarded lines were every bit as eloquent, as sonorous, as the ones he kept. But then he came to see that eloquence and sonorousness were mere accessories to the main task, which was the telling of a particular tale in a way that most directly illuminated its inner meaning.

And then, when he had brought the tale of Lord Stiamot to its conclusion, Furvain was startled to find that the Divine was not yet done with him. Without pausing even to question what he was doing, he drew a line beneath the last of the Stiamot stanzas and began to inscribe a new verse – beginning, he saw, right in the middle of a stanza, with the triple-rhyme passage – that dealt with an earlier event entirely, the project of Lord Melikand to import beings of species other than human to help with the task of settling the greatly underpopulated world that was Majipoor.

He continued in that project for another few days. But then, while the Melikand canto was yet unfinished, Furvain discovered himself at work on a passage that told still another story, that of the grand assembly at Stangard Falls, on the River Glayge, where Dvorn had been hailed as Majipoor's first Pontifex. At that moment Furvain realized that he was writing not simply an account of the deeds of Lord Stiamot, but an epic poem embracing nothing less than the whole of Majipoor's history.

It was a frightening thought. He could not believe that he was the man for such a task. It was too much for a man of his limitations. He thought he saw the shape that such a poem must take, as it traversed the many thousands of years from the coming of the first settlers to the present day, and it was a mighty one. Not a single great arc, no, but a series of soaring curves and dizzying swoops, a tale of flux and transformation, of the constant synthesis of opposites, as the early idealistic colonists tumbled into the violent chaos of anarchy, were rescued from it by Dvorn the law-giver, the first Pontifex, spread out in centrifugal expansion across the huge world under the guidance of Lord Melikand, built the great cities of Castle Mount, reached across into the continents of Zimroel and Suvrael, came inevitably and tragically into collision with the Shapeshifter aboriginals, fought the necessary though appalling war against them under the leadership of Lord Stiamot, that man of peace transformed into a warrior, that defeated and contained them, and so onwards to this present day, when billions of people lived in peace on the most beautiful of all worlds.

There was no more splendid story in all the universe. But was he, Aithin Furvain, such a small-souled man, a man flawed in so many ways, going to be able to encompass it? He had no illusions about himself. He saw himself as glib, lazy, dissolute, a weakling, an evader of responsibility, a man who throughout his whole life had sought the path of least resistance. How could he, of all people, having no other resource than a certain degree of cleverness and technical skill, hope to contain such a gigantic theme within the bounds of a single poem? It was too much for him. He could never do it. He doubted that anyone could. But certainly Aithin Furvain was not the one to attempt it.

And yet he seemed somehow to be writing it. Or was it writing him? No matter: the thing was taking shape, line by line, day by day. Call it divine inspiration, call it the overflowing of something that he had kept penned unknowingly within him for many years, call it whatever one wished, there was no denying that he had already written one full canto and fragments of two others, and that each day brought new verses. And there was greatness in the poem: of that he was certain. He would read through it over and over again, shaking his head in amazement at the power of his own work, the mighty music of the poetry, the irresistible sweep of the narrative. It was all so splendid that it humbled and bewildered him. He had no idea how it had been possible to achieve what he had done, and he shivered with dread at the thought that his miraculous fount of inspiration would dry up, as suddenly as it had opened, before the great task had reached its end.

The manuscript, unfinished though it was, became terribly precious to him. He came to see it now as his claim on immortality. It troubled him that only one copy of it existed, and that one kept in a room that could be locked only from outside. Fearful now that something might happen to it, that it might be blotted into illegibility by the accidental overturning of his ink-stand, or stolen by some prying malicious denizen of the fortress jealous of the attention paid to Furvain by Master Kasinibon, or even taken out of his room as trash by some illiterate servant and destroyed, he copied it out several times over, carefully hiding the copies in different rooms of his little suite. The main draft he buried each night in the lowest drawer of the cupboard in which he kept his clothing; and, a few days later, without really knowing why, he fell into the habit of painstakingly arranging three of his pens in a star-shaped pattern on top of the pile of finished sheets so that he would know at once if anyone had been prowling in that drawer.

Three days after that he saw that the pens had been disturbed. Furvain had taken care to lay them out with meticulous care, the central pen aligned each time at the same precise angle to the other two. This day he saw that the angle was slightly off, as though someone had understood that the purpose of the arrangement was the detection of an intrusion and had replaced the pens after examining the manuscript, but had not employed the greatest possible degree of accuracy in attempting to mimic Furvain's own grouping of the pens. That night he chose a new pattern for the pens, and the next afternoon he saw that once again they had been put back almost as he had left them, but not quite. The same thing happened over the succeeding two days.

It could only have been the doing of Kasinibon himself, Furvain decided. No member of Kasinibon's outlaw band, and certainly not any servant, would have taken half so much trouble over the pens. He is sneaking in while I am elsewhere, Furvain thought. He is secretly reading my poem.

Furious, Furvain sought Kasinibon out and assailed him for violating the privacy of his quarters.

To his surprise, Kasinibon made no attempt to deny the accusation. 'Ah, so you know? Well, of course. I couldn't resist.' His eyes were shining with excitement. 'It's marvellous, Furvain. Magnificent. I was so profoundly moved by it I can hardly begin to tell you. The episode of Lord Stiamot and the Metamorph priestess – when she comes before him, when she weeps for her people, and Stiamot weeps also –'

'You had no right to go rummaging around in my cupboard,' said Furvain icily.

'Why not? I'm the master here. I do as I please. All you said was that you didn't want to have a discussion of an unfinished work. I respected that, didn't I? Did I say a word? A single word? For days, now, I've been reading what you were writing, almost since the beginning, following your daily progress, practically participating in the creation of a great poem myself, and tears came to my eyes over the beauty of it, and yet not ever once did I give you a hint – never once –'

Furvain felt mounting outrage. 'You've been going into my room all along?' he sputtered, astounded.

'Every day. Since long before you started the thing with the pens. Look, Furvain, a classic poem, one of the great masterpieces of literature, is being born under my own roof by a man I feed and shelter. Am I to be denied the pleasure of watching it grow and evolve?'

'I'll burn it,' Furvain said. 'Rather than let you spy on me any more.'

'Don't talk idiocy. Just go on writing. I'll leave it alone from now on. But you mustn't stop, if that's what you have in mind. That would be a monstrous crime against art. Finish the Melikand scene. Do the Dvorn story. And continue on to all the rest.' He laughed wickedly. 'You can't stop, anyway. The poem has you in its spell. It possesses you.'

Glaring, Furvain said, 'How would you know that?'

'I'm not as stupid as you want to think I am,' said Kasinibon.

But then he softened, asked for forgiveness, promised again to control his overpowering curiosity about the poem. He seemed genuinely repentant: afraid, even, that by intruding on Furvain's privacy this way he might have jeopardized the completion of the poem. He would never cease blaming himself, he said, if Furvain took this as a pretext for abandoning the project. But also he would always hold it against Furvain. And then, once more with force: 'You *will* go on with it. You *will*. You could not possibly stop.'

Furvain was unable to maintain his anger in the face of so shrewd an assessment of his character. It was clear that Kasinibon perceived Furvain's innate slothfulness, his fundamental desire not to involve himself in anything as ambitious and strenuous as a work on this scale. But also Kasinibon saw that the poem held him in thrall, clasping him in a grip so powerful that even an idler such as he could not shrug off the imperative command that each day was willing the poem into being. That command came from somewhere within, from a place beyond Furvain's own comprehension; but also, Furvain knew, it was reinforced by Kasinibon's fierce desire to have him bring the work to completion. Furvain could not withstand the whiplash force of Kasinibon's eagerness atop that other, interior command. There was no way to abandon the work.

Grudgingly he said, 'Yes, I'll continue. You can be sure of that. But keep out of my room.'

'Agreed.'

As Kasinibon began to leave Furvain called him back and said, 'One more thing. Has there been any news yet from Dundilmir about my ransom?'

'No. Nothing. Nothing,' replied Kasinibon, and went swiftly from the room.

No news. About what I expected, Furvain thought. Tanigel has thrown the note away. Or they are laughing about it at court: can you believe it, poor silly Furvain, captured by bandits!

He felt certain that Kasinibon was never going to hear from Tanigel. It seemed appropriate, then, to draft new ransom requests – one to his father at the Labyrinth, one to Lord Hunzimar at the Castle, perhaps others to other people, if he could think of anyone who was even remotely likely to be willing to help – and have Kasinibon send his messengers forth with them.

Meanwhile Furvain continued his daily work. The trance state came ever more easily; the mysterious figure of Lord Valentine appeared whenever summoned, and gladly led him back through time into the dawn of the world. The manuscript grew. The pens were not disturbed again. After a little while Furvain ceased taking the trouble to lay them out.

* * *

Furvain saw the overall shape of the poem clearly now.

There would be nine great sections, which in his mind had the form of an arch, with the Stiamot sequences at the highest part of the curve. The first canto would deal with the arrival of the original human settlers on Majipoor, full of the hope of leaving the sorrows of Old Earth behind and creating a paradise on this most wonderful of all worlds. He would depict their tentative early explorations of the planet and their awe at its size and beauty, and the founding of the first tiny outposts. In the second, Furvain would portray the growth of those outposts into towns and cities, the strife between the cities that arose in the next few hundred years, the spreading conflicts that caused in time the breakdown of all order, the coming of turbulence and general nihilism.

The third canto would be Dvorn's: how he had risen up out of the chaos, a provincial leader from the west-country town of Kesmakuran, to march across Alhanroel calling upon the people of every town to join with him in a stable government uniting all the world under its sway. How by force of personality as well as strength of arms he had brought that government into being – the non-hereditary monarchy under the authority of an emperor to whom he gave the ancient title of Pontifex, 'bridge-builder', who would choose a royal subordinate, the Coronal Lord, to head the executive arm of his administration and ultimately to succeed him as Pontifex. And Furvain would tell how Dvorn and his Coronal, Lord Barhold, had won the support of all Majipoor and had established for all time the system of government under which the world still thrived.

Then the fourth canto, a transitional one, depicting the emergence of something resembling modern Majipoor out of the primordial structure devised by Dvorn. The construction of the atmosphere-machines that made possible the settling of the thirty-mile-high mountain that later would be called Castle Mount, and the founding of the first cities along its lower slopes. Lord Melikand's insight that the human population alone was insufficient to sustain the growth of a world the size of Majipoor, and his importation of the Skandars, the Vroons, the Hjorts and the other various alien races to live side by side with humankind there. The exacerbation of human-Metamorph conflicts, now, as the relatively sparse aboriginal population found itself being crowded out of its own territories by the growth of the settlements. The beginnings of war.

Lord Stiamot's canto, already completed, would be the fifth one, the keystone of the great arch. But reluctantly Furvain realized that

Stiamot required more space. The canto would have to be expanded, divided perhaps into two, or more likely three, in order to do justice to the theme. It was necessary to limn Stiamot's moral anguish, the terrible ironies of his reign, the man of peace compelled for his people's sake to wage a ghastly war against the original inhabitants of the world, innocent though those inhabitants were of anything but the desire to retain possession of their own planet. Stiamot's construction of a castle for the Coronal at the highest point of the Mount, symbolizing his epic victory, would be the climax of the middle section of the poem. Then would come the final three cantos, one to show the gradual return to general tranquillity, one to portray Majipoor as a fully mature world, and one, a visionary ninth one not entirely shaped yet in Furvain's mind, which would, perhaps, deal somehow with the healing of the unresolved instabilities – the *wound* – that the war against the Metamorphs had created in the fabric of the planet's life.

Furvain even had a name for the poem, now. *The Book of Changes* was what he would call it, for change was its theme, the eternal seasonal flux, the ceaseless ebb and flow of events, and in counterpoint to that the steady line of the sacred destiny of Majipoor beneath. Kings arose and flourished and died, movements rose and fell, but the commonwealth went ever onwards like a great river, following the path that the Divine had ordained for it, and all its changes were but stations along that path. Which was a path marked by challenge and response, the constant collision of opposing forces to produce an inevitable synthesis: the necessary triumph of Dvorn over anarchy, the necessary triumph of Stiamot over the Metamorphs, and – some day in the future – the necessary triumph of the victors over their own victory. That was the thing he must show, he knew: the pattern that emerges from the passage of time and demonstrates that everything, even the great unavoidable sin of the suppression of the Metamorphs, is part of an unswerving design, the inevitable triumph of organization over chaos.

Whenever he was not actually working on the poem Furvain felt terrified by the immensity of the task and the insufficiency of his own qualifications for writing it. A thousand times a day he fought back the desire to walk away from it. But he could not allow that. *You have to change your life*, the Lady Dolitha had told him, back there on Castle Mount, what seemed like centuries ago. Yes. Her stern words had had the force of an order. He *had* changed his life, and his life had changed him. And so he must continue, he knew, bringing into being this great poem that he would give to the world as his atonement for all those wasted years. Kasinibon, too, goaded him mercilessly towards the same goal: no longer spying on him, never even inquiring after the poem, but for ever watching him, measuring his progress by the gauntness of his features and the bleariness of his eyes, waiting, seeking, silently demanding. Against such silent pressure Furvain was helpless.

He worked on and on, cloistered now in his rooms, rarely coming forth except for meals, toiling each day to the point of exhaustion, resting briefly, plunging back into trance. It was like a journey through some infernal region of the mind. Full of misgivings, he travelled by wandering and labourious circuits through the dark. For hours at a time he was certain that he had become separated from his guide and he had no idea of his destination, and he felt terrors of every kind, shivers and trembling, sweat and turmoil. But then a wonderful light would shine upon him, and he would be admitted into pure meadow lands, where there were voices and dances, and the majesty of holy sounds and sacred visions, and the words would flow as though beyond conscious control.

The months passed. He was entering the second year of his task now. The pile of manuscript steadily increased. He worked in no consecutive way, but turned, rather, to whichever part of the poem made the most insistent call on his attention. The only canto that he regarded as complete was the central one, the fifth, the key Stiamot section; but he had finished much of the Melikand canto, and nearly all of the Dvorn one, and big pieces of the opening sequence dealing with the initial settlement. Some of the other sections, the less dramatic ones, were mere fragments; and of the ninth canto he had set down nothing at all. And parts of the Stiamot story, the early and late phases, were still untold. It was a chaotic way to work, but he knew no other way of doing it. Everything would be handled in due time, of that he felt sure.

Now and again he would ask Kasinibon whether any replies had come to his requests for ransom money, and invariably was told, 'No, no, no word from anyone'. It scarcely mattered. Nothing mattered, except the work at hand.

Then, when he was no more than three stanzas into the ninth and final canto, Furvain suddenly felt as though he stood before an impassable barrier, or perhaps an infinite dark abyss: at any rate that he had come to a point in the great task beyond which he was incapable of going. There had been times in the past, many of them, when Furvain had felt that way. But this was different. Those other times what he had experienced was an *unwillingness* to go on, quickly enough conquered by summoning a feeling that he could not allow himself the shameful option of not continuing. What he felt now was the absolute *incapacity* to carry the poem any further, because he saw only blackness ahead.

Help me, he prayed, not knowing to whom. *Guide me.*

But no help came, nor any guidance. He was alone. And, alone, he had no idea how to handle the material that he had intended to use for the ninth canto. The reconciliation with the Shapeshifters – the expiation of the great unavoidable sin that humankind had committed against them on this world – the absolution, the redemption, even the amends – he had no notion whatever of how to proceed with that. For here was Majipoor, close to ten thousand years on beyond Dvorn and four thousand years beyond Stiamot, and what reconciliation, even now, had been reached with the Metamorphs? What expiation, what redemption? They were still penned up in their jungle home in Zimroel, their movements elsewhere on that continent tightly restricted, and their presence anywhere in Alhanroel forbidden entirely. The world was no closer to a solution to the problem of the Shapeshifters than it had been on the day the first settlers landed. Lord Stiamot's solution – conquer them, lock them up forever in southern Zimroel and keep the rest of the world for ourselves – was no solution at all, only a mere brutal expedient, as Stiamot himself had recognized. Stiamot had known that it was too late to turn back from the settlement of the planet. Majipoor's history could not be unhappened. And so, for the sake of Majipoor's billions of human settlers, Majipoor's millions of aborigines had had to give up their freedom.

If Stiamot could find no answer to the problem, Furvain thought, then who am I to offer one now?

In that case he could not write the ninth canto. And – worse – he began to think that he could not finish the earlier unfinished cantos, either. Now that he saw there was no hope of capping the edifice with its intended conclusion, all inspiration seemed to flee from him. If he tried to force his way onwards now, he suspected that he would only ruin what he had already written, diluting its power with lesser material. And even if somehow he did manage to finish, he felt now in his hopelessness and despair that he could never reveal the poem to the world. No one would believe that he had written it. They would think that some sort of theft was involved, some fraud, and he would become a figure of scorn when he was unable to produce the real author. Better for there to be no poem at all than for that sort of disgrace to descend upon him in his final years, he reasoned.

And from that perception to the decision that he must destroy the manuscript this very day was a short journey indeed.

From the cupboards and crannies of his apartment in Kasinibon's fortress he gathered the various copies and drafts, and stacked them atop his table. They made a goodly heap. On days when he felt too tired or too stale to carry the poem onwards, he had occupied his time in making additional copies of the existing texts, in order to lessen the risk that some mischance would rob him of his work. He had kept all his discarded pages, too, the deleted stanzas, the rewritten ones. It was an immense mound of paper. Burning it all would probably take hours.

Calmly he peeled an inch-thick mass of manuscript from the top of his stack and laid it on the hearth of his fireplace.

He found a match. Struck it. Stared at it for a moment, still terribly calm, and then brought it towards the corner of the stack.

'What are you doing?' Kasinibon cried, stepping swiftly into the room. Briskly the little man brought the heel of his boot down on the smouldering match and ground it out against the stone hearth. The pile of manuscript had not had time to ignite.

'What I'm doing is burning the poem,' said Furvain quietly. 'Or trying to.'

'Doing *what?*'

'Burning it,' Furvain said again.

'You've gone crazy. Your mind has snapped under the pressure of the work.'

Furvain shook his head. 'No, I think I'm still sane. But I can't go on with it, that I know. And once I came to that realization, I felt that it was best to destroy the incomplete poem.' In a low, unemotional tone he laid out for Kasinibon all that had passed through his mind in the last half-hour.

Kasinibon listened without interrupting him. He was silent for a long moment thereafter. Then he said, looking past Furvain's shoulder to the window and speaking in a strained, hollow, barely audible tone, 'I have a confession to make, Furvain. Your ransom money arrived a week ago. From your friend the Duke. I was afraid to tell you, because I wanted you to finish the poem first, and I knew that you never would if I let you go back to Dundilmir. But I see that that's wrong. I have no right to hold you here any longer. Do as you please, Furvain. Go, if you like. Only – I beg you – spare what you've written. Let me keep a copy of it when you leave.'

'I want to destroy it,' Furvain said.

Kasinibon's eyes met Furvain's. He said, speaking more strongly now, the old whiplash voice of the bandit chieftain, 'No. I forbid you. Give it to me freely, or I'll simply confiscate it.'

'I'm still a prisoner, then, I see,' said Furvain, smiling. 'Have you really received the ransom money?'

'I swear it.'

Furvain nodded. It was his time for silence, now. He turned his back on Kasinibon and stared out towards the blood-red waters of the lake beyond.

Was it really so impossible, he wondered, to finish the poem?

Dizziness swept over him for an instant and he realized that some unexpected force was moving within him. Kasinibon's shamefaced confession had broken things open. No longer did he feel as though he stood before that impassable barrier. Suddenly the way was open and the ninth canto was in his grasp after all.

It did not need to contain the answer to the Shapeshifter problem. Since Stiamot's day, forty centuries of Coronals and Pontifexes had failed to solve that problem: why should a mere poet be able to do so? But questions of governance were not his responsibility. Writing poetry was. In *The Book of Changes* he had given Majipoor a mirror that would show the world its past; it was not his job to provide it with its future as well. At least not in any explicit way. Let the future discover itself as its own time unfolds.

Suppose, he thought – suppose – suppose – I end the poem with a prophecy, a cryptic vision of a tragic king of the years to come, a king who is, like Stiamot, a man of peace who must make war, and who will suffer greatly in the anguish of his kingship. Fragmentary phrases came to him: 'A golden king . . . a crown in the dust . . . the holy embrace of sworn enemies . . .' What did they mean? He had no idea. But he didn't need to know. He needed only to set them down. To offer the hope that in some century to come some unimaginable monarch, who could unite in himself the forces of war and peace in a way that would precisely balance the suffering and the achievement of Stiamot, would thereby put an end to the instability in the Commonwealth that was the inevitable consequence of the original sin of taking this planet from its native people. To end the poem with the idea that reconciliation is possible. Not to explain how it will be achieved: merely to say that achieving it is possible.

In that moment Furvain knew not only that he could go on to the finish but that he *must* go on, that it was his duty, and that this was the only place where that could be accomplished: here, under the watchful eye of his implacable captor and guardian. He would never do it back in Dundilmir, where he would inevitably retrogress into the shallowness of his old ways.

Turning, he gathered up a copy of the manuscript that included all that he had written thus far, and nudged it across the table to Kasinibon. 'This is for you,' he said. 'Keep it. Read it, if you want to. Just don't say a word to me about it until I give you permission.'

Kasinibon silently took the bundle from him, clutching the pages to his breast and folding his arms across them.

Furvain said, then, 'Send the ransom money back to Tanigel. Tell the Duke he paid it too soon. I'll be staying here a little while longer. And send this with it.' He pulled one of his extra copies of the finished text of the Stiamot canto from the great mound of paper on the table. 'So that he can see what his old lazy friend Furvain has been up to all this time out in the east-country, eh?' Furvain smiled. 'And now, Kasinibon, please – if you'll allow me to get back to work –'

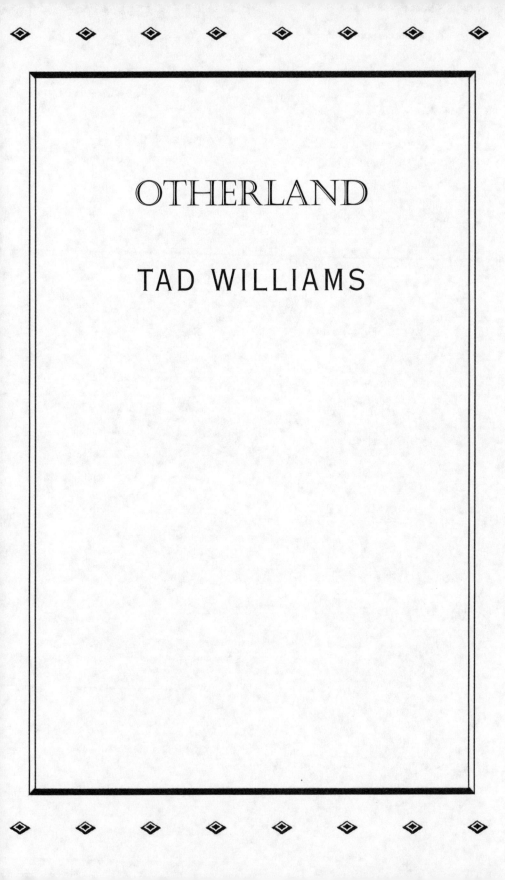

OTHERLAND

TAD WILLIAMS

OTHERLAND
TAD WILLIAMS

City of Golden Shadow (1997)
River of Blue Fire (1998)
Mountain of Black Glass (1999)
Sea of Silver Light (2001)

The characters in the four volumes of Tad Williams's Otherland, set in the extremely near future, discover a universe that exists side by side with our own – a fantastical, artificial universe hidden within the worldwide information net. And in that universe there are worlds within worlds within worlds.

That universe is the Otherland network, the creation of some of the world's richest and most powerful people, an amoral assembly known as the Grail Brotherhood. The Otherland network contains hundreds of virtual worlds, the best that money and top-flight programming can produce. Many are near-perfect re-creations of historical eras, others are famous stories like the *Oz* books or Tolkien's *Lord of the Rings* brought to life, and some, like the endless House or the cartoon Kitchen, are unique to the network. The magnates of the Grail Brotherhood intend not only to visit these expensive playgrounds, but actually to live in them – to shed their ageing bodies and live online forever as the immortal gods of this pocket universe.

However, something about the Otherland network is sending children in the real world into comas. The Grail Brotherhood will go to any lengths to cover this up, including murder, so a group of ordinary people from all parts of the globe are secretly brought together online by a mysterious figure known as Mr Sellars; their goal is to enter the Otherland network and find out what is happening to the children. But once inside the virtual network, these volunteers make a terrifying discovery: something in the network will not permit their minds to return to their bodies – not only that, but their real bodies (which are locked in comas now, just like the children they are trying to save) have become vulnerable to the perils of the virtual worlds. If they are killed in the Otherland network, they will truly die. Thus they find themselves trapped in ultra-realistic worlds full of monsters and madness, one moment fleeing for their lives from one of Lewis Carroll's jabberwocks, the next besieged inside the walls of Troy or chased across the desert by an angry Egyptian god.

The real mysteries of the system turn out to be even stranger than the mechanism that keeps the explorers trapped there. As these accidental heroes penetrate deeper and deeper into its unexplored places they begin to realize that the network is not only more complex than they had guessed, there is something alive at the heart of it – something with plans of its own.

In the end these ordinary people find themselves the centre of the most extraordinary events imaginable, struggling not just against the wealthy, powerful Grail Brotherhood and its hired murderer John Dread, as well as all the bizarre dangers of the virtual worlds, but also against their own fears and failings. The teenager Orlando Gardiner, an invalid with an incurable disease who feels truly alive only when adventuring on the net, battles right up to the moment of his own death to protect his friend Sam Fredericks and the others caught with him in the toils of the Otherland network, and in large part because of him, these ordinary people win an unexpected victory. It has come at a great cost, of course. Orlando and others have given their lives for it.

But in the Otherland network, even death is far from straightforward.

THE HAPPIEST DEAD BOY
IN THE WORLD

BY TAD WILLIAMS

Tharagorn the Ranger was deep in conversation with Elrond Half-elven in the quiet shadows of the Hall of Fire. The man of the west had just returned from roaming through the world, and he and the elven lord had not spoken together in a long time. Things of moment were in their minds, not least of which a sudden rash of goblin raids near the Misty Mountains. Thus it was that the elven messenger, with the graceful diffidence of his kind, waited for some long moments in the doorway before either of them noticed him.

'A visitor is here who wishes to speak to Tharagorn,' the elf replied to Elrond's question. 'It seems to be a halfling.'

'Yeah, that would be me.' The voice was louder and, it had to be said, a bit less cultured than what was normally to be heard in the Last Homely House. The figure in the doorway was half the size of anyone else present, his feet covered in hair so thick and matted he appeared to be standing ankle-deep in the corpses of two small mountain goats. 'Bongo Fluffernutter, at your service,' he said with a sweeping bow. 'Nice place you got here, Elrond. Love the old-world craftsmanship. Tharagorn, can you spare a second?'

'Oh, for God's sake, Beezle,' the ranger said under his breath. 'I am truly sorry,' he told the master of the house. 'Will you excuse me for a moment?'

'Of course.' Elrond looked a little puzzled, although the simulation was adept at incorporating or simply ignoring anomalies. 'Is it really a halfling? We have not seen such a one, I think, since Gandalf brought his friend Bilbo Baggins to us from the Shire some years ago.'

'Yes, well, this . . . this is a different sort of hobbit.' Tharagorn lowered his voice. 'A less successful branch of the species, if you get my drift.'

'Hey! I heard that!'

Elrond and the messenger withdrew, leaving Tharagorn, also known as Orlando Gardiner, alone in the high-raftered hall with his small, shabby visitor.

'Beezle, what the hell are you doing?'

'Don't blame me, boss, you're the one who said I couldn't show up here unless I was in character.' He lifted a foot and admired it. 'Whaddaya think? Nice pelt, huh?'

'Bongo Fluffernutter?'

'Isn't that the kind of name they all have? Jeez, I've only got so much room for Tolkien trivia, y'know.'

Orlando stared at the pint-sized horror in front him. Whether it was a better fit with the simulation than Beezle Bug's normal, multi-legged, cartoonish appearance was open to debate, but there was no doubt he was looking at the world's ugliest hobbit. Orlando was beginning to suspect the software agent's sense of humour had moved on a bit beyond what was covered by the original warranty. Maybe he'd given Beezle a bit too much freedom over the years for self-programming off the net.

'I mean, really,' Beezle said, 'look at which pot's calling which kettle black, boss – Tharagorn? *Tharagorn?* Are you just waiting around here for the Return of the Thking or something?'

'Ha ha. Oh, you're one funny piece of code. I picked it because it sounds like Thargor.' Who had been, of course, Orlando's online avatar for most of his childhood, the brawny barbarian swordsman who had conquered so many gameworlds back in the old days, when Orlando Gardiner had still had a real world to return to at the end of the adventure. Not that he wasn't a little embarrassed by it all now. 'Look, I wanted something easy to remember. Do you know how many names I have on this network?' He realized that he was justifying himself to an entity that had once been a birthday present, and not even the most expensive present he had received that year. 'What was it you wanted, anyway?'

'Just to do my job, boss.' Beezle actually sounded hurt. 'I'm just serving as a furry-footed link to your busy social calendar. We already talked about dinner with your folks, so I know you remember that. You know you've got Fredericks scheduled in first, right?'

'Yeah. She's meeting me here.'

'Oh, good, I'm sure that'll be fun for everyone. May I recommend the Hall of Endless Nostalgic Singing? Or perhaps the Silvery Giggling Lounge?'

'Your sarcasm is noted.' It wasn't as though Orlando didn't harbour occasional less-than-reverent thoughts about the Tolkien world himself, but it was still the closest thing he had to a home, after all. Back in the beginning of his full-time life on the network, when

Orlando was overwhelmed by all that had happened to him, Middle-earth – and Rivendell in particular – had been a blessed haven for him, a familiar, much-loved place where he could relax and heal and come to terms with his responsibilities and even with the possibilities of immortality, a subject that surrounded him on every side in Elrond's ancient residence.

'By the way, tonight's also the first Friday of the month in Wodehouse World,' Beezle went on. 'Did you remember that too?'

'Oh, *fenfen*. No, I forgot. How long do I have?'

'Meeting's in about three hours.'

'Thanks. I'll be there.' But Beezle just stood, waiting expectantly, forcing Orlando to ask, 'What is it now?'

'Well, if I have to stay in character and walk out of this overgrown bed and breakfast and all the way across the bridge just so I can leave the simulation, you could at least say, "Fare thee well, Bongo Fluffernutter!" or something.'

Orlando glowered. 'You're joking.'

'It's only polite.'

'Fenfen.' But Beezle showed no signs of leaving without it. 'Chizz, then. Fare thee well, Bongo Fluffernutter.'

'Don't forget, "And may your toes grow ever more curly."'

'Just get out of here.'

'OK. Fare thee well, also, Tharagorn, Cuddler of Elves.'

It turned out Beezle could move quickly on those furry feet when he had to.

Sam Fredericks was almost an hour late, but that was all right: guests could get something to eat and drink at pretty much all hours in Rivendell if they didn't mind the limited menu. The people who had programmed this simworld years ago – a team from the Netherlands, as Orlando had discovered – had stuck to the original very carefully. There was no specific mention in the books of meat being served in Imladris, the elven name for Elrond's sumptuous house, so what the kitchen offered was pretty much limited to bread, honey, fruit, vegetables, and dairy products. Orlando, who had spent a lot of time in the Tolkien simulation during his early days living in the network, could remember more than a few times when he would have been willing to crawl to Mordor for some pepperoni.

When she showed up, she looked exactly the same as she had on her last visit, dressed in the manner of a male elf, her coffee-and-cream skin radiant, her frizzy hair a glorious confusion held only by a cloth band that made her look slightly piratical. She and Orlando hugged. Sam let go first.

'Something to eat?'

'I'm not really hungry,' she said. 'You go ahead if you want to.'

'Sam, the food here won't fill you up, and I don't need to eat at all. It's just social.' He led her on to one of the covered balconies instead. They could hear the river ringing in the valley below them, although the lanterns of Rivendell illuminated only the tops of the trees.

Sam slid on to a bench. Orlando sat down beside her and stretched his long legs. That was one of the holdovers from his illness that even he recognized: he was never going to be in a sick or crippled body again if he could avoid it. 'So, you,' he asked. 'Are you OK?'

'I'm fine. How are you?'

'Oh, you know. Getting around, keeping an eye on things. This whole job has turned out a lot different from what I expected. When I first agreed to be the sort of head park ranger, I thought I'd be, I don't know, stopping wars or something.'

Sam smiled. 'Like Superman?'

'Or God, yeah. I try not to limit my ambitions.' He waited; Sam's laugh was a little late. 'But since Sellars and Kunohara convinced all the others to let it go free-range, I'm kind of more like an anthropologist or something.' Patrick Sellars had brought together the group of people who had prevented the network from being used for its original purpose, which had been to give immortality within its confines to the Grail Brotherhood, a group of people as unpleasant as they were rich. Kunohara, a former minor member of the Grail who had turned against them, had joined Sellars at the end in saving the network – and in essence, saving the lives of all the network's complex sims, as well as Orlando himself, who had been copied into the network before his physical death and now existed only as information. Sellars, too, had soon after left his dying body behind to take up existence on the Otherland network, but unlike Orlando, his move had been voluntary.

'Anthropologist?' Sam prompted.

'Yeah, well, except for fixing obvious code errors, which don't happen much, I mostly make a lot of reports and keep an eye on the interesting, unexpected stuff. But since Sellars is gone now and Kunohara's so majorly busy, I kind of wonder who I'm making reports for.'

'The rest of us, I guess. And other people who might study it some day.' Sam shrugged. 'Do you miss him? Sellars?'

'Yeah. I can't say we were utterly friends or anything, not like you and me.' He hoped to see her smile, but she only nodded. 'He was just too . . . something. Old. Smart. But I liked him a lot once I got to know him. And he was the only person who lived here with me, Sam. I knew he wasn't going to be around for ever – that he was tired, that he wanted to follow those information-people out into the great whatever. But I sort of thought we'd get to have him for few more years.' He was playing it down, of course, for Sam's benefit. It had been even more devastating than he had expected when Sellars moved on: Orlando had felt deserted, bereft. After all, the crippled ex-pilot had been the only other person in the universe truly to understand the strangeness of knowing you were alive only on a network, that your real body was ashes now, that most of the people who had known you thought you were dead . . . and were more or less right.

Also, Sellars had been a kind person, and – either because or in despite of his own suffering – a good listener. He had been one of the few people who ever saw Orlando Gardiner cry. That had been back in the earliest days of living on the network, of course. Orlando didn't cry any more. He didn't have the time for things like that.

Sam and Orlando sat on the Rivendell balcony another half an hour, talking about all manner of things, even sharing a few jokes, but there continued to be something awkward in his friend's behaviour. It touched Orlando with something he so much did not expect to feel around Sam Fredericks that it took him long minutes to recognize it as fear: he was almost terrified by the idea that she might not want to be here with him, that their friendship had finally become no more than an obligation.

They had wandered back to the subject of the network. To his surprise, she seemed to think he was the one who needed cheering up. 'It's still an amazing job you have – the ranger for a whole universe. All those worlds, your responsibility.'

'Three hundred and ninety-eight at the moment, but a few others have just temporarily collapsed and they'll cycle back on again. That's like a quarter of what there used to be, but Sellars just switched a bunch of them off because they were too scanny, too violent or creepy or criminal.'

'I know, Orlando. I was at that meeting, too.'

'Are you sure you're OK, Sam? You seem . . . I don't know, sad.' He looked her up and down. 'And now that I think about it, you haven't changed sims in like a year's worth of visits.'

'So? Jeez, Gardiner, you're the one who wants everyone to dress up all elfy-welfy here.'

'I don't mean the clothes.' He almost told her about Beezle's version of Rivendell chic, but he could not get past what was suddenly bothering him. 'Sam, what's going on? Is there a reason you won't change your sim? You must have something more up-to-date you use for remotes and friendlines and all back home.'

She shrugged – she was doing it a lot – but would not meet his eyes. 'Yeah. But what does it matter? I thought you were my friend, Orlando. Is it really that important to see if . . . if my breasts have developed since the last time you saw me?'

He flinched. 'You think that's why I want to see the real you?'

'No. I don't know. What's *your* problem?'

He swallowed down the anger, as much because of the resurgence of fear as anything else. There were times when it felt as if his friendship with Salome Fredericks was the only thing that kept him connected to the world he had been forced to leave behind. His parents were different – they were his parents, for God's sake, and always would be – and the other survivors of the Otherland network would always be his friends as well, but Sam . . .'Damn it, Fredericks, don't you get it? You're . . . you're part of me.'

'Thanks a lot.' Despite the mocking words, she looked more unhappy than angry. 'All my life I wanted to be something important, but part of Orlando Gardiner? I never even hoped . . . !'

'That's not what I mean and you know it. Fenfen, I mean you're in my . . . OK, you're in my heart, even though that sounds utterly drooly. You're why I still feel like I'm a living person when, well, we both know I'm not.'

Now she was the one to flinch, but there was still some kind of wall between them. 'What does that have to do with my sim? When you first met me, you thought I was a boy!'

'But this is different, Sam.' He hesitated, then put his hand on her arm. The world's most powerful simulation engine made it feel just as it was supposed to feel, the warm skin on her wrist, the velvety folds of her sleeve over muscle and tendon and bone. 'I know I'm never going to grow up, not in the normal way. I may not have a real body any more, but that doesn't mean I expect everyone else to play with me for ever here in the Peter Pan Playground. Look at me, Sam.' He knew it was mostly guilt that kept her eyes on him, but just now he was willing to use whatever he had. 'If you hide things from me, especially the normal stuff, because you think I can't take it – well, that's the worst thing I can think of. I was a cripple my whole life. Having progeria wasn't just knowing I was going to die young, it was having every single person who saw me for the first time look at me and then look away real fast, like I was some kind of horrible human car accident. Even the decent ones who tried to treat me like anyone else . . . well, let's just say it was obvious they were working at it. I don't want to be pitied ever again, Sam.'

She looked miserable and ashamed. 'I still don't understand, Orlando. What does that have to do with my sim?'

'You don't want me to see the way you look now, but it's not because you've got a zit or something and you're embarrassed. It's because you know you look different, that you're growing or changing or whatever. Tell me I'm wrong. Jeez, Fredericks, I've been living on this network almost three years, do you think I expect things not to change? It's not going to hurt me. But if you can't show me, then . . . well, it's like you don't trust our friendship. Like we can only be the kind of kid-buddies we used to be back in the Middle Country game.'

She looked at him with something of the old Sam on her face, amused even though she was irritated. 'Same old Gardiner. You still know everything.' She took a long breath. 'OK, you want to see how I look now? Fine.' For a moment her Rivendell-self froze as she reselected her appearance, the new information passing through the series of blind relays that kept the very private Otherland network isolated from the real-world net. Then, suddenly, like a hardcopy picture dropped on to the top of a stack, Sam's image changed. 'Satisfied?'

'You don't look that different,' he said, but it wasn't really true. She was an inch or two taller, but also more curved and womanly – she had wider hips now that the elven breeches only emphasized. The Sam he had known had been a greyhound-slender athlete. There was also suddenly a length to her face he hadn't seen before. She was really lovely, and not just because she was the Sam he loved. He also realized he hadn't told the truth about something else: seeing her suddenly a year older, seventeen instead of sixteen, did hurt. It hurt like hell. 'Thanks.'

'Oh, Orlando, I'm sorry. I'm being utterly jacked. It's not that, it's not any of that.' She slumped on the bench, leaned forward until she could rest her elbows on her knees. She had stopped meeting his eye again. 'It's just . . . I'm seeing somebody.'

For a moment he didn't understand what she meant, thought she was still talking about sims and images. 'Oh. Is it . . . serious?'

'I don't know. Yeah, I guess. We've been going around together for a couple of months.'

Orlando took a breath. 'Well, I hope it works out. Fenfen, Frederico, is that what's been bothering you all day? We've been past that jealousy stuff for a long time.' In part, he had to admit, because Sam had made it clear from the beginning of their real friendship, after he knew she was a girl and she knew about his illness, that although she loved him as much as he loved her, it was never going to be the romantic kind. Which was just as well, he had decided, because what they had was going to last their whole life and not be messed up by sex.

He often wondered if real, living teenagers told themselves the same kind of pathetic lies he did.

'I don't know, it just . . . scares me. Sometimes I feel like . . .' She shook her head. 'Like I'm not a very good friend for you. *To* you,' she amended hurriedly. 'I don't see you as often as I should. You must think I'm terrible.'

He laughed, surprised. 'It never even occurred to me. You know, Sam, no offence, but it's not like when you're not here I just sit around waiting for your next visit. Two days ago I was dodging arrows in Edo while a bunch of warlords tried to overthrow the Tokugawa shogunate. The week before I spent a few days with Captain Nemo exploring some undersea ruins.'

'So . . . so you're OK? With everything? Not bored or . . . or lonely?'

He gave her arm another squeeze before letting go. The elves were singing again in the Hall of Fire, a meditation on the light of the Two Trees. The voices seemed almost to belong to the valley itself, to the night and the forest and the river singing together. 'Bored? Not when I consider the alternatives. No, don't fret about me, Frederico – I always have places to go, things to do, and people to see. I must be the happiest dead boy in the whole wide world.'

It wasn't really so much that Sam was dating someone that was bothering him, he thought as he got ready to connect to his parents' house, or even that she'd kept it a secret for a while. In fact, now that he thought of it, he *still* didn't know if her new soulmate was male or female. Sam had always been funny that way, not wanting to talk about those sorts of things, irritated by questions, as if Orlando might think differently about her if she ever clarified her gender and sexual issues. No, it wasn't so much that she was dating someone, or even that she was growing up. He loved her, he really did, and he wanted her to have a happy life no matter what. Instead, it was the sudden worry that he might not be growing up himself, as he had always assumed he was, however weird his situation. He felt a kind of chill as he thought about it, and wondered whether he was becoming irrelevant to everything, not just to Sam, whether despite the fact that years were passing for him in Make-Believe Land just as they did for her in the real world, his experiences here might not be the same as growing up at all.

Maybe you have to be real to do it. Maybe you have to do real things, make a fool of yourself at a party, trip and skin your knee, fall in love, or just . . . just . . . have a heartbeat. Maybe I'll never really change. I'll be like one of the sims – a sim of a fourteen-year-old kid. For ever. He pushed away the sickening thought. Right now, it was Family Night, which was hard enough to get through at the best of times.

It didn't really seem fair, being dead and still having to go home for visits. Not that he didn't love Conrad and Vivien. In fact, it was because he loved them so much that it could be so difficult.

He took a deep breath, in a metaphorical sort of a way – he felt as if he was taking a deep breath, anyway – and as he did so, he remembered that his mother and father apparently had a surprise for him tonight. They had asked him to connect to a different location in the house for his visit instead of the wallscreen. '*Well, actually, it's really Conrad's surprise,*' his mother had explained. She had smiled, but she hadn't seemed entirely pleased with whatever it was going to be. Orlando had seen that expression before: she had worn it when Conrad had given him the bike for his eleventh birthday. Anyone, even Orlando himself, could have told his father that his bones were too brittle and his muscles too weak even to think of riding a bicycle, but Conrad Gardiner had insisted that his son should have every chance to be normal.

When he had become more or less bedridden in the last year, they had finally got rid of it to make more room in the garage for medical equipment, spare filters and oxygen pods. He had never ridden it, of course. Progeria, the disease that had ruined and eventually ended his previous life, was a condition that turned children into doddering ancients and then killed them, mostly before they had even reached their teenage years.

As he made the connection, Orlando wondered why he couldn't just join them through the wallscreen, as usual. He liked doing that, because it felt no different from an ordinary kid-to-parents call, as though he were simply away at school in a different state instead of living in what was functionally a different universe.

Maybe Conrad swapped in the old screen for one of those deep-field things. He was talking a while back about investing in one of the solid-crystal ones.

The connection opened and he was looking at his parents, who looked back at him. His mother was teary-eyed, as she always was when they first saw each other. His father was beaming with what looked like pride. But there was also something unusual about the way they both appeared; it took him a moment to process what it was.

I'm looking through a different imager, he decided. *I guessed right – it's a new screen.* But if his parents had indeed bought a new unit, he suddenly realized, they had installed it in the dining room instead of the living room: he could see the old oak sideboard behind their heads, and the poster of the French can-can dancers next to it that had hung on the wall there for years.

'Hi. What's up – new screen?' Without thinking, he raised his hand to blow his mom a kiss as he always did – yes, it was embarrassing, but you had to do things differently when you couldn't actually touch – and something shadowy rushed towards him. Even after years without a real body, he could not help flinching a little. The new thing stopped and hung in his view in the same way a simulated hand would.

It *was* a hand, but not being simulated on his end. Instead, it seemed to be looming in front of his parents' screen and thus effectively hanging in front of his eyes, a weird-looking, smooth, maroon hand made of what appeared to be shiny plasteel. Half-forgetting his bodiless state, he reached out to touch it. The hand reached out too, extending away from his viewpoint, just as if it were his own hand, responding to his thoughts. Fascinated and troubled as he began to catch on, he tried to make the fingers wiggle as he would with one of his own simulated hands. The fingers wiggled. But these fingers weren't on one of his sims, and weren't even in the network – they were in Conrad and Vivien's dining room in the real world.

'What the hell is this?'

'Do you like it?' His father was nodding, the way he used to nod when someone was trying out his home-brewed beers, back when they had still had visitors.

Well, that's one thing, Orlando thought. *Now that I'm gone, at least they can have people over again.* 'Like it? What is it? Some kind of robot arm attached to the new screen?'

'It's not a new screen, it's a whole body. So you can, you know, be here. Inside the house with us. Whenever you want.'

Orlando had discovered the other arm. He flexed it, held the two hands up together, then looked down. The viewpoint swivelled, showed him the cylindrical, beet-coloured torso, the jointed legs. 'A . . . body?'

'I should have thought of it before,' his father said. 'I don't know why I didn't – your software agent used to have that little body with all the mechanical legs so it could crawl around the house, remember? I looked around until I found something that seemed like it would work. It's a remote figure they use for certain kinds of reconnaissance operations – I think it was built for Antarctica originally, maybe military or something. I found a collector and bought it. I had to get different feet put on it – it kind of had hands at the end of the legs.' He was clearly a little nervous: when he was nervous, he babbled. 'Better for climbing and moving on ice or something. I'm surprised they weren't skis or tractor-treads or maybe . . .'

'Conrad,' Vivien said, 'that's enough. I don't want to hear about hands on legs. It's . . . disturbing.' She darted a quick look at Orlando, who was more than a little stunned.

'What . . . what am I looking out of?'

'The face,' his father said. 'Well, it should be, but we'll have to change what you're putting out from your end. I didn't want to spoil the surprise, so right now there's a whole little Orlando standing there in the face-screen.'

'I'm still trying to figure this out. You mean, I'm supposed to . . . move around in this?'

'Sure, go ahead!' Conrad was delighted by the question. 'Walk! You can go anywhere in the house!'

'He doesn't have to if he doesn't want to,' said his mother.

Orlando flexed his muscles, or performed the mental actions that flexed muscles in the real world and the better virtual worlds. The cartoon fingers reached out and gripped the tabletop. He put his feet under him and stood; the point of view rose, not altogether steadily. Now that he was listening for it, he could hear the faint wet hiss of fibromotors bunching and relaxing.

'Do you need some help?'

'No, Conrad. I'll be OK.' He got up and took a few swaying steps, then stopped to look down at the feet – they were huge ovals, like Mickey Mouse shoes. It was strange to be in a body as clumsy as this: his Otherland network bodies all responded exactly as though they were his own, and made him stronger, faster and far more nimble than he had ever been in real life.

He hadn't been in the bathroom since his death. It was interesting, even strangely touching, to have movement around his old house restored to him, but he wasn't certain about any of this. He looked at his reflection in the mirror, the strange stick-figure shape of the thing. The screen in the faceplate showed Orlando's full-body sim, so that he looked like one of those giant Japanese robot-monsters with a human controller rattling around inside its head. He scaled his sim's output so that only the face appeared, and suddenly, even though it wasn't his real face, not by a long shot – no one including Orlando himself had seen that since his physical body had been cremated – it made the whole thing more real and also far more disturbing.

Is this what they want for me? This . . . thing? He knew that Conrad meant well, that his parents were only trying to find a way to make his continued presence in their lives more real, more physical, but he didn't know if he could stand to live for even short periods as this stalking, plasticized scarecrow.

He looked at the face he used with his parents, a teenage face appropriate to his age, made with help from various police forensic illustration nodes, scaled up from scans of his own skull and incorporating features from both his mother and his father. *The face of the kid they should have had,* he thought. *Stuck on this thing like a lollipop on a stick.*

Orlando did his best. He sat through dinner and tried to concentrate as his parents told him things about friends and relatives, about their jobs and the small annoyances of life in security-walled Crown Heights Community, but he felt even more like an alien than he usually did. The servo-muscles on the body were clumsy and the tactors less advanced than what he was used to: he knocked over his mother's glass twice and almost tipped the table over when he stood up at the end of the meal.

'I'm going to have to make it an early night,' he said.

'Are you all right?' his mother asked. 'You seem sort of down.'

'I'm fine, I've just got a meeting to go to at the Drones Club.'

'That's that 1920s English place you told us about?' Conrad asked. 'That must be interesting. Didn't you say there was a war there?'

'Sort of.' It was still hard to make his parents understand about John Dread, about the terrible destruction the killer had wrought in so many of the Otherland network worlds in the brief days he had ruled over the system as a kind of evil god. 'The simulation is coming back, but we're letting things sort themselves out instead of just wiping out what's happened and starting the cycles over, so there's some pretty scanny stuff going on in some of them. Adaptations, almost like after a forest fire has changed an ecosystem. Very barky.' He noticed their puzzled faces. 'Barky? It means funny. The weird kind of funny.'

'You know so much about these things,' his mother said. 'This complicated network. You've learned so much. And you've really worked hard to make something out of . . .' Vivien Fennis was about to say something like *your terrible situation*, but of course she was too much of an old hand for that, too smart and too kind to mess up this proud-mom moment she was giving him. 'Out of your life in this new world. New universe, really. It's still so hard to believe or even understand.'

'You have the makings of a first-class scientific education there,' Conrad chimed in. 'Even if it's not the accredited type. Life experience has to count for something, doesn't it? Maybe some day . . .'

'This all has to stay secret – me, the Otherland network, everything. If it ever becomes public, there will be lawsuits for decades over who owns the network. It's worth gazillions – it'll be torn apart by the military looking for weapons-quality code, at the very least. You know that.' Orlando tried to puncture his dad's fantasies gently, but they did have to be punctured: Conrad came up with hopeful, impractical plans every few months, and some of them made the maroon robot-body seem positively normal. 'Look, the chances are that I'm not ever going to live in the real world again. I'm sorry. I wish I could have had a grown-up life here and done all the things you guys wanted for me.' He took a breath: he found himself getting angry and he didn't want to. But why did everyone keep projecting ridiculous expectations and ideas on to him? He more or less figured on getting it from his parents, but Sam's lack of trust in him was still hurting. 'Anyway, it doesn't matter. This is a lot better than being dead. Don't worry about me. Like you said, the network's a whole new universe and I'm the one who gets to explore it. I'm happy.'

Happy or not, he was beginning to feel he couldn't breathe. He did his best to be cheerful as he said his goodbyes, even allowing his mother and father to give the robot-body a hug, although it was a weird and uncomfortable experience, probably even for Conrad. As he sat the mechanical form down in a chair so it wouldn't fall over when he was no longer animating it, Orlando was finding it harder and harder to hide his ugly mood. Getting out of that horrible, whirring prison and back into the freedom of the network was like finally being allowed to take off a scratchily ill-fitting Christmas sweater after the aunt who gave it to him had finally gone home.

He had half an hour to kill before the meeting of the Worldwalkers Society. He wandered the streets of P. G. Wodehouse's London, thinking.

Before Dread, this simulation world had been a shiny little confection of unadulterated good cheer, a London where the poor were content to be that way and the unguilty rich could concentrate on important things, like eating a really good breakfast and avoiding dragon-ish aunts (who could pop up and spoil the aforementioned breakfast, not to mention zillions of other innocent pastimes, with amazing swift-ness). Now this particular London had become a much different place. Like some Socialist demagogue that even the most paranoid Tory could barely have imagined, John Dread had first enraged and then armed the city's working class – a group in short supply in Wodehouse, but not entirely absent. A horde consisting mostly of gardeners, butlers, chauffeurs, delivery men, maids and cab drivers had stormed the haunts of the upper crust, besieging and attacking the rich in their mansions, Kensington flats, and clubs. Whole blocks had been put to the torch as some of Wodehouse's wild-eyed Socialists and anarchists, rumoured but scarcely ever seen, turned out to be more than merely rumour, and a few turned out to be dab hands at arson as well. There had even been some massacres, public slaughters of the class enemies – the class of the victims depending on which side was top of form at that particular moment of the struggle – although because of the happy-go-lucky nature of the Wodehouse world, even Dread's malign influence had waned quickly once his direct supervision ended. Still, by the time Sellars and Kunohara had got round to shutting down the particulars of Dread's intervention, some weeks after Dread himself had been dethroned, the city had descended into a sort of weird twilight state, something that combined the ruination of post-Blitz London with the freewheeling lawlessness of its earlier Elizabethan incarnation and more than a touch of the fearful shadows that had clung to the nineteenth-century city during the Jack the Ripper crimes.

Curzon Street was full of horses and waggons these days – very few cars had survived the Unpleasantness, as the reign of terror was referred to – and Orlando had to watch what was under his feet as he made his way to Hyde Park. The squatter camps that had appeared in the first few weeks of the upheaval had become more or less permanent settlements, and with the chill evening coming down, bonfires burned everywhere. It didn't do to walk too obliviously through the park – desperately cold and hungry people had long ago obliterated the park squirrels and the waterfowl of the Serpentine, and chopped down most of the beautiful old trees for fuel. Many wealthy folk who supposed that now the Unpleasantness had ended they could return to riding along Rotten Row had discovered that although horsemeat might come into the park on its own hooves as in the old days, the only way it was leaving again was inside someone's stomach.

However, if anyone could walk heedless of personal safety in Hyde Park these days, it was Orlando Gardiner, the system's bashful demigod, and the demigod had a lot to consider.

Is it just me? Conrad and Vivien mean well. Why is it so hard to humour them? After all, I'm their only kid and it's pretty obvious things aren't going to work out the way they hoped – no graduation, no girlfriends, no marriage, no grandkids . . . But no matter how he thought about it, he couldn't feel anything but resentful horror at the idea of wearing that remote body. Instead of making him feel more natural it did the opposite, made the distance between his new life and his old one more acute, as though the real world had become some kind of alien planet, a toxic environment he could only enter dressed in a clanking robot-suit. The fact that the real world had become exactly that for him, and had been that way for going on three years, didn't matter: as long as he only visited his folks by phone he could half-pretend he was just putting in a year in Africa with the UN Service Corps or something, but now Conrad's compulsion to fix things was going to put a serious crimp in Orlando's hard-earned denial.

It was the stuff with Sam, though, that really got to him. He didn't want to be someone who never grew up, never changed no matter what he experienced. That was worse than the suit – that was like being truly dead. He would be a sort of ghost.

A ghost in a dead world. Nothing changing, not me, not these worlds.

He turned back across the park towards Dover Street and the club. Crews of young toughs were gathered around rubbish-bin bonfires, singing mocking serenades to their rivals. It sounded as if they might be working up to a reading, as in a 'read and write', local slang for a gangfight.

They're free-range, he reminded himself. *None of my business. Happens all the time, anyway, and I couldn't be here to stop them all.*

He looked at the laughing young men in scarves and fingerless gloves and stolen top hats, dapper as Dickensian urchins. Some were openly sharpening knives and razors. In the simworld's more normal operation they would be prone to no worse mischief than flinging snowballs at unsuspecting vicars and fat uncles, but even this evidence of a certain flexibility of ambition allowed by the system didn't change Orlando's feelings. They might have adjusted to the high level of local chaos, but these hooligans were still essentially the same kind of minor characters they had been in the world's earlier incarnations. It was becoming obvious that for all Kunohara's and Sellars's florid early predictions, a certain depth of reality, a flare of unpredictability, had gone out of the Otherland network for good with the death of the operating system. What was left was still fabulously complex, but ultimately lifeless.

No wonder everyone keeps asking if I'm OK. It's not me that's the problem, it's this network. Nothing really changes, or if it does, it's just like ivy growing wild in someone's yard or something – the same kinds of changes over and over and over. It's not an evolving universe, it's a big, broken toy, and even if it's more complicated than anything anyone ever made before, it's still never going to be like living in the real world. It wasn't so much a lack of other people that was depressing him, he realized – the sims who inhabited the various worlds were astonishingly diverse and self-actualized, their interactive programming so flexible and their canned histories so comprehensive that in most cases you could never get to know any of them well enough to see the gaps in their near-perfect mimicry of life. But Orlando *knew* they weren't real, and that was a very big part of the problem. He was also the most powerful person in this pocket universe now that Sellars was gone and Hideki Kunohara was so frequently absent, which added to the imbalance between himself and his cohabitants.

Yeah, that's it – that's who I am, he realized. *I'm not Aragorn or the Lone Ranger, I really am Superman, like Sam said. I'm one of a kind in these worlds and I'm going to spend my life doing things for people who are lesser beings – who won't ever seem quite real to me. And that's a long time to do something, because I just might live for ever.*

For the first time since he had been reborn into the system, his potential immortality felt more like a burden than a gift.

The meeting was under way, but a few other latecomers were still wandering into the Bertram W. Wooster Memorial Salon – a chamber dedicated, Orlando had gathered, to a former Drones Club member who had been smothered to death by a mob of crazed railway porters during the Unpleasantness. Orlando took his Coca Cola and sat at the back of the room. His first requests for the beverage had baffled the club's bar staff, but the proprietor had stepped in and now a bottle of syrup and a siphon of soda water were waiting for him whenever he dropped in.

That was only on meeting nights, of course – the Wodehouse simulation was not really his kind of world in the first place, and Orlando had never been interested in joining clubs even when he was alive, but the Society was different.

'Before we welcome tonight's speaker,' the chairman was saying, 'we have a few orders of business – messages sent by members who were not able to attend tonight, but who nevertheless have information of importance to share.' The chairman, Sir Reginald de Limoux, was a handsome man in his middle thirties, hawk-nosed, lean and tanned in a way that proclaimed him in this world as a labourer or an adventurer. He was clearly not a labourer. 'The gateway between Chrysostom's Byzantium and Toyland is no longer safe. Toyland is still unstable, and some kind of military group has captured the shop where the portal operates and made it their headquarters. They are wooden soldiers, I am told, so unless you are a termite, it is suggested you avoid that gateway for now.' A few of the club members laughed politely. 'Visitors to Toyland can still use the forest gate, which is protected by factions more sympathetic to free travel. Now, still on the subject of gateways, we have a report of a new one discovered in Benin, at an oasis just outside the city . . .'

As de Limoux continued with the announcements, Orlando sipped his Coke and studied him. He wondered how much of the chairman's source personality remained. He was one of the Jongleur-shadows, based on copies that had been made of Felix Jongleur, the Otherland network's original master at a time when the ancient industrialist was planning to live for ever within its circuits, a god ruling over many worlds. Jongleur had indeed achieved immortality of a sort, as had many of the network's other wealthy, powerful and largely amoral founders from the Grail Brotherhood, but not in the way he or any of them hoped.

Instead of serving the purpose for which they had been intended, these copies, meant to be the basis for what would be immortal information-based incarnations, had been warped and changed during the last mad days of the original operating system, then the copies had been allowed to scatter and disperse through the system. Nobody knew how many of them there were, or what they had become, since there was no foolproof way to track individual sims in the huge network. One of the reasons Orlando Gardiner, in his role as the network's conservator, had become involved with the Worldwalkers Society was so that he could keep tabs on these various Grail Brotherhood clones, many of which seemed drawn to the club by a compulsion that might have been subconscious.

Orlando had been surprised at first that Kunohara and Sellars, the two men who best understood the Otherland system, had not even tried to remove these remnants of the network's original masters, but they had pointed out to him that even if all the shadow-copies could be found and identified, they were not automatically criminal themselves any more than the children of a thief could be assumed to be inherently dishonest, and that even the least pleasant of the Grail Brotherhood originals were no worse than other nasty sim personalities that were original inhabitants of some of the network worlds. It had been the Grail masters' personal wealth and power, and also their control over the network from the outside, that had made them dangerous. Inside the network these clones and imitations started over from scratch, some with admitted personality defects which cropped up in most incarnations, but others with a surprising capacity to become decent citizens. As he watched the Society's chairman at work, Orlando thought that this particular version of Jongleur, Sir Reginald de Limoux, seemed somewhere in the middle – sharp-tempered and obviously ambitious, but certainly no out-and-out villain.

The other legacy granted to the Grail shadows and a few similar beings that the old operating system had created – some based on Orlando's real friends and acquaintances, like the Englishman Paul Jonas – was that they alone of all the simulated souls on the network could travel with relative freedom between the network worlds, or even knew that there were worlds outside the simulation in which they lived. Unlike Orlando, these travellers did not understand what they were, or what kind of universe they lived in, but they did have a freedom of thought that set them apart from the rest of the sims. In fact, they were the closest thing to equals Orlando Gardiner had these days. Sitting around in the Drones Club bar after a Worldwalker meeting, listening to the humorous stories and impossible boasts of Society members, was the closest thing to the happiness he had once found in the adventurers' taverns of his old Middle Country game.

And, of course, even in their wildest stories, these walkers-of-worlds brought back gems of information that Orlando found very useful. He might be a ranger with godlike powers, but he still couldn't stamp out every untended campfire in four hundred different worlds.

When the chairman had finished his announcements, the featured speaker took the lectern and began to describe the findings from his most recent expedition. This gentleman seemed to have spent most of his time in Troy and Xanadu, two simworlds Orlando knew well, so he let his attention drift to other things. He became so caught up in wondering how to reconnect with Sam that he did not realize for several moments that someone who had harrumphed significantly several times behind him was now tapping on his shoulder.

'Mr Roland? Someone urgently wishes to speak with you.' The tapper was the proprietor of the Drones Club, a tall, poker-faced fellow named Jeeves who, rumour suggested, had been in some kind of domestic service before the Unpleasantness but had risen very high, very quickly during those unstable times. 'Did you hear me, Mr Roland?'

It took Orlando another long moment to recognize his local pseudonym. 'Sorry, sorry. Someone to see me?' Could it be Beezle again, dressed for maximum embarrassment value in a cummerbund or pith helmet? But it was only when Orlando was in Rivendell, the closest thing to a refuge he had, that the agent wasn't allowed to contact him directly: it was hard to relax and enjoy the peaceful singing of the elves and the flickering of firelight when you were getting four or five calls an hour from an agent with the raspy voice and abrupt manners of an old-school Brooklyn cabbie.

'Yes, a visitor, sir,' Jeeves said, leaning close. 'A young lady. Very attractive, if I may say so, but perhaps a bit . . . confused. I've taken the liberty of installing her in one of the unused lounges – some of the older members are less than open-minded about women in the club, even now. I beg pardon for interrupting you. She said it couldn't wait, and it seemed from her conversation that it might be something with which you would wish to deal . . . discreetly.'

Orlando looked at the man's sombre mouth, his tall, intelligent brow. Jeeves was not supposed to know who the Worldwalkers really were – on the surface, they were only a stuffily ordinary club of travellers and adventurers who met at the Drones Club once a month – let alone have even an inkling of Orlando Gardiner's true nature, but he had always treated Orlando with extra care and a certain glint in the eye, as though he suspected him of being more than he appeared. Orlando in turn had often wondered whether the club's new owner weren't a Worldwalker himself, albeit an undiscovered one. If so, he had found the perfect place to hide, right under the Society's nose.

He made a mental note to do some research on this Jeeves fellow when he had some spare time and turned back to survey the room. The Society members had fallen into civilized but contentious discussion about a proposed new expedition. Orlando knew they would be batting it around for at least half an hour, and probably wouldn't finish the discussion this month. Expeditions took resources, and those Worldwalkers who were independently wealthy in one simworld could seldom move valuables or tangible resources from one simulation to another. In fact, the only really certain, completely portable capital was knowledge, and that was one of the reasons most Society members valued their membership above anything except their lives. He rose, certain there was nothing going on tonight he couldn't pick up later, in the bar.

Jeeves led him to the doorway of the lounge before sliding away down the corridor, silent as a cat burglar. Orlando stepped into the snug room and almost knocked over a young woman dressed in a pale frock who was warming herself before the coal fire. It was only as he put out a hand to steady himself he realized he was still carrying his Coca Cola.

'Sorry,' he said and balanced the glass on the narrow mantel. 'My name is Roland. I'm told you were looking for me.'

She was pretty, as Jeeves had suggested, in a wide-eyed, consumptive sort of way, the darkness of her curly hair and the blush on her cheek only emphasizing the almost translucent pallor of her skin. She returned his stare a little wildly, as though at any moment he might lunge at her – or, worse, laugh at her.

'Perhaps I am mistaken. I was told . . . I understood the person I was seeking could be found here. The name Roland was given to me. I'm looking for Orlando Gardiner.' She peered at him as though she might be near-sighted, or as though she were looking for a resemblance in a newly met, very distant relative, then her face fell. 'But you are not him. I have never seen you before.'

He was astonished to hear his real name spoken aloud by a sim, and almost equally surprised to be told he was not himself, but hearing her voice confirmed what he had guessed when he had first seen her. This young woman was another Avialle Jongleur-shadow, either one of the original copies of Felix Jongleur's dead daughter or a variant coined from those copies in the last days of the operating system. The original Avialle had been obsessively in love with the Englishman Paul Jonas, and most of the copies, certainly all those that had been made from the living Avialle after she met Jonas, had continued this infatuation. They had popped up in numerous guises during Jonas's amnesiac wanderings through the Otherland network, sometimes encouraging him, sometimes actively aiding him, other times brokenly pleading for his love or understanding.

But none of them had ever had much or anything to do with Orlando, and he had no idea why one should be seeking him now, especially under his real name.

'You say you haven't seen me before.' He gestured for her to sit down – she seemed prepared to bolt like a rabbit at the slightest noise, and he was curious now. 'I have to admit, I don't recognize you either. I do know someone named Orlando Gardiner, however, and I might be able to get a message to him. Can you tell me something of your problem?' The surroundings were beginning to get to him, he realized. He was starting to sound like one of the simworld's native characters.

'Oh. You . . . you know him?' She looked a little more hopeful, but it was a miserable sort of hope, as though she had been told that instead of torture she would be given a mercifully swift death. 'Where can I find him?'

'You can give me a message. I promise he'll hear it.'

She brought a hand to her mouth, hesitating. She was very pale, shaking a little, but Orlando could see now that there was a determination behind the doe-eyes that belied her outward appearance. *She's taken some risk to come here,* he thought. *She must want to get this message to me very badly.* 'Very well,' she said at last. 'My shame could not be any greater. I will trust to your discretion, Mr Roland. I will trust you to behave like a gentleman.

'Please tell Mr Gardiner that I need to see him as soon as possible. I am in terrible straits. Terrible. If he does not come to me I do not know what I shall do.' Her reserve suddenly fell apart; tears welled in her eyes. 'I am desperate, Mr Roland!'

'But why?' Orlando hunted vainly for a handkerchief, but she had already produced one of her own from her sleeve and was dabbing at her face. 'I'm sorry, Miss . . . Mrs. . . . I'm afraid I don't know your name. Look, I don't want to make things worse, but I really do have to know why you want to speak with him before I can pass along your message.'

She looked at him, eyes still wet, and seemed to come to a decision. Her lip stopped trembling. She spoke with self-mocking dignity. 'It is not such an unusual story in this wicked world of ours, Mr Roland. My name is Livia Bard. I am an unmarried woman and I am with child. The child is Mr Gardiner's.'

Then, as though they had reached the climax of a particularly good magic trick, the young woman simply vanished into thin air.

Find one single woman in only four hundred or so different simworlds, each world with life-size geography, maybe a few million simulated citizens, and no central tracking system? Yeah, problem not. Piece of cake. He couldn't even amuse himself these days. 'Beezle? Any word back on that Amazon place, that Lost World thing with the dinosaurs? What's it called?'

'Maple White Land, boss. Yeah, we got a confirmed sighting. It seems like another Avialle Jongleur-shadow, awright, but she looks different and she's using a different name – Valda Jackson, something like that.

Older, too, if our informant's right. And she don't act much like a pregnant lady, either. She leads expeditions into the interior and she drinks like a fish.'

'Fenfen.' He looked around the spacious room, frowning. The river was loudly musical outside and the air smelled of green things, but it wasn't as soothing as it usually was. He was beginning to find Rivendell less comfortable than it had been, and even though he now permitted Beezle to contact him inside the simulation without having to make an actual appearance, it seemed less and less like the best place for this kind of work. After all, he didn't want to turn the Last Homely House, the ideal of his childhood, into the permanently busy capitol of Orlando Land. Maybe he needed to think about moving his base of operations. 'Three months now and this woman might as well have been drezzed right out of the network code for all I can find out about her. Where is she?'

'It's just a search operation, boss. Like you always say, there ain't no central registry office. It takes time. But seems to me, time's one thing you definitely got plenty of.'

'When I want philosophy, I'll buy a plug-in module. When you get hold of Sam, ask if we can meet somewhere different this time. Her choice.'

'Your wish is my command, O master.'

'It's really pretty, isn't it? I always liked Japanese teahouses and stuff.'

Orlando wrinkled his nose. 'I think that's the first time I ever heard you use the word "pretty" except when you're on something like, "That's a pretty stupid idea, Gardiner."'

Sam Fredericks frowned a little, but her samurai sim turned it into a scowl that might have graced a Noh mask. 'What's that supposed to mean? That I'm turning all girlie or something?'

'No, no.' He was depressed, now. He had had only a few brief visits with Sam since the whole Livia Bard thing had started, and he had missed her, but they still seemed to be out of rhythm with each other. 'I just didn't expect you to pick a place like this for us to meet.'

'You're always talking about how much you like it.' She looked out from the teahouse. Beyond the open panels of the wall and beyond the tiny, orderly garden of rocks and sand and small trees, the wooden roofs of the city stretched away on all sides. On the far side of the Nihon-Bashi, the stately wooden arch across the Sumida, Edo Castle loomed proudly.

'Well, I like the war part, although that's mostly over for this cycle – the shogun has pretty much settled in for good. The armour is *ho dzang*, too.'

'*Ho dzang!* I haven't heard anyone say that for a long time.' She saw the look on his face and went on with nervous haste, 'Yeah, that armour is great, especially those helmets with the sticking-up things – makes your elves almost look dull. I'm not crazy about the music, though. I always thought it sounded like unhappy cats.'

Orlando clapped his hands and sent away the geisha who had been quietly playing *Jiuta* on her shamisen. The only singing now was the hoarse chant of a water-seller that drifted up from the street below. 'Better?'

'I guess.' She looked at him carefully. 'Sorry I've been so hard to get hold of. How's your noble quest?'

'Noble quest? Like the kind we used to have back in the Middle Country?' He fought off a moment of panic – did she think he hadn't changed at all? 'You mean about the pregnant woman.'

'Yes.' She made herself smile. 'And it is a noble quest, Orlando, because you're a noble quest kind of guy.'

'Except that apparently I impregnated this poor girl and then deserted her. Not really the kind of thing people usually call noble.'

Sam frowned, but this time because she was irritated with his flippancy. 'But you didn't do it. Just because there's some evil clone version of you running around . . .'

'Maybe, but I don't think so. There's never been any other sign of another version of me, or even a hint. Believe me, I've had Beezle combing every record since we started up the network again.'

'I thought there wasn't any main archive or whatever.'

'There isn't, but there's the informal one that Kunohara started when he and Sellars got the system running again, and most of the individual worlds have their own records that are part of the simulation. For instance, the Wodehouse place where I met this woman started out pretty much like the real early twentieth-century London, so there are birth records and death records and telephone directories and everything. The data are a bit hinky sometimes because it's sort of a comedy world, but there certainly wasn't any mention of a Livia Bard in any of those.'

'So you think she must come from somewhere else. She's one of those travellers, then, the ones that can cross from one world to another. I can't remember – were all the Jongleur girl's shadows like that?'

He shook his head, felt the topknot bob. 'I don't know. They've always been the weirdest of all the shadows because the operating system jacked around with them so much.' He sat back, toying with his bowl of tea. It was easy to believe his mystery woman could think she was pregnant – many of the Avialle-shadows thought they were pregnant, because the original had been, at least for a little while. Orlando had gone back and forth through Sellars's history and Kunohara's margin notes trying to make sense of it, even though he'd heard some of the story from Paul Jonas's own mouth – it was a bizarre bit of history and hard to figure out.

'Orlando?'

'Sorry, Sam. I was thinking about something.'

'I just wanted to ask you . . . are you absolutely sure that . . . that you didn't do it?'

'Do what . . . ? Fenfen, Fredericks, you mean get her pregnant?' He felt his cheeks reddening in a most unsamurai manner.

Sam looked worried. 'I didn't mean to embarrass you.'

He shook his head, although he definitely was embarrassed. He had been a fourteen-year-old invalid when he died, a boy denied a normal childhood or adolescence. Gifted with a life after death, with health and vigour beyond anything he had ever known, not to mention an almost complete lack of adult supervision, he had of course experimented. At first the knowledge that his partners were in some ways no more real than what you could rent on the crudest kind of interactive pornodes hadn't bothered him, any more than the literal two-dimensionality of women in girlie magazines disturbed earlier generations, but the novelty had worn off fast, leaving him lonely and more than a little disgusted with the whole situation. Also, because he was uncomfortable with their origins, he had made a personal rule never to get involved with any of the Worldwalker Society's female members, so he found himself more or less unable to date anyone with actual free will.

Of course, love and sex weren't things he'd ever been very comfortable talking to Sam Fredericks about, anyway. 'Let's just put it this way,' he said at last. 'If I had been in a situation where it could have happened, I'd remember. But, Sam, that doesn't even matter. This isn't a real person and it's not a real pregnancy – she's a construct!'

'Didn't all those What's-her-name Jongleur girls have a pregnancy thing, anyway? They all thought they were, or some of them did, or something?'

'Avialle Jongleur. Yes, and like I said, they aren't real pregnancies.

But that's not the point. The question is, why does this one know my real name and why does she think it's my baby?'

Sam slowly nodded. 'Yeah, that all barks pretty drastically. So what are you going to do?'

'I wish I knew. I've been looking for months, but she's just vanished. Beezle wants me to authorize a bunch of mini-Beezles so we can search the system more effectively – not just for this one woman, but any time we need to. It's not a bad idea, really, but I'm not sure I want to be the Napoleon of an army of bugs.'

Sam Fredericks sat back, toying with her bowl of tea. 'You seem . . . I don't know, a little more cheerful than the last couple of times I saw you.'

He shrugged. 'I keep busy. I thought you were the one who was depressed.'

'Scanmaster. I was probably locked off with you for some reason.'

Orlando smiled. 'Probably.'

Sam stirred. 'I brought you something. Can you import it into the network? It's on the top level of my system, labelled "Orlando".'

'You brought me something?'

'You don't think I'd forget your birthday, do you?'

He had half-forgotten, himself. 'Actually, it's tomorrow.' It was strange how little something like a birthday meant when you didn't go to school and you had hardly any friends – any normal friends, that is.

'I know that, but I won't see you tomorrow, will I?'

'Seventeen years old. I'm an old man, now.'

'Old man – hah! You're younger than me, so six that noise.' A small, gift-wrapped package appeared on the low table. 'Good, you found it. Open it.'

He took off the lid and looked at the thing nestled on virtual cotton in the virtual box. 'It's really nice, Sam.'

'Happy birthday, Gardino. Don't just stare at it – it's a friendship bracelet, you idiot. You have to read what it says.'

He turned the simple silver bracelet. The inscription said, *To Orlando from Sam. Friends For Ever.* For a moment he didn't trust his voice. 'Thanks.'

'I know there are places you go where you can't wear it, but I spent a lot of time thinking, like, what can you get someone who can have anything in the whole world – rocket cars, a live pet dinosaur, you name it? All I've got to give you that you can't get in one of these worlds is me. We're friends, Gardiner, and you remember that. No matter what. As long as we both live.'

Orlando was very grateful that this sim was too *bushi* to cry – the blushing had been bad enough. 'Yeah,' he said. 'No matter what.' He took a deep breath. 'Hey, you want to go for a walk before you have to go? I'll show you a little of the Tokaido – that's kind of the main road. It's the best place to sightsee. If we're lucky, a few of the daimyos will still be coming into town. They're the nobles, and they have to make a pilgrimage here twice a the year. Some of them come in with thousands of retainers and soldiers, horses and flags and concubines and all that fen, a big parade. It's like Samurai Disneyland.'

'You really know this place!'

'I keep busy.'

'You left tonight open, didn't you?' Beezle asked as Orlando reanimated his Rivendell sim. 'Your parents have got plans.'

'Oh, jeez, right, my birthday dinner. That means they'll want me to wear that *tchi seen* robot-body. Conrad's probably hooked it up with an air-hose so I can blow out the candles on my cake.' He resented tromping around in that thing so much that he had been avoiding seeing his parents because of it. Still, in just three visits he'd broken a table-leg and several vases, and pulled a door off its hinges by accident. The thing had very delicate hand-responses, but the rest of it was meant for slogging around in mine shafts or in the holds of sunken ships and was about as graceful as an elephant on roller skates. Orlando didn't want to hurt their feelings, and Conrad was so proud of his idea, but he just hated it.

It's not as if I didn't have enough to deal with. Just at the moment, two Society members were stuck in the House simulation in the middle of an armed uprising and unable to escape, there was a programming glitch or something like it causing mutations in the plant life of Bronte World so that Haworth Parsonage was under siege by carnivorous cacti, and he still had no idea of where Livia Bard might be, let alone any explanation for her weird accusation. *Yeah, I keep busy.*

'Any decision yet on letting me whip up some sub-agents, boss?'

'I'm still thinking about it.'

'Well, don't hurt yourself – I hear that thinking stuff ain't for beginners. You ready to go to your folks? 'Cause you got an urgent message from that Elrond guy you gotta deal with first. He needs you downstairs right now.'

'Jeez, it never stops. Make the connection to that locking toy robot at my parents', will you? After I finish downstairs I'll duck into a closet or something and go directly.'

'Yeah, wouldn't want to screw up the continuity.' It sounded suspiciously like sarcasm. 'Don't worry, boss. I'm on it. Just go see Elrond.'

He was halfway down the delicate wooden staircase between the small house that he called his home and the central buildings when the thought occurred to him, *Why the hell would Beezle be passing messages for Elrond? Rivendell doesn't work that way.*

All questions were answered when he walked into the main hall and discovered his mother, father and several score elves, dwarves and assorted other Middle-earthers waiting for him.

'Surprise!' most of them shouted. 'Happy birthday!'

Orlando stopped just inside the doorway, dumbfounded. The hall was strung with cloth-of-gold bunting, and candles burned everywhere. Huge trestle tables were covered with food and drink. His mother came up and threw her arms around him, kissed him and hugged him. When she leaned back she looked at him worriedly, but she was also flushed with excitement. 'Is this OK? You said your network can deal with incongruities. This won't spoil anything, will it?'

'It's fine, Vivien. I'm just . . . well, surprised.'

She was wearing elven costume, a long dress in shades of butter yellow and pale beige, and had piled her hair up on top of her head, where it was held by diamond pins. 'Do I look funny?' she asked. 'That nice Arwen girl gave me these hair things. I think that's her name – I don't remember her from when I read the books, but it was a long time ago.'

'That nice Arwen girl?' Orlando couldn't help smiling. 'Yeah, you look great.'

Conrad came up with a goblet in one hand. 'Those dwarves like to drink, don't they? What do you think? Did we surprise you?'

Orlando could only nod, appalled and touched. The party already seemed in high gear. Someone put a cup of ale in his hands. Elrond came up and bowed to Orlando's parents. 'Regards to you on this festive day, Tharagorn,' the elf said. 'You are always an ornament to our house.'

Vivien started to flirt with Elrond, to Orlando's horror, but the master of the house accepted it with good humour. Even more fortunately, Conrad had already wandered off to look more closely at the ceiling joists – he was a hobbyist carpenter – so at least Orlando didn't have to worry about his father picking a jealous fight with an elven lord.

Arwen Undómiel, Elrond's daughter – the one his mother had referred to as a 'nice girl' – was standing with her love, Aragorn, who was dressed in a tattered cloak and seemed to have come straight in

off the road. The man whose name Orlando had more or less borrowed
for his incarnation in this world left his betrothed's side long enough
to come and clasp Orlando's hand. 'Good wishes, cousin. We have not
met in many a long year. I did not know anyone outside the halfling
lands celebrated the day of their birth in this manner.'

'Blame my parents.'

'There is no blame. They are noble folk.' Aragorn embraced him,
then returned to Arwen's side, where her brothers Elladan and Elrohir
now also stood, as travel-worn as Aragorn, as though they had all
ridden fast and far to be here. The elven princess raised her glass
towards Orlando in a silent salute. He would have been flattered if he
hadn't known it was all make-believe, just programming.

'I don't even want to know how you arranged this, Vivien,' he said
to his mother.

'Beezle helped.' She pointed to a small, disreputable and extremely
hairy-footed figure on the far side of the room, who was busy
outdrinking three dwarves from Dale. 'He's almost human, isn't he?'

'Who isn't?' He hugged her again. 'Thanks. I really didn't expect it.'

Vivien was asking Elrond something domestic – he thought he heard
her use the phrase 'finding kitchen help' – when Orlando's attention
was suddenly drawn to a pale shape moving through the throng at
the centre of the hall. For a moment he could only stare, wondering
which Tolkien character this was, why she looked so familiar.

'Oh my God,' he said. 'It's *her*!'

He was across the room before Vivien finished asking him where
he was going and caught the woman in white as she stepped into the
Hall of Fire. The unsteady light of the flames made her seem a phantom,
but if it was not Livia Bard herself who stood before him, it was her
exact duplicate.

She looked up at his approach, startled and even a little frightened.
'What do you want?'

He realized the look on his face might very well be something that
would frighten anyone. After months of searching, to have her simply
walk past him . . . ! 'Miss Bard. Livia. I've been looking for you.'

She turned to face him and he had a second shock. Beneath the
flowing white gown, she was very obviously several months pregnant. 'Who are you?' She stared, then blinked. 'Can it be? Are you
truly him . . . ?'

And then she disappeared again.

'Beezle!' he bellowed. 'That was her! Right here, then she disappeared! Where did she go?'

'Couldn't tell you boss. Hang on, let me just roll Snori here off me and I'll be right with you.'

By the time his parents and his faithful software agent reached him, Orlando was down on his knees on the floor of the Hall of Fire, pounding on the boards in frustration. Conrad and Vivien suggested calling off the feast, but Orlando knew it was for them as much as himself, so he climbed to his feet and let himself be led back to the party. Still, despite all the diversions and distractions offered by Rivendell in holiday mode, he hardly noticed what was going on around him. As soon as he could decently manage it he made his excuses and headed for bed, pausing on his way up to his rooms to have a word with Beezle.

'OK, you have my permission – I've run out of ideas. Put together your little army of sub-agents. But do me a favour and don't make them bugs, huh? I'm going to have to see Kunohara, and I'll get enough of the things there to last me for years.'

'Will do, boss.'

Orlando went to bed. Beezle stayed up late drinking with the dwarves from Dale. He showed them how it was possible to belch several whole stanzas of the Lay of Queen Berúthiel, and also that there is a point at which even dwarves should stop drinking.

Elves don't complain, but Elrond's folk had a terrible mess to deal with the next morning.

'Mr Gardiner, it is always a pleasure to see you, but I hope you will be understanding.' Kunohara gestured for him to sit on one of the chairs that looked out from the balcony across the expanse of forest-high grass and the undergrowth that loomed beyond it like a frozen tsunami wave. He was a small, trim man in a modern-style kimono who appeared to be in early middle age, or at least his sim always looked that way, his black hair and beard both grey-flecked. 'My time is very limited these days. A nephew of mine – barely out of adolescence, or so it seems – is leading a hostile takeover against me. They claim too much of the family company's money has been spent on what they call "the amusements of the chairman". Who would be me, and this simulation would be one of the amusements, except they do not know it still exists.' He glowered. 'A company built with my patents, and they think to take it away from me. I will crush them, of course, but it is sad for the family and irritating for me. It wastes a great deal of my resources.'

Orlando nodded. 'I appreciate you making time for me.' He had never quite warmed to Hideki Kunohara, not having known him as well as some of his other companions had; there were ways in which Kunohara never made himself really available, even when he was sitting right in front of you, chatting in a seemingly amiable, open way. Orlando had always wondered what the man was really thinking, and because of that had never entirely trusted him, but with Sellars gone, Kunohara understood the system's underlying logic better than anyone alive.

If there is such a thing as logic involved, Orlando thought sourly.

'I've reviewed your messages,' Kunohara said, then stopped suddenly to watch a striking black and orange butterfly the size of a small plane flit down into their field of view, almost touch the ground, then lift away again, wings flashing in the sunshine. 'A heleconid,' he announced. '*Numata*, it looks like. Nice to see them so near the station.'

Hideki Kunohara's house was a recycled building far too large to make a satisfactory dwelling for anything less substantial than a king's household, or at least it would have been in the real world, where people were limited by various petty annoyances like the laws of physics, but size was not such an issue in a private node where travel could be instantaneous. The house had formerly been a scientific station that Kunohara had leased to governments and the biology departments of universities because all visitors to Kunohara's world found themselves smaller than most of the insects and other invertebrate fauna. It was a fascinating if occasionally terrifying perspective: the research station had been destroyed by soldier ants and all the human sims in it killed during the upheavals of the network. Kunohara's own house had also been ruined. The balcony on which he and Orlando sat now had originally been one of the raised viewing stations which ran all along the southern face of the complex's main building; as they talked Orlando could watch all kinds of monstrous animals feeding and being fed upon in the field sloping away below them, including birds the size of passenger jets tugging worms that seemed long as subway trains out of the damp morning ground.

'Anyway, I've read your messages and I don't really have much to say, Mr Gardiner. Have you considered the possibility she's someone from outside the network? A real person who discovered your name somewhere, or even someone who knows you and is playing a trick?'

'That would be worse than the mystery we have,' said Orlando. 'Because unless it was one of my friends, and I can't quite picture any of them thinking this was funny, it would mean that our security is compromised. This network is supposed to be a secret.'

'We have a few people on the outside who actively help us maintain it as a distributed network.'

'Yeah, but even those people don't know about me.'

Kunohara nodded. 'The possibility of this being the work of some outsider does not seem likely, I grant you.'

'I think there must be a shadow-Orlando, although I've never seen one or heard even a hint of one before now.'

'That raises questions, too, Mr Gardiner. It is possible that a duplicate of you might exist, and also possible that it could have escaped our notice for almost three years – it is a big network after all. It is even possible that this duplicate uses your real name, still without attracting our attention. But there still remains one question that would have to be answered before we could accept this hypothesis as a valid theory.'

'I know.' Orlando squinted at a pair of what looked like flies chasing each other across the tops of the tree-tall grass, iridescent objects the size of taxis performing a mid-air *pas de deux*, their glassy wings sparking light. He wasn't nuts about bugs in the first place, let alone bugs that were a lot bigger than he was, but there were moments like this when he could almost understand Kunohara's world, if not Kunohara himself. 'The problem with the shadow-Orlando theory is how she knew *I* had something to do with Orlando Gardiner when she found me in the Wodehouse world – and how she found me again in the Tolkien world. How could she track me like that?'

'The copies derived from Felix Jongleur's daughter really are remarkable, as you know,' said Kunohara. 'Some of the Avialle-shadows seem able to move at will from one simulation to another. Others can travel between simulations, but only in the workaday manner that your Worldwalkers employ, using the gateways. And some of the Avialles do not seem to move out of their home simulations at all, although those versions usually end up holding some powerful or unusual position in their worlds.'

'Yeah, like the one we met in the freezer in the cartoon Kitchen world. I guess the original Avialle – the real person – was utterly important to the old operating system, so maybe all her shadows are still kind of important to the system.' Something tugged at him, an idea that would not quite form. 'But why? I mean, we've got a whole different operating system now, right?'

'In part, but it's far more complicated than that.' Kunohara clicked his tongue against his teeth. 'Not all the remnants of the old operating system, that poor tortured creature known as the Other, could be removed from the network. That is one of the reasons we suspected that some of its attempts to create a kind of life, as it did once already with raw materials from Sellars's own experimentation, might have permeated the entire network and changed it into another order of thing entirely. A sort of living, evolving entity.'

'But it didn't turn out to be that way. That's what you're always saying.'

'It's true, there's been no evidence of it. We've seen no other information-creatures like the ones it grew before, which are now gone. Neither has there been any sign of the evolutionary process beginning again in some other manner – not a one. You can trust me on that, Mr Gardiner – the permutations of life, and now of pseudo-life, are my passion, and I have looked long and hard for any evidence of it on the current network. It is a fantastically complex creation, but essentially it has become what any other network is – an unliving artefact. I'm afraid that with the death of the Other and the escape of its information-creatures into space, the network is now effectively dead.'

Orlando had more or less known this – after all, the flatness of things, the lack of real change, had been troubling him for months – but being told it in such a categorical manner by Kunohara was a bit like being punched in the stomach. 'But the sims themselves reproduce within their simworlds. They have babies. The animals have little animals. Look at your bugs here – they lay eggs, don't they? Make little giant baby bugs?'

'Yes, but only within the matrix of the simulations. It is part of the program for the sims to appear to reproduce, but it is not true life, any more than it would be if you wrote a story in which someone gave birth. New life in this system is a construct. Look at your Avialle-shadows – some of them have perpetual pregnancies, as is probably the case with the one you are seeking. That is no real pregnancy, it is a programmed trait, like the colour of a sim's hair or how fast it can run.'

'But the last time I saw her, she looked really pregnant! None of the Avialle-shadows ever get to the point of showing their pregnancy. I read that in your own notes.'

Kunohara shook his head. 'Mr Gardiner, you are a smart young man and a very fine conservator of the network worlds and I'm sure that wherever he now is, Patrick Sellars is proud that he chose you, but you are not a scientist – not yet, anyway. Do you know for certain that she really *did* have the belly of a woman several months pregnant, or are you basing this entirely on what you think you saw from a distance of several metres for a period of just a few seconds? The simulated people can be nearly as psychologically complex as real people. Perhaps she feels herself to be with child but her belly does not grow – it never will grow, but she does not know this – so she pads herself with a pillow or some similar object, out of anxiety, perhaps. No, Mr Gardiner, my friend, when you or I can examine her and see that she truly does have an advancing pregnancy, then we can begin to wonder about how she differs from the other Avialle Jongleur-shadows. Until that time, I urge you not to jump to conclusions.'

Orlando didn't particularly like being lectured. 'So you're saying that this whole weird mess is just another hysterical Avialle-clone who's stumbled on my name somehow – nothing more, nothing less.'

'I am saying nothing about what it *is*, Mr Gardiner, because I do not have enough information.' Kunohara steepled his fingers and slowly shook his head. 'I am sharing what I suspect, and also what I strongly doubt. People spent trillions of credits on this network to make things *appear* as real as possible, but please do not confuse appearance with reality, and especially do not mistake the appearance of reproduction and other symptoms of life, however sophisticated, with real reproduction and actual life. Life is a very stubborn phenomenon that uses an astonishing number of strategies to perpetuate itself. What this network does is mimic those processes for the benefit of its human users, to create a realistic environment – an experience not tremendously different from an amusement-park ride. But the gap between the simulated thing and the actual process it imitates is vast indeed. Now, forgive me, but I have kept my lawyers waiting for half an hour.'

Orlando thanked him, but Kunohara was already making his call and only nodded. Orlando left him talking to himself, or so it appeared, as he gazed out across his super-sized domain. Flowers tall as redwoods creaked and swayed in the freshening breeze.

Beezle Bug was waiting for Orlando back in his bedroom at Rivendell. Out of the elven public eye and with the rules now relaxed, the agent wasn't even bothering to masquerade as a hobbit, but was back in his usual form, something that could have been a black dustmop with eyes, a cartoon spider, or even a particularly disturbing Rorschach ink blot. Beezle's natural good looks were enhanced today by a floppy, striped top hat. He grinned toothily as Orlando came in and did a little hairy-legged dance.

'You're in a good mood.'

'You don't sound like you are, boss. Any luck with Kunohara?'

'Nothing that cleared anything up. I think he thinks I'm over-reacting.'

'Well, I know what will cheer you up. You can meet my crew.'

'Your what? Oh, the sub-agents. Look, Beezle, I don't think I'm up to having a bunch of bugs crawl all over me . . .'

'No bugs – you already told me.' The agent swept off his hat and a horde of small shapes began to jump out of it. Within seconds they were filling the floor all around him. 'I kind of swiped the idea from the Dr Seuss world. Meet Little Cats A1 through A99, B1 through B99, C1 through C99 . . .'

'I get the drift.' Already Orlando was ankle-deep in a lagoon of tiny, hatted cats. 'I don't need to meet all 2,600 of them. I suppose I should count my blessings you didn't steal your idea out of *Hop on Pop*.' He squinted at the little cats which were now clambering up the bedclothes and trampolining across his pillow. 'How the hell are these things going to get the kind of information we need discreetly? They're not exactly inconspicuous, are they?'

'Boss, boss.' If Beezle had a neck, he would have been shaking his head. Instead, he was doing a sort of hairy hula. 'They're my sub-agents. You don't think I go out looking for information looking like this, do you? Looking like anything, for that matter. I'm gear – good gear. I just interface with the stuff directly at machine level, and so will they. I just thought the reports would be more fun this way.'

'Great.' Beezle was the second person in an hour – second thing, anyway – to tell him that he was making the mistake of judging matters by face value. The network was seductive that way – so much time and money spent to make the worlds seem like real places. Reminded, he looked at his virtual wrist, his Tharagorn wrist since he was in Rivendell, and at the virtual friendship bracelet he now wore on it. It seemed like a real bracelet, but it wasn't; it hadn't ever been real, but it meant as much as or more than any actual pieces of shaped metal, because the friendship it represented *was* real.

There was the core of an idea there, something that he needed to think about, but he was distracted as the living cat-carpet abruptly swirled up into a spinning cloud of miniature felines, then vanished back into Beezle's hat with a loud *pop*. 'Hey, boss, I forgot to tell you. They need you back in that P. G. Wodehouse simulation – someone left a note in your box at the club.'

'But the next meeting's not for weeks.'

'Emergency get-together of the steering committee, and you're in the rotation.'

'I don't have time. Send an excuse for me.'

'Actually, you might want to go. They're trying to get rid of whatsisname, de Limoux, the chairman.'

'What for?'

'Seems a couple of the women members are going to have babies and they say he's the daddy.'

'I had nothing to do with it!' Sir Reginald was almost white with anger. 'With either of them! I scarcely even know Mrs Hayes, and I despise Maisie Macapan. Everyone knows that.'

Orlando himself only barely recognized the first name: she was a quiet, colourless woman who seemed to owe her sim existence to some early equipment tests by one of the Grail Project's female engineers. The second was a shadow of Ymona Dedoblanco, who had been the only woman in the Grail Brotherhood's inner circle. The real woman could fairly be termed a monster, but her shadow merely seemed to incorporate some of her less murderous, albeit still irritating, faults, namely self-absorption almost to the point of megalomania. Like her template, she also had a full measure of ambition, which was why she and the Jongleur-shadow, Sir Reginald, often found themselves at cross-purposes.

'Why aren't the two women here?' Orlando asked. 'Shouldn't de Limoux have a chance to confront his accusers?'

'Roland, you are an honourable man,' said Sir Reginald. 'Yes, where are they? Why this star-chamber inquisition, based on accusations that are ridiculous on their face. Everyone knows I am a happily married man, with a wife and family in Third Republic Paris.'

'Happily married men may stray,' suggested a moustached traveller named Renzi whom Orlando suspected of being the shadow of another of the network's early engineers, or possibly even a much-degraded version of his friend Paul Jonas.

'But not with that Macapan woman!' De Limoux seemed more offended by that idea than by the accusation itself. 'I would sooner throw myself into a cage with a hungry lioness.'

'The women are both unwell, Mr Roland,' Renzi explained to Orlando. 'And their stories, it must be admitted, are a bit confusing. But they both swear that their charges are accurate, and although Miss Macapan is known to bear Sir Reginald some ill feeling, Mrs Hayes does not seem like the type to invent such a thing.'

'Unless the Macapan bitch bribed her,' snarled de Limoux. 'She would do anything to steal the chairmanship away.'

'If she could bribe one, she could bribe two,' Orlando said. 'If she's only trying to ruin your reputation, Sir Reginald, it seems strange she should make herself one of the victims, since everyone knows she has a grudge or two against you.'

'Surely you are not suggesting you believe this twaddle, Mr Roland?'

'I'm not saying I believe or disbelieve anything, Sir Reginald. I don't have enough information. I'm just thinking out loud.'

After that he let the others talk while the idea began to form. Even in its earliest shape, it was a very strange idea.

He had the travel records of the Worldwalkers Society members in hardcopy form – leather-bound books handwritten in ink, in keeping with the simulation – spread all over the wooden table that served as his desk in Rivendell. A year earlier, Orlando himself had covertly lobbied for and helped to push through the particular Society rule that mandated all members to keep diaries of their travels and make them available in the Society library inside the Drones Club, and just now he was glad that he'd done it.

Orlando had noticed something very interesting about de Limoux and his two accusers and had drawn a small chart for himself to try to make sense out of their comings and goings. He had just confirmed his suspicion and was staring at the chart, chewing the end of his pencil in something like astonishment, when he heard his agent speaking in his ear.

'*Boss?*'

'Let me guess, Beezle. You've got some news for me. There's another pregnancy at the Society and another denial of responsibility.'

After a moment's pause, the agent said: '*Hey, that's pretty good, boss. How did you know about the Society thing?*'

'I'm just starting to get a few ideas.'

'*Do you want to know who's involved?*'

'If the ideas I'm starting to get are right, it doesn't really matter. Let me go back to what I'm doing, Beezle. I'll let you know when I need you, and I'll probably need you soon.'

'*Boss?*'

'Beezle, I'm really trying to concentrate here. Thanks for bringing me the information, now get lost, OK?'

'*It's important, boss.*'

Orlando sighed. 'What is it?'

'Well, it's about Little Cats N42 and N45 – two of my sub-agents, remember? I think you might want to see about getting them a little treat. A year's supply of fish heads or something.'

'Fish heads . . . ? Beezle, you are making me crazy. What the hell are you talking about?'

'Just as a reward, maybe. Because they found your girlfriend.'

'They . . .' He sat up. 'Are you sure?'

'Avialle-shadow, dark, curly hair, visibly pregnant. Yeah, pretty much.'

'Fish heads for everyone. No, give 'em the whole fish. Where?'

'Living in an apartment in Old Chicago, of all places. We don't think she's been there long. I've sent you the address, but it's easy to find. It's over a club on Thirty-seventh Street at Giles.'

'I'm there.'

And he was, a subvocalized command taking him to the heart of the simworld more swiftly and certainly than any magic carpet. Sometimes it was OK being a sort of god.

Thirty-seventh Street was loud and lively. There were no Al Capone-type gangsters in sight, which was what Orlando usually associated with Old Chicago, but the sidewalks were crowded with quite a lot of ordinary people of several colours. Everybody seemed to be dressed up to go somewhere important, all the men in ties, the women in dresses. The apartment was above a club called Toothy's Free-For-All, which had a buzzing neon mouth grinning above the door. A half-dozen black men in handsome, big-shouldered suits stood underneath the overhang, smoking and talking and looking up at the overcast sky, and coincidentally blocking the apartment building's stairway next to the club's front door. Orlando wondered if the men might be gangsters. He wasn't even sure if they had African-American gangsters back in those days, but he didn't want to waste time on trouble. Unfortunately, he was wearing his only prepared sim for the Chicago world, which was inarguably Caucasian and, although reasonably tall and strong, meant more to be inconspicuous than to scare people into leaving him alone. But the men in front of the doorway seemed much more interested in the cigarette they were sharing; they hardly looked at him as he angled through and started up the narrow staircase.

'Looks like Missy got a gentleman caller,' one said to Orlando's retreating back.

'He ain't the first caller for that little girl,' said another, and the men laughed quietly.

The corridor smelled faintly of mildew, and the hall carpets were so dark with years of dirt that he couldn't make out the pattern, although he was pretty sure there was one. He knocked on the door with the number on it that Beezle had given him.

She opened it on the chain. Her eyes widened. She let him in, but almost as if she were sleepwalking: she was clearly frightened and confused. She wore a quilted, pale blue housecoat and her hair was unbound, spilling over her shoulders.

'Who are you?' she asked.

If she was confused, he was even more so. 'Who are *you*?' But he knew who she was, she was an Avialle Jongleur-shadow – the dark curly hair, the big eyes and especially the voice had removed all doubt. And, as Beezle had noticed, she was quite visibly pregnant. The problem was, she wasn't *his* Avialle Jongleur-shadow, and the differences weren't subtle. Other than a similarity in the hair and eyes, this was a completely different woman.

'My . . . my name is Violet Jergens.' She seemed on the verge of tears. 'What do you want? You look familiar.'

He had no other ideas, so he went for broke. 'I'm Orlando Gardiner.'

For a moment her face almost seemed to light up, a child's Christmas-morning face of wonder and joy, then her smile faltered and was replaced by bafflement and anxiety once more. 'I've . . . I've dreamed of the day Orlando would come back to me, when we would be a family. But I've never seen you before.' She backed away, raising her hands. 'Please, whoever you are, don't hurt me.'

Orlando shook his head. He had been working on a theory that seemed very promising, but now he was confused again. 'I'm sorry. I mean you no harm.' Perhaps his original idea could still make sense. He decided to ask her the same question he would have put to Livia Bard. 'Just tell me one thing. What does Orlando Gardiner look like?'

The question seemed to anger her, but after a moment her face changed. 'I . . . it has been such a hard time for me, lately. It is all . . . I would . . .'

'You don't remember, do you?'

She was crying now. 'I haven't been well.'

He saw a chance to add another piece of information. 'You're going to have to trust me now. May I . . . may I feel your stomach?'

'What?'

'I swear I won't harm you or the baby, Miss Jergens. Please. I promise I'll be gentle.'

She didn't assent, but she did not back away as he moved closer. He slowly extended his hand and put it on the curve of her belly where it made her housecoat swell like a wind-filled sail. The bump was firm and, as far as he could tell, warmly alive.

He was not at all surprised this time when Violet Jergens abruptly disappeared from her own apartment like a soap-bubble popping. He did not bother looking for her on Thirty-Seventh Street or anywhere else. He didn't need to find her, he was beginning to feel certain, because the chances were he'd be seeing her again, and others just like her.

Kunohara, he thought, *you owe me an apology.*

'I don't get it,' Sam said. 'So now *another* of those Avialles thinks you're the father of her child?' She was talking to him on the phone because she was in the middle of finals and couldn't leave her studying very long. It was kind of nice, Orlando decided, just talking face to face from different places. It was a bit like being back in the real world, except Sam Fredericks was in West Virginia and he, at the moment, was in Atlantis, or rather hovering above its watery grave, tidying up a wave-motion problem before the city rose out of the ocean and started its cycle again. 'What's going on?'

'I went back to see Kunohara. We think we've finally got the whole thing figured out.' He couldn't help adding: 'I figured it out myself, mostly, but he agrees, and he came up with the one part I couldn't wrap my head around. It was the Worldwalkers Society pregnancies that tipped me off – there's about a half-dozen of them now, by the way. I haven't figured out yet how to straighten out that part of the mess. They're all utterly scanned about it, accusations, denials, meetings falling apart and people threatening legal action. And the thing is, just like with me and the Avialle-shadows, everybody's right.'

'Hang on.' Sam put her book down. 'I've been in, like, a death-struggle with colligative properties all day for my chemistry final, but this is worse. What do you mean, everybody's right? You said you never saw her before, let alone played bumper cars with her.'

Orlando shook his head. 'I hadn't and I didn't. Or with the other one, and there'll almost certainly be more. And the Society chairman de Limoux didn't suddenly get sweet on his arch-enemy Maisie Macapan and give her the gift of motherhood, either – except he did, in a way.'

'That's it – you've gone way far scanbark, Gardiner. You are barking to the moon and back, then taking a little side trip to Bark Island. I have no idea what you're talking about.'

'Kunohara got me thinking about it first. He was telling me off about mistaking appearance for reality, and he said something like, "Never underestimate how many strategies Life will use to perpetuate itself, Mr Gardiner," in that kind of irritating way he has. Well, it irritates me, anyway. And that made me think about how this network has always been so complex. The Other, the original operating system, actually bred life from information viruses and antiviruses. And it made imitation children, based on real children. They may not have been alive, but they weren't just normal sims, either'

'Not it, *him*. The Other was a person, Orlando, despite all the horrible things the Grail people did to him. But he's gone now.'

'Yeah, but the system was built around his brain, so his original impulses have an effect on everything about the network. And especially – and this is where I started to get my idea – his influence is utterly strong in the shadow-people, all those copies that he made and then released into the system.'

'Like your Society folks, the ones who can travel from world to world through the gateways. And the Avialle-shadows.'

'Who don't need gateways, although they can use them. In fact, other than me, the Avialle-shadows are the only sims who can travel freely throughout the network. That makes them the most advanced of all the copies, really, even if a lot of them are a bit mental. So, me and the Avialle-shadows are pretty much the most advanced things in the network. Are you starting to get the picture yet?'

Sam frowned. 'Don't be all Professor Mysterioso. I was up practically all night last night studying *Chemistry: The Central Science* and I have a drastic headache.'

'Well, I've been up several nights in a row studying biology, so who's zoomin' now?'

'Just explain.'

'How about if I said that instead of "most advanced", you could also call me and the Avialle-shadows the fittest creatures on the network. As in "survival of the fittest"?'

'You mean it's like an evolution thing?'

'Yeah, in a sense, it's beginning to look that way. Somehow, even without the original operating system, this network still has a tendency towards . . . well, if not actually being alive, then to lifelike behaviour. It wants to reproduce. In fact, now that the original brain of the network is gone, it may be more like a true organism. It's just trying things and if some of them work, it will continue. See, in some ways the people in the network, at least those like me and the Society people who are more or less alive, we really are people. We think, we feel, we make plans. But to the network, we're more like cells in a single organism – or maybe like individuals, but in a hive culture. The network is the hive, and we're the drones and workers and all that. That's the example that Kunohara kept using, anyway. He's utterly excited about all this, by the way, even though it means he was wrong about the network being dead.'

'He would like it, if it's got hives in it. But I still don't get this, Orlando. Are you saying that the system wanted you and the Avialle-shadows to reproduce together? But you'd never seen each other and she's already pregnant. That doesn't make sense.'

'It does if you remember what Kunohara said, that we shouldn't confuse appearance and reality, that Life has lots of strategies. Just because we look like humans and the women appear to be pregnant in the ordinary, human way doesn't really mean it has to be anything like the same process. Think about flowers. They reproduce too, but sometimes the genetic information comes from two plants that are miles apart – they certainly don't ever see each other. But when humans or us humanoid sims think they're pregnant, the natural assumption is that it happened the old-fashioned way.' He frowned. 'Unlike normal human reproduction, I have to say the network's model is a little lacking in the motivations department – you know, the *we-do-it-because-it's-fun* stuff.'

'Slow down, Sherlock. So the system is just . . . throwing together genetic material from you and other people in the system to make new people? But you don't *have* any genetic material.' She suddenly looked horrified. 'I'm sorry, Orlando, I didn't mean . . .'

'Don't worry, I've been thinking about this stuff for days. This game is weird and different and even a dead guy like me can play. See, it's not genetic material in the normal sense, it's what Kunohara calls the network's codification of us – the blueprints of us copies, which is the closest to genes we're going to have. It's just found a way to mix them up.' She still looked worried, so he smiled. 'As far as throwing the stuff together – yes, more or less, but not so random. A good reproductive system usually has some component of winners-get-to-mate in it. That's why my material showed up first, and it was paired with an Avialle-shadow – the fittest parents, remember? – and why more than one of the Avialles is pregnant by me. We have the most mobility, and in my case I have the most power – I'm not sure the network really factors that in, though – so my material . . . I'm going to need a new word, "material" just doesn't do it . . . my infor-mation is the most attractive. There's only one me, but there are more than a few Avialle-shadows, and they'll tend to select for my information if they can get it.'

'How? Does the network just . . . impregnate them with it?'

'No. This is another weird touch. I began to get a hint of it with the Society members. Two women got pregnant, and the Jongleur-shadow said he didn't do it. After my own experience, I wondered if he might not be telling the truth. So I went through the travel diaries of the three people involved and found out they almost hadn't ever been in the same worlds at the same time, let alone shacked up. In fact, they were only near each other during Worldwalkers meetings in the Wodehouse version of London, and the Jongleur-shadow had travelled back to his own home world right afterwards, which meant there wasn't much chance for a regular, old-fashioned simulated conception and pregnancy. But they all *had* travelled through a lot of the same gateways between the network worlds, de Limoux first – he's the man – and then the women.'

'Gateways? You mean it was the gateways?'

'We think so, yeah. Like the way bees brush up against pollen and then take it to another flower, or even the way some fish or insects sort of go to the same spot to deposit sperm and eggs, but they don't have to be there at the same time. The system is making male information – from people like me and de Limoux – reproductively active in some way, and then receptive females can pick it up as they pass through the gateways. In fact, me and Kunohara are going to have to turn down the success rate of the connections or the Society women are going to be pregnant all the time.'

Sam was now waggling her hands in the way she did when she was having problems. 'You mean you're going to let it happen? But . . . but what kind of babies are these women going to *have*? This is far scanny, Orlando! I mean, if these pregnancies are like fish or insects or something, maybe they'll have . . . uck! . . . *swarms* of babies.' For the second time in a few minutes, she looked stricken. 'Will they even look like human children?'

'We think so. Even if the methodology is more like a hive or something, the network seems to be using a lot of human-type models for the actual pregnancies – it was programmed to simulate things like that already, remember. They seem to be moving along at the right rate, and the doctors in Wodehouse World who've checked the Society women only hear one baby heartbeat per mother. Also, there's a couple of other clues that kind of suggest they'll be human babies – or as close to it as the system can manage, considering that they're not working with real humans as parents, but copies, some of them pretty imperfect. One is that it seems like a lot of trouble to use the human sims within the system as information-donors – parents – if you're going to change the information a whole bunch afterwards. It's easier just to use the human models of parents and children that are already built in, see? But the other reason is the answer to one of the questions that was bothering me even after I started to figure all this out. I couldn't get it, but Kunohara did.'

'Go ahead. I'm just trying to swallow all this.' Sam really did look as though she had been thumped on the head. 'Dozens of women lining up all over the network to have your babies, Gardiner. You must be living on Aren't I Special Street.'

'It'd be a lot more flattering if it was happening the old-fashioned way. Anyway, while we were putting this all together, I told Kunohara that two questions were still burning up my brain. One was why the Avialle-shadows knew my name even though we'd never actually met. Kunohara figures that's another proof we'll have human-type babies. Higher mammals, especially humans, have long childhoods, and they need lots of parental care. It was in the interest of the network's reproductive strategy to give both donors a chance of bonding together to raise the children, so the females get implanted with not just the male genetic information, but also the knowledge of who the father is and an ability to locate him, even if they don't really know how the pregnancy itself happened. That's how the Society women knew de Limoux was the daddy, and how the Avialle-shadows know they're carrying my children – I guess I have to call them that, even if I didn't really have anything to do with it.'

'But that doesn't make sense, Orlando. I mean it does in a sort of way, but if the network really wants you to be involved with these children like a father, why would the mothers keep disappearing every time you hooked up with them?'

'See? Even after hours of rubbing your poor, sore brain against honours chemistry, Frederico, you're still smarter than you think you are. That was exactly my other question. Kunohara figured that one out, too. It's kind of embarrassing, really.'

'Chizz. Do tell.'

'Well, among higher mammals, especially the ones like us that need both parents, there's usually an elaborate courtship strategy that helps to bind the father to the mother and the coming offspring. Since there isn't anything remotely like courtship before the pregnancy in the network's reproductive strategy . . . well, the system came up with a substitute. Kind of courtship *after* the pregnancy. Like a mating dance, or – what did Kunohara call it, bees do it? A nuptial flight.'

'Huh?'

'It only works really well for the Avialle-shadows because they can travel instantaneously – just vanish – but some of the Society women have also dropped out and disappeared in more conventional ways. This woman named Maisie Macapan has taken off for Imperial Rome, for instance. All this running away is supposed to keep the father interested. He chases after them, see?' He shook his head. 'Boy, did it work on me.'

This was the hardest bit, and Orlando knew he was stalling. He thought about the last thing Sam had said before they disconnected.

'*I guess it's good,*' she'd told him, '*because you look utterly excited and interested. I was really beginning to worry about you – you seemed so depressed for a while. But what does it mean? How are you going to deal with being a father to all these babies, if that's how it really turns out? What are you going to do, Orlando?*'

And the truth was, he didn't know – in fact, there were still hundreds of questions to be answered. How had the system arrived at this point, seemingly all at once? Had it been trying things out in some evolutionary laboratory-world hidden in the folds of the network? Was it conscious, as the old operating system had been, or was it simply working out old tendencies left over from the original system? Or was it actually moving towards a new kind of consciousness – would Orlando and the other sims eventually become cells in some greater living thing? Some of the questions were downright scary. The elation of solving the mystery hadn't entirely faded, but he knew the reality of this wasn't going to be anywhere near as simple as explaining it to people. Not that explaining it was ever going to be easy – especially the explanation he was about to give, which was why he was stalling.

If there are dozens of children just from me, I can't be a full-time father, obviously. We may have to turn the process off after this first group, at least as far as my own information – otherwise, what if the network plans to keep doing this all the time, generation after generation? Like I'm the queen bee, the king bee, whatever, and it's going to make thousands of kids with me as a parent? He had some time to think about that, at least, to discuss the problem with Kunohara, since there were a limited number of potential mothers and the pregnancies seemed to be lasting as long as in the real world. The entomologist was in rapture with these new developments, and was hurrying to settle his court case so that he could throw himself into investigating the new paradigm.

Easy for him – his information isn't copied into the system. He's not going to be a dad to dozens of kids, to have all that responsibility. But if there was ever anyone in a position to protect his children, it was Orlando Gardiner, network ranger. After all, like they used to say about the sheriffs in the Wild West, *I'm all the law there is this side of reality.*

God, I don't know. I'll figure it out. I've got friends. It'll be weird, but I'm dead and I'm on my way to visit my folks, so how much weirder can things get? It'll be an adventure.

I'm going to be a father! Me! He couldn't get over it. It was terrifying and exciting. What would the children be like? What would happen to the network as this first generation grew and then reproduced themselves, creating ever more complex patterns of inheritance? No one in the history of humanity had ever experienced anything like this. *Unknown country. It's all unknown country ahead.*

'I'm going now, Beezle,' he announced. 'I don't want to be interrupted unless the universe as we know it is actually collapsing, OK? Take messages.'

'No problem, boss. I'll just hang out here in imaginary space and play with the cats.'

Orlando summoned up the connection for his parents' house. This time he would even be willing to wear that horrid plasteel scarecrow. After all their work arranging that surreal and touching birthday party at Rivendell, he felt he owed Conrad and Vivien a little something. Even more importantly, he wanted them in a good mood when he told them that against all logic, they were apparently going to be grandparents after all.

Maybe forty or fifty times.

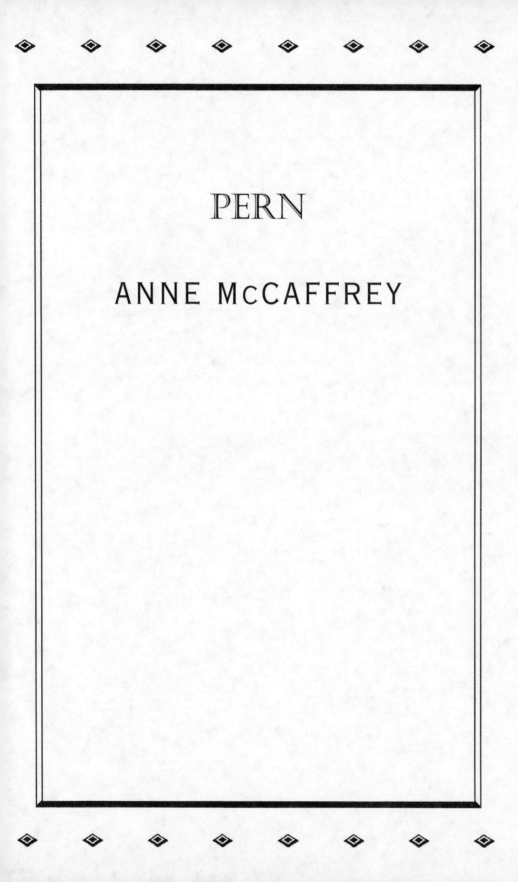

PERN

ANNE McCAFFREY

PERN
ANNE McCAFFREY

THE DRAGONRIDERS OF PERN TRILOGY:
Dragonflight (1969)
Dragonquest (1971)
The White Dragon (1978)

THE HARPER HALL TRILOGY:
Dragonsong (1976)
Dragonsinger (1977)
Dragondrums (1978)

OTHER PERN NOVELS:

Moreta, Dragonlady of Pern (1983)
Nerilka's Story (1986)
Dragonsdawn (1988)
The Renegades of Pern (1989)
All the Weyrs of Pern (1991)
The Chronicles of Pern (1992)
The Dolphins of Pern (1994)
Dragonseye (1996)
The Masterharper of Pern (1998)
Skies of Pern (1999)
Gift of Dragons (2002)
Dragon's Kin, with Todd McCaffrey (December 2003)

Dissatisfied with life on technologically advanced Earth, hundreds of colonists travelled through space to the star Rukbat, which held six planets in orbit around it, five in stable trajectories, and one that looped wildly around the others. The third planet was capable of sustaining life, and the spacefarers settled there, naming it Pern. They cannibalized their spaceships for materiel and began building their homes.

Pern was ideal for settlement, except for one thing. At irregular intervals, the sixth planet of its system would swing close to it and release swarms of deadly mycorrhizoid spores, which devoured anything they touched and rendered the ground where they landed fallow for years. The colonists immediately began searching for a way to combat the Thread, as the spores were named. For defence, they turned to the dragonets, small flying lizards that the colonists had tamed when they first landed. The fire-breathing ability of these reptiles had been a great help in the first Threadfall. By genetically enhancing and selectively breeding these reptiles through the generations, the colonists created a race of full-sized dragons.

With the dragons and their riders working together, the Pern colonists were able to fight Thread effectively and establish a firm hold on the planet. They settled into a quasi-feudal agricultural society, building Holds for the administrators and field workers, Halls for the craftsmen, and Weyrs for the dragons and riders to inhabit.

Many of the Pern novels detail the politics of the Holds and Weyrs between Threadfalls. The entire line of books spans over 2,500 years, from the first landing of the settlers to their descendants' discovery of the master ship's computer centuries later. *Dragonflight*, the first of the Dragonriders of Pern books, tells of a time 2,500 years after the initial landing. The Thread has not been seen in four centuries, and people are starting to be sceptical of the old warnings. Three dragonriders, Lessa, F'lar and F'nor, believe that the Thread is coming back, and try to mobilize the planetary defences. Lessa, knowing that there are not enough dragons to combat the Thread effectively, time-travels back four hundred years to a point just after the last Threadfall, when that era's dragonriders are growing restless and bored from lack of activity. Lessa convinces most of them to come back with her to combat Thread in her time. They arrive and fight off the Thread.

Dragonquest, the second book, picks up seven years after the end of the first book. Relations between the Oldtimers, as the time-travelling dragonriders are called, and the current generation are growing tense. After getting into a fight with one of the old dragonriders, F'nor is sent to Pern's southern continent to recover from his wound. There he discovers a grub that neutralizes the Thread after it burrows into the ground. Realizing they have discovered a powerful new weapon against Thread, F'nor begins planning to seed the grubs over both continents.

Meanwhile, an unexpected Threadfall is the catalyst for a duel between F'lar, the Benden Weyrleader, and T'ron, the leader of the

Oldtimers. F'lar wins and banishes all dragonriders who will not accept his role as overall Weyrleader. The banished go to the Southern Continent. The book ends with the grubs being bred for distribution over Pern.

The third book, *The White Dragon*, chronicles the trials of young Jaxom as he raises the only white dragon on Pern, a genetic anomaly. Jaxom encounters prejudice and scorn from other dragonriders because his dragon is smaller than the rest. He is also scheduled to take command of one of the oldest Holds on Pern, and there are those who doubt his ability to govern. Both Jaxom and his dragon Ruth rise to the challenges and succeed in proving that bigger is not necessarily better. Jaxom commands his Hold, gets the girl, and all is set right with the world.

The Harper Hall trilogy (*Dragonsong, Dragonsinger, Dragondrums*) is aimed at young readers, and deals with a girl named Menolly and her rise from unappreciated daughter to Journeywoman Harper and keeper of fire-lizards.

In many subsequent novels, and in the short novel published here, McCaffrey has examined various other aspects of life on Pern from the earliest days of its colonization by humans.

BEYOND BETWEEN

BY ANNE McCAFFREY

Foreword

When human colonists first settled on Pern, the third planet of the sun Rukbat, in the Sagittarian Sector, they paid little attention to the eccentric orbit of the sister planet they called the Red Star. After all, the star system had been surveyed and declared safe, and the Earth-born colonists, all war veterans, were more concerned with building a peaceful, low-tech, agrarian society for themselves and their children. So they were ill prepared when disaster struck, eight years later, in the form of a menace from space – a mindless organism that fell from the sky in thin strands, consuming all organic matter in its way. The colonists called it 'Thread', and although it could be destroyed by water or fire, and could not penetrate stone or metal, it fell so relentlessly that it seemed virtually unstoppable.

Then a solution was found: using their old-world ingenuity and genetic engineering, the settlers altered an indigenous life-form that resembled the dragons of legend. The resulting enormous 'dragons' became Pern's most effective weapon against Thread. Able to chew and digest a phosphine-bearing rock, the dragons could literally breathe fire and sear the airborne Thread before it could reach the ground. Able not only to fly but to teleport, as well, the dragons could manoeuvre quickly to avoid injury during their battles with Thread. And their telepathic bond with their human riders – a bond forged at the moment of hatching – enabled dragons and humans to work in perfect harmony in their campaigns against Threadfall.

The dragonriders became the heroes of Pern, and it was many a child's dream to grow up to be a dragonrider, to share that incredible mental and emotional bond with one of the great dragons. But that bond had a downside, as well: death was a separation neither could endure alone. If the rider died, the dragon would commit suicide. If the dragon died, the rider might likewise attempt to take his own life or, at best, would be doomed from then on to lead but half a life.

Once the first fifty-year-long attack of Thread ended, three disparate societies developed on Pern: Holds, where strong-minded men managed the bounty of the land and kept people safe during the Falls of Thread; Halls, where crafts were practised and perfected; and Weyrs, where dragons and their riders lived.

During the Sixth Pass of Thread, in 1543, on the third day of the tenth month, an unusual situation occurred for which the carefully kept records in the Harper Hall and individual Weyrs could find no precedent. A plague had raged across the continent and the Healers had developed a preventative vaccine that needed to be administered as soon as the dragons and their riders brought it to every individual Hall and Hold from sea to sea. In an effort to perform this unusual delivery, dragons and their riders relied on a little known, or understood, ability in the dragons to teleport not just any*where* their riders could visualize, but any*when*. It was very dangerous to cross not only distance but also time and, when tired and confused, even the best-trained dragon and rider could make mistakes.

When the runnerbeasts first started acting up, Thaniel wasn't paying much attention. As happened so often, he was dreaming fondly of his beloved wife, gone these long turns and still missed. The two of them had been like two halves: once united they became a perfect whole. He pulled a worn little kerchief from his pocket and fingered it fondly, feeling the blue and green embroidered flowers in one corner – the careful stichery so typical of his wife's work. He sighed heavily. Death seemed so unfair – and so frighteningly final.

'Why should trees and plants always come back to life after every cold season when *we* only have this one short time?' he'd rail when thoughts of death overwhelmed him.

Thaniel was in his late middle turns, honed to a wiry frame from decades of riding and working runnerbeasts. Three turns before, a sharp hoof to the knee had left him with a permanent limp. No longer quick enough on his feet to handle the runnerbeasts, he had been forced to let his children take over the endless routine of hold chores while he took over much of the work his wife used to perform, keeping the hold in proper order, and cooking the meals for his family. The youngest was Bill, whose difficult birth had cost his mother's life. Maynar was the oldest and most competent in breaking and schooling the runnerbeasts. Jerra was a solid young woman who would soon, Thaniel hoped, make a match with one of the nearby holder lads.

Brailli, the younger of the two girls, was quite clever and would go to the Weaver Hall for training once the plague was under control. Destry, the dreamer of his kids, aimed at BeastMaster training.

The high-pitched squeals of his favourite riding beast, old Rusty, distracted him, and with a shake of his head he dragged his attention back to the present. What could be upsetting the old runner like this? Nothing terrified Rusty like dragons, but the likelihood of dragons coming here was distant at best. Then Thaniel remembered: his hold was due to receive vaccine for the plague that was spreading across the continent. He knew that *someone* would deliver the vaccine with instructions on how to use it. A dragonrider?

With the cup of hot, sweet klah he had just poured in hand, Thaniel left the kitchen and went out the front door of his hold. Scanning the scenery, he saw nothing amiss, just the rolling plains of grass spotted with copses of the hardy trees that could survive in the wind-swept, often freezing open lands. Nearby was their modest beasthold – not a 'real' stone beasthold such as could easily be built in Crom or Nabol with the stones some of the holders said was their only crop, but it was sufficient for birthing animals. Beside it, a stretch of fence led to the nearest paddock: sturdy wood palings on posts that had taken an entire day for a strong man to situate in the dense soil. Beside the gate, there was a watering trough that some ingenious ancestor had rigged to be continuously supplied with water from the Waterhole twelve dragonlengths away. Sure enough, a dragon was sweeping in to land in the open space by the watering trough. Good old Rusty never missed a trick, Thaniel thought, mentally chuckling at the runner's uncanny ability to sense dragons.

Thaniel quickened his pace to meet the newcomers, careful not to spill hot klah on his hand. What first struck him as odd was that the dragon was a very pale gold and her head sagged, which suggested she was very tired. As she landed, her nose almost touched the ground, but she pulled herself up and regained her balance with a long sigh of relief. Queen dragons were the strongest and largest of the Pernese dragons, and he'd never seen one so ungainly, not even after the fatigue of a long Threadfall.

'Thaniel,' said the rider, and his amazement was complete, for he recognized her as Moreta, the Weyrwoman of Fort Weyr. He knew her from Gathers, to which people often came from all over to celebrate, but Ista was the Weyr Thaniel was beholden to, and it was Ista that was usually responsible for keeping Thread from dropping on his land.

Moreta reached into the sack slung across her dragon's neck and held out two packages to him. He hurried to take them and to offer his cup of klah to her.

'I just poured it, and you look like you need it more'n I do,' he said.

'You've no idea how much I appreciate this,' she said, giving him a grateful smile as she sipped the hot beverage. After her first swallow, she seemed to shake her shoulders as if to release the tension in them. She looked out at the westering sun and sighed again deeply, this time from a satisfaction she did not explain to him. Not that queen riders and Weyrwomen were required to explain their actions or share their thoughts with mere holders like himself.

'That's the vaccine for your runnerbeasts and you and your holders, Thaniel. There should be a healer coming if you don't want to inject it yourself.'

The word 'inject' made Thaniel shudder, but he took the package and thanked her.

'It must be done, better today, definitely tomorrow,' she said, and told him how to press the needlethorn into the fleshy part of the upper arm or thigh. She looked around at the large yard, as if she expected to see more people. Thaniel understood her curious glance.

'They're all out, checking on yearlings,' he said, as he peered into the smaller of the two packets at the nest of carefully padded vials that would protect him and his family from the plague. 'There's exactly enough here for all in my holding.' He glanced up at her with gratitude and then realized that she was utterly exhausted. He remembered her as a very pretty woman, with short blonde hair and deep-set eyes. Now her eyes were underscored by dark circles of fatigue, her body was listless, and her skin was tinged slightly grey, making her look far older than he knew her to be. It was Leri who was the old Weyrwoman at Fort, not Moreta. Maybe it was just the light of the setting sun shining on her face. But there was no question that the dragon was tired. Her skin drooped and sagged on her withers and haunches, and the light of life barely shone from the many facets of her eyes.

'Why are you doing a green's work, Weyrwoman?' he asked, allowing his tone to be critical. Surely others less important than a gold could have delivered the vaccine to a small hold like his.

'I grew up in Keroon. I've been here to Waterhole Hold before. None of the Ista riders would know the area as well as I. Just use the vaccine as soon as you get back to your hold, Thaniel.' As she held the empty cup out to him to take, he noticed that her other hand was gripping the neck ridge in front of her as if to prevent her from plunging forward off the dragon. 'That was just what I needed, Thaniel. My thanks.'

'And my thanks to you, Weyrwoman.' He stepped back, aware even if she did not seem to be, that her queen was shaking under her.

'This is our last stop, Holder Thaniel,' she said as she stroked the old queen's neck and smiled at him. 'We have delivered all the vaccine on our run.' She looked again at the westering sun.

'Fly in safe skies, Weyrwoman. The light is surely fading fast.'

'One last jump *between*, that's all we have to take, Holth,' she said encouragingly and kneed the dragon to the right.

Thaniel heard the relief resonant in her voice and it seemed to give energy to the queen as well, for she sprang into the air and disappeared. Rather close to the ground, he thought, but who was he to judge? He took the cup and the packets of vaccine back to his hold, carefully placing the medicine in the centre of the big table where his brood took their meals.

He poured himself another cup of klah, sweetened it, and felt a glow of pride for having served the Weyrwoman himself from a pot of his own brewing. He brewed a good cup: everyone said so, and now the Weyrwoman had praised him, too. He sat down, work-worn hands around the warm pottery cup, easing his finger joints.

'Holth?' He said the name aloud now in surprise. Now that was odd! Not that everything about this day wasn't unusual – like a queen dragon delivering a parcel – but there was nothing wrong with either his memory or his understanding of Hold and Weyr. Fort's Weyrwoman, Moreta, rode Orlith, not Holth.

But Orlith had clutched recently, which might be one reason why Moreta wasn't riding her own queen. Gold dragons tended to be very proprietorial about their eggs. And the report was that the clutch numbered twenty-five, one of which was likely to be a queen.

Holth, now, was old Leri's queen. He was sure of that, as she had been Weyrwoman ever since he had taken hold of his family's land. He'd heard that she suffered badly from joint-ail and her physical condition had deteriorated past the point where she could lead the Weyr against Threadfall. And, if Moreta was riding Holth, maybe that was why the dragon had looked so pale and tired: separated from her life-long rider who would never, he was sure, have pushed the old queen past her strength.

Just then the herd, which had settled back to grazing, spooked again, racing to the eastern side of the paddocks. Old Rusty gave another of his back-chilling shrieks as if a field snake were squeezing him. Oddly enough, the big flat-bodied plain snakes never frightened Rusty. He even seemed to enjoy trampling them to death under his large hooves.

But this time Rusty's shriek made Thaniel shudder, as if something terrible had happened that he didn't understand.

Thaniel could see no dust in any direction to suggest that his children were on their way back home, or anything strange in the sky to account for Rusty's shriek. He looked out at the wide, flat, shallow lake from which his hold derived its name. The lake never went dry – water bubbled up in the middle of it from some subterranean source – and so he was able to supply water to any who came looking for it. There was always the Keroon River, but the Waterhole was closer for some of his western neighbours. And everyone said the water was sweeter.

He shrugged off the sensation of malaise he had felt when Rusty shrieked and returned to his hearth to give the stew a stir; the pot was warming up nicely. He poured himself more klah and mused over the event of the day.

Ever the worrier, Thaniel clasped his fingers tighter around the cup. Why was Moreta doing delivery duty anyhow? And why was she riding another's dragon? Holth she had said, too clearly for him to mistake the name of the queen she rode.

Oh well, it was not his place to criticize queen riders. Maybe when the healer came, he'd have an answer for that. He stirred the stew, inhaling the meaty odours with pleasure and eager for the return of his family so he could tell them what had happened.

Maynar, Jerra, Brailli, Destry and Bill all arrived back just as twilight was beginning to fade. They were full of news of well-grown, healthy-looking yearlings, and had made good notes of landmarks so the smaller herds could be easily found. Thaniel explained how Moreta herself had brought the vaccine. His tale was greeted by amazement at the very idea of a queen rider delivering to their small hold, but after a brief, lively discussion, he drew their attention back to the packages of vaccine on the table. As soon as a healer arrived to do the necessary, they would all be safe against the plague.

'Nonsense, Father,' said Jerra, 'I will inject the vaccine. We're not supposed to wait.' She added: 'The plague could come on the next wind, and wouldn't we look stupid with the medicine sitting on the table and useless to us.'

We wouldn't look stupid, we'd just look dead, Thaniel thought. 'We will eat, and then I will inject us all,' Jerra continued in an imperious tone. 'I've seen how the healer does it. Just jab it in the flesh of the arm.'

Maybe Jerra was a trifle domineering at times – so unlike her mother – but she always had the good of the family at heart, Thaniel reminded himself. So he nodded acceptance of her offer and the entire family set to eating, though no one looked away from the little parcel all during the meal.

Rusty's shrill shriek nearly toppled Thaniel off his stool.

'*What* is going on?' he exclaimed. 'That poor animal has been spooking all day.'

Maynar, closest to the window, jumped off his stool to look outside. Thaniel joined him.

'Visitors? And we've not enough supper left to fill the bottom of even the smallest bowl,' Jerra said, embarrassed.

'It's more dragons,' Thaniel said. He took the glowbasket from its hook and, opening the door, strode forth to make proper welcome to their guests. He was astonished to see three dragons and riders, each with a passenger, descending to the ground.

'Waterhole Hold? Is this Waterhole?' cried a man.

'It is, and who might you all be?'

'I am MasterHarper Tirone, here with Kamiana, queen rider of Pelianth, and Desdra of the Healer Hall . . . And with us are A'dan, Tigrath's rider, and D'say and Critith. We must know if Moreta came here sometime this afternoon!'

'She did, just at sundown, and left us the vaccine,' Thaniel replied, his voice carrying easily in the dark. 'Come to the hold. We have wine and klah.'

As he waved them towards him, all Thaniel could think of was that one of these people was from the Healer Hall and could possibly inject them, saving the entire family from Jerra's well-meant but inexperienced attempts. Fortunately there was fresh klah being brewed, and Jerra and her siblings had found their hold's precious glasses in which to serve a hastily uncorked bottle of wine: a drinkable red made in the Crom hills.

'You are kind, Thaniel, Jerra, but we have no time to spare, though we appreciate your hospitality,' Tirone said as he and the others entered the hold. 'Only tell us what you know of Moreta and Holth.' His eyes, and those of his companions, were dull with grief.

Fear struck Thaniel to the heart, for Moreta and Holth should long have been back at Fort Weyr. Hours ago! And so he said.

'I gave her a cup of klah to help her on her way,' he added, hoping he had done the right thing.

'What did she say?' asked Kamiana.

'She thanked me,' Thaniel replied.

'Did she say anything as she and Holth went off?'

'Oh, aye, and I felt sorry for the poor queen. She was quite faded with fatigue and she looks so old, you know.' Thaniel worried that his observation was irrelevant. 'She said, and my memory's good, "Just one last jump *between*, Holth, that's all we have to take." I thought that was odd, as I'm sure Moreta's queen is Orlith.' No one contradicted him.

'Surely she visualized Fort Weyr?' Desdra murmured to the others in the silence that had fallen. The visitors looked nervously at one another.

'But they would have been exhausted by the time they reached here,' Kamiana said. 'Moreta had been riding all morning on Orlith. And riding all the stops here in Keroon would have been a lot for an old queen like Holth to do.'

Ever the Healer, Desdra pulled the smaller bundle of vaccine to her and looked inside. 'Would you object to my giving you the injection?'

'No, no,' Thaniel said quickly. 'We have no idea when our own Healer will drop by – we are out of the way of most paths – although my daughter said she's seen the Healer do this sort of thing.'

If Jerra was upset to have to forgo the pleasure of inoculating her family, she gave no sign, hurriedly unbuttoning her sleeve and rolling it up.

'Thaniel, was Holth's leap-off steady?' Kamiana asked anxiously.

'Oooh, I'd say steady enough, but they were both of them very tired, as I said.'

Kamiana breathed out a sigh. 'Very tired. Maybe too tired to do that one more thing that a rider must always do with her dragon, especially an unfamiliar one.'

'Moreta knew Holth very well,' MasterHarper Tirone protested.

Kamiana dismissed that. 'As a friend, since Moreta was so often in Leri's weyr, but *not* as a rider. I think that has made more of a difference than we thought it would.'

'And all the timing they must have done. It would be enough to scramble anyone's wits,' Desdra said, pressing the little piece of cotton firmly to Jerra's arm now that the deftly made injection was complete. The visitors lapsed into worried silence at her words.

Thaniel and his brood hardly noticed, however; their attention was fixed firmly on the thornneedles and the vaccine. Thaniel took Jerra's seat close to the MasterHealer, his sleeve rolled up. Desdra pinched the skin of his arm and jabbed him. He winced just a trifle as the thornneedle punctured him and then sighed as the vaccine coursed into his arm. How lucky they all were that a Healer journeywoman had come with the others.

Once all the injections had been given, the visitors rose, apologizing for their haste and thanking the holders for their hospitality and time.

'I think they have died *between*.' Thaniel heard Kamiana say unsteadily as he lit their way back to the dragons. 'The dragons have keened them.'

'Such a waste,' Master Tirone said. 'You must protect others from the same fate, Kamiana.'

'Never fear. The weyrs will take immediate steps. I just can't understand why an experienced rider like Moreta was unable to visualize her destination. Or why Holth wouldn't automatically head for Leri. Their mission was done.'

'Where do we go now?' Tirone asked quietly, settling himself behind the blue rider.

'Back to Fort Hold, for you must be exhausted yourselves, Master Tirone, Journeywoman Desdra,' Kamiana said, 'I would see you safely back to your halls.'

As the dragonriders clearly spoke their destination, the dragons rose from the ground. In a moment they winked out, going *between*, leaving Thaniel alone with the rising moon and the shrieking runnerbeasts.

The night after Moreta disappeared, Thaniel was alone at Waterhole Hold. His children had been out vaccinating their runnerbeast stock and would be late returning home. Suddenly Rusty shrieked louder than ever. Wondering if a wherry was attacking his old runnerbeast, Thaniel cautiously drew back the curtain to look out the window. Rusty was the only beast upset; all the others were calm, although curious about Rusty's behaviour. Thaniel wondered if Rusty was just getting too old, and was perhaps a little addled in the head. He might have to put the old runner down.

A strange shiver of apprehension palpably shook Thaniel. Gripped by a huge sense of terror, he dropped the curtain. Breathing hard, heart pounding, he went to the door, opened it a crack, and peeked out. He saw nothing untoward save for the terrified Rusty. He opened the door wide and stepped out into the night.

'Who is it? Who goes there?' Thaniel called out, walking toward the paddock.

Rusty shrieked again and he turned towards the beast.

'Stupid beast. There's no one here.' He swept his hand, indicating empty space.

Rusty continued shrieking, showing the whites of his eyes and flaring his nostrils as he galloped around the enclosure in terror.

'Shut your bawling!' Thaniel shouted loudly at Rusty. 'The riders looking for Moreta have all gone back to their weyrs. There's not a sign of a dragon in the sky.'

Suddenly Thaniel felt as if he'd been touched on the arm by a shaft of sheer ice. He pulled his arms to his body, muttering quietly, 'What was that to make me shiver as if this were midwinter and me catching a cold?' And then more loudly, as a horrifying thought hit home, he said, 'Am I getting the plague after all?'

Trembling violently, Thaniel turned and ran, terrified, to his hold, slamming the door shut behind him.

Some time later, Jerra, Maynar, and the others returned to the hold and found their father noticeably distraught. He was sitting by the fire on the edge of his seat; his hands, palms together, were clenched tightly between his knees.

'What's wrong, Da?' Jerra asked, concern stamped on her face.

'It's nothing, nothing.'

'Did you see something?' Maynar asked.

'I saw nothing,' Thaniel replied sharply, and stared intently into the fire.

The following day two dragonriders visited Waterhole to check that all the holders and runnerbeasts had, indeed, been vaccinated and that no one had suffered any ill effects from the injection. Their arrival was, of course, punctuated by Rusty's shrieks of terror. Assuring them that all in his hold had been injected by none other than the Journeywoman Healer, Desdra, Thaniel wanted to add that the only ill effect was his old runnerbeast shrieking from the appearance of dragons every day. But he held his tongue instead, conscious of the grief the dragonfolk endured. He couldn't help but think that he was the last person to have seen Moreta and Holth. That thought preyed on his mind and he grew anxious.

His anxiety did not go unnoticed by his children, so that night and the following day one of Thaniel's daughters or sons stayed with him in the hold while the others went about the routine of checking stock. But, then, just before dusk, Bill came charging back on his little runner, self-important with the news that a beast had trapped itself in a narrow gully and couldn't find enough foot-purchase to get free. All hands were needed to hoist the animal to safety so Jerra, attending her father that day, would have to go back with her brother. Thaniel and Bill assembled ropes, straps and lanterns and stowed them carefully on Bill's runner. Jerra and the boy were clearly reluctant to leave their father alone, but Thaniel reassured them that he would be quite all right and, after all, the animal must be rescued.

The dust kicked up by Bill's and Jerra's mounts had only just settled when Thaniel was overcome by a terrible sinking feeling that was punctuated by a frightful scream from Rusty. Heart skipping several beats, Thaniel crept to the door, holding a thick stick as long as a man's arm. He opened the door and scanned the horizon for any sign of dragons. All he saw was Rusty rearing on his hind legs, striking out with his forefeet at some invisible foe. Within a few moments the runner started to calm down, only to start shrieking again. He was so frightened that he backed away from the fence as fast as his feet could move. Then he stopped, firm in his tracks, starring intently ahead of him – at nothing. Concern overriding fear as the terrified beast started pawing the ground, Thaniel left the safety of his hold doorway and approached the enclosure, beckoning Rusty to him. The animal ignored him, his ears pricked forward and his eyes fastened on to something in front of him that only he could see.

'What is it, old fellow? What's bothering you?' Thaniel asked as he watched the muscles on Rusty's shoulders quivering. Rusty pawed the ground again. Thaniel passed a hand over his eyes, rubbing them, before he peered again at the empty space that transfixed Rusty. Suddenly, the runnerbeast took a huge step backwards, nearly sitting on his hindquarters in his attempt at high-speed retreat. Then, after kicking his hind legs high behind him and prodding the ground with his forelegs, the distraught animal tore around the enclosure like an unbroken yearling, wheeling and rearing as if Thread or some other unthinkable terror were engulfing him.

Thaniel's jaw dropped.

'He only does that when there's dragons about,' he said to himself. 'Maybe Rusty's just beyond it, and the kindest thing would be to put the old fellow down. Can't have him screaming like that every night!' Shaking his head, he turned away from the runnerbeast and walked back into his hold.

And so Rusty's wild behaviour continued, night after night, until the fifth evening after Moreta had vanished into *between*. That night, Thaniel was watching at the right time. To his utter amazement, the full moon illuminated the ethereal forms of a dragon and rider.

Hollering louder than Rusty, Thaniel dropped his club, turned, and fled back to his hold where he slammed the door quickly behind him.

Five days earlier . . .

Moreta felt the better for the klah the old holder had given her. She couldn't remember when she had last eaten, though she must have, as her stomach didn't feel all that empty. But she was so tired, and even the longest Fall had never seemed so endless and draining. Just this one last jump *between* and then Holth could rest, too, for the old queen had been valiant. As she sprang from the ground on this last leg of their day's journeying, Moreta began her litany against her fear of *between*. 'Black, blacker, blackest . . .'

Never had *between* felt so cold to her, even with the warmth of klah seeping into her veins. Hugging herself with her arms to ward off the chill, she closed her eyes against the unrelenting blackness of *between*. Then she opened them again, as out of the corner of her eye, her brain registered something different about her surroundings, something unexpected.

'*Is that a light?*' She turned towards it, shaking her head, waiting for the darkness to greet her eyes once again. Instead, a greyness lay before her, imperceptibly blending with the black of *between*. Somehow, she did not feel so cold any more. She felt an overwhelming desire to move away from the greyness and suddenly realized that Holth was motionless. Surely more than the usual eight seconds had passed. She had nearly finished the verse of her litany and they were still – immovably – *between* . . .

Holth? she cried. *What has happened? We are not back at Fort Weyr!*

We are between. *I did not 'see' where we should go,* replied Holth in a querulous tone, bugling in distress.

Panic welled in Moreta's chest and she tried to think back to what she had said to Holth as the tired old dragon had lurched off the ground. She shook her head.

I had to have visualized Fort Weyr for you, Holth! she protested, forcing her time-wearied mind to recall exactly what she had said. *I've been a rider too long to make such a weyrling mistake.*

We are both tired, Holth replied blandly. *We went* between, *as you said. That is all we did.*

Why didn't you ask me where? Moreta demanded sharply, wondering how a dragon so experienced could have forgotten something so basic.

You have been telling me where to go, and at what time to get there, all day. You always gave me the directions. Specific directions, according to the sun. This time you only told me to go between. Despair crept into the dragon's mental tone.

Frantically quelling her own mounting panic, Moreta recalled that she had indeed only told weary old Holth to go *between*, assuming that the dragon had also heard her say that this was the last time she'd have to jump. Meaning, of course, for them to jump between to 'home', Fort

Weyr, where they could both rest after the arduous day; home to Leri and home to Orlith and her eggs. She hugged herself tightly and looked longingly behind her, as if she were looking at her past. A past she could not change. *Move, Holth! Maybe we can find our way back.* Holth uttered a disbelieving noise and made no move with either wing or leg.

I cannot go anywhere. There was just the slightest emphasis on 'go'.

'What do you mean, you can't "go"?' Moreta cried out loud.

Not yet, and not with you, was Holth's cryptic reply.

We must go home. They are expecting us. Leri will be worried about you, and Orlith will be frantic.

I know, the dragon replied. *I cannot reach them,* she added after a brief pause.

Frightened, Moreta pushed her thoughts out for the comforting touch of Orlith, ever present at the back of her mind and often stronger when they were separated. For the first time, it was not there, and Moreta gasped. This couldn't be happening! she thought as, unbidden, tears flowed down her cheeks. Overwhelming grief consumed her.

Orlith! she cried.

Just then, she saw something moving, grey against greyer, but shaped like a dragon with its rider on its withers.

'Hallo there!' a male voice called. And he waved an arm at her. Moreta momentarily froze and then desperately wiped at her wet face. This was an impossible nightmare, and now she was hearing things as well as seeing – in *between*! 'Wait for me!' the man called out.

Stunned, Moreta numbly waited while an unusually small, brown dragon halted neatly just a nose away from Holth. The old dragon put her nose forward and made the expected courtesy touch with a newcomer. Then Holth backed up with far more energy than she had previously shown.

Duluth? the gold dragon asked, surprised.

'What's happening? Who are you? Why can I hear and see you?' Moreta cried. The panic was rising in her again. The old queen backed up a further step.

'I'm Marco Galliano,' the young rider said in a measured, calming tone. Or at least Moreta thought he was young. He had to be a new rider, for she didn't know of a brown dragon named Duluth.

'Don't worry, I can help you. Are you cold? You're both shivering.'

'Not from the cold,' Moreta said, trying to control the panic in her voice, but what else would one feel, stuck in *between*?

'Look, I know you're new to all this, up here in the fold. Duluth and I do the rounds every day to look for strays.'

'Do rounds? Look for strays?' Moreta echoed, incredulous. She felt as if the greyness was closing in around her and clutched at her riding harness, fearful that she was losing consciousness. If she fell off Holth now, she'd be falling into *between*. A whimper, unbidden, surged up her throat.

'C'mon, I'll take you where it's warm.'

His dragon turned.

'Wait! Where are you going?' she yelled.

Just follow me. It's easy, said the dragon.

'I don't know why it works,' Marco said casually, 'but I can always get back to Paradise.'

Duluth took off on a good run and in a moment was so competently airborne that Moreta quickly urged Holth to follow. Holth took off at speed, as if she, like Moreta, wanted to get anywhere but here, no matter where that might be. Moreta's vision blurred again as panic continued to exert its grip on her. She felt totally disoriented.

They flew straight for what seemed a long time, and then suddenly, unexpectedly, Marco and Duluth suddenly dropped, flattened out, and dived down through the dark floor of *between*. A hole appeared to engulf them, and Moreta urged Holth to follow.

They broke out over a very blue sea, facing a spit of white sand and tall frond-waving trees along a shore. The sound of the water washing onto the shore rushed into Moreta's ears. Duluth landed on the beach, followed by Holth, who, sighing mightily as she instinctively kept her wings open to absorb the heat all dragons enjoyed, dug her feet down into the warm sand. The hot sun slapped Moreta in the face and she gasped with relief.

We're safe! We can go home now, Holth! she cried with relief. Holth didn't answer her. Quickly, Moreta tried to get her bearings, but the heat, combined with the complete exhaustion she felt, was too much to bear. She began to slide off Holth's neck, but fell halfway down, landing on all fours on the hot sands.

'Look, you're both awfully tired now. Your dragon has the right idea. C'mon,' Marco said, lifting her to her feet with great ease. Moreta wanted to correct him, tell him that Holth was not her dragon, but her mouth wouldn't form the words. He put a hand gently under her elbow and started to propel her towards the shade. The heat was enervating and she unconsciously opened her heavy flying jacket. Mute from shock and fatigue she followed Marco's lead, looking over her shoulder to be sure that Holth was comfortable in the sand. The old queen snorted once, wriggled her shoulders, let her tail fall down on the sand, and exhaled noisily into a snore.

'Here, sit down for a while; you'll feel better if you have a little rest.' Marco swept away some dry fronds from the tough grass that grew under the shading trees.

His hand changed position and practically forced her to the ground. She had no strength left. When he took her jacket from her limp hand and made a pillow of it on the grass, she lay down. Closing her eyes, Moreta hoped that when she opened them, she'd be back in her own weyr and that this was all a terrible dream.

The strange young rider murmured a gentle reassurance she didn't hear as she fell almost instantly into a deep sleep.

When Moreta roused, suddenly alert to the noise Holth made while changing position in the sand, Marco was still there. He placed a hand on her shoulder and spoke to her with all the calm assurance of a man five times his age. Strangely, the panic she had felt before she slept did not rise in her again. A calmness now pervaded her senses.

'It wasn't a dream, much as you would like it to have been. This is real. You went *between* and didn't come out. But I found you,' he said reassuringly.

Marco gestured for her to sit up and lean against a tree trunk. She noticed for the first time that he was clad in odd flying gear; but concern for Holth had her eyes swiveling to the dragon, who was resettling herself on the sand.

'She's fine,' Marco said. 'I think she needs to get the other side warm, too. This is the first she's moved since she lay down, except to snore. Which she does loudly, as you must know.'

Marco was an attractive young man – but nowhere near as handsome as Alessan, she thought to herself. But she put thoughts of her lover away. This frightening situation was hard enough to comprehend without being tortured by thoughts of being lost to him.

'Where are we, Marco?' she asked imploringly. 'And, if we didn't make it out of *between*, then what is all of this?' She gestured to the beach and the water lapping gently at the shore.

'Holth says your name is Moreta and that you're the Fort Weyrwoman,' he said calmly, looking at her with respect. 'Duluth is impressed.'

'Which weyr did you say you were from?'

'I didn't, because Duluth and I were never in a weyr. You don't know your dragonrider history?' He looked disappointed.

Moreta, startled to be so accused, glared at him. 'Of course I do.'

'Then who,' he asked very quietly, 'were the first riders?'

She was aware that her jaw dropped as she stared up at him. She knew who the first riders were and . . . she tried to grasp the concept.

'You and Duluth . . .' she said, dragging the facts from memory, 'were the first pair to go *between*, to avoid a collision with an air sled at Paradise River Stake . . .' She paused, glancing around.

'Of course, the mechanics of going *between* safely were learned later,' Marco went on. 'Duluth and I just acted out of instinct.'

'And you've been in – *between* – ever since?' Moreta asked, a large knot clenched deep in her gut.

'More or less. It took me a while to realize that I could return to Paradise River whenever I wanted to. Of course, by the time I figured that out and got back here, everyone in Jim Tillek's armada had moved on. I flew east in the direction I knew they were headed, but a fierce storm blew up and damned near knocked me off Duluth's back, so I quit following. Duluth had strained a ligament in his right pinion. Fortunately I had enough numbweed left to ease the injury. By the time we could follow on, we figured they'd been hit pretty badly by the storm, too. There were even some pieces of wrecked ships among the debris washed ashore. No bodies – we looked. So we came back to Paradise and made it our headquarters. There are some buildings back there. At first I stored the things that washed up on the beach there, just in case anyone came back looking for them. No one ever did. And then, I sort of found others caught the same way.'

'Others? Where are they?'

'Probably hunting. The dragons still like to hunt, you know. It's instinctive. But once they've made the kill, they don't even bother to blood it. There were a lot of fine cattle that had to be let loose for the Second Crossing. Not enough room for any but the prime breeding stock on the boats going to the new settlement. They've multiplied, and the cats . . .'

'Cats?' Moreta exclaimed nervously.

'Yes, cats. The big felines that Ted Tubberman bred and let loose down here.'

'Oh! But they're the creatures that brought us the plague. Don't let any of them come near you!'

Marco laughed, and the knot of tension gripping Moreta's innards gently dissolved. 'Not ruddy likely, Moreta. For one thing, they're usually scared of dragons; and two: we have no weapons' – he opened his hands wide – 'so we keep our distance. How could they spread a plague?'

Moreta said, 'Believe me, they can. I don't know how many people have died. But Healers managed to develop a vaccine.'

'How did cats get to the north?' Marco wondered.

Moreta clicked her tongue. 'Some seamen who'd been shipwrecked on the coast found the animal and brought it back, thinking they'd make a mark or two displaying it at Gathers. Before we traced the disease back to the cat, too many people had been infected.'

'Don't your people know about quarantines?' Marco asked, taken aback.

'Of course we do, but the plague spread too fast. At first no one knew what had started it. We get contagious diseases now and then, but they're usually just seasonal and only affect a small number of folk. This plague affected almost everyone.'

'Riders and dragons died, too?'

'Yes,' she replied sadly. 'How did you know that?'

'I saw quite a few of them,' he said, grimacing. 'Far more than would have been accounted for in a heavy Threadfall.'

'But if you saw them in *between*, then you must have seen where they went!' Moreta felt a rush of hope.

He shook his head slowly. 'I don't know where they went. I haven't been there yet.' A curious expression touched his face as he talked. Duluth warbled gently to his rider.

Moreta stared at him, having figured out that he and the first riders had all been about nineteen or twenty turns at the time they Impressed those first dragons. Why, he must be over fifteen hundred turns old! That is, if he really existed at all! She wanted to reach out and touch him.

'I still don't understand . . .' Her voice quavered with uncertainty and she felt fresh tears behind her eyes.

'How I could be here *and between*?' He shook his head. 'I don't understand either, but demonstrably I am. *Cogito, ergo sum.*'

'I beg your pardon?'

'That's a very old Earth language, called Latin. It translates as "I think, therefore I am."'

'Oh.'

'A double big O, Moreta. What year – I mean, turn – is this?'

Moreta stared at him for a moment even as she said the words. 'Fifteen hundred and forty-three. We're nearly through the Sixth Pass.'

He nodded his head, staring at some far distant spot on the horizon. A gentle sigh passed his lips.

'But *how* have you survived?'

'I'm not sure, but I've decided that time must be different in *between*.

Which supports my notion that it's another dimension or level, or something.'

'Aren't you –' Moreta stopped, reluctant to hurt this gentle young man with her prying. '– lonely?' she asked.

'I have Duluth.' He looked towards his dragon, lounging next to Holth on the sand. As he made mental contact with his life partner, Moreta saw his eyes shining with the bond that all dragonriders knew. It made her long even more for Orlith.

Duluth rumbled with affection for his rider, and Holth stirred briefly as she lay in the warm sands.

'What happened to you and Holth?'

'Bad luck, bad imaging. Ours, I can candidly say, was due to fatigue and too many time changes.'

'Time changes?'

Moreta took a deep breath, composing herself before she began her story. As she recounted the events of the last few days, the pervading calmness that had overcome her faded. With the conclusion of her tale, her emotions welled up.

'All I said to her was "we only have to take one last jump *between*, Holth, that's all." And then we were stuck until you found us.' Moreta broke down in tears at her failure to give a clear picture of where she and Holth should have gone. Through sobs she cried, 'I never said goodbye to Orlith.'

'This is where I help,' Marco said gently, as he shifted his position so he could put an arm around her shoulders. He rocked her slightly until she was calm again. 'You delivered parcels to forty different places in the space of an afternoon?' He couldn't help sounding incredulous. 'But taking off and landing take up a lot of time.'

'Well, we made each hour work for two, or maybe three. Dragons can go *between* time, too, you see.'

'Dragons can go *between* time?' Marco asked, astonished.

'Well, as you can see, it can be very dangerous and totally disorient the rider. I've done it before, and even gone to the future, but only because the necessities of fighting this plague made that unavoidable. But we were short of riders. Since I was the most familiar with Keroon plains and holds, I offered to make the circuit. I used the position of the sun to guide me, but in order to get the medicine to everyone today, as promised, I had to backtrack. We were both exhausted by the time we made the last delivery.'

He touched her shoulder, studying her face with such a look of understanding that she blinked in surprise.

'Marco, why have you been here so long?'

He shrugged. 'No place else we can go or come back to.'

'But haven't you tried to follow any of the other dragons and riders when you see them in *between*?' she asked.

'Yes, we've tried. But it's all just endless greyness. We've flown for hours, no, days! But it's always been the same. At first, I thought I could see an end to it, and tried to get to it, but I never could. It always receded as fast as Duluth and I approached.'

He took another breath and said in a rush, 'Sometimes though . . . I see dragons, usually with their riders, just heading away – sometimes heading up . . .' He waved his hand in some inexplicit overhead direction. 'They aren't heading for *between*, because they are already *between*. They are aiming for some destination . . . *beyond between*.'

'Beyond *between*?' A shiver ran down her spine. 'But there's nothing beyond *between*.'

A heavy silence fell over them and it was quite some time before either one spoke.

'Are you sure?' Marco asked quietly.

'You should know. You arrived here in a spaceship, so you should have seen all there was to see of Pern.'

'You better believe it.' His tone was nostalgic. 'They put the forward view up on all the screens so we could watch it getting closer. Most of us were awake, preparatory to landing, and I don't think many of us bothered to eat or sleep. We couldn't get enough of watching.' His eyes glowed. 'Prettier than Earth, beautiful blue seas and green lands, and some desert spots, too. But beautiful – *and ours!*'

'And did you see *between*?

He gave her a very thoughtful look before he shook his head slowly. '*Between* was something we needed the dragons to find for us. It's something *they* do. We don't. Their own special place.'

'Dragons go *between* to die,' Moreta said flatly.

'They may go through *between*,' he retorted, 'but they don't stay there. No bodies. I've gone to check when I see a dragon in the greyness.'

'You're sure?'

'I'm sure.'

Moreta wasn't sure of anything any more, but she said nothing. She knew that dragons would go *between* if their riders had died. She knew that sometimes riders and dragons went *between* together if the life of one of them had become insupportable. Her head snapped back as she was gripped by an overwhelming sense of urgency.

'I have to be with Orlith and get Holth back to Leri somehow,' she blurted.

'I understand,' Marco said.

'Didn't you say I could go back to the place I came from? Waterhole?' She stood up, dusting sand from her clothing.

He looked up at her, almost expressionlessly. 'You can go back to Waterhole, yes, but I'm not sure it will do you any good.'

'If I can get back to Waterhole maybe I can get back to Fort Weyr.' He tilted his head sideways, a wry look on his face.

'Now that may be the problem. You see, you're dead.'

She stared at him with a combination of horror and disbelief.

'By the shards of my dragon's egg! Then why am I here with *you?*' She tilted her head to one side, looking intently at his eyes, and reached out her hand to pull him to his feet. He stared at her outstretched hand and then, clenching and unclenching his jaw, he returned her unwavering gaze. Moreta held her breath but did not break eye contact.

'You're not with the right dragon. You should have gone *between* with Orlith, not Holth!' he said, and in one smooth movement he gripped her forearm and pulled himself to his feet.

'Couldn't I find a way to get a message to Leri?'

He gave her an odd smile. 'I don't think they'll see you,' he said in a measured tone. 'And I'm not sure writing a message will work either.'

'Why not?'

He sighed. 'It's the problem of making it visible.'

She looked frantically at the sun, which was very low on the horizon. 'I must go now,' she said, shrugging into her riding jacket.

She was about to call to Holth when Marco put a heavy hand on her shoulder to prevent her moving.

'I should have gone right back and waited,' she said, ducking her shoulder from under his grasp.

'No!' he said in a loud, firm voice. Holth raised her head and Duluth looked over at him from where he was drowsing in the sun, a peaceful green color in his many-faceted eyes. 'It wouldn't have done you any good. I'm positive of that.'

She subsided, more out of confusion than because he had prevented her. There's something he knows that he won't tell me, Moreta thought. Marco stared hard at Moreta's face.

'I've had a great deal of time to think, Moreta. More than any man should have. And I've begun to believe that dragons can be immortal. I think that's why I'm still here with Duluth.'

'Immortal?'

'I mean, they do not age, as we do, nor do their bodies decay. They can live hundreds of turns.'

'But dragons can get injured in Threadfall and get sick,' Moreta protested, seizing on the one fact she did understand.

'Sure, but their organs don't degenerate, so technically, they could last as long as they want to. Usually, they last as long as their rider; because the bond between the two is so strong they don't wish to live after the rider is gone.' Marco paused and then, taking a deep breath, struggling to find the right words, continued. 'Dragonmen and, I guess other folk on Pern, have rules and beliefs they live by. Where I came from we had quite a few belief systems. Some were very useful; some were very misused. I won't go into all *that* now. But beyond everything, the one tenet the people of my world cherished was that there is a part of us that's more than bones and blood.'

When Moreta shook her head, more confused than ever, he went on.

'Don't you think we all have something about us that is special, different?' Marco asked. 'An essence that makes you different from everyone else?'

'I'm not very different from everyone else I know,' she said, almost defensively.

'Well, you are a queen rider,' he said, 'and your essence – power – and that of your dragon are eternally interlocked. You will never be parted.'

A tortured expression marred Moreta's pretty face. Marco's words were confusing her. All his talk of beliefs and blood and bones made her head reel. She needed to do something. Now! She feared she was wasting time.

'I'm apart from my dragon right now,' she said and walked toward Holth. 'If I can get back to Waterhole, I must go now.'

He followed her, glancing over at Duluth, who immediately struggled out of his comfortable sand wallow. Holth woke, startled, her eyes beginning to whirl with the orange-red of alarm.

What is wrong?

'No, dear, no dear, it's all right,' Moreta said. 'We're going back to Waterhole. I have to try to get back to Orlith. Somehow I'll get a message to Leri to join us.'

Leri. Holth echoed, a piteous tone tingeing her mental voice.

Moreta turned to Marco. 'You're sure I can make the journey back?'

Marco nodded slowly. 'Every one of us here can get back to their last point of entry. Just nowhere else – except of course Paradise River, because I can lead them in.' Heaving a sigh, he touched her arm in sympathy. 'You can't jump *now* to where you intended to go *then*.'

He shrugged into his worn riding jacket. 'We'll come with you – to guide you through.'

Holth moved slowly until Duluth leaned toward her, touching her muzzle. That revived the old queen. Moreta made much of her, patting her neck and murmuring suitable reassurances and endearments as she hauled herself onto the dragon's back.

'Now, you'd best visualize Waterhole just after dusk,' he said, securing his helmet and giving it a brief rub to settle over his hair. 'Me and Duluth will wait for you in *between* to help you get back here.'

Moreta held the landscape firm in her mind: the way the fences came to a point for the three fields and the hold off to the left; the way the lowering sun had caught sparkles from the grey-blue roof slates.

'Go on,' Marco said, showing her both hands with his thumbs pointed up.

'Let's go to Waterhole, Holth,' she said, and the queen, slithering a bit in the sand underfoot, managed a much more energetic ascent than her last two.

'Black, blacker, blackest,' Moreta mumbled out of habit as she felt the dragon's body lifting.

'You're ready to drop, Moreta,' Marco shouted and, before she could draw another breath, she and Holth dropped through the greyness and were out into fresh crisp air. Above them, Timor, the smaller moon, was just rising. A runnerbeast was shrieking at the top of its lungs, a grey-muzzled roan animal, his unusual markings gleaming in the moonlight. The other runners in the paddock were galloping around him in mindless terror. With neither Marco nor Duluth nearby Moreta was afraid.

Holth managed a graceful glide to their destination of the intersecting fence lines. Lights, warm and yellow from glowbaskets, were visible in the nearby hold. Moreta heard sudden shouts of fright. All the lights went out, as the hold door was slammed tight by whoever looked out to see why the runnerbeasts were shrieking. She was just about to nudge Holth to walk to the hold and see why they had been so frightened when the doorway opened again, a mere crack and a figure was silhouetted in the light.

'Who is it? Who goes there?' Moreta recognized the voice as Thaniel's.

'Moreta, of course, Thaniel,' she called, but he didn't seem to see her. Rusty shrieked again and Thaniel turned towards the sound.

'Stupid beast! There's no one here.' He swept his hand in a wide gesture as if he saw nothing but empty space. An empty space that Moreta was sure she filled.

'Thaniel! I'm here. Can't you see me?' she shouted as loud as she could, urging Holth to move forward.

Rusty increased his complaints, racing up and down the fenced enclosure, showing the whites of his eyes in terror.

'Shut your bawling!' Thaniel roared at Rusty. 'The riders looking for Moreta have all gone back to their weyrs. There's not a sign of a dragon in the sky.'

Moreta was stunned. She ought to have returned earlier. If he could hear that wretched creature, surely he could hear her shouting? She dismounted Holth quickly and ran up to Thaniel, to stand right in front of him. In fact, when he turned his head back in her direction, she had to take a step back or their noses would have touched. She reached out to grab his arm, and Thaniel immediately gave a visible shudder that ran from his dusty boots to his long hair.

He mumbled something Moreta couldn't hear and wrapped his arms about himself. 'Am I getting the plague after all?' he cried out loud.

'No, you old fool. I'm trying to make you see me,' Moreta answered. But he did not appear to hear her, though Rusty continued bawling and wheeling around his enclosure, stirring up the other animals. Thaniel turned abruptly, trembling, and ran back to his hold, slamming the door firmly behind him.

'Marco was right. How can I possibly communicate with him if he doesn't see or hear me? Moreta exclaimed as she marched back to Holth, and then vaulted to the dragon's back.

In the lights from the front window of the hold, Moreta could see that Thaniel still had his arms crossed in front of him – a recognizable stance of warding off fear.

They don't see us, Moreta, Holth said mournfully. *We went* between *but never arrived.*

Think hard about Fort Weyr, then, Holth, and take us there. Think of the mountain range behind the weyr. Think of the ledge on which you have lain so long, protecting Leri. Think of home, Holth. Take us there.

Moreta's last sentence was a wish as well as an order. Summoning strength from deep within, Holth leapt from the ground, her wings valiantly stroking her body upwards, and then they went *between*. It was cold and . . . grey, but not as bone-numbingly cold as before. And Moreta's litany did nothing to reassure her that they would come out at sunset above Fort Weyr, with the range of familiar mountains, the familiar bowl, and the ledges where dragons lay basking in the sunlight.

A vast shiver caught Moreta at the back of her neck, ran down her spine and to her toes. She leaned forward on Holth's neck, feeling the warmth of the dragon through her gloves and the cheek she laid against a neck ridge. They remained in between, and greyness stretched around her, merging in the distance with black.

'No luck, huh?' Marco appeared before them, edging Duluth forward.

'Thaniel was talking to himself, or his terrified runnerbeast, perhaps. He said riders had come back to look for me,' she said, trying to keep the panic she felt out of her voice. 'But he didn't see me.' She shivered again.

'Then let's go back to Paradise River – it's warmer there. We'll figure out what we can do,' Marco said, an air of optimism in his voice.

'What do you mean?' Moreta tried to keep the tension out of her tone.

'You said Thaniel was talking to himself, or his runnerbeast. And the beast was terrified?'

Moreta nodded her head.

'Although Thaniel didn't see you,' Marco continued, 'maybe his runnerbeast *did*. If you keep returning to Waterhole, terrifying the poor runner, Thaniel might start to wonder why.' He sounded as if he was containing some private amusement. .

'Keep returning to Waterhole?' Moreta repeated. 'Why?'

'Let me explain. On Earth some people believed they saw the "essence", if you will, of a person who had died. Some even claimed that the "essence" or "ghost" would return, again and again, to a favourite place.' He paused again as Moreta regarded him with incomprehension. 'Ghosts, they claimed, appeared in order to make the living do their bidding.'

'I don't know a thing about ghosts. But I know *I* don't want to go around scaring people,' she said dogmatically.

'Hell's bells, woman, you've done half the job already! You've scared the runnerbeast, probably scared Thaniel half to death, too. They know you're dead! You *have* to keep going back.'

'What?'

'You keep going back and maybe Thaniel will see you. Then maybe you can find a way to let him know what you want. It's the only option I can think of to reunite you with your dragon.'

'Should I go back to Waterhole now?'

'Hmmm, no, I think not. You should return at the same time every day – or night, better yet. Otherwise Thaniel will think his runner is quite mad. Go back tomorrow, same time. Now, you and Holth should come back to the beach.'

Moreta couldn't imagine how Marco's plan would work, but she followed him nonetheless. Marco urged his dragon aloft and then, with all the assurance of a long-term wingleader, pointed downwards and disappeared through the uneven floor of *between*.

'Tired, yes, she must have been very tired,' Leri said, and Kamiana wondered how many times the old Weyrwoman would have to go over the tragic events which had left her without her beloved dragon. This tragedy had aged the old Weyrwoman terribly. 'The plague was so virulent and we were short of dragons and riders. Orlith was fretting over her eggs and I was weary from the ache in my joints. They were both willing to complete the deliveries and I encouraged them. But,' and now her eyes flashed with a anger as well as tears, 'they *both* should have made it back to Fort, of all places.'

Leri groaned and reached for the cup that was always close to her badly twisted right hand. She sighed before she sipped – a long swallow, and then waited until it began to ease her pain.

'I do so completely desire all this to be over,' Leri said wearily. 'I'm tired of this old body. Orlith says if I stay until her clutch is ready to hatch, then she'll take me with her *between*.'

Kamiana bowed her head; she had no words of reply. She sat silently, a gentle hand resting on Leri's arm.

Footsteps sounded along the stone passageway outside Leri's quarters, and Kamiana heard someone clearing their throat. She rose quietly from her seat next to Leri's bed and went to the door.

'We have come to see Leri,' said Sh'gall. He gestured to Desdra, Lidora, Levalla, and the MasterHarper Tirone, all of whom stood quietly behind Sh'gall, concern and anxiety clearly stamped on their faces.

'Please, come in.' Kamiana gestured for them to enter. 'She is weary from the pain, tired of life, yet I think your visit would be welcome – to help pass the time . . .' She led the group into Leri's quarters, and the old Weyrwoman greeted them with a wave of her hand.

'I have been berating myself.' Leri said to those gathered around her. 'I should not have encouraged Moreta and Holth to deliver those vaccines. High Reaches was to cover Tillek and the small holds on the Telgar plains. But M'tani refused and so we split up the remaining loads. With all the queens flying in and out of the weyr, Orlith grew defensive of her eggs and would not leave them . . .' She paused, the terrible pain of her loss making her unable to continue.

'And Holth . . .' Kamiana continued for Leri, dropping her head in respect, 'volunteered.'

'At my urging,' Leri said sharply, and Kamiana nodded respectfully. 'Holth said she could do it. She knew I ached from our morning's runs and was eager to help Moreta finish the deliveries. She insisted!' She frowned at the memory. 'And I wished her well.' Tears overflowed her eyes and trickled down her lined face until Kamiana passed her a soft kerchief. 'Holth may have been old, but she was sure and steady.'

Kamiana exchanged looks with Tirone and Desdra. No one would ever know exactly what had happened to Moreta and Holth. Whatever the reason, both were now gone.

Leri straightened her bowed shoulders, not wanting the others to think her last statement was one of criticism. 'Not that Moreta wasn't one of the finest riders in our weyr. Remember the time she saved Kordeth when his dragon was so badly wing-scorched? Why, she and Orlith got so close to the pair that V'sen only had to swing over Orlith's back from his dragon. And they were able to ease Kordeth to the ground, too. No one but a top-flight rider could have done that!'

Everyone agreed: that mid-air rescue had been a sheer triumph. Both the rider and his blue dragon were still serving the weyr.

Leri fretted at her bed linens, fresh tears in her eyes. 'Will I for ever be lost to Holth, and Orlith to Moreta?' The beseeching look the old queen rider cast about her was too much for the assembled group to bear. The men shuffled their feet and the women hastily dabbed at their eyes; Kamiana was not the only person trying hard not to weep.

'It is something I have thought often about,' Sh'gall said quietly. 'When our lives as dragonriders are over, do we go on with our dragons to something else, or is this all we are?'

'I like to think that there is more for us, somewhere else.' Leri said wistfully, through her unchecked tears. 'Another part to this life. But I am just a foolish old woman, hoping I'll find my beloved *between*.'

'As to that,' Master Tirone cleared his throat, rocking back on his heels as he assumed an academic stance, 'we know only that it is an area of nothingness separating here from there. But there is –' He paused dramatically. 'More to it than we will ever know. Another dimension, perhaps, through which only the dragons may travel.'

'Another dimension?' Lidora looked startled.

'As height and width and depth are dimensions. *Between* may be another such.'

'But we don't know, do we?' Levalla, the Benden Weyrwoman, said in a puzzled tone.

'No, we don't and I'm not sure how that applies to this . . . situation,' said Sh'gall.

'Has Orlith heard Moreta?' Tirone asked hopefully, whipping his head around to stare in the direction of the Hatching Ground.

'She says not,' Leri replied. 'I asked her first,' she added in a tone that suggested Tirone shouldn't have intimated that Orlith hadn't been asked. 'She is devastated.' Then Leri drew a deep breath. 'Orlith and I shall go *between* as soon as the eggs are ready to hatch.'

There was furious dispute from everyone in the room.

'And why should I stay?' Leri demanded when Sh'gall had waved for silence. 'I had planned to leave anyway. Without my own dragon, I have no reason to stay, and much more for going.'

'Dear Leri, if your pain has worsened, I can increase the dose of fellis juice in your cup,' Desdra said, but Leri met her eyes.

'You haven't a palliative strong enough to ease my loss of Holth,' she said, almost angrily. 'It is no time to mourn,' she added, glancing at Lidora, who was weeping openly. 'There is a queen egg to hatch, and twenty-four others. They are our future and deserve all our care and devotion. Your care and devotion.' She stared hard at Kamiana, whose eyes were dimmed by the tears she did not shed. The younger Weyrwoman gently folded sympathetic arms about the old woman, careful not to squeeze her sore body.

'You have more courage than the rest of us, dear Leri.'

The second night Moreta and Holth returned to Waterhole, she tried a new tactic. Dismounting, she made her way directly to Rusty's paddock, where he was standing, front legs splayed, as he trumpeted his usual announcement about the proximity of a dragon.

'Boo!' Moreta shouted, leaning over the fence towards the runner.

Letting out a piercing squeal that made Moreta grab tightly to the top rail, Rusty kicked away from her, shooting pieces of dirt in all directions in his haste to flee.

Hearing the commotion, Thaniel appeared in the doorway. Rusty was rearing on his hind legs and striking out at some menace only he could see.

Now that Moreta had an audience, she took several steps backwards and then stood very still, waiting for Rusty to calm down. Then, aware that Thaniel might go back inside the house, she ran forward again until she was right under Rusty's nose.

'Boo!' she shouted again. He screeched, backing up as fast as he could move his feet. Then Moreta stepped back, which so confused the trembling old runner that he just watched her intently, evidently afraid of what she might do next.

He pawed the ground in front of him, as if daring her to come closer. But it was Thaniel who came closer, and he beckoned the runner-beast over.

'G'wan. Rusty, do your stuff!' Moreta shouted loudly. 'Can't you see Holth over there? You always shriek when there are dragons about. Let's hear it for old Holth!'

Quite willing to oblige, Holth moved from where she was standing. That did it. Rusty almost sat on his hindquarters in an effort to put distance between him and what his instincts told him was the bane of his existence. He cut some very fancy shapes on the ground and above it as he protested the dragon's presence.

Moreta saw Thaniel's incredulous expression.

But with that, he turned and walked back into his hold.

Moreta believed that Rusty had felt her presence and had looked at her, not through her. So there had to be some way to get Thaniel to understand what she wanted.

This time Marco wasn't waiting for her *between*. She took a few deep breaths to stifle her concern, but a twinge of fear added to the cold she was already feeling.

Holth, do you sense Duluth anywhere near?

Holth's concern doubled Moreta's. What would happen to them if they were forced to remain *between*? Where was Marco?

Holth, can you get us back to Paradise River? Moreta asked, already knowing the answer.

No, was the glum reply. *If I could go* between *as I used to do with no trouble, I could take us there by flying straight, but it's a long way from Waterhole.*

Moreta began to shiver, earnestly wanting the warmth at Paradise River to revive her. What would she and Holth do if Marco didn't come?

Then abruptly, she sensed movement in the air to her right and a dark shape loomed towards them.

'Sorry. You didn't take as long as I thought you would.' Marco said.

'Where were you?' she demanded. Then, contritely, she added: 'I was scared.'

'Ah, now, Moreta, you know I wouldn't leave you here.' Marco gestured expansively at the darkness around them. 'I went to check on some movement I saw.' He pointed over his shoulder in the direction from which he had come. 'Nothing.' He shrugged. 'I'm sorry for giving you and Holth a fright.'

With a nod, she accepted his apology.

'So how'd your haunting go today?' Marco asked when they had landed back at Paradise River Cove.

'Haunting?'

'That's a word we used on my homeworld to describe what you're trying to do.'

'Oh, I see,' she replied, and proceeded to fill him in. He was highly amused by her tale of saying 'boo' to Rusty and chided her for being so mean to a poor old runnerbeast.

'Right now, I'm glad that anything sees me.' She rubbed at her face. 'If only I could just give Thaniel a message.'

They were both watching their dragons sprawling in the hot white sands. He gestured for her to sit on the rocks surrounding the fire pit, where, he told her, he lit a fire every night because it was comforting.

'If I could just get him to see me once, Marco, I might get him to send a message of some sort,' she said as she jabbed aimlessly at the sand with a charred, broken stick.

'I wonder what will work.'

'Something has to. I can't keep "haunting" him forever. Thaniel is supposed to be smarter than Rusty.'

Marco leaned across and took the stick from her hand. With the end of it, he wrote a large M in the sand. 'I've never experienced anything like this before. No rider has ever been stuck *between* with the wrong dragon.' He rubbed his eyes, and continued. 'I really don't know if it'll work, but you *could* try writing a message for Thaniel in the dirt. What do you want to tell him?'

'Get Leri. Moreta.'

'That's short, sweet, and to the point. Let's hope he sees it,' Marco said.

And so Moreta returned again and again, every evening at the same time, until it became such a routine that Thaniel came out of his hold to stand by Rusty's enclosure as if he were waiting for her. And each evening Moreta performed the same scare tactics with Rusty and then scratched her message in the ground. It was obvious to Moreta that the runnerbeast saw her, stared straight at her, while she gouged her message in the dirt, but Thaniel still looked through her, oblivious to the message she wanted him to see.

She was at her wits' end by the fifth evening when the full moon suddenly burst from behind windswept clouds, outlining her form just long enough for Thaniel to see her as she scratched her message in the dirt.

'Moreta!' the old man gasped, then ran, shrieking as loudly as Rusty ever had, back to his hold and slammed the door shut.

'Now I think I've got him,' she said with great satisfaction as she remounted Holth.

How long are we going to have to keep doing this, Moreta? Holth asked plaintively.

Not for much longer, Holth. She caressed the old dragon's neck affectionately. *Let's go back to Marco in* between.

After Marco had guided them back to Paradise River Cove, she told him of her progress.

'You probably scared him so much he thinks he's going as mad as his runnerbeast.' Marco grinned. 'I think you're nearly there.'

It was the Runner Stationmaster himself who carried the message immediately to the weyr, for Leri from Thaniel of Waterhole Hold. Everyone read it: 'She comes every evening at the same time, just after sundown, when it's growing dark. She asks for Leri. What can I do?'

'Ha! We *are* stupid folk!' Leri said scathingly. 'Orlith! Aren't your eggs hard enough yet?'

A grumble echoed back from the Hatching Ground from Orlith, who was still fussing over a proper little mound of sand to raise her queen egg higher than the rest. She moved so slowly and carefully that it seemed as if she were putting each grain of sand in place individually. This, however, made her task seem too sadly pathetic to watch for very long.

'It's her way of passing time,' Leri had remarked when this was pointed out to her.

Now she thanked the Runner Stationmaster graciously for the personal delivery and slipped him a full Harper Hall credit for his trouble.

'My pleasure, Weyrwoman. May I send back a message for you?'

'That would be most kind of you,' Leri said with great dignity, and hastily the Stationmaster took out a small pad and writer.

'Give him my thanks and say we shall be there soon. He can do nothing, like us, but wait until Orlith decides the eggs are ready to hatch. My thanks for your trouble.'

The Stationmaster bowed himself out of the weyr.

It was before dawn one morning not long after, that Orlith informed Leri that her eggs would undoubtedly hatch that day. With gentle wing strokes, she rolled the queen egg to its special mound, while Leri waited in her weyr, dressed in her warmest clothing.

'Not that warm clothing will do much good in *between*,' she remarked in her acerbic way, and hobbled to the entrance to her weyr without a backwards glance. She looked up towards the skies; a magnificent dawn would soon break. 'Just the day to start the rest of my journey,' she said.

I hope this day is not marred by any unnecessary sadness, Orlith. A Hatching Day is to look to the future, not to regret the past.

Thaniel had remained at Waterhole Hold that day to bake bread. He needed to keep busy. The whole affair had already turned his hair white but, nonetheless, when the Stationmaster brought back Leri's reply, he felt his ordeal might soon be over. Ignoring his children's pleas to join them on their rounds to check the herds, Thaniel was determined to remain by his hold waiting for Leri. At his father's suggestion, Maynar saddled Rusty and rode off with his siblings.

With Rusty gone, Thaniel was not aware that a dragon and rider had landed at the nearby waterhole. But when he looked up from his work, he saw the great gold queen, and Leri, huddled in furs, on the dragon's back. Quickly he took a piece of fresh, hot bread and a cup of klah to the waiting Weyrwoman, who thanked him and ate willingly. He was sorry to see how gnarled the old woman's fingers were and how awkwardly she held her body.

'If there is aught else I may do for you, Weyrwoman, you have but to call me and I will come,' Thaniel said.

'I am well enough as I am,' Leri replied in her brisk way, returning the empty plate to the holder.

Thaniel went back to his work, but kept an eye on the pair from the window as he kneaded the second batch of dough. He was clearing off the last of the flour from the worktop when he noticed that the sun was beginning to sink. So he poured himself another cup of klah, wondering whether he should bring more out to the old rider before he realized he had already poured two. He took one out to Leri, who thanked him for his thoughtfulness but sipped so slowly that Thaniel, whose bad leg was aching after the day's baking, returned to his house, to rest himself for what else might happen on this unusual day.

It was about an hour later when the second dragon appeared. Thaniel let out a deep sigh when he heard the glad cries from the women, and the loud trumpeting of the dragons

The reunions brought tears to Thaniel's eyes as he looked on from the doorway. Moreta leapt from the back of Holth and ran to Orlith. She caressed her queen's head, touching the pale gold neck with great tenderness as she gazed adoringly into faceted eyes that whirled bright blue with happiness. Leri dropped her cup and walked as quickly as she was able to meet Holth; she hugged her dragon's neck fervently, as a newly Impressed weyrling would. Thaniel later said that he thought his heart would break at the old Weyrwoman's joy.

'I never thought I'd see you again, dear heart,' Leri said amid tears of joy, while her fingers remembered the texture of Holth's wattling hide.

The two weyrwomen spoke quietly to each other in the first light of the rising moon. What they said Thaniel would never know, but when he saw Leri settled, with some difficulty, on her dragon, he hurried out to them.

'Thank you, Holder Thaniel, for having the wit to know what we needed. The Weyrs will always be grateful to you and your family, as will Orlith and I.' Moreta's voice, though faint, was full of warmth as she spoke to the old holder, regarding him intently. Then she turned her attention back to Leri.

'Now, we are matched correctly,' she said with an air of intense satisfaction.

Just then, Orlith jerked her head upright, swinging her eyes around in the direction of Fort Weyr. She gave a triumphant bugle, which Holth echoed.

'The queen egg has hatched; her name is Hannath and her rider is Oklina! Oh, I am pleased! Good news makes even the longest journey easier.'

'Young Alessan's sister has Impressed?' Leri said. 'I told you there was rider blood in Ruatha Hold.'

'Well, I am glad,' Moreta repeated. She squared her shoulders, putting all other thoughts from her head. She could not think of Alessan now. She turned to Leri. 'We can go now, together, you and I, Orlith and Holth.'

She urged her dragon into motion. 'Just the one more trip *between*, Orlith,' she said. 'And I mean that.'

The dragon nodded her head once and, wheeling away from Holth, trotted a few paces to spring upwards. Holth was right behind her, a front foot clipping the klah mug that Leri had dropped, scattering the pieces about. The tired old queen just managed to clear the ground and was into the air, urged on by her own eager rider. Both dragons were soon high enough so that their wings could sweep downwards in a magnificent ascent. Emblazoned in the full moonlight, the two queen riders raised their right arms high above their heads, punching the air with clenched fists. Thaniel held his breath as suddenly both dragons disappeared *between*.

Thaniel wished them well, as his tears at last brimmed over. He bent to pick up the handle that was all that remained of the mug. He suddenly felt reassured for the first time in many years. Perhaps there was some other place he would go eventually; some place he did not yet know. Some place where he might even see his beloved wife again. He slipped the broken handle into his apron pocket and patted it – a keepsake by which to remember Moreta.

THE RIFTWAR

RAYMOND E. FEIST

THE RIFTWAR
RAYMOND E. FEIST

THE RIFTWAR SAGA:
Magician (1982, revised edition 1992)
Silverthorn (1985)
A Darkness at Sethanon (1986)

THE EMPIRE TRILOGY (with Janny Wurts):
Daughter of the Empire (1989)
Servant of the Empire (1990)
Mistress of the Empire (1992)

STAND-ALONE RIFTWAR-RELATED BOOKS:
Prince of the Blood (1989)
The King's Buccaneer 1992)

THE SERPENTWAR SAGA:
Shadow of a Dark Queen (1994)
Rise of a Merchant Prince (1995)
Rage of a Demon King (1997)
Shards of a Broken Crown (1998)

THE RIFTWAR LEGACY:
Krondor: the Betrayal (1998)
Krondor: the Assassins (1999)
Krondor: Tear of the Gods (2000)

CONCLAVE OF SHADOWS:
Tales of the Silver Hawk (2003)
King of Foxes (2004)
Magician's Son (2005)

Raymond E. Feist's Riftwar fantasy series begins with the adventures of two boys, Pug and Tomas, each wishing to rise above his lowly station in life. Pug desires to become a magician, Tomas a great warrior. Each achieves his dream through outside agencies and his own natural abilities; Pug is kidnapped during the Riftwar, discovered to have magic abilities, and is trained to greatness. Tomas stumbles upon a dying dragon who gives him a suit of armour imbued with an ancient magic, turning him into a warrior of legendary might.

As Pug and Tomas undergo their transformations and become more adept at controlling the powers that have been granted them, the scope of the novel expands to reveal more about the two worlds upon which the conflict known as the Riftwar takes place: Midkemia and Kelewan. Midkemia is a young world, vibrant and conflict-ridden, while Kelewan is ancient and tradition-bound, but no freer of conflict. The militaristic Tsurani, from Kelewan, have invaded the Kingdom of the Isles on Midkemia to expand their domain and seize metals common on Midkemia but rare at home. The only way open between these worlds is a magic Rift, and through that portal in space-time the invaders have established a foothold in the Kingdom. Gradually Tomas learns that he has become invested with the power of a Valheru, one of the mystical creatures who are legends in Midkemia. The Dragon Lords were near-godlike beings who once warred with the gods themselves. The action in the first trilogy comes to a climax in *A Darkness at Sethanon*, with the resolution of the war between the Kingdom and the invading Tsurani, Tomas gaining control over the ancient magic that sought to conquer him, and Pug returning to the homeland of his youth.

The Empire Trilogy concerns itself with conflict back on the Tsurani homeworld, where for much of the first and second book we see 'the other side of the Riftwar'. Lady Mara of the Acoma, a girl of seventeen in the first book, is thrust into a murderous game of politics and ritual, and only through her own genius and ability to mprovise does she weather unrelenting attacks on all sides. Aided by a loyal group of followers, including a Kingdom slave named Kevin, whom she comes to love more than any other, Mara rises to dominate the Empire of Tsuranuanni, even facing down the mighty Great Ones, the magicians who are outside the law.

The Serpentwar Saga is the story of Erik, the bastard son of a noble, and Roo, a street boy who is his best friend. The Kingdom again faces invaders, but this time from across the sea. The story of the two young men is set against the Kingdom's hurried preparation for and resistance against a huge army under the banner of the Emerald Queen, a woman who is another agent of dark forces seeking dominion over the world of Midkemia. More of the cosmic nature of the battle between good and evil is revealed and Pug and Tomas again have to take a hand in the struggle.

The Riftwar Legacy series contains three novels regarding events taking place a few years following the Riftwar, featuring more adventures of Jimmy Locklear, Prince Arutha and other characters from the original series.

Legends of the Riftwar are novels set in the period of the original Riftwar series, but featuring new characters in different locations, revealing more intimate stories that took place during that epic conflict.

Feist sees Midkemia as an objective, virtual world, even though a fictional one. He regards all the tales set in Midkemia as historical novels and stories of this fantastic realm. 'The Messenger' is a tale from the middle years of the Riftwar, when the war had turned into a struggle along a stable front.

THE MESSENGER

BY RAYMOND E. FEIST

The wind whipped the trees.

Their branches swayed and creaked in protest as the last brown leaves of the fall were sent flying. The shushing sound of the pines and firs as their needle-laden branches seemed to wave in protest was a forlorn harbinger of long winter nights and frigid days rapidly approaching.

Outside the command tents, soldiers huddled close to their camp-fires. Snow should be weeks away, but many of the local men could sense an early winter was coming. The cold cut through padded over-jackets like a blade of ice. Soldiers who had put all their undergarments on as well as two or even three pairs of stockings – forcing their feet into their boots – were complaining of numb toes if their feet got wet. Locals knew it was going to be a bad winter. Many turned their eyes skywards, anticipating the first flakes that would surely fall soon. This winter would come early, would come hard and linger too long.

The foothills of the Grey Tower Mountains were rarely forgiving to men caught exposed when the weather turned suddenly, and the soldiers of the Kingdom of the Isles were equipped to deal with all but this harshest of seasons. They expected to be back in the cities of Yabon province when winter's full fury was unleashed, billeted in barracks and houses, warm before fireplaces and protected from the snow piling up outside their windows. But the experienced veterans knew that unless the weather turned a more gentle aspect their way soon, the columns of soldiers soon leaving the front would be marching through thigh-high drifts of snow as they reached LaMut City, Ylith and Yabon. Some wounded who might make it back home in a more normal season would surely not survive such a march.

All around the camp a sense of anticipation was building, for surely the Dukes conducting this war would realize an early and hard winter was soon upon them and the fighting would stop. The commissary chief and his cooks and helpers, the Quartermaster and the boys in the luggage who were inspecting the scant remaining weapons and clothing available to the soldiers, all paused from time to time to look at the sky, to sense the coming weather and to ask, is it time to go home? The armourer held up a dented cavalryman's breastplate to inspect what could be done to mend it, while his apprentice fed coal into the hearth; both wondered if the armour would be needed, for it must be time to go home, wasn't it? Soldiers nursing wounds in the infirmary tents, the cavalry in their tents and the mercenaries in their bedrolls and bundles who slept in whatever shelter they could find, all wondered, is it time to go home?

Inside the command tent, Vandros der LaMut looked at the orders that had just arrived and nodded in agreement.

He looked to his senior captain, Petir Leyman, and said, 'We're going home for the winter. Orders from Dukes Brucal and Borric.'

'About time,' said the rangy captain. He blew on his hands for emphasis, even though his heavily padded gauntlets kept his fingers warm enough. Then he grinned. 'I'll ensure we have ample firewood put by back at the castle, m'lord.' He lost his smile. 'This is feeling like a bad winter coming.'

The Earl of LaMut looked out the open tent flap, past the brazier which kept him relatively warm and said, 'We'll have plenty of snow to push through by the time I'm called to the Commander's Muster up in Yabon.' He sighed, barely audible, but a sign nevertheless. 'Assuming I can get there. This feels like a bad winter, indeed.'

Leyman nodded.

Vandros stood up and said, 'I need a messenger to ride to the forward positions.'

He crossed to the field map on his command table and pointed, 'These three positions, Gruder here, Moncrief here, and Summerville there.' His finger stabbed each location. 'I need them to withdraw in order. It's cold enough the Tsurani should be pulling back to their own winter billets.'

'Should is a dangerous word, m'lord.'

'Agreed, but they've never moved against us once the snows start. They're just as cold out there as we are, and they've been around long enough to know that snow is only days away. They'll retreat to their own winter camps.'

'They should do us all a favour and stay there come spring, m'lord.'

Vandros nodded. 'Send word to Swordmaster Argent we're starting the withdrawal. I'll follow in a day or two with the rear guard.'

'And tell whomever you send to be careful,' Vandros added. 'I've got a report of a Minwanabi patrol-in-force that's somehow wandered off course and got itself lost east of the King's Highway, north of LaMut. No one's sure where they've gone, but they're certain to turn up at the most inconvenient time.'

Leyman said, 'Yes, m'lord.'

'And send a messenger to me,' he added as the captain left the tent.

Vandros reflected while waiting for the messenger. He had been a young officer in his father's court, a Captain of Calvary, the Light Horse, the most dashing unit of soldiers in Yabon. Vandros remembered with a sense of age beyond his years the harsh education the Tsurani had provided. After years of bloody warfare, all illusions of war's glory were dispelled.

The Tsurani, aliens from another world – though it had taken a long time for more than one Kingdom noble to finally accept the reality of that fact – had reached the world of Midkemia via a rift, a magic doorway though space, that brought them to the Kingdom of the Isles. As fortune had it, they had landed in a high valley, up in the Grey Tower Mountains. The good news was that that made it difficult for the Tsurani to strike quickly outside the valley. The bad news had been that it made it nearly impossible for the Kingdom to dig them out of their foothold high among the peaks.

Tough, unrelenting fighters, the Tsurani wore brightly coloured armour made of some alien material, bone or hide or something unknown on Midkemia, fashioned by unknown crafts to a hardness near that of metal. They had attacked without warning the first spring of the war, seven years earlier, and had swept down from the mountains to claim a large area of both the Kingdom of the Isles and the Free Cities of Natal.

The war had been a veritable stalemate for all its seven years, since the first campaign. Vandros shook his head slightly as he considered the seemingly endless fight. He had been Earl for five of those years, and things had gone from bad to worse. Three years earlier the Tsurani had launched an offensive against Crydee, to the west, attempting to wrest the entire Far Coast from the Kingdom, by moving down from the northernmost stronghold, but the siege had failed. Since then, a stalemate.

While they were holding their own militarily, the cost was staggering, with taxes rising every year and fewer soldiers to be recruited. It was so bad this last year Vandros had been forced to hire mercenaries to supplement his levies to the Duke of Yabon. A few had proven worthwhile, but most of them were little more than bodies to throw in front of Tsurani swords.

And the weather. He had lived here all his life and he knew this was going to be a punishing winter. Blizzards were not uncommon during the coldest months of winter in the region, but today the air felt as if a blow could come at any moment. The Duke's order to withdraw to winter billets was coming none too early, in Vandros's opinion.

The messenger appeared at the tent door. 'M'lord?' he said as a means to announce himself.

'Come in, Terrance.'

The young man came to stand before the Earl and snapped to attention. He wore the traditional LaMutian uniform of the Messenger Corps. A round fur cap, flat on top, sporting a shining golden badge of the corps on one side, perched on his head at just the correct, jaunty angle. The forest-green jacket was cut at the waist, and bedecked with gold braid at the shoulders and sleeves, with six pairs of golden buttons down the front. The messengers wore tight-fitting grey riding trousers with a full leather seat, tucked into low riding boots of black leather. Each man carried a cavalry sabre and a belt knife, but little else. Vandros knew the rider would have a heavy coat he'd wear over the rig, once he was on the trail, but otherwise he carried only one ration of oats for his horse, and a water skin. Speed was the hallmark of the Messenger Corps.

Vandros looked at this particular messenger with a slight twinge of irritation. He was a distant cousin, his grandfather's great-nephew, and had used his relationship to the Earl to worm his way into the army at what Vandros considered too young an age, despite the objections of his mother. The boy was just too young and inexperienced. Still, he was here, and there was nothing the Earl could do about it that wouldn't dishonour the family. Terrance was barely sixteen years of age, one of those children born just weeks before the Midsummer's Day when his first birthday was celebrated. He still didn't need to shave.

But there were boys younger serving, Vandros reminded himself, and the Messenger Corps was not the same as serving with the Light Horse or the Heavy Lancers. The boy was a fair swordsman on or off horseback, so he could have been easily assigned to a unit at the front. Only his exceptional skill as a rider elevated him out of the cavalry, for only the finest riders in Yabon served in the Duke's Messenger Corps.

'Your turn?'

'Yes, m'lord,' said Terrance. 'Captain Leyman sent for two of us, and Williamson Denik was next, so he's riding to LaMut, and I was after, so here I am.'

Messengers served in rotation, and no captain or noble could change that without earning the messengers' ire. Every group within the army had its traditions. And this one made sense, for without it, certain senior messengers would take only the easy runs, along safe roads, leaving the more hazardous duty to newer riders.

Vandros said nothing for a moment. He wished he had known his young, if distant, cousin had been near the top of the rotation, for he could have instructed Petir to order Williamson to the command tent, then sent Terrance on to LaMut and relative safety.

Vandros pushed aside these thoughts and pointed to the map. Terrance knew the map as well as the Earl did: it was a section map, showing the entire campaign area and some of the surrounding countryside.

No one knew why, exactly, the Tsurani had invaded. Attempts at parley had been repulsed, and the best reasons for the invasion were still only speculation. The one finding the most favour among the nobles of the Kingdom was a Tsurani desire for metal. From the scant intelligence gathered from captured Tsurani slaves – the soldiers died fighting or killed their wounded before retreating – metal was very rare in most forms on their homeworld. Still, Vandros found that explanation lacking. Too many men had died without strategic gain for it to be over something as simple as metal. There had to be another reason; they just didn't know what it was.

Terrance looked at the map, each mark and line memorized already. The region shown was bordered on the west by the Grey Tower Mountains. To the west lay the Duchy of Crydee, and the shores of the Endless Sea. But those areas were under the command of Prince Arutha and the barons of Carse and Tulan, and of no concern to Earl Vandros. His area of operation was limited to the border between the Duchy of Yabon, along the former border of the Free Cities, and into the foothills of the Grey Towers.

Vandros's index finger stabbed at three locations on the map, one to the south west of their present locations, another due south of that, and one slightly south west of the second. Those three bases, along with Vandros's headquarters camp, were the foundation of the Kingdom's defensive line throughout the region. Forces from any of the four camps could quickly respond to any Tsurani offensive.

But they were impossible to supply during the harsh winters of the region, forcing the Kingdom to withdraw each season as the snows came.

'Messages to Barons Gruder, Moncrief and Summerville: inform them it's time to withdraw.' He gave specific instructions on who was to pull out first, how he wanted the order of march, and when he expected them to reach their designated city for billeting during the winter.

Terrance studied the map, committing his route to memory, and said, 'Yes, m'lord. I have it memorized.'

Vandros knew better than to ask him to repeat the orders, for he knew he would hear them back exactly as he had given them. Besides being a good rider, having an accurate memory was a requirement for the corps. While some reports and documents were sent by messenger, all military orders were given orally, so documents might not fall into the enemy's hands should a rider be killed.

'Staged, orderly withdrawal. Defensive combat only,' said the Earl. That meant an order to the field commanders to avoid conflict with any Tsurani units if possible while they retreated eastwards. The assumption being the Tsurani would not be looking to gain territory this late in the season; rather, they would be seeking out warm winter shelter for themselves.

'Staged, orderly withdrawal. Defensive combat only,' repeated the messenger.

Vandros said, 'You sound a bit stuffy, there? Are you fit to ride?'

'Just a bit of a cold, m'lord. Nothing to speak of.'

'Then go,' said Vandros. 'And, Terry?'

'Yes, m'lord,' said the youngster at the tent flap.

'Stay alive. I have no wish to have to explain to your mother how I got you killed.'

With a boyish grin, he replied, 'I'll do my best, sir.'

Then he was gone.

Vandros pondered sending someone so young into harm's way, then resigned himself to the fact that this was the essence of command, and that he had sent many young men and boys into harm's way in the five years he had been Earl. And while he would rather Terrance was riding to LaMut, there was probably little danger of his being exposed to enemy action this late in the year. The Tsurani were probably trying to stay warm as much as his own men were. He stopped worrying about Terrance, and started thinking about the order of march for the bulk of his army, billeted right outside this tent.

He could hear them talking and laughing as he sat down at his table.

As was usual, Terrance endured the taunting jokes and laughter of the regulars in the camp as he walked towards his tent. 'Isn't that one pretty!' exclaimed a grizzled veteran. 'I think I'll keep it as me pet!'

The men around the campfire laughed, and Terrance resisted the impulse to say anything. He had been cautioned by the older messengers when he had first joined the corps the previous spring that such taunting was common. The messengers were seen to have what the others thought was a 'cushy' billet, for often they could be seen sitting around their tents for days, waiting for orders to ride. Of course in a battle they could be riding constantly, with little or no sleep and scant food, having to negotiate their way though the heart of combat to take messages to field commanders. But then the other soldiers were too busy keeping alive to notice the comings and goings of the messengers.

Terrance was tall for his age, a little more than six feet in height and just starting to develop a man's broad shoulders and back. But he was blond and blue-eyed, and his beard refused to do more than dust his lips and chin with a faint blond fuzz, much to his irritation, for it was tradition among the Messenger Corps to grow a moustache and chin beard, what they called a 'goatee'. Terrance had attempted to grow one, but had started shaving again after a month, as his looked ridiculous. The other messengers had not spared him from their teasing, but several had said privately that the beard would come and not to worry. Shaving would even encourage it to grow faster, several had suggested.

Terrance found keeping silent and his expression blank served him well, for he hated the thought that anyone might see how uncertain he felt at times. He knew after his first month in service that he had overreached himself, but throughout the seven months he had been with the corps, he had faced little true danger. Still, he couldn't shake the constant worry that he might break under pressure or somehow fail, both justifying his family's condemnation of his enlisting in the service so young and bringing disgrace to them all, including the Earl. He just hadn't thought of that responsibility at the time, and now he regretted having acted rashly.

Perhaps with a successful year under his belt, spending the winter with his family on their estate outside LaMut, he might gain the confidence he feigned. At least with a safe return home, his mother might stop her constant message writing and demand he return at once.

Terrance reached the tent he shared with Charles McEvoy, from Tyr-Sog, and found Charles lying on his bedroll, on the cold ground, reading a message.

'From Clarise?' asked Terrance as he entered.

'Yes,' said the other young man, four years Terrance's senior. 'You've got the run?'

'It's my turn,' said Terrance.

'Where to, Terry?'

With a grin, the younger boy leaned over and said, 'The three staging points. Orders to the barons for home. You'll be back with Clarise in a couple of weeks. Winter withdrawal.'

The older rider sat up. 'About time. It's cold enough to freeze my manhood off! Then what use would I be to her?'

Terrance laughed. Charles had wed the winter before and had been away from his wife since the last spring thaw. 'The question is, what use are you to her now?'

'Get out of here!' said the older rider with a playful swipe of his hand.

Terrance said, 'Just need to get my coat and ride.'

'Ride safe, Terry,' said Charles in the traditional farewell of the messengers.

'Ride safe, Charlie,' Terrance returned as he departed his tent.

He hurried to where his horse was staked at the picket. She was a nine-year-old bay, with a sure foot and quick response. She wasn't the fastest animal in the corps, but Terrance loved her even temper and stamina. She would run all day if he asked her, and collapse without complaint. He called her Bella.

She picked up her head as he neared, and while a couple of the other mounts nickered in question, she knew it was her rider approaching and that it would be her turn to run today. He patted her neck and said, 'Let's be off, girl.'

He moved to the saddle rack, under a shed roof on four poles a few yards behind the picket, and got his saddle. He quickly tacked up the horse and made sure he had a full water skin and a bag of oats. The trip should take only two days, one out to the first staging point, where he would sleep the night and get whatever food the camp had to offer, then one day back, circling to the south west, then south east, stopping at the other two staging points on the way back. He glanced at the sky. It was only two hours after sunrise, so the trip should be an easy one if he didn't encounter any troubles. He should be back by sundown tomorrow.

He untied his horse, mounted up and started riding west. Once outside the camp, after Bella had warmed up, he settled into a rocking canter and let her do the work.

*   *   *

The wind was cutting through his greatcoat and his face was numb. His nose was running freely, and he had given up wiping it with the back of his sleeve. Now it was completely stuffed and he was forced to breath through his mouth, which was starting to irritate his lungs. His chest felt tighter than it had early in the day. He knew he could have begged off riding for a serious illness, but to have stepped aside for something as simple as a cold was unthinkable. Yet there was a nagging doubt that this was what he should have done, simply told the Captain of Messengers he was too ill to ride and stayed in his tent.

Terrance had stopped twice since midday to take shelter while he rested Bella. He stood shivering behind a stand of birch trees, which cut the wind a little, while the horse rested. It wasn't good to linger too long in those conditions, as Bella would stiffen up and that increased the chance of her pulling up lame.

Still, she was a fine horse, reliable and level-headed, the perfect mount for a messenger. She would obey his commands and react quickly. And she was calm; earlier in the summer he had paused on trail and looked down to see a viper slithering towards the horse. Many animals would have responded with panic, yet Bella had calmly lifted one hoof and crushed the snake before it could react.

He mounted up after she was rested and headed towards his first destination. Glancing skywards, he realized he had fallen behind schedule and resisted the urge to gallop. He would reach the camp a few hours later than anticipated, but the message would still arrive in a timely fashion and he would have a hot meal and a relatively warm billet. He knew that if the wind didn't relent, tomorrow's ride would be more punishing, for he had two camps, higher in the foothills and closer to the enemy lines, to visit.

He kept his mind on the task at hand, getting through the woodlands, avoiding the few Tsurani patrols sweeping the frontier before the winter snows fell, and not letting his horse come to harm. On foot he would risk freezing to death during the night, for it would take him until midday tomorrow to reach the first camp.

After two hours of steady riding, he again rested Bella, though she snorted in protest at having to endure walking with him in the lead, when she knew oats, hay and the relative warmth behind a windbreak with other horses were waiting at the end of this ride.

A half-hour's walk and he mounted up again. He urged Bella to a steady canter and kept his eyes moving around the landscape. It was easy to be lulled into daydreaming or drawn into looking at one feature of the landscape. A messenger was nearly the most vulnerable member of the Duke's army, second only to the boys who rode in the luggage and served with the commissary. Two or three armed men in ambush and the Earl's orders would never reach his barons.

Three hours before sunset he saw movement to the north. A hint of colour in the tree line and nothing more, but it was enough. A Tsurani patrol, without a doubt, for the bright orange trim used by those invaders called Minwanabi on their black armour was found in no natural plant in these forests, as was the scarlet and yellow of those called Anasati. He urged Bella to a faster pace and sought more signs of the invaders, but the forests revealed nothing.

He kept alert the remainder of the day, and didn't relax until he was within minutes of his first objective.

As he approached the first camp, he could smell the smoke from the campfires, as the wind blew right into his face. He welcomed the acrid sting of it, and knew he was only a few minutes from rest.

He heard a sentry shout, 'Rider coming in!'

Had he been on foot, Terrance most probably would have been challenged a half-dozen times since leaving the contested woodlands and entering Kingdom-held territory, but the Tsurani had no horses, so a rider was never challenged. Terrance wondered why over the years the Tsurani had never trained riders to use captive horses, but as no one he knew had spoken to a living Tsurani, he was left to wonder.

Terrance knew the location of the commander's tent, and rode there. The frontier was being held by soldiers from Yabon province, bolstered by levies from as far south as the Southern Marches. This commander was Baron Gruder, one of Duke Sutherland's men put under the Earl's command. Terrance had spoken with him three times since becoming a messenger and found him a no-nonsense type, very straight to the point, and utterly lacking in any social skills.

A guard ushered him into the command tent, while another took Bella to the windbreak where the remounts were kept. LaMutian lancers were billeted here, as well as a company of light cavalry from Zun. Two companies of heavy foot from Ylith and Tyr-Sog rounded out this army, and they had spent a long hard year fighting the Tsurani and their Cho-ja allies, or 'Bugs' as the men from the south had come to call them.

Terrance came to stand before the Baron and said, 'Orders from the Earl, m'lord.'

'Well, are we to withdraw?' said the stout Gruder, his face showing that he already anticipated the order.

'Yes, m'lord. You're to withdraw in orderly stages, to the winter billets assigned to you by the Duke.' The politics of the Kingdom's Western Realm made minor nobles jealous of their prerogatives, and this Gruder had been voluble about being seconded to a 'foreign' Earl, so the messengers had learned to refer to orders coming from Dukes Brucal and Borric as often as they could, to keep the Baron from another rant. Terrance was nearly frozen, and starving, and was eager to avoid another long diatribe regarding Vandros's leaving Gruder here without enough men, food, weapons, gold and anything else he judged necessary to the conduct of his portion of the war. 'Defensive combat only.'

'Anything else?'

'About three hours ago I glimpsed movement in the trees north of the trail from the east. The colours were Tsurani.'

'Could you tell who?'

'Minwanabi and Anasati, my lord.'

Gruder considered this silently for a moment. 'From what our intelligence tells us, those two Houses don't like each other very much. They must be up to something to be marching under a unified command. I'll have to keep an eye out.'

'Sir,' said Terrance, as neutrally as possible. He wondered how the Kingdom had come to learn anything about the Tsurani, given that they preferred death to capture, but kept his curiosity in check; he was there to carry messages, not to interpret or understand them.

The Baron looked at the messenger as if realizing he was still there and said, 'Very well. Get some food and rest, then carry on. We'll begin the withdrawal at first light.'

As Terrance left the command tent, he heard the Baron shout for an orderly. The page would be carrying word to the officers along the line in minutes. Terrance glanced skywards as the light faded. Clouds were coming in fast from the west and while sunset was just commencing, it was rapidly getting dark.

That meant the clouds were heavy with moisture and judging from the cold, it wouldn't be rain that came down that night, but snow. Terrance wanted a hot meal and to rest, but first he would check the remounts to see how Bella was being cared for, and then he would take care of himself.

As he headed towards the remounts, moisture touched his cheek and again he glanced skywards. A scattering of flakes was beginning to fall. He paused a moment, while soldiers hurried past him and the activity in the camp increased as word to prepare to withdraw for the winter was passed.

As the mood of the men around him brightened, for many would be home for the winter within a few days, Terrance felt a dark concern rise up inside; if the snows fell heavily tonight, his second day would be difficult, and he might have to remain at the third camp before returning to the Earl's command position. Silently he wished Killian – the goddess of nature – would hold off the snows for another day at least. Glancing at the faces of the men eager to be home, he amended that thought; a week would be better.

He brought himself out of his reflection and moved off to find his horse.

The groom had taken good care of Bella, and she snorted a greeting as she looked up from a pile of hay. Terrance still went through the process of inspecting her feet, ensuring she was properly dried, and was pleased she had been afforded a relatively warm spot behind the windbreak rather than being tied to the picket line at the ends, outside the shelter.

Then Terrance realized there were fewer horses than should have been tied down. He turned to the groom. 'Big patrol out?'

'No,' said the old soldier. 'We've just lost a lot of lads this year.' He motioned with his chin at the far end of the line. 'Lot of horses, too.'

Terrance nodded, and patted Bella's neck. 'Thank you for taking care of her.'

'That's the job,' he said, moving off.

Terrance smiled, and turned away. He hurried to the mess tent and got into line behind a young officer of horses. He was handed a wooden plate and a metal cup by a kitchen boy as it was obvious from Terrance's uniform who he was; most of the soldiers in the line had their own plate and cup which they kept with their gear in their tents.

The food was hot and filling, if unremarkable, and the tea was bitter, but also hot. He ate alone, sitting on the ground under the lee side of the tent. As was usual, most of the soldiers ignored him. When he was finished, he returned the plate and cup to the boy in the tent, then set out to find a place to sleep.

As a messenger, he was expected to find a billet where he could, and often that meant sleeping on the ground with only a saddle for a pillow and his greatcoat for a blanket. Most of the year that was acceptable, but the cold tonight would make it impossible.

As he was approaching the row of tents used by the cavalry, Terrance coughed and suddenly found himself unable to control a wracking attack. He reached out and gripped the bole of a tree, half bent over, and forced himself to breathe deeply, then brought up a large amount of nasty green phlegm. He spat and grimaced at the bitter sulphur taste at the back of his throat and the itching that had turned into a hot soreness. 'Damn,' he said softly. He was getting far sicker than he had thought and he still had a day's ride ahead, perhaps more if the weather turned worse, before he could return to the Earl's camp and get a cure from the apothecary who served in the infirmary. Still, there was nothing for it but to soldier on.

He moved to the first line of tents, and began asking, 'Have you room?' The first half-dozen queries netted him negative replies, but at the seventh tent he found a single cavalryman who looked at him for a moment, then nodded.

Terrance moved into the tent and looked down at the empty bedding, separated from the reclining cavalryman by the tent's support pole. 'Go ahead,' said the man, his words accompanied by a slight shrug. 'He won't need it.'

Terrance didn't ask who 'he' was, as it was obviously a fallen comrade. He sat down and exchanged glances with the cavalryman. The man was at least ten years Terrance's senior, but looked twice that. His eyes were sunken and rimmed with red, as if he hadn't slept in days, and dark circles accentuated the appearance of a deep-in-the-bones fatigue.

Terrance said, 'Just get in?'

'Yesterday,' said the man. 'Caught a Tsurani patrol-in-force out in the open . . .' His voice trailed off and he felt back on his own sleeping mat. 'Our captain didn't realize we'd charged just the vanguard until the rest of them came roiling out of the trees. It was a close thing.'

'Combined force? More than one House?'

The man nodded. 'Our thirty against their hundred or more. It wasn't pretty.' He sighed. 'Don't think me rude, but I need sleep. We ride out again tomorrow.'

Terrance resisted the impulse to tell the man he would get new orders in the morning, for it wasn't his place to do so. He just said, 'Sleep well,' but the man was already breathing deeply and evenly.

Terrance untied the cord that kept the tent flap open, letting the flap fall into place; he then pulled the thick blanket around him as he settled down on the thin sleeping mat. The blanket was sour with another man's sweat and dirt, and the ground underneath was cold and uneven, but Terrance had slept on worse and, moreover, was young and tired. He had two attacks of coughing, and both times looked to see if he had disturbed his tent companion. He hadn't. Like most soldiers, the cavalryman had learned to sleep soundly no matter what noise was made nearby.

Terrance closed his own eyes and tried to relax. He felt perspiration running down his neck and back despite the cold, and pulled the blanket tightly around him. His mind seem to race with images of home and family, but nothing was coherent. After a few fitful moments, sleep came quickly.

Morning saw a flurry of snow. As Terrance made his way to the mess the pace in the camp quickened, as word spread the order was to leave the front for winter camp. Men who were grim with anticipation that this day might bring another battle breathed deeply, hardly able to contain smiles or tears of relief as they realized they were almost certain to live until next spring.

Terrance's body ached and he felt as if he'd got no rest. Still, he had a mission to finish, so he grabbed a quick meal of hot bread, fresh from the oven, honey, butter, some dried fruit and a long cut of beef that had been cooked the night before. The cook was being generous, for the more the men ate this morning, the less he had to pack up and transport back to LaMut.

As he finished his morning meal, Terrance was approached by a sergeant, a scarred veteran with a patch over his left eye. 'Baron wants you,' he said. Without another word he turned, expecting Terrance to fall in behind, which the messenger did.

Terrance announced himself at the tent flap and was ordered into the pavilion. Baron Gruder held out a packet of messages. 'Add this to your pack, boy,' he said. 'It's for the Earl. Barons Moncrief and Summerville will no doubt also have reports for you to carry back.'

Terrance nodded. 'Yes, m'lord.'

Gruder muttered to himself, 'Defensive combat, indeed. What is Vandros thinking?' As if needing someone to voice his opinion to, he added, 'I've got word of another outpost being overrun just four days ago! The Tsurani aren't just sending out patrols, they're moving large numbers of men; they're up to something.

'If we're to ever win this war, we need to carry the fight to them.' He looked down at a map on a table to his right and his eyes darted from mark to mark, as if trying to read the future in it.

He looked up and said, 'Some of the lads ran into a Tsurani patrol-in-force day before yesterday, and it wasn't the one you saw, so keep your eyes open. I think our playmates on the other side of the line might be thinking of trying to move in behind us as we withdraw.

They'll dig in and establish fortifications, so they'll have expanded their territory come spring when we return. Pass that along to the other barons, if you will, and advise them I'm withdrawing in stages, ready to turn and fight if I need. Defensive combat, indeed.' He waved at the packet in Terrance's hand. 'And make sure Earl Vandros gets my messages, boy.'

Terrance nodded, committing all the Baron's remarks to memory. He waited to see if there was anything else. Finally, Gruder realized Terrance was waiting to be dismissed and waved him away.

Terrance saluted, turned and left the tent, heading straight for the picket line. In less than fifteen minutes, Bella was tacked and he mounted, moving through the roil of men breaking camp around him. He moved with purpose, but slowly, letting the cold horse get her feet under her and getting her warmed up before he would pick up speed.

The ground was not frozen, and the night's snow was being quickly churned to mud by the army breaking camp. Terrance knew he would have to stop several times and pick out his mare's hooves, but at least it wouldn't be the thick, forelock-deep goop that could suck the shoes off a horse or the boot off a rider come the spring thaw.

He was thankful for small blessings as he turned his horse south-westward and urged her to a light trot. He felt her twitch when he broke into a fit of coughing, but he patted her on the neck when he was finished and she relaxed. Then he set her to a canter, and watched as the miles fell behind.

Terrance reined in Bella. The air was still, as if the weather held its breath in anticipation of the next assault. The snow flurries had halted an hour after he had left camp, but Terrance knew there would be more, soon. The hazy sun hung in the sky, its slight touch on his face taunting him with the promise of warmth that would be withheld. The frigid air was starting to freeze the ground, and Bella's hooves were crushing ice crystals more often with every passing minute. The cold bit through Terrance's coat and Bella's breath formed clouds of steam. And in the west more clouds were approaching.

Since leaving Gruder's camp Terrance had encountered nothing out of the ordinary, but he had to be constantly alert. The fever that was gripping him made it difficult to keep his attention focused as much as he would have liked, but for the most part he could ignore the misery that was now seeping into every bone in his body.

He let Bella rest a moment while he regarded the landscape. He rode along a trail that hugged a line of trees spreading southwards. To the north the land fell away into a large meadow. In the distance Terrance took stock of landmarks, for he carried no maps against the possibility of enemy capture. Like all messengers he had committed local maps to memory and could recognize where he was given any sort of significant feature to use as a reference point.

Something caught his eye at the far end of the meadow. A group of figures emerged, moving slowly towards his position. At first he thought it might be a Tsurani patrol, but then he quickly discarded that notion. There were approximately two dozen people, moving in ragged fashion, with no order or apparent purpose other than to move south as quickly as possible, all of them lacking the colourful armour that marked the Tsurani.

Terrance waited. The time spent investigating this group would be well spent if they had any reasonable intelligence regarding Tsurani movements to the north or west. As they approached, the figures resolved themselves into a group of villagers, looking to be farmers or woodcutters by their dress. Men, women and a few children, all carrying bundles, approached.

One man saw Terrance and pointed and the others started waving and shouting. He turned his horse and urged her down the slope in their direction. By the time he reached them, they were in the middle of the meadow, obviously fatigued. They children clung to adults and everyone was short of breath.

'Hello!' shouted one man as Terrance came within hearing range. 'Are you a soldier?' The man spoke the language of the Free Cities, Natalese. As a native of Yabon, Terrance could understand most of it; his Yabonese dialect was closely related, though the King's Tongue was the predominant language in his household.

'Yes,' said Terrance. 'Who are you?'

'We are from the village of Ralinda, seven miles to the north.'

Terrance nodded. He knew where it was. 'I thought it was in Tsurani hands.'

'They pulled out yesterday,' answered a woman standing next to the man. 'Every one of them. Last year they left a handful of soldiers to keep us working, but not this year. So we ran.'

Terrance nodded. He turned and pointed upslope. 'Once you reach that high ground, turn north east and follow the ridge. That will take you to a trail in the woods leading to where Baron Gruder's camp is breaking to head back to LaMut. You can go with them and find shelter for the winter.' He turned to the man. 'Where did the Tsurani go?'

'South west.'

Terrance did a momentary calculation in his head, then said, 'Thank you. Good luck.' He turned Bella and spurred her up the slope to the ridge, feeling sudden urgency. If the entire garrison billeted in that village wasn't returning to their staging area, north west in the Grey Towers Mountains, that meant they were joining other units for a last assault and from the direction they were heading, that could mean only Baron Moncrief's position. For a brief instant, he considered turning to tell the villagers to carry word to Baron Gruder, but even if they reached Gruder's camp before nightfall, any battle at Moncrief's camp would be decided long before Gruder sent reinforcements.

Besides, he thought, he was only speculating and it could be he was wrong.

But in his gut he knew he wasn't.

He got Bella to a fast canter and hoped he could get to Moncrief before the Tsurani.

Bella laboured to keep galloping. Terrance had tried to keep her pace as fast as possible without ruining her. He had alternated long gallops with canters and trots, but had not let her rest since receiving word of the Tsurani pull-out from the village of Ralinda. As much as he treasured the horse he knew he would be duty-bound to sacrifice her to bring warning to Baron Moncrief.

He could hear Bella's breathing, the raspy, deep huffing that warned him she was close to her end. She had heart and would run until she collapsed under him, he knew. He faced a terrible test, balancing the necessity for speed with the need to keep Bella alive. His chances of reaching Moncrief before the Tsurani were close to non-existent if he were forced to cover even the last two miles on foot.

He reined her in and let her slow until she was walking, her laboured breathing recovering slowly after five minutes at that pace. He wiped his forehead with the back of his gloved right hand and could feel the chilled perspiration run off his neck and down inside his tunic. He felt a strange detachment as he realized he was drenched under his coat, despite the freezing air. His throat was dry no matter how much water he choked down, and his lungs felt constricted, making it difficult to take in a deep breath. Fits of coughing had forced him to rein in three times, leaning over the saddle to spit fluid. His ribs ached.

He ignored his own discomfort and glanced around, seeking landmarks, and realized he was entering a narrowing valley, three or four miles long, that came to a 'V' in the south west, entering the last pass he would encounter before reaching Moncrief's position.

Movement along a tree line to the north caught his eye and he halted Bella for a moment. Raising himself up in the stirrup irons, he studied the trees. Just beyond the first line of trees he could see movement, faint hints of colours among the shadows of the deeper woods, blue, green, red.

He knew it was the Tsurani, and from the variety of colours he glimpsed, a combined command. Gruder was right and the Tsurani were poising themselves to sweep in behind the retreating Kingdom forces and establish larger areas of control.

The Tsurani had ceased trying to expand their holdings since the first year of the invasion, letting a stable front develop over the last six years, the attack on Crydee and the attempt to reach Port Natal and the Bitter Sea being the only two exceptions.

But it didn't mean they weren't trying now.

Terrance urged the tired horse forward.

He knew as well as most that the Tsurani were among the finest infantry ever seen in Midkemia, able to march fifty miles though a day and night and still fight when they reached their destination. And twenty miles a day was a stroll for them.

He judged the distance from the trees to where he knew the entrance of the pass was and realized he would have to hurry to get there before the Tsurani vanguard. He kicked hard at the sides of his fatigued mount, and the valiant Bella responded.

At first she ran nearly as fast as she would when rested, but Terrance felt her energy wane by the minute. When he had halved the distance to the gap, she could barely maintain a weak canter, and when he was nearing the trees, she fell into a stumbling walk.

He leaped from her, and quickly stripped off his greatcoat. It was too bulky to run in. With the cold slicing through his light jacket, the chill doubled by the perspiration running down his skin, he secured the pouch around his shoulder carrying Baron Gruder's report to the Earl, and bade a silent goodbye to Bella. He turned her head back towards the route they had travelled, said a silent prayer to Ruthia, goddess of luck, and slapped the horse hard on the flanks. She moved away and then stopped, her sides heaving as she struggled for breath. She looked back at him and he said, 'Home, Bella!' She almost seemed to nod as she turned and started walking slowly back the way they had come.

Setting his sight on the gap less than two miles ahead, he started a steady trot. The ground was icy enough that any attempt to run could be disastrous. He could not chance an injury that would keep him from finishing his assigned mission. And should he fall now, he would almost certainly be captured or killed by the Tsurani.

A few times he felt his boots slip an inch, but for the most part, the trot kept him moving quickly towards his goal while giving him firm footing. As he reached a smaller clearing before the woodlands leading to the pass, shouts in the distance told him the Tsurani had spied him making his way. Disregarding the icy ground, Terrance started to run.

He glanced to his right and saw a half-dozen Tsurani soldiers, dressed in the black and orange of House Minwanabi set out to cut him off. He judged the angle and decided he could make it to the trees before they could reach him. He hoped those chasing him hadn't got to know the area as well as he, for there were a couple of places he could gain some time if they didn't know their way around.

If they did, he was most likely to be killed.

He lowered his head and sprinted.

A hundred yards short of the first line of trees, Terrance could hear the sound of the Tsurani sandals crunching the icy ground as they ran to intercept him. At fifty yards, he could hear their ragged breath as they drew near. At twenty-five yards, a single arrow sped past his head, missing him by less than a yard, and he ducked, reaching the trees as another struck the bole he had passed behind.

He dodged to his left, and down a narrow path between a half-dozen larger boles. His lungs burned and he could feel his legs grow shaky, but he kept his mind focused on getting free of the Tsurani. His heart pounded and he felt fear so near to overwhelming him that he had to blink away tears. He kept his eyes focused on the path. It was a game trail that led to a small pond two hundred yards farther along. At fifty yards, he started to move back to his right, up a slight rise. He knew that if the Tsurani lost track of him, they would be likely to continue down the trail towards the pond and he would gain valuable minutes.

But even if he lost the half-dozen chasing him, there was the bulk of the Tsurani force heading for the same destination he was, and if he didn't get there at least five minutes before they did, the chances were high one of their bowmen would bring him down, for there was a clearing before the pass that afforded a running man no cover whatsoever.

For the first time since taking service, Terrance cursed the need for high riding heels. He felt his ankles wobble and almost give out several times as he dashed through the woods. Absently he wondered if he could have a bootmaker cut the fronts at the ankles and add grommets and laces so he could tighten them. Then he realized the far wiser choice was to avoid having to run in the first place.

He hit the small clearing in full stride, electing to run as fast as possible rather than dodging from side to side, hoping to be into the rocks a short distance away before a Tsurani bowman might stop, draw, take a bead on him, and let fly.

Something, the hint of a bowstring being released, the sound of pursuing footfalls diminished by one, or just intuition caused him to dart to the left at the last instant. A black arrow sped past him, missing his back by less than six inches. He darted right, then cut into the gap in the rocks, hugging the left side.

The gap was narrow enough so that only two men on horses could ride abreast, and Terrance knew it was a logical choke point for the defenders to the south west. There would be at least a small squad of Kingdom soldiers at the other end and he would be safe if he could negotiate the mile of rocky trail before the Tsurani overtook him.

He prayed they would become cautious and slow down as they entered the gap, perhaps fearing he had turned to stage an ambush. But moments later the sounds of running men echoed from behind and he realized the Tsurani were anything but cautious. They had seen one man, armed only with a sword, running for his life.

Terrance felt his legs burn with fatigue and his lungs didn't seem to take in enough air. He forced himself to breathe as deeply as he could, blowing out all the air, then breathed normally. He felt an attack of coughing begin and he exhaled sharply, overcoming the urge. He felt as if he were losing strength by the moment and felt a desperate dread that he might collapse before reaching safety. He battled panic and knew it would kill him faster than anything else. He was tired and sick, but he kept focused and moved as quickly as he could, knowing death was only fifty yards behind.

The gap curved and turned, preventing the Tsurani from unleashing another shot at him. Terrance also knew that the trail straightened for a hundred and fifty yards as it also broadened at the south-west mouth of the pass. He prayed Kingdom archers would be alert enough to recognize his uniform, and then recognize who was chasing him.

Then he was there, rounding a curve and looking at a hundred-and-fifty-yard-long trail leading down to what could only be a Kingdom barricade. A chest-high redoubt had been built across the gap since the last time he had ridden through. Shouts from the redoubt told Terrance he had been seen, and he waved his right hand in a signal as he ran.

He knew he looked nothing like a Tsurani, but hoped it was that obvious to the bowmen facing him. Then as he neared the redoubt he saw them draw their bows and let arrows fly.

The shafts sped over Terrance's head and he heard a cry of pain from behind and realized the Tsurani were now in sight. Terrance didn't chance a look back, in case the Tsurani were ignoring the covering fire and still chasing him.

As he reached the redoubt he leaped into the air, landing atop the four-foot barricade, letting his body go limp as Kingdom soldiers grabbed his jacket and pulled him over.

The man who yanked him to his feet was a grizzled sergeant nursing a nasty scar on his face, less than a week old and badly sewn from the look of it. 'Cutting it close, aren't you, boy?' he said.

'No . . . choice,' said Terrance between gasps and a sudden, wracking cough. 'My horse . . . was all out . . . and I had to get . . . my messages to Baron Moncrief.'

'Yes,' said a soldier nearby who was crouching low behind the breast-work, 'but did you have to bring them with you?' He pointed to where the Tsurani bowmen were trading shots with the Kingdom archers.

'It wasn't my idea,' said Terrance, getting to his feet, but keeping his head low. Suddenly he exploded into a fit of coughing, his body wracked and his ribs hurting from the effort. He hacked up fluid from his lungs, turned his head and spat.

'You going to live?' asked the sergeant.

'I'll live,' said Terrance. 'Just a nasty chest cold. Nothing to speak of.' He rested a moment, hands on knees, then stood upright. 'Sergeant, I need a horse.'

'Go get one from the picket,' said the sergeant. 'We've lost a few lads in the last week. What do we have coming?'

'A lot of Tsurani from the look of things,' said Terrance. 'I'll tell the Baron. Looks like a last-minute push to take this whole region.'

'Wonderful,' said the sergeant, pulling out his sword. 'Get ready, boys!' he shouted as Terrance hurried away from the defensive position.

A dozen small tents were pitched a hundred yards south of the barricade, and the soldiers who had been resting there were now running towards the defensive point; the sergeant must have sent word when he saw Terrance running out of the gap. Terrance did a quick calculation and judged there were about a hundred men at the barricade. With archers they should be able to hold the Tsurani for an hour, perhaps two. That should be enough time for Terrance to reach the

Baron's camp and for reinforcements to come to the sergeant's relief.

Terrance quickly evaluated the horses at the picket and selected a grey gelding, barrel-chested and sound in all four legs. It had the look of an animal with endurance and strength, and he needed that more than he needed the speed some of the other horses might possess.

Just to be sure, he quickly inspected the animal's hooves and found the feet well cared-for and without thrush or any other problems. He examined the saddles resting on the row of racks and picked one that was almost as light as the one he used on Bella. Twice he had to pause while he experienced coughing fits, but after spitting up more fluid, he felt better and could breathe a little easier. Maybe the cold was burning itself out, he thought. He inspected the saddle he had picked. It was probably a scout's saddle, as the rest were heavy-duty rigs designed for those who fought from horseback. The company here was mounted infantry, but they also were used as support cavalry at times and their saddles reflected that.

Terrance tacked up the animal and mounted, keeping his mind on his work. He kept from thinking how frightened he had been when running and turned his mind away from the fear, for to embrace it, he knew, would cripple him. If he didn't ignore the fear, it would keep him from continuing with his mission and he couldn't abide the thought of the disgrace that would bring.

With a snort, the animal headed along the trail, away from the pending battle, and Terrance let it settle into a quick trot for a few minutes, to warm up, then set his heels to the animal's barrel and got him into a gallop.

The Baron's camp was less than four miles away, so it took only a few minutes for him to cover the distance. Without a word, Terrance dismounted and threw the reins of the mount to a guard outside the Baron's tent. To the guard on the opposite side of the tent entrance, he said, 'Orders from the Earl!'

The guard nodded and stuck his head inside, said something, and a moment later stood aside, holding open the entrance for Terrance. Terrance stepped in and said, 'Messages from the Earl and Baron Gruder, m'lord.'

Moncrief was an older man, perhaps nearing seventy years, and the war had made him look older. His grey hair hung to his shoulders and his eyes were deep-set and underlined with dark circles. 'Go on,' he said in a soft voice.

'From the Earl: you're to withdraw to winter quarters. Orderly withdrawal. Defensive combat only.

'From Baron Gruder: he expects a large Tsurani push to occupy these territories as you withdraw, so the Tsurani can expand their holdings in the spring.

'And, sir, as I arrived, your barricade at the northern pass was being attacked by what I judge to be company strength or better, at least two major Houses, Anasati and Minwanabi.'

The Baron blinked. 'What?'

'Your northern barricade at the pass is under assault right now and your sergeant in command respectfully requests reinforcements.'

'Why didn't you say so first thing?' demanded the Baron, but he didn't wait for an answer, rather he began shouting orders for the camp to get ready to move north in response to the Tsurani attack.

Terrance was waiting, as he hadn't been dismissed. When the Baron had finished issuing orders the Baron turned to Terrance. 'Anything else?'

'Sir, I lost my horse on the way here and took one from the remounts at the barricade. May I keep him so I may continue my mission?'

'Yes,' said the Baron, waving away the question.

'Do you have any messages you wish me to carry, m'lord?'

'Normally I would pen a report to the Earl, but under the circumstances, I will be too busy.' His orderly entered the room, followed by two other servants, holding the Baron's armour. The old man obviously intended to lead the relief column to the barricade himself. 'I'll give my report to the Earl in person when I return to LaMut. Just tell Baron Summerville what's going on up here and ask him to use best judgement in how to withdraw while protecting his flank.'

'Sir,' said Terrance.

'You're dismissed,' said the Baron.

Terrance left the tent and took the reins of the horse. He was sick, famished and tired, and more than anything, thirsty. He worked his way through a camp in uproar as hundreds of soldiers raced to form companies and get ready to march to the north. Even the reserves who would remain to protect the camp or rush to reinforce other positions along the line were marshalling.

He reached the commissary tent and found the cooks and their boys frantically preparing to feed men at the front. He grabbed a boy hurrying to load a basket with still hot bread on to a waggon and said, 'Water skin?'

The boy shook off his hand and said, 'Don't have any. Ask the commissary chief.'

Terrance grabbed a loaf of bread off the top of the basket over the boy's protest. He shouldered his way past another pair of boys carrying a half-filled barrel of apples and snatched up one from it before they noticed. The fruit was already showing age, but he ignored the brown spots and bit into it.

He found the commissary chief overseeing the loading of supplies and said, 'I'm the Earl's messenger. I have need of a water skin, and a coat if there's one to be had.'

The commissary chief glanced at Terrance and saw the tunic and braid. 'Lose yours?'

'With my horse.'

'A little thoughtless, don't you think?'

Terrance ignored the remark. 'Do you have them?'

The man motioned towards a pile of clothing at the edge of the commissary area, towards which two boys were driving an empty waggon. 'You might find a cloak or coat in there, if you don't mind the blood.' He turned and rummaged though a stack of canvas bags. 'And here's a water skin for you.'

Before Terrance could ask, the commissary chief said, 'And you'll find the water barrels over there.' He pointed to the centre of the camp where men were filling their skins in preparation for the march. 'I'd hurry if I were you.'

Terrance took the man's meaning; with the conflict at the barricade erupting, the luggage and commissary would be moved up in support of the reinforcements. The luggage boys were hurrying to load waggons, hitch up the horses and get supplies up to the site of the battle as quickly as possible.

Terrance gulped down bites of the apple and bread as he led the horse to the mound of clothing waiting to be disposed of. At some point before the chaos erupted, the boys in the luggage would have gone through the clothing taken from the dead, and determined what was salvageable, cleaned it, and returned it to the Quartermaster. The coats, cloaks, jackets and trousers too damaged to be repaired would be burned.

But now the two boys who had driven up were frantically loading everything into the back of the waggon. Terrance shouted, 'Wait a minute!'

They paused in their labour and one said, 'What?'

'I need a coat. Mine was lost to the Tsurani.'

'Be quick about it,' said the other boy, a short, broad-shouldered lad who would probably be in the army next year. 'We've got word that we're taking all this back to LaMut and we'll sort it out there.'

Terrance ignored the stench of dried blood, sweat, urine and faecal matter that was the hallmark of clothes stripped from the battlefield dead. He quickly tossed aside a half-dozen coats and cloaks until he caught sight of a familiar grey design.

He pulled a messenger's coat out from under a bundle of blood-soaked trousers and inspected it. Except for an arrow hole that signalled a shaft had found a rider between the shoulderblades, it was undamaged. He threw it over his arm and said, 'I'll take this one.'

The boys said nothing, returning to their labours.

Terrance walked away from the tattered remnants of men lost in war, leading the horse slowly to the southern edge of the camp. He filled his skin from a water barrel and as he mounted, a half-dozen porters came and picked up the barrel and turned it over. Streams were plentiful in this area so there was no need to lug water back to LaMut.

He took two steps and suddenly found himself doubled over, wracking coughs forcing him to breath deep, hack up ropy phlegm, and spit. He repeated it until his ribs ached, but finally he could breathe a bit better. He stood upright and his head swam for a moment. Then he regained his bearings.

He took a slow, deep breath and felt a tickle, but no urge to cough. He took a second breath, then let out a slow sigh. Terrance finished his bread and apple and donned the coat. He tried to ignore the smell, and knew he would soon stop noticing it, but he couldn't help but think of who the former owner might be. Three messengers had been lost in the last six months, so it could have been worn by any of them. For a moment he pondered which was most likely. Jack Macklin had been riding this way when he was killed, so it might have been his.

Terrance wondered if he would ever know. He climbed up into the saddle and urged the gelding forward, heading for Baron Summerville's camp. He glanced skywards and knew he'd lost half a day and would have to sleep one more night on the ground before returning to the Earl's camp.

Without thought he patted the pouch hanging at his hip to ensure Baron Gruder's messages were still with him. He took a deep breath and had his mount pick up speed as he didn't want to be on the trail after dark.

The horse was no Bella, but he was obedient and trail-wise. He responded nicely and Terrance felt that he might actually see the end of this seemingly interminable day. He knew it was only eight hours since he had left Gruder's camp, but it felt like days. Terrance was tired to his bones and aching from too little rest after a murderous ride and running from the Tsurani.

The afternoon passed slowly, and twice he felt a heat rush up his body that caused perspiration to break out all over him, run down his face and turn to a freezing mask in the cold wind. He fought to keep his mind on his task and off his overall misery. At sundown, he rode within sight of Baron Summerville's camp. The soldiers on picket waved him through without comment and he reached the Baron's command tent as darkness fell.

One of the Baron's guards announced Terrance's arrival and then took the reins of his mount while the young messenger went inside to make his report.

Baron Summerville was the only commander of the three whom Terrance knew well; he was the son of another distant cousin and served as a court Baron in Krondor. 'Terry!' he said, pleased to see his distant kinsman. 'What news?'

'Sir, the Duke sends orders we're home for the winter.'

'Wonderful,' said Summerville, indicating Terrance should take a seat. Taking in Terrance's appearance fully for the fist time, the Baron said, 'You look like hell. Are you ill?'

'A chest cold, m'lord. Nothing to speak of.'

'Wine?'

'A little, m'lord.' Terrance's throat was sore and he thought the wine might soothe it a little.

The baron signalled and his personal servant poured a mug for each of them. Terrance welcomed the full, warming drink and then said, 'Orders from the Earl. Orderly withdrawal; defensive fighting only.

'From Baron Gruder: he thinks the Tsurani will push in behind the withdrawal and seize lands to hold until spring.

'From Baron Moncrief: the Tsurani are attacking his position from the north.'

Baron Summerville stood and went to a map. He studied it for a moment, then said, 'I think Gruder is right. The bastards are trying to push Moncrief out, forcing him to the south east. That would cut us off from Gruder, whose only option would be to fall back straight to LaMut.' He rubbed his chin, resplendent with a blond beard he took great pains to keep neatly trimmed, even in the field. 'We're untroubled here, and our scouts have seen no signs of the Tsurani. I think I can follow the Earl's instructions and still move in support of Moncrief. If we "withdraw" together, in an orderly fashion of course, we can push the Tsurani back behind their own positions, then swing east while Gruder holds his ground, then all leave.' He nodded. 'Yes, that would do it. It would be too bloody cold and nasty for them to try another push in a few weeks, and it would take them that long to regroup and return in force, which they would be forced to do, just in case we left a garrison behind. Yes, that is what I'll do.'

He turned to face Terrance. 'I'm afraid I've got to ask you to take the long way back, Terry.'

'Sir?'

'At first light I want you to head back to Moncrief and tell him I'm "withdrawing" in his direction. I'll move the bulk of my forces up in support of his position by noon tomorrow. The rest will serve as a harassing rear guard in case there are more Tsurani circling around to flow in behind us.'

'Yes, sir.'

With a smile, Baron Summerville said, 'How's your family, Terry?'

'Well enough, m'lord. I had a letter from Mother a month ago. All's calm back home, thank the gods. Father's still serving up with Duke Brucal's army in northern Yabon, but she had word from him he was all right just before she wrote to me. My brother Gerald is still commanding a company of cavalry from Tyr-Sog under Father.'

'Best to assume things are well until you hear otherwise,' said Baron Summerville. 'Else you have trouble keeping down the meals, if you know what I mean?'

'Yes, sir,' said Terrance.

'Speaking of meals, I'd invite you to stay and dine, kinsman, but as we're going to be at march on daybreak, I have much to do. Find the commissary and get what you need. No need to see me again before leaving. Be on the trail at dawn, then, will you?'

'Yes, m'lord,' said Terrance. Understanding he was dismissed, he bowed then left.

As he reached the tent flap, the Baron said, 'And Terry . . .'

'Yes, m'lord?

'Don't get yourself killed: that's a good lad.'

'Sir,' said Terrance with a smile and he left.

Terrance took his horse and walked him through the camp, towards the commissary tent. Before he reached it, the tone of the camp changed and again he felt the quickening pace of activity as word was passed they'd be pulling out the next morning, early, to support Moncrief and then home!

He found the cook tent, got his meal and sat behind the tent as close to the cooking fire on the other side as he could get; the warmth from the fire seeped through the canvas and was welcome comfort to his back, as was the food he wolfed down. There was even a fair drink of wine in the bottom of a bottle left over from the Baron's supper the night before, which the cook was kind enough to give the obviously exhausted boy. He was halfway through his meal when another attack of coughing struck him and he spat until his body ached. His ribs felt as if he had wrestled the Duke's champion and had been subjected to a massive bear-hug. He could barely breathe without feeling pain. He sat back and took slow, shallow breaths. He felt fatigue in every joint, and closed his eyes to rest them a moment.

Terrance suddenly felt the toe of a boot gently nudging his leg. 'Here, now, lad. You'll freeze to death if you don't move along.'

The messenger looked up and saw the cook had come around to throw out scraps and had found Terrance sleeping, the plate of food still in his lap and a wooden spoon still clutched in his right hand.

'Got a place to sleep?' asked the cook.

'Haven't found one, yet,' said Terrance.

'You most likely won't. Not much fighting here since the last batch of reinforcements showed, so there's no empty tents to speak of.' The old cook rubbed his chin. 'The commissary chief won't mind if you sleep near the fires, long as you don't mind getting up before dawn – that's when we'll cook the last meal before we pull out.'

'I don't mind,' said Terrance. 'I have to be on the road before dawn, anyway.'

'Good, then come along.'

Terrance followed the cook to the far side of the commissary tent, where boys were banking the fires for use in the morning. Two boys were lifting large shovels of ash, with which they covered the flaming wood and coal. Terrance realized he had never bothered to notice that they used both. He then realized there were many things about the commissary he didn't pay close attention to.

There were earthenware jars and pots in all sizes and shapes heaped beside one tent. Near another stood stacks of bowls and platters, some nearly as tall as a man.

A dozen brick ovens stood nearby and boys were using large wooden paddles to pull out steaming loaves of hot bread. Despite having eaten a short time before, Terrance found the smell of fresh bread nearly overwhelming and his mouth was watering. He asked, 'Do you take the ovens back to LaMut?'

'We could,' said the cook. 'We'd need a waggon and team for each, but they can be lifted up by a rope and block, and dragged into the bed of a stout waggon. But why bother? We leave them here and they'll be waiting come spring. The snow doesn't hurt them. We just shoo away any animal or bird that's decided to nest in one and with a little cleaning they're ready to go. If this camp is ever relocated, we can transport one or two a day to the new camp.

'Here you go,' he said, pointing to two dozen waggons that formed the luggage of the army. 'Work your way in there and grab a blanket. The boys will be crawling under there when the bread is done for the morning. They're a lice-ridden lot of little bastards, but they won't bother you. And you'll find having a bunch of them around you will keep you warm enough. You'll be roused an hour before dawn.'

Terrance said his thanks and crawled down under the first waggon. He had to negotiate a veritable maze of waggon wheels, crockery holding personal belongings, bundles of dirty clothing, and a few sleeping boys who appeared to be ill. He found a spot on a dirty blanket next to a bundle of other dirty blankets and pulled one over himself.

Terrance considered the lot of the boys in the luggage and the commissary. It was already after dark and most of the soldiers were sleeping, yet these boys were busy packing up the camp's extras, arms, clothing, bandages and the rest, or working in the kitchen tents making bread, cooking meat and preparing whatever was left to feed the men before the early march to the north east. The boys might manage five hours of sleep before starting their next work day. Terrance realized that they grabbed naps during the morning and early afternoon, but still it was a bone-grinding schedule.

He felt perspiration running off his body, and despite the blanket and the proximity of the fire, was wracked with chills. He fought off a coughing fit, then succumbed to another, and finally relaxed enough to try to sleep.

Terrance remembered one soldier, during his first week in the Earl's camp, who had told him, 'Learn to sleep any chance you get, boy. You never know how long it'll be before you have another chance.'

Terrance understood the wisdom of that advice and was quickly asleep.

For a moment he didn't realize where he was. The sound of boys protesting about the need to get up after too little sleep and his own profound fatigue confused his senses. He sat up and banged his head hard against the underside of a waggon.

It was still dark.

'Here, now,' said a boy next to him. 'Go easy, else you'll brain your-self.'

Rubbing his sore pate, Terrance said, 'Thanks. I'll be more cautious.'

The boys crab-walked out from under the waggons and hurried to their various tasks. Terrance paused to let the exodus of boys finish, then made his way out from under the waggons. He was more than usually stiff from sleeping on the ground, and he felt tired and miserable, despite the night's sleep. He was visited by another coughing fit and spat and spat until his ribs protested and he found tears forming in his eyes from the pain.

For a long moment he felt the urge just to sit on the ground and cry. He had never felt this tired or hopeless before in his life. His body seemed to fight him as much as the elements, and the thought of the ride before him was almost more than he could bear.

There was an apothecary in the Earl's camp who had a potion he brewed, herbs and roots, which would hasten recovery from coughs and chest congestion, even things far nastier. By his original plan, he should be back there this afternoon and he could chase down the apothecary and take care of this, but as fate would have it, he had to return the way he came, and there was certainly an army of Tsurani between Moncrief and Gruder's camps, which would mean another day and night on the trail.

Terrance conceded that he'd be flirting with pneumonia by the time he reached the Earl's camp if his luck didn't hold. He almost gave in to despair, but realized he had no choice. He just set his mind to doing each thing needed as it came, and was determined not to dwell on how much more effort lay beyond the task at hand.

He wandered through the turmoil of boys readying the final meal in this camp and those already intent upon packing up the last of the stores so the commissary and luggage could follow quickly behind the advancing army. Terrance saw order emerge from the apparent confusion and admired the way in which each boy appeared to know what was expected of him. There was a fair amount of jostling and bumping involved, but they were boys and they didn't let it distract them from the tasks at hand.

Camp boys had a hard lot, Terrance judged, but no worse than the homeless urchins in the cities. At least here they had a meal or two a day and a place to sleep where they would be untroubled. Boys might be abused by drunken soldiers in other armies, but since before Terrance was born, battery or rape had been hanging offences in the King's army.

Some grew up to be soldiers, while others found positions as cooks' helpers, teamsters, or luggage supervisors. Terrance saw a pair of luggage supervisors, boys almost grown to manhood, perhaps only two or three years younger than himself, who quickly moved through the crowds imparting instructions and helping along some boys with a smack to the back of the head or a cuff to the ear.

At the cooking tent he saw that the kitchen was already being disassembled. While the brick hearths would be left to await the army's return in the spring, the metal cooking stoves were being taken apart and readied for transport.

Food was resting on wooden tables across the compound, and Terrance hurried over to grab something to eat before the trumpets blew the soldiers to assembly. He saw a few soldiers, those coming off guard duty, already lined up to eat. He fell in behind a rangy infantryman wearing the tabard of Questor's View and moved along. As he reached the end of the first table, the trumpets sounded, and he could hear fatigued men cursing as the soldiers in nearby tents responded to the call.

Terrance grabbed up some fresh bread, a pear that didn't look too damaged and a slice of hard cheese. He stuffed the pear in his pocket to eat on the road. He looked in vain for a water skin, and hoped the one that had rested on his saddle horn was still there when he retrieved his horse from the remounts.

He didn't bother to sit with the soldiers and eat. He chewed his food while he went to the horses. He found cavalrymen inspecting their mounts before going to eat, for they knew their lives depended on the horses being sound. The grooms were too busy to help him, so he stuffed what was left of his food inside his unbuttoned tunic and found his horse. The animal had been poorly cared for. He took a few minutes to pick out the hooves and find his saddle. As he feared, the water skin was nowhere in sight.

He went to the stores and found a nosebag and a near empty bag of oats, but enough for his mount. He filled the nosebag and returned to his horse and fitted it over the animal's nose. He would let the horse eat while he went in search of a water skin.

It took him almost a quarter-hour to find a skin and fill it, and when Terrance returned to the remounts, he found a stocky groomsman removing the nosebag from the horse's snout.

'Here! What are you doing?' Terrance asked.

The groom, a large-shouldered young man with a nose flattened in many brawls, turned and said, 'I'm takin' this here bag off. No one told me to feed this horse, an' this part o' the line is mine, see?'

'That's my horse and I need him fed.'

'So does them what's going to fight, fancy pants, so you can wait until they's done, got it?'

Terrance knew a bully when he saw one and realized this idiot was spoiling for a fight. He didn't hesitate. He took one step forward and kicked the groom as hard as he could in the groin. With a grunt of pain, the man fell to his knees, clutching himself as his eyes widened and he fought to catch his breath.

Terrance was forced to admit he was a tough one, for he shook off the blow in a fraction of the time most men would have been rendered unable to move. But as the groom regained his wits he realized Terrance had his sabre out and had the point levelled at his throat.

'Now, you buffoon. You'll leave that nosebag alone until my horse is done. You'll go over there and retrieve that scout saddle and bridle from the rack and tack up the horse. If you think you've got a problem now, see what kind of trouble you'll see if the Baron finds out you're interfering with his orders. I'm supposed to be riding out *now*! So, what are you going to do?'

'Tack up the horse . . . sir.'

Terrance put away his sword. The groom struggled to his feet, still obviously tender and hobbled over to get the saddle.

Terrance turned to find a cavalryman watching him. The tall soldier said, 'So what would you have done without a sabre?'

Terrance said, 'Wasted a lot of time finding an officer to bully him into obeying me. I certainly am not going to scare him.'

The man studied Terrance a moment then smiled. 'A man who knows his limits. I like that.'

Terrance started to cough, and the cavalryman said, 'Are you ill?'

'Nothing to speak of,' said Terrance, gasping for a moment, then regaining his composure.

The soldier shrugged. 'Ride well,' he offered. He didn't wait for a response, but finished inspecting his own horse, then left to get his morning meal.

The groom tacked up the horse under Terrance's watchful eye. There would be no loosely fastened girths or uncomfortable bits on this horse. Terrance finished eating and hung his water skin on the horse's saddle, then mounted and rode off.

His chest was getting tighter by the moment, and he felt achy all over and he had to ride a good pace to carry word to Baron Moncrief from Baron Summerville. Even the little bit of exertion needed to cow the groom had caused him to break out in drenching perspiration.

Then it started to snow.

'Gods,' said Terrance under his breath, 'this is turning into a lousy morning.' For a brief moment he considered returning to the Baron's tent. He would report to the infirmary and rest for a day or two, then travel by waggon behind the army. He was obviously ill and Summerville was a kinsman, even if a distant one. He would let the family know that Terrance had given it his very best. Then he wondered, but would it be my best?

For a long minute he sat motionless, considering his options. Then he admitted he had none and kicked the horse into motion.

It was near noon when Terrance came into view of the Baron's camp. The guards were on alert, for there was only a small squad left behind to guard the tents, equipment and animals. They waved him through and he rode to the command tent. The guard shouted as he rode near, 'The Baron's up at the barricade, leading the defence himself.'

'How goes it?'

'Close,' was all the man said.

Terrance rode on, wishing he could spare the time to rest the horse. He had become fond of the tough little gelding. He wasn't as sturdy an animal as Bella, but he was willing and obedient.

Terrance himself was miserable. Every step the horse took caused his aching body to protest, and he knew he was in the grips of a high fever, for despite the freezing air, he was perspiring under his heavy cloak and alternately felt flushed with heat, then chills that caused him to shudder. He paused to refill his water skin then moved on and relieved himself. He knew that his only choice was to drink as much water as possible, until he returned to the Earl's camp and found the apothecary.

The four miles to the battlefront were marked by a few signs of battle, a dead horse and rider off to one side of the road, a pair of wounded men walking with arms around one another, slowly making their way to the infirmary back at the main camp. Within a mile of the barricade, he could hear the sounds of battle.

When he came into view of the barricade, he saw hundreds of men apparently milling about behind the wall, until he got close enough to see the ordering of the men. Companies stood ready to rush forward and man the barricade, while engineers were frantically loading up trebuchets and letting fly their deadly cargo of rocks on the attackers. The sounds of battle echoed off the rockface. It was a deafening cacophony that made hearing anyone more than a few yards away impossible.

Other men were spreading out, obviously protecting the flanks of the army from any elements of the Tsurani forces that might have wended their way through the rocks above, in an attempt to outflank the Kingdom defenders. And everywhere he looked, he saw men too wounded to move, and the dead.

On one side of the road, the men had been laid out in a row, three dozen or more, while on the other side, the boys from the luggage and the infirmary were carrying bodies away from the battlefront.

Terrance reached the rear of the barricade and shouted to a sergeant upon the wall, 'Where is the Baron?' The effort brought on a coughing fit.

The sergeant looked down and said, 'With the dead. What news?'

Terrance swallowed hard and forced himself to breathe as deeply as he could. 'Baron Summerville comes in haste.' His voice came out thin and strangled, but he was heard.

'How long?'

'No more than an hour, two at the most.'

'We can hold,' shouted the sergeant, 'if but barely.'

'Do you need me to carry word back?'

'Only if there's need to tell the Baron to hasten faster.'

'There is no need. He comes as swiftly as conditions allow.'

'Then I have nothing for you, messenger, save carry news to the Earl that Baron Moncrief died bravely, repulsing the invaders at a breech. He gave his life for King and country.'

'I will do that, Sergeant. May the gods save you.'

'May the gods save us all,' said the sergeant, returning his attention to commanding the defence of the barricade.

Terrance turned his horse around and moved back down the road. He called up from memory the map of the area, and realized he would have to ride miles to the east, to find a small trail through the mountains, one that rose up more than a thousand feet higher than the summit of this road, before he could loop around the invaders and return to the Earl's camp.

The snow continued to fall, and Terrance hoped the pass wasn't snowed in completely by the time he reached there. He patted his horse on the neck and said, 'No rest for either of us until we get safely back to the Earl, I'm afraid.' The thought of the next few hours of riding almost caused him to break down, and tears formed in his eyes, but he blinked them back.

Shivering now from the cold and his fever, Terrance tried to huddle down deeper in his coat as he turned his animal and rode east. His head pounded and his throat was sore beyond anything he had experienced as a boy. He couldn't breathe through his nose and the cold air savaged his throat each time he breathed. He realized he had no choice; behind him a battle raged and there was no place for him to rest. If he must strive, then let him do so attempting to finish his mission. He rode on.

The horse laboured up the pass, slipping on the icy rocks from time to time. Terrance fought to keep his mind focused, which was becoming more and more difficult as he felt his fever turn worse. He knew that any mishap here would mean his death, for he could not possibly walk out from these icy heights. Yet while such thoughts caused him great fear only hours before, now he felt a fey detachment, as if whatever the outcome might be, it really didn't matter. He had no other option but to press on.

The pass where Moncrief and Summerville's forces were locked in combat with the Tsurani was a bit more than three thousand feet in elevation, but this pass was nearly five, and the snow had been falling steadily up here for days. It hadn't begun to drift yet, so he felt confident he would breast the summit soon, yet there was always the chance of an accident.

If the wind below had been knives cutting into his face, razors were now being administered to every inch that was exposed. Not for the first time did he wish for more gear, a heavy pair of trousers, a heavy wool muffler, heavier gloves, but now he wished more fervently than before. He understood the need to keep as much weight off the horse as possible, but right now he would have given up two hours' travel time for a pair of fur-lined gloves.

Cresting the summit brought a sudden sense of relief, even though the wind now raked him like the claws of a predator. He urged the horse on as it half-walked, half-staggered down the icy trail, thinking that every second moving was a second closer to safety.

An hour later he found a cut through the rocks that was relatively sheltered from the wind and there he paused to let the horse rest. He dismounted and moved between the horse's neck and the rocks, letting the animal's body heat give him a slight respite from the brutal cold. He patted his pockets and found the pear, which he gave to the horse. It wasn't much, but the little bit of food seemed to revive the animal slightly and Terrance felt better for it.

After a half-hour in the lee of the rocks, Terrance judged the animal was now taking more punishment from the cold than from moving, so he mounted up and they again descended the mountain.

It was almost night when he reached the foothills and the lightly forested path that would take him back around to the main road to the Earl's camp. He would have either to keep moving throughout the night, or make a camp and light a fire.

It was a difficult choice, for to keep moving meant dangerous footing and the chance for the horse to be injured. A fire was equally dangerous, for the Tsurani might have flanking units out looking for passes like the one he had just used.

He decided to press on and stop only if he found a clearly safe campsite. He was moving through a lightly wooded area when he noticed a small trail leaving the one on which he rode. It might be a game trail, but it also might be a forester's track, leading him to a shelter. He decided he was at no more risk for investigating and moved the horse slowly along the new trail.

A half-mile along he saw a low shape in the gloom, for almost no light was coming from the cloud-shrouded moons. Only the presence in the sky of both large moon and middle moon gave him any illumination.

He identified the mount as a low hut, built into the side of a hillock. Either a charcoal burner's or forester's hut, he judged.

He dismounted and investigated. The hut was abandoned, but it had a stone hearth and he quickly set about building a fire. If the Tsurani blundered this far off the main trail it meant only that the gods had fated his death and he had best resign himself to it.

He took flint and steel from his belt pouch and found some very dry wood near the hearth that sprang easily to flame. He then went outside and found some damp logs that he carefully fed to the fire and watched clouds of steam and smoke rise, as the damp wood resisted the flames.

When he was satisfied the fire would not go out, he went back outside and tended the horse. He tried to rub it down with a handful of stale straw he had pulled off the floor of the hut, and then poured water into his hand and let the animal drink. He would look around in the morning to see if there was any fodder, but suspected he and the animal would both arrive in the Earl's camp starving.

Once he had finished caring for the horse, he went back inside and fell on the hard stones before the fire. The warmth felt wonderful on his face, and he found a ragged blanket tossed into the corner, which he rolled up for a pillow, letting his coat serve as his blanket.

His breath came raggedly and he could not breathe deeply without coughing, and his body ached from hair to toes. But he was tired to the point of numbness and quickly fell into a troubled, fevered sleep.

Terrance could hardly move when he awoke. The fire had died down to glowing embers and what little warmth it generated was offset by the painful cold he felt on the side of his body turned away from the fire. He rolled over with effort and felt his freezing side drink in the heat.

His head swam as he tried to stand. His legs shook and he felt his head pounding. His stomach was tied in knots and he felt himself start to heave; he swallowed hard and fought down his nausea. He reached out and held the door jamb, his head down a moment, eyes closed, and he let his aching body reach a point of balance. He took a long slow breath, and opened his eyes.

Looking out through the partially open door, he judged the morning half over. He knew he was sick to the point of danger, and his only hope was in getting to the Earl's camp before he lost all ability to ride.

He staggered outside and found his horse standing patiently where Terrance had tied him, in the lee of the hut. Terrance had to concentrate to the point of perspiration breaking out on his forehead to tack up the animal.

He judged there was enough water left in the skin, so he didn't have to go looking for any. He also knew he'd cross a stream halfway between here and the Earl's camp, so there he'd refill the skin if needed.

Terrance almost lost consciousness when he mounted, his head swimming for nearly a minute from the exertion. He didn't need a healing priest or chirurgeon to tell him he was burning up from a raging fever, and his lungs gurgled when he breathed deeply. He had pneumonia and wouldn't last another day without attention.

He directed the horse back to the trail and started towards the Earl's camp.

The morning ride was a haze of imaginings and, Terrance knew, hallucinations. He felt fine for moments, only to come awake with a lurch as he almost pitched from the saddle, and realized he had been dreaming of being well. He found it odd that he was now without fear. He simply knew he would either die on the road or reach safety. It didn't bother him any more to consider the risk.

The horse walked as slowly as he permitted, so he constantly had to urge it to a faster pace, only to discover he had lost focus and the horse had slowed to a walk.

More than once he had regained his wits to find the horse had wandered off the trail to nibble at what scant foliage it could find. By midday he was barely able to keep in the saddle.

Terrance knew that to stop would mean his death. If he fell from his horse, he would lose consciousness and freeze to death. He undid the strap of the message pouch and retied it around his waist, running it through two metal rings on the saddle, effectively tying himself to the saddle. The pouch flapped behind him with every step the horse took.

His head pounded and his throat was swollen and hot. His lungs protested with every breath he took and he couldn't feel his hands and feet.

Twice more during the day he gained enough lucidity to see he had wandered off course. He barely had enough wits to get back to the small trail.

Sometime in the seemingly endless hours he spent hanging on to the saddle, he noticed he had left the small trail from the mountains and was back on the main trail to the Earl's camp. That recognition perked him up a little and for the better part of the next hour he felt more focused and aware of his surroundings.

Through endless minutes of jerking awake and dozing he wandered over the countryside, until a jolt of alarm shot though him. The horse had stiffened and snorted and the sudden sense of danger brought him to full awareness.

He was a hundred yards or more south of the road, once again wandering, but despite the fever and his aching body, he rose up in the stirrups. The pouch leather he had tied around his waist pulled against him, but he scanned the horizon in all directions, looking for the cause of the horse's alarm.

Then he saw them, a line of figures less than a hundred yards to the south, crouching and advancing quickly. A flash of green colour told him all he needed to know: Tsurani.

He didn't know if this was a detachment sent far to the left on a flanking move in support of those attacking Moncrief's position, or if this was simply a unit deep behind the lines trying to get back to their own camps before the first blizzard hit.

He didn't debate which was more likely, but turned the horse and kicked hard against the animal's barrel. The horse needed little urging, sensing danger in the approaching men. He leaped forward, heading back to the trail. In less than ten seconds he was on the trail and racing.

Terrance bent low over the horse's neck, his buttocks out of the saddle, in a racing stance, his toes barely in the irons of the stirrups. He fought against fever and fear and kept his horse guided up the road, praying another band of Tsurani weren't waiting for him ahead.

Those who had been approaching him shouted and others appeared along his line of march, but none was close enough to intercept him. He sped past the closest enemy soldier, who let fly with an arrow more out of frustration than any real hope of striking the speeding rider.

With the last of its strength, the horse stretched out, tearing along the road for three miles, then fatigue caught up with horse and rider and Terrance let the animal slow.

Struggling to hold a rocking canter, Terrance realized suddenly where he was, and knew that once he crested a small rise less than a half-mile ahead, he would be within sight of the first sentry post on the road.

Suddenly Terrance felt as he had once when running a race at home, during the Midsummer's Day festival. He had been among the very youngest boys in the race and had been pressed to finish, let alone be among the winners. At the end of the long run, nearly five miles, he had seen the finish line in the distance. Another boy was a few yards ahead, and Terrance had vowed not to be the last across the line. By sheer focus and will he had pressed on and on, until he had crossed the line a step ahead of the older boy. Then he had collapsed and had had to be carried away to his father's house.

He reached deep inside and pulled up that same resolve. He focused and by will kept his horse moving along the road at a canter. In the distance he saw the first sentry and as he approached they waved him through.

He rode along another quarter-mile until the first tents appeared, white shapes seen between the boles of the trees that lined each side of the road. Then suddenly he was in the clearing that housed the Earl's camp.

He started to rein in his horse and the animal slowed as he reached a line of picketed horses. A groom came up and taking one look at Terrance shouted, 'Help me!'

Two soldiers close by hurried over to see what was the matter, as Terrance lost all grip on consciousness and started to slide from the saddle. Only the strap he had tied kept him from falling and then he felt hands upon him, as someone held him up while other hands undid the strap.

Then he felt himself carried, and he wondered why he was no longer cold.

Then darkness.

Suddenly pain.

It felt as if his skin were being peeled off, from the crown of his head, an inch at a time, down his entire body until it reached his toes.

Terrance sat up and screamed.

Strong hands restrained him as he tried to flip himself out of the cot upon which he had rested. Then he went weak and felt those hands push him back on to the cot.

'He'll be fine.'

Terrance felt his head swim, and perspiration drenched his skin with a wetness that stank of poisons leaching out of his body. He could feel his skin burn, as if the sweat were acid and he expected blisters to form, but suddenly he felt his senses return and the pain vanished. He felt weak, but well. He blinked and the room came into focus. He ran his hand across his forehead and it came away dry. He looked at a circle of concerned faces above him and said, 'I'll be fine.'

Terrance sat up slowly, turning to put his feet on the dirt floor. He glanced around. He was in the infirmary tent. Next to him stood a pair of orderlies, and behind them the apothecary and a healing priest. The priest nodded, while the apothecary said, 'That was a close thing, boy. Another hour or two and we'd be putting you on the funeral pyre.'

Terrance took a deep breath. He still felt weak, but far better than he had in days. 'What happened?'

'You rode into camp at sunset, then fell off your horse, and they hauled you in here. We worked on you all night. I gave you some of this,' – he held up a flask – 'and Father William said a prayer, and it worked. Your fever broke and you're back to health.'

'I could use a meal,' said Terrance as he stood up. He expected to feel light-headed, but he didn't. He sniffed at himself and said, 'And a bath.'

'That's the poisons from your body, son,' said the priest. 'My spell held your spirit in your flesh while the apothecary's draught purged your body of the sickness.'

'Your body needs nourishment. The magic in my drug doesn't replenish the body, just heals it,' said the apothecary.

'Thank you,' said Terrance.

The apothecary said, 'I had little choice. It seems the Earl would look upon me with little favour if I let a cousin die.'

'A distant cousin,' said Terrance.

'Still, a relative. In any event, I do what I can for whoever I can.' He looked around the tent at the dying men who would not see home and said, 'Often it is not enough.'

Terrance nodded. He motioned for a infirmary boy to bring over a basin and cloth. The air was frigid, so he raised gooseflesh and he sponged off his skin, and then he dressed. Looking at the apothecary, he said, 'I need to report in.'

'Then get some food and sleep,' cautioned the apothecary. 'I don't want to try to save you twice in two days.'

'I will,' said Terrance. He saw his message pouch was on the ground next to the cot, so he bent over and retrieved it.

He left the tent and looked around. His horse was nowhere in sight. Some groom must have taken it to the remounts. He wondered if Bella had found her way back.

He moved slowly, still weak and not wanting to appear clumsy before the other soldiers. He marvelled he was alive. He had been so fearful just the day before. Now he realized that every time he went on a mission he might face death. He *understood* that fact, rather than just thought he knew. He had faced his own weaknesses and he had overcome them. He felt positively buoyant when he reached the Earl's tent. He said to the guard, 'I have messages for Earl Vandros.'

He had to wait only a few moments before he was admitted. The Earl looked up from a conversation he was having with one of his captains and said, 'Ah, Terry. I expected you back two days ago.'

'A slight delay, m'lord.'

'Messages?'

Terrance handed the pouch to an orderly, who took it. 'A report from Baron Gruder, m'lord.'

'What else?'

'The Tsurani moved in force against Baron Moncrief. He repulsed them for a day and was relieved by Baron Summerville.' He filled in the Earl with the rest of the report then added, 'Baron Moncrief fell during the battle.'

'Shame,' said Vandros. 'He was a good man. It'll put the Duke of Bas-Tyra in a foul mood. Moncrief was one of his barons. Anything else?'

'Yesterday, I saw a unit of Tsurani to the south making their way westwards.'

'I'll send out a patrol to see what they're up to.'

'That's all I have to report, sir.'

Vandros looked at Terrance. His uniform was filthy, and his grey coat had blood on it. 'Any difficulties along the way?'

'Nothing to speak of, m'lord.'

'Then go and get some food and rest. And send another messenger in. Dismissed.'

Terrance left the tent and Vandros turned to the captain. 'Glad I kept that boy with the messengers. Much safer for him there.'

Terrance voraciously wolfed down a hunk of hot bread and clutched a small half-wheel of cheese and a bottle of wine he had purloined from the commissary on his way from the Earl's tent. He felt fit, but he was starving. He reached the messengers tent, where an older messenger lay on a dry mat, his arm across his eyes. 'William,' said Terrance as he stuck his head in the tent.

'Terry?'

'Your turn.'

The man nodded and put on his boots. Terrance sat down to finish his food and William said, 'Much trouble?'

With a smile and a nod, he answered, 'Nothing to speak of.'

William returned the smile. 'I understand. See you soon.'

'Ride safe, William.'

'Ride safe, Terry,' was the reply and William departed.

The young messenger sat down to eat, hoping he could manage a full night's sleep before he was sent out again. But rested or not, if it was his turn, he'd go.

THE SYMPHONY OF AGES

ELIZABETH HAYDON

THE SYMPHONY OF AGES
ELIZABETH HAYDON

THE RHAPSODY TRILOGY:
Rhapsody: Child of Blood (1999)
Prophecy: Child of Earth (2000)
Destiny: Child of the Sky (2001)

Requiem for the Sun (2002)
Elegy for a Lost Star (2003)

The Symphony of Ages is written as a history in which the eras of time in the universe are recounted in seven distinct ages. The debut trilogy, *Rhapsody*, *Prophecy* and *Destiny*, and the subsequent sequels, are set at the end of the Fifth Age, the age of Schism, and the beginning of the Sixth Age, the age of Twilight.

A giant tree stands at each of the places, known as the birthplaces of Time, where the five primordial elements – air, fire, water, earth and ether – first appeared in the world. The oldest of these World Trees is Sagia, which grows on the Island of Serendair, the birthplace of ether. It is through the interconnected roots of Sagia that three people, all half-breeds, running from different pursuers, escape the cataclysm that destroys the Island and find themselves on the other side of the world, sixteen centuries later.

The three companions are initially antagonistic. Rhapsody, a woman of mixed human and Lirin blood, is a Namer, a student of lore and music who has learned the science of manipulating the vibrations that constitute life. She is on the run from an old nemesis, and is grudgingly rescued from his henchmen by two men. The Brother is an irritable and hideously ugly assassin with a bloodgift that makes him able to identify and track the heartbeats of any victim. His only friend, Grunthor, is a giant Firbolg Sergeant-Major with tusks, an impressive weapons collection and a fondness for singing bawdy marching cadences. The two men are fleeing the demon of elemental fire who has control of the Brother's true name. Rhapsody accidentally changes the Brother's name to Achmed the Snake, breaking the control the demon has over him, and making his escape possible. The Three make the trek along the roots of the World Trees through the belly of the Earth, passing through the fire at the centre with the help of Rhapsody's ability to manipulate names. In the process, the distrustful adversaries become grudging friends. When they emerge on the other side they find themselves transformed; time appears to have stopped for them. In addition, they discover the story of their homeland's destruction and that refugees from Serendair, alerted to the impending cataclysm by a king's vision, travelled across the world to the place they have emerged, built a new civilization and destroyed it in war in the intervening centuries. Now the people from their homeland, knows as Cymrians, are hiding or quiet about their ancestry. It becomes clear to the three companions that a demon known as a F'dor accompanied the refugees away from the Island, and is clinging to an unknown host, biding its time and sowing the seeds of destruction. *Rhapsody* chronicles the journey of the Three as they cope with the loss of their world and build a new life in this new land, and the rise of the Firbolg, the demi-human nomads that they eventually come to make a life with, and Achmed comes to rule, in the kingdom of Ylorc, the ruins of the Cymrian civilization carved into forbidding mountains. In *Prophecy*, the discovery of a dragon's claw in the ancient library of Ylorc leads Rhapsody to travel overland with Ashe, a man who hides his face, to find the dragon Elynsynos and return the claw before she destroys the Bolg in revenge. More of the F'dor's plot is uncovered, though its identity remains a mystery. Achmed discovers a child of living earth that slumbers endlessly in the ruins of a colony of Dhracians, tended to by the Grandmother, the only survivor of the colony. He realizes that the F'dor is seeking this Sleeping Child because her rib, made of Living Stone, would form a key like the one with which he opened Sagia – but in the demon's hand would be used to unlock the Vault of the Underworld and loose the remaining fire demons, who only seek destruction and chaos. *Destiny* follows the tale to its conclusion, the unmasking of the demon, the battle that ensues and the reformation of the Cymrian alliance.

The sequels, *Requiem* and *Elegy*, pick up the story three years later, and show the factors that eventually led to intercontinental war. With each new book, more of the history is laid bare, more of the secrets revealed, and more of the tale told in the style of a musical rhapsody.

The novella in this anthology is set in the Third Age, and chronicles the destruction of Serendair, telling the story of those who remained behind after the exodus.

THRESHOLD

BY ELIZABETH HAYDON

Two Ages ago, the doomed island of Serendair survived one cataclysm, when the burning star that came to be known as the Sleeping Child fell from the sky into the sea, taking much of the coastline, but sparing the middle lands. This time, as the Child that has slept beneath the waves for centuries signals its awakening, the earth and sea prepare for it to rise, and Gwylliam, the prescient king of the Island, foresees Serendair's obliteration in a vision of a second cataclysm.

Nearly everyone has left, the Nain of the northern mountains, the Lirin of the central forests and plains, and the humans, following their king in three great fleets to rebuild their civilization on another continent. The unbelieving, the foolish, the stubborn, the resigned, and a few truly abandoned souls remain, awaiting the end.

By the command of the king, a small detail of guards remains as well, to maintain order and protect those that stayed behind, and to keep some shred of the king's authority intact, just in case there is no second cataclysm. Condemned as they are, there is no way they could foresee what can happen when one pauses on the threshold between life and death.

This is their story, otherwise lost to history.

Hot vapour covered the sea, making it appear as calm and still as a misty morning.

There is more steam above the northern islands today, Hector thought, shielding his eyes from the stinging glare of the midday sun that blazed in rippling waves off the water, blinding in its intensity. *Most definitely.*

He glanced to his right, where Anais stood, staring into the impenetrable fog. The expression in his friend's silver eyes was calm, contemplative, as always; it had rarely varied since childhood. Hector knew he had made note of the thickening as well.

He watched a moment longer as the plumes of mist ascended, then stood and wiped the sweat from his forehead with the back of his sleeve, his gaze still affixed on the rising steam.

'Still unable to make out the increase, Sevirym?' he asked facetiously. He already knew the young soldier's answer.

'I see no difference from yesterday,' Sevirym replied rotely. 'Or the day before.'

Jarmon, older than the other men by twice over, took his hand down from his eyes as well and exhaled in annoyance.

'And so he will continue to insist, until the waves fill his mouth and the sea closes over his head,' he said. 'His eyes work perfectly, but he is blind as a mole nevertheless. Do not ask him any more, Hector. It sorely tries what is left of my patience.'

Sevirym spat into the sea and rose to follow Hector, who had turned and now ambled away from the abandoned dock.

'I am not under false illusions, despite what you believe, Jarmon,' he muttered. 'I just see no need to accept the inevitability of doom. Perhaps the king's vision was wrong, or he misinterpreted it. Or perhaps the Sleeping Child *is* destined to rise, but the sea won't consume the entire island; that didn't even happen when the star fell to Earth in the first place. Certainly we will lose some coastline, but if we go to higher ground, as we have been telling all the others to do –'

'I pray thee, cease,' Cantha said.

The raspy dryness of her voice sliced through the wind, causing Sevirym to fall immediately silent. Cantha used words sparingly, as if doing so pained her. It was difficult not to obey whatever she said.

Hector stopped, turning to look carefully for the first time in as long as he could remember at his companions, four completely different souls with one thing in common: they had each willingly sacrificed whatever remaining time life would have given them to stay behind on the Island, assisting in his futile mission.

He was surprised by how much they had changed physically since the exodus of the Fleets, but was even more shocked by the fact that he had failed until now to notice. Jarmon's beard, a famous shade of burnt red all his life, had gone grey enough to blend into the fog in which he stood; Cantha's body, always thin and dark as a shadow, had withered to little more than a whisper on the wind. Her eyes stared unflinchingly back at him from the haze; the strength of her will was such that it held the space her physical presence had once taken in the air.

Sevirym was staring at the ground, the sting of Cantha's words evident in his expression. Little more than a boy when he had rashly thrown his lot in with Hector, he had aged a score of years in the last five months, still maintaining an intermittent idealism that drove Jarmon to distraction. With each disappointment, each rebuke from an elder, the life seemed to seep a little more out of him, leaving him visibly older.

Hector inhaled slowly, then caught the look of understanding aimed at him by Anais as if it were a ball tossed to him. His closest friend, a brother in all but blood, Anais had always understood his thoughts without needing to hear them spoken aloud; perhaps it was their shared Lirin heritage that made their minds one while granting them opposite physical traits. Anais had been born with the traditional features of the Liringlas race, the silver eyes, the rosy skin and smooth hair that reflected the sun; Hector had favoured his mother's kin, dark of eye and hair, the crown of curls atop his head only reaching to Anais's brow. Now they looked remarkably similar – both had faded, their features dulled to grey colourlessness by circumstance and exhaustion and the heat of the boiling sea.

He watched for a moment more, still in the thrall of the silence that Cantha had commanded, unable to feel anything about the changes he had noticed. Then he signalled wordlessly for them to head out.

That silence held sway for the duration of the walk along the rocky shore until the group reached the spot where the horses waited, oblivious to the changes in the morning wind. Then Anais cuffed Sevirym across the back of the head.

'I discern the reasons for your reluctance now!' he joked. 'You wish to get out of sandbag duty.'

Sevirym mustered a slight smile. 'Can you blame me?'

'Certainly not,' Anais said agreeably. 'I just might form an alliance with you, Sevirym; we can mutiny and call for abandoning this mind-numbing task.'

Hector chuckled as he mounted his roan. 'A waste of time, that would be. The destruction of the Island may not be foregone, but sandbag duty remains as inevitable as death.'

'You are decorating the wind, Hector,' Jarmon said sourly. 'But if it occupies your mind while we wait, I suppose there is nothing to be said against it.'

Anais pulled himself into the saddle. 'Speak for yourself. *I'll* gainsay it. If I had known this is how you were to going to put us to use, I would not have stayed. It's one thing to agree to face certain death with one's best friend. It is altogether another to have one's carefully cleaned fingernails *ruined* playing in the dirt in the never-ending pursuit of useless sandbag fortifications. It is too onerous to be borne. You owe me a night of very expensive drinking, Hector.'

Hector chuckled again and spurred the roan to a canter.

They rode without speaking down the north-western shoreline to the outskirts of the abandoned fishing village and dismounted, to begin combing through what remained of the thatched huts and broken docks. Little effort had been needed to evacuate this place; fishermen knew the sea, and had been among the first to realize what was coming.

The five walked in silence through the packed sand and crushed shell streets, leading their mounts, the only sound the whine of the coastal wind, the cracking of thatch or the groaning of wood, the skittering of dock rats and the occasional snorting of the horses.

At the remains of each building one of the group peeled off from the others and poked through the fragments; little was left, as fishermen were practical people and had harvested whatever was usable in their village before packing their vessels and heading out in one of the earliest flotillas to the northern continent, the nearest haven.

On two earlier occasions they had found squatters, wild-eyed men, women and children who had come from places inland, seeking passage off the Island after the Fleets had already gone. These lost souls had taken shelter in the shells of the huts that remained, praying for miracles or wandering in aimless dementia. Luck had it that places for them could be found on the few remaining rescue ships that came in the wake of the exodus of the Fleets. Hector himself prayed that he would never again have to tell a living soul that the time had passed when escape was possible; the wailing that resulted was too reminiscent of the sobbing he had heard upon breaking other such news.

As always, his mind wandered to Talthea and the children. If he closed his eyes he could almost see her, her belly great with child, her hand on the shoulder of his son –

'Body,' Cantha called from within the ruins of the old salting shed.

Jarmon and Anais made their way over the litter of tin lantern shells and rusted iron hinges in the sand and opened the door. Cantha stood just over the threshold, her arms crossed, staring at the corpse, that of an old man who had curled up beneath what at one time had been the skinning table, its longboard missing. Flies swarmed in the heat.

'Wasn't here the last time we passed through – that was less than a fortnight ago, was it not, Hector?' Anais asked.

Hector only nodded, pulling forth his tinderbox as the others stepped out of the shed. He struck the flint against the steel and set the spark to the fragment of brittle twigs that remained in the roofing bundles.

'Whoever you are, I commit your body to the wind and your soul to the care of God, the One, the All,' he said blandly, a chant he had intoned many times in the last few weeks. It was a Namer's benediction, but without a name.

Cantha, Kith by birth and thus a child of the aforementioned wind, blew gently on the sparks as she passed. They glowed brighter, then kindled, igniting a moment later into a thin flame.

When the remnants of the shed began to fill with smoke, and the flames had started to consume the roof, the group turned away and continued their task. Finding no one else in the empty village, they mounted again and rode south, not looking back at the billowing smoke and flames behind them.

The cobbled streets of Kingston, the great port city that lay south along the coast of the fishing village, introduced the element of noise back into the journey as the horses' hooves clattered loudly over the stones, echoing off the empty alleyways leading to the town square.

The stoicism that had beset the faces of the travellers seemed to wane somewhat whenever they returned to the capital city of the west-lands, resolving into a quiet communal dismay. With each turn of the cycle, the shining jewel of the western seacoast looked more shabby, more broken, a desolate haven for ghosts and vermin that had once been a glistening city built by a visionary king centuries before.

Upon reaching the dry fountain in the square, the group dismounted. Sevirym's feet landed on the cobblestones first, followed by the muffled thuds from the others' boots.

'Damnation,' he murmured, looking up at the place where the statue of that long-dead king riding a hippogriff had once towered over the mosaic inlaid in the fountain's bed. The figure had been battered savagely, the formerly outstretched wings of the king's mount shattered into marble shards that lay scattered in the dry basin. The statue's stone head had been smashed from its shoulders and now lay in the street just outside the cap stones, the pupil-less eyes staring blindly at the hazy sky.

Jarmon had given a lifetime's service to the descendants of that king. He waded through the dust and gravel to the statue's base and numbly brushed the grit from the inscription:

> *An empire built by slaves crumbles in the despot's lifetime;*
> *A city built in freedom stands a thousand years.*

'Fell short by half, Your Majesty,' the elderly guard said softly, running his calloused finger over the letters.

'What was the purpose in this?' demanded Sevirym of no one in particular. 'What was the need? Did they not have enough to concern them that they had time for *this*? Is there not enough destruction coming that they needed more? Bloody *animals*.'

'Peace,' said Hector quietly. 'It is but a statue. It doesn't matter now. The ideal remains.'

Sevirym choked back a bitter laugh and seized the reins of his mount, leading the animal away from the dusty fountain.

'Must be hard on you westlanders, riding this continuous loop,' Anais said after a moment, once Jarmon and Cantha had followed Sevirym away from the town square and were now combing through the remains of their assigned streets. 'At least those of us who dwelt to the east beyond the Great River are spared watching the gradual destruction of our homelands.'

Hector said nothing but clicked to his roan. He and Anais fell into routine, joining the others in their search through the empty city.

He walked numbly past the abandoned shops where as a child he had delighted to linger, manoeuvring his horse around the mounds of broken glass and grit that had once been the window of the Confectionary; the bakeshop had produced baked goods so exceptional that the populace believed them to be imbued with magic. He allowed himself to linger again, one last time, trying to recall the scent of the flaky pastries, the sight of the castles rendered entirely in cookies and sweetmeats, the chocolate carvings of winged horses and dragons with strawberry scales, but he could see only the hollowed shell of the building with patches of light on the floor sinking in from the holes in the roof, could smell only the odour of pitch and oil and destruction.

How long he had stood, staring futilely back into the past, he did not know, but when Anais's voice finally reached his consciousness, it was like a bell rousing him from a deep sleep.

'Nothing save some stray dogs and a murder of crows that has taken refuge in the eaves of the old prelate's office.'

'A murder of crows?'

Anais adopted an aspect of mock seriousness. 'Aye, big uglies, too. One of them may have been the prelate's wife.'

Hector smiled. 'She certainly had quite a caw to her, but alas, none of the birds could be she. May God the One, the All, help my father – she sailed on his ship.'

Anais shook his head in sympathy. 'Poor MacQuieth. As if he did not have enough to contend with.'

Hector nodded, abandoning the attempt to summon better memories of the Confectionary. 'My father's greatest burden in the last days before the exodus was the irony of it all. He spent his youth fighting the Seren War to spare the Island from the fires of the Underworld, to keep the demons born of that fire from destroying Serendair. And now that the F'dor are defeated, the last of their kind sealed for ever in the Vault of the Underworld, the Island is going to succumb to fire after all – fire from the sky long lodged in the sea.'

'Somehow I doubt that the irony was your father's greatest burden,' Anais said, kicking the broken storefront sign away from the cobbled street.

'Did you look in on the stable?'

'Aye.'

'Are any of the horses still alive?'

'Remarkably, all of them are, the poor beasts. Most have withered to skin and bones. Cantha is feeding them the last of the hay.'

Hector loosed a deep sigh. 'I think we should deviate from our regular route, Anais. Before we leave here, let's take them out of the city to the fields at the crossroads and turn them loose. Surely it is kinder than leaving them in their paddocks, to be fed only when we come through. They can find grass and water there.'

'Agreed,' Anais said. 'The human population is gone now. What's a delay in a route that guards no one, anyway?'

Hector looked back over his shoulder up the main street that led at its terminus to the entrance of the Gated City in the north of Kingston.

'Not all of the human population is gone,' he objected quietly. 'Only those that were free to leave.'

Anais followed his gaze, then exhaled deeply.

As the sea wind blew through Kingston's desolate streets, whipping sand into their eyes, both men thought back to earlier days, after the exodus of the Fleets but before the rescue ships from other lands had stopped coming to Serendair. The young king, Gwylliam, newly crowned and the architect of the evacuation that had saved most of his subjects from death in the cataclysm that was still to come, had sailed on the last ship of the last Fleet, and so believed that every Seren citizen who wanted to leave had done so.

He had forgotten completely about the Gated City.

It was really not surprising that the City had been missed in the inventory of Gwylliam's conscious thought. Though it occupied geographical space in his realm, it was a world unto itself, a former penal colony of petty thieves and cutpurses that had evolved into its own entity, a dark and colourful society with layers of governance and threat that were incomprehensible to any but those who lived within its locked gates.

Despite the appearance of being contained, the Gated City clearly had as many tunnels out into the world beyond its fortifications as a beaver dam or a nest of rats. Even in the days prior to the Seren War that had ended two hundred years before, the City had been divided into the Outer Ring and the Inner Ring. The Outer Ring contained a flourishing market of exotic goods and eccentric services that citizens of the outside world could visit as long as they were checked through the gates.

They entered on the middle day of the week, known as Market Day, at the sound of the great brass bell, to shop in the bazaar, clutching the token that would allow them passage back out of the City again when the bell sounded again at closing time, buying perfumes that could transport the mind to places beyond the horizons of reality, linens and silks of indescribable colours, jewels and potions and soothing balms and myriad other wares from the far corners of the earth. The mere existence of these exotic goods was a broad hint at how porous the thick walls of the Gated City really were.

The Inner Ring was even more mysterious, a dark place to which none but the permanent residents of the City had access. Within its windowless buildings, in its shadowy alleys, another sort of business was conducted that those who lived outside the Gated City could only imagine in the course of their nightmares.

When Hector and his companions first realized that the Gated City had been overlooked, they had sought to offer its residents refuge on the first of the ships that had come in the wake of the exodus. He had gone to the City himself – its massive gates no longer were guarded from the outside. He had sprung the lock and thrown the gates open wide, issuing an invitation to the startled population he found on the other side to flee, to save themselves from the destruction that was surely to come when the Sleeping Child awakened and rose, taking the Island of Serendair back beneath the waves of the sea with it, as the king had prophesied it soon would.

The Gated City was teeming with people then. They stared at him as if he were mad, then turned away, averting their eyes, and went about their business as if he were not there.

The next day, when he returned to try and entreat them once again to reconsider, to explain once more the cataclysm that was coming, he found the gates closed again. A polite note was pinned to the outside of the gate, declining his offer with thanks and wishing him well.

The thought of the thousands of souls on the other side of those gates had haunted Hector for weeks afterwards, as he and the others carefully packed the remaining stragglers that came from the lands east of the Great River, or had somehow missed the exodus, on to the last of the rescue ships. Ofttimes he found himself walking outside the City's walls, wishing he had a way to make whatever governing force within them change its mind and spare its people.

After a while the point became moot. The ships stopped coming as the temperature of the sea over the gravesite of the Sleeping Child grew increasingly warmer, causing bilgewater to boil in the heat and some of the ships to burst at the seams. Hector no longer could summon the strength to think about those who might still be on the other side of the wall, condemned now to remaining on the Island to the end, just as the populations east of the Great River who had chosen to stay were condemned.

Just as he and his four companions were condemned.

It was far too late to worry about it now.

Hector blinked; the afternoon sun had shifted, blinding him. He shaded his brow and looked over at Anais, who nodded towards the docks.

'Come,' his Liringlas friend said, his silver eyes glinting in the light.

Without a word, Hector clicked to his horse and followed.

Bonfires burned along the wharf, the ashes mixing with the steam from the sea. Cantha, Jarmon and Sevirym must have found more bodies, human or otherwise, Hector knew, or something festering that warranted the spending of precious fuel in making the pyres.

The irony of the infernos no longer choked him. In the weeks since the last ship had come and departed, there had been many such bonfires along the route they travelled, a long south–north loop of the lands to the west of the Great River. They had ventured into the eastern territories only once – that wide expanse of land held the subkingdoms that had chosen to stay, either because they did not believe the king's vision, or, even in accepting it, preferred to remain in their birthlands to the end. Because the final departure of the Third Fleet had been launched from the port of Kingston, it was to the westlands that the stragglers had come late, and so it was this part of the realm that Hector had seen fit to guard, to maintain a futile sense of order in the last days. The rioting and looting had dwindled as starvation and disease had set in, and the western coast burned with cleansing pyres that would have made marvellous signal fires, beacons of distress, had there been any ship out on the sea to answer them.

The clouds of smoke swirled and danced, buffeted by the inconstant sea winds. Hector could see the black shadows of his friends moving silently in the haze, raking the ashes over, tossing driftwood on to the pyres.

On the docks a shade that must have been Anais beckoned to him.

Hector walked through the acidic mist, his eyes stinging from the smoke, to the end of the pier where his childhood friend waited and stood beside him, staring off into the lapping sea and the impenetrable fog. It was a ritual they both had observed many times since the Second Fleet had departed, this silent vigil. In standing there, together, as they had stood on that horrific day when together they bound over their wives and children into the hands of MacQuieth for safekeeping, for a moment there was a connection, a link back in Time, to the last place where life still held meaning for them.

'I no longer dream of them,' Anais said, gazing into the steam. His voice was muffled by the whine of the wind.

'No?'

'No. You?'

Hector inhaled deeply, breathing in the salt and the heavy scent of ash, thinking of Talthea and their son, and their unborn child. 'Yes. Each night.' He broke his gaze away and looked down through the mist at the waves cresting under the pier. 'Of nothing else.' It was the only thing that made the day bearable, the knowledge that the night would come, bringing such dreams.

Anais nodded thoughtfully. 'When awake, I can summon their faces if I try,' he said, 'but at night I dream of the World Tree.'

Hector blinked and turned to face his friend. 'Sagia?'

Anais nodded again. 'And the forest Yliessan where I was born.'

In the heat of the afternoon sun, Hector felt suddenly cold at his friend's mention of the great tree; it was the sacred entity of Anais's people, the Lirin, the children of the sky. Sagia was one of the five birthplaces of Time, where the element of Ether was born, and its power was the heart'sblood of the Island.

'What do you see in these dreams, Anais?'

Anais inclined his head as if to facilitate recall of the vision. 'I am standing in Yliessan at the base of the Tree, staring up its massive trunk to the lowest limbs that stretch out over the canopy of the other trees in the forest. Its silver bark is gleaming. Around the Tree are lines of Lirin of all strains, Lirindarc, the forest dwellers; Lirinved, the In-between, the nomads who live in both forest and field, making their home in neither; the Lirinpan from the cities – they are all waiting. The Liringlas, my own people, the skysingers, are at the end of the line, weaving flower garlands as they wait.

'One by one, they climb into the lowest branches, then higher, building shelters of sorts, nests, for lack of a better word. The Liringlas are adorning the trunk of Sagia with the floral garlands.' Anais closed his eyes, concentrating on the vision. 'They are singing. The Lirin are taking refuge in Sagia, awaiting the end in Her arms.'

Sevirym's voice shattered the stillness of the docks.

'Hector! Hector! Ship! A ship is coming into port!'

The men at the dock's end turned in surprise and stared harder into the mist.

At the outer reaches of their vision they could see it after a moment, sails spilling wind as it approached the lower landing at the southern tip of the main jetty. Hector ran back down the pier, followed a moment later by Anais, where they met up with the other three.

Jarmon was shaking his head. 'Fools,' he muttered, watching the vessel as it disappeared into the steam rising off the seawall. 'Must be lost. Can't be a ship's captain in the world who doesn't know the peril at this point.'

Cantha shook her head too. 'Not lost. Deliberate in its movements.'

'Hoay!' Sevirym called, jogging towards the jetty and waving his arm in the swirls of floating black ash from the bonfires. 'Hoay! Here!'

Nothing but the sea wind answered them.

They stood in the heavy mist for what seemed a half-hour or more, until finally Anais spotted a dim light making its way over the waves in their direction, bobbing up and down near the water's surface.

'They've launched a longboat,' he said, pointing out the approaching glow. 'A lantern lights its prow, low to the water.'

'The ship's a two- or three-masted schooner,' Jarmon reported. 'Brigantine, mayhap – I can't make it out. Big monster, she is. Must have dropped anchor just outside the seawall. Can't say as I blame her. Wouldn't want to navigate this harbour in the fog now that the light towers have gone dark.'

'Sevirym, light a brand and wave it,' Hector called as he walked to the end of the jetty. He strained to see through the smoke and mist, but caught only occasional sight of the tiny lantern that bobbed nearer on the wide bay.

'Madness,' Jarmon muttered under his breath as Sevirym climbed to the top of the massive wall of sandbags that they had erected along the coastline and held the firebrand aloft for light. 'It has been more than two full turns of the moon since the last one – why is a ship coming now? Can they not see the rising steam? It must reach well into the sky; how can they miss that from open sea?'

'Perhaps they have the same sort of eyes as Sevirym,' Anais suggested. 'Let us wait and see.'

They watched in impatient silence for a long while, then simultaneously made their way down the long pier through the brightness of the fog that had swallowed Hector, who waited at its end.

The light from the lantern on the longboat's prow was now in close sight, its radiance diffused by the glow of the sun in the steam that blanketed the coast. Over the sound of the waves slapping the pier they heard a ragged voice calling.

'Hoay!'

Farther out in the harbour, a score of voices picked up the hoarse cry.

'Hoay! Anyone there? Hoay!'

Before the eyes of the five companions, twinkling lights appeared, spread in an arrowpoint formation behind the first beacon. A longboat guided by a boatswain and steered by four rowers emerged from the fog, followed a moment later by five others that followed it.

In the first boat a man was standing; they could see his shadow begin to take on form and definition as the longboat neared the pier.

'Hoay! I am looking for Sir Hector Monodiere! Be any of you he?'

'I am he,' Hector said, grasping the pylon and leaning out over the end of the pier to get a better look at the man in the longboat through the hazy light. 'Why have you come here?'

The man shielded his eyes. 'I am Petaris Flynt, captain of the *Stormrider*, sailing under the flag of Marincaer. I bear news; toss me a line.'

Jarmon and Anais set about mooring the lead longboat, while Cantha went back to assist Sevirym in guiding the remaining ones to the pier with the firebrand. Hector offered the captain his hand and discovered upon pulling the man on to the dock how weak his grip had become, how much flesh had been lost from his arm.

The captain was a burly man, stout and barrel-chested, with a full grey beard and eyes as black as the depths of the sea. He looked up at Hector, half a head taller, then allowed his eyes to wander to the others and beyond to the empty wharf. He shook his head and sighed.

'Who could ever have imagined the great light tower of Kingston would go dark in my lifetime?' he mused. 'I had thought the rising of the sun was more in doubt than the presence of that beacon. Alas and alack.' He signalled to the sailors in the longboat to be at ease, then met Hector's eye again.

'We are here to take one last load, Sir Hector – whatever stragglers remain, whoever may have missed the last ship out – this truly *is* the final chance they will have. The sea above the Northern Isles is roiling in the heat; the bilge in any ship now boils within ten leagues of Balatron. We don't know if we will make it out ourselves – we sail with the tide at sunset, heading south west as fast as the wind will carry us until we hit the Icefields, then looping back to the north. Anyone on board at sunset can come with us. All others remain – no exceptions.'

'May God the One, the All forgive my ingratitude, but why did you come here?' Hector asked incredulously. 'The shipping lanes have been closed to this place for more than two months now. The exodus was completed three months before that; the Third Fleet left in mid-spring. There is no one left to save – everyone who was willing to leave is already gone.'

Flynt's brow furrowed. 'I came by the order of the king of Marincaer, who was asked to send me by Stephastion, one of the barons of Manosse.'

'Manosse?' Hector glanced at Jarmon and Anais, who shrugged. Manosse was a great nation half a world away on the eastern coast of the Northern Continent, far from the lands to which the refugees that had refused to sail with the Fleets had fled.

'Aye,' said Flynt. 'It is from Manosse that the news comes as well. Your father's fleet landed there.'

'In Manosse?' Hector asked in concern. 'Why? What happened? That is not to where they were bound.'

'Apparently they were beset by a great storm,' Flynt replied, speaking rapidly. 'Sundered at the Prime Meridian. Many ships were lost. Part of the surviving flotilla landed at Gaematria, the Isle of the Sea Mages, though it is a forbidden place to most. Your father led the remainder of the fleet back to Manosse, probably because he knew the weakened ships would not survive the rest of the voyage east to the Wyrmlands, where they were originally headed. They plan to stay there, I'm told.'

Hector nodded. 'What of the First Fleet? And the Third?'

The captain shook his head. 'No word. But if they were going to the Wyrmlands, I fear there will never be word from them again. That place is not part of the Known World for a reason.' He glanced around nervously.

'Do you have word of my family?' Hector asked.

'I am told your wife and son are safe in Manosse. And your daughter as well – your child has been born, safe and healthy, I am to tell you.'

'Do you know what name she was given?'

'No, but your wife apparently said that you do.'

'And my father – he is well? And his ship?'

Flynt looked away. 'He survived the trip. His ship remained intact, I am told.'

Hector and Anais exchanged a glance of relief; the news boded well for Anais's family, who had travelled with Hector's, though it was clear the captain was leaving something out.

'Tell me of my father, whatever it is you have not said,' Hector asked. 'Is he ill?'

'Not to my knowledge.' The sea captain gestured nervously to the crew of his longboat, who took up oars and rowed towards the shore, then turned his attention back to the young man.

'Your father stands vigil in the sea, Sir Hector. Once what remained of the Second Fleet was docked, and his duty discharged, he went to the peninsula of Sithgraid, the southernmost tip of Manosse, and waded into the surf. It is said that he stands there, night into day into night again, refusing sustenance and company from any but your wife and son. When the baron asked your wife what he is doing, she merely said that he is waiting.'

Hector absorbed the words in silence, gazing off to the eastern horizon. 'Thank you.'

Impatience won its battle for control of the sea captain. 'All right, then, Sir Hector; I've delivered my news. As I have told you, I have come to take the last souls who wish to leave before the Island succumbs. Gather them.'

As if hearing the words for the first time, Hector turned and looked intently at Flynt, then nodded.

'Very well.'

'Open the gate, Sevirym.'

The young soldier looked doubtful as his gaze ran up the massive entranceway to the empty guard towers on either side. He stared at the wall that encircled the Gated City, and, noting no one walking atop it, grasped hold of the rusted handle and pulled with all his strength.

The heavy wooden gate, bound in brass, swung open silently.

'Would you look at that,' Jarmon muttered bitterly. 'For four hundred years it took three men to spring those brass locks, seven to open that gate into this nest of thieves. Now it swings open like my mother's kitchen door. Truly I have lived too long.'

Hector stepped through the entranceway past the thick walls reinforced internally with iron bars, trying to absorb the sight beyond them.

The Gated City was empty.

Or perhaps it only appeared that way. From every street corner, every boarded window and alleyway, he could sense the presence of shadows, could feel the weight of eyes on him, even though there was no one visible.

Through the silent thoroughfares they walked, stepping over the detritus of the bazaar that littered the streets, shreds of cloth and broken market carts, sparkling glass fragments and streaks of soot from long-cold roasting fires. At each street corner Hector stopped and peered into the recesses of the Outer Ring, but saw nothing; called, but received no answer.

Finally they came to the great well at the centre of the Gated City, a place that a revered historian had described in his writings as the 'upspout of a warren of Downworlders, people who lived entirely in the darkness beneath city streets, in lairs with more tunnels that a queendom of ants'. Hector didn't know if he believed the lore of those mythical human rats, and didn't care; he only knew that sound in the well would reverberate throughout the city. He leaned over the edge and shouted.

'Hullo! Come out now, all you within the sound of my voice! I command you, in the name of Gwylliam, High King of Serendair, quit this place at once! The last ship that will ever come waits in the harbour, and sails with the tide at sunset. Come! The Sleeping Child rises in the north west – save yourselves!'

His words resounded off the stones of the alleyways, echoed down the well and through the streets. Hector waited.

There was no answer.

'Anais,' Hector said without turning, maintaining his watch on the streets and alleys before him, 'go back to the gate and ring the Market Day bell.'

'Are you certain it is there still?' Anais asked doubtfully. 'Most of Kingston's bells were melted down for ship fittings when the exodus began.'

'That bell was within the Gated City, which was overlooked in the planning of the exodus. It was too large to be taken by those who have already scurried out of here through whatever holes there may be in the walls. Keep ringing it until the walls start to give way.'

Unconsciously the other three moved into a circle with their backs to Hector, watching at the compass points for signs of response. Aside from a shifting of shadows and a flutter here and there in the darkness, there was none.

They stood thus, crossbows nocked but pointed at the cobblestones, still as those stones, even as the great bell sounded loudly from atop the wall at the gate.

Waves of harsh brass sound rippled through the empty streets as Anais struck again and again. A wild flapping rose from the eaves of a boarded mudbrick building near the well; a flock of roosting pigeons started and took to the sky, squawking angrily.

For fifteen long minutes the great bell kept sounding, the clanging trailing off into silence after a few sustained moments, only to resume in its ear-splitting furore again and again. Hector continued to stare into the darkened alleyways, enduring the cacophony without wincing, until finally a dark outline of a man appeared at the end of a street near the well. The man waited until Anais paused in his pounding of the bell, then shouted down the empty street.

'Have him stop immediately, or I will order him shot.'

'It would be an unwise order to give,' Hector shouted back, as the three that surrounded him levelled their crossbows, 'and your last.'

A ragged chuckle came from the bony figure, and the man at the alley's end came forward, limping slightly into the afternoon light as the bell began to crash once more.

'Hold, Anais,' Hector yelled as the thin man stepped into the square the same moment the ringing paused again. He watched impatiently as the man leaned on his walking stick and turned his head to the south to scan the distant wall. The others did not lower their weapons.

'What, pray tell, do you think you are doing?' the ragged man asked in a mixture of annoyance and inquisitiveness. 'Besides disturbing the pigeons and my afternoon nap.'

'A final rescue ship has come into the harbour. I am here to make one last attempt to save what remains of the king's people.'

The bony man broke into a wide smile graced intermittently by teeth.

'Ah,' he said smugly, running a thin hand over the grey stubble on his face. 'Now the source of our misunderstanding is clear. You are merely confused.' His tone turned conciliatory, with a hint of exaggerated condescension, as if he were speaking to children. 'You see, these are not the king's people; they never were. The king forgot about this place long ago, just as his father and his grandfather before him did. I am king of this place now – well, they call me the Despot, actually – now that anyone with actual power has long ago left. These are *my* people. *I* say whether they come or go, live or die.' He leaned forward on his walking stick, his patchy smile growing brighter. 'And I say they are staying. So go about your business, sir knight; run along and board your ship. We do thank you for your kind offer, but respectfully, as king of those that remain, I decline.'

'You are king of nothing,' Jarmon shouted scornfully.

The Despot laughed. 'Well, I have something in common with Gwylliam, then. How repulsive. I am more king than he ever was, he who frightened the people with his visions, his predictions of cataclysm, and then left them, a king who abandoned his birthright to save his own hide. At least I stayed with my people – held my post. Unlike Gwylliam, I am not a coward.'

Jarmon's expression blackened and he raised his bow sight to his eye.

'Give the word, Hector,' the old guard said angrily. 'I want this one.'

'There is no time for your games, your foolishness,' Hector said tersely to the Despot, raising a cautionary hand to Jarmon.

'Then stop wasting what time you have left here,' the Despot said, his tone flattening. 'Do you not know the origins of this place? What is there here worth saving?'

Before answering, Hector sized him up. He had always been told that the city beyond the gates was full of tricks, but the scrawny man before him had no weapons he could detect, and he saw no open doors or windows that might conceal bowmen. He could not be certain that Anais's position was clear a block or so down.

'Them,' he said simply, gesturing into the dark streets and alleyways. 'Anyone who did not have the chance to choose life; anyone who was condemned as an afterthought. One man. One woman. One child. Any and all that want to leave, whatever their crimes, whatever their innocence. In the name of Gwylliam, the king, I am here to offer them that chance. Now, move aside! We have no time for this! We stand on the threshold of death.'

The eyes of the Despot darkened as well, revealing a soulless depth.

'By all means, step over, then,' he said icily. 'It's rude to hover in doorways.'

'After you, Your Majesty,' Hector replied.

He dropped his hand.

Three bolts were unleashed simultaneously, piercing the ragged man in the eye, heart and forehead, tearing through him as if he were parchment. The Despot fell back on to the broken cobblestones of the square with a thud, sending another bevy of pigeons skywards. The noise of his fall and their rise echoed through the empty streets, followed by a deafening silence.

'Anais, ring the bell thrice more,' Hector called over his shoulder.

The metallic crashing resumed, then ceased, dying away slowly.

'Now, come!' Hector shouted into the Outer Ring. 'Come with us if you want to live!'

For a long moment nothing answered him. Then, at the outer edges of his sight in the dark alleyways, Hector saw the shadows thicken a bit, then move.

Slowly, one and two at a time, figures began to move into the light of the square, like ghosts in the haze of the sun, squinting as if in pain. Thin men, emaciated women and a few tattered children came forward, hovering close to one another, their eyes hollow and downcast. Hector loosed his breath; until this moment, he could not have been certain that there was anyone in the dark city left to save.

'Sevirym,' he said to the young soldier, 'lead these people to the pier and get them aboard the ship. Send Anais back when you pass through the gate; we will go quickly house to house, and into the Inner Ring.'

Sevirym nodded curtly at the mention of the dark interior of the Gated City, then turned and gestured excitedly to the two dozen or so human shadows wandering slowly toward the gates.

'Come,' he shouted. 'Follow me to the ship – and to a chance at living another day.'

Street after street, building after mudbrick building revealed no one living, only broken remains. There were decidedly more bodies in the Gated City than they had found elsewhere in the westlands, too many to burn or even pray over.

As they ran from lintel to lintel, from post to pillar, they called into the empty corridors and banged on the walls and stairs to rouse anyone in the upper floors or lofts, but only managed to disturb nests of rats, roosting birds and packs of feral cats ripping out what little they could scrounge from the charnel.

Finally Anais, who had clambered from rooftop to rooftop through much of the city, climbed down and stood in the middle of the street before an interior wall that ran perpendicular to the rest of the buildings, sealing the Outer Ring from the dark streets that lay beyond it. A black wrought-iron gate shaped like a giant keyhole was broken off its hinges, the metal twisted with a savage ferocity. Anais bent over at the waist, panting from exertion and frustration.

'The Inner Ring must begin here,' he said between breaths. 'You are going to want to go in, aren't you, Hector?'

'Yes.'

Anais sighed. 'Of course. A waste of valuable air to have asked in the first place. Be so good as to allow me a moment to catch my breath. I am growing too old for this nonsense.'

Hector said nothing. *What I would give if only you had the chance to grow old, Anais,* he thought.

'Sun's descending,' Cantha said, shading her eyes with her long-fingered hand and staring into the all-but-impenetrable mist. 'Two hours and 'twill be beyond the horizon.'

'Right; thirty minutes' more search at most, then,' Hector said, nodding his head at Jarmon to pull the twisted portal open. 'And let us stay together in here. This was, in its day, a largely evil enclave, the closest place to the Vault of the Underworld that existed on this Island; we don't want to make a misstep.'

Quickly they pulled themselves through the portal, avoiding the jagged metal, and stepped for the first time in any of their lives into the streets of the Inner Ring.

It was stunning in its dullness.

The buildings in what had once been one of the darkest corners of the world were no different from the ones in the Outer Ring, or even in the more populated parts of the westlands, for that matter. The streets here were, if possible, even quieter than they had been in the outside world, even more devoid of anything valuable left behind. The buildings stood, unmolested, appearing for all the world as pedestrian as the buildings of Kingston's residential area. The only discernible difference was the proximity of them; they crowded each other for space, squeezing next to each other on narrow streets. Ropes hung intermittently from windows, tying the streets closely together in the air above the ground as well.

Hector pulled aside a half-door that hung from only one hinge and peered into the recesses of a dilapidated shop.

'My father walked these streets many times,' he mused aloud. 'He said there was a darkness that hung over the place, that was present in the very air itself. It must have been extant in the nefarious population that lived here; it appears they took it with them when they left.'

'Good,' Jarmon muttered. 'Perhaps it obscured their path on the sea and they sank without a trace.'

They combed each street, each alley, calling rotely as they had in the Outer Ring, but within this smaller, closer section of the Gated City their words were swallowed in the devouring silence that reigned here.

At one street corner halfway in, Cantha stopped and turned down the thoroughfare; the others followed her past a stand of dark buildings to a place where one appeared to be missing. A grey hole of cold ash held its place amid the otherwise unscathed structures, like a missing tooth in a dull smile.

The Kith woman inclined her head into the wind and inhaled.

'The Poisoner's,' she said. It was the only building in the Inner Ring that had been razed.

'They took their secrets with them as well,' said Anais.

'There's no one here, Hector,' Jarmon called impatiently from further up the street, his voice muted. 'Can we quit this place now? We have searched as well as God, the One, the All could possibly ask; let us be out of here before we set off a trap or discover some other sign of contempt left behind for the forces of His Majesty.'

Hector glanced around at the desolate streets, the hollow buildings, silent witnesses to acts that would have defied description even if their stones could talk. *Another trove of mystery enters the annals of Time,* he thought bemusedly, then turned back to the others who watched him intently from further up the street.

'Yes,' he said at last. 'We've searched enough. Let's be off.'

The second longboat was preparing to depart when Hector and the others returned to the pier in Kingston's harbour.

Sevirym waved for the boatswain to wait and jogged back up the dock, looking behind his friends in the mist.

'Anyone else?'

'No one,' Hector said flatly. 'The City is empty.'

The captain of the *Stormrider* came forward hastily out of the fog.

'We are not even two-fifths laden with this boatload,' he said sombrely. 'Surely this is not all?'

'I'm afraid it is.'

'Hardly worth the risk, the effort,' Petaris Flynt muttered. 'A score of ragged human rats – for this we chanced boiling and splitting?'

Hector's brow darkened in the dimming light of the setting sun.

'If you rescue but one soul, it will have been worth the effort,' he said bitterly. 'Would that I had the chance to do so. Take to your ship, captain, and set sail. Hurry home to whomever you love, bearing your human cargo. Quit this place while you can.'

The captain nodded sharply. 'Very well. Climb aboard, then, Sir Hector, and we'll be off for the Icefields.'

Five pairs of eyes stared at him stonily through the mist.

'You misunderstand,' Anais said finally after a long and awkward moment. 'We are not leaving.'

'I am sworn to stay here,' Hector interrupted, waving Anais into silence. 'By command of my king and lord, I am to remain to keep order in the last days, and hold the line of succession.'

'Madness!' puffed Flynt. 'The king is gone, Sir Hector; the exodus has passed, and passed successfully. There is nothing left to guard. Surely your king did not mean for you to remain to your death, now that your duty is fully discharged! Come aboard.'

'I thank you, but I cannot.'

'By the king's command?'

'By the king's command, yes.'

'Then your king was a fool,' said the sea captain contemptuously. 'If there is nothing left to guard, to what end does a sovereign condemn good men to certain death standing watch over *nothing*? What sort of man, what sort of king, would do that?'

'My king,' growled Jarmon, his eyes blazing in fury as he elbowed his way between Anais and Hector, stopping a hairbreadth from the captain's face. 'Our king. And you would be well advised not to gainsay him again, if you do not wish to face certain death yourself.'

'Think of your family, man,' the captain said desperately, ignoring the old guard and turning to Hector once more.

Hector leaned closer. 'I do, with each breath,' he said, gently pulling Jarmon back. 'But I am sworn to my king, and they –' he nodded at the other four, 'are sworn to me. I thank you for your concern, Captain Flynt, and for your heroic efforts on behalf of the remaining population of this land. But only one of us will be going with you.'

The captain blinked; the tension that had run in the air like steel bands a moment before vanished, replaced with shock as the four others looked askance at each other, bewilderment on their faces.

Hector turned and signalled to his companions, nodding down the pier. Together they walked halfway back to the dock, shaking their heads, exchanging glances of confusion, until Hector stopped out of earshot of the captain, and pointed through the mist to shore, where the dark mountain of sandbags loomed.

'Cantha, Jarmon, walk on,' he said softly. 'You too, Anais.'

'Me?!' Sevirym shouted, too overwrought to catch the words before they exploded from his lips. 'You are sending *me* away? No, Hector. I'll not leave.'

Hector signalled again to his puzzled friends, urging them away from the pier.

'Yes, Sevirym,' he said quietly, laying a hand on Sevirym's arm. The young soldier shrugged it off angrily. 'Yes, you will.'

'Why? Has my loyalty to you been any less than theirs? Have I dishonoured you, failed you –'

'Never,' Hector interrupted him, taking his arm again. 'Hear me, Sevirym; time is short and words should be used sparingly, so that their meaning is undiluted. No man could have asked for a more loyal companion and a better friend than you have been to me, to the others – to this dying land. But I need you to go with the captain now, to guard the refugees, and to make certain they are not combative.' Involuntarily he winced at the sight of the pain on his friend's face.

'I want to remain here, Hector.'

Hector sighed. 'Well, that makes one of us, Sevirym. I do not – but what I want is not at issue. Nor is what you want. We are both prisoners of what needs to be done, as decided by the one who commands us.' His tone softened. 'You are fulfilling the same order of the king that the rest of us are – "Keep my people safe in the last days." These ragged refugees – they are the king's subjects as much as you or I. They need our protection. Get them out of here, Sevirym. Take them to safety.'

Sevirym dropped his eyes, unable to maintain a calm mien any more.

'You are commanding me to do this, against my will and my vow?' he said, his voice choked with anguish.

'Only if you force me to,' Hector replied gently. 'Rather, I am asking you to do this for me, as my friend and brother. You swore to stand by me, to help me in this task that was commanded of me. In leaving with the ship, you are helping me far more than by staying.'

For a long moment, Sevirym continued to stare at the rotting planks of the pier, listening to the splash of the waves beneath the mist. Then finally he nodded.

In turn Hector nodded to the three standing on the docks and turned to walk with Sevirym back to the end of the pier. Anais raised his hand; Sevirym lifted his half-heartedly in return. Jarmon bowed his head, then turned away. Only Cantha remained still, her eyes staring sharply through the fog, her face expressionless.

'I am abandoning them, and you,' Sevirym muttered as they walked back to where the longboats and the ship's captain waited. 'I may live, but you are sentencing me to life as a coward.'

Hector stopped suddenly, dragging Sevirym to a harsh halt by the arm.

'Damn your tongue if it utters such a thing again,' he said sharply. 'And damn your mind if it believes it. What I ask of you requires more bravery than staying behind, Sevirym; I am asking you to live. Dying is easy; any fool can do it – it's living that requires courage. Now get on that damned ship and do your duty to the king, to me, and to yourself.'

After a moment Sevirym lifted his eyes and met Hector's. 'Why me?' he asked softly. 'I go, Hector, but I just want to know why you chose me, and not Anais, or Jarmon or Cantha.'

Hector exhaled. 'Because you have never really believed that you were going to die, Sevirym. Unlike the rest of us, you kept hoping that the Island could be spared, that death was not inevitable – and perhaps that is a sign from God, the One, the All, that for you it is not.'

Sevirym continued to stare at him for a long time, then finally nodded, acceptance in his eyes.

'I will find Talthea and your children, Hector, and guard them until my last breath.'

Hector embraced him. 'Thank you, my friend. Tell Talthea that they were in my thoughts until the last, and what happened here. Everything, Sevirym, tell her everything; do not spare her. She is stronger than any of us.' His grip tightened. 'I will say this to you, Sevirym, and it is something I have not said, nor will I say, to any other living soul.' He leaned closer and whispered into his friend's ear.

'None of us should have had to stay.'

Sevirym, unable to form words, nodded again.

They walked to the end of the pier, swathed in impenetrable vapour. The shade of the captain was waiting still. Hector watched as the boatswain lifted the lamp from the prow of the longboat to light Sevirym's way aboard, then raised a hand in final salute.

In the misty glow of the longboat's lantern, Sevirym held up his hand in return.

Hector stared, trying to keep his eyes focused until the shadow had slipped away into the sea mist, then turned to the captain again.

'Thank you,' he said.

'Is that all, then?' Petaris Flynt said regretfully. 'I cannot change your mind, Sir Hector?'

'That is all,' Hector answered. 'Can you take some of the horses from the livery? Those mounts served the king with their lives as well; if you have room for them, it would gladden my heart to see you spare them.'

Flynt nodded dully. 'Such a waste,' he muttered. 'A handful of human rats, some skeletal horses and one soldier, while good men stay behind to their doom. Proffer my apologies for my insult to your elderly friend, Sir Hector; any king who inspires so much loyalty and devotion in such obviously true men must have been a very great king indeed.'

Hector exhaled evenly. 'He was our king,' he said simply.

'I understand,' said Flynt. He glanced towards the setting sun. 'Have your companions round up those animals and get them into the long-boats – we can only make one last trip back to the ship before we sail.' The captain prepared to descend into the closest of the five remaining longboats.

Hector stopped him. 'I have found that each life I spare saves my own a little bit,' he said, shaking the man's hand. 'Thank you for helping me in this way, Captain Flynt.'

The captain nodded. 'I'm sorry I won't have the chance to know you longer, Sir Hector,' he said. Then he stepped into the longboat, shouted orders to the crew, and disappeared into the devouring fog.

As the sun slipped below the horizon, the four remaining companions stood atop the ramparts of sandbags, watching the dark masts of the *Stormrider* become part of the twilight beyond the heavy mist, listening to the crashing of the waves and the howling of the sea wind.

'That be it, then,' said Jarmon finally when night took hold, casting the last of the light from the sky.

The others said nothing. Anais climbed down from the sandbag wall, handed Jarmon the firebrand, and jogged to the end of the pier, letting the fog swallow him. When he reached the edge he peered out into the blackness but saw nothing.

'Godspeed, Sevirym,' he shouted into the wind. 'Mind the ice!'

Hector descended from the wall as well. 'I suppose we should put an hour or so into reinforcing the sandbags,' he said, brushing the grit from his hands. 'The burlap is long gone, but we can continue spading and packing around the base of the –' His words choked off as his eyes came to rest on the two shadows that hovered at the edge of the darkness behind them.

A woman was standing at the far end of the wharf that bordered the town, clutching the remains of a tattered shawl around her thin shoulders. More wraith than human, she said nothing, but stared out into the fog with hollow eyes.

Beside her was a child, a boy, it appeared, long of hair and slight, young enough still to warrant the holding of his hand, though he stood alone. Like his mother's, his eyes were large and appeared dark in the light of the brand, but unlike her he still showed signs of life behind those eyes.

The firelight flashed for a moment as Jarmon's hand quivered.

'Aw, *no*,' he muttered. 'No.'

For a moment the only sound at the edge of the pier was the ever-present howling of the wind. A spattering of icy rain blew across the deserted wharf, stinging as it fell. Then Hector turned to the others, angrily brushing the hair from his eyes.

'Jarmon, Cantha – find me a longboat. There must be something still around here, a rowboat, a fisherman's skiff, something –'

'Hector –' Anais said quietly.

'Give me the brand,' said Hector frantically, motioning to Jarmon. 'I'll row them out quickly. The ship will see the light –'

'Stop it, Hector,' Anais said more firmly.

The young knight's eyes held the bright gleam of desperation in the fireshadows.

'For God's sake, find me a bloody *boat* –'

'Cease,' said Cantha. Her voice cut through the wind. The others turned to see her face impassive, her eyes glinting either from sympathy or, more likely, from the rivulets of cold water that were now insistently strafing her eyelashes. 'Get them out of the rain.'

The companions watched their leader silently, intently, oblivious to their increasingly sodden clothes and heads. Hector bent over at the waist and put his hands on his knees, as if suddenly winded. He stood thus for a long moment, then nodded, gulping for air.

'We will take shelter in the livery stable until the storm passes,' Anais said, squeezing Hector's shoulder as he passed on his way to the woman and the child. 'It's the only building left with most of a roof.'

Hector nodded, still bent over.

'We will take them with us to the inn at the crossroads for the night,' he said when he could speak again.

The woman did not move as Anais approached, but the child's eyes widened in fear and he dashed behind her. The Liringlas soldier stopped, then turned back to the others.

'Hector, you had best deal with this,' he said, his voice flat in the wind. 'I don't think he has seen one of my race before.'

Hector straightened and shook the rain from his shoulders and head. 'I am part Liringlas too, Anais.'

Anais gestured impatiently. 'Aye, but you look more human, because you *are*. Come over here.'

Hector exhaled deeply, then walked quickly to Anais's side. 'Come with us,' he said to the woman, but she did not appear to be listening; if she were not standing erect, he would have believed that the life had already fled her body. He crouched down and put out his hand to the child.

'Come with me,' he said in the same tone he had used to coax his own son, only a year or so older than this one. 'We will take you where it is dry.'

The child stared out from behind the woman, water dripping from his hair.

Hector beckoned to him with his hand. 'Come along,' he said again.

The boy considered a moment more, then took the woman's hand and led her, still clutching her now-sodden shawl, to where the men stood.

With a sizzle, the brand in Jarmon's hand extinguished in the rain.

The child slept all the way to the crossroads, leaning against Hector, sitting before him in the saddle. The woman, who rode behind Anais, slept as well, or at least seemed to; her hollow eyes remained open, glassy and unfocused, but her breathing took on a more even rhythm after a mile or so.

Neither had spoken a word the entire time the six people had huddled in the livery. The insistent rainshower had given way quickly to a full-blown storm, tempestuous and drenching; the sheets of rain rattled what remained of the stable's roof and poured in small water-falls through the openings.

'Well, at least the horses got out,' Jarmon had observed sourly, shifting to avoid a new leak.

'Something to be grateful for,' Anais had said. Hector had said nothing.

After the worst of the storm had passed, leaving great clouds of mist blanketing the cold ground, the travellers had taken to the road leading east out of Kingston, through the broken city archway that had once been an architectural marvel but now lay in pieces in the roadway. In the dark the destruction was not as apparent as it was by day, and once the city was behind them there was little indication that anything at all was wrong with the world on this rainy night. The horses trotted easily over the muddy roadway, seemingly invigorated, perhaps relieved to be away from the cleansing pyres and out in the cool mist of rolling fields again.

A hour's ride put them at the crossroads, where the legendary inn stood, abandoned and empty of most of its furnishings. The Crossroads Inn had been a place of historical impact beyond any a building should have a right to possess; a critical meeting place and refuge of blessed ground in the Seren War two centuries before and even after it, famous for its hospitality, safety and the vast stone hearth where the fire was never extinguished. Now it was dark, hollow as the woman's eyes. Its door, once gilded with a golden griffin and said to be the talisman by which the inn remained untouched even in the times when enemies occupied the westlands, was missing, taken over the sea with the First Fleet. Its entrance yawned open like a dark cave.

The inn's hospitality may have been intrinsic, because it remained in the place even now, shell that it was. It was their favourite resting place, a refuge still, even in the absence of innkeeper, barkeep, house-hold spirits or door.

Jarmon dismounted, lit a brand and went inside, scouting to ascertain whether anything had come to call since the last time they had been here. While he quickly checked the empty tavern and rooms, Cantha assisted Hector and Anais from their horses with their human cargo.

'Where did they come from?' Hector asked as the boy sleepily wound his thin arms around the knight's neck.

'From the market, I'd wager,' said Anais, helping the woman down from the saddle.

'How could we have missed them?'

His friend shrugged. 'I don't know that we did. They might have walked from east of the Great River, or a village along the river itself. We can't save everyone, Hector, though you certainly insist upon trying. Surely you must know that by now.'

Hector passed his hand gently over the sleeping boy's back, thinking of another child like him. 'I do, Anais.'

Cantha strode off into the darkness; both men took note of her passing but did not comment. They had become accustomed to her nightly disappearances as she went to commune, as all members of her race did, with the wind.

'Clear inside,' Jarmon called from within the flickering light of the inn.

'Good. Get a fire going, Jarmon. Anais, go below to the stores and bring up victuals if there are any left.' He stepped through the dark opening and into the cold tavern.

Anais, following behind, nodded. 'There should be, unless the vermin got to them. Sevirym laid in an estimable supply down there.' He led the woman inside, then released her hand and crossed to the stairway, starting down to the hidden passage where the food was kept, chuckling softly. He turned in the dark on the stairs, his silver eyes twinkling. 'Remember how he'd say that there was no point in surviving a cataclysm only to starve to death?'

Hector smiled slightly in return. 'Yes.'

'It was a good thing you did, sending him with the *Stormrider*, Hector,' Anais called over his shoulder as he headed down the steps.

'I'm glad you think so, Anais,' said Hector.

'Aye,' agreed Jarmon sourly as he blew on the sparks of the hearth flame. 'Now we can at least die in peace.'

The boy woke when the tendrils of smoke that carried the scent of ham reached his nostrils; he was eating greedily in the flickering firelight by the time Cantha returned.

Anais ceased chewing long enough to prod her.

'Well, what does the wind have to say this night, Cantha?' he asked jokingly, pushing the plate they had saved for her nearer on the heavy table board. He waited for the withering stare that he alone in the group relished.

'Much,' Cantha replied flatly, tossing her vest on to the hearth to dry and sitting down beside it. 'None of it clear.'

The eyes of the three men locked on to her as she picked up her plate and settled in to eating. They waited in pensive, almost tense silence to hear her elaborate, but the Kith woman merely finished her supper and took a deep draught of Sevirym's prized cider.

For a long time the only sound in the cavernous inn was that of the crackling fire. Finally Hector handed the boy his mother's untouched supper and silently urged him to convince her to eat.

'Cantha,' he said, watching the woman take a piece of hard cheese from her plate and stare at it in her hand, 'what did the winds say?'

Backlit by the hearth fire, Cantha's eyes were blacker than the darkness that surrounded them. The chestnut skin of her thin face glowed orange in the reflected light of the flames.

'Something comes,' she said simply.

'What?' demanded Jarmon. 'What comes?'

Cantha shook her head. 'When the winds speak, most times they speak as one,' she said, her raspy voice clear.

Then it changed, scratching against all of their ears. In it was the howling of many toneless voices, a cacophony of shrieks, rising and falling in intermittent discord.

'Now, they do not,' she said, speaking in the discordant sound of the wind. 'They moan wildly, as if in terror. What they say is like a maelstrom; unclear. But whatever is coming, the winds fear it.'

The men exchanged a glance. In Cantha's voice they could hear the wail of sea winds, the rumblings of thunder, the nightmarish cadence of destruction as gusts in a gale battered buildings to their ruin. It was almost like the sound of battle, the confusion, the shouting, the utter sense of being lost in the fury of war. The wind was foretelling something dire, but that was not unexpected.

Anais wanted her to give voice to it anyway.

'So what, then, do you believe is coming?' he asked.

'The end,' Cantha said.

Once the chill of emptiness had been driven from the great rooms of the inn by the steady hearth fire, the travellers began dropping off to sleep one by one. Jarmon first; as a lifelong member of the King's Guard, he had learned to stay awake and watchful for days on end, and thereby had learned to take his repose the instant it was offered him. His bedroll lay behind what had once been the tavernkeeper's bar as a courtesy to the others; Anais had once complained that Jarmon's prodigious snoring was causing his bow to warp and his sword to rust.

The woman, who still had not responded to a single salutation, had drifted off into unconsciousness soon after Jarmon. The boy had played a merry game of mumblety-peg with Anais and had spent more than an hour on Hector's lap, taking turns making shadow puppets on the wall in the firelight before finally curling up beside her under Hector's cloak.

Cantha eventually took her place near the open doorway where the wind could wash over her in her slumber, standing a watch of a sort, though there was little chance that even the brigands that still remained in the doomed land would approach the inn. Its reputation as a refuge of good and a bastion of those who defended it had survived the evacuation into these latter days.

After the others had fallen asleep, the two childhood friends passed a skin of wine between them, musing in mutual silence. Finally Anais looked up at Hector, who was staring pensively into the fire, and leaned forward, his silver eyes bright but solemn.

'A girl, then,' he said softly.

Hector nodded.

'The twins must be happy with that,' Anais said, thinking of his own daughters. 'They were a mite put out when your Aidan turned out to be a boy.'

'The three of them made fine playmates nevertheless,' Hector said, leaning back and crossing his feet on the hearthstones. 'It gives me comfort to know that our friendship has been passed along to another generation.'

'What is her name? Flynt said you would know it.'

Hector nodded again. 'We agreed if the child were to be born a girl, and Talthea did not sense after seeing her that it was a misnomer, she would be named Elsynore.'

Anais took another swig from the wineskin.

'A fine namesake,' he said, lifting the skin in a comical toast in the direction of the fire. 'Elsynore of Briarwood. A fine Seren role model.'

'Yes, but that is not the only thought behind the name,' said Hector, watching the flames dance and pulse over gleaming coals in the old hearth. 'The wyrm who opened her lands to the king and the refugees –'

'Ah, of course, Elynsynos, yes? You named your daughter to honour her.'

'With the aid of a Liringlas Namer. We gave the child both names we had chosen, male and female, so that it could be named before birth.'

Anais chuckled. 'Were you expecting that giving her a name similar to the wyrm's own would give the dragon pause about eating her?'

Hector's eyes lost their warmth and he turned away, watching the shadows twist and writhe in the darkness behind them. He stared at the dark form of Cantha, sleeping on the open threshold, then glanced over to where the child and his mother slept. He could not see Jarmon, but the grinding snore that rose and fell in regular rhythm, almost like a marching cadence, signalled that he slept still.

'I confess that learning my father and the Second Fleet had been diverted to Manosse was heartening news for me,' he said finally. 'Manosse is an ocean away from the Wyrmlands; it is a long-civilized nation with a healthy shipping trade, an army, a mercantile – all signs that it is a stable place. Binding them over to his care when we all believed they would end up in uncharted lands beyond the known world, lands that are ruled by an ancient dragon whose hospitality is only attested to by Merithyn, was possibly the hardest thing I have ever had to do. Now at least I know they will be safe.'

'As long as they stay in Manosse,' Anais said seriously. 'Each refugee pledged fealty to the king on the horn as they boarded, remember? They are charged with the duty to come should the horn ever sound, generation unto generation. If Gwylliam calls, they will have no choice but to set sail again for the Wyrmlands.' He saw his friend's shoulders sag somewhat. 'But it should reassure you that Merithyn believes the place to be a safe and bountiful paradise. When he set out with the king's other explorers to find a place for our people to emigrate to, no one had ever broached the Wyrmlands and lived to tell about it. As he was the only one of Gwylliam's explorers to return, and with a generous offer of asylum at that, I would hazard he knows about which he speaks.'

'Who knows?' Hector said dully. 'Who knows whether any of them made it to the Wyrmlands? Flynt said there had been no word whatsoever from the First and Third Fleets. Who knows? But God, the One, the All, has granted us a sweet boon in our final days. We know at least that our own families are safe in Manosse. When they left, I never expected to hear word of them again. And now, as Jarmon is so fond of saying, I can die in peace.'

Anais rose from the hearth and stretched lazily. 'Yes, but most likely not tonight,' he said. 'What are the plans now, Hector? Is there any reason to go back to our guard route? If, as Cantha believes, the end is what is coming, why not spend it here? There is food, and firewood, and shelter, and, above all else, ale. Seems like a good place to spend one's final days.'

'Yes,' Hector agreed. 'I think there is wisdom in that, even though I suspect your love of fine ale might have more than a little to do with the suggestion.' He glanced over at the woman and the boy. 'And it would be folly to attempt to ride our regular watch with them. The woman is a walking corpse, and cannot properly care for the child alone. We may as well make them, and ourselves, as comfortable as we can.' He shook out his own camp blanket and laid it, and himself, down before the hearth to sleep.

'And besides, we are close enough to town to do two shifts of sandbag duty daily.'

Anais groaned and rolled over towards the fire.

And so they remained, wrapped in dreams of the World Tree and of faces they would never see again, still asleep before the coals, until the stillness was broken by the harsh metal sound of Cantha unsheathing her sword.

In one fluid movement that belied her age, the ancient Kith soldier rose, drew and crossed the threshold to the doorstep of the inn, where foredawn had turned the sky to the smoky grey that signals morning is nigh.

'Halt and declare,' she called sharply into the gloom.

The men were behind her a moment later. They peered through the doorway, drawn as she was, searching the semi-darkness for the sound that had summoned her attention.

At the crossroads a horse stood, dancing exhaustedly in place. Atop it a rider, bent with strain, was struggling to remain upright in the saddle.

'Help me,' called an old man's voice. 'I am Brann, from the village of Dry Cove on the northern seacoast at Kyrlan de la Mar. I seek the soldiers of the king.'

'Jarmon, bring me a lantern,' Hector ordered.

He stepped out into the cold grey air, watching closely as the rider slid from his mount, took a wobbly step, then collapsed in the centre of the roadway. As the rider dropped, the horse took several steps away from him, which Hector took to be a sign of its poor training or the rider's lack of skill. Once he had the lantern in his hand, he signalled to Anais to wait with the boy and the woman, then beckoned to Cantha and Jarmon to follow him.

'What do you want?' he called as he approached.

'I – I seek the soldiers of – the king,' the old man wheezed again.

Hector held up the lantern better to illuminate the man in the roadway. He was human, by the look of him in the shadows, and aged, with white hair that hung around his wrinkled face like dry leaves hanging from a dormant tree.

'I am Hector Monodiere, in the service of His Majesty, Gwylliam, High King of Serendair. What do you seek from me?'

'Your assistance, sir knight,' the man croaked, waving away the water flask that Jarmon held out to him. 'The Sleeping Child is awakening.'

'I well know it. What would you have me do about it?'

The old man's eyes, bloodshot with exhaustion, held a desperate light that was visible even in the grey foredawn. 'There may be a way to contain it – or at least to stem part of the flooding that is sure to come in its wake.'

The three companions exchanged a glance, then Jarmon spat on the ground.

'Madness,' he muttered as Hector reached behind the man's shoulder and helped him rise. 'You rode all the way from the northern coast to tell us this? Why did you not flee with the rest to high ground in the east, or into the High Reaches?'

In the lantern light they could better make out the man's features. As they had seen a moment before, he was human, dark-eyed and aged, though much of that ageing had clearly come from the hardship of life in the northern clime, a rough seascape of rocky beach and heavy surf where only the stoutest of heart continued to ply the rough waters near the Great River's mouth. He was dressed in the tattered oilcloth garb of a fisherman. Rot and decay clung to his clothing and breath, much as it did to the rest of the population they had encountered after the Fleets had left; it was beginning to cling to their own clothing and breath now as well. The man's malodour was particularly strong, coupled with the stale, fishy smell of a life on the sea that never completely washed clean of a fisherman's hands and clothes.

'My people are old,' he said. 'What you ask may seem simple, and perhaps it would be to those younger, haler of body. But we have lived at the sea's edge for a very long time, Sir Hector. We are frail. Fleeing would be an arduous undertaking, something many of us would not survive. If the Awakening is to determine our fate, we are ready to meet it.'

'Then why have you come here?' Jarmon asked crossly. 'There are others like you all across this doomed island – Liringlas, Bolg, Bengard, Gwadd, human – all who chose, for reasons of their own, to disregard the king's vision and stay behind. We cannot help you now. You were offered passage, all of you. You refused it. You have already sealed your own fate.'

'Peace, Jarmon,' said Hector quietly. He turned to the old man, whose arm he was still supporting. 'Come inside and warm yourself. We have food and drink that we are happy to share with you.'

The old man shook his head. 'No, no, Sir Hector. There is no time. You must help me – I – I believe – we have found a way –'

'Cantha, summon Anais,' Hector said. He waited until the Liringlas soldier was within earshot, then asked again, 'What would you have me do?'

From the centre of the pool of illumination cast by the lantern, Brann pointed into the darkness to the south east where the horizon was beginning to lighten.

'Go to the castle Elysian,' he said, his voice stronger. 'I know you guard the symbol of the king – his sceptre, Sir Hector. I – have need of it.'

Jarmon's arm shot out and grasped the man by the shirt, pulling him off the ground with little more resistance than the wind.

'Impudent *dog*,' he snarled into the old man's face, his fury straining the limits of its bridle. 'We stand on the brink of the death of this nation; we gave up all we had to stay behind with the imbeciles and the unbelievers who chose death over the life offered you by your king, and now you actually believe we would dishonour ourselves by yielding something like that to the likes of *you*?'

'Release him, Jarmon,' Hector commanded angrily. 'Get hold of your-self.' The guard dropped the old man to the ground contemptuously. Hector crouched down next to the fisherman, who was now quivering in fright, and steadied the man by the shoulder. 'What need? I ask you again, what is it you would have me do?'

For a moment the man's eyes darted around at the faces staring down at him. Finally he focused on Hector's, and seemed to be calmed by what he saw in it.

'From the highest point of our village, one has always been able to see across the strait that covers the grave of the Sleeping Child to the Northern Isles, on clear days, at any matter,' he said haltingly. His words faltered; Hector nodded silent encouragement. 'The sea now boils; much of the coastline has receded as the star awakens, gathering heat and power to itself. What was once the tidal basin of Dry Cove is now sand, sir knight. And as the sea has receded for the moment, it has revealed something vast, something dating back to another age of Time.'

'What?' Anais asked.

The old man swallowed as his eyes went to the Liringlas soldier, then focused on Hector again.

'It appears to be an ancient mine, Sir Hector – silver, who knows, though in the First Age, the Day of the Gods, before the star fell to earth, there were mines of every sort delving into the crust of the world, where men of ancient races drew forth riches the way men now draw forth fish from the sea. This one's vastness cannot be described in words, at least not in my words, except to say that we can see the ridges and depressions which define some of its edges, but not all of them, revealed now by the drawing of water away from the tidal areas of the sea as the Child prepares to awaken. Those ridges and depres-sions stretch for as far as the eye can see.'

Hector shrugged. 'I still do not see what this has to do with me, or with the king's sceptre.'

The man named Brann spoke slowly, cautiously, his eyes nervously moving from soldier to soldier.

'It is said that in the days before the end of the First Age, much of what now rests beneath the sea was dry land. When the falling star Melita, now known as the Sleeping Child, struck Serendair from the sky, it took much of the Island with it, Sir Hector. What are now the Northern Isles, Balatron, Briala and Querel, were mountaintops then; almost half of the tillable fields of the realm went into the sea in the flooding that ensued. For centuries Serendair was known as Halfland, so much of it was consumed by the ocean in the wake of the impact.

'In those days, before the first cataclysm, this mine, if that's what it is, once it was expended was probably locked by whatever king ruled the ancient race that quarried it. A mine of that size would be a hazard because of its vastness alone, but it may have been for other reasons as well – mines that are expended run with rivers of acid, and burn with fires that can be extinguished only by time; they contain treacherous precipices, deep shafts. One this size would have been an extremely dangerous place, and so it was shut, its great doors sealed and locked, seemingly for ever.' The old man's voice, hoarse from exertion, dropped low, and he leaned forward to be certain Hector could hear him. 'We believe we have found those doors, Sir Hector.'

'And you believe the king's sceptre would unlock them?'

'Yes,' said Brann, his dark eyes kindling with excitement. 'In the hand of the king – or he who stands in his place. It could be the key – certainly it is the last remaining vestige of the king's authority here, the only symbol of his dominion that he did not take with him. Those doors face the Child's gravesite, and are bound more by a king's command than by a physical lock. Perhaps, as the king's regent, you could exercise his authority to bid them open. If you can throw open the doors before the Awakening, perhaps – and only perhaps – the mine can act as a natural levy of sorts, a dam, a dike – it is a mammoth underground cave at the sea's edge. Surely it is reasonable to think that some of the destruction may be averted if the swell of the sea is contained, or at least limited, by this great hole in the earth.' The man fell silent, watching the knights intently as they stepped away from him to confer.

'Ridiculous,' Jarmon muttered under his breath. 'You can't hold back the sea with a hole in the ground any more than you can with a teacup.'

'That's not necessarily so,' said Anais, considering. 'The fisherman is right in that what spared the Island the first time was the natural levies – mountains, reefs, low-lying areas – that ringed the larger Serendair. The sea took some of the coastline, but not all of it.'

'You sound like Sevirym,' Jarmon scoffed. 'Please tell me, Anais, that the rigours of sandbag duty have not addled your brain that much.' He turned to Hector to see their leader lost in thought. 'You as well, Hector. This is folly – utter nonsense.'

'What if it isn't, Jarmon?' Hector interjected. 'What if, in these final days, God, the One, the All, has provided us with an answer? Is it so hard to believe, to hope, that we might be spared, or partially spared, by His grace?'

'Do you now doubt the king's vision?' Jarmon demanded, his voice agitated.

'The *king himself* doubted it,' said Hector softly. 'Had he been more assured that the cataclysm he foresaw on the day of his coronation meant the complete destruction of the Island, he would never have left us – left *me* – behind to maintain his line of succession on the throne.' He looked to Cantha, whose eyes were narrow with suspicion. 'Is that not correct, Cantha? I stand in the shadow of the king. I am of his line, and his regent, named so that his power over the land would hold sway. Should the Island survive the Awakening, because I remained here, in Gwylliam's name, his line of succession will have remained unbroken. He can return and reclaim the throne without contest.'

'Aye,' Cantha said curtly.

'So if the king himself entertained the possibility that complete destruction was not inevitable, is it so far beyond reasonability that we entertain it, too?'

Anais touched Hector's elbow. 'Is it also possible that you are only now more willing to hope for it because of those who missed the *Stormrider*?' he asked in the Liringlas tongue.

Hector fell silent for a moment, then shrugged. 'I no longer know my own motivations,' he said bluntly. 'I am not even able to ascertain what my father would do in these circumstances, and that has always been my touchstone, my guide. Like the wind that Cantha described last night, my senses are lost in a maelstrom of confusion. I have very little clarity any more, Anais. I can only tell you that this possibility rings with promise in my head, probably because, if nothing else, it is doing *something*. As comfortable as spending the last days supping and imbibing in the inn might be, the thought does not sit well with me. The glory is in the trying. I would rather go to my death doing something futile, trying, than miss the chance to have saved what I could.'

The other three fell silent, contemplating. Finally Anais spoke.

'Well, even in your confusion, you are still our leader, to whom we are sworn, Hector. If you wish to make the attempt, we are with you.' He glanced at Cantha and Jarmon. 'Are we not?'

'We are,' Jarmon said. Cantha nodded imperceptibly.

Hector considered for a moment longer, then turned to the old man in the middle of the road.

'I will do as you ask,' he said finally. 'But let us be clear – the sceptre does not leave my hand.'

The man's face crumpled in relief. 'Understood. None of my people would wish it any other way. And know, sir knight, that whether or not you are successful, the people of my homeland will be eternally grateful for whatever you attempt on our behalf.'

Even Cantha, suspicious by nature, could hear the undeniable truth in the man's words.

It was full-sun, the moment the sun had just crested the horizon completely, when the group of seven set out into the east, following the brightening morning. Mist enveloped the ground, making it seem as if they were riding a golden pathway into the clouds.

The boy, who still had not spoken his name, sat before Hector in the saddle, drinking in the fresh breeze and the autumn splendour that was beginning to claim the countryside. A child of sooty city streets, he was transfixed by the sight of meadow wildflowers dried by the first signs of frost, of rolling fields that undulated in great waves like a grassy sea, of still-green trees along the roadway or in the distance, their leaves turning the colour of fire.

Elysian castle lay to the south east, across the Great River that bisected the western end of the Island from north to south. It stood perched atop high cliffwalls that overlooked the southern seacoast ten miles away. On clear days the ocean was visible from its tallest towers, rolling gently to the leeward shores, in marked contrast to the angry, billowing breakers that battered the beaches in the north from whence Brann had come.

As they came within a league of the river, Anais and Hector exchanged a glance of confusion. The river was really a tidal estuary this far south, and roared grandly along its shores, swollen with the waters from the north sea joined by the runoff of every major river and stream on both sides of it. Its deep, abiding song could be heard for miles; now it was silent, the wind carrying no sound at all save the nervous twittering of birds and its own howl.

'The river was low the last time we crossed it, but I don't recall it being so quiet,' Anais said, drawing the woman's arm more tightly around his waist when she tilted alarmingly to one side.

'It is all but dry now,' Brann said, his voice thin with strain. 'There are places along it where there are nothing but great muddy pools in the midst of a waterless, rocky bed. I rode the eastern shore on my way to you, and when I passed the stone mill at Hope's Landing, the wheel was still.'

'The heat of the star is drawing the seawater back into its grave,' Hector said, pointing out a circling hawk to the boy.

'The shoreline in the north has receded by more than a league, Sir Hector,' said the fisherman. 'Elsewise the doors would never have been revealed.'

As soon as the words left his lips the ground rumbled.

The soldiers spurred their mounts on. Even before the exodus, the Sleeping Child had made its presence felt in this manner, loosing tremors through the earth as if stretching in slumber that was coming to an end. Those tremors were growing stronger.

They rode the rest of the way to the river in silence. The bridge at Pryce's Crossing was the largest in the land, and loomed before them, its timbers dark against the morning sun, now halfway up the firmament of the sky.

'Did you bring any bread for the trolls, Hector?' Anais asked jokingly as they slowed to cross. Tradition had long held that a scrap of biscuit or bread be tossed into the river for good luck to assuage the legendary beasts that lived beneath the centuries-old structure.

'No,' Hector said, smiling slightly. 'We should be saving every last crumb now, Anais. After all, there is no point in surviving a cataclysm only to starve to death.'

'The trolls sailed with the Second Fleet anyway,' said Jarmon. The fresh air of the open country seemed to have lifted his spirits.

'That would explain why the prelate's wife was on your father's ship,' said Anais.

'To call the prelate's wife a troll is an insult to trolls,' said Jarmon.

The horses' hooves clattered over the wooden planks that spanned the all-but-dry riverbed, drowning out the sound of their voices. As they passed out of the westlands for the last time, they looked over the edge of the Pryce's Crossing bridge; they could see the rocky bottom, normally more than a man's height in depth, tiny tributaries still running defiantly through the stony bed, as if to prove that the river was not quite dead yet.

The sun had reached the pinnacle of the firmament when the towers of Elysian castle came into sight. As many times as they had seen it, the soldiers could not help but slow to a halt for a moment to take in the distant majesty of it, white marble still gleaming against the blue of the autumn sky atop the crags from which it rose like a beacon, triumphant.

Hector had been born in that palace, as had his mother before him. He watched in silence for a moment, then urged his mount forwards, cantering with a speed that delighted his small passenger.

It was not long before melancholy returned. They rode through the endless apple orchards that had once surrounded the castle's lands, now sparse and bare. The trees of the lowlands, west from Kingston across the Wide Meadows to Anais's birthplace, Yliessan, the Enchanted Forest in the east, had been harvested quickly and brutally to provide wood for the exodus. Even the apple trees, whose flesh was useless in the actual making of ships, had been stripped and used for chests, barrels, even firewood to stoke the forges that smelted steel for fittings, arrowheads and thousands of other uses. Those few trees that remained bore a stunted crop, but it was worthy enough to merit a pause to be collected.

Harder to bear was the ride through Earthwood, the stone forest that had once led up to the base of the cliffs on which the palace stood. The ground from which the ancient trees had sprung was said to have been Living Stone, the pure element of earth left over from the Before-Time, the era prior to the first age of history, when the world was new. The seeds of the forest's trees had been scattered over the living earth, as the legend said, and had grown into mammoth redwoods, heveralts and oaks, alive with magic. Those trees, their bark rich in shades of green, purple, vermilion and gold, were as Living Stone themselves, and had never split or fallen in high wind, had never burned in fire, had never rotted with disease, but stood, stalwart and unchanging, their ancient saps coursing through their bark and leaves in an endless, mystical symphony of ages. Anais and Hector had spent their childhood in the stone forest, and so it was painful on a soul-deep level to see it razed to nothing more than broken stumps, its choice wood reaped to make hulls and masts and planks of ships that would not rot, nor burn, nor split in the high winds of a sea voyage.

Those ships bore our families to safety, Hector reminded himself as they passed the desolate forest ruin. *To safety.*

On the other side of Earthwood the ramparts of the castle walls could be seen, atop the three hundred steps that led up to them. Hector reined his horse to a halt, then looked to the others, observing the silent dismay on the face of the exhausted old fisherman.

'You needn't despair, Brann,' he said reassuringly. 'It's too much of a climb for most, now that the waggon-ramps are gone. Stay here, Jarmon, Anais. Cantha and I will return forthwith.'

The two soldiers, one old, one young, inhaled deeply but said nothing.

For all the years he had spent in the palace, the design and construction of the place had been a constant source of fascination to Hector. As he and his father's oldest friend hurriedly climbed the stone steps hewn from the rock, passing through the empty gardens and loggia that had long beautified the terraces leading to Elysian, they both unconsciously glanced back at the ramparts hidden beneath them. In its time, more than ten thousand soldiers were routinely garrisoned within the palisaded battlements that scored, in ascending rings, the crags on which the palace stood. That they had been hidden so decoratively was tribute to Vandemere, the king who had designed and built the place as a shining monument to a new era of peace, knowing all the while that war loomed, ever watchful, in the distance.

The king riding the hippogriff whose broken statue was now rubble in the dry fountain bed of Kingston's square.

Hector's grandfather.

'Did you know him, Cantha?' Hector asked as they hurried over the granite walkways past beds of dried flora and dying topiary. 'Vandemere?'

'Aye.' The Kith woman kept her eyes focused directly on the great doors that marked the side entrance of the palace, now unguarded. One stood slightly open, a testament to the completeness of the evacuation. In its time, never fewer than a score of soldiers held watch over those doors.

Through the towering hallways they ran, keeping their eyes fixed on the corridors ahead of them, rather than see the emptiness of the once beautiful stronghold. Their footsteps echoed through the cavernous rooms, bare and dull in the dark.

Hector knew this place blind; it was only the urgency he had heard in the fisherman's voice and the stirrings of a long-denied hope that prevented him from taking the time to stop and gaze one last time at the rooms, alcoves and nooks he had loved from childhood. Most of the tapestries still lined the walls; much of the art remained in place, unmolested by the looters and thieves that had picked the rest of the countryside clean. There was something sacred about Elysian that kept it sacrosanct, a power that protected it, even with no king on the throne.

Entering the corridor that led to the Great Hall, Hector realized what it was.

In a way, there was a king on the throne still. Gwylliam had named Hector the king's shadow, born of the same bloodline, and therefore in a way, the king had not left, not completely.

'This was a remarkable place to spend time as a child,' Hector said, passing the doors to the nursery where his mother and her siblings had played while their parents held court. 'There were so many alcoves to explore, so many places to hide. The palace guards were more than once called out to find me. I had made a nest beneath the drape of a pedestal in the Hall of History, and had fallen asleep in there. It was great fun – until I had a child of my own and Aidan started doing it.' He drew deeper breath. 'I still don't know where that boy and his mother could have been secreted that allowed us to miss them.'

'In the City's necropolis,' Cantha said, her eyes fixed on the enormous mahogany doors of the Great Hall before them. 'In one of the crypts.'

'Why do you think so?'

'They had the smell of death about them.' The Kith woman grasped the massive brass handle. 'They still do, but it be different now.'

The dark, cavernous room revealed the throne from which the unmarried last king had held court, a wide marble chair with blue and gold giltwork channels running through up the arms to the back. Hector walked the long carpet to the foot of the dais, mounted the steps quickly and sat down unabashedly in the king's seat. He took a moment to look up at Vandemere's motto, inscribed for the ages on the wall directly before his eyes, where each subsequent king was bound to see it at every moment while enthroned: *He whom all men serve bears the greatest duty to serve all men.*

Then he stretched his hand out over the right arm of the throne.

'Traan der, singa ever monokran fri,' he commanded softly, speaking in the tongue of the Ancient Seren, the mystical race of Firstborn beings born of the element of ether, the first people of the Island. *Come forth, in the name of the king.*

The marble arm of the chair cracked open along a hidden fault, and split away. From beneath the dais a mechanical arm rose to an even height with the chair, the royal sceptre of Serendair in its metallic grasp.

The symbol of state was simple in its design, a curved piece of dark wood the length of a man's thigh, gilt and inscribed with intricate runes. Beneath the golden overlay the thin striations of purple and green, gold and vermilion could still be vaguely made out, the colours of the stone trees in Earthwood, from which it had probably been harvested. Atop its splayed pinnacle a diamond the size of a child's fist was set; it gleamed dully in the darkness of the Hall.

Hector stared at the sceptre for a moment, encased within the mechanism of the king's design. Then he seized it, plucking it from the metal arm, pulling it free.

Cantha's dark eyes were watching with a gleam he had not seen before. He looked at her questioningly, inviting her to speak, and was surprised when she did. Cantha guarded her thoughts jealously.

'Had the crown passed to the first of Vandemere's children, rather than the last, this might have been a sight seen long ago; thee, Hector, on the throne as king.'

Hector rose from the throne and started back out of the palace.

'I suppose that means I am foreordained to meet my end in this way, then,' he said as they retraced their steps. 'For if I had been king, I would not have left. You, however, Cantha, you and Jarmon, Anais and Sevirym, would have been sent off with the others, to guard them in the new world, and live on. For that reason, and only that one, I am sorry that the line of succession did not fall to me.'

The Kith woman said nothing.

They hurried from the palace in silence. At the brink of the battlements, Hector touched her arm.

'Tell me one thing, Cantha, now that the time for niceties is past, and there is nothing left to be gained in politeness,' he said. 'When you announced that the king of the Kith had decided you would stay behind as a representative of your race, I believe it was because you had volunteered to do so. You are my father's dearest friend. It was for him that you stayed with me, wasn't it?'

The Kith woman's eyes narrowed in displeasure. 'MacQuieth would never have asked such of thing of me. Of anyone.'

Hector smiled. 'I know. But he didn't have to ask.'

Cantha exhaled, frowning at him. Finally she assented.

'Nay,' she said. 'He did not have to ask. Aye, 'twas for him that I stayed, to stand with his son when he could not.' She looked over the grassy fields, falling into shadows of gold as the sun began to set. ''Twas as good a choice of end as any.'

'Thank you,' Hector said. 'For staying, and for telling me.'

The Kith woman merely nodded.

'I have one more boon to ask of you,' Hector said as they descended the stone steps. 'We will part company now. To take the woman and child north with us would only slow us down, and end any chance they have to survive. Elysian is the highest point on the southern half of the Island. If any ground is to be spared by the sea, it would be here. Stay with them, Cantha, in these last days; keep them safe, especially the boy. We will leave your supplies, and you can scavenge the orchards for fruit. If we succeed in containing the sea, and you run short of stores, you can go back to the inn.' Cantha nodded, and Hector took her elbow, drawing her to a halt for a moment. 'If the wave comes, though, get to the highest ground you can. I'd advise you stay near the vizier's tower.' He nodded behind them to the tallest of the palace's spires, where Graal, the king's adviser and seer, had once dwelt. Cantha nodded again.

Jarmon had prepared the horses to leave as soon as Hector returned. As the men mounted, Hector heard a screech from below him.

'No,' the child was screaming, struggling in Cantha's firm grasp. 'No!' He turned to Hector, his eyes pleading. 'No! Stay w'chyou! Stay w'chyou!'

The words echoed in Hector's mind; they were the same as the ones uttered by Aidan on the docks the day he bound his family over to his father for sailing.

Stay w'chyou! Da! Stay w'chyou!

His throat tightened, remembering Talthea, so strong and brave, dissolving into tears at the pain in their son's voice. He reached down and gently caressed the head of the writhing child, then nodded to Cantha. His last sight of the boy was seeing him struggling violently in her arms as she restrained him. He continued to kick and fight with a wilfulness that finally collapsed into a visibly broken spirit once the horses were out of sight.

Just as Aidan had.

They rode north along the river now, following the mule-road where barges had long travelled, laden with goods from the northern isles and distant ports that were traded at every crossing and village until the flat-bottomed boats finally reached Southport, the enormous city at the river's delta.

The rocks at the mule-road's edge trembled as they passed; tremors in the north had intensified in strength and frequency, and viewing the sky above was now almost impossible through the mist. Patches of blue became fewer and farther between.

The men rode in silence. Each day that passed brought the mist down even more heavily, making first joking, then speaking, too weighty to bother with.

Finally they arrived in Hope's Landing, the largest milltown on the Great River, where the east–west thoroughfare had crossed. In its time Hope's Landing had been the heart of the river, a bustling city where the westlands met the east, with waggons lining up as far as the eye could see to unload grain for the mills, foodstuffs bound for markets in the south, and then to reload with every kind of good imaginable from the barges. Now the city stood empty, the wheels of the great mills lodged in the mud or jammed by rocks where the water had once flowed freely.

Pratt's Mill had been the largest of all, spanning the river at its deepest and swiftest place. Bridges at one time had connected the east and west banks, with the mill between, an esplanade over which travellers could pass, observing the river's currents beneath them. The western span was gone, but the eastern bridge was still there, they noted, then rode past as the heat of the sun beat down from overhead, the only sign that it was now midday.

Just past the silent mill, where the roadway led off to the east, Hector signalled to the party to stop and let the horses graze. He scooped up a handful of smooth river stones, then beckoned to Anais, and together they walked to the banks of the Great River, dry now except for a thin stream that pooled and trickled in the wide riverbed.

'Remember when this river seemed a mile wide?' he mused, watching the water wend its way around the rocks and broken barrels that now lined its bed.

'Aye,' Anais agreed. ''Twas death to fall in up here. That millstone ground day and night; if you took a tumble north of it, you'd be bread the next day.'

'And now we could cross easily, with feet barely wet. It's as if the river never divided the Island at all.' Hector examined the stones in his hand. 'My father once said something to me that is finally taking hold in my mind.' He fell silent for a moment, trying to remember the words correctly. 'He was a Kinsman, one of a brotherhood of soldiers whose patron was the wind, and thus had learned to pass through doors in the wind that would take him great distances in a short time. When I asked him by what magic this could happen, he said that it was not magic, but merely understanding that distance was an illusion.

'There are ties between us, Anais, all of us, friend and foe, that transcend what is normally seen as the space in the world. That distance, that space, is merely the threshold between one realm and another, one soul and another; a doorway, a bridge if you will. The stronger the connection between the two places, the smaller the threshold; the more easily crossed, anyway. The physical distance between the two becomes secondary. It was in making use of this that MacQuieth was able to win his greatest battle, his destruction of the fire demon, the F'dor Tsoltan. His hatred of that demon, and that primordial race, was a tie that could not be outrun. There was not enough space in the world to keep them apart.' He sighed deeply. 'I believe it is also the reason that my family is only as far away as my next breath, that I can see them in my dreams, see them as they are now, not as a memory. Why you dream of the World Tree, and the place where you were born.'

Anais nodded, and they stood in companionable silence for a while, watching the trickling stream.

'How does the weather appear to be taking shape for the next few days?' Hector asked finally, tossing a stone into what was left of the water.

'Aside from the likelihood of catastrophic destruction, it looks to be a fine week,' Anais answered jokingly. 'Why do you ask?'

Hector lobbed another pebble into the stream. 'I just wanted to know how you would fare on your journey, if you would be dry or sodden with rain.'

Anais's face lost its smile. 'Journey?'

Hector exhaled and nodded. 'I'm sending you home now, Anais. There is no need for you to go on with us from here. Either we will prevail in this undertaking or we will fail, but your being with us will not make that difference. The dreams you are having of Yliessan is Sagia calling to you to come home. If the World Tree is beckoning to you, it would be wrong to keep you from her.'

His friend's silver eyes reflected sadness and understanding in the same gleam.

'I have come to accept many things I could not have fathomed would be possible a year ago, Hector, many tragic and horrific things, but until this moment, it had never occurred to me that I might not meet my end at your side.'

Hector tossed the rest of the stones into the riverbed and wiped the grit from his hand on his shirt.

'We have lived in each other's company all our lives, Anais, and lived well,' he said, his voice steady. 'There is no need to die in each other's company, as long as we die well.'

Anais turned away.

'Perhaps if Sevirym was right, or you prevail, we will not die at all,' he said.

'Perhaps,' Hector said. 'But go home anyway.'

Beneath their feet the ground rumbled, stronger than before, as if in confirmation.

On the way back to camp, Hector stopped his friend one last time.

'Know that wherever we are when the end comes, you will be with me, Anais,' he said simply.

The Liringlas knight smiled. 'Beyond the end, Hector. Not even death can separate you from me.' He clapped his friend's shoulder. 'You still owe me a night of very expensive drinking.'

Once Anais had gone, the days and nights ran together.

In the distance, the sky had begun to glow yellow through the mist above the Northern Isles. The rumblings had increased in sound and frequency, making the men nervous and edgy without respite. Sleep seemed a luxury that they could ill afford, and yet exhaustion threatened to drive them off course, bleary-eyed in the dense fog.

When at last the sea could be heard in the distance and splashing fire could be seen far away above the horizon, they determined they were near enough to Dry Cove and made camp for what they decided was the last time. Hector stirred the remains of their stores in a pot above their fire while the old fisherman and Jarmon tended to the horses before setting down to a last meal at rest.

'Brann,' Hector said, trying to break the awkward silence with conversation, 'have you lived in Dry Cove all your life?'

The old man shook his head. 'No. I was born there, but I had not been back until recently.'

'Oh?' Jarmon asked, setting down his tankard. 'That's odd for a fishing village, isn't it? It seems that most families in such places remain there for generations.'

Brann nodded. 'True. But long ago, I had the chance to leave, and I took it. I travelled the wide world, doing a variety of things, but my birthplace has never been far from my mind. When it became apparent that the Child was awakening, I wanted nothing more than to return home, to help in any way that I could.'

'You do know the chances that we can do anything at all, let alone save your village, are very small?' Jarmon said seriously. 'This is a fool's errand.'

'No, it's not,' Hector said quickly, seeing the light in the fisherman's eyes dim slightly. 'It is a slim chance. But it is a chance, none the less. Trying is never foolish.'

'That is all I ask, so that my people might live.' Brann mumbled, drawing his rough burlap blanket over his shoulders and settling down to sleep.

When the old man's breathing signalled he had fallen into the deepest part of slumber, Jarmon took a well-used wallet of smoking blend from his pack and tamped nearly the last of it into his pipe.

Beneath them the earth trembled. It seemed to Hector that the quakes were lasting longer, and it was undeniable that they were coming more frequently. Anais had observed, just before he rode east, that even Sevirym would have been hard pressed to ignore it.

Hector looked up into the dark sky, missing the stars. 'You and me, Jarmon; we are the last ones left,' he mused, watching the clouds of thickening haze race along in the dark sky on the twisting wind.

'And Brann,' the guard said, blowing out a great ring of smoke that blended with the mist around them.

'And Brann. Perhaps you should be kinder to him – he is obviously terrified of you.'

The old guard smiled. 'Good.' He leaned forward over the firecoals. 'I trust no one any more, Hector, especially those too stupid or selfish to have taken the chance they were given and now want to be saved in the last hour. Better that they fear me. They have reason to.'

Hector turned the sceptre of the king in his hands. 'You needn't be on guard against him, Brann. The king's sceptre is formed of an ancient element of power; it rings true in the hand of the one who holds it. I would be able to discern if the old fisherman was lying, and thus far he has told us nothing but the truth.'

Jarmon shrugged. 'What does it matter anyway?' he said nonchalantly. 'You and he are the only ones who remain with something to lose.' Hector signalled for him to explain, but the old guard just shrugged again.

'You say you believe that the glory is in the trying,' Jarmon said, puffing contentedly on his pipe. 'But in truth, you fear failure. You have all along – as if there was anything you could do to ward it off. This situation was doomed to failure from the beginning, Hector, but only you struggled with that. The rest of us are followers, not leaders. We know that even in inevitable failure, there is glory. In the end, to a soldier it matters not what the outcome of the battle is. What matters is how he fought, whether he stood his ground nobly, or whether, in the face of death, he faltered. A soldier does not decide who to fight, or when, or where. Deciding to remain behind with you was the only real choice I have ever made. It's a choice I do not regret.

'You have struggled in silence with the king's decision to leave you behind, and with our decisions to remain with you. You could cease that and live out your days in some semblance of peace if you were not born to lead. Unlike you, I know my opinion of His Majesty's decision doesn't matter. How I live between now and the end – that is what matters.'

Hector stared out into the darkness. 'I stand in the shadow of the king. I am of his line; I am his regent, named so that his power over the land would hold sway. His responsibilities are mine now. If I let go of them, then I have failed.'

'Don't deceive yourself, lad,' Jarmon said seriously, automatically stowing the wallet where it had come from. 'The king's power that mattered left when he left – the Sleeping Child began its rise as his ship crested the horizon and sailed out of sight of Serendair. While I don't deny that his claim to the throne is in place because you are here, in the end it will mean nothing. The power that once reigned in this land undisputed is broken. The protection it proffered is all but gone. There are holes in it, Hector, gaping holes that were once solid in the king's time, and that of all the rulers before him; an iron-strong dominion that is now rusted and pitted. You cannot plug those holes, no matter how much you struggle to. It's already been decided. You try to protect the Island in its last days by virtue of your vow, but your authority does not mean anything.'

He took the pipe from his mouth and looked directly at the younger man. 'But that doesn't mean your sacrifice was not worthy. You may never achieve greatness in itself, but when one has been groomed for greatness, to surrender the chance to prove it, now there's a sacrifice. On the word of your king to yield, give way in a battle you felt you could win, that's the most terrible sacrifice. It dwarfs all others.' Jarmon settled down into a pile of leaves by the fire. 'Except perhaps for having to serve sandbag duty.'

On that last night Hector dreamt, as he always did, of Talthea and the children. The rocky ground beneath his ear burned with the rising heat from the north, making his night visions dark and misty where once they had been clear.

In his dreams he was holding his daughter, playing with his son, basking in quiet contentment with his wife when he felt a shadow beckon to him. When he looked up, the shade that was summoning him took form. It was the spectre of a long-dead king, a forebear he had never known. The headless statue, broken in pieces in Kingston Square, whole once more. His grandfather.

Vandemere.

Wordlessly the king beckoned to him again. Hector looked down to find his arms empty, his wife and son gone.

He followed the shade of the king through a green glade of primeval beauty, back through Time itself. In this dream he trod the path of history, unspooling it in reverse as he walked deep into the silent forest through a veil of sweet mist.

All around him the world turned, undoing what had gone before as it did so. The present, the Third Age in which history was now marked, unwound before his eyes. He could see the Fleets returning to the docks from which they had been launched in anticipation of the second cataclysm, watched the disassembly of the new empire into the broken one that was the result of the Seren War, and the war itself. He saw bloody fields strewn with broken bodies turn green again, saw the ages slipping by, unhurried, remaking history as Time passed in reverse.

Hector looked ahead; the shade of the king was farther away now, disappearing into the mist.

He started to run, and as he did, the unspooling history sped back faster and faster. From the Seren War back to the racial wars that preceded it, the coming of the races of man to Serendair in the Second Age, time hurried crazily backwards. He called to the king, or tried, but no sound came out in this drowsy place, the misty vale of cool, rich green.

Racing now, compelled to find out the purpose of this visitation or command, he barely noticed when the Second Age slipped back to the First, the Day of the Gods, when the Elder races walked the earth. From the corner of his eye Hector saw the first cataclysm reverse itself, saw the waters that had covered much of the Island recede, the star rise back into the sky, saw the Vault of the Underworld where the F'dor had once been imprisoned sealed shut again, containing once more the formless spirits that, upon its rupturing, had escaped and taken human hosts, like Tsoltan, the one his father had vanquished.

With each undone event, the world through which he ran grew greener, newer, more peaceful, more alive. It was in watching the turning back of Time that Hector began to realize how much of the magic had been gone from the world he had known, how much it had been present at one time, long before, when the world was new.

As the First Age melted away into the Before-Time, the prehistory, he saw the birth of the primordial races that sprang from the five elements themselves – the dragons, great wyrms born of living earth; the Kith, Cantha's race, children of the wind; the Mythlin, water-beings who were the forebears of humans, building the beautiful undersea city of Tartechor; the Seren, the first of the races born, descended of the stars; and the F'dor, formless demons sprung from ancient fire, destructive and chaotic, sealed by the four other races into the Vault to spare the earth from obliteration at their hands.

He saw the primeval world, glorious and unspoiled, and quiet. And even that slipped from his view as he watched; the land disappeared into the sea as the wind died away, leaving the surface of the world burning with fire, until it was nothing more than a piece of a glowing star that had broken off and streaked across the heavens on its own. That glowing ball sped backwards, joining the burning body from which it had come.

Leaving nothing around him but starry darkness and the shade of the long-dead king.

Finally the shadow of Vandemere turned around and stared at him sadly.

What, Grandfather? Hector asked, no sound coming from his lips, but echoing none the less in the dark void around them. *What is it you are trying to show me?*

Eternity, the king said. His voice did not sound, but Hector heard the word anyway.

What of eternity? Hector asked, struggling to breathe in the heavy mist of the dark void.

The king's shadow began to fade.

There is no time in eternity. Vandemere's voice echoed in the emptiness. *In staying behind, you fought to give them more time. Instead, you should be fighting to keep from losing eternity.*

Hector woke with a start.

The ground beneath his head was splitting apart, a great fissure ripping the earth asunder.

In a heartbeat he was on his feet, grasping the startled fisherman next to him and dragging the old man back from the brink of the chasm as Jarmon made a dive to untie the horses.

A roar like thunder shivered the scorched trees around them, and the fisherman shouted something that Hector could not hear. They backed away, pulling the frightened beasts with all their strength, running blindly north into the fire-coloured mist, until the ground beneath their feet stopped shaking, settling into a seething rumble that did not cease.

'You all right, Brann?' Hector asked, trying to settle the roan and failing; the animal whinnied in fear and danced in place, her ears back and eyes wild.

The old man's eyes were as glassy as the horse's, but he nodded anyway.

'The Awakening – it's coming,' he whispered, his voice barely audible above the rumbling ground. 'There is no more time for sleep, Sir Hector. We are not that far away; if we hurry, we will be in Dry Cove before morning. Let us make haste, I beg you! My people await rescue.'

'Your people are fools if they haven't quit the village by now, old man,' Jarmon muttered. 'The heat is searing from here. If they be closer, they have already cooked in the belching fire.'

Hector took the trembling fisherman by the shoulders and helped him mount.

'We go,' he said. 'We will stop no more until we are there, or we are in the Afterlife.'

Through the lowlands that had once been the towns and villages near the Great River's mouth they rode, the air thick with black smoke that obscured their vision of anything but the riverbed.

The horses, ridden ceaselessly and deprived of frequent stops for fresh water, began to show signs of faltering. When Brann's mount finally collapsed into a quivering mass on the mule-road, Jarmon pulled the fisherman, grey of face from exhaustion and fear, behind him in the saddle and spurred his own mount onwards.

'Sorry, Rosie, old girl,' he muttered, patting the animal's neck. His hand was covered with flecks of sweat and horse sputum. 'It will soon end, and then you can rest.'

Finally the sound of the sea crashing in the distance broke through the screaming wind.

'Here! We are here!' Brann whispered, tugging roughly on Jarmon's sleeve. 'The sea has drawn back a goodly distance, but you can hear it still.'

Hector reined the roan to a halt. Off to the north sparks of molten flame, like iridescent fireflies, shot haphazardly into the wind above the sea, swirling in menacing patterns against the blackening sky. He strained to see through the smoke, and thought he made out the silhouettes of shacks and docks, charred timbers blending into the darkness.

They dismounted, abandoning the horses at the shoreline, and waded into the wet sand, every now and then passing what was probably once a body, now buried beneath a thick coating of ash.

Hector glanced at Brann, but the fisherman's gaze did not waver; rather, the old man shielded his eyes, trying to peer through the grey and black fog to where he had seen what he thought were the doors to the mammoth mine.

'This way,' the fisherman said, his voice stronger now. 'It was just north of that failed land bridge, past the tip of the peninsula, where once the water met on three sides.'

As if to punctuate his words, the sandy ground shook violently.

'Lead onwards,' Hector shouted, following the fisherman into the sand bed.

Blindly they made their way across the tidal wasteland, where the sea had once swelled to the land, now nothing but a desert of ocean sand. The sea's retreat had laid bare the bones of ships, broken reefs, shells of every imaginable kind, broken and jagged in the wet grit where the water once broke against the shore.

A plume of fire shot into the black sky in the near distance, then fell heavily back into the sea.

Over the broken land bridge for a mile, then another, and another, the three men limped hurriedly across the wet sand, burning now through their boots. Finally, when they reached a place where the smoke blackened the air almost completely, Brann stopped near a small, intact fishing boat wedged in the seabed, dropped to his knees, and pointed beneath the low-hanging smoke down into the distance.

'There,' he whispered.

Hector crouched down and followed the old man's arthritic finger with eyes that burned from the heat and ash.

At first he could see nothing save for the endless sand and black smoke. But after a moment, his eyes adjusted, and his breath caught in his raw throat.

They were standing on what appeared to be a great ridge in the seabed, a towering wall that led down into a crevasse a thousand or more feet deep, at the bottom of which the remnants of seawater pooled. Hector followed the perimeter with his eyes, and could not see its beginning, nor its end. The depression seemed to stretch to the horizon; the cliffwall beneath them made the seabed seem as if they were standing in a vast meadow atop a mountain. Whatever the actual dimensions of the ancient mine, it was clear that a man could not see all of it at once even in clear air; it stretched out beneath the sand, hidden for millennia by the sea, into the place to which the water had retreated. He finally now understood Brann's insistence that enough of the sea could be diverted into such a mammoth space that at least a part of the Island might be spared.

'Where are the doors?' he shouted over the thundering roar that came forth from within the sea to the north.

'At the bottom,' Brann shouted in return, struggling to remain upright in the burning wind.

'Can we scale the cliff face, Hector?' Jarmon asked, looking for a foothold and finding none. 'If we fall from this height there will be no stopping; 'twill be a quick end at least.'

'There looks to be a path of a sort, or at least a place where the cliffwall slants,' Hector said, ducking again so that he could see more clearly.

Brann was eyeing the sky nervously. 'We must hurry!' he urged as liquid fire shot aloft again, spewing ash and making the ground lurch beneath their feet. He scurried over the rim and began sliding down the wall that Hector had indicated, followed a moment later by the two soldiers.

Down into the crevasse, running and slipping they ran, falling, sliding on knees or even on their backs, only to rise, driven by necessity and the imminence of the Awakening. The seabed was thick here, like rock beneath the sand, but the debris that they had seen in the higher ground at the shoreline was absent.

Finally, when they had fallen far enough down to have descended a small mountain, they found themselves at the base of a sheer cliffwall, their feet wet in the dregs of the sea that had covered this place a short time before, staring up at a solid wall of rock.

The wind howled and shrieked above them, but stayed at the level of the sea, only venturing down into the canyon long enough to whip sand into their eyes. 'Where are the doors?' Hector asked again, his voice quieter in the near-silence.

Brann pointed to a towering slab to the north. 'There,' he said, in a trembling. tone.

Crawling now, the three men made their way over the scattered rock of the sea floor, scaling outcroppings, climbing over dips and hollows, until at last they stood where the fisherman had indicated.

Above them towered what appeared to be two massive slabs of solid earth, smooth as granite and white as the rest of the sea sand. There was a slash of thin darkness between them; otherwise they appeared in no way different from the rest of the rocky undersea hills.

Beneath their feet the ground trembled again, more violently than before. The winds atop the canyon screamed, rising into an atonal wail that fell, discordant. Distant fire shot into the sky, turning the clouds the colour of blood.

From his pack Hector drew forth the sceptre. It glowed brightly in his hand, the gilt shaft shining beneath the diamond which sparkled almost menacingly.

Before them the slabs of stone seemed to soften. The three men watched, transfixed, as the sand that had covered them for time uncounted began to slide away, pooling at the base, revealing towering doors of titanic size bound in brass, with massive handles jutting from plates of the same metal, a strange keyhole in the rightmost one. The gigantic doors were inscribed with ancient glyphs and wards, countersigns and runes the like of which Hector had never seen before.

Brann was watching the northern sky nervously over his shoulder. 'Make haste, sir knight,' he urged.

Hector stared at the ancient key in his hand. It appeared different from how it had been a moment before; the dark shaft of once living wood that he thought was the branch of a stone tree now more closely resembled a bone, the diamond perched atop it on the rim of where a joint would connect. Carefully he held it next to the keyhole, trying to ascertain the angle which would fit it.

'Viden, singa ever monokran fri,' he said. *Open, in the name of the king.*

The glyphs on the doors glowed with life.

The gilding began to fall from the sceptre's shaft, sliding off in sandy golden flakes.

Hector pushed the key into the lock and slowly turned it counterclockwise.

Beneath his hand he more felt than heard an echoing thud. Ever so slightly the crack between the stone doors widened. Hector pushed on the rightmost of the two, but could only cause it to move infinitesimally. He attempted to look inside. He could see very little.

The darkness was devouring in its depth. Gingerly Hector pushed the door open a little further, straining against the wedge of sand that had built up at the door's base over the ages. Brann took up a place beside him, adding the remains of his strength to the effort.

Behind him the flares of fire from the Awakening rose suddenly higher, burning more intensely, casting shadows into the black cavern beyond the doors. Hector peered through the crack.

The immensity of the place was more than Hector could fathom. From the small vista he had gained there seemed to be no border to it, no walls below limiting it to edges, but rather was more like opening a door into the night sky, or the depths of the universe.

'Again, sir knight,' Brann whispered, pale with exertion. 'We must open it wider. Hurry; there is no time left.'

Jarmon leaned with all his strength against the door as well. With a groan that made Hector shudder, the rightmost of the two doors swung further into the endless darkness.

Hector looked in again. At first he saw nothing, as before. Then, at the most distant edge of his vision, he thought he could make out tiny flames, perhaps remnants of the mine fires that could still be burning thousands of years later. But when those flames began to move, he felt suddenly weak, dizzy, as his head was assaulted from within by the cacophony of a thousand rushing voices, cackling and screeching with delight.

Like fire on pine, the living flames began to sweep down distant ledges within the mammoth pit, some nearer, some farther, all dashing towards the door, churning the air with the destructive chaos of mayhem.

Hector, his head throbbing now with the gleeful screaming that was drawing rapidly closer, could only watch in horror as the fire swelled, burning intensely, a legion of individual flames scrambling down the dark walls towards the doors.

His mind reeled for a moment as the sickening realization of what they had done crashed down on him. Time stood still as the truth thundered around his ears, louder than the tremors from the Sleeping Child.

He had just broken the one barrier that separated life from void, that stood between the earth and its destruction, and more.

That threatened even the existence of the Afterlife.

'My God,' he whispered, his hand slick with sweat. 'My sweet God! Jarmon – This is the Vault! We've opened the Vault of the Underworld!'

Jarmon's guttural curse was lost in the sound of oncoming destruction and the orgiastic screaming of the approaching fire demons, long entombed, now rushing towards freedom.

The soldiers seized the door handle and together they pulled on it with all their strength. They succeeded in dragging the door shut most of the way, but they were able to close it only as far as was possible with the obstacle of the fisherman's body in the way.

Brann had interposed himself in the doorway, straddling the threshold.

Jarmon reached over to shove the old man out of the way. 'Move, you fool!' he shouted. And gagged in pain when his arm was crushed against the door, so that it was clasped in a withering grip.

They looked at the old man. His face had hardened, had become an almost translucent mask of undisguised delight. Its wrinkled skin now was tight over a feral smile, above which a pair of dark eyes gleamed, their edges rimmed in the colour of blood.

'I,' Brann said softly. 'I am what the winds forewarned you of, Sir Hector. I am what comes.'

'No,' Hector whispered raggedly. 'You – you –'

The demon in the old man's body clucked disapprovingly, though his smile sparkled with amusement. 'Now, now, Sir Hector,' he said with exaggerated politeness. 'This is a historic moment, one to savour! Let us not spoil it with recriminations, shall we?' He let go of Jarmon's arm.

The soldiers dragged on the heavy door again, but the F'dor only wedged himself in tighter, preventing it from closing with a strength that was growing by the moment. Hector pulled with all his might, but managed only to strip the skin from his sweating palms against the hot metal handles.

Jarmon stepped back angrily and drew his sword, but the fisherman merely gestured at him. Dark fire exploded from his fingers and licked the weapon; the blade grew molten in Jarmon's hand, melting away in a river of liquid steel. It drew a scream of agony from the guard, who fell heavily away into the sand.

'The sceptre –' Hector choked.

'Would help you to discern the truth?' the demon asked solicitously, glancing at his approaching fellows, who were drawing nearer now. 'Indeed, you were not wrong. Everything I told you was the truth. My people *have* lived at the sea's edge for a very long time; we *are* frail in body, though we are strong in spirit. Without a host, or someone to give us aid, we could never open the door alone. And I was most sincere when I assured you that none of my people would dream of touching the sceptre; for one of our kind to touch an object of Living Stone crowned with a diamond would be certain death. That's why we needed you; we thank you for your service.'

'Blessed ground,' Hector whispered, pulling futilely at the door and fighting off the screaming voices that swelled inside his head. 'The inn is blessed ground –'

'I never broached the inn,' said the F'dor. 'Nor the palace, if you recall. No, Sir Hector, I never crossed the threshold of either place; you met me at the crossroads and left me at the foot of the castle. Kind of you.' The demon laughed again. 'And what I told you of my life was the truth as well. Long ago I had the chance to leave my birthplace – that was in the old days, during the first cataclysm, when the star first ruptured the Vault. Many of us escaped before it was sealed again, only to have been hunted throughout history, having to flee from host to host, hiding, biding our time. But now, once again, we will be out in the world, thanks to you, Sir Hector. You wished to rescue whomever you could from the cataclysm, and here you are! You have spared an entire race from captivity! And not only have you freed us from the Vault, but our master – the one who has long watched the doors, waiting for this day – you will be his host! What could be more edifying than that?'

The fire in the demon's eyes matched the intensity of that in the sky.

'When the old fisherman rowed out in his little boat to examine what the retreat of the sea had revealed, I was waiting, formless. I had come home when I heard of the upcoming Awakening, just as I said I had.' The demon sighed. 'A younger, stronger host might have been preferable, but one takes what one is offered in the advent of cataclysm. Isn't truth a marvellous thing? The art is in telling it so that it is interpreted the way one wishes to have it heard.

'Finally, I told you that we would be eternally grateful, sir knight. And we are. We are. Eternally.'

Jarmon rose shakily to his feet and met Hector's eye.

'Hector,' he said quietly, 'open the door.'

In his dizziness, the words rang clear. Hector's gaze narrowed a moment, then widened slightly with understanding.

With the last of his strength, he threw himself against the rightmost door of the Vault, shoving it open even farther than it had been before. His head all but split from the frenzied screaming of the demonic horde that was virtually within reach of the door; he tried to avert his eyes from the horror of the sight, but found his gaze dragged to the approaching fire that burned black with excitement as it rushed forward to freedom.

At the same moment, Jarmon threw himself into Brann and locked his arms around his knees. The frail form of the demon's host buckled in the strong arms of the guard and the momentum thrust both of them over the threshold and into the Vault.

Which gave Hector just enough time to drag the mammoth door shut before the multitude of F'dor that had been sealed away since the First Age crossed the threshold into the material world.

He pulled the key from the hole and tossed it behind him. Then he wrapped his arms through the huge brass handles, holding on with all the leverage he could muster as the gleaming doors darkened and settled back into lifeless stone once more.

Hector's mind buckled under the screaming he could hear and feel beyond those doors. The stone shook terrifyingly as the demons pounded from the other side, causing tremors that shook his entire body. He bowed his head, both to brace the closure and to try and drown out the horrifying sounds that scratched his ears. Within the demonic screeches of fury he thought he could hear Jarmon's voice rise in similar tone, the unmistakable sound of agony of body and soul ringing harshly in it.

As he clutched at the burning doors that seared the flesh from his chest and face, the sky turned white above him.

With a thundering bellow that cracked the vault of the heavens, the Sleeping Child awoke in the depths of the sea and rose in fiery rage to the sky.

The sound of the screaming on the other side of the door faded in the roar of the inferno behind him. All he could feel now was searing heat, heat that baked his body to the core from behind, and radiated through the stone doors before him, as molten volcanic fire rained down, sealing him eternally in an ossified shell to the brass handles.

As he passed over the threshold of death, from life to Afterlife, Hector finally saw what his father had told him of, and what he had relayed to Anais. Just beyond his sight, closer than the air of his last breath, and at the same time half a world away, he could see his friend in the branches of the World Tree, could see his father in knee-deep surf, standing vigil, Talthea and Aidan behind him on the shore, the baby in her arms. MacQuieth's eyes were on him, watching him from the other side of the earth, the other side of Time.

As his spirit fled his body, dissipating and expanding to the farthest reaches of the universe at the same time, Hector willed himself to hold for a moment to the invisible tether, paused long enough to breathe a final kiss on his wife and children, to whisper in his father's ear across the threshold over which they were bound to each other by love.

It's done, Father. You can cease waiting; go back to living now.

His last conscious thought was one of ironic amusement. As the sea poured in, sealing the entrance to the Vault once more beneath its depths, his body remained behind, fired into clay, forming the lock that barred the doors, vigilant to the end in death as he had been life.

The key of living earth lay behind him, buried in the sand of the ocean floor, just out of reach for all eternity.

'Apple, Canfa, peez.'

The daughter of the wind looked down solemnly into the earnest little human face. Then she smiled in spite of herself. She reached easily into the gnarled branches of the stunted tree that were beyond the length of his spindly arms and plucked a hard red fruit, and handed it to the boy.

She glanced to her left, where the woman sat on the ground of the decimated orchard, absently eating the apple she had been given a moment before and staring dully at Cantha's silver mare grazing on autumn grass nearby.

A deathly stillness fell, like the slamming of a door.

The winds, howling in fury as they had been for weeks uncounted, died down into utter silence.

And Cantha knew.

She stood frozen for a moment in the vast emptiness of a world without moving air, poised on the brink of cataclysm. And just before the winds began to scream, she seized the child by the back of the shirt and lifted him through the heavy air, bearing him to the horse as the apple fell from his hand to the ground.

She was dragging the startled woman to her feet and heaving her on to the horse as well when the sky turned white. She had mounted and was spurring the beast when the horizon to the north west erupted in a plume of fire that shot into the sky like a spark from a candle caught by the wind, then spread over the bottom of the melting clouds, filling them with light, painful in intensity. Cantha uttered a single guttural command to the horse and galloped off, clutching the woman and the boy before her.

Even at the southern tip of the Island they could feel the tremors, could see the earth shuddering beneath the horse's hooves. Cantha could feel the child's sides heave, thought he might be wailing, but whatever sound he made was drowned in the horrifying lament of the winds. She prayed to those winds now to speed her way, to facilitate her path and her pace, but there was no answer.

At the foot of the battlements she pulled the humans from the horse's back, slashed the saddle girdings and turned it loose, silently wishing it Godspeed. Then she seized the woman by the hand and tucked the boy beneath her arm as she began the daunting climb up the steps of the rock face.

She was halfway up, her muscles buckling in exertion, when the winds swelled, rampant, heavy with ash and debris. They whipped around her, dragging the air from her lungs, threatening her balance. Finally she had to let go of the woman lest she lose her grip on the boy.

'Climb!' Cantha shouted to the woman, but the woman merely stopped, rigid, where she was. Cantha urged her again, and again, pushing her futilely, finally abandoning her, running blindly up the steps as the sky turned black above her.

Through the dark halls and up the tower steps, two at a time, Cantha carried the child, in her arms now, clinging around her neck. The tower shuddered beneath them, swaying in the gale, the stone walls that had stood for five hundred years, stalwart, unmoving, buffeted by the winds of hurricanes and of war, trembling around them.

Finally they reached the pinnacle of the topmost tower, the dusty room lined with bookshelves and jars that had once been the abode of the royal vizier. Cantha, spent, set the boy down, took his hand and ran through the study, throwing open the doors that already banged in the wind, running heedlessly through the shards of broken glass scattered across the stone floor, up the final flight of wooden steps, and pushed open the trapdoor to the utmost top of the parapets. She held tight to the boy as they stepped out on to the platform from which the vizier had once communed with the lightning, and stared down at the world below her.

Across the wide meadows and broken forests that surrounded Elysian dust was gathering in great spiral devils, loose earth driven upwards by the chaos of the winds. In the distance she could see the silver horse running, galloping free, saddled no more. She looked around for the woman, but could not see the battlement steps.

Beside her she felt the boy move; she looked down to see him pointing north.

A wall of water the height of the tower was coming, dark grey in the distance, sweeping ahead of it a conundrum of debris that had once been towns and cities, bridges and mills.

It was but the forewave.

Behind it the real wave hovered, the crest of which Cantha could not see, rising to meet the dark sky.

Shaking, she reached down and lifted the child to her shoulders, mostly to give him as much height as possible, but also to avoid having to see again the expression in his eyes. Her own gaze was riveted on the vertical sea as it swelled forward across the Island, swallowing the river, the fields, the broken orchard as she watched. Just before it took the tower, sweeping forth to rejoin itself at the southern coast, she thought of the legends of enclaves of Lirin who had lived along the shore at the time of the first cataclysm, whose lands had been subsumed when the Child first fell to earth. The lore told of how they had transformed, once children of the sky, now children of the sea, coming to live in underwater caves and grottos, building entire civilizations in the sheltering sands of the ocean, hiding in the guardian reefs, breathing beneath the waves. *If such a fairy tale be possible, may it be possible for thee, child*, she thought, patting the leg that dangled over her shoulder.

All light was blotted out in a roaring rush of grey-blue fury.

'Hold thy breath, child,' Cantha said.

From the aft deck of the *Stormrider*, Sevirym watched the fire rise in the distance. The Island was so far away now, here at the edge of the Icefields at the southern end of the world, that at first he barely noticed; the Awakening resembled little more than a glorious slash of colour brought on by the sunset. But as the clouds began to burn at the horizon, and the sea winds died at the same moment, he knew what he was beholding.

He was unable to tear his eyes away as the fire blazed, a white-hot streak in the distance brighter than the sun. And then, oblivious to the crew and passengers around him, staring east as well, he bowed his head and gave in to grief as the fire faded and disappeared into the sea.

The wave swelled to the outer edges of the Island, spilling over the charred land, swallowing the High Reaches in the north all the way down to the south-eastern corner. It poured over what had once been great rolling fields and forests, largely blackened now or swollen with gleaming lava, all the way to Yliessan, where it seemed to hover for a moment above Sagia, her boughs adorned with flowers, sheltering the children of the sky who had sought final refuge there. Then it crashed down, meeting the sea at the land's edge on all sides.

As the tide rose to an even height, taking in the overflow, the crest of the waves closed above the Island, the first birthplace of Time, swallowing it from sight.

And then peace returned.

Hot vapour covered the sea, making it appear as calm and still as a misty morning.

AMERICAN GODS

NEIL GAIMAN

AMERICAN GODS
NEIL GAIMAN

American Gods (2001)
Anansi Boys (forthcoming)

American Gods tells the story of a man called Shadow, who, when the story begins, is in prison, having served out his sentence for a crime he did commit.

He's looking forward to getting out of prison, rejoining his wife, getting his old job back: but his wife's tragic death in a car accident puts paid to that, and he soon finds himself working as a bodyguard and driver for an elderly grifter who calls himself Mr Wednesday.

Shadow learns that when people came to America they brought their gods with them. Some gods have done well; most of the gods and mythical creatures have had to eke out a bare living on what scraps of belief they could find. Working for Wednesday, Shadow meets many of them: Czernobog, the Slavic death god, and Mr Nancy, the African trickster-god Anansi, and sundry fates and mythical figures, some remembered and many forgotten.

Wednesday is the American aspect of the old Norse god Odin, and he is apparently attempting to start a war between the old gods and the new ones who are taking up people's minds and hearts – gods of television, of technology, of money.

Shadow survives, although Wednesday does not. Shadow dies on a tree, and rises again. He even manages to end the war. And then, no longer entirely human, but not a god, he leaves America.

Gaiman says, 'I always conceived of *American Gods* as a backdrop to tell stories with. The next novel, the one I'm writing now, is called *Anansi Boys*, and is the story of Mr Nancy and his sons, Spider and Fat Charley. Until Robert Silverberg called and asked about an *American Gods* novella, I had thought of Shadow as someone I would come back to a long time from now, someone I could use to tell a different story about America. But a story started twining in my head: something with Shadow in northern Scotland, and various old stories and archaeological books I'd read started to twist and shape.

'I wrote the story, and I realized as I wrote it that there were a number of other stories waiting to be told about Shadow in the United Kingdom and on his journey back to the United States. And I knew what the next *American Gods* book would be.'

THE MONARCH OF THE GLEN

BY NEIL GAIMAN

*She herself is a haunted house. She does not possess herself; her ances-
tors sometimes come and peer out of the windows of her eyes and that
is very frightening.*

Angela Carter, The Lady of the House of Love

I

'If you ask me,' said the little man to Shadow, 'you're something of a
monster. Am I right?'

They were the only two people, apart from the barmaid, in the
bar of a hotel in a town on the north coast of Scotland. Shadow
had been sitting there on his own, drinking a lager, when the man
came over and sat at his table. It was late summer, and it seemed
to Shadow that everything was cold, and small, and damp. He had
a small book of Pleasant Local Walks in front of him, and was
studying the walk he planned to do tomorrow, along the coast,
towards Cape Wrath.

He closed the book.

'I'm American,' said Shadow, 'If that's what you mean.'

The little man cocked his head to one side, and he winked, theatri-
cally. He had steel-grey hair, and a grey face, and a grey coat, and he
looked like a small-town lawyer. 'Well, perhaps that is what I mean,
at that,' he said. Shadow had had problems understanding Scottish
accents in his short time in the country, all rich burrs and strange
words and trills, but he had no trouble understanding this man.
Everything the little man said was small and crisp, each word so
perfectly enunciated that it made Shadow feel that he himself was
talking with a mouthful of oatmeal.

The little man sipped his drink and said, 'So you're American.
Oversexed, overpaid and over here. Eh? D'you work on the rigs?'

'Sorry?'

'An oilman? Out on the big metal platforms. We get oil people up here, from time to time.'

'No. I'm not from the rigs.'

The little man took out a pipe from his pocket, and a small penknife, and began to remove the dottle from the bowl. Then he tapped it out into the ashtray. 'They have oil in Texas, you know,' he said, after a while, as if he were confiding a great secret. 'That's in America.'

'Yes,' said Shadow.

He thought about saying something about Texans believing that Texas was actually in Texas, but he suspected that he'd have to start explaining what he meant, so he said nothing.

Shadow had been away from America for the better part of two years. He had been away when the towers fell. He told himself sometimes that he did not care if he ever went back, and sometimes he almost came close to believing himself. He had reached the Scottish mainland two days ago, landed in Thurso on the ferry from the Orkneys, and had travelled to the town he was staying in by bus.

The little man was talking. 'So there's a Texas oilman, down in Aberdeen, he's talking to an old fellow he meets in a pub, much like you and me meeting actually, and they get talking, and the Texan, he says, Back in Texas I get up in the morning, I get into my car – I won't try to do the accent, if you don't mind – I'll turn the key in the ignition, and put my foot down on the accelerator, what you call the, the –'

'Gas pedal,' said Shadow, helpfully.

'Right. Put my foot down on the gas pedal at breakfast, and by lunchtime I still won't have reached the edge of my property. And the canny old Scot, he just nods and says, Aye, well, I used to have a car like that myself.'

The little man laughed raucously, to show that the joke was done. Shadow smiled, and nodded, to show that he knew it was a joke.

'What are you drinking? Lager? Same again over here, Jennie love. Mine's a Lagavulin.' The little man tamped tobacco from a pouch into his pipe. 'Did you know that Scotland's bigger than America?'

There had been no one in the hotel bar when Shadow came downstairs that evening, just the thin barmaid, reading a newspaper, and smoking her cigarette. He'd come down to sit by the open fire, as his bedroom was cold, and the metal radiators on the bedroom wall were colder than the room. He hadn't expected company.

'No,' said Shadow, always willing to play straight man. 'I didn't. How'd you reckon that?'

'It's all fractal,' said the little man. 'The smaller you look, the more things unpack. It could take you as long to drive across America as it would to drive across Scotland, if you did it the right way. It's like, you look on a map, and the coastlines are solid lines. But when you walk them, they're all over the place. I saw a whole programme on it on the telly the other night. Great stuff.'

'OK,' said Shadow.

The little man's pipe-lighter flamed, and he sucked and puffed and sucked and puffed until he was satisfied that the pipe was burning well, then he put the lighter, the pouch and the penknife back into his coat pocket.

'Anyway, anyway,' said the little man. 'I believe you're planning on staying here through the weekend.'

'Yes,' said Shadow. 'Do you . . . are you with the hotel?'

'No, no. Truth to tell, I was standing in the hall, when you arrived. I heard you talking to Gordon on the reception desk.'

Shadow nodded. He had thought that he had been alone in the reception hall when he had registered, but it was possible that the little man had passed through. But still . . . there was a wrongness to this conversation. There was a wrongness to everything.

Jennie the barmaid put their drinks on to the bar. 'Five pounds twenty,' she said. She picked up her newspaper, and started to read once more. The little man went to the bar, paid, and brought back the drinks.

'So how long are you in Scotland?' asked the little man.

Shadow shrugged. 'I wanted to see what it was like. Take some walks. See the sights. Maybe a week. Maybe a month.'

Jennie put down her newspaper. 'It's the arse-end of nowhere up here,' she said, cheerfully. 'You should go somewhere interesting.'

'That's where you're wrong,' said the little man. 'It's only the arse-end of nowhere if you look at it wrong. See that map, laddie?' He pointed to a fly-specked map of northern Scotland on the opposite wall of the bar. 'You know what's wrong with it?'

'No.'

'It's upside down!' the man said, triumphantly. 'North's at the top. It's saying to the world that this is where things stop. Go no further. The world ends here. But you see, that's not how it was. This wasn't the north of Scotland. This was the southernmost tip of the Viking world. You know what the second most northern county in Scotland is called?'

Shadow glanced at the map, but it was too far away to read. He shook his head.

'Sutherland!' said the little man. He showed his teeth. 'The South Land. Not to anyone else in the world it wasn't, but it was to the Vikings.'

Jennie the barmaid walked over to them. 'I won't be gone long,' she said. 'Call the front desk if you need anything before I get back.' She put a log on the fire, then she went out into the hall.

'Are you a historian?' Shadow asked.

'Good one,' said the little man. 'You may be a monster, but you're funny. I'll give you that.'

'I'm not a monster,' said Shadow.

'Aye, that's what monsters always say,' said the little man. 'I was a specialist once. In St Andrews. Now I'm in general practice. Well, I was. I'm semi-retired. Go in to the surgery a couple of days a week, just to keep my hand in.'

'Why do you say I'm a monster?' asked Shadow.

'Because,' said the little man, lifting his whisky glass with the air of one making an irrefutable point, 'I am something of a monster myself. Like calls to like. We are all monsters, are we not? Glorious monsters, shambling through the swamps of unreason . . .' He sipped his whisky, then said, 'Tell me, a big man like you, have you ever been a bouncer? "Sorry mate, I'm afraid you can't come in here tonight, private function going on, sling your hook and get on out of it," all that?'

'No,' said Shadow.

'But you must have done something like that?'

'Yes,' said Shadow, who had been a bodyguard once, to an old god; but that was in another country.

'You, uh, you'll pardon me for asking, don't take this the wrong way, but do you need money?'

'Everyone needs money. But I'm OK.' This was not entirely true; but it was a truth that, when Shadow needed money, the world seemed to go out of its way to provide it.

'Would you like to make a wee bit of spending money? Being a bouncer? It's a piece of piss. Money for old rope.'

'At a disco?'

'Not exactly. A private party. They rent a big old house near here, come in from all over at the end of the summer. So last year, everybody's having a grand old time, champagne out of doors, all that, and there was some trouble. A bad lot. Out to ruin everybody's weekend.'

'These were locals?'

'I don't think so.'

'Was it political?' asked Shadow. He did not want to be drawn into local politics.

'Not a bit of it. Yobs and hairies and idiots. Anyway. They probably won't come back this year. Probably off in the wilds of nowhere demonstrating against international capitalism. But just to be on the safe side, the folk up at the house've asked me to look out for someone who could do a spot of intimidating. You're a big lad, and that's what they want.'

'How much?' asked Shadow.

'Can you handle yourself in a fight, if it came down to it?' asked the man.

Shadow didn't say anything. The little man looked Shadow up and down, and then he grinned again, showing tobacco-stained teeth.

'Fifteen hundred pounds, for a long weekend's work. That's good money. And it's cash. Nothing you'd ever need to report to the tax man.'

'This weekend coming?' said Shadow.

'Starting Friday morning. It's a big old house. Part of it used to be a castle. West of Cape Wrath.'

'I don't know,' said Shadow.

'If you do it,' said the little grey man, 'you'll get a fantastic weekend in a historical house, and I can guarantee you'll get to meet with all kinds of interesting people. Perfect holiday job. I just wish I was younger. And, uh, a great deal taller, actually.'

Shadow said 'OK,' and as soon as he said it, wondered if he would regret it.

'Good man. I'll get you more details as and when.' The little grey man stood up, and gave Shadow's shoulder a gentle pat as he walked past. Then he went out, leaving Shadow in the bar on his own.

II

Shadow had been on the road for about eighteen months. He had backpacked across Europe and down into northern Africa. He had picked olives, and fished for sardines, and driven a truck, and sold wine from the side of a road. Finally, several months ago, he had hitchhiked his way back to Norway, to Oslo, where he had been born thirty-five years before.

He was not sure what he had been looking for. He only knew that he had not found it, although there were moments, in the high ground, in the crags and waterfalls, when he was certain that whatever he needed was just around the corner: behind a jut of granite, or in the nearest pine-wood.

Still, it was a deeply unsatisfactory visit, and when, in Bergen, he was asked if he would be half of the crew of a motor-yacht, on its way to meet its owner in Cannes, he said yes.

They had sailed from Bergen to the Shetlands, and then to the Orkneys, where they spent the night in a bed and breakfast in Stromness. Next morning, leaving the harbour, the engines had failed, ultimately and irrevocably, and the boat had been towed back to port.

Bjorn, who was the captain and the other half of the crew, stayed with the boat, to talk to the insurers and field the angry calls from the boat's owner. Shadow saw no reason to stay: he took the ferry to Thurso, on the north coast of Scotland.

He was restless. At night he dreamed of freeways, of entering the neon edges of a city where the people spoke English. Sometimes it was in the Midwest, sometimes it was in Florida, sometimes on the east coast, sometimes on the west.

When he got off the ferry he bought a book of scenic walks, and picked up a bus timetable, and he set off into the world.

Jennie the barmaid came back, and started to wipe all the surfaces with a cloth. Her hair was so blonde it was almost white, and it was tied up at the back in a bun.

'So what is it people do around here for fun?' asked Shadow.

'They drink. They wait to die,' she said. 'Or they go south. That pretty much exhausts your options.'

'You sure?'

'Well, think about it. There's nothing up here but sheep and hills. We feed off the tourists, of course, but there's never really enough of you. Sad, isn't it?'

Shadow shrugged.

'Are you from New York?' she asked.

'Chicago, originally. But I came here from Norway.'

'You speak Norwegian?'

'A little.'

'There's somebody you should meet,' she said, suddenly. Then she looked at her watch. 'Somebody who came here from Norway, a long time ago. Come on.'

She put her cleaning cloth down, turned off the bar-lights, and walked over to the door. 'Come on,' she said, again.

'Can you do that?' asked Shadow.

'I can do whatever I want,' she said. 'It's a free country isn't it?'

'I guess.'

She locked the bar with a brass key. They walked into the reception hall. 'Wait here,' she said. She went through a door marked PRIVATE, and reappeared several minutes later, wearing a long brown coat. 'OK. Follow me.'

They walked out into the street. 'So, is this a village or a small town?' asked Shadow.

'It's a fucking graveyard,' she said. 'Up this way. Come on.'

They walked up a narrow road. The moon was huge and a yellowish brown. Shadow could hear the sea, although he could not yet see it.

'You're Jennie?' he said.

'That's right. And you?'

'Shadow.'

'Is that your real name?'

'It's what they call me.'

'Come on then, Shadow,' she said.

At the top of the hill, they stopped. They were on the edge of the village, and there was a grey stone cottage. Jennie opened the gate, and led Shadow up a path to the front door. He brushed a small bush on the side of the path, and the air filled with the scent of sweet lavender. There were no lights on in the cottage.

'Whose house is this?' asked Shadow. 'It looks empty.'

'Don't worry,' said Jennie. 'She'll be home in a second.'

She pushed open the unlocked front door, and they went inside. She turned on the light switch by the door. Most of the inside of the cottage was taken up by a kitchen sitting room. There was a tiny staircase leading up to what Shadow presumed was an attic bedroom. A CD player sat on the pine counter.

'This is your house,' said Shadow.

'Home sweet home,' she agreed. 'You want coffee? Or something to drink?'

'Neither,' said Shadow. He wondered what Jennie wanted. She had barely looked at him, hadn't even smiled at him.

'So did I hear right? Was Doctor Gaskell asking you to help look after a party on the weekend?'

'I guess.'

'So what are you doing tomorrow and Friday?'

'Walking,' said Shadow. 'I've got a book. There are some beautiful walks.'

'Some of them are beautiful. Some of them are treacherous,' she told him. 'You can still find winter snow here, in the shadows, in the summer. Things last a long time, in the shadows.'

'I'll be careful,' he told her.

'That was what the Vikings said,' she said, and she smiled. She took off her coat and dropped it on the bright purple sofa. 'Maybe I'll see you out there. I like to go for walks.' She pulled at the bun at the back of her head, and her pale hair fell free. It was longer than Shadow had thought it would be.

'Do you live here alone?'

She took a cigarette from a packet on the counter, lit it with a match. 'What's it to you?' she asked. 'You won't be staying the night, will you?'

Shadow shook his head.

'The hotel's at the bottom of the hill,' she told him. 'You can't miss it. Thanks for walking me home.'

Shadow said good-night, and walked back, through the lavender night, out to the lane. He stood there for a little while, staring out at the moon on the sea, puzzled. Then he walked down the hill until he got to the hotel. She was right: you couldn't miss it. He walked up the stairs, unlocked his room with a key attached to a short stick, and went inside. The room was colder than the corridor.

He took off his shoes, and stretched out on the bed in the dark.

III

The boat was made of the fingernails of dead men, and it lurched through the mist, bucking and rolling hugely and unsteadily on the choppy sea.

There were shadowy shapes on the deck, men as big as hills or houses, and as Shadow got closer he could see their faces: proud men and tall, each one of them. They seemed to ignore the ship's motion, each man waiting on the deck as if frozen in place.

One of them stepped forward, and he grasped Shadow's hand with his own huge hand. Shadow stepped on to the grey deck .

'Welcome to this accursed place,' said the man holding Shadow's hand, in a deep, gravel voice.

'Hail!' called the men on the deck. 'Hail sun-bringer! Hail Baldur!'

The name on Shadow's birth certificate was Balder Moon, but he shook his head. 'I am not him,' he told them. 'I am not the one you are waiting for.'

'We are dying here,' said the gravel-voiced man, not letting go of Shadow's hand.

It was cold in the misty place between the worlds of waking and the grave. Salt spray crashed on the bows of the grey ship, and Shadow was drenched to the skin.

'Bring us back,' said the man holding his hand. 'Bring us back or let us go.'

Shadow said, 'I don't know how.'

At that, the men on the deck began to wail and howl. Some of them crashed the hafts of their spears against the deck, others struck the flats of their short swords against the brass bowls at the centre of their leather shields, setting up a rhythmic din accompanied by cries that moved from sorrow to a full-throated berserker ululation . . .

A seagull was screaming in the early-morning air. The bedroom window had blown open in the night, and was banging in the wind. Shadow was lying on the top of his bed in his narrow hotel room. His skin was damp, perhaps with sweat.

Another cold day at the end of the summer had begun.

The hotel packed him a tupperware box containing several chicken sandwiches, a hard-boiled egg, a small packet of cheese-and-onion crisps, and an apple. Gordon on the reception desk, who handed him the box, asked when he'd be back, explaining that if he was more than a couple of hours late they'd call out the rescue services, and asking for the number of Shadow's mobile phone.

Shadow did not have a mobile phone.

He set off on the walk, heading along the coast. It was beautiful, with a desolate beauty that chimed and echoed with the empty places inside Shadow. He had imagined Scotland as being a soft place, all gentle heathery hills, but here on the north coast everything seemed sharp and jutting, even the grey clouds that scudded across the pale blue sky. He followed the route in his book, across scrubby meadows and past burns, up rocky hills and down.

Sometimes he imagined that he was standing still and the world was moving underneath him, that he was simply pushing it past with his legs.

The route was more tiring than he had expected. He had planned to eat at one o'clock, but by midday his legs were tired and he wanted a break. He followed his path to the side of a hill, where a boulder provided a convenient windbreak, and he crouched to eat his lunch. In the distance, ahead of him, he could see the Atlantic.

He had thought himself alone.

She said, 'Will you give me your apple?'

It was Jennie, the barmaid from the hotel. Her too-fair hair gusted about her head.

'Hello, Jennie,' said Shadow. He passed her his apple. She pulled a clasp-knife from the pocket of her brown coat, and sat beside him. 'Thanks,' she said.

'So,' said Shadow, 'from your accent, you must have come from Norway when you were a kid. I mean, you sound like a local to me.'

'Did I say that I came from Norway?'

'Well, didn't you?'

She speared an apple-slice, and ate it, fastidiously, from the tip of the knife-blade, only touching it with her teeth. She glanced at him. 'It was a long time ago.'

'Family?'

She moved her shoulders in a shrug, as if any answer she could give him was beneath her.

'So you like it here?'

She looked at him and shook her head. 'I feel like a *hulder*.'

He'd heard the word before, in Norway. 'Aren't they a kind of troll?'

'No. They are mountain creatures, like the trolls, but they come from the woods, and they are very beautiful. Like me.' She grinned as she said it, as if she knew that she was too pallid, too sulky and too thin ever to be beautiful. 'They fall in love with farmers.'

'Why?'

'Damned if I know,' she said. 'But they do. Sometimes the farmer realizes that he is talking to a *hulder* woman, because she has a cow's tail hanging down behind, or worse, sometimes from behind there is nothing there, she is just hollow and empty, like a shell. Then the farmer says a prayer, or runs away, flees back to his mother or his farm.

'But sometimes the farmers do not run. Sometimes they throw a knife over her shoulder, or just smile, and they marry the *hulder* woman. Then her tail falls off. But she is still stronger than any human woman could ever be. And she still pines for her home in the forests and the mountains. She will never be truly happy. She will never be human.'

'What happens to her then?' asked Shadow. 'Does she age and die with her farmer?'

She had sliced the apple down to the core. Now, with a flick of the wrist, she sent the apple core arcing off the side of the hill. 'When her man dies . . . I think she goes back to the hills and the woods.' She stared out at the hillside. 'There's a story about one of them who was married to a farmer who didn't treat her well. He shouted at her, wouldn't help around the farm, he came home from the village drunk and angry. Sometimes he beat her.

'Now, one day she's in the farmhouse, making up the morning's fire, and he comes in and starts shouting at her, for his food is not ready, and he is angry, nothing she does is right, he doesn't know why he married her, and she listens to him for a while, and then, saying nothing, she reaches down to the fireplace, and she picks up the poker. A heavy black iron jobbie. She takes that poker, and, without an effort, she bends it into a perfect circle, just like her wedding ring. She doesn't grunt or sweat, she just bends it, like you'd bend a reed. And her farmer sees this and he goes white as a sheet, and doesn't say anything else about his breakfast. He's seen what she did to the poker and he knows that at any time in the last five years she could have done the same to him. And until he died, he never laid another finger on her, never said one harsh word. Now, you tell me something, Mister every-body-calls-you-Shadow, if she could do that, why did she let him beat her in the first place? Why would she want to be with someone like that? You tell me.'

'Maybe,' said Shadow, 'maybe she was lonely.'

She wiped the blade of the knife on her jeans.

'Doctor Gaskell kept saying you were a monster,' she said. 'Is it true?'

'I don't think so,' said Shadow.

'Pity,' she said. 'You know where you are with monsters, don't you?'

'You do?'

'Absolutely. At the end of the day, you're going to be dinner. Talking about which, I'll show you something.' She stood up, and led him up the hill. 'See. Over there? On the far side of that hill, where it drops into the glen, you can just see the house you'll be working at this weekend. Do you see it, over there?'

'No.'

'Look. I'll point. Follow the line of my finger.' She stood close to him, held out her hand and pointed to the side of a distant ridge. He could see the overhead sun glinting off something he supposed was a lake – or a loch, he corrected himself, he was in Scotland after all – and above that a grey outcropping on the side of a hill. He had taken it for rocks, but it was too regular to be anything but a building.

'That's the castle?'

'I'd not call it that. Just a big house in the glen.'

'Have you been to one of the parties there?'

'They don't invite locals,' she said. 'And they wouldn't ask me. You shouldn't do it, anyway. You should say no.'

'They're paying good money,' he told her.

She touched him then, for the first time, placed her pale fingers on the back of his dark hand. 'And what good is money to a monster?' she asked, and smiled, and Shadow was damned if he didn't think that maybe she *was* beautiful, at that.

And then she put down her hand and backed away. 'Well?' she said. 'Shouldn't you be off on your walk? You've not got much longer before you'll have to start heading back again. The light goes fast when it goes, this time of year.'

And she stood and watched him as he hefted his rucksack, and began to walk down the hill. He turned around when he reached the bottom of the hill, and looked up. She was still looking at him. He waved, and she waved back.

The next time he looked back she was gone.

He took the little ferry across the kyle to the cape, and walked up the lighthouse. There was a minibus from the lighthouse back to the ferry, and he took it.

He got back to the hotel at eight that night, exhausted but feeling satisfied. It had rained once, in the late afternoon, but he had taken shelter in a tumbledown bothy, and read a five-year-old newspaper while the rain drummed against the roof. It had ended after half an hour, but Shadow had been glad that he had good boots, for the earth had turned to mud.

He was starving. He went into the hotel restaurant. It was empty. Shadow said 'Hello?'

An elderly woman came to the door between the restaurant and the kitchen and said, 'Aye?'

'Are you still serving dinner?'

'Aye.' She looked at him disapprovingly, from his muddy boots to his tousled hair. 'Are you a guest?'

'Yes. I'm in room eleven.'

'Well . . . you'll probably want to change before dinner,' she said. 'It's kinder to the other diners.'

'So you *are* serving.'

'Aye.'

He went up to his room, dropped his rucksack on the bed, and took off his boots. He put on his sneakers, ran a comb through his hair, and went back downstairs.

The dining room was no longer empty. Two people were sitting at a table in the corner, two people who seemed different in every way that people could be different: a small woman who looked to be in her late fifties, hunched and birdlike at the table, and a young man, big and awkward and perfectly bald. Shadow decided that they were mother and son.

He sat down at a table in the centre of the room.

The elderly waitress came in with a tray. She gave both of the other diners a bowl of soup. The man began to blow on his soup, to cool it; his mother tapped him, hard, on the back of his hand, with her spoon. 'Stop that,' she said. She began to spoon the soup into her mouth, slurping it noisily.

The bald man looked around the room, sadly. He caught Shadow's eye, and Shadow nodded at him. The man sighed, and returned to his steaming soup.

Shadow looked at the menu without enthusiasm. He was ready to order, but the waitress had vanished again.

A flash of grey; Dr Gaskell looked in at the door of the restaurant. He walked into the room, came over to Shadow's table.

'Do you mind if I join you?'

'Not at all. Please. Sit down.'

He sat down, opposite Shadow. 'Have a good day?'

'Very good. I walked.'

'Best way to work up an appetite. So. First thing tomorrow they're sending a car out here to pick you up. Bring your things. They'll take you out to the house. Show you the ropes.'

'And the money?' asked Shadow.

'They'll sort that out. Half at the beginning, half at the end. Anything else you want to know?'

The waitress stood at the edge of the room, watching them, making no move to approach. 'Yeah. What do I have to do to get some food around here?'

'What do you want? I recommend the lamb chops. The lamb's local.'

'Sounds good.'

Gaskell said loudly, 'Excuse me, Maura. Sorry to trouble you, but could we both have the lamb chops?'

She pursed her lips, and went back to the kitchen.

'Thanks,' said Shadow.

'Don't mention it. Anything else I can help you with?'

'Yeah. These folk coming in for the party. Why don't they hire their own security? Why hire me?'

'They'll be doing that too, I have no doubt,' said Gaskell. 'Bringing in their own people. But it's good to have local talent.'

'Even if the local talent is a foreign tourist?'

'Just so.'

Maura brought two bowls of soup, put them down in front of Shadow and the Doctor. 'They come with the meal,' she said. The soup was too hot, and it tasted faintly of reconstituted tomatoes and vinegar. Shadow was hungry enough that he'd finished most of the bowl off before he realized that he did not like it.

'You said I was a monster,' said Shadow to the steel-grey man.

'I did?'

'You did.'

'Well, there's a lot of monsters in this part of the world.' He tipped his head towards the couple in the corner. The little woman had picked up her napkin, dipped it into her water-glass, and was dabbing vigorously at the spots of crimson soup on her son's mouth and chin with it. He looked embarrassed. 'It's remote. We don't get into the news unless a hiker or a climber gets lost, or starves to death. Most people forget we're here.'

The lamb chops arrived, on a plate with overboiled potatoes, underboiled carrots, and something brown and wet that Shadow thought might have started life as spinach. Shadow started to cut at the chops with his knife. The Doctor picked his up in his fingers, and began to chew.

'You've been inside,' said the Doctor.

'Inside?'

'Prison. You've been in prison.' It wasn't a question.

'Yes.'

'So you know how to fight. You could hurt someone, if you had to.'

Shadow said, 'If you need someone to hurt people, I'm probably not the guy you're looking for.'

The little man grinned, with greasy grey lips. 'I'm sure you are. I was just asking. You can't give a man a hard time for asking. Anyway. *He's* a monster,' he said, gesturing across the room with a mostly chewed lamb chop. The bald man was eating some kind of white pudding with a spoon. 'So's his mother.'

'They don't look like monsters to me,' said Shadow.

'I'm teasing you, I'm afraid. Local sense of humour. They should warn you about mine when you enter the village. Warning, loony old doctor at work. Talking about monsters. Forgive an old man. You mustn't listen to a word I say.' A flash of tobacco-stained teeth. He wiped his hands and mouth on his napkin. 'Maura, we'll be needing the bill over here. The young man's dinner is on me.'

'Yes, Doctor Gaskell.'

'Remember,' said the doctor to Shadow. 'Eight-fifteen tomorrow morning, be in the lobby. No later. They're busy people. If you aren't there, they'll just move on, and you'll have missed out on fifteen hundred pounds, for a weekend's work. A bonus, if they're happy.'

Shadow decided to have his after-dinner coffee in the bar. There was a log fire there, after all. He hoped it would take the chill from his bones.

Gordon from reception was working behind the bar. 'Jennie's night off?' asked Shadow.

'What? No, she was just helping out. She'll do it if we're busy, sometimes.'

'Mind if I put another log on the fire?'

'Help yourself.'

If this is how the Scots treat their summers, thought Shadow, remembering something Oscar Wilde had once said, *they don't deserve to have any.*

The bald young man came in. He nodded a nervous greeting to Shadow. Shadow nodded back. The man had no hair that Shadow could see: no eyebrows, no eyelashes. It made him look babyish, and unformed. Shadow wondered if it was a disease, or if it were perhaps a side-effect of chemotherapy. He smelled of damp.

'I heard what he said,' stammered the bald man. 'He said I was a monster. He said my ma was a monster too. I've got good ears on me. I don't miss much.'

He did have good ears on him. They were a translucent pink, and they stuck out from the side of his head like the fins of some huge fish.

'You've got great ears,' said Shadow.

'You taking the mickey?' The bald man's tone was aggrieved. He looked like he was ready to fight. He was only a little shorter than Shadow, and Shadow was a big man.

'If that means what I think it does, not at all.'

The bald man nodded. 'That's good,' he said. He swallowed, and hesitated. Shadow wondered if he should say something conciliatory, but the bald man continued, 'It's not my fault. Making all that noise.

I mean, people come up here to get away from the noise. And the people. Too many damned people up here anyway. Why don't you just go back to where you came from and stop making all that bluidy noise?'

The man's mother appeared in the doorway. She smiled nervously at Shadow, then walked hurriedly over to her son. She pulled at his sleeve. 'Now then,' she said. 'Don't you get yourself all worked up over nothing. Everything's all right.' She looked up at Shadow, birdlike, placatory. 'I'm, sorry. I'm sure he didn't mean it.' She had a length of toilet paper sticking to the bottom of her shoe, and she hadn't noticed yet.'

Everything's all right,' said Shadow. 'It's good to meet people.'

She nodded. 'That's all right then,' she said. Her son looked relieved. *He's scared of her,* thought Shadow.

'Come on pet,' said the woman to her son. She pulled at his sleeve, and he followed her to the door.

Then he stopped, obstinately, and turned. 'You tell them,' said the bald young man, 'not to make so much noise.'

'I'll tell them,' said Shadow.

'It's just that I can hear everything.'

'Don't worry about it,' said Shadow.

'He really is a good boy,' said the bald young man's mother, and she led her son by the sleeve, into the corridor and away, trailing a tag of toilet paper.

Shadow walked out into the hall. 'Excuse me,' he said.

They turned, the man and his mother.

'You've got something on your shoe,' said Shadow.

She looked down. Then she stepped on the strip of paper with her other shoe, and lifted her foot, freeing it. She nodded at Shadow, approvingly, and walked away.

Shadow went to the reception desk. 'Gordon, have you got a good local map?'

'Like an Ordnance Survey? Absolutely. I'll bring it into the lounge for you.'

Shadow went back into the bar and finished his coffee. Gordon brought in a map. Shadow was impressed by the detail: it seemed to show every goat-track. He inspected it closely, tracing his walk. He found the hill where he had stopped and eaten his lunch. He ran his finger south west.

'There aren't any castles around here are there?'

'I'm afraid not. There are some to the east. I've got a guide to the castles of Scotland I could let you look at – '

'No, no. That's fine. Are there any big houses in this area? The kind people would call castles? Or big estates?'

'Well, there's the Cape Wrath Hotel, just over here,' and he pointed to it on the map. 'But it's a fairly empty area. Technically, for human occupation, what do they call it, for population density, it's a desert up here. Not even any interesting ruins, I'm afraid. Not that you could walk to.'

Shadow thanked him, then asked him for an early-morning alarm call. He wished he had been able to find the house he had seen from the hill on the map, but perhaps he had been looking in the wrong place. It wouldn't be the first time.

The couple in the room next door were fighting, or making love. Shadow could not tell, but each time he began to drift off to sleep raised voices or cries would jerk him awake.

Later, he was never certain if it had really happened, if she had really come to him, or if it had been the first of that night's dreams: but in truth or in dreams, shortly before midnight by the bedside clock-radio, there was a knock on his bedroom door. He got up. Called, 'Who is it?'

'Jennie.'

He opened the door, winced at the light in the hall.

She was wrapped in her brown coat, and she looked up at him nervously.

'Yes?' said Shadow.

'You'll be going to the house tomorrow,' she said.

'Yes.'

'I thought I should say goodbye,' she said. 'In case I don't get a chance to see you again. And if you don't come back to the hotel. And you just go on somewhere. And I never see you.'

'Well, goodbye then,' said Shadow.

She looked him up and down, examining the tee shirt and the boxers he slept in, at his bare feet, then up at his face. She looked worried.

'You know where I live,' she said, at last. 'Call me if you need me.'

She reached her index finger out and touched it gently to his lips. Her finger was very cold. Then she took a step back into the corridor and just stood there, facing him, making no move to go.

Shadow closed the hotel room door, and he heard her footsteps walking away down the corridor. He climbed back into bed.

He was sure that the next dream was a dream, though. It was his life, jumbled and twisted: one moment he was in prison, teaching himself coin tricks and telling himself that his love for his wife would get him through this. Then Laura was dead, and he was out of prison; he was working as a bodyguard to an old grifter who had told Shadow to call him Wednesday. And then his dream was filled with gods: old, forgotten gods, unloved and abandoned, and new gods, transient scared things, duped and confused. It was a tangle of improbabilities, a cat's cradle which became a web which became a net which became a skein as big as a world . . .

In his dream he died on the tree.

In his dream he came back from the dead.

And after that there was darkness.

IV

The telephone beside the bed shrilled at seven. He showered, shaved, dressed, packed his world into his backpack. Then he went down to the restaurant for breakfast: salty porridge, limp bacon and oily fried eggs. The coffee, though, was surprisingly good.

At ten past eight he was in the lobby, waiting.

At fourteen minutes past eight, a man came in, wearing a sheep-skin coat. He was sucking on a hand-rolled cigarette. The man stuck out his hand, cheerfully. 'You'll be Mister Moon,' he said. 'My name's Smith. I'm your lift out to the big house.' The man's grip was firm. 'You *are* a big feller, aren't you?'

Unspoken was, 'But I could take you,' although Shadow knew that it was there.

Shadow said, 'So they tell me. You aren't Scottish.'

'Not me, matey. Just up for the week to make sure that everything runs like it's s'posed to. I'm a London boy.' A flash of teeth in a hatchet-blade face. Shadow guessed that the man was in his mid-forties. 'Come on out to the car. I can bring you up to speed on the way. Is that your bag?'

Shadow carried his bag out to the car, a muddy Land-Rover, its engine still running. Shadow dropped his backpack in the back, climbed into the passenger seat. Smith pulled one final drag on his cigarette, now little more than a rolled stub of white paper, and threw it out of the open driver's side window, into the road.

They drove out of the village.

'So how do I pronounce your name?' asked Smith. 'Bal-der or Borl-der, or something else? Like Cholmondeley is actually pronounced Chumley.'

'Shadow,' said Shadow. 'People call me Shadow.'

'Right.'

Silence.

'So,' said Smith. 'Shadow. I don't know how much old Gaskell told you about the party this weekend.'

'A little.'

'Right, well, the most important thing to know is this. Anything that happens, you keep *shtum* about. Right? Whatever you see, people having a little bit of fun, you don't say nothing to anybody, even if you recognize them, if you take my meaning.'

'I don't recognize people,' said Shadow.

'That's the spirit. We're just here to make sure that everyone has a good time without being disturbed. They've come a long way for a nice weekend.'

'Got it,' said Shadow.

They reached the ferry to the cape. Smith parked the Land-Rover beside the road, took their bags, and locked the car.

On the other side of the ferry crossing, an identical Land-Rover waited. Smith unlocked it, threw their bags in the back, and started the car along the dirt track.

They turned off before they reached the lighthouse, drove for a while in silence down a dirt road that rapidly turned into a sheep-track. Several times Shadow had to get out and open gates; he waited while the Land-Rover drove through, closed the gates behind them.

There were ravens in the fields and on the low stone walls, huge black birds that stared at Shadow with implacable eyes.

'So you were in the nick?' said Smith, suddenly.

'Sorry?'

'Prison. Pokey. Porridge. Other words beginning with a P, indicating poor food, no nightlife, inadequate toilet facilities, and limited opportunities for travel.'

'Yeah.'

'You're not very chatty, are you?'

'I thought that was a virtue.'

'Point taken. Just conversation. The silence was getting on my nerves. You like it up here?'

'I guess. I've only been here for a few days.'

'Gives me the fucking willies. Too remote. I've been to parts of Siberia that felt more welcoming. You been to London yet? No? When you come down south I'll show you around. Great pubs. Real food. And there's all that tourist stuff you Americans like. Traffic's hell, though. At least up here, we can drive. No bloody traffic lights. There's this traffic light at the bottom of Regent Street, I swear, you sit there for five minutes on a red light, then you get about ten seconds on a green light. Two cars max. Sodding ridiculous. They say it's the price we pay for progress. Right?'

'Yeah,' said Shadow. 'I guess.'

They were well off-road now, thumping and bumping along a scrubby valley, between two high hills. 'Your party guests,' said Shadow. 'Are they coming in by Land-Rover?'

'Nah. We've got helicopters. They'll be in in time for dinner tonight. Choppers in, then choppers out on Monday morning.'

'Like living on an island.'

'I wish we were living on an island. Wouldn't get loony locals causing problems, would we? Nobody complains about the noise coming from the island next door.'

'You make a lot of noise at your party?'

'It's not my party, chum. I'm just a facilitator. Making sure that everything runs smoothly. But yes. I understand that they can make a lot of noise when they put their mind to it.'

The grassy valley became a sheep-path, the sheep-path became a driveway running almost straight up a hill. A bend in the road, a sudden turn, and they were driving towards a house that Shadow recognized. Jennie had pointed to it, yesterday, at lunch.

The house was old. He could see that at a glance. Parts of it seemed older than others: there was a wall on one wing of the building built out of grey rocks and stones, heavy and hard. That wall jutted into another, built of brown bricks. The roof, which covered the whole building, both wings, was a dark grey slate. The house looked out on to a gravel drive, and then down the hill on to a small loch. Shadow climbed out of the Land-Rover. He looked at the house and felt small. He felt as though he were coming home, and it was not a good feeling.

There were several other four-wheel-drive vehicles parked on the gravel. 'The keys to the cars are hanging in the pantry, in case you need to take one out. I'll show you as we go past.'

Through a large wooden door, and now they were in a central court-yard, partly paved. There was a small fountain in the middle of the courtyard, and a lot of grass, a ragged green, viperous swath bounded by grey flagstones.

'This is where the Saturday-night action will be,' said Smith. 'I'll show you where you'll be staying.'

Into the smaller wing through an unimposing door, past a room hung with keys on hooks, each key marked with a paper tag, and another room filled with empty shelves. Down a dingy hall, and up some stairs. There was no carpeting on the stairs, nothing but white-wash on the walls. ('Well, this is the servants' quarters, innit? They never spent any money on it.') It was cold, in a way that Shadow was starting to become familiar with: colder inside the building than out. He wondered how they did that, if it was a British building secret.

Smith led Shadow to the top of the house, and showed him into a dark room containing an antique wardrobe, an iron-framed single bed that Shadow could see at a glance would be smaller than he was, an ancient washstand, and a small window which looked out on to the inner courtyard.

'There's a loo at the end of the hall,' said Smith. 'The servant's bath-room's on the next floor down. Two baths, one for men, one for women, no showers. The supplies of hot water on this wing of the house are distinctly limited, I'm afraid. Your monkey-suit's hanging in the wardrobe. Try it on now, see if it all fits, then leave it off until this evening, when the guests come in. Limited dry-cleaning facilities. We might as well be on Mars. I'll be down in the kitchen if you need me. It's not as cold down there, if the Aga's working. Bottom of the stairs and left, then right, then yell if you're lost. Don't go into the other wing unless you're told to.'

He left Shadow alone.

Shadow tried on the black tuxedo jacket, the white dress shirt, the black tie. There were highly polished black shoes, as well. It all fitted, as well as if it had been tailored for him. He hung everything back in the wardrobe.

He walked down the stairs, found Smith on the landing, stabbing angrily at a small silver mobile phone. 'No bloody reception. The thing rang, now I'm trying to call back it won't give me a signal. It's the bloody stone age up here. How was your suit? All right?'

'Perfect.'

'That's my boy. Never use five words if you can get away with one, eh? I've known dead men talk more than you do.'

'Really?'

'Nah. Figure of speech. Come on. Fancy some lunch?'

'Sure. Thank you.'

'Right. Follow me. It's a bit of a warren, but you'll get the hang of it soon enough.'

They ate in the huge, empty kitchen: Shadow and Smith piled

enamelled tin plates with slices of translucent orange smoked salmon on crusty white bread, and slices of sharp cheese, accompanied by mugs of strong, sweet tea. The Aga was, Shadow discovered, a big metal box, part oven, part water heater. Smith opened one of the many doors on its side and shovelled in several large scoops of coal.

'So where's the rest of the food? And the waiters, and the cooks?' asked Shadow. 'It can't just be us.'

'Well spotted. Everything's coming up from Edinburgh. It'll run like clockwork. Food and party workers will be here at three, and unpack. Guests get brought in at six. Buffet dinner is served at eight. Talk a lot, eat, have a bit of a laugh, nothing too strenuous. Tomorrow, there's breakfast from seven to midday. Guests get to go for walks, scenic views, all that, in the afternoon. Bonfires are built in the courtyard. Then in the evening the bonfires are lit, everybody has a wild Saturday night in the north, hopefully without being bothered by our neighbours. Sunday morning we tiptoe around, out of respect for everybody's hangover, Sunday afternoon the choppers land and we wave everybody on their way. You collect your pay packet, and I'll drive you back to the hotel, or you can ride south with me, if you fancy a change. Sounds good?'

'Sounds just dandy,' said Shadow. 'And the folks who may show up on the Saturday night?'

'Just killjoys. Locals out to ruin everybody's good time.'

'What locals?' asked Shadow. 'There's nothing but sheep for miles.'

'Locals. They're all over the place,' said Smith. 'You just don't see them. Tuck themselves away like Sawney Beane and his family.'

Shadow said, 'I think I've heard of him. The name rings a bell . . .'

'He's *historical*,' said Smith. He slurped his tea, and leaned back in his chair. 'This was, what, six hundred years back – after the Vikings had buggered off back to Scandinavia, or intermarried and converted until they were just another bunch of Scots, but before Queen Elizabeth died and James came down from Scotland to rule both countries. Somewhere in there.' He took a swig of his tea. 'So. Travellers in Scotland kept vanishing. It wasn't that unusual. I mean, if you set out on a long journey back then, you didn't always get home. Sometimes it would be months before anyone knew you weren't coming home again, and they'd blame the wolves or the weather, and resolve to travel in groups, and only in the summer.

'One traveller, though, he was riding with a bunch of companions through a glen, and there came over the hill, dropped from the trees, up from the ground, a swarm, a flock, a pack of children, armed with daggers and knives and bone clubs and stout sticks, and they pulled the travellers off their horses, and fell on them, and finished them off. All but this one geezer, and he was riding a little behind the others, and he got away. He was the only one, but it only takes one, doesn't it? He made it to the nearest town, and raised the hue and cry, and they raise a troop of townsfolk and soldiers and they go back there, with dogs.

'It takes them days to find the hideout, they're ready to give up, when, at the mouth of a cave by the seashore, the dogs start to howl. And they go down.

'Turns out there's caves, under the ground, and in the biggest and deepest of the caves is old Sawney Beane and his brood, and carcasses, hanging from hooks, smoked and slow-roast. Legs, arms, thighs, hands and feet of men, women and children are hung up in rows, like dried pork. There are limbs pickled in brine, like salt beef. There's money in heaps, gold and silver, with watches, rings, swords, pistols and clothes, riches beyond imagining, as they never spent a single penny of it. Just stayed in their caves, and ate, and bred, and hated.

'He'd been living there for years. King of his own little kingdom, was old Sawney, him and his wife, and their children and grandchildren, and some of those grandchildren were also their children. An incestuous little bunch.'

'Did this really happen?'

'So I'm told. There are court records. They took the family to Leith, to be tried. The court decision was interesting – they decided that Sawney Beane, by virtue of his acts, had removed himself from the human race. So they sentenced him as an animal. They didn't hang him or behead him. They just got a big fire going and threw the Beanies on to it, to burn to death.'

'What happened to his family?'

'I don't remember. They may have burned the little kids, or they may not. Probably did. They tend to deal very efficiently with monsters in this part of the world.'

Smith washed both their plates and mugs in the sink, left them in a rack to dry. The two men walked out into the courtyard. Smith rolled himself a cigarette expertly. He licked the paper, smoothed it with his fingers, lit the finished tube with a Zippo. 'Let's see. What d'you need to know for tonight? Well, basics are easy: speak when you're spoken to – not that you're going to find that one a problem, eh?'

Shadow said nothing.

'Right. If one of the guests asks you for something, do your best to provide it, ask me if you're in any doubt, but do what the guests ask as long as it doesn't take you off what you're doing, or violate the prime directive.'

'Which is?'

'Don't. Shag. The posh totty. There's sure to be some young ladies who'll take it into their heads, after half a bottle of wine, that what they really need is a bit of rough. And if that happens, you do a *Sunday People.*'

'I have no idea what you're talking about.'

'*Our reporter made his excuses, and left.* Yes? You can look, but you can't touch. Got it?'

'Got it.'

'Smart boy.'

Shadow found himself starting to like Smith. He told himself that liking this man was not a sensible thing to do. He had met people like Smith before, people without consciences, without scruples, without hearts, and they were uniformly as dangerous as they were likeable.

In the early afternoon the servants arrived, brought in by a helicopter that looked like a troop carrier: they unpacked boxes of wine and crates of food, hampers and containers with astonishing efficiency. There were boxes filled with napkins and with tablecloths. There were cooks and waiters, waitresses and chambermaids.

But, first off the helicopter, there were the security guards: big, solid men with earpieces and what Shadow had no doubt were gun-bulges beneath their jackets. They reported, one by one to Smith, who set them to inspecting the house and the grounds.

Shadow was helping out, carrying boxes filled with vegetables from the chopper to the kitchen. He could carry twice as much as anyone else. The next time he passed Smith he stopped and said, 'So, if you've got all these security guys, what am I here for?'

Smith smiled affably. 'Look, son. There's people coming to this do who're worth more than you or I will ever see in a lifetime. They need to be sure they'll be looked after. Kidnappings happen. People have enemies. Lots of things happen. Only with those lads around, they won't. But having them deal with grumpy locals, it's like setting a landmine to stop trespassers. Yeah?'

'Right,' said Shadow. He went back to the chopper and picked up another box marked *baby aubergines* and filled with small, black eggplants, and put it on top of a crate of cabbages and carried them both to the kitchen, certain now that he was being lied to. Smith's reply was reasonable. It was even convincing. It simply wasn't true. There was no reason for him to be there, or if there was it wasn't the reason he'd been given.

He chewed it over, trying to figure out why he was in that house, and hoped that he was showing nothing on the surface. Shadow kept it all on the inside. It was safer there.

V

More helicopters came down in the early evening, as the sky was turning pink, and a score or more smart people clambered out. Several of them were smiling and laughing. Most of them were in their thirties and forties. Shadow recognized none of them.

Smith moved casually but smoothly from person to person, greeting them confidently. 'Right, now you go through there and turn right, and wait in the main hall. Lovely big log fire there. Someone'll come and take you up to your room. Your luggage should be waiting for you there. You call me if it's not, but it will be. 'Ullo your ladyship, you do look a treat – shall I 'ave someone carry your 'andbag? Looking forward to termorrer? Aren't we all.'

Shadow watched, fascinated, as Smith dealt with each of the guests, his manner an expert mixture of familiarity and deference, of amiability and cockney charm: aitches, consonants and vowel sounds came and went and transformed according to who he was talking to.

A woman with short dark hair, very pretty, smiled at Shadow as he carried her bags inside. 'Posh totty,' muttered Smith, as he went past. 'Hands off.'

A portly man who Shadow estimated to be in his early sixties was the last person off the chopper. He walked over to Smith, leaned on a cheap wooden walking stick, said something in a low voice. Smith replied in the same fashion.

He's in charge, thought Shadow. It was there in the body language. Smith was no longer smiling, no longer cajoling. He was reporting, efficiently and quietly, telling the old man everything he should know.

Smith crooked a finger at Shadow, who walked quickly over to them. 'Shadow,' said Smith. 'This is Mister Alice.'

Mr Alice put out his hand, shook Shadow's big, dark hand with his pink, pudgy one. 'Great pleasure to meet you,' he said. 'Heard good things about you.'

'Good to meet you,' said Shadow.

'Well,' said Mr Alice, 'carry on.'

Smith nodded at Shadow, a gesture of dismissal.

'If it's OK by you,' said Shadow to Smith, 'I'd like to take a look around while there's still some light. Get a sense of where the locals could come from.'

'Don't go too far,' said Smith. He picked up Mr Alice's briefcase, and led the older man into the building.

Shadow walked the outside perimeter of the house. He had been set up. He did not know why, but he knew he was right. There was too much that didn't add up. Why hire a drifter to do security, while bringing in real security guards? It made no sense, no more than Smith introducing him to Mr Alice, after two dozen other people had treated Shadow as no more human than a decorative ornament.

There was a low stone wall in front of the house. Behind the house, a hill that was almost a small mountain, in front of it a gentle slope down to the loch. Off to the side was the track, by which he had arrived that morning. He walked to the far side of the house, and found what seemed to be a kitchen garden, with a high stone wall and wilderness beyond. He took a step down into the kitchen garden, and walked over to inspect the wall.

'You doing a recce, then?' said one of the security guards, in his black tuxedo. Shadow had not seen him there, which meant, he supposed, that he was very good at his job. Like most of the servants, his accent was Scottish.

'Just having a look around.'

'Get the lay of the land, very wise. Don't you worry about this side of the house. A hundred yards that way there's a river leads down to the loch, and beyond that just wet rocks for a hundred feet or so, straight down. Absolutely treacherous.'

'Oh. So the locals, the ones who come and complain, where do they come from?'

'I wouldnae have a clue.'

'I should head on over there and take a look at it,' said Shadow. 'See if I can figure out the ways in and out.'

'I wouldnae do that,' said the guard. 'Not if I were you. It's really treacherous. You go poking around over there, one slip, you'll be crashing down the rocks into the loch. They'll never find your body, if you head out that way.'

'I see,' said Shadow, who did.

He kept walking around the house. He spotted five other security guards, now that he was looking for them. He was sure there were others that he had missed.

In the main wing of the house he could see, through the french windows, a huge, wood-panelled dining room, and the guests seated around a table, talking and laughing.

He walked back into the servants' wing. As each course was done with, the serving plates were put out on a sideboard, and the staff helped themselves, piling food high on paper plates. Smith was sitting at the wooden kitchen table, tucking into a plate of salad and rare beef.

'There's caviar over there,' he said to Shadow. 'It's Golden Osetra, top quality, very special. What the party officials used to keep for themselves in the old days. I've never been a fan of the stuff, but help yourself.'

Shadow put a little of the caviar on the side of his plate, to be polite. He took some tiny boiled eggs, some pasta and some chicken. He sat next to Smith, and started to eat.

'I don't see where your locals are going to come from,' he said. 'Your men have the drive sealed off. Anyone who wants to come here would have to come over the loch.'

'You had a good poke around, then?'

'Yes,' said Shadow.

'You met some of my boys?'

'Yes.'

'What did you think?'

'I wouldn't want to mess with them.'

Smith smirked. 'Big fellow like you? You could take care of yourself.'

'They're killers,' said Shadow, simply.

'Only when they need to be,' said Smith. He was no longer smiling. 'Why don't you stay up in your room? I'll give you a shout when I need you.'

'Sure,' said Shadow. 'And if you don't need me, this is going to be a very easy weekend.'

Smith stared at him. 'You'll earn your money,' he said.

Shadow went up the back stairs to the long corridor at the top of the house. He went into his room. He could hear party noises, and looked out of the small window. The french windows opposite were wide open, and the partygoers, now wearing coats and gloves, holding their glasses of wine, had spilled out into the inner courtyard. He could hear fragments of conversations that transformed and reshaped themselves; the noises were clear but the words and the sense were lost. An occasional phrase would break free of the susurrus. A man said, 'I told him, judges like you, I don't own, I sell . . .' Shadow heard a woman say, 'It's a monster, darling. An absolute monster. Well, what can you do?' and another woman saying, 'Well, if only I could say the same about my boyfriend's!' and a bray of laughter.

He had two alternatives. He could stay, or he could try to go.

'I'll stay,' he said, aloud.

VI

It was a night of dangerous dreams.

In Shadow's first dream he was back in America, standing beneath a streetlight. He walked up some steps, pushed through a glass door, and stepped into a diner, the kind that had once been a dining car on a train. He could hear an old man singing, in a deep gravelly voice, to the tune of 'My Bonnie Lies Over the Ocean',

> 'My grandpa sells condoms to sailors
> He punctures the tips with a pin
> My grandma does back-street abortions
> My God how the money rolls in.'

Shadow walked along the length of the dining car. At a table at the end of the car, a grizzled man was sitting, holding a beer bottle, and singing, 'Rolls in, rolls in, my God how the money rolls in'. When he caught sight of Shadow his face split into a huge monkey grin, and he gestured with the beer bottle. 'Sit down, sit down,' he said.

Shadow sat down opposite the man he had known as Wednesday.

'So what's the trouble?' asked Wednesday, dead for almost two years, or as dead as his kind of creature was going to get. 'I'd offer you a beer, but the service here stinks.'

Shadow said that was OK. He didn't want a beer.

'Well?' asked Wednesday, scratching his beard.

'I'm in a big house in Scotland with a shitload of really rich folks, and they have an agenda. I'm in trouble, and I don't know what kind of trouble I'm in. But I think it's pretty bad trouble.'

Wednesday took a swig of his beer. 'The rich are different, m'boy,' he said, after a while.

'What the hell does *that* mean?'

'Well,' said Wednesday. 'For a start, most of them are probably mortal. Not something *you* have to worry about.'

'Don't give me that shit.'

'But you *aren't* mortal,' said Wednesday. 'You died on the tree, Shadow. You died and you came back.'

'So? I don't even remember how I did that. If they kill me this time, I'll still be dead.'

Wednesday finished his beer. Then he waved his beer bottle around, as if he were conducting an invisible orchestra with it, and sang another verse:

> *'My brother's a missionary worker,*
> *He saves fallen women from sin*
> *For five bucks he'll save you a redhead,*
> *My God how the money rolls in.'*

'You aren't helping,' said Shadow. The diner was a train carriage now, rattling through a snowy night.

Wednesday put down his beer bottle, and he fixed Shadow with his real eye, the one that wasn't glass. 'It's patterns,' he said. 'If they think you're a hero, they're wrong. After you die, you don't get to be Beowulf or Perseus or Rama any more. Whole different set of rules. Chess, not checkers. *Go*, not chess. You understand?'

'Not even a little,' said Shadow, frustrated.

People, in the corridor of the big house, moving loudly and drunkenly, shushing each other as they stumbled and giggled their way down the hall.

Shadow wondered if they were servants, or if they were strays from the other wing, slumming. And the dreams took him once again . . .

Now he was back in the bothy where he had sheltered from the rain, the day before. There was a body on the floor: a boy, no more than five years old. Naked, on his back, limbs spread. There was a flash of intense light, and someone pushed through Shadow as if he was not there and rearranged the position of the boy's arms. Another flash of light.

Shadow knew the man taking the photographs. It was Dr Gaskell, the little steel-haired man from the hotel bar.

Gaskell took a white paper bag from his pocket, and fished about in it for something that he popped into his mouth.

'Dolly mixtures,' he said to the child on the stone floor. 'Yum yum. Your favourites.'

He smiled and crouched down, and took another photograph of the dead boy.

Shadow pushed through the stone wall of the cottage, flowing through the cracks in the stones like the wind. He flowed down to the seashore. The waves crashed on the rocks and Shadow kept moving across the water, through grey seas, up the swells and down again, towards the ship made of dead men's nails.

The ship was far away, out at sea, and Shadow passed across the surface of the water like the shadow of a cloud.

The ship was huge. He had not understood before how huge it was. A hand reached down and grasped his hand, pulled him up from the sea on to the deck.

'Bring us back,' said a voice as loud as the crashing of the sea, urgent and fierce. 'Bring us back, or let us go.' Only one eye burned in that bearded face.

'I'm not keeping you here.'

They were giants, on that ship, huge men made of shadows and frozen sea-spray, creatures of dream and foam.

One of them, huger than all the rest, red-bearded, stepped forward. 'We cannot land,' he boomed. 'We cannot leave.'

'Go home,' said Shadow.

'We came with our people to this southern country,' said the one-eyed man. 'But they left us. They sought other, tamer gods, and they renounced us in their hearts, and gave us over.'

'Go home,' repeated Shadow.

'Too much time has passed,' said the red-bearded man. By the hammer at his side, Shadow knew him. 'Too much blood has been spilled. You are of our blood, Baldur. Set us free.'

And Shadow wanted to say that he was not theirs, was not anybody's, but the thin blanket had slipped from the bed, and his feet stuck out at the bottom, and thin moonlight filled the attic room.

There was silence, now, in that huge house. Something howled in the hills, and Shadow shivered.

He lay in a bed that was too small for him, and imagined time as something that pooled and puddled, wondered if there were places where time hung heavy, places where it was heaped and held – cities, he thought, must be filled with time: all the places where people congregated, where they came and brought time with them.

And if that were true, Shadow mused, then there could be other places, where the people were thin on the ground, and the land waited, bitter and granite, and a thousand years was an eyeblink to the hills – a scudding of clouds, a wavering of rushes and nothing more, in the places where time was as thin on the ground as the people . . .

'They are going to kill you,' whispered Jennie, the barmaid.

Shadow sat beside her now, on the hill, in the moonlight. 'Why would they want to do that?' he asked. 'I don't matter.'

'It's what they do to monsters,' she said. 'It's what they have to do. It's what they've always done.'

He reached out to touch her, but she turned away from him. From behind, she was empty and hollow. She turned again, so she was facing him. 'Come away,' she whispered.

'You can come to me,' he said.

'I can't,' she said. 'There are things in the way. The way there is hard, and it is guarded. But you can call. If you call me, I'll come.'

Then dawn came, and with it a cloud of midges from the boggy land at the foot of the hill. Jennie flicked at them with her tail, but it was no use; they descended on Shadow like a cloud, until he was breathing midges, his nose and mouth filling with the tiny, crawling stinging things, and he was choking on the darkness . . .

He wrenched himself back into his bed and his body and his life, into wakefulness, his heart pounding in his chest, gulping for breath.

VII

Breakfast was kippers, grilled tomatoes, scrambled eggs, toast, two stubby, thumb-like sausages and slices of something dark and round and flat that Shadow didn't recognize.

'What's this?' asked Shadow.

'Black pudden,' said the man sitting next to him. He was one of the security guards, and was reading a copy of yesterday's *Sun* as he ate. 'Blood and herbs. They cook the blood until it congeals into a sort of a dark, herby scab.' He forked some eggs on to his toast, ate it with his fingers. 'I don't know. What is it they say, you should never see anyone making sausages or the law? Something like that.'

Shadow ate the rest of the breakfast, but he left the black pudding alone.

There was a pot of real coffee, now, and he drank a mug of coffee, hot and black, to wake him up and to clear his head.

Smith walked in. 'Shadow-man. Can I borrow you for five minutes?'

'You're paying,' said Shadow. They walked out into the corridor.

'It's Mr Alice,' said Smith. 'He wants a quick word.' They crossed from the dismal whitewashed servants' wing into the wood-panelled vastness of the old house. They walked up the huge wooden staircase, and into a vast library. No one was there.

'He'll just be a minute,' said Smith. 'I'll make sure he knows you're waiting.'

The books in the library were protected from mice and dust and people by locked doors of glass and wire mesh. There was a painting of a stag on the wall, and Shadow walked over to look at it. The stag looked haughty, and superior: behind it a valley filled with mist.

'The Monarch of the Glen,' said Mr Alice, walking in slowly, leaning on his stick. 'The most reproduced picture of Victorian times. That's not the original, but it was done by Landseer in the late 1850s as a copy of his own painting. I love it, although I'm sure I shouldn't. He did the lions in Trafalgar Square, Landseer. Same bloke.'

He walked over to the bay window, and Shadow walked with him. Below them, in the courtyard, servants were putting out chairs and tables. By the pond in the centre of the courtyard other people, party guests Shadow could see, were building bonfires out of logs and wood.

'Why don't they have the servants build the fires?' asked Shadow.

'Why should *they* have the fun?' said Mr Alice. 'It'd be like sending your man out into the rough some afternoon to shoot pheasants for you. There's something about building a bonfire, when you've hauled over the wood, and put it down in the perfect place, that's special. Or so they tell me. I've not done it myself.' He turned away from the window. 'Take a seat,' he said. 'I'll get a crick in my neck looking up at you.'

Shadow sat down.

'I've heard a lot about you,' said Mr Alice. 'Been wanting to meet you for a while. They said you were a smart young man who was going places. That's what they said.'

'So you didn't just hire a tourist to keep the neighbours away from your party?'

'Well, yes and no. We had a few other candidates, obviously. It's just you were perfect for the job. And when I realized who you were. Well, a gift from the gods really, weren't you?'

'I don't know. Was I?'

'Absolutely. You see, this party goes back a very long way. Almost a thousand years, they've been having it. Never missed a single year. And every year there's a fight, between our man and their man. And our man wins. This year, our man is you.'

'Who . . .' said Shadow. 'Who are *they*? And who are *you*?'

'I am your host,' said Mr Alice. 'I suppose . . .' He stopped, for a moment, tapped his walking stick against the wooden floor. '*They* are the ones who lost, a long time ago. *We* won. We were the knights, and they were the dragons, we were the giant-killers, they were the ogres. We were the men and they were the monsters. And *we won*. They know their place, now. And tonight is all about not letting them forget it. It's humanity you'll be fighting for, tonight. We can't let them get the upper hand. Not even a little. Us versus them.'

'Doctor Gaskell said that I was a monster,' said Shadow.

'Doctor Gaskell?' said Mr Alice. 'Friend of yours?'

'No,' said Shadow. 'He works for you. Or for the people who work for you. I think he kills children, and takes pictures of them.'

Mr Alice dropped his walking stick. He bent down, awkwardly, to pick it up. Then he said, 'Well, I don't think you're a monster, Shadow. I think you're a hero.'

No, thought Shadow. *You think I'm a monster. But you think I'm your monster.*

'Now, you do well tonight,' said Mr Alice, '– and I know you will – and you can name your price. You ever wondered why some people were film stars, or famous, or rich? Bet you think, he's got no talent. What's he got that I haven't got? Well, sometimes the answer is, he's got someone like me on his side.'

'Are you a god?' asked Shadow.

Mr Alice laughed then, a deep, full-throated chuckle. 'Nice one, Mister Moon. Not at all. I'm just a boy from Streatham who's done well for himself.'

'So who do I fight?' asked Shadow.

'You'll meet him tonight,' said Mr Alice. 'Now, there's stuff needs to come down from the attic. Why don't you lend Smithie a hand? Big lad like you, it'll be a doddle.'

The audience was over, and as if on cue, Smith walked in.

'I was just saying,' said Mr Alice, 'that our boy here would help you bring the stuff down from the attic.'

'Triffic,' said Smith. 'Come on, Shadow. Let's wend our way upwards.'

They went up, through the house, up a dark wooden stairway, to a padlocked door, which Smith unlocked, into a dusty wooden attic, piled high with what looked like . . .

'Drums?' said Shadow.

'Drums,' said Smith. They were made of wood and of animal skins. Each drum was a different size. 'Right, let's take them down.'

They carried the drums downstairs. Smith carried one at a time, holding it as if it was precious. Shadow carried two.

'So what really happens tonight?' asked Shadow, on their third trip, or perhaps their fourth.

'Well,' said Smith. 'Most of it, as I understand, you're best off figuring out on your own. As it happens.'

'And you and Mr Alice. What part do you play in this?'

Smith gave him a sharp look. They put the drums down at the foot of the stairs, in the great hall. There were several men there, talking in front of the fire.

When they were back up the stairs again, and out of earshot of the guests, Smith said, 'Mr Alice will be leaving us late this afternoon. I'll stick around.'

'He's leaving? Isn't he part of this?'

Smith looked offended. 'He's the host,' he said. 'But.' He stopped. Shadow understood. Smith didn't talk about his employer. They carried more drums down the stairs.When they had brought down all the drums, they carried down heavy leather bags.

'What's in these?' asked Shadow.

'Drumsticks,' said Smith.

Smith said, 'They're old families. That lot downstairs. Very old money. They know who's boss, but that doesn't make him one of them. See? They're the only ones who'll be at tonight's party. They'd not want Mr Alice. See?'

And Shadow did see. He wished that Smith hadn't spoken to him about Mr Alice. He didn't think Smith would have said anything to anyone he thought would live to talk about it.

But all he said was, 'Heavy drumsticks.'

VIII

A small helicopter took Mr Alice away late that afternoon. Land-Rovers took away the staff. Smith drove the last one. Only Shadow was left behind, and the guests, with their smart clothes, and their smiles.

They stared at Shadow like a captive lion who had been brought for their amusement, but they did not talk to him.

The dark-haired woman, the one who had smiled at Shadow as she had arrived, brought him food to eat: a steak, almost rare. She brought it to him on a plate, without cutlery, as if she expected him to eat it with his fingers and his teeth, and he was hungry, and he did.

'I am not your hero,' he told them, but they would not meet his gaze. Nobody spoke to him, not directly. He felt like an animal.

And then it was dusk. They led Shadow to the inner courtyard, by the dusty fountain, and they stripped Shadow naked, at gunpoint, and the women smeared his body with some kind of thick yellow grease, rubbing it in.

They put a knife on the grass in front of him. A gesture with a gun, and Shadow picked the knife up. The hilt was black metal, rough and easy to hold. The blade looked sharp.

Then they threw open the great door, from the inner courtyard to the world outside, and two of the men lit the two high bonfires: they crackled and blazed.

They opened the leather bags, and each of the guests took out a single carved black stick, like a cudgel, knobbly and heavy. Shadow found himself thinking of Sawney Beane's children, swarming up from the darkness holding clubs made of human thigh-bones . . .

Then the guests arranged themselves around the edge of the court-yard and they began to beat the drums with the sticks.

They started slow, and they started quietly, a deep, throbbing pounding, like a heartbeat. Then they began to crash and slam into strange rhythms, staccato beats that wove and wound, louder and louder, until they filled Shadow's mind and his world. It seemed to him that the firelight flickered to the rhythms of the drums.

And then, from outside the house, the howling began.

There was pain in the howling, and anguish, and it echoed across the hills above the drumbeats, a wail of pain and loss and hate.

The figure that stumbled through the doorway to the courtyard was clutching its head, covering its ears, as if to stop the pounding of the drumbeats.

The firelight caught it.

It was huge, now: bigger than Shadow, and naked. It was perfectly hairless, and dripping wet.

It lowered its hands from its ears, and it stared around, its face twisted into a mad grimace. 'Stop it!' it screamed. 'Stop making all that noise!'

And the people in their pretty clothes beat their drums harder, and faster, and the noise filled Shadow's head and chest.

The monster stepped into the centre of the courtyard. It looked at

Shadow. 'You,' it said. 'I told you. I told you about the noise,' and it howled, a deep throaty howl of hatred and challenge.

The creature edged closer to Shadow. It saw the knife, and stopped. 'Fight me!' it shouted. 'Fight me fair! Not with cold iron! Fight me!'

'I don't want to fight you,' said Shadow. He dropped the knife on the grass, raised his hands to show them empty.

'Too late,' said the bald thing that was not a man. 'Too late for that.'

And it launched itself at Shadow.

Later, when Shadow thought of that fight, he remembered only fragments: he remembered being slammed to the ground, and throwing himself out of the way. He remembered the pounding of the drums, and the expressions on the faces of the drummers as they stared, hungrily, between the bonfires, at the two men in the fire-light.

They fought, wrestling and pounding each other.

Salt tears ran down the monster's face as he wrestled with Shadow. They were equally matched, it seemed to Shadow.

The monster slammed its arm into Shadow's face, and Shadow could taste his own blood. He could feel his own anger beginning to rise, like a red wall of hate.

He swung a leg out, hooking the monster behind the knee, and as it stumbled back Shadow's fist crashed into its gut, making it cry out and roar with anger and pain.

A glance at the guests: Shadow saw the blood-lust on the faces of the drummers.

There was a cold wind, a sea-wind, and it seemed to Shadow that there were huge shadows in the sky, vast figures that he had seen on a boat made of the fingernails of dead men, and that they were staring down at him, that this fight was what was keeping them frozen on their ship, unable to land, unable to leave.

This fight was old, Shadow thought, older than even Mr Alice knew, and he was thinking that even as the creature's talons raked his chest. It was the fight of man against monster, and it was old as time: it was Theseus battling the Minotaur, it was Beowulf and Grendel, it was every hero who had ever stood between the firelight and the darkness and wiped the blood of something inhuman from his sword.

The bonfires burned, and the drums pounded and throbbed and pulsed like the beating of a thousand hearts.

Shadow slipped on the damp grass, as the monster came at him, and he was down. The creature's fingers were around Shadow's neck, and it was squeezing; Shadow could feel everything starting to thin, to become distant.

He closed his hand around a patch of grass, and pulled at it, dug his fingers deep, grabbing a handful of grass and clammy earth, and he smashed the clod of dirt into the monster's face, momentarily blinding it.

He pushed up, and was on top of the creature, now. He rammed his knee hard into its groin, and it doubled into a foetal position, and howled, and sobbed.

Shadow realized that the drumming had stopped, and he looked up.

The guests had put down their drums.

They were all approaching him, in a circle, men and women, still holding their drumsticks, but holding them like cudgels. They were not looking at Shadow, though: they were staring at the monster on the ground, and they raised their black sticks and moved towards it in the light of the twin fires.

Shadow said, 'Stop!'

The first club-blow came down on the creature's head. It wailed and twisted, raising an arm to ward off the next blow.

Shadow threw himself in front of it, shielding it with his body. The dark-haired woman who had smiled at him before now brought down her club on his shoulder, dispassionately, and another club, from a man this time, hit him a numbing blow in the leg, and third struck him on his side.

They'll kill us both, he thought. *Him first, then me. That's what they do. That's what they always do.* And then, *She said she would come. If I called her.*

Shadow whispered, 'Jennie?'

There was no reply. Everything was happening so slowly. Another club was coming down, this one aimed at his hand. Shadow rolled out of the way awkwardly, watched the heavy wood smash into the turf.

'Jennie,' he said, picturing her too-fair hair in his mind, her thin face, her smile. 'I call you. Come now. *Please.*'

A gust of cold wind.

The dark-haired woman had raised her club high, and brought it down now, fast, hard, aiming for Shadow's face.

The blow never landed. A small hand caught the heavy stick as if it were a twig.

Fair hair blew about her head, in the cold wind. He could not have told you what she was wearing.

She looked at him. Shadow thought that she looked disappointed.

One of the men aimed a cudgel-blow at the back of her head. It never connected. She turned . . .

A rending sound, as if something was tearing itself apart . . .

And then the bonfires exploded. That was how it seemed. There was blazing wood all over the courtyard, even in the house. And the people were screaming in the bitter wind.

Shadow staggered to his feet.

The monster lay on the ground, bloodied and twisted. Shadow did not know if it was alive or not. He picked it up, hauled it over his shoulder, and staggered out of the courtyard with it.

He stumbled out on to the gravel forecourt, as the massive wooden doors slammed closed behind them. Nobody else would be coming out. Shadow kept moving down the slope, one step at a time, down towards the loch.

When he reached the water's edge he stopped, and sank to his knees, and let the bald man down on to the grass as gently as he could.

He heard something crash, and looked back up the hill.

The house was burning.

'How is he?' said a woman's voice.

Shadow turned. She was knee deep in the water, the creature's mother, wading towards the shore.

'I don't know,' said Shadow. 'He's hurt.'

'You're both hurt,' she said. 'You're all bluid and bruises.'

'Yes,' said Shadow.

'Still,' she said. 'He's not dead. And that makes a nice change.'

She had reached the shore now. She sat on the bank, with her son's head in her lap. She took a packet of tissues from her handbag, and spat on a tissue, and began fiercely to scrub at her son's face with it, rubbing away the blood.

The house on the hill was roaring now. Shadow had not imagined that a burning house would make so much noise.

The old woman looked up at the sky. She made a noise in the back of her throat, a clucking noise, and then she shook her head. 'You know,' she said, 'you've let them in. They'd been bound for so long, and you've let them in.'

'Is that a good thing?' asked Shadow.

'I don't know, love,' said the little woman, and she shook her head again. She crooned to her son as if he were still her baby, and dabbed at his wounds with her spit.

Shadow was naked, at the edge of the loch, but the heat from the burning building kept him warm. He watched the reflected flames in the glassy water of the loch. A yellow moon was rising.

He was starting to hurt. Tomorrow, he knew, he would hurt much worse.

Footsteps on the grass behind him. He looked up.

'Hello, Smithie,' said Shadow.

Smith looked down at the three of them.

'Shadow,' he said, shaking his head. 'Shadow, Shadow, Shadow, Shadow, Shadow. This was not how things were meant to turn out.'

'Sorry,' said Shadow.

'This will cause real embarrassment to Mr Alice,' said Smith. 'Those people were his guests.'

'They were animals,' said Shadow.

'If they were,' said Smith, 'they were rich and important animals. There'll be widows and orphans and god knows what to take care of. Mr Alice will not be pleased.' He said it like a judge pronouncing a death sentence.

'Are you threatening him?' asked the old lady.

'I don't threaten,' said Smith, flatly.

She smiled. 'Ah,' she said. 'Well, I do. And if you or that fat bastard you work for hurt this young man, it'll be the worse for both of you.' She smiled then, with sharp teeth, and Shadow felt the hairs on the back of his neck prickle. 'There's worse things than dying,' she said. 'And I know most of them. I'm not young, and I'm not one for idle talk. So if I were you,' she said, with a sniff, 'I'd look after this lad.'

She picked up her son with one arm, as if he were a child's doll, and she clutched her handbag close to her with the other.

Then she nodded to Shadow, and walked away, into the glass-dark water, and soon she and her son were gone beneath the surface of the loch.

'Fuck,' muttered Smith.

Shadow didn't say anything.

Smith fumbled in his pocket. He pulled out the pouch of tobacco, and rolled himself a cigarette. Then he lit it. 'Right,' he said.

'Right?' said Shadow.

'We better get you cleaned up, and find you some clothes. You'll catch your death, otherwise. You heard what she said.'

IX

They had the best room waiting for Shadow, that night, back at the hotel. And, less than an hour after Shadow returned, Gordon on the front desk brought up a new backpack for him, a box of new clothes, even new boots. He asked no questions.

There was a large envelope on top of the pile of clothes.

Shadow ripped it open. It contained his passport, slightly scorched, his wallet, and money: several bundles of new fifty-pound notes, wrapped in rubber bands.

My God, how the money rolls in, he thought, without pleasure, and tried, without success, to remember where he had heard that song before.

He took a long bath, to soak away the pain.

And then he slept.

In the morning he dressed, and walked up the lane next to the hotel, that led up the hill and out of the village. There had been a cottage at the top of the hill, he was sure of it, with lavender in the garden, a stripped pine counter-top, and a purple sofa, but no matter where he looked there was no cottage on the hill, nor any evidence that there ever had been anything there but grass and a hawthorn tree.

He called her name, but there was no reply, only the wind coming in off the sea, bringing with it the first promises of winter.

Still, she was waiting for him, when he got back to the hotel room. She was sitting on the bed, wearing her old brown coat, inspecting her fingernails. She did not look up when he unlocked the door and walked in.

'Hello, Jennie,' he said.

'Hello,' she said. Her voice was very quiet.

'Thank you,' he said. 'You saved my life.'

'You called,' she said dully. 'I came.'

He said, 'What's wrong?'

She looked at him, then. 'I could have been yours,' she said, and there were tears in her eyes. 'I thought you would love me. Perhaps. One day.'

'Well,' he said, 'maybe we could find out. We could take a walk tomorrow together, maybe. Not a long one, I'm afraid, I'm a bit of a mess physically.'

She shook her head.

The strangest thing, Shadow thought, was that she did not look human any longer: she now looked like what she was, a wild thing, a forest thing. Her tail twitched on the bed, under her coat. She was very beautiful, and, he realized, he wanted her, very badly.

'The hardest thing about being a *hulder*,' said Jennie, 'Even a *hulder* very far from home, is that, if you don't want to be lonely, you have to love a man.'

'So love me. Stay with me,' said Shadow. 'Please.'

'You,' she said, sadly and finally, 'are not a man.'

She stood up.

'Still,' she said, 'everything's changing. Maybe I can go home again now. After a thousand years I don't even know if I remember any *norsk*.'

She took his hands in her small hands, that could bend iron bars, that could crush rocks to sand, and she squeezed his fingers very gently. And she was gone.

He stayed another day in that hotel, and then he caught the bus to Thurso, and the train from Thurso to Inverness.

He dozed on the train, although he did not dream.

When he woke, there was a man on the seat next to him. A hatchet-faced man, reading a paperback book. He closed the book when he saw that Shadow was awake. Shadow looked down at the cover: Jean Cocteau's *The Difficulty of Being*.

'Good book?' asked Shadow.

'Yeah, all right,' said Smith. 'It's all essays. They're meant to be personal, but you feel that every time he looks up innocently and says "This is me," it's some kind of double-bluff. I liked *La Belle et la Bête*, though. I felt closer to him watching that than through any of these essays.'

'It's all on the cover,' said Shadow.

'How d'you mean?'

'The difficulty of being Jean Cocteau.'

Smith scratched his nose.

'Here,' he said. He passed Shadow a copy of the *Scotsman*. 'Page nine.'

On the bottom of page nine was a small story: retired doctor kills himself. Gaskell's body had been found in his car, parked in a picnic spot on the coast road. He had swallowed quite a cocktail of painkillers, washed down with most of a bottle of Lagavulin.

'Mr Alice hates being lied to,' said Smith. 'Especially by the hired help.'

'Is there anything in there about the fire?' asked Shadow.

'What fire?'

'Oh. Right.'

'It wouldn't surprise me if there wasn't a terrible run of luck for the great and the good over the next couple of months, though. Car crashes. Train crash. Maybe a plane'll go down. Grieving widows and orphans and boyfriends. Very sad.'

Shadow nodded.

'You know,' said Smith, 'Mr Alice is very concerned about your health. He worries. I worry too.'

'Yeah?' said Shadow.

'Absolutely. I mean, if something happens to you while you're in the country. Maybe you look the wrong way crossing the road. Flash a wad of cash in the wrong pub. I dunno. The point is, if you got hurt, then whatsername, Grendel's mum, might take it the wrong way.'

'So?'

'So we think you should leave the UK. Be safer for everyone, wouldn't it?'

Shadow said nothing for a while. The train began to slow.

'OK,' said Shadow.

'This is my stop,' said Smith. 'I'm getting out here. We'll arrange the ticket, first class of course, to anywhere you're heading. One-way ticket. You just have to tell me where you want to go.'

Shadow rubbed the bruise on his cheek. There was something about the pain that was almost comforting.

The train came to a complete stop. It was a small station, seemingly in the middle of nowhere. There was a large black car parked by the station, in the thin sunshine. The windows were tinted, and Shadow could not see in.

Mr Smith pushed down the train window, reached outside to open the carriage door, and he stepped out on to the platform. He looked back in at Shadow through the open window. 'Well?'

'I think,' said Shadow, 'that I'll spend a couple of weeks looking around the UK. And you'll just have to pray that I look the right way when I cross your roads.'

'And then?'

Shadow knew it, then. Perhaps he had known it all along.

'Chicago,' he said to Smith, as the train gave a jerk, and began to move away from the station. He felt older, as he said it. But he could not put it off for ever.

And then he said, so quietly that only he could have heard it, 'I guess I'm going home.'

Soon afterwards it began to rain: huge, pelting drops that rattled against the windows and blurred the world into greys and greens. Deep rumbles of thunder accompanied Shadow on his journey south: the storm grumbled, the wind howled and the lightning made huge shadows across the sky, and in their company Shadow slowly began to feel less alone.

SHANNARA

TERRY BROOKS

SHANNARA
TERRY BROOKS

The Sword of Shannara (1977)
The Elfstones of Shannara (1982)
The Wishsong of Shannara (1985)

THE HERITAGE OF SHANNARA:
The Scions of Shannara (1990)
The Druid of Shannara (1991)
The Elf Queen of Shannara (1992)
The Talismans of Shannara (1993)

First King of Shannara (1996)

THE VOYAGE OF THE JERLE SHANNARA:
Ilse Witch (2000)
Antrax (2001)
Morgawr (2002)

HIGH DRUID OF SHANNARA:
Jarka Ruus (2003)
Tanequil (forthcoming)

The time of the Shannara follows in the wake of an apocalypse that has destroyed the old world and very nearly annihilated its people as well. A thousand years of savagery and barbarism have concluded at the start of the series with the emergence of a new civilization in which magic has replaced science as the dominant source of power. A Druid Council comprised of the most talented of the new races – Men, Dwarves, Trolls, Gnomes and Elves, names taken from the old legends – has begun the arduous task of rebuilding the world and putting an end to the racial warfare that has consumed the survivors of the so-called Great Wars since their conclusion.

But the wars continue, albeit in a different form. Magic, like science, is often mercurial and can be used for good or evil and can have a positive or negative effect on those who come in contact with it. In *The Sword of Shannara*, a Druid subverted by his craving for magic's power manipulated Trolls and Gnomes in his effort to gain mastery over the other races. He failed because of Shea Ohmsford, the last of an Elven family with the Shannara surname. Shea, with the help of his brother and a small band of companions, was able to wield the fabled Sword of Shannara to destroy the Dark Lord.

Subsequently, in *The Elfstones of Shannara*, his grandson Wil was faced with another sort of challenge, one which required the use of a magic contained in a set of Elfstones. But use of the Stones altered Wil's genetic makeup, so that his own children were born with magic in their blood. As a result, in the third book of the series, *The Wishsong of Shannara*, Brin and her brother Jair were recruited by the Druid Allanon to seek out and destroy the Ildatch, the book of dark magic that had subverted the Warlock Lord and was now doing the same with the wraith-like Shadowen.

The story that follows takes place several years after the conclusion of *The Wishsong of Shannara* and again features Jair Ohmsford, who must come to terms with his obsession with the past and his use of magic that his sister has warned him not to trust.

INDOMITABLE

BY TERRY BROOKS

The past is always with us.

Even though he was only just of an age to be considered a man, Jair Ohmsford had understood the meaning of the phrase since he was a boy. It meant that he would be shaped and reshaped by the events of his life, so that everything that happened would be in some way a consequence of what had gone before. It meant that the people he came to know would influence his conduct and his beliefs. It meant that his experiences of the past would impact his decisions of the future.

It meant that life was like a chain and the links that forged it could not be severed.

For Jair, the strongest of those links was to Garet Jax. That link, unlike any other, was a repository for memories he treasured so dearly that he protected them like glass ornaments, to be taken down from the shelf on which they were kept, polished, and then put away again with great care.

In the summer of the second year following his return from Graymark, he was still heavily under the influence of those memories. He woke often in the middle of the night from dreams of Garet Jax locked in battle with the Jachyra, heard echoes of the other's voice in conversations with his friends and neighbours, and caught sudden glimpses of the Weapons Master in the faces of strangers. He was not distressed by these occurrences; he was thrilled by them. They were an affirmation that he was keeping alive the past he cared so much about.

On the day the girl rode into Shady Vale, he was working at the family inn, helping the manager and his wife as a favour to his parents. He was standing on the porch, surveying the siding he had replaced after a windstorm had blown a branch through the wall. Something about the way she sat on her horse caught his attention, drawing it away from his handiwork. He shaded his eyes against the glare of the sun as it reflected off a metal roof when she turned out of the trees. She sat ramrod straight astride a huge black stallion with a white blaze on its forehead, her dark hair falling in a cascade of curls to her waist, thick and shining. She wasn't big, but she gave an immediate impression of possessing confidence that went beyond the need for physical strength.

She caught sight of him at the same time he saw her and turned the big black in his direction. She rode up to him and stopped, a mischievous smile appearing on her round, perky face as she brushed back loose strands of hair. 'Cat got your tongue, Jair Ohmsford?'

'Kimber Boh,' he said, not quite sure that it really was. 'I don't believe it.'

She swung down, dropped the reins in a manner that suggested this was all the black required, and walked over to give him a long, sustained hug. 'You look all grown up,' she said, and ruffled his curly blond hair to show she wasn't impressed.

He might have said the same about her. The feel of her body against his as she hugged him was a clear indication that she was beyond childhood. But it was difficult to accept. He still remembered the slender, tiny girl she had been two years ago when he had met her for the first time in the ruins of the Croagh in the aftermath of his battle to save Brin.

He shook his head. 'I almost didn't recognize you.'

She stepped back. 'I knew you right away.' She looked around. 'I always wanted to see where you lived. Is Brin here?'

She wasn't. Brin was living in the Highlands with Rone Leah, whom she had married in the spring. They were already expecting their first child; if it were a boy, they would name it Jair.

He shook his head. 'No. She lives in Leah now. Why didn't you send word you were coming?'

'I didn't know myself until a little over a week ago.' She glanced at the inn. 'The ride has made me tired and thirsty. Why don't we go inside while we talk?'

They retreated to the cool interior of the inn and took a table at a window where the slant of the roof kept the sun off. The innkeeper brought over a pitcher of ale and two mugs, giving Jair a sly wink as he walked away.

'Does he give you a wink for every pretty girl you bring into his establishment?' Kimber asked when the innkeeper was out of earshot. 'Are you a regular here?'

He blushed. 'My parents own the inn. Kimber, what are you doing here?'

She considered the question. 'I'm not entirely sure. I came to find you and to persuade you to come with me. But now that I'm here, I don't know that I have the words to do it. In fact, I might just not even try. I might just stay here and visit until you send me away. What would you say to that?'

He leaned back in his chair and smiled. 'I guess I would say you were welcome to stay as long as you like. Is that what you want?'

She sipped at her ale and shook her head. 'What I want doesn't matter. Maybe what you want doesn't matter either.' She looked out of the window into the sunshine. 'Grandfather sent me. He said to tell you that what we thought we had finished two years ago isn't quite finished after all. There appears to be a loose thread that needs snipping off.'

'A loose thread?'

She looked back at him. 'Remember when your sister burned the book of the Ildatch at Graymark?'

He nodded. 'I'm not likely to forget.'

'Grandfather says she missed a page.'

They ate dinner at his home, a dinner that he prepared himself, which included soup made of fresh garden vegetables, breads and a plate of cheeses and dried fruits stored for his use by his parents, who were south on a journey to places where their special healing talents were needed. They sat at the dinner table and watched the darkness descend in a slow curtain of shadows that draped the countryside like black silk. The sky stayed clear and the stars came out, brilliant and glittering against the firmament.

'He wouldn't tell you why he needs me?' Jair asked for what must have been the fifth or sixth time.

She shook her head patiently. 'He just said you were the one to bring, not your sister, not your parents, not Rone Leah. Just you.'

'And he didn't say anything about the Elfstones either? You're sure about that?'

She looked at him, a hint of irritation in her blue eyes. 'Do you know that this is one of the best meals I have ever eaten? It really is. This soup is wonderful, and I want to know how to make it. But for now, I am content just to eat it. Why don't you stop asking questions and enjoy it, too?'

He responded with a rueful grimace and sipped at the soup, staying quiet for a few mouthfuls while he mulled things over. He was having difficulty accepting what she was telling him, let alone agreeing to what she was asking. Two years earlier, the Ohmsford siblings had taken separate paths to reach the hiding place of the Ildatch, the book of dark magic that had spawned first the Warlock Lord and his Skull Bearers in the time of Shea and Flick Ohmsford and then the Shadowen in their own time. The magic contained in the book was so powerful that the book had taken on a life of its own, becoming a spirit able to subvert and ultimately re-form beings of flesh and blood into monstrous undead creatures. It had done so repeatedly and would have kept on doing so had Brin and he not succeeded in destroying it.

Of course, it had almost destroyed Brin first. Possessed of the magic of the wishsong, of the power to create or destroy through use of music and words, Brin was a formidable opponent, but an attractive ally, as well. Perhaps she would have become the latter instead of the former had Jair not reached her in time to prevent it. But it was for that very purpose that the King of the Silver River had sent him to find her after she had left with Allanon, and so he had known in advance what was expected of him. His own magic was of a lesser kind, an ability to appear to change things without actually being able to do so, but in this one instance it had proved sufficient to do what was needed.

Which was why he was somewhat confused by Kimber's grandfather's insistence on summoning him now. Whatever the nature of the danger presented by the threat of an Ildatch reborn, he was the least well-equipped member of the family to deal with it. He was also doubtful of the man making the selection, having seen enough of the wild-eyed and unpredictable Cogline to know that he wasn't always rowing with all his oars in the water. Kimber might have confidence in him, but that didn't mean Jair should.

An even bigger concern was the old man's assertion that somehow the Ildatch hadn't been completely destroyed when Brin had gone to such lengths to make certain that it was. She had used her magic to burn it to ashes, the whole tome, each and every page. So how could it have survived in any form? How could Brin have been mistaken about something so crucial?

He knew that he wasn't going to find out unless he went with Kimber to see the old man and hear him out, but it was a long journey to Hearthstone, which lay deep in the Eastland, a draining commitment of time and energy. Especially if it turned out that the old man was mistaken.

So he asked his questions, hoping to learn something helpful, waiting for a revelation. But soon he had asked the old ones more times than was necessary and had run out of new ones.

'I know you think Grandfather is not altogether coherent about some things,' Kimber said. 'You know as much even from the short amount of time you spent with him two years ago, so I don't have to pretend. I know he can be difficult and unsteady. But I also know that he sees things other men don't, that he has resources denied to them. I can read a trail and track it, but he can read signs on the air itself. He can make things out of compounds and powders that no one else has known how to make since the destruction of the Old World. He's more than he seems.'

'So you believe that I should go, that there's a chance he might be right about the Ildatch?' Jair leaned forward again, his meal forgotten. 'Tell me the truth, Kimber.'

'I think you would be wise to pay attention to what he has to say.' Her face was calm, but her eyes troubled. 'I have my own doubts about Grandfather, but I saw the way he was when he told me to come and find you. It wasn't something done on a whim. It was done after a great deal of thought. He would have come himself, but I wouldn't let him. He is too old and frail. Since I wouldn't let him make the journey, I had to make it myself. I guess that says something about how I view the matter.'

She looked down at her food and pushed it away. 'Let's clean up, and then we can sit outside.'

They carried off the dishes, washed them and put them away, and then went out on to the porch and sat together on a wooden bench that looked off towards the south west. The night was warm and filled with smells of jasmine and evergreen, and somewhere off in the darkness a stream trickled. They sat without speaking for a while, listening to the silvery sound of the water. An owl flew by, its dark shape momentarily silhouetted by moonlight. From down in the village came the faint sound of laughter.

'It seems like a long time since we were at Graymark,' she said quietly. 'A long time since everything that happened two years ago.'

Jair nodded, remembering. 'I've thought often about you and your grandfather. I wondered how you were. I don't know why I worried, though. You were fine before Brin and Rone found you. You've probably been fine since. Do you still have the moor cat?'

'Whisper? Yes. He keeps us both safe from the things we can't keep safe from on our own.' She paused. 'But maybe we aren't as fine as you think, Jair. Things change. Both Grandfather and I are older. He needs me more; I need him less. Whisper goes away more often and comes back less frequently. The country is growing up around us. It isn't as wild as it once was. There is an Elven village not five miles away and Gnome tribes migrate from the Wolfsktaag to the Ravenshorn and back again all the time.' She shrugged. 'It isn't the same.'

'What will you do when your grandfather is gone?'

She laughed softly. 'That might never happen. He might live for ever.' She sighed, gesturing vaguely with one slender hand. 'Sometimes, I think about moving away from Hearthstone, of living somewhere else. I admit I want to see something of the larger world.'

'Would you come down into the Borderlands, maybe?' He looked over at her. 'Would you come and live here? You might like it.'

She nodded. 'I might.'

She didn't say anything else, so he went back to looking into the darkness, thinking it over. He would like having her here. He liked talking to her. He guessed that over time they might turn out to be good friends.

'I need you to come back with me,' she said suddenly, looking at him with unexpected intensity. 'I might as well tell you so. It has more to do with me than with Grandfather. I am worn out by him. I hate admitting it because it makes me sound weak. But he grates on me the older and more difficult he gets. I don't know if this business about the Ildatch is real or not. But I don't think I can get to the truth of it alone. I'm being mostly selfish by coming here and asking you to come to Hearthstone with me. Grandfather is set on this happening. Just having you talk with him might make a difference.'

Jair shook his head doubtfully. 'I barely know him. I don't see what difference having me there would make to anything.'

She hesitated, then exhaled sharply. 'My grandfather was there to help your sister when she needed it, Jair. I am asking you to return the favour. I think he needs you, whether the danger from the Ildatch is real or not. What's bothering him is real enough. I want you to come back with me and help settle things.'

He thought about it a long time, making himself do so even though he already knew what he was going to say. He was thinking of what Garet Jax would do.

'All right, I'll come,' he said finally.

Because he knew that this is what the Weapons Master would have done in his place.

He left a letter with the innkeeper for his parents, explaining where he was going, packed some clothes and closed up the house. He already knew he would be in trouble when he returned, but that wasn't enough to keep him from going. The innkeeper loaned him a horse, a steady, reliable bay that could be depended on not to do anything unexpected or foolish. Jair was not much for horses, but he understood the need for one here, where there was so much distance to cover.

It took them a week to get to Hearthstone, riding north out of Shady Vale and the Duln Forests, around the western end of the Rainbow Lake, then up through Callahorn along the Mermidon River to the Rabb Plains. They crossed the Rabb, following its river into the Upper Anar, then rode down through the gap between the Wolfsktaag Mountains and Darklin Reach, threading the needle of the corridor between, staying safely back from the edges of both. As they rode, Jair found himself pondering how different the circumstances were now from the last time he had come into the Eastland. Then, he had been hunted at every turn, threatened by more dangers than he cared to remember. It had been Garet Jax who had saved his life time and again. Now, he travelled without fear of attack, without having to look over his shoulder, and Garet Jax was only a memory.

'Do you think we might have lived other lives before this one?' Kimber asked him on their last night out before reaching Hearthstone.

They were sitting in front of a fire in a grove of trees flanking the south branch of the Rabb, deep within the forests of Darklin Reach. The horses grazed contentedly a short distance off, and moonlight flooded the grassy flats that stretched away about them. There was a hint of a chill in the air this night, a warning of autumn's approach.

Jair smiled. 'I don't think about it at all. I have enough trouble living the life I have without wondering if there were others.'

'Or if there will be others after this one?' She brushed at her long hair, which she kept tied back as they rode, but let down at night in a tumbled mass. 'Grandfather thinks so. I guess I do, too. I think every-thing is connected. Lives, like moments in time, are all linked together, fish in a stream, swimming and swimming. The past coming forward to become the future.'

He looked off into the dark. 'I think we are connected to the past, but mostly to the events and the people that shaped it. I think we are always reaching back in some way, bringing forward what we remember, sometimes for information, sometimes just for comfort. I don't remember other lives, but I remember the past of this one. I remember the people who were in it.'

She waited a moment, then moved over to sit beside him. 'The way you said that – are you thinking about what happened two years ago at Heaven's Well?'

He shrugged.

'About the one you called the Weapons Master?'

He stared at her. 'How did you know that?'

'It isn't much of a mystery, Jair. You talked about no one else after-wards. Only him, the one who saved you on the Croagh, the one who fought the Jachyra. Don't you remember?'

He nodded. 'I guess.'

'Maybe your connection with him goes farther back in time than just this life.' She lifted an eyebrow at him. 'Have you thought about that? Maybe you were joined in another life as well, and that's why he made such an impression on you.'

Jair laughed. 'I think he made an impression on me because he was the best fighter I have ever seen. He was so . . .' He stopped himself, searching for the right word. 'Indomitable.' His smile faded. 'Nothing could stand against him, not even a Jachyra. Not even something that was too much for Allanon.'

'But I might still be right about past lives,' she persisted. She put her hand on his shoulder and squeezed. 'You can grant me that much, can't you, Valeman?'

He could, that and much more. He wanted to tell her so, but didn't know how without sounding foolish. He was attracted to her, and it surprised him. Having thought of her for so long as a little girl, he was having trouble accepting that she was now full-grown. Such a transition didn't seem possible. It confused his thinking, the past conflicting with the present. How did she feel about him, as changed in his own way as she was in hers? He wondered, but could not make himself ask.

In late afternoon of the following day, they reached Hearthstone. He had never been here before, but he had heard Brin describe the chimney-shaped rock so often that he knew at once what it was. He caught sight of it as they rode through the trees, a dark pinnacle over-looking a shallow, wooded valley. Its distinctive, rugged formation seemed right for this country, a land of dark rumours and strange happenings. Yet that was in the past, as well. Things were different now. They had come in on a road, where two years before there had been no roads. They had passed the newly settled Dwarf village and seen the houses and heard the voices of children. The country was growing up, the wilderness pushed back. Change was the one constant in an ever-evolving world.

They reached the cottage shortly afterwards. It was constructed of wood and timber with porches front and back, its walls grown thick with ivy and the grounds surrounding it planted with gardens and ringed with walkways and bushes. It had a well-cared-for look to it; everything was neatly planted and trimmed, a mix of colours and forms that were pleasing to the eye. It didn't look so much like a wilderness cottage as a village home. Behind the house, a paddock housed a mare and a foal. A milk cow was grazing there as well. Sheds lined the back of the paddock, neatly painted. Shade trees helped conceal the buildings from view; Jair hadn't caught even a glimpse of roofs on the ride in.

He glanced over at her. 'Do you look after all this by yourself?'

'Mostly.' She gave him a wry smile. 'I like looking after a home. I always have, ever since I was old enough to help do so.'

They rode into the yard and dismounted, and instantly Cogline appeared through the doorway. He was ancient and stick-thin beneath his baggy clothing, and his white hair stuck out in all directions, as if he might have just come awake. He pulled at his beard as he came up to them, his fingers raking the wiry hairs. His eyes were sharp and questioning, and he was already scanning Jair as if not quite sure what to make of him.

'So!' He approached with that single word and stood so close that the Valeman was forced to take a step back. He peered intently into Jair's blue eyes, took careful note of his Elven features. 'Is this him?'

'Yes, Grandfather.' Kimber sounded embarrassed.

'You're certain? No mistake?'

'Yes, Grandfather.'

'Because he could be someone else, you know. He could be *anybody* else!' Cogline furrowed his already deeply lined brow. 'Are you young Ohmsford? The boy, Jair?'

Jair nodded. 'I am. Don't you remember me? We met two years ago in the ruins of Graymark.'

The old man stared at him as if he hadn't heard the question. Jair could feel the other's hard gaze probing in a way that was not altogether pleasant. 'Is this necessary?' he asked finally. 'Can't we go inside and sit down?'

'When I say so!' the other replied. 'When I say I am finished! Don't interrupt my study!'

'Grandfather!' Kimber exclaimed.

The old man ignored her. 'Let me see your hands,' he said.

Jair held out his hands, palms up. Cogline studied them carefully for a moment, grunted as if he had found whatever it was he was looking for, and said, 'Come inside, and I'll fix you something to eat.'

They went into the cottage and seated themselves at the rough-hewn wooden dining table, but it was Kimber who ended up preparing a stew for them to eat. While she did so, directing admonitions at her grandfather when she thought them necessary, Cogline rambled on about the past and Jair's part in it, a bewildering hodge-podge of information and observation.

'I remember you,' he said. 'Just a boy, coming out of Graymark's ruins with your sister, the two of you covered in dust and smelling of death! Hah! I know something of that smell, I can tell you! Fought many a monster come out of the netherworld, long before you were born, before any who live now were born and a good deal more who are long dead. Might have left the order, but didn't lose the skills. Not a one. Never listened to me, any of them, but that didn't make me give up. The new mirrors the old. You can't disconnect science and magic. They're all of a piece, and the lessons of one are the lessons of the other. Allanon knew as much. Knew just enough to get himself killed.'

Jair had no idea what he was talking about, but perked up on hearing the Druid's name. 'You knew Allanon?'

'Not when he was alive. Know him now that he's dead, though. Your sister, she was a gift to him. She was the answer to what he needed when he saw the end coming. It's like that for some, the gift. Maybe for you, too, one day.'

'What gift?'

'You know, I was a boy once. I was a Druid once, too.'

Jair stared at him, not quite knowing whether to accept this or not. It was hard to think of him as a boy, but thinking of him as a Druid was harder still. If the old man really was a Druid – not that Jair thought for a moment that he was – what was he doing here, out in the wilderness, living with Kimber? 'I thought Allanon was the last of the Druids,' he said.

The old man snorted. 'You thought a lot of things that weren't so.' He shoved back his plate of stew, having hardly touched it. 'Do you want to know what you're doing here?'

Jair stopped eating in mid-bite. Kimber, sitting across from him, blinked once and said, 'Maybe you should wait until he's finished dinner, Grandfather.'

The old man ignored her. 'Your sister thought the Ildatch destroyed,' he said. 'She was wrong. Wasn't her fault, but she was wrong. She burned it to ash, turned it to a charred ruin and that should have been the end of it, but it wasn't. You want to sit outside while we have this discussion? The open air and the night sky make it easier to think things through sometimes.'

They went outside on to the front porch, where the sky west was turning a brilliant mix of purple and rose above the treetops and the sky east already boasted a partial moon and a scattering of stars. The old man took possession of the only rocker, and Jair and Kimber sat together on a high-backed wooden bench. It occurred to the Valeman that he needed to rub down and feed his horse, a task he would have completed by now if he had been thinking straight.

The old man rocked in silence for a time, then gestured abruptly at Jair. 'Last month, on a night when the moon was full and the sky a sea of stars, beautiful night, I woke and walked down to the little pond which lies just south. I don't know why, I just did. Something made me. I lay in the grass and slept, and while I slept, I had a dream. Only it was more a vision than a dream. I used to have such visions often. I was closer to the shades of the dead then, and they would come to me because I was receptive to their needs. But that was long ago, and I had thought such things at an end.'

He seemed to reflect on the idea for a moment, lost in thought. 'I was a Druid then.'

'Grandfather,' Kimber prodded softly.

The old man looked back at Jair. 'In my dream, Allanon's shade came to me out of the netherworld. It spoke to me. It told me that the Ildatch was not yet destroyed, that a piece of it still survived. One page only, seared at the edges, shaken loose and blown beneath the stones of the keep in the fiery destruction of the rest. Perhaps the book found a way to save that one page in its death throes. I don't know. The shade didn't tell me. Only that it had survived your sister's efforts and been found in the rubble by Mwellrets who sought artefacts that would lend them the power that had belonged to the Shadowen. Those rets knew what they had because the page told them, a whisper that promised great things! It had life, even as a fragment, so powerful was its magic!'

Jair glanced at Kimber, who blinked at him uncertainly. Clearly, this was news to her as well. 'One page,' he said to the old man, 'isn't enough to be dangerous, is it? Unless there is a spell the Mwellrets can make use of?'

Cogline ran his hand through this wiry thatch of white hair. 'Not enough? Yes, that was my thought, too. One page, out of so many. What harm? I dismissed the vision on waking, convinced it was a malignant intrusion on a peaceful life, a groundless fear given a momentary foothold by an old man's frailness. But it came again, a second time, this time while I slept in my own bed. It was stronger than before, more insistent. The shade chided me for my indecision, for my failings past and present. It told me to find you and bring you here. It gave me no peace, not that night or after.'

He looked genuinely distressed now, as if the memory of the shade's visit was a haunting of the sort he wished he had never encountered. Jair understood better now why Kimber felt it so important to summon him. Cogline was an old man teetering on the brink of emotional collapse. He might be hallucinating or he might have connected with the shades of the dead, Allanon or not, but whatever he had experienced, it had left him badly shaken.

'Now that I am here, what am I expected to do?' he asked.

The old man looked at him. There was a profound sadness mirrored in his ancient eyes. 'I don't know,' he said. 'I wasn't told.'

Then he looked off into the darkness and didn't speak again.

'I'm sorry about this,' Kimber declared later. There was a pronounced weariness in her voice. 'I didn't think he was going to be this vague once he had the chance to speak with you. I should have known better. I shouldn't have brought you.'

They were sitting together on the bench again, sipping at mugs of cold ale and listening to the night. They had put the old man to sleep a short while earlier, tucking him into his bed and sitting with him until he began to snore. Kimber had done her best to hasten the process with a cup of medicated tea.

He smiled at her. 'Don't be sorry. I'm glad you brought me. I don't know if I can help, but I think you were right about not wanting to handle this business alone. I can see where he could become increasingly more difficult if you tried to put him off.'

'But it's all such a bunch of nonsense! He hasn't been out of his bed in months. He hasn't slept down by the pond. Whatever dreams he's been having are the result of his refusal to eat right.' She blew out a sharp breath in frustration. 'All this business about the Ildatch surviving somehow in a page fragment! I used to believe everything he told me, when I was little and still thought him the wisest man in the world. But now I think that he's losing his mind.'

Jair sipped at his ale. 'I don't know. He seems pretty convinced.'

She stared at him. 'You don't believe him, do you?'

'Not entirely. But it might be he's discovered something worth paying attention to. Dreams have a way of revealing things we don't understand right away. They take time to decipher. But once we've thought about it . . .'

'Why would Allanon's shade come to Grandfather in a dream and ask him to bring you here rather than just appearing to you?' she interrupted heatedly. 'What sense does it make to go through Grandfather? He would not be high on the list of people you might listen to!'

'There must be a reason, if he's really had a vision from a shade. He must be involved in some important way.'

He looked at her for confirmation, but she had turned away, her mouth compressed in a tight, disapproving line. 'Are you going to help him, Jair? Are you going to try to make him see that he is imagining things or are you going to feed this destructive behaviour with pointless encouragement?'

He flushed at the rebuke, but kept his temper. Kimber was looking to him to help her grandfather find a way out of the quicksand of his delusions, and instead of doing so, he was offering to jump in himself. But he couldn't dismiss the old man's words as easily as she could. He was not burdened by years and experiences shared; he did not see Cogline in the same way she did. Nor was he so quick to disbelieve visions and dreams and shades. He had encountered more than a few himself, not the least of which was the visit from the King of the Silver River, two years earlier, under similar circumstances. If not for that visit, a visit he might have dismissed if he had been less open-minded, Brin would have been lost to him and the entire world changed. It was not something you forgot easily. Not wanting to believe was not always the best approach to things you didn't understand.

'Kimber,' he said quietly, 'I don't know yet what I am going to do. I don't know enough to make a decision. But if I dismiss your grandfather's words out of hand, it might be worse than if I try to see through them to what lies beneath.'

He waited while she looked off into the distance, her eyes still hot and her mouth set. Then finally, she turned back to him, nodding slowly. 'I'm sorry. I didn't mean to attack you. You were good enough to come when I asked, and I am letting my frustration get in the way of my good sense. I know you mean to help.'

'I do,' he reassured her. 'Let him sleep through the night, and then see if he's had the vision again. We can talk about it when he wakes and is fresh. We might be able to discover its source.'

She shook her head quickly. 'But what if it's real, Jair? What if it's true? What if I've brought you here for selfish reasons and I've placed you in real danger? I didn't mean for that to happen, but what if it does?'

She looked like a child again, waif-like and lost. He smiled and cocked one Elfish eyebrow at her. 'A moment ago, you were telling me there wasn't a chance it was real. Are you ready to abandon that ground just because I said we shouldn't dismiss it out of hand? I didn't say I believed it either. I just said there might be some truth to it.'

'I don't want there to be any. I want it to be Grandfather's wild imagination at work and nothing more.' She stared at him intently. 'I want this all to go away, far away, and not come back again. We've had enough of Shadowen and books of dark magic.'

He nodded slowly, then reached out and touched her lightly on the cheek, surprising himself with his boldness. When she closed her eyes, he felt his face grow hot and quickly took his hand away. He felt suddenly dizzy. 'Let's wait and see, Kimber,' he said. 'Maybe the dream won't come to him again.'

She opened her eyes. 'Maybe,' she whispered.

He turned back towards the darkness, took a long, cool swallow of his ale and waited for his head to clear.

The dream didn't come to Cogline that night, after all. Instead, it came to Jair Ohmsford.

He was not expecting it when he crawled into his bed, weary from the long journey and slightly muddled from a few too many cups of ale. The horses were rubbed down and fed, his possessions were put away in the cupboard and the cottage was dark. He didn't know how long he slept before it began, only that it happened all at once, and when it did, it was as if he were completely awake and alert.

He stood at the edge of a vast body of water that stretched away as far as the eye could see, its surface grey and smooth, reflecting a sky as flat and colourless as itself, so that there was no distinction between the one and the other. The shade was already there, hovering above its surface, a huge dark spectre that dwarfed him in size and blotted out a whole section of the horizon behind it. Its hood concealed its features, and all that was visible were pinpricks of red light like eyes burning out of a black hole.

Do you know me?

He did, of course. He knew instinctively, without having to think about it, without having been given more than those four words with which to work. 'You are Allanon.'

In life. In death, his shade. Do you remember me as I was?

Jair saw the Druid once again, waiting for Brin and Rone Leah and himself as they returned home late at night, a dark and imposing figure, too large somehow for their home. He heard the Druid speak to them of the Ildatch and the Shadowen. The strong features and the determined voice mesmerized him. He had never known anyone as dominating as Allanon – except, perhaps, for Garet Jax.

'I remember you,' he said.

Watch.

An image appeared on the air before him, gloomy and indistinct. It revealed the ruins of a vast fortress, mounds of rubble against a backdrop of forest and mountains. Graymark destroyed. Shadowy figures moved through the rubble, poking amid the broken stones. Bearing torches, a handful went deep inside, down tunnels in danger of collapse. They were cloaked and hooded, but the flicker of light on their hands and faces revealed patches of reptilian scales. Mwellrets. They wound their way deeper into the ruins, into fresh-made catacombs, into places where only darkness and death could be found. They proceeded slowly, taking their time, pausing often to search nooks and crannies, each hollow in the earth that might offer concealment.

Then one of the Mwellrets began to dig, an almost frantic effort, pulling aside stones and timbers, hissing like a snake. It laboured for long minutes, all alone, the others gone elsewhere. Dust and blood soon coated its scaly hide, and its breath came in gasps that suggested near exhaustion.

But in the end, it found what it sought, pulling free from the debris a seared, torn page of a book, a page with writing on it that pulsed like veins beneath skin . . .

Watch.

A second image appeared, this one of another fortress, one he didn't recognize right away, even though it seemed familiar. It was as dark and brooding as Graymark had been, as thick with shadows and gloom, as hard-edged and rough-hewn. The image lingered only a moment on the outer walls, then took the Valeman deep inside, past gates and battlements and into the nether regions. In a room dimly lit by torches that smoked and steamed in damp, stale air, a cluster of Mwellrets hovered over the solitary book page retrieved from Graymark's ruins.

They were engaged in an arcane rite. Jair could not be certain, but he had the distinct feeling that they were not entirely aware of what was happening to them. They were moving in concert, like gears in a machine, each one in synch with the others. They kept their heads lowered and their eyes fixed, and there was a hypnotic sound to their voices and movements that suggested they were responding to something he couldn't see. In the gloom and smoke, they reminded him of the Spider Gnomes on Toffer Ridge, come to make sacrifice of themselves to the Werebeasts, come to give up the lives of a few in the mistaken belief that it was for the good of the many.

As one, they moved their palms across the surface of the paper, taking in the feel of the veined writing, murmuring furtive chants and small prayers. Beneath their reptilian fingers, the page glowed and the writing pulsed. It was responding to their efforts. Jair could feel the raw pull of a siphoning, a leaching away of life.

The remnant of the Ildatch, in search of a way back from the edge of extinction, in need of nourishment that would enable it to recall and put to use the spells it had lost, was feeding.

The image faded. He was alone again with Allanon's shade, two solitary figures facing each other across an empty vista. The gloom had grown thicker and the sky darker. The lake no longer reflected light of any sort.

In the aftermath of the visions, he had realized why the second fortress had seemed so familiar. It was Dun Fee Aran, the Gnome prisons where he had been taken by the Mwellret Stythys to be coerced into giving up his magic and eventually his life. He remembered his despair on being cast into the cell allotted to him, deep beneath the earth in the bowels of the keep, alone in the darkness and silence. He remembered his fear.

'I can't go back there,' he whispered, already anticipating what the shade was going to ask of him.

But the shade asked nothing of him. Instead, it gestured and for a third and final time, the air before the Valeman began to shimmer.

Watch.

'I knew it!' Cogline exclaimed gleefully. 'It's still alive! Didn't I tell you so? Wasn't that just what I said? You thought me a crazy old man, Granddaughter, but how crazy do I look to you now? Hallucinations? Wild imaginings? Hah! Am I still to be treated as if I were a delicate flower? Am I still to be humoured and coddled?'

He began dancing about the room and cackling like the madman which, Jair guessed, he was as close as possible to being while still marginally sane. The Valeman watched him patiently, trying not to look at Kimber, who was so angry and disgusted that he could feel the heat radiating from her glare. It was morning now, and they sat across from each other at the old wooden dining table, bathed in bright splashes of sunlight that streamed through the open windows and belied the darkness of the moment.

'You haven't told us yet what the shade expects of you,' Kimber said quietly, though he could not mistake the edge to her words.

'What you have already guessed,' he answered, meeting her gaze reluctantly. 'What I knew even before the third image showed it to me. I have to go to Dun Fee Aran and put a stop to what's happening.'

Cogline stopped dancing. 'Well, you can do that, I expect,' he said, shrugging aside the implications. 'You did it once before, didn't you?'

'No, Grandfather, he did not,' Kimber corrected him impatiently. 'That was his sister, and I don't understand why she wasn't sent for, if the whole idea is to finish the job she started two years ago. It's her fault the Ildatch is still alive.'

Jair shook his head. 'It isn't anybody's fault. It just happened. In any case, Brin's married and pregnant and doesn't use the magic any more.'

Nor would she ever use it again, he was thinking. It had taken her a long time to get over what happened to her at the Maelmord. He had seen how long it had taken. He didn't know that she had ever been the same since. She had warned him that the magic was dangerous, that you couldn't trust it, that it could turn on you even when you thought it was your friend. He remembered the haunted look in her eyes.

He leaned forward, folding his hands in front of him. 'Allanon's shade made it clear that she can't be exposed to the Ildatch a second time – not even to a fragment of a page. She is too vulnerable to its magic, too susceptible to what it can do to humans, even one as powerful as she is. Someone else has to go, someone who hasn't been exposed to the power of the book before.'

Kimber reached out impulsively and took hold of his hands. 'But why you, Jair? Others could do this.'

'Maybe not. Dun Fee Aran is a Mwellret stronghold, and the page is concealed somewhere deep inside. Just finding it presents problems that would stop most from even getting close. But I have the magic of the wishsong, and I can use it to disguise myself. I can make it appear as if I'm not there. That way, I can gain sufficient time to find the page without being discovered.'

'The boy is right!' Cogline exclaimed, animated anew by the idea. 'He is the perfect choice!'

'Grandfather!' Kimber snapped at him.

The old man turned, running his gnarled fingers through his tangled beard. 'Stop yelling at me!'

'Then stop jumping to ridiculous conclusions! Jair is not the perfect choice. He might be able to get past the rets and into the fortress, but then he has to destroy the page and get out again. How is he to do that when all his magic can do is create illusions? Smoke and mirrors! How is he to defend himself against a real attack, one he is almost sure to come up against at some point?'

'We'll go with him!' the old man declared. 'We'll be his protectors! We'll take Whisper – just as soon as he comes back from wherever he's wandered off to. Dratted cat!'

Kimber ran a hand across her eyes as if trying to see things more clearly. 'Jair, do you understand what I am saying? This is hopeless!'

The Valeman didn't answer right away. He was remembering the third vision shown him by Allanon's shade, the one he hadn't talked about. A jumble of uncertain images clouded by shadowy movement and wildness, it had frightened and confused him. Yet it had imbued him with a certainty of success, as well, a certainty so strong and unmistakable that he could not dismiss it.

'The shade said that I would find a way,' he answered her. He hesitated. 'If I just believe in myself.'

She stared at him. 'If you just believe in yourself?'

'I know. It sounds foolish. And I'm terrified of Dun Fee Aran, have been since I was imprisoned there by the Mwellret Stythys two years ago on my way to find Brin. I thought I was going to die in those cells. And maybe worse was going to happen first. I have never been so afraid of anything. I swore, once I was out of there, that I would never go back, not for any reason.

He took a deep breath and exhaled slowly. 'But I think that I have go back anyway, in part because it's necessary if the Ildatch is to be stopped, but also because Allanon made me feel that I shouldn't be afraid any more. He gave me a sense of reassurance that this wouldn't be like the last time, that it would be different because I am older and stronger now – better able to face what's waiting there.'

'Telling you all this might just be a way to get you to do what he wants,' Kimber pointed out. 'It might be a Druid trick, a deception of the sort that shades are famous for.'

He nodded. 'It might. But it doesn't feel that way. It doesn't feel false. It feels true.'

'Of course, it would,' she said quietly. She looked miserable. 'I brought you here to help Grandfather find peace of mind with his dreams, not to risk your life because of them. Everything I told you I was afraid was going to happen is happening. I hate it.'

She was squeezing his hands so hard she was hurting him. 'If I didn't come, Kimber,' he said, 'who would act on your grandfather's dreams? It isn't something we planned, either of us, but we can't ignore what's needed. I have to go. I have to.'

She nodded slowly, her hands withdrawing from his. 'I know.' She looked at Cogline, who was standing very still now, looking distressed, as if suddenly aware of what he had brought about. She smiled gently at him. 'I know, Grandfather.'

The old man nodded slowly, but the joy had gone out of him.

It was decided they would set out the following day. It was a journey of some distance, even if they went on horseback. It would take them the better part of a week to get through the Ravenshorn Mountains and skirt the edges of Olden Moor to where Dun Fee Aran looked out over the Silver River in the shadow of the High Bens. This was rugged country, most of it still wilderness, beyond the spread of Dwarf settlements and Gnome camps. Much of it was swamp and jungle, and some of it was too dangerous to try to pass through. A direct line of approach was out of the question. At best, they would be able to find a path along the eastern edge of the Ravenshorn. They would have to carry their own supplies and water. They would have to go prepared for the worst.

Jair was not pleased with the thought that both Kimber and Cogline would be going with him, but there was nothing he could do about that, either. He was going back into country that had been unfamiliar to him two years earlier and was unfamiliar to him now. He wouldn't be able to find his way without help, and the only help at hand was the girl and her grandfather, both of whom knew the Anar much better than anyone else he would have been able to turn to. It would have been nice to leave them behind in safety, but he doubted that they would have permitted it even if he hadn't had need of them. For reasons that were abundantly apparent, they intended to see this matter through with him.

They spent the remainder of the day putting together supplies, a process that was tedious and somehow emotionally draining, as if the act of preparation was tantamount to climbing to a cliff ledge before jumping off. There was not much conversation exchanged, and most of what was said concerned the task itself. That the effort helped pass the time was the best that could be said for it.

More often than he cared to admit, Jair found himself wondering how far he was pressing his luck by going back into country he had been fortunate to escape from once already. He might argue that this time, like the last, he was going because he had no choice, but in fact he did. He could walk away from the dreams and their implications. He could argue that Kimber was right and that he was being used for reasons that he did not appreciate. He could even argue that efforts at reviving the Ildatch were doomed in any case, its destruction by his sister's magic so complete that trying to re-create the book from a single page was impossible. He could stop everything they were doing simply by announcing that he was going home to ask help from his parents and sister. It would be wiser to involve them in any case, wouldn't it?

But he would not do that. He knew he wouldn't even as he was telling himself he could. He was just new enough at being grown up not to want to ask for help unless he absolutely had to. It diminished him in his own mind, if not in fact, to seek assistance from his family. It was almost as if they expected it of him, the youngest and least experienced, the one they all had been helping for so long. There was an admission of failure written into such an act, one that he could not abide. This was something he could do, after all. He had gone into this country once, and dangerous or not, he could go into it again.

His mood did not improve with the coming of nightfall and the realization that there was nothing else to be done but to wait for morning. They ate the dinner Kimber made them, the old man filling the silence with thoughts of the old days and the new world, of Druids past and a future without them. There would be a time when they would return, he insisted. The Druids would be needed again, you could depend on it. Jair kept his mouth shut. He did not want to say what he was thinking about Druids and the need for them.

He dreamed again that night, but not of the shade of Allanon. In his dream, he was already down inside the fortress at Dun Fee Aran, working his way along corridors shrouded in damp and gloom, hopelessly lost and searching for a way out. A sibilant voice whose source he could not divine whispered in his ear, *Never leavess thiss plasse.* Terrifying creatures besieged him, but he could see nothing of them but their shadows. The longer he wandered, the greater his sense of foreboding, until finally it was all he could do to keep from screaming.

When a room opened before him, its interior as black as ink, he stopped at the threshold, afraid to go further, knowing that if he did so, something terrible would happen. But he could not help himself because the shadows were closing in from behind, pressing up against him, and soon they would smother him completely. So he stepped forward into the room – one step, two, three – feeling his way with a caution he prayed might save him and yet feared wouldn't.

Then a hand stretched towards him, slender and brown, and he knew it was Kimber's. He was reaching for it, so grateful he wanted to cry, when something shoved him hard from behind and he tumbled forward into a pit. He began to fall, unable to save himself, the hand that had reached for him gone, his efforts at escape doomed. He kept falling, waiting for the impact that would shatter his bones and leave him lifeless, knowing it was getting closer, closer . . .

Then a second hand reached out to catch hold of him in a grip so powerful it defied belief, and the falling stopped . . .

He woke with a start, jerking upright in bed, gasping for breath and clutching at the blanket he had kicked aside in his thrashings. It took him a moment to get out of the dream completely, to regain control of his emotions so that he no longer feared he might begin to fall again. He swung his legs over the side of the bed and sat with his head between his knees, taking long, slow breaths. The dream had made him feel frightened and alone.

Finally, he looked up. Outside, the first patch of dawn's brightness was visible above the trees. Sudden panic rushed through him.

What was he doing?

He knew in that moment that he wasn't equal to the task he had set himself. He wasn't strong or brave enough. He didn't possess the necessary skills or experience. He hadn't lived even two decades. He might be considered a man in some quarters, but in the place that counted, in his heart, he was still a boy. If he were smart, he would slip out the door now and ride back the way he had come. He would give up on this business and save his life.

He considered doing so for long moments, knowing he should act on his instincts, knowing as well that he couldn't.

Outside, the sky continued to brighten slowly into day. He stood, finally, and began to dress.

They departed at mid-morning, riding their horses north out of Hearthstone towards the passes below Toffer Ridge that would take them through the Ravenshorn and into the deep Eastland. A voluble Cogline led the way, having mapped out a route that would allow them to travel on horseback all the way to Dun Fee Aran barring unforeseen weather or circumstances, a fact he insisted on repeating at every opportunity. Admittedly, the old man knew the country better than anyone save the nomadic Gnome tribes and a few local Trackers.

What worried Jair was how well he would remember what he knew when it counted. But there was nothing he could do about Cogline's unpredictability; all he could do was hope for the best. At present, the old man seemed fine, even eager to get on with things, which was as much as Jair could expect.

He was also upset that Whisper had failed to reappear before their departure, for the moor cat would have been a welcome addition to their company. Few living creatures, man or beast, would dare to challenge a full-grown moor cat. But there was no help for this either. They would have to get along without him.

The weather stayed good for the first three days, and travel was uneventful. They rode north to the passes that crossed down over Toffer Ridge, staying well below Olden Moor, where the Werebeasts lived, traveling by daylight to make certain of their path. Each night, they would camp in a spot carefully chosen by Cogline and approved by Kimber, a place where they could keep watch and be reasonably certain of their safety. Each night, Kimber would prepare a meal for them and then put her grandfather to bed. Each night, the old man went without complaining and fell instantly asleep.

'It's the tea,' she confided in Jair. 'I put a little of his medication in it to quiet him down, the same medication I used at Hearthstone. Sometimes, it is the only way he can sleep.'

They encountered few other travellers, and there was an ordinariness to their journey that belied its nature. At times it felt to Jair as if he might be on nothing more challenging than a wilderness outing, an exploration of unfamiliar country with no other purpose than to have a look around. At such times, it was difficult to think about what was waiting at the end. The end seemed far away and unrelated to the present, as if it might belong to another experience altogether.

But those moments of complacency never lasted, and when they dissipated he reverted to a dark consideration of the particulars of what would be required when he arrived at Dun Fee Aran. His conclusions were always the same. Getting inside would be easy enough. He knew how he would use his magic to disguise himself, how he would employ it to stay hidden. Unlike Brin, he had never stopped using it, practising constantly, testing its limits. So long as he remembered not to press himself beyond those limits, he would be all right.

It was being caught out and exposed once he was inside that concerned him. He did not intend for this to happen, but if it did, what would he do? He was older and stronger than he had been two years ago, and he had studied weapons usage and self-defence since his return to the Vale. But he was not a practised fighter, and he would be deep in the centre of an enemy stronghold. That his sole allies were a young woman and a half-crazed old man was not reassuring. Kimber carried those throwing knives with which she was so lethal and the old man his bag of strange powders and chemicals, some of which could bring down entire walls, but Jair was not inclined to rely on either. When he wasn't thinking about turning around and going home – which he found himself doing at least once a day – he was thinking about how he could persuade Kimber and her grandfather not to go with him into Dun Fee Aran. Whatever his own fate, he did not want harm to come to them. He was the one who had been summoned and dispatched by Allanon's shade. The task of destroying the Ildatch fragment had been given to him.

His fears and doubts haunted him. They clung to him like the dust of the road, tiny reminders that this business was not going to end well, that he was not equal to the task he had been given. He could not shake them, could not persuade himself that their insistent little voices were lies designed to erode his already paper-thin confidence. With every mile travelled, he felt more and more the boy he had been when he had come this way before. Dun Fee Aran was a fire-pit of terror and the Mwellrets were the monsters that stirred its coals. He found himself wishing he had his companions from before – Garet Jax, the Borderman Helt, the Elven Prince Edain Elessedil, and the Dwarf Foraker. Even the taciturn, disgruntled Gnome Slanter would have been welcome. But except for the Gnome, whom he had not seen since their parting two years earlier, they had all died at Graymark. There was no possibility of replacing them, of finding allies of the same mettle. If he was determined not to involve Cogline and Kimber as more than guides and travelling companions, he would have to go it alone.

On the fourth day, the weather turned stormy. At dawn, a dark wall of clouds rolled in from the west, and by mid-morning it was raining heavily. By now they were through the Ravenshorn and riding south east in the shadow of the mountains. The terrain was rocky and brush-clogged, and they were forced to dismount and walk their horses through the increasingly heavy downpour. Cloaked and hooded, they were effectively shut away from one another, each become a shadowy, faceless form hunched against the rain.

Locked away in the cold dampness of his water-soaked coverings, Jair found himself thinking incongruously that he had underestimated his chances of succeeding, that he was better prepared than he had thought earlier, that his magic would see him through. All he had to do was get inside Dun Fee Aran, wait for his chance, and destroy the Ildatch remnant. It wasn't like the last time, when the book of magic was a sentient being, able to protect itself. There weren't any Shadowen to avoid. The Mwellrets were dangerous, but not in the same way as the walkers. He could do this. He could manage it.

He believed as much for about two hours, and then the doubts and fears returned, and his confidence evaporated. Slogging through the murk and mud, he saw himself walking a path to a cliff edge, taking a road that could end only one way.

His dark mood returned, and the weight of his inadequacies descended anew.

That night they made camp below Graymark on the banks of the Silver River, settled well back in the concealment of the hardwoods. They built a fire in the shelter of oaks grown so thick that their limbs blocked away all but small patches of the sky. Deadwood was plentiful, some of it dry enough to burn even after the downpour. Closer to Dun Fee Aran and the Mwellrets, they might have chosen not to risk it, but the most dangerous creatures abroad in these woods were of the four-legged variety. This far out in the wilderness, they were unlikely to encounter anything else.

But not long after they had cooked and eaten their dinner, they were startled by a clanking sound and the sharp bray of a pack animal. Then a voice called to them from the darkness, asking for permission to come in. Cogline gave it, grumbling under his breath as he did so, and their visitor walked into the firelight leading a mule on a rope halter. The man was tall and thin, cloaked head to foot in an old great-coat that had seen hard use. The mule was a sturdy-looking animal bearing a wooden rack from which hung dozens of pots and pans and cooking implements. A pedlar and his wares had stumbled on them.

The man tethered his mule and sat down at the fire, declining the cup of tea that was offered in favour of one filled with ale, which he gulped down gratefully. 'Long, wet day,' he declared in a weary voice. 'This helps put it right.'

They gave him what food was left over, still warm in the cooking pot, and watched him eat. 'This is good,' he announced, nodding in Kimber's direction. 'First hot meal in a while and likely to be the last. Don't see many campfires out this way. Don't see many people, for that matter. But I'm more than ready to share company this night. Hope you don't mind.'

'What are you doing way out here?' Jair asked him, taking advantage of the opening he had offered.

The pedlar paused in mid-bite and gave him a wry smile. 'I travel this way several times a year, servicing the places other pedlars won't. Might not look like it, but there are villages at the foot of the mountains that need what I sell. I pass through, do my business, and go home again, out by the Rabb. It's a lot of travelling, but I like it. I've only got me and my mule to worry about.'

He finished putting the suspended bite into his mouth, chewed it carefully, and then said, 'What about you? What brings you to the east side of the Ravenshorn? Pardon me for saying so, but you don't look like you belong here.'

Jair exchanged a quick glance with Kimber. 'Travelling up to Dun Fee Aran,' Cogline announced before they could stop him. 'Got some business ourselves. With the rets.'

The pedlar made a face. 'I'd think twice about doing business with them.' His tone of voice made clear his disgust. 'Dun Fee Aran's no place for you. Get someone else to do your business, someone a little less . . .'

He trailed off, looking from one face to the next, clearly unable to find the words that would express his concern that a boy, a girl and an old man would even think of trying to do business with Mwellrets.

'It won't take long,' Jair said, trying to put a better face on the idea. 'We just have to pick something up.'

The pedlar nodded, his thin face drawn with more than the cold and the damp. 'Well, you be careful. The Mwellrets aren't to be trusted. You know what they say about them. Look into their eyes, and you belong to them. They steal your soul. They aren't human and they aren't of a human disposition. I never go there. Never.'

He went back to eating his meal, and while he finished, no one spoke again. But when he put his plate aside and picked up his cup of ale again, Kimber filled it anew and said, 'You've never had any dealings with them?'

'Once,' he answered softly. 'An accident. They took everything I had and cast me out to die. But I knew the country, so I was able to make my way back home. Never went near them again, not at Dun Fee Aran and not on the road. They're monsters.'

He paused. 'Let me tell you something about Dun Fee Aran, since you're going there. Haven't told this to anyone. Didn't have a reason and didn't think anyone would believe me, anyway. But you should know. I was inside those walls. They held me there while they decided what to do with me after taking my wares and mule. I saw things. Shades, drifting through the walls as if the stone were nothing more than air. I saw my mother, dead fifteen years. She beckoned to me, tried to lead me out of there. But I couldn't go with her because I couldn't pass through the walls like she could. It's true. I swear it. There was others, too. Things I don't want to talk about. They were there at Dun Fee Aran. The rets didn't seem to see them. Or maybe they didn't care.'

He shook his head. 'You don't want to go inside those walls again once you've got out of them.'

His voice trailed off and he stared out into the darkness as if searching for more substantial manifestations of the memories he couldn't quite escape. Fear reflected in his eyes with a bright glitter that warned of the damage such memories could do. He did not seem a cowardly man, or a superstitious one, but in the night's liquid shadows he had clearly found demons other men would never even notice.

'Do you believe me?' he asked quietly.

Jair's mouth was dry and his throat tight in the momentary silence that followed. 'I don't know,' he said.

The man nodded. 'It would be wise if you did.'

At dawn, the pedlar took his leave. They watched him lead his mule through the trees and turn north along the Silver River. Like one of the shades he claimed to have seen in the dungeons at Dun Fee Aran, he walked into the wall of early morning mist and faded away.

They travelled all that day through country grown thick with scrub and old growth and layered in grey blankets of brume. The world was empty and still, a place in which dampness and gloom smothered all life and left the landscape a tangled wilderness. If not for the Silver River's slender thread, they might easily have lost their way. Even Cogline paused more than once to consider their path. The sky had disappeared into the horizon and the horizon into the earth, so that the land took on the look and feel of a cocoon. Or a coffin. It closed about them and refused to release its death grip. It embraced them with the chilly promise of a constancy that came only with an end to life. Its desolation was both depressing and scary and did nothing to help Jair's already eroded confidence. Bad enough that the pedlar had chilled what little fire remained in his determination to continue on; now the land would suffocate the coals as well.

Cogline and Kimber said little to him as they walked, locked away with their own thoughts in the shadowy coverings of their cloaks and hoods, wraiths in the mist. They led their horses like weary warriors come home from war, bent over by exhaustion and memories, lost in dark places. It was a long, slow journey that day, and at times Jair was so certain of the futility of its purpose that he wanted to stop his companions and tell them that they should turn back. It was only the shame he felt at his own weakness that kept him from doing so. He could not expose that weakness, could not admit to it. Should he do so, he knew, he might as well die.

They slept by the river that night, finding a copse of fir that sheltered and concealed them, tethering the horses close by and setting a watch. There was no fire. They were too close to Dun Fee Aran for that. Dinner was eaten cold, ale was consumed to help ward against the chill, and they went to sleep sullen and conflicted.

They woke cold and stiff from the night and the steady drizzle. Within a mile of their camp they found clearer passage along the river-bank, remounted and rode on into the afternoon until, with night descending and an icy wind beginning to blow down out of the mountains, they came in sight of their goal.

It was not a welcome moment. Dun Fee Aran rose before them in a mass of walls and towers, wreathed in mist and shrouded by rain. Torchlight flickered off the rough surfaces of ironbound gates and through the narrow slits of barred windows as if trapped souls were struggling to breathe. Smoke rose in tendrils from the sputtering flames, giving the keep the look of a smouldering ruin. There was no sign of life, not even shadows cast by moving figures. Nor did any sounds emanate from within. It was as if the keep had been abandoned to the gloom and the pedlar's ghosts.

The three travellers walked their horses back into the trees some distance away and dismounted. They stood close together as the night descended and the darkness deepened, watching and waiting for something to reveal itself. It was a futile effort.

Jair stared at the keep's forbidding bulk with certain knowledge of what waited within and felt his skin crawl.

'You can't go in there,' Kimber said to him suddenly, her voice thin and strained.

'I have to.'

'You don't have to do anything. Let this go. I can smell the evil in this place. I taste it on the air.' She took hold of his arm. 'That pedlar was right. Only ghosts belong here. Grandfather, tell him he doesn't have to go any farther with this.'

Jair looked at Cogline. The old man met his gaze, then turned away.

He had decided to leave it up to the Valeman. It was the first time since they had met that he had taken a neutral stance on the matter of the Ildatch. It spoke volumes about his feelings, now that Dun Fee Aran lay before them.

Jair took a deep breath and looked back at Kimber. 'I came a long way for nothing if I don't at least try.'

She looked out into the rain and darkness to where the Mwellret castle hunkered down in the shadow of the mountains and shook her head. 'I don't care. I didn't know it would be like this. This place feels much worse than I thought it would. I told you before – I don't want anything to happen to you. This,' she gestured towards the fortress, 'looks too difficult for anyone.'

'It looks abandoned.'

She gave him a withering look. 'Don't be stupid. You don't believe that. You know what's in there. Why are you even pretending it might be something else?' Her lips compressed in a tight line. 'Let's go back. Right now. Let someone else deal with the Ildatch, someone better able. Jair, it's too much!'

There was a desperation in her voice that threatened to drain him of what small resolve he had left. Something of the pedlar's fear reflected now in her eyes, a hint of dark places and darker feelings. She was reacting to the visceral feel of Dun Fee Aran, to its hardness and impenetrability, to its ponderous bulk and immutability. She wasn't a coward, but she was intimidated. He couldn't blame her. He could barely bring himself to consider going inside. It was easier to consider simply walking away.

He looked around, as if he might be doing exactly that. 'It's too late to go anywhere tonight. Let's make camp back in the trees, where there's some shelter. Let's eat something and get some sleep. We'll think about what to do. We'll decide in the morning.'

She seemed to accept that. Without pursuing the matter further, she led the way into the woods, beyond sight and sound of the fortress and its hidden inhabitants, beyond whatever might choose to go abroad. The rain continued to fall and the wind to blow, the unpleasant mix chasing away any possibility of even the smallest of comforts. They found a windbreak within a stand of fir, the best they could expect, tethered and unsaddled their horses, and settled in.

Their stores were low, and Jair surprised the girl and her grandfather by bringing out an aleskin he told them he had been saving for this moment. They would drink it now, a small indulgence to celebrate their safe arrival and to ward off bad feelings and worse weather. He poured liberally into their cups and watched them drink, being careful only to pretend to drink from his own.

His duplicity troubled him. But he was serving what he perceived to be a greater good, and in his mind that justified far worse.

They were asleep within minutes, stretched out on the forest earth. The medication he had stolen from Kimber and added to the ale had done its job. He unrolled their blankets, wrapped them tightly about, tucked them in under the sheltering fir boughs, and left them to sleep. He had watched Kimber administer the drug to her grandfather each night since they had set out from Hearthstone, his plans already made. If he had judged correctly the measure he had dropped into their ale, they would not wake before morning.

By then, he would be either returned or dead.

He strapped on his short sword, stuck a dagger in his boot, wrapped himself in his greatcloak, and set off to find out which it would be.

He did not feel particularly brave or confident about what he had decided to do. Mostly, he felt resigned. Even if Kimber thought he had a choice in the matter, he did not. Jair was not the kind to walk away from his responsibilities, and it didn't matter whether he had asked for them or not. The shade of Allanon had summoned him deliberately and with specific intent. He could not ignore what that meant. He had travelled this path before in his short life, and by doing so he had come to understand a basic truth that others might choose to ignore, but he could not. If he failed to act, it was all too likely no one else would either.

In his mind, the matter had been decided almost from the outset, and his doubts and fears were simply a testing of his determination.

He took some comfort in the fact that he had managed to keep Kimber and her grandfather from coming with him. They would have done so, of course, well meaning and perhaps even helpful. But he would have worried for them, and that would have rendered his efforts less effective. Besides, it would be all he could do to conceal himself from discovery. To conceal two others while gaining entry into Dun Fee Aran was taking on too much.

Mist and rain obscured his vision, and he was forced to make his way cautiously, unable to see more than a few yards in any direction. Ahead, the dull yellow glow of Dun Fee Aran's torches reflected through the gloom as through a gauzy veil. Beneath his boots, the ground was spongy and littered with deadwood and leaves knocked down by the wind. The air was cold and smelled of damp earth and wet bark. The

sharp tang of burning pitch cut through both, a guide to his destination.

Then the trees opened before him, and the massive walls of the
fortress came into view, black and shimmering in the rain and mist.
He slowed to a walk, studying the parapets and windows carefully,
searching for movement. He was already singing, calling up the magic
of the wishsong. Unlike Brin, he welcomed it as he would an old
friend. Perhaps that had something to do with why he was the one
who was here.

Ahead, the main gates to the keep loomed, thick oak timbers
wrapped in iron and standing well over twenty feet high. A forbidding obstacle, but he had already seen the smaller door to one side,
the one that would be used to admit a traveller on nights such as this
when it was too dangerous to chance opening the larger gates. He
walked towards that door, still singing, no longer cloaking himself in
invisibility but in the pretence of being someone he wasn't.

Slowly, he began to take shape, to assume the form that would gain
him entry.

When he reached the smaller doors, he sent a whispered summons
to the sentry standing watch inside. He never doubted that someone
was there. Like Kimber, he could feel the evil in this place and knew
that its source never slept. It took only moments for a response. A slot
opened in the iron facing, and yellow-slitted eyes peered out. What
they saw wasn't really there. What they saw was another Mwellret,
drenched and angry and cloaked in an authority that was not to be
challenged. A decision was quickly reached, the door swung outwards
with a groan of rusted hinges, and a reptilian face appeared in the
opening.

'Sstate what bringss . . .'

The sentry choked hard on the rest of what he was going to ask.
The Mwellret he had expected was no longer there. What waited instead
was a black-cloaked form that stood seven feet tall and had been
thought dead for more than two years.

What the sentry found waiting was the Druid Allanon.

It was a bold gamble on Jair's part, but it had the desired effect.
Hissing in fear and loathing, the sentry stumbled backwards into the
gatehouse, too traumatized even to think to resecure the doors. Jair
stepped through at once, forcing the Mwellret to retreat even further
into the small gatehouse. Belatedly, the ret snatched at a pike, but a
single threatening gesture was sufficient to cause him to drop the pike
in terror and back away once more, this time all the way to the wall.

'You hide a fragment of the Ildatch,' the Druid's voice thundered out of Jair. 'Give it to me!'

The Mwellret bolted through the back door of the gatehouse into the interior of Dun Fee Aran, crying out as he went, his sibilant voice hoarse before he reached the central tower and disappeared inside. He did not bother to look back to see if Allanon was following, too intent on escaping, on giving warning, on finding help from any quarter. Had he done so, he would have found that the Druid had vanished and the Mwellret he had thought to admit in the first place had reappeared. Cloaked in his new disguise, Jair pursued the fleeing sentry with an intensity that did not allow for distraction. When other rets scurried past him, bound for the gatehouse and the threat that no longer existed, he either stepped back into the shadows or gave way in deference, a lesser to superiors, of no interest or concern to them.

Then he was inside the main stronghold, working his way along hallways and down stairs, swimming upriver against a sudden flow of traffic. The entire fortress had come alive in a swarm of reptilian forms, a nest of vipers with cold, gimlet eyes. *Don't look into those eyes!* He knew the stories of how they stole away men's minds. He had been a victim of their hypnotic effect once and did not intend to be so ever again. He avoided the looks cast his way as the Mwellrets passed, advancing deeper into the keep, leaving behind the shouts and cries that now came mostly from the main courtyard.

He felt time and chance pressing in on him like collapsing walls. Where was the sentry?

He found him not far ahead, gasping out his news to another Mwellret, one that looked to be a good deal more capable of dealing with the unexpected. This second ret listened without comment, dispatched the frightened sentry back the way he had come, and turned down a corridor that led still deeper into the keep. Jair, mustering his courage, followed.

His quarry moved with purpose along the corridor and then down a winding set of stairs. He glanced back once or twice, but by now Jair had changed his appearance again, no longer another Mwellret, but a part of the fortress itself. He was the walls, the floor, the air, and nothing at all. The Mwellret might look over his shoulder as many times as he chose, but he would have to look carefully to realize that there was something wrong with what he was seeing.

But what concerned Jair was that the ret might not be leading him to the Ildatch fragment after all. He had assumed that the sentry would rush to give warning of the threat from Allanon and by doing so lead

Jair to those who guarded the page fragment he had come to destroy. Yet there was nothing to indicate that the ret was taking him to where he wanted to go. If he had guessed wrong about this, he was going to have trouble of a sort he didn't care to contemplate. His ability to employ the magic was not inexhaustible. Sooner or later, he would tire. Then he would be left not only exposed, but also defenceless.

Torchlight flooded the corridor ahead. An ironbound door and guards holding massive pikes blocked the way forward. The Mwellret he followed signalled perfunctorily to the watch as he stepped out of the darkened corridor into the light, and the guards released the locks and stepped aside for him. Jair, still invisible to those around him, took advantage of the change of light, closed swiftly on his quarry at the entry and slipped into the chamber behind him just as the door swung closed again.

Standing just inside, he glanced quickly at the cavernous, smoke-filled chamber and its occupants. Seven, no eight, Mwellrets clustered about a huge wooden table on which rested bottles, vials and similar containers amid a scattering of old books and tablets. At their centre, carefully placed on a lectern that kept it raised above everything, was a single piece of aged paper, its edges burned and curled. A strange glow emanated from that fragment, and the writing on its worn surface pulsed steadily. The aura it gave off was so viscerally repellent, that Jair recoiled in spite of himself, a sudden wave of nausea flooding through him.

There was no question in his mind about what he was seeing. Forcing his repulsion aside, he gathered up the fraying threads of his determination and threw the bolt that locked the door from the inside.

Nine heads turned as one, scaly faces lifting into the light from out of shadowy hoods. A moment of uncertainty rooted the Mwellrets in place, and then the one the Valeman had followed down from the upper halls started back for the door, a long knife appearing in his clawed hand. Jair was already moving sideways, skirting the edges of the chamber, heading for the table and its contents. The Mwellrets had begun to move forward, placing themselves between the door and their prize, their attention focused on what might be happening outside in the hallway. All the Valeman needed was a few moments to get behind them and seize the page. He could feed it into one of the torches before they could stop him. If he were quick enough, they would never even realize he was there.

Stay calm. Don't rush. Don't give yourself away.

The Mwellret at the entry released the lock and wrenched open the door. The startled sentries turned in surprise as he looked past them wordlessly into the corridor beyond, searching. Jair had reached the table and was sliding along its edge towards the page fragment, a clear path ahead of him. The Mwellrets were muttering now, glancing about uneasily, trying to decide if they were threatened or not. He had only a few seconds left.

He reached the lectern, snatched up the page fragment and dropped it with a howl as it burned his fingers like a live coal.

Instantly the Mwellrets swung around, watching their precious relic flutter in the air before settling back on the table amid the debris, steaming and writhing like a living thing. Shouts rose from its protectors, some snatching out blades from beneath their cloaks and beginning to fan out across the chamber. Furious with himself, terrified by his failure, Jair backed away, fighting to stay calm. Magic warded the Ildatch fragment as it had warded the book itself. Whether this was magic of the book's own making or of its keepers, it changed what was required. If he couldn't hold the page, how was he going to feed it into the fire? How was he going to destroy it?

He backed against the wall, sliding away from the searching rets, who were still uncertain what they were looking for. They knew something was there, but they didn't know what. If he could keep them guessing long enough . . .

His mind raced, his fading possibilities skittering about like rats in a cage.

Then one of the Mwellrets, perhaps guessing at his subterfuge, snatched up a round wooden container from the table, reached into it, and began tossing out handfuls of white powder. Everything the powder settled on, it coated. Jair knew what was coming. Once the powder was flung in his direction, he would be outlined as clearly as a shadow cast in bright sunlight. The best he could hope for was to find a way to destroy the Ildatch fragment before that happened, and he was likely to get only one more chance.

He glanced over his shoulder to where a torch burned in its wall mount behind him. If he snatched it up and rushed forward, he could lay it against the paper. That should be enough to finish the matter.

Steady. Don't rush.

The Mwellrets were moving back around the table now, hands groping the empty air as they attempted to flush out their invisible intruder. The Mwellret with the powder continued to toss handfuls into the air, but he was still on the other side of the table and not yet close enough to threaten. The Valeman kept the wishsong steady and his concentration focused as he edged closer to his goal. What he needed was another distraction, a small window of opportunity to act.

Then the ret with the powder turned abruptly and began throwing handfuls in his direction.

The immediacy of the threat proved too much for the Valeman to endure. He reacted instinctively, abandoning the magic that cloaked him in the appearance of invisibility for something stronger. Images of Garet Jax flooded the room, black-cloaked forms wielding blades in both hands and moving like seasoned fighters. It was all Jair could come up with in his welter of panic and need, and he grasped at it as a drowning man would a lifeline.

At first, it appeared it would be enough. The Mwellrets fell back in terror, caught off guard, unprepared for so many adversaries appearing all at once. Even the sentries who now blocked the doorway retreated, pikes lifting defensively. Whatever magic was at work, it was beyond anything with which they were familiar, and they did not know what to do about it.

It was the distraction Jair required, and he took immediate advantage of it. He reached for one of the torches set in wall brackets behind him, grasped it by the handle and wrenched at it. But his hands were coated in sweat and he could not pull it loose from its fitting. The Mwellrets hissed furiously, seeing him clearly now behind his wall of protectors, realizing at once what he intended. Under different circumstances, they might have hesitated longer before acting, but they were driven by an irrational and overwhelming need to protect the Ildatch fragment. Whatever else they might countenance, they would not stand by and lose their chance at immortality.

They came at the images of Garet Jax in a swarm, wielding their knives and short swords in a glittering frenzy, slashing and hacking without regard for their own safety. The fury and suddenness of their onslaught caught Jair by surprise, and his concentration faltered. One by one, his images disappeared. The Mwellrets found not real warriors facing them, but men made of little more than coloured vapour.

The Valeman gave up on his effort to free the recalcitrant torch and turned to face the Mwellrets. They were all around him and closing in, their blades forming a circle of sharp-edged steel that he could not get past. He had been too slow, too hesitant. His chance was gone. Despairing, he drew his own sword to defend himself. He thought fleetingly of Garet Jax, trying to remember the way he had moved when surrounded by his enemies, trying to imagine what he might do now.

And as if in response, a fresh image formed, unbidden and wholly unexpected. In a shimmer of dark air, the Weapons Master reappeared, a replication of the images already destroyed, black-cloaked and wielding one of the deadly blades he had carried in life. But this image did not separate itself from Jair as the others had. Instead, it closed about him like a second skin. It happened so fast that the Valeman did not have time to try to stop it.

In seconds, he had become the image.

Instantly, this hybrid version of himself joined to the Weapons Master vaulted into the Mwellrets with a single-mindedness of purpose that was breathtaking. The rets, thinking it harmless, barely brushed at it with their weapons. Two of them died for their carelessness in a single pass. Another fell on a lunge that buried his blade so deep it had to be wrenched free. Belatedly, the Mwellrets realized they were faced with something new. They slashed and cut with their own blades in retaliation, but they might as well have been wielding wooden toys. Jair heard sharp intakes of breath as his knives found their mark; he felt the shudder of bodies and the thrashing of limbs. Mwellrets stumbled, dying on their feet, stunned looks on their faces as he swept through them, killing with scythe-like precision.

It was horrific and exhilarating, and the Valeman was immersed in it, living it. For a few stunning moments, he was someone else entirely, someone whose thoughts and experiences were not his own. He wasn't just watching Garet Jax – he *was* Garet Jax. He was so lost to himself, so much a part of the Weapons Master, that even though what he was experiencing was dark and scary, it filled him with satisfaction and deep longing for more.

Now the ret guards rushed to join the battle, pikes spearing at him. The guards were trained and not so easily dispatched. A hooked point sliced through his sword arm, sending a flash of jagged pain into his body. He feinted and sidestepped the next thrust. The guards cut at him, but he was ready now and eluded them easily. A phantom sliding smoothly beneath each sweep of their weapons, he was inside their killing arc and on top of them before they realized they had failed to stop him.

Seconds later, the last of the rets lay lifeless on the floor.

But when he wheeled back to survey the devastation he had left in his wake, he saw the young Valeman who had remained on the far side of the table. Their eyes met, and he felt something shift inside. The Valeman was fading away even as he watched, turning slowly transparent, becoming a ghost.

He was disappearing.

Do something!

He snatched free a torch mounted on the wall behind him and threw it into the powders and potions on the table. Instantly, the volatile mix went up in flames, white-hot and spitting. The Ildatch fragment pulsed at its centre, then rose from the table into the scorched air, riding the back of invisible currents generated by the heat.

Escaping . . .

He snatched the dagger from his boot and leaped forward, spearing the hapless scrap of paper in mid-air and pinning it to the wooden tabletop where the flames were fiercest. The paper curled against his skin in a clutching motion and his head snapped back in shock as razor-sharp pains raced up his arm and into his chest. But he refused to let go. Ignoring the pain, he held the paper pinned in place. When the inferno finally grew so intense that he was forced to release his death grip on the dagger and back away, the Ildatch fragment was just barely recognizable. He stood clutching his seared hand on the far side of the burning table, watching the scrap of paper slowly wither and turn to dust.

Then he walked back around the table and through the image of the Valeman and he was inside his own body again. Feeling as if a weight had been lifted from his shoulders, he looked over to where the shadowy, black-cloaked figure he had been joined to was fading away, returning to the ether from which it had come, returning to the land of the dead.

He fled the chamber, skittering through the sprawl of Mwellret bodies and out the door, hugging the walls of the smoke-filled corridors and stairwells that led to safety. His mind spun with images of what he had just experienced, leaving him unsteady and riddled with doubt. In spite of having the use of the wishsong to disguise his passing, he felt completely exposed.

What had happened back there?

Had Garet Jax found a way to come back from the dead on his own, choosing to be Jair's protector one final time? Had Allanon sent him through a trick of Druid magic that transcended the dictates of the grave?

Perhaps.

But Jair didn't think so. What he thought was that he alone was responsible, that somehow the wishsong had given that last image life.

It was impossible, but that was what he believed.

He took deep, slow breaths to steady himself as he climbed out of Dun Fee Aran's prisons. It was madness to think that his magic could give life to the dead. It suggested possibilities that he could only just bear to consider. Giving life to the dead violated all of nature's laws. It made his skin crawl.

But it had saved him, hadn't it? It had enabled him to destroy the Ildatch fragment, and that was what he had come to Dun Fee Aran to do. What difference did it make how it had been accomplished?

Yet it did make a difference. He remembered how it had felt to be a part of Garet Jax. He remembered how it had felt to kill those Mwellrets, to hear their frantic cries, to see their stricken looks, to smell their blood and fear. He remembered the grating of his blade against their bones and the surprisingly soft yield of their scaly flesh. He hadn't hated it; he had enjoyed it – enough so that for the brief moments he had been connected to the Weapons Master, he had craved it. Even now, in the terrible, blood-drenched aftermath when his thoughts and body were his own again, he hungered for more.

What if he had not looked back at the last moment and seen himself fading away?

What if he had not sensed the unexpectedly dangerous position he had placed himself in, joined to a ghost out of time?

He found his way up from the prisons more easily than he had expected he would, moving swiftly and smoothly through the chaos. He did not encounter any more Mwellrets until he reached the upper halls, where they were clustered in angry bands, still looking for something that wasn't there, still unaware that the Druid they sought was an illusion. Perhaps the sounds had been muffled by the stone walls and iron doors, but they had not discovered yet what had happened below ground. They did not see him as he passed, cloaked in his magic, and in moments, he was back at the gates. Distracting the already distracted guards long enough to open the door one last time, he melted into the night.

He walked from the fortress through the rain and mist, using the wishsong until he reached the trees, then stopped, the magic dying on his lips. His knees gave way, and he sat on the damp ground and stared into space. His burned hand throbbed and the wound to his arm ached. He was alive, but he felt dead inside. But how he felt inside was his own fault. Wasn't bringing Garet Jax back from the dead what he had wanted all along? Wasn't that the purpose of preserving all those memories of Graymark and the Croagh? To make the past he so greatly prized a part of the present?

He placed his hand against the cool earth and stared at it.

Something wasn't right.

If it was the Weapons Master who had fought against the Mwellrets and destroyed the fragment of the Ildatch, why was his hand burned? Why was his arm wounded?

He stared harder, remembering. Garet Jax had carried only one blade in his battle with the Mwellrets, rather than the two all of the other images had carried.

Jair's blade.

His throat tightened in shock. He was looking at this all wrong. The wishsong hadn't brought Garet Jax back from the dead. It hadn't brought Garet Jax back at all. There was only one of them in that charnel house tonight.

Himself.

He saw the truth of things now, all of it, what he had so completely misread. Brin had warned him not to trust the magic, had cautioned him that it was dangerous. But he had ignored her. He had assumed that because his use of it was different from her own, less potent and seemingly more harmless, it did not threaten in the same way. She could actually change things, could create or destroy, whereas he could only give the appearance of doing so. Where was the harm in that?

But magic had evolved. Perhaps it had done so because he had grown. Perhaps it was just the natural consequence of time's passage. Whatever the case, sometime in the past two years it had undergone a terrible transformation. And tonight, in the dungeons of Dun Fee Aran, responding to the unfamiliar urgency of his desperation and fear, it had revealed its new capabilities for the first time.

He hadn't conjured up the shade of Garet Jax. He hadn't given life to a dead man in some mysterious way. What he had done was to remake himself in the Weapons Master's image. That had been all him back there, cloaked in his once-protector's trappings, a replica of the killing machine the other had been. That was why he had felt everything so clearly, why it had all seemed so real. It was. The Garet Jax in the chambers of Dun Fee Aran was a reflection of himself, of his own dark nature, of what lay buried just beneath the surface.

A reflection, he recalled with a chill, into which he had almost disappeared completely.

Because risking that fate was necessary if he was to survive and the Ildatch to be destroyed.

Then a further revelation came to him, one so terrible that he knew almost as soon as it occurred to him that it was true. Allanon had known what his magic would do when he had summoned him through Cogline's dreams. Allanon had known that it would surface to protect him against the Mwellrets.

Kimber Boh had been right. The Druid had used him. Even in death, it could still manipulate the living. Circumstances required it, necessity dictated it, and Jair was sacrificed to both at the cost of a glimpse into the blackest part of his soul.

He closed his eyes against what he was feeling. He wanted to go home. He wanted to forget everything that had happened this night. He wanted to bury the knowledge of what his magic could do. He wanted never to have come this way.

He ran his fingers through the damp leaves and rain-softened earth at his feet, stirring up the pungent smells of both, tracing idle patterns as he waited for his feelings to settle and his head to clear. Somewhere in the distance, he heard fresh cries from the fortress. They had discovered the chamber where the dead men lay. They would try to understand what had happened, but would not be able to do so.

Only he would ever know.

After long moments, he opened his eyes again and brushed the dirt and debris off his injured hand. He would return to Kimber and her grandfather and wake them. He would tell them some of what had happened, but not all. He might never tell anyone all of it.

He wondered if he would heed his sister's advice and never use the magic again. He wondered what would happen if he chose to ignore that advice again or if fate and circumstances made it impossible for him to do otherwise, as had happened tonight. He wondered what the consequences would be next time.

The past is always with us, but sometimes we don't recognize it right away for what it is.

He got to his feet and started walking.